Summer Rain

Summer Rain

Jon Konrath

Writers Club Press
San Jose New York Lincoln Shanghai

Summer Rain

All Rights Reserved © 2000 by Jon Konrath

No part of this book may be reproduced or transmitted in any form or by any means, graphic, electronic, or mechanical, including photocopying, recording, taping, or by any information storage retrieval system, without the permission in writing from the publisher.

Writers Club Press
an imprint of iUniverse.com, Inc.

For information address:
iUniverse.com, Inc.
620 North 48th Street, Suite 201
Lincoln, NE 68504-3467
www.iuniverse.com

This is a work of fiction. All of the characters and incidents, except for incidental references to public figures, products, or services, are imaginary and are not intended to refer to any living persons or to disparage any company's products or services.

ISBN: 0-595-13494-7

Printed in the United States of America

Acknowledgements

First and foremost, many great thanks to fellow writer and vomitologist Ray Miller for innumerous discussions, support, Death Metal research, and friendship during the five years it took to write this book and the last 15 years in general. I'm sorry there weren't any Godzilla references. Don't worry, next time I'm in Elkhart, we'll go to 7-Eleven and fuck some sluts.

Many thanks go to fellow author Michael Stutz for his great support, friendship, and his first novel, *Sunclipse*, which made me realize I wasn't the only one who came of age in the Midwest and survived to write about it. Thanks much for the dsl.org interview, the Linux help, a place to crash in Cleveland, and all of the editorial review over the years.

Thank you to my favorite (favourite?) Canadian-American, Andrea Donderi, for being my most diligent reader, and for all of the help during the "changing of Amy" debacle. Without your input, this book (and life in general) would be much more boring.

Much thanks to Marie Mundaca, for helping me beyond the call of duty, giving me a place to write for most of 1999, taking the photo on the rear cover, and listening to all of my incessant babbling. Also thanks to Mungo Baguette for all of his wake-up calls and unsolicited editing assistance, and Henrey Lucat for all of the black cat fireworks and advice at the OTB.

Thanks also to Larry Falli, my unofficial legal counsel and good friend. From firing your civil war cannon across the parking lot to driving aimlessly around half of the country, you made my last year in Bloomington much more survivable. May HB2A.JPG live forever.

Thanks and hello: Lisa Franchina, Penny Alano, Steph Ingle, Sean Sowder, Erika Hopper, Julius Cooper, Alison Bachman, Tara Culbertson, Chris Hagen, Larry Falli, Bill Perry, Scott Boggan, Virginia Lore, Chris Blanc, and Aaron Renn. And Sonya Gamargo, thank you for the jacket.

Thank you to the Indiana University Office of the Bursar (I never thought I'd say that) for their research assistance. Also many thanks to the two wonderful books on the subject, *Indiana University: Midwestern Pioneer*, by Thomas D. Clark and *Indiana University: A Pictorial History*, by Dorothy C. Collins and Cecil K. Byrd.

Thank you to Tom Sample for giving me a couch to sleep on in Indianapolis for a week in 1995, when this whole idea was starting to fall into shape. Green hell!

Thanks to David Gulbransen (david@gulbransen.net) for the cover photo and the stuff for the website. Also thanks again to Marie Mundaca for the rear cover author photo.

And thank you for buying and reading this book. Check out my web site at **www.rumored.com** for updates and information on upcoming projects.

No thanks to Evergreen Ford in Issaquah.

Book One

1

I pulled the VW Rabbit off the road and killed the engine. The familiar smell of diesel fumes from the beat-up Volkswagen mingled with the Indiana springtime air outside. For a split-second I enjoyed the first moment of peace that day, maybe that whole week. This is just the calm before the storm, I thought. I cranked shut the moonroof, shut down everything in the car, and got ready to head into campus.

5:15 PM, Friday evening—the spring semester officially ended fifteen minutes ago. I finished a four-hour shift in solitary confinement, babysitting an empty computer lab with thirty-six Macs in the colossal Student Union building. With work done, classes over, and finals flunked, I now made my last stop, a visit to Collins Quad to see my old buddy Max. He graduated the next morning and would be in a car for New Jersey by noon. This would be our last chance to talk before the real world swallowed him whole.

The door of the rusty VW closed with a thud. I left the car halfway in the grass by the side of the road and headed toward Collins. The walk downhill took me through a student ghetto, a neighborhood built by slum landlords and filled with battered, identical two story houses. Battalions of college students rented the flats to avoid the tiny dorm rooms and no-alcohol policy, so the places weren't built for style. Most off-campus houses resembled the before picture of a Bob Vila project, but as long as the rents were cheap, they filled with new students every year. Similar neighborhoods filled every area bordering the campus that wasn't owned by the university or one of the major corporate rental companies. Some modern apartment buildings sprang up next to the old saltshaker houses, but the low-cost, low-maintenance postwar clones were standard issue. Almost every student rented, subletted, or partied in these houses during their stay at Indiana University. Walking down this street made me feel great about the last twelve months I spent off-campus, drinking beer, flunking out, and trying to score with women who probably didn't know I existed.

Every house had the same front porch, with a sweeping roof extending past the house and resting on pillars. For decades, these were the places of keg parties, barbecues and lazy gatherings. Rusted lawn chairs, dented beer kegs and mountain bikes populated the awnings, along with charcoal grills that hadn't been cleaned since the Korean War. Each block had a dormant VW bus plastered with Phish, "Mean People Suck" and "Fuckengroovin" bumper stickers, and a few motorcycles parked amidst many old Honda Civics. Most of the sidewalk recycling bins overflowed with the amber and green of MGD and Bud Lite bottles, and layers of rain-streaked, photocopied band fliers covered every telephone pole.

It looked like another subdued and lazy Friday night for the people lounging in front of their houses. Most folks, locked into full-year leases, would rather pay rent all summer than move home to mommy and daddy, like the on-campus students. A changing of the guard occurred in some houses, where dorm residents dragged their stuff into houses and made the leap to off-campus living, filling spots vacated by graduates and dropouts skipping town. But for most of the district, tonight was the first Friday night of the summer, the end of finals, and a time for beer to pour.

During the walk, a feeling of summer surrounded me for the first time that year. The smell of May trees, flowers, and freshly mowed grass, and the gentle temperature bombarded my senses like they hadn't all semester. During the stress, depression and confusion of the last few weeks, I drowned my feelings with a walkman, erasing the sounds of springtime when I walked on campus. I'd try to forget about the money, women, broken cars, dropping grades, and nagging parents by listening to loud music, but I also never saw the world around me. These few minutes alone made me think about the end of spring and beginning of summer for the first time in a real, physical way, not just in terms of dollars and classes and sublets and finals and jobs.

At the bottom of the hill, the traffic light at Tenth and Woodlawn marked the northern boundary of campus. On the corner across the street stood a nineteenth century limestone building, an archetypal college structure with narrow, tall windows and ivy vines creeping on the walls. I walked past the building to a courtyard, bounded on three sides by Cravens, Edmondson, and Smith halls. The trio of sand-white buildings formed Collins Quad, allegedly the oldest operational dorm in the country, with a long tradition of artists, poets, revolutionaries and humanities scholars, and flunkies like me.

The courtyard flowed with parents arguing with their children, people hefting disassembled lofts, and students dragging portable fridges and trunks from their rooms. Moving vans circled the block, trying to find a parking spot within ten blocks of the loading zones of the buildings. Usually at five o'clock on a Friday, long-hairs played Frisbee, spiked and leathered punks convened, asking what bands would be playing that weekend, and resident watercolor artist or folk-singing guitarist sat on the large veranda in front of the center building. Today, a handful of stray hippies dodged annoyed and confused glances of parents who tried to load boxes into minivans and station wagons before the traffic got worse.

Edmondson, the center building and largest of the three, sported a huge veranda. Today, it served as a staging area for crates, appliances and hand carts, as people unloaded belongings extricated from the only dorm without elevators. I navigated around the chaos, through the large keystone portal into the building, and into the main lobby. So many memories rushed into my head, from the mailboxes on the wall to the center desk where I used to buy stamps and sign for packages. Everything made me feel like I was a freshman again, coming home from classes for a good nap before dinner in the cafeteria downstairs.

Climbing the familiar stairs to Ed 2, my old floor, felt just like the walk I made many times each day, when I came up from the lounge, cafeteria, or elsewhere. The paint, carpet, and fliers on the walls all looked different, but dragging my feet up each step felt as familiar as sitting in a favorite easy chair. The second floor looked just like it did when I was a freshman, first dragging my Led Zeppelin albums and dorm fridge to a new chapter of life. Tall ceilings, thick, ornate wood trim pecked with cigarette burns, wide hallways and hundred-year-old windowsills made this building look more like a bed and breakfast than the prison-like dorm towers built in the sixties all over the campus.

That evening, the halls filled with people dividing CD collections with roommates, trying to get posters from the walls without ruining paint, and fixing closet doors that were broken back in October. However, the floor still felt like an old home to me, preserved in time for the last few years while I was away.

"Hey John," yelled a thick New Jersey accent. "Come on in, we're fucking stuff up before the moveout." The six-and-a-half foot tall giant looked like Marine, holding a cigarette lighter in one hand and a bottle of beer in the other.

"Mad Max," I said. "Mad fuckin' Max. Glad I caught you before you left this pit."

I met Max in this same hallway almost three years ago, when he lived in a suite across from my room. He introduced himself as the resident non-freshman, and synthesized folklore about hazing rituals, urban legends and impossible professors. But during my first lonely experiences away from home, family, friends, and everything else I knew, he took me in as his disciple and educated me in the ways of the collegiate. We spent two semesters burning away late nights with deep discussion about music, hometowns, women, and stealing stuff from McDonald's. With cheap delivery pizzas and Cokes from the center store, his suite became a communal room where everyone from the hall would swap stories about their ex-girlfriends or escapades, and newcomers to any situation would come to ask questions about calculus, women, clothes, cars or life. Max helped me find things on campus, taught me how to make prank phone calls, and entertained me by heckling people from his second story window. His combination of humor and care helped me survive a difficult part of my life. Now, I lived off-campus, and he was loading his shit into cardboard boxes and moving back to New Jersey with a degree and no job.

"It's good to see you," he said, ushering me into his room. Boxes half-filled with books and clothes littered the floor, and the wooden closet looked half-disassembled, with toiletries and school supplies scattered on the floor. "Grab a seat if you can find one," he said. "Beer? I've gotta empty out this fucking fridge before my parents show up." He pulled an amber bottle from the fake-wood cube and tossed it to me.

"Thanks man," I said, grabbing the container. "Hey, isn't this a dry campus?" I joked.

"Fuck man, my RA is already in Kansas. I'm hoping somebody shows up and kicks me out."

"You did a good job of fixing this place up," I said.

"Yeah, I finished it just in time to tear it down and put it into boxes." He grabbed his beer from a dresser, took a drag, and sat on the bed. "That's the pisser about living in the dorms for five years—you never really live in them," he said. "You unpack your shit, sleep in a room for a few months, and then pack it up again."

I took a hit from the beer, and looked around the room in an uncomfortable silence, as Max dumped books and class notes into a box. "So, it's all over, huh?" I asked.

"I guess so," he said. "I didn't really expect it to end like this. I thought I'd stick with ROTC, be an Air Force pilot, get married, have a business degree. But shit, I'm single, I'm gonna be living in my mom's basement, with a management degree and no job." He stopped packing the books and took the last hit from his beer before grabbing another. "Fuck! You think about shit like that, and it'll really throw a wrench in you."

"No shit, that's all I've been doing lately." I took another pull of beer. "Right before I graduated high school, me and the folks drove down for one of those prospective freshman brainwashing sessions in the winter. You know, you take their tour, see a dorm room, eat lunch in a cafeteria, and get nothing but fucking chrome and polish from the tour guides. After that weekend, I felt like I'd be living the life of the coeds in that *Breaking Away* movie—all of the women would be wearing tight sweaters and coming over to my dorm to study, the guys would invite me to drink beer and watch football, and I'd meet hundreds of friends and date all kinds of women and eventually find one that I'd want to marry. I had such a strong image of the ideal woman in my head, and thought she'd cross my path after a year or two. And here I am, shuffling from one dating disaster to another. Shit, I just fucked up another relationship this week."

"What, that one chick you just started seeing? The music major?"

"Yeah, Tammy. It went okay for a couple of months, and it looked long term, but..." I swigged back more beer. "She's moving back to Pennsylvania for the summer and she wants a cease-fire until fall, because of the distance thing."

"You seeing her this summer?"

"Probably not. My car won't make the trip, and she can't afford to fly back or anything."

"That blows. At least you can fuck around for a few months. You moving back to Elkhart again?"

"Nope," I said. "I couldn't deal with this split and my parents too. I'll be here, taking classes both sessions."

"That's cool. You'll dig it here in the summer," he said. "Hey dude, I have this tape of these guys in New York, they recorded all of these prank calls. Real works of art, better than the shit we used to do" Max said. He set down the sticks and went to the stereo, stopped the CD and put in a tape.

"Yeah, auto mechanic! Lookin' for a job!" The thick New York accent cut through the poor recording, dozens of generations of noise and static distorting the phone call. The person on the other line, some Indian-sounding guy at a mechanic's office, asked "You have experience?" and got the excited reply of, "Seven years! I work on racecars!" After the office asked where the prankster currently worked, he said, "Right now, I just had to leave a job because of my FUCKING boss!" While Max and I rolled in laughter, the band of three misfits called NYC businesses asking about jobs, complaining about bad pizza, or griping about fictitious, outlandish counts of poor service.

The level of insanity and humor topped Max's wild antics, which included trying to rob a pizza joint over the phone, pretending to be his suitemate's academic advisor and then hitting on him, and conducting fake condom surveys to random phone numbers. Several years later, I'd find out the tape contained the raw versions of the first two Jerky Boys albums, uncensored and uncut. After we heard a few calls, he popped in a blank tape and high-speed dubbed the whole thing for me.

We chatted more, and fell back into the pattern of staggering discussion we followed during late nights during the school year. We always babbled about non sequiturs, going from our pasts to the future to the obvious. These rings of discourse often had me explaining all about my family, life in Elkhart as a kid, distant memories I had almost forgotten, and what I thought of college so far. It also taught me about Max's life in Jersey, his family, stories of a summer on the road with a drum corps and ROTC tales. Often, others would join in on the speech marathons; suitemate Paul told stories of living in Germany as Ian from down the hall combated this with tales of Paris; the other suitemate Markus discussed Judaism versus Christianity, amidst heavily falsified tales of one night stands. The stories always integrated around TV shows, visits from other people and fast food deliveries, but kept going well into the night.

After another hour of rambling and prank calls on tape, I announced I had to split and let him continue his cleaning tasks. "That's cool dude, if you're ever in Jersey, look me up. Call my mom's, she will probably know where I am if I'm not still living in her basement."

Max scribbled down an address and phone for his mother's house and promised to get ahold of me after he got settled in. I left him hauling the remainder of his perishables to the incinerator chute and scuffled down the stairs to the courtyard. I knew I'd never make it to Jersey. It felt like visiting a favorite restaurant that would be closing forever. Mad Max. Mad fuckin' Max.

Commotion and chaos still filled the dorm courtyard as parents fist-fought over parking spaces and bitched at kids for having beer in their fridges. It reminded me of my escape from campus after my freshman year: a four hour lecture about my moral and academic shortcomings, followed by a summer of slave labor at an ungodly hour of the morning. That was nothing compared to spending the next year living in my mom's basement and driving 45 minutes each way to a commuter college. And I took some pleasure in knowing I wouldn't have to pack, move, and unpack everything I owned two times this year.

The goodbye with Max stuck in my head like a bad lunch in my stomach. I hated good-byes and funerals because they always seemed like emotional busy work to me. Long ago, I accepted the fact that I'd never be living around the same people for the rest of my life. Worrying when a person left was something for people who lived in one-horse towns. In college, everyone moved every semester. My address book became obsolete after every semester, because every single phone number changed. And some of my mail showed up with layers of yellow address-correction labels half an inch thick. Thinking about all of the people coming and going would blow my mind ten times over. At the end of every semester, or any other time people drifted from my life, all I did was hope I'd cross paths with them again in this tiny world. It's all you can do, really.

Before I even left the courtyard, my mind shifted from thoughts of Max to everything else that happened that week, the turmoil of the bigger goodbye with Tammy. I'd hoped a few minutes of Max's antics would ease the depression for a while. It helped, but I knew it would take a bigger diversion to put all of this behind me.

I crossed the traffic light and headed back up the hill on Woodlawn, toward my car. During the uphill walk, I heard a familiar voice yell at me from the sorority house on the corner. "John! John Conner!" In the parking lot of a sorority house, I saw my friend Tricia, wearing a baggy sorority sweatshirt with her long, thick, brunette hair in a ponytail. The huge trunk and doors of her powder blue Mercedes were propped open, with the interior packed full of boxes.

I walked to her car and wrapped my arms around her. The warmth in her touch calmed me, the smell of perfume in her hair and her sweater pressing against me. For half a second, I almost forgot about everything that happened that week, and bathed in the comfort of her embrace.

"I'm really glad I caught you." I said.

"It's good to see you," she said. "I haven't talked to you all week! What's been up? Is Tammy still around?" Tricia met me during the worst of my depression and slowly nursed me back into the dating game. Since I was her pet cause, she held a strong vested interest in my relationship with Tammy.

"Actually, no," I said. "We sort of broke up last night."

"Oh my god, what happened?"

"Well, we sort of split for the summer," I said. "She'll be gone, and we don't want to kill each other with the long distance thing..."

"I knew you were completely in love with this one...What's the real story? Is it her or you?"

"I...I don't know." I paused for a second, and tried to hold back the stock answer I'd been repeating all day. "It's her. She wanted to split up, just for the break. I don't know what to believe. I want to believe her, wait out the summer, and get back together in the fall. But you know how I handle these things. I really do love her, but I don't know how I can live without her."

She grabbed my hand and held it tight. "John, I don't know what to tell you. I know you deserve to find someone who loves you, but I also know everything you've gone through with women lately. I don't like to see you upset about this, you've been doing so well since you met her," she said. "I hope she comes back to you...or I hope something else happens this summer. There are a lot of women out there, John..." She smiled, and messed up my hair with her free hand. "Hey, when are you moving back to Elkhart?" she asked.

"I'm not," I said. "I can't find a sublettor, and I need some classes because I'm flunking out, so I decided to stay."

"That's good! You'll like it here in the summer, I was here last year. It'll help you get through this. The summers are different here. Lots of beautiful babes in shorts to keep you busy..."

"Yeah, yeah," I said. "When are you leaving for Europe?" I asked. She landed an internship as a flight attendant for an airline based in the UK, and would be spending the summer working all over the continent.

"I'll be home for a week, then I fly over. I'm so excited about going out there!" she said. "I'll be back here the week before classes."

"Well, send me a postcard. You've got my address."

"Okay, I will. She gave me a hug again, and held me tight. "Hang in there this summer, okay? I'll really miss you and worry about you, but I won't be able to help you out like this semester. I'll be back in August, okay?"

"Okay, I'll try not to shoot up any fast food restaurants," I joked.

She gave me a friendly kiss on the cheek as she released the hug. "I do worry about you. Will you be good?"

"I'll try."

"Promise?"

"Promise I'll try. You know my luck with women."

"Yes I do. Just be careful. Bye John."

"Bye Tricia. Good luck this summer."

"You too!"

I left Tricia to her packing and kept heading up the hill to find my car. Tricia helped me so much last semester with my depression, and now that everything was hitting the fan at the same time, she was gone. I'm gonna miss her, I thought.

2

The boxy VW slept on the shoulder of a side street ahead, waiting for my return. I opened the thin door and climbed into the cockpit, an almost toyish blue interior worn and faded from years of roadtrips and sunlight. The diesel glow plugs lit with the turn of the key, and I waited for a dash light to go out so I could crank the engine. I clicked the blue-gray seat belt in place, and slapped Max's tape into the stereo. Maybe the offbeat humor would distract me from the day's morbidity, I thought. Even with the volume cranked, it was hard to discern the crackling and distorted voices on the tenth-generation copy. Better than nothing, though. The engine burst to life when I turned the key, and I pulled onto the road heading east through the heart of the university.

The drive across campus felt like a trip through South Vietnam, 1975. Trucks full of furniture blocked the roads, U-Hauls and Ryders circling lost or ignoring the maze of one way streets and navigating with pure anarchy. A clusterfuck of people without cars ran down sidewalks carrying boxes and lofts, trying to move from dorm to summer sublet on foot. The people who flew home couldn't take more than luggage on the plane, and gave away refrigerators, old TVs, secondhand couches, and rugs, or threw them into overfilled dumpsters. People scrambled to take everything they could and destroy everything else, before the dorms locked down for the summer.

The desperation of people trying to be anywhere but on campus pulled the happiness and energy of spring from the air. I imagined being one of the Vietnamese who stayed in Saigon and watched American GIs burning

US Embassy records en masse and pushing helicopters off the decks of aircraft carriers. People were almost killing themselves to leave the same place I would call home for the next few months. Every other year, I was filling nail holes with toothpaste and selling hundred dollar bookcases for five bucks. But this time, I'd be cruising the dumpsters for a new stereo.

Past the Main Library, I hung a right down Jordan Street, one of the main thoroughfares of campus, and headed toward my apartment. Big mistake—campus police with batons waved traffic through the intersection of Seventh and Jordan, causing more pile-ups and slowdowns than they prevented. In the long line of cars, my mind burned with the feeling of desolation. Soon, there would be parties, sunny days, cool nights, easy classes, women, friends, and everything else I hoped for in a summer. But right now, all of the people moving away just reminded me of Tammy.

Gravel crunched under the tires as I guided the VW from Mitchell Street to the wide driveway in front of my apartment. I lived in a monstrosity of a house, cobbled together from what looked like spare pieces of several demolished structures added to the side of an older condemned duplex and coated with a sickly gray paint. The architectural catastrophe held eleven people in dorm-sized rooms with twenty-year-old paneling and firewood quality, third-hand furniture covered with dozens of layers of paint barely covering deep gashes and scars. Everyone shared three unsterile bathrooms with leaky plumbing and broken mirrors, and two communal kitchens, with 1950's appliances encrusted in grease and filth. The house had no other common areas or living rooms; every square foot other than the bathrooms, kitchens and hallways had been converted into sleeping quarters.

Today, half of the tenants loaded their cars and went AWOL. The boardinghouse contract forced people to pay three months of rent in advance, an open invitation for people to abandon their rooms for the last quarter of their lease. This worked to my advantage, since three months of paid rent meant I could stay in town with almost no income. And because utilities were included with the rooms, I only had to scrape together the cash for food, the phone bill, and keeping the VW in one piece. If I could hold any part-time job, it would mean money in the bank.

Walking to the front door, I saw my roommate Deon, a huge black guy that looked like a former linebacker that now spent his time telling goofy stories and walking around with a perpetual grin on his face. "Hey John, I thought you were moving home or something," he yelled from the alcove just inside the front door.

"No, I'll be here for the summer." I opened the squeaky door and entered the alcove. "I'm going home tomorrow for a visit, but I'll be back Sunday night." I looked through a pile of mail on a shelf for recent deliveries, finding nothing but junk mail and "Have you seen this child?" fliers.

"Right on! We can hang out this summer, drink some beers. This house gets hotter than hell, but we'll find some cool parties."

"Hey man, you got like 100 CDs, but I sold them all and bought some ganja," echoed a voice from behind me. Yehoshua tumbled down the stairs, a blur of long hair and thin, gangly limbs. "Just kidding man," he said. "Don't kill me or anything." Yehoshua lived upstairs; he studied guitar in the music school, and stayed randomly employed. The name sounded foreign, but he was really just a white hippie-freak from Indianapolis. His main hobbies besides jazz guitar were drinking forties of cheap beer and bumming pot from other people in the music school. Like a Kramer with long hair, he provided humor, strange conversation, and a constant burden on my grocery bill.

"Hey man, when are you moving?" Yehoshua asked in his slow, perpetually stoned voice. "Can I have your room?"

"I'm not leaving. I'm going home for a couple of days, but I'll be here all summer."

"Far out, maybe we can drink some beers or something."

"Sounds cool," I said. I ducked past Yehoshua to get to my room at the end of the hall. One of four fridges stood outside my bedroom, and I opened its grimy brown door and pulled out a can of Coke before fumbling with keys and opening my room.

"Hey man, is Tammy staying here this summer?" Yehoshua asked.

"No, she's back East," I told him, setting my stuff down in the room.

"Is she coming back? Are you going to visit her and shit?" asked Deon.

"Probably not. We sort of broke up last night."

"No way! What happened?" he asked.

"I don't wanna go into it right now. Hey, I'll catch you guys later with the full details," I mumbled. "I need to crash or something," I said, shutting the door behind me.

I hit the lights, and a pair of overhead fluorescent tubes bombed me with eerie fake-light illumination, like a 7-Eleven at three in the morning. Two dissimilar spaces formed the room: a large, square area with a high ceiling and a long but thin rectangular piece joining on one of its small sides. Because the house had been a family duplex, a big house, an apartment building, and who knows what else in the last few decades, most of the rooms were cobbled together with disparate pieces of other rooms, hence the two ceiling heights in my small abode.

The square piece functioned as an office/living room. On a card table, my computer, dishes from my last weeks' meals, and several dozen empties formed the nucleus of my working life. To the right of the table, a bookcase held a few dozen computer manuals and texts I couldn't sell back to the bookstore, plus a Kenwood stereo and about 100 CDs. The square part of the room also housed milk crates full of food I didn't want Yehoshua to steal, cassettes, homework, more dirty dishes, and everything else I owned, which wasn't much. The narrow rectangle served as my living/sleeping quarters. A twin bed set on blocks wedged between the walls almost perfectly, blocking a doorless closet full of dirty laundry. A beaten and worn dresser stood next to the bed, and also functioned as a vanity.

The air in the room broiled during the day, and made me wonder how I'd survive a summer in the tiny closet of a bedroom. I went to the window by the bookcase, and turned on the box fan to get air circulating again. With considerable force, I pried open the smaller window near the bed.

I sat at the command console, the captain's chair of the room, and fired up the computer, a Frankenstein beast parted together from used pieces bought over the last year. After the squeal of a modem yielded a solid connection to the university, I logged on and checked my account for anything new and interesting. I found no new mail, no friends online, and less than 30 people using the VAXcluster, the five central machines that usually housed over five hundred active logins at a time during a busy day of the school year. No solace here, I thought, logging off and shutting down the PC.

I dug my wallet out of my pants, and checked my cash situation: thirty seven dollars and a pocketful of change. Lunch came and went during the confusion today, and I realized I hadn't eaten anything in 24 hours, unless Max's beer counted as food. Aside from picking up dinner, I'd need to fuel up the Rabbit for tomorrow's trip north. I cringed when I thought about the visit to my parents: driving 250 miles to get in an argument. Fuck. I turned off the lights, and hit the door for a run to McDonald's.

The VW spun down Third Street, now back to the cool traffic levels of a typical Friday night in Bloomington. I cruised toward the mall and thought more about how weird it was to be in Bloomington during a summer. The year before, I dated someone in town when I was living in my mom's basement in Elkhart. Every time I stole away for a weekend and took the roadtrip to campus, it felt like I entered some kind of wormhole or holodeck fantasy. For weeks, I'd be hunched over a punch press in my grimy work clothes, working on the line with a bunch of union-member codgers. Six hours later, like a jail break, I'd be in a Denny's, wearing a t-shirt of Bart Simpson smoking a bong and surrounded by young, cool, hip college students. It always felt so good, the feeling that I didn't belong—almost like wandering through a dream. Then on Monday morning, I'd return to my life of packing copper pipe fittings in boxes.

I went to a McDonald's equidistant from the highway entrance, in hopes of avoiding any U-Hauls and family gatherings. My hunch proved correct—the restaurant was almost dead, and I didn't attract stares as I gulped down a quarter pounder meal alone. The food tasted great after a day of starvation, but I couldn't take my mind off the strange feeling of displacement I felt by staying on campus. Maybe once classes and work started and I got into a routine, it wouldn't feel so alien. Then again, living on a campus designed for 35,000 and occupied by 5,000 would always feel more than weird.

My scheme ran through my mind all week, the plan I formulated to survive the summer. Tomorrow, I'd need to justify myself to my mom, explain how I'd survive and why I wasn't returning. No matter how many times I repeated the story to myself, I knew the slightest problem would throw it all off course. I inhaled the last of my fries and took a long drag off the large Coke while thinking of this, running through the script in my mind. I kept repeating it to myself because I thought it would work. But the worst contingency had already happened—Tammy left. How the fuck would I pull this off?

I gathered my pile of nonbiodegradable packaging, threw it in the garbage, and wandered the dusk-lit streets in the VW. Sleeping tonight will be an exercise in futility, I thought. I contemplated picking up a cold six and a bottle of sleeping pills, but decided to head home.

2:47 AM. The clock's bastard face taunted me as I turned sleepless in the bed. I knew this wouldn't be easy. Thoughts about every facet of my life tore through my head: money, love, parents, school, everything. I knew if I didn't get in a few hours of sleep before 9 AM, I'd spend the afternoon nodding off during the drive north. But I still couldn't let go, even for a few minutes. Fuck it. I got out of bed, quickly dressed, grabbed my wallet and keys, and left the house for a walk.

The late-night walks were a tradition of mine over the last year. Insomnia possessed me almost every evening, and weather permitting, I'd stray the campus to kill time. Sometimes I'd stop in the computer lab to check my email, or swing past the Village Pantry on Third and Jordan to grab a snack. Other walks had no destination, and I'd wander in depression for hours. The cool air and barren desolation of the early morning were a better place to let thoughts race through my mind than my claustrophobic bedroom.

It was easier to stay awake all night when my depression was heaviest, do some work on the computer, and then skip classes and sleep through the next day. The swarms of people on campus all morning and afternoon killed me—people with their lives in line, pushing to graduate in three years and kill everyone in their path. I needed to be away from them, hidden in the darkness of my apartment with only the computer tying me to reality. But at three or four in the morning, the power students went to sleep, and I owned the campus. I could got to the corner store, buy a Coke and a hot dog, and sit on the limestone steps of some huge abandoned building by myself.

When depressed and alone, I could revel in the emptiness, the suicidal isolation of nothing and nobody. I could play and replay the hurt and savor in the bitterness. Even though I didn't want to be depressed, I somehow felt the need to take the long journeys and think of nothing except my short-term failures. I hated life, and the night was as far from life as I could be.

I carried a walkman with me at all times I wasn't driving—the Conner sound system. I'd listen to Death Metal as loud as the Aiwa tape player would pump it into my ear canals. Morbid Angel, Dismember, Obituary, Terrorizer, Entombed, whatever kept me in my own world became my personal soundtrack. But sometimes at night, I'd save my batteries and listen to nothing. The sounds of the vacant campus, mixed with my own thoughts of misery propelled my steps.

I crossed Atwater and cut through the parking lot behind the Chinese grocery. This was my first long walk since she left. I had a feeling I'd be taking many more over the course of the summer. When Tammy came into my life, I got back into the regular schedule for a while. She'd stay over, and I'd wake at the crack of dawn to bring her back to her dorm for breakfast. Sometimes I'd go back to bed for a few more hours, but other times, I'd stay up and start my day at 6 AM. At the latest, I'd end up awake and functional before noon. But now, depression and insomnia would relapse the missed classes, missed work, and more missed sleep as the shoebox apartment roasted in the summer daytime heat.

I slipped past the pizza places and down a long alley, next to Aristotle's books. I knew this walk so well, the few blocks between the house and the campus. I walked through this pass every day, every night. It looked different in darkness, more solitary, but felt the same under my feet.

Third Street. Third and Jordan, Village Pantry, and the Monroe County Bank ATM were all landmarks I saw more than my own bed. The green and red Papa John's Pizza sign blazed over the parking lot, but inside, a lone clerk scrubbed the ovens and prepared to close for the night. Even pizza sleeps. I walked through the middle of the intersection, the red and yellow lights blinking in the signals above my head, and headed north on Jordan.

Ten minutes later, past the soon-to-be-decommissioned Education building, the Musical Arts Center, and Read quad, I passed Seventh and Jordan. In front of me: the Main Library, an unprecedented pile of limestone, usually lit by Bat-signal-like spotlights until midnight. Now, in resting, it looked like some kind of Stanley Kubrick-designed obelisk, with only a few lights glimmering on the first floor. An eleven-story block on the right made up the graduate stacks, and met with a smaller and more rectangular block of stone on the left, the undergraduate library. I scaled the mountain of steps at the back entrance, leading to the main lobby between the two pieces.

The glass doors opened to the lobby, a Valhalla-sized hall filled with wooden study tables and chairs older than time. Typically crammed with hundreds of grad students researching papers, fraternity pledges at study tables, and undergrads locked into all-night study sessions, tonight the lobby only housed a few transient students sleeping on the benches against each wall.

I took a left and went to Lib102A, the 24 hour PC lab. Under harsh fluorescent lighting, a handful of people checked email or played games sans consultant supervision. I scanned the room, and found my pal Eric Fournier hunched over a Zenith keyboard, madly working on something. Eric was a straight-laced finance major who decided in his last year to teach himself everything about programming, and as a result, turned into a coding machine. While dealing with 400-level business courses during the day and working for University Computing Services in the evening, he spent his sleep time hacking away at the C programming language on a unix box or the VAX cluster. I snagged the machine next to him, to sneak a peek at his latest project.

"Hey Eric, happy hacking?"

"As happy as you can get in VAX Pascal," he said, rubbing his reddened eyes. "I'm working on an NNTP newsreader for VMS that isn't as brain-dead as CNEWS. Check this out..." He pulled up a session, typed a few keystrokes, and ran the program. "It's just handshaking with the news server, then pulling in headers on a bunch of groups and displaying them in TPU. I've still got a lot of work done, but at least they're talking to each other." I tried to hide my amazement at the hack that I always wanted to do, but deemed too insane and time-intensive.

"So are you staying this summer or not?" he asked, still staring at his code and typing. "I got your junk mail saying you were leaving, but you're still here."

I fired up a telnet session at my computer. "Yeah, I'm here, both summer sessions. I had a last-second change in plans. You?"

"My four years are up—Disneyland is over. I have a couple of finance job leads, but I'm trying to find a consulting firm that will take me with no computer degree and no experience."

"You know COBOL?"

"That's not funny, man."

I logged on to see what was going on. No new mail. Nobody on except Eric and me. Absolutely no concentration or patience to sit down and hack C code for a few minutes or hours.

"Shit, there's nothing going on," I said.

"You didn't have to get out of bed and come here to find that out," he said.

"Speaking of which, I've gotta get some sleep, dude. I'm driving to Elkhart tomorrow morning."

"You mean this morning."

"Don't fuck with me man. I'll catch you later."

"Later," he said, waving bye without moving his eyes from the monitor.

The light switch clicked off, and the overhead fluorescents flickered to a deep sleep, leaving only a faint 40-watt glow in the corner of the room. Tripping through the darkness with a plastic tumbler of fresh water, I sifted toward the light, on top of the chest of drawers. On top of the dresser, stripped of paint from years of abuse, lived the remnants of my daily routines: change, keys, ticket stubs, floppy discs, deodorant, prescription bottles, and the minimalist hair care products a guy with a no-style shoulder-length mane of hair needs to face to world every day.

A cracked piece of mirror screwed the paneling wall leaked a weary image of the stranger rummaging with hairbrush, then throwing wallet, spare change, and keys into a plastic tray. I looked up at the reflection and smirked. "Glad to see you haven't left, too."

I pulled a plastic prescription bottle from the dresser and push-twisted open the lid. Tipping back two lithium tablets, I knocked them back with the cool water from the glass. Twice a day, every day for the last three years, I thought. I've changed cities, majors, cars, women, diets, jobs, religions and hobbies, but I've always had the same diagnosis.

Then she looked back at me. Her picture. I pulled the three by five snapshot from the mirror, something I'd forgotten to hide, remove or return since she left that morning. The photo became part of my daily routine in the last few months. When she was at class, I'd stare at it for hours, prying apart every detail of the image. I'd imagine the smell of the red on white Indiana sweater, the feel of her hair, the hug I'd give her if she really existed in front of me. I'd cherish the photo when she wasn't with me, knowing she'd be in bed in the same dorm room, sleeping before her early morning classes. And I'd sleep, pretending she was still with me.

And I still did. As I held the picture under the dim desk lamp, I wondered what she thought now. Was I still in her dreams?

I carefully set the photo on the dresser of junk, and crawled to bed. The events of the day, the week cycled through my head, faster and faster. None of it made sense. None of it would ever make sense.

After clicking off the light, I stared into the darkness, no longer mentally tired. My body still felt underwater, sunken from a day of extreme depression and grief. And when my thoughts weren't focusing and refocusing and repeating on her, they moved to tomorrow's mission of returning home, or my summer plans, or a thousand other issues and problems. In a few hours, I'd have to emerge from bed and drive hundreds of miles in the battered VW to face a chaotic and unnerving scenario with my parents. And I knew I needed to be awake for it. But that wouldn't make me sleep.

The alarm nagged and buzzed for what seemed like hours. I rose from the bed just before nine and beat the clock back into silence. The semester of missed classes and night shifts at work did nothing to condition me for the ritual wakeup at an hour any earlier than two or three in the afternoon, but today I had to get moving and point the car north toward my Mom's house. I never looked forward to the four-hour drive, and since this short visit would be filled with lectures and arguments, it felt more like a trip to the gallows pole.

After trying to rinse the sleep out of my head with a quick shower, I turned on the stereo and stumbled around the small room, packing a weekend's worth of supplies into a gray gym bag. As a Rush CD spun away, Geddy Lee's voice singing about New World Men, I went through a mental checklist of what to bring. A couple pair of jeans, shorts just in case it warmed up...all of them went from dresser to bag. A nice shirt, from the closet, and a couple of black t-shirts to wear when hanging out, also went in the bag, along with a few pair of underwear and socks. Cologne and hairbrush from the dresser, toothbrush shampoo from my toiletries, all fit in the side pockets of the satchel. And just in case, I grabbed a handful of evil and offensive CDs from the stereo, for good luck. I checked my email, grabbed a pillow and a few tapes with my gym bag and headed down the long corridor to the front door, to board my car and leave for the north.

3

A thin mist covered the morning, droplets of haze teasing the air as the crimson morning sun awakened. Rays of spring ignited the green-speckled gold and brown fields of southern Indiana, the thick hedges of hearty forest dividing the valleys of farmers' crops from the ridges and foothills in the distance. Twin ribbons of asphalt twisted through the terrain, following the gentle creases to cut through the state map.

My battered VW buzzed northward on State Road 37, toward my first stop, Indianapolis. Before departing, I wiped the May dew from the windows, and arranged my cargo in the compartment, in a meticulous layout. A large pile of random cassettes rode on the passenger seat, accessible with ease while driving at high speed. My light jacket rested on the floor and the gym bag of supplies slept in the rear hatch. The task of arranging the small Mercury capsule of a car for the voyage seemed secondhand, after so many trips to Bloomington last summer.

Elletsville crept past, a tiny city only a dozen miles outside of Bloomington. The tiny four-cylinder engine whirred with smooth precision at high RPM, pulling the rusty box up the blacktop slopes. The VW revved too high, with a four-speed transmission that felt like a five speed with a missing top gear. With practice, I found I could push the car well above the speed limit by building momentum and blocking fears that the high-whining engine would explode. Last fall, the oil rings failed and the engine did explode, which didn't help my paranoia. But now, with a new rebuild on the old engine, I felt safe pushing it to a high whir.

A cheap tape-only deck sat in a too-big hole in the faded blue dash. The ugly but functional black box churned the Dead Kennedys tape *Give Me Convenience or Give Me Death*. The hour-long compilation of the old punk band's songs drowned most of the road noises and hypnotized me with memories and energy of a period several years before, when the band was new to me and I spent a whole summer devouring their stuff. The music made the road scroll past my windows faster, the grinding guitars and funny satire biding my time.

The driving became more monotonous, the straight road ahead putting my mind on autopilot. My thoughts wandered from the current tape in the deck and the scenery around me, and back to the situation with Tammy. Still confused and overloaded from the events of the week before, I couldn't focus on anything else, no matter what loud and offensive cassette ran through the car's sound system. Thoughts of seeing my friends Peter and Nick, daydreams of summer, and mirages of computer code didn't block the pain, depression and anxiety etched into my mind. I tried to make sense of the jumble of images of my relationship with her, to find a way to deal with it, but I couldn't. Flashbacks of her invaded every waking moment alone. I wanted to figure out if it was my fault, or otherwise come to some sort of closure. With another four hours of isolation in the Volkswagen's cockpit ahead of me, I decided to replay all of it from start to finish, a painful exercise in self-analysis, a jury trial of one to investigate what really happened.

It all started that spring. A turgid and destructive relationship with a snooty pianist named Lauren consumed the prior year, and broke apart right after Christmas. The fiasco started as a one-night stand and evolved into a yearlong nightmare of arguments, misunderstandings and infidelity. The last few months featured nightly shouting matches, both of us threatening to leave forever and then somehow getting things back to a neutral point before the evening's end. After a messy split, I spent a month engaged in mind games with her, wasting my limited energy and wearing down my patience with human beings. During the pitiful battles, I locked my email account so anyone but her could send me mail. It pissed her off that she couldn't send me hourly messages telling me what a jerk I was, and she stopped talking to me entirely.

After things cooled down, I conducted my first experiments in alcohol abuse as a coping tool. January brought my 21st birthday, and for the first time, I could legally buy booze on demand, no questions asked. I found that drinking alone, while not a socially acceptable behavior, distracted me from the post-breakup solitude. When I eased up from the bottle, the loneliness kicked in. The lack of a daily routine with a partner created a hole in my life I couldn't fill with classwork, friends, or alcohol. I missed having a default person to spend my time with, even if their daily activities included throwing all of my shit out of a third story window until the cops showed up.

Despite my obvious esteem issues, I started the alien procedure of casual dating with a series of drive-by relationships, trying to meet as many women as I could. With the aid of the computer and friends who set me up with random matches, I talked to a dozen women a week and made informal dates with half of them, for meetings on campus, for lunch, or over coffee. I spent countless hours on the phone, talking to a voice and hoping it would be a go. Usually it wasn't; she'd be into dropping LSD daily, or had an old boyfriend she was perpetually in love with, or only liked the underwear ad fashion model types, or would have some other fatal flaw. And although I mastered the casual telephone conversation with women, I failed miserably in person due to bad karma.

The more times I got shot down, the faster I evaluated potential match-ups. The information flowed through my head like a giant IBM computer scanning job applications: age, major, hometown, grades, experiences, family, religion, interests, charisma, looks, sexual experience, musical tastes, favorite foods, allergies, hobbies. As I spent time in the standard phone conversation with a new woman, I'd pry the questions from our talk, like a psychiatrist checking through the DSM-3R to categorize a new patient. The statistics ran through a complicated equation, and within seconds, I'd hit a result: yes or no, in our out, sink or swim. As the cynicism built, the equation changed, and my answers always came up negative. I would always spot a flaw within a few moments of evaluation and give up before hurting myself more.

This game consumed my life, and I started theorizing ways to change the odds by changing myself. Maybe I was the problem. Maybe I needed to wallpaper my real feelings, emotions, or appearance long enough to attract a woman. So the numbers started churning, as I thought of possibilities for modification. Should I be a nice guy? A gigolo? A friend? Friends first, then date? Just go for it? Ask out strangers? Friends? Classmates? Coworkers? Dress casual? Hip? Expensive? Punk? Crossdress? Grow my hair? Cut it off? Light it on fire? Date one woman? Date many? Fuck many? Stay monogamous? Keep celibate? Cut off my penis and just get it over with? Add salt petre to my food so my hormones would go away? Move to the middle of Idaho and never be heard from again? The endless nights of critical self-analysis and destruction drove me further into depression and loneliness.

And as I plunged further into solitude, I tried harder to escape. I spent time in therapy, got my psychiatrist to increase my lithium levels, and read dozens of self-help books. But when I tried to keep going, I tried too hard, and faced more failures and rejection, slipping even further into depression. My desolation got worse, and I pass my time drinking away the pain. After many a failed date, I'd the night alone in my tiny apartment, slamming beers or shots of rum, repeating mantras about why it was all so unfair. But the next day, I'd be back to looking, because if I never looked, I'd never find. And it felt vaguely more productive than spending the weekends alone.

This cycle of death led to a Saturday night, a week before spring break, where I found myself driving to the library at 10 PM. I had a date like most others that spring. It involved me making dinner, and then the conversation floundering to the point of mutually assured destruction. I got her back to her dorm before the food even cooled off. With the rest of the evening to kill, I went to the library to mope on a computer and hope for someone to entertain me.

The library's giant and empty lobbies served as a painful reminder that most people had lives away from school, and didn't spend Saturday nights in front of a computer. When I got to a PC, my list of friends online came up completely blank, so I scanned and re-scanned the full list of users online for anyone who might be interesting to talk to. The high tech equivalent to looking at a phone book for interesting names to dial at random, the scanning of people logged on turned up usernames of people who were awake and maybe as bored as me.

After hours of nothing, I started talking to someone. Her name was Tammy, and she was killing time, playing on the computer in her dorm while her friend typed a paper. The conversation spooled out, and we chatted for hours. She had to leave with her friend, but I convinced her to call me at home. I rushed back to my apartment, and by 4 AM, we were talking on the phone and enjoying ourselves. We joked, chatted, and I invited her to breakfast with me that morning (which was now only a few hours away.) She agreed, and we planned to both get to sleep and hook up for breakfast at my place in about three hours. And that's how I got my first date with Tammy.

In the distance, a tall red and white striped smokestack pointed up from the hills, breaking the dreary horizon of trees and hills. Indianapolis—the colossal needle jutted up from the southern industrial area of the city, part of town inhabited only by industry. City-sized truck stops filled the region, with slogans like "clean showers" and "trailer drop off" on their billboards. Fuel price signs with the disclaimer "tax-exempt only" lined the highway, as did giant diesel tanks, storage buildings holding entire armies inside their corrugated aluminum walls, and warehouse sized diners that advertised their pancakes on fifty foot high signs. I seldom ventured off the main roads in this part of Indianapolis, but then I almost never went anywhere in the city. Just a giant tree in my way, Indy was an obstacle I had to circumvent to get up to US 31.

37 climbed its last hill to a clover with I-465, the six-lane loop around the city. Before the graft with 465, I stopped at a monolithic truck stop to fill the tank with some lower-priced fuel. With only two places selling diesel in Bloomington, the prices were jacked to extraordinary levels. The truck stop fuel would be cheaper because of volume and competition, even if I did have to pay tax on it. When I pulled the tiny, boxy Rabbit to the pumps, it sat next to a towering semi truck, the roof of my car below the running boards of the semi. The awning over the fuel island hovered twenty feet above my car, and the hoses on the pumps stretched four or five times longer than the length of the VW. The tiny silver machine looked like an HO scale truck on an O scale train set, and it was unbelievable that both the giant Mack truck and my baby German toy ran on the same fuel.

I filled up the car, the high-pressure pump spewing eight gallons into the thimble of a tank in a matter of seconds. Inside, I paid the cashier and went to use the restroom before refueling myself with another Coke. An arsenal of CB radios, radar detectors, car parts, fluids, cleaners, oils, food of every sort, drinks and sodas and teas and coffees in a wall-to-wall icehouse, books, tapes, books on tape, bumper stickers, soaps, shampoos, and almost anything that someone on the road might need lined the walls of the store. Dean Moriarty would've been impressed.

On the way out, the sun broke into view, and approached the crest of the sky. The cheerful glow made it feel good to whip the car through the maze of on-ramps to the interstate for the navigation around the city. Quiet traffic, nice weather, a full tank of diesel, a Coke at my side and smooth six lane highways would make the trip almost automatic. I made the final merge, looked ahead, and drifted back to my daydream.

After sleeping an hour the Saturday night I first talked to Tammy, I woke up in excitement, and launched into house preparation mode for our impromptu meeting. My head thick with sleep, I showered at lightning speed, then dressed and cracked the room back into A-1 shape for her visit. Most days, I slept 10 hours and then felt too lazy to go to class, but after sixty minutes of slumber, I surged with energy. She called to announce her readiness, and after a few moments of conversation, I bolted to the car for the rendezvous.

With the tragedy of the previous night still fresh in my mind, I didn't know what to expect from the meeting. As I drove the few blocks to her dorm, my mind raced through the possibilities, imagining everything from a perfect woman to another psychotic episode only humorous after 10 years of pain. When I pulled into the lot, I saw a young brunette with shoulder length hair, medium height, dressed in a casual sweatshirt and jeans, patiently waiting under the awning of the women's' dorm. I still remember her innocent gaze and warm smile, the positive aura of the little girl cuteness in her face mixed with the prompt and anxious excitement of the situation. Without doubt, I thought this was IT, the soulmate I had been spending the last decade wishing for. My usual formulas of evaluation and rejection spun in my head, and for the first time, the equation produced a resounding yes. The look, her walk, her face, the phone conversation, her voice, and everything else made me think, for the first time in a long time, that it was a definite in.

We drove back to my house in nervous conversation, and I tried to whip together a functional breakfast with the little amount of food I possessed. Scrambled eggs, toast, milk and even some bacon graced the kitchen that morning, with my flatware and nice plates on the table. She looked angelic sitting at my kitchen table, watching me cook at my worn and grease-encrusted stove. She giggled shyly as I joked about the ancient appliances, trying to look knowledgeable as I pushed around the yellow scrambled egg mush with a spatula and stumbled with the pots and pans in the random cooking area. I apologized for the shoddy facilities, but she didn't seem to mind.

We sat across from each other at the Formica table, picking at the food as I tried to keep the conversation going. She stayed quiet and shy, gracefully hiding her smile and listening to my stories. But when she talked, she sounded articulate and levelheaded, instead of nervous or remissive. I felt that her shyness was not because of bashfulness or insecurity, but because of a sense of awe or respect. It was a situation unlike most I'd been in, where the female had absolutely no regard for me and I had to fester for some sort of stability to keep the date going through the evening. With her, things flowed. It felt natural.

After we finished eating, I rinsed the plates and suggested we go for a walk. A beautiful sunny March day graced the campus, with a cool breeze, bright blue skies and only a few puffy white clouds in the distance. It seemed like a perfect way to spend more time with her, talk for a while, and do something that didn't involve my house. As we started down my street, our arms awkwardly collided, and I pulled her hand to mine. My nervousness faded as she looked up and smiled, and we strolled down the road, hand in hand. I didn't know if things would become romantic with her or if she was just one of those people who casually held hands with anyone, but because of her shy, reserved behavior, I assumed she liked me.

We spent the day wandering across campus, playing with the computers in one of the labs in the Student Building and enjoying the beautiful sun and breeze of the afternoon. Our walk looped through the brick sidewalks weaving around the old crescent of buildings on campus. Thick green grass pulling upward in the sun surrounded the old limestone castles, with hundreds of colorful, blooming flowers everywhere.

Eventually, we wandered back to my house, and decided to lounge around the room after the long walk and listen to some relaxing music. With the lights off and the shades halfway down, the studio glowed from the available light, and the refreshing outside air filtered through the windows, making the room smell pure and tranquil.

After almost an hour of lying on the bed and holding her in my arms, we awkwardly shifted around and I carefully and gently kissed her for the first time. She smiled and said, "I've been waiting for you to do that since breakfast." We kissed more, a slow series of cautious embraces. We kept things calm, enjoying the romantic mood of the spring air and relaxed afternoon.

The perfect afternoon ended when my eight-hour shift at the computer lab approached at three o'clock. Before work, I walked her back to her dorm, and gave her a goodnight kiss on the steps of Forest. On the short stroll back, the entire experience felt surreal, like it didn't happen because it was too perfect. Usually, my dates were complete crash-and-burn, and I couldn't even remember what it felt like to be in total bliss because everything went great. She told me to call her after my shift and maybe we could hang out for a bit more. If I didn't have to work that night, it would have been a perfect day.

Consulting in the Student Union computer cluster after such a triumphant day combined the anticipation of a child waking up at four on the morning of Christmas and the boredom of a semester of third-semester calculus. I ignored the regular commotion of printing problems, stupid user questions and queries for help in the cluster, and floated above the din with the thoughts of everything else that happened earlier.

I shut down the cluster in record time, jetted back home in the trusty VW, and called her first thing after bolting into my apartment. We chatted for a few minutes, then decided to skip the phone and see each other again. She had a morning class and couldn't stay too late, but we both wanted to continue the earlier comfortable situation my job interrupted.

A few minutes later, she was in my arms again. We listened to music by candlelight, and curled up in each others' arms. After a few hours, we both fell asleep fully clothed, on top of the made bed. I woke up in the middle of the night, set the alarm, and took off her shoes, trying not to wake her. She stirred a bit and asked what time it was. "I've set the alarm for six, go back to sleep," I whispered. I cuddled next to her, and she pulled me tight. As I wrapped my arm around her, I kissed her forehead and went back to sleep.

465 sped behind me fast. I managed to cruise past the airport and jump to US 31 before 11:30. 31 stretched like a straight line across the center of the state, barren of hills, curves, or features. The summer before, I made the Elkhart to Bloomington trip so much I memorized the location and details of every Mom and Pop gas store, big truck rest area and fast food joint along the entire circuit. At any given point in the four-lane ribbon, I knew how many miles it was to the next fuel stop, turnoff, or rest area. With the precise gas intake of the little diesel engine, a trip odometer zeroed in at each fill-up, and some quick mental arithmetic, I could calculate my cruising range, when I'd need more gas, where I could stop, what stations sold diesel, and how much time remained in the journey. The system served as another way to kill time, like counting days in prison. I didn't do it out of planning or foresight, just anticipation and monotony.

Kokomo, the halfway point in the journey, would roll by in just over an hour. In about three, I'd hit Elkhart. With the car pointed north on the twin strands of asphalt, I put my brain back on autopilot, and continued my mental drifting.

After the first night, I was unofficially in love with Tammy. During the next week, we met every evening, and I entered the phase where nothing mattered except the relationship forming before our eyes. Even though I didn't get to sleep until after midnight and had to wake before six, it didn't matter because my infatuation made sleep insignificant. With no funds until next payday, money suddenly didn't matter because falling in love was free.

Midterms week hit the week after we met, and as she studied for tests, it influenced me to get my act together with my coursework. She got me out of bed earlier than my usual wakeup call of noon, and I forced myself to attend lectures. For months before, I wandered the streets at three in the morning half-drunk and mourning my own life instead of getting out of bed early to learn about calculus and economics. Teachers didn't recognize me when I went to classes after six-week absences, taking quizzes and tests on material I couldn't even begin to comprehend.

By Thursday, I found that I would flunk half of my classes. Even if I pulled a half-semester of straight A's, it would only guarantee C's and D's in the remaining courses. I bailed from the bad classes, destroying any chance of passing a full-time load in the spring. This put my $2000 a year scholarship in danger, unless I could make up the classes during the summer. But, I didn't care—all I could think and talk about was the beautiful woman I loved.

She spent every night that week with me, both of us curled up in my single bed, talking or just enjoying the novelty of being in love. We'd wake at a ludicrous hour and I'd drive her back to the dorm so she could shower and prepare for her 8:00 classes. My mornings were now free, since I withdrew from most of my classes. Some days I'd fall back asleep, or just screw around for three or four hours before taking a shower and starting the day. But some days I'd pick up an extra shift at work, do some cleaning around the house, read computer books, work on computer programs, write her long, rambling email, or talk to more people, telling them that I was in love and the world was just great. And even though I was in the library at seven in the morning, slamming together insane projects in VAX C, I thought the world was great.

On Wednesday, I finally told her that I was falling in love with her. She said she felt the same, and for that moment, I couldn't think of anything wrong in my life. That evening, we consummated our newly declared love. After a half-year of celibacy and months of fantasy, things were difficult, but felt better than ever.

Kokomo. Joke-amo. The city of a million factories, a sprawl of one-story warehouses that probably had more bowling alleys and monster truck parts stores per capita than any city in the country. The town was known to any US 31 voyager as "stoplight alley." After an extensive surgery to bypass 31 around the city, the highway department still broke the stretch of road with at least 20 stoplights. You could keep a solid 60 miles an hour through the entire state of Indiana, except here. Maybe they wanted everyone to get a good look at their Chrysler transmission plant.

It was past noon, so I stopped at a Rax and got a beef, bacon and cheddar sandwich, some fries and a Coke. With the straight drive ahead, eating the BBC at the wheel would be no problem. Before I pulled back into traffic, I took everything out of the bag and staged it on the seat for easier access at high speed. After a quick check of the instruments and a mental calculation on gas mileage and the distance to the next place that sold diesel, I turned back to stoplight alley and continued.

Over spring break, I went to Elkhart to piss away the week hanging out with my pal Nick, and Tammy flew to Pittsburgh to suffer with her parents. I got nervous while she was gone, but when we returned, she gave me a 16-page letter, spilling her guts about how much she was in love and how she was treated badly in the past, but I was different. Our relationship flourished and helped me get my act together as a whole. She got me to go to classes and work on programming projects, and I had the energy to sort out more of my finances and academic trouble. Self-confidence surged through me, probably because I was having sex on a frequent basis for the first time in months. On the weekends, I spent evenings with her, and when she was with her friends, I programmed like mad. Our typical night together entailed the simple dinner and movie date, but other times, we took long walks, went on picnics, or found other things to do.

One night we sat in my room (which was a disaster, my cleaning was still very hit and miss) and drank wine from a cheap set of fluted glasses I bought at Target. The dark room flickered with the light from a half dozen candles, and a Shadowfax CD played from the stereo as we sat close together on the bed with the wine. Even something simple held so much magic, because I felt like I was finally winning. Tammy was younger than me, and I felt that things worked well because she looked up to me, but I still respected her greatly. Nobody controlled the relationship, which allowed for a great deal of mutual comfort and fun. It wasn't like one person ran the other or one person consented to the arrangement while the other bowed down to them. Both of us enjoyed the comfort of each other, and it allowed for a manageable situation.

Tammy also gave me something to be proud of. I loved her, and was not afraid to talk about that to other people. She made me feel very confident in the relationship, because of her level of affection. She called me on a regular basis, talked to me for hours, sent me email, wrote me notes, and visited me at work. It wasn't in an obsessive way either—it felt natural and healthy. And with the summer weather and occasional money from the extra hours I pulled made the end of the semester feel more balanced than I'd felt in a long time. Even years later I would say this was the happiest point in my life.

Between Kokomo and South Bend stretched a no-mans' land devoid of cities, gas stations, fast food, and almost any other roadside landmark. The highway barreled ahead, straight and flat, with a very occasional sign marking a village far from the main road, probably without a McDonald's or open restroom. This part of the trip required a tight bladder and something interesting in the stereo. As the endless grassland clicked past, I tried to bruise my mind into semi-consciousness by cranking Bolt Thrower's *Warmaster* album, slamming the drum parts on the steering wheel and yelling the words aloud. About a third of the way up the stretch, I passed Peru, although no city whatsoever was visible from the road, just Grissom Air Force Base. A large chain link fence and miles of runway blurred by the left side of the road, with three tiers of razor wire and giant government warning signs every ten feet.

The deafening war cry of high-output jet engines tore apart the air, drowning my stereo in an instant and shaking the small car. Overhead, through the moonroof's rectangle of blue and puffy white, a KC-135 refueling jet swept over. Its sprawling silhouette filled the sky with its Desert Storm green paint scheme as it passed, gear down, at an approach altitude of a few hundred feet. It appeared to almost hover during its slow, final pass to one of the long ribbons of asphalt marked with strobe lights. I kept my car on the two lanes of blacktop ahead of me, lining up for my final approach as well.

The end of the spring semester arrived with sorrow and confusion, mostly because I knew Tammy would have to leave for Pittsburgh for the summer. Lauren and I dated from opposite ends of Indiana the summer before, and I was confident that I could hold out for three months, with a trip or two east to break up the detachment. But Tammy spent the beginning of the school year dating someone from home, and ended it because the distance made her physically sick, and almost destroyed her grades that semester. With that experience still fresh in memory, she didn't want to repeat it. Over the next few weeks we fought almost every day, with her trying to convince me that it wouldn't work and me trying argue that we could make it happen. We came to no conclusions by the time of finals week.

The night her parents were to arrive and move her back east, she came over after my shift at work. We started with the usual conversation, when she point blank said we should break things off, or at least suspend them for the summer. I wanted more than this, but knew more arguing wouldn't make my voice heard. She explained that she still loved me, and wanted things to happen, but the summer would cause more difficulty and pain. I didn't want to accept this, but I did.

We laid on the bed, holding each other in a strange state of shock, knowing that emotions had to take priority to real life. Although everything worked out—the relationship, the love, the sex, the personalities—one thing still had to go wrong: the cities we lived in.

Friday morning, we stood in front of her dorm, in the exact spot I first saw her for the first time. Now surrounded by moving trucks and people returning lofts and trying to back their stationwagons to the curb to load boxes, I tried to think of something to say that didn't sound stupid, but stumbled with sadness and grief. We kissed, and I pulled her close, hugging her tight, smelling her hair and holding back my tears and wondering how long it would be until I could hold her again, if ever.

Walking away, I turned back to see her one last time. She stood by the glass doors of the building, with the same innocence and karma in her brown eyes as the first time I saw her. The image burned in my mind, a permanent slide etched forever in my brain, the last glance of a drowning friend that slipped through my fingers, the only photo of a dead sibling, the last look in a coffin before it is lowered in the ground. The reserved tears flowed after I crossed the street, and I stumbled home to bury my face in the pillows of my bed and cry uncontrollably in the confusion and loss.

I forgot about the new bypass for US20 that would cut from my trip. I used to take US6, a two-lane road through Amish country where a horse cart or old lady would always pull on ahead of me and block traffic for a mile back. The new road, a super-hi-tech divided four lane made with bright white concrete, let me scream across St. Joe County and half of Elkhart County until I got to Mishawaka road, which dumped out a few miles from my Mom's

I cruised down Mishawaka road, toward the Concord Mall. The lane's bordering trees, farmland and occasional industrial warehouses transformed to more yogurt stores, little satellite malls, and the massive farm of asphalt parking lots that made up the main shopping solution of Elkhart. Fifteen-year-old mall punks cruised around on BMX bikes as sixty year old women with Day-Glo blue eyeliner bought clothes for their poodles. Pickup trucks belonging to toothless man sat in the K-mart lot as they shopped inside for gun racks, beef jerky, and 500-pound bags of dog food for their hounds. Town cars in handicapped spots waited for their owners, who were inside the Montgomery Ward bitching at the help because a lawnmower they bought didn't run after they kept it underwater for a month. And a dozen stores closed since Christmas, because Wal-Mart drove them out.

Concord Mall, heart of the metropolis known as Elkhart. And my parents wondered why I didn't want to come back.

4

Past the Concord Mall's fields of asphalt, the scenery drifted from the fast-food restaurants, gas stations and video rental stores to a world of cloned subdivisions, quaint neighborhoods of older houses, and more than occasional southern Baptist or evangelical churches. Near the mall, smaller tract housing lined the back roads, with tiny unkempt yards and weeds twisting around chain link fences. As I drove deeper into suburbia, the structures became more uniform, with green yards, majestic shade trees, and expensive cars in the driveway.

After passing three or four identical subdivisions, I whipped the Rabbit into a two-lane boulevard with a huge brick entrance monument sporting a placard that said Cedar Manor. I plowed down the lane, even rows of trees in the center divider strip whipping past me. I carefully zipped around center circles in the intersections. Curvy, flowing streets flowed from the tributary, the kind of layout that facilitated maximum yard layout and lot size instead of coherent navigation. With similar, artificial names like River Oak Way and Bent Fir Drive and the jigsaw street scheme, almost everyone got lost within moments of entering the division.

Thick, ancient oaks shaded decade-old tri-level homes in the older parts of the development, and newer ranch houses rested on freshly-cleared lots with only a few token trees and thick new carpets of sod. In addition to the similarity of the structures, the residents fought a bitter war, striving for the perfect lawn, the best landscaping, and the most immaculate cars in their driveways. It gave me good reason to stop calling the place home when I moved away.

Even though I hadn't driven down Cedarwood drive in months, it felt like high school revisited—back from classes and returning to my basement room to sleep an hour before my job at the mall. I instinctively cruised past the other houses and landmarks I knew for most of my childhood. My mother's blue tri-level approached on the left, on top of a gentle hill. From the road, everything looked untouched by time.

I gunned up the driveway and parked the Rabbit in a dirt space next to the garage. The diesel engine whined to a stop after I clicked off the ignition, and pinged after the long afternoon of travel. I rolled shut the moonroof and grabbed my bag from the rear seat.

Like clockwork, my mom appeared from the kitchen, to greet me and rope me inside for the first round of interrogation. Climbing from the car, I set the gym bag on the roof, making small talk and trying to avoid eye contact. I made a beeline for my room in the basement. "We need to sit down and talk about your plans for the summer," she yelled.

"I know, we'll do it later. I just got here," I mumbled. I continued down to the basement and my bedroom. The summer before my freshman year of high school, I constructed two walls, some wiring, and the requisite glossy wood paneling that defines a basement room. The rest of the basement remained unfinished, filled with boxes of junk and old clothes from the seventies.

Opening the door to my old room felt like stepping into a photograph of my high-school past. A twin bed and small endtable were the only furniture left, my old shelves and dresser bare. I dropped my gear on the floor and crashed on the bed. After pounding out the lumpy pillow, I kicked my legs up on the bed and stretched, gazing at the unfinished ceiling of heater ducts and joists and enjoying the feel of something other than a VW driver's seat.

Years before, posters of Pink Floyd and Iron Maiden covered the bare concrete walls, and a mural of college acceptance letters and other senior year mementos stretched from wall to ceiling on the naked paneling by the door. The now-barren bookshelves held sci-fi paperbacks, technical books, and hardcover copies of all the old classics. I could almost hear the first Metallica album and see the piles of dirty laundry and empty Coke cans on the floor. But now, the stripped walls and missing personal goods made the room look more like a warehouse than a bedroom, which made temporary stays even less bearable.

A knock on the door interrupted my daydream, and my mom appeared. "Are you staying for dinner?" The invite sounded more like an insult.

"No, I've got plans," I lied.

"If you change your mind, we're ordering pizza. And we need to talk about your money situation." She vanished, and left the door open, echoing the sound of the sump pump into the room.

I leaned over the edge of the bed, picked up the phone and dialed Peter's parents' house. One of his sisters picked up, when she set down the phone to find him, I heard the screams, laughs, cries and voices of the Ford household, full of kids and their friends and mischief. His mom had six or seven kids; it took me years to remember all of the names. The constant flow of neighbors and kids they were babysitting and friends and everything else made their house a perpetual lineup of rug-rats.

"Yo man. What's going down?" he said.

"You know that Thin Lizzy song, 'Tonight there's gonna be a jail-break...?' I feel like that," I said, almost whispering in the phone. "I've only been here two minutes, and she's already starting with the 'we need to talk' bullshit."

"Okay, okay, get your butt over here. We'll head out to South Bend and hang out for a while. I've got some cash, we can catch some food later."

"Sounds cool. I've gotta meet up with Nick at his store," I said. I knew this was a snag, because Peter didn't entirely get along with Nick and his pseudo-macho image. "We'll catch up with him long enough to see what's up and then head out."

"Okay, but I don't want to be driving around for seven hours looking for women to jump on the hood of the car and screw us."

"Yeah, I'm with you," I agreed. "Lemme light off some grenades or something so I can sneak out of here undetected, and we'll go from there."

"Okay cool, see you in a couple."

After carefully arranging my stuff in the room and memorizing the location to notify me of any tampering or cursory searches, I bolted back upstairs. "I'm leaving!" I said, not looking into the kitchen as I jetted through the front door.

"Where are you going? When will you be back?" she squawked, as I opened up my car door and crawled in.

I slammed the door and rolled open the window and moonroof. "I'm going to Peter's. I'll be back late." I cranked the engine, slammed the tape in the player (Morbid Angel, *Blessed are the Sick*) and opened the roof as she continued asking me questions. I ignored her and slammed down the driveway. The insane, ultra-Christian neighbor lady and her two kids were playing in the middle of the street while I shifted from reverse to first and gunned the engine. She started to yell at me to slow down, so I kept it in first, gave the diesel everything it had, and flipped her off through the moonroof as I rounded the curve.

The ten minute drive to Peter's led out of the suburbs and weaved through a hard-ass industrial district, packed with rusted warehouses and corrugated factories producing car parts, mobile homes, and RV pieces at peak capacity, thanks to the post-Gulf War economy. Workers and welders and packers lived in this hard-working section of town. They filled beaten houses with years of neglect, abandoned cars, appliances on the front porch, and trash burning in barrels. Thousands of coats of chipping and peeling low-grade paint hid the faded framework of the identical fifties-style structures.

Even though the buildings changed hands, changed colors, or changed companies, the entire drive felt the same to me as it did years before. I started hanging out with Peter in my freshman year of high school, when I worked at a department store job at the mall, selling paint and wallpaper and trying to get into the pants of the girls in the housewares department. An odd part-time schedule left many summer days with nothing to do, no money, and nothing but a car and maybe a few bucks in change. Peter worked sporadic hours also, and we'd spend off-time driving, listening to old Black Flag or Led Zeppelin or whatever it was that week, and chip together enough loose change and bills for a few hamburgers and enough gas to keep my old Camaro running.

Now, in a car with a fifth the horsepower and none of the fury or style, I watched the same brick warehouses and vacant lots pass. I'd pick up Peter, our minds would lock after months apart, and we'd be on our way to another adventure of doing nothing just to keep ahead of the game. We spent time apart at our respective colleges, and didn't do a good job of keeping in touch, other than a few token phone calls. He spent last fall in China, where he was "bored out of my mind and ready to shit white from all the rice I've been eating," according to his three or four letters on thin paper with weird airmail envelopes and alien-looking stamps. He never made it to Bloomington, and the only reason I spent any time at his school was because it was in Goshen, only ten miles down the road from Elkhart. Despite all of this, our link would instantly form when we did meet over holidays, and within moments, we were joking, finishing each others' sentences, and remembering joint memories like it was 1987 again. I hoped the same process would happen tonight, since I hadn't talked to anybody in confidence about the Tammy situation, and I still didn't have any good advice on how to continue with my life.

The factories slowly morphed into a more urban setting, with rows of small houses and smaller front yards. Spraypainted walls, bombed-out cars, and bars on windows defined an unwritten darkness in this part of town. At Wolf Street, I hung a left and weaved into an alley behind a row of garages. Sitting on a twenty-year-old black Plymouth's trunk, Peter played with the laces on his aquamarine Chuck Taylor Reeboks, his bleached-blonde mop of hair draped over his round John Lennon specs.

He jumped into action when he saw the familiar silver Rabbit. Launched from the trunk of the car, he jumped into the road, in my path. "JOOOOHNNNN!" he screamed, with arms outspread and a wild, wide-eyed look of insanity on his face. I dropped anchor in the narrow roadway, and he pried open the VW door and climbed into the copilot's seat. "Dude! Good to see you," he said, raising his hand for a high five.

I slapped his outstretched palm before shifting into gear. "I'm still alive. Finished another semester."

"You pass?"

"Fuck no. I doubt I finished any of my classes. But I'm still here."

"That's the spirit, man. So, where we going? U.P. mall?" he asked.

"U.P. it is," I said. "Let's roll." I hit the gas and the diesel engine launched us down the alley. University Park, a.k.a. U.P., was a large shopping mall just north of the Notre Dame campus, about fifteen miles west of Elkhart. We adopted the South Bend-Mishawaka region as our stomping ground when we got cars and grew tired of the tamer Concord Mall in our own backyard. The stores weren't much better, but they were different, and that gave us some hope that we'd eventually meet women (although we didn't.)

"You're looking good," Peter said, as I zoomed the car through traffic. "You working out?"

I laughed. "No, just walking everywhere. And I'm too damn poor to eat."

"I fucking hear that one, dude," he laughed. "I'm glad China taught me how to starve. After all that fucking rice, Ramen noodles are like steak fucking fillet!"

"How's the woman situation in Goshen?" I asked. "You bag any hairy-legged Mennonites?"

"Some of them shave, you know..."
"Dude, some of them NEED to shave, more than I do."
"Which isn't much, you motherfucker!" We both laughed.
"What about you? What's up with the lady in Bloomington?"
"Dude..." I hesitated. "It's off. She left yesterday, and I got the 'break up for summer' bullshit."
"Shit man...I thought..."
"Yeah, me too. Hey, this is bumming me out—I want to talk about it later in more detail. For now, find me a tape from the case in back."

Peter grabbed the red nylon cassette bag, and dug through it before producing a copy of Iron Maiden's classic *Piece of Mind*. Within seconds of the weird, backtracked message on the second side that led into the song "Still Life," Peter recalled one of the first times he heard the album, which was within my old Camaro, on one of our first trips to U.P. with two other guys, on a Friday we had off of school. He continued reminiscing, and I added facts and laughed along, while thinking about how much it really helped to have him in the passenger seat right now.

The year before, I commuted from Elkhart to IUSB every day, and could navigate the route without thinking, even with a foot of snow on the windshield. The path still felt like a dream to me, and I could describe every foot of my drive during the 1990-1991 school year. It reminded me not only of the mind-numbing commutes, but also of the times Peter and I used to nomad around the area in my old car. The summers, the voyages with no destination—it all jumped back like I never left.

We motored out of Elkhart County on US 20 and into the no-man's-land between Elkhart and Mishawaka. Subtle changes occurred on the route, even in the year since I drove it daily. Gas station names mutated, restaurants changed owners, and vacant lots gave birth to new superstores, with prefab buildings, large parking lots, giant neon signs and all-glass storefronts.

We wound past the AM General plant, a city-sized factory of ominous proportions, with a parking lot that looked larger than Elkhart itself. Home of the Hummer, the next-generation Jeep/military tool/sport utility vehicle, it brought Mishawaka its 15 minutes of fame during their big marketing blitz otherwise known as the Gulf War. Now they built the beasts with leather interiors for yuppies that had to get a mile a gallon to impress their friends.

We crossed the line into Mishawaka, where US 20 became McKinley Road, a major five-lane thoroughfare with a high density of fast food joints, new car dealers, strip malls and video stores. Nick worked in a small record store called Around the World Records, named because of the large volume of 'import' bootlegs they sold from Europe. He hated every aspect of the job except for the fact that he got a discount, and it kept him from working at a grocery store or factory. Oh, and he didn't have to cut his hair.

I cruised into the lot of his strip mall and parked the VW in a spot by a neighboring hobby store. Peter and I walked up to the small storefront, the glass windows and door covered with promo posters and displays of new releases. I pulled open the door and the sound of a large PA system playing rap rushed forward. We peered around for any sign of Nick, and saw Carl, one of the assistant managers, at the counter. A younger lady stood at the counter, trying to hold two smaller children in line and struggle with her purse at the same time, while Carl rang up her cassette singles. "Psycho!" Carl yelled to me while scanning the tapes. "I think Nick's in the back," he said.

"Cool, how's life?" I yelled over the beat of the rap music. "Oh, this is my friend Peter," I said, pointing to my sidekick.

"I'm still alive. That's punishment enough," Carl answered. "Hey Peter," he replied without looking up from the register transaction.

The inside of the shop resembled a narrow alley, with a tiny area of storefront but a lot of depth to the building. CD and tape racks lined both walls, and a self-standing set of bins ran down the length of the sales floor, holding thousands of used CDs. By the front counter, magazines, patches and drug paraphernalia ("It's 'tobacco accessories,'" Nick had to claim) lived in various racks and glass cases. T-shirts wallpapered the back of the store, and more bins held used LPs. Posters and banners hung from the high ceilings, suspended over the center racks, and promotional placards and record label displays covered almost every other square foot of the free wall space.

"Hey you goat-fuckers," echoed a voice from behind the vinyl section. "What the fuck's up?"

"Nick! Hey man, sorry we're late," I said, walking back to the record section. "Did you already go to dinner?"

Nick stood in a doorway, holding open a portal with a one-way mirror in the top half. Sporting long, straight, blonde hair and wearing a black Rotting Christ t-shirt with a graphic of a gory, dismembered Jesus crucified on an inverted cross, he didn't look much like the type of person who would work at a record store that catered primarily to top-40 music. But, it paid the bills.

"Yeah, I had to go to Arby's," he said. "I also spent most of the afternoon convincing a customer that we could not give him a refund on a used bong because 'it was the wrong color,'" he said. "I finally had to beat him to death with a lava lamp."

Peter and I laughed, wondering if his story was true. Nick spent hours bitching about how the average customer was a complete idiot who burned away most of their functional brain cells with dope and then got steered into the worst music marketing strategies like sheep. That month, people were showing up in droves to buy a record by some little kid from France who sang horrid renditions of Frank Sinatra songs. Next month, it might be a Swedish goat farmer yodeling and playing the accordion to a rap beat and synths, and people would be lined up out the door as long as the record labels marketed it as the next big thing.

"Hey Nick, are you still doing the zine?" Peter asked. He referred to Cursed Metal, Nick's fanzine detailing his love of extreme Death and

Thrash Metal. Tons of bands and some cool record labels sent demos and albums that he reviewed, plus he got hooked up at shows and interviewed some cool people. I occasionally wrote for him, and watched the zine go from something we photocopied at his mom's office to a slick publication read all over the world and respected by the metal community.

"Fuck yeah I'm still doing it. I have some copies on display—go ahead and grab some, on the house."

"Hey that's cool," Peter said.

"Where's that Virus 100 tape? I want to buy a copy," I said.

Nick grabbed a tape, snapped it out of the plastic alarm device, and rang it up with a 20% discount. I dug through my wallet for the cash, while Peter examined the cassette.

"What is this?" Peter asked.

"It's the 100th release on Jello Biafra's record label," Nick said. "They got a bunch of cool bands to record fucked up versions of Dead Kennedys songs. Napalm Death does a version of 'Nazi Punks Fuck Off.'"

"Cool, I'll have to check it out," Peter said, wary of Nick's enthusiasm.

"How long are you in town? Do you wanna go out tonight and fuck some sluts?" Nick asked me.

"I'm leaving tomorrow. We've already got some stuff going on tonight, and I've gotta get the fuck out of Dodge before my mom regains consciousness from the beating I gave her."

"Have it your way dude," he said. "Hey, when can I come back to Bloomington again? I had fun last time when that stupid fucking bitch you called a girlfriend wasn't around." He referred to Lauren—they got in a shouting match in the College Mall parking lot over whether or not M.C. Hammer wrote his own songs.

"Yeah, I killed her. You should come down again," I said. "It would be pretty cool. The women are more desperate because the frathouses are all closed."

"That sounds awesome. I'll figure out how to get some time off and I can drive down there and we can fuck some sluts."

"Sounds like a plan. I'll give you a call when I'm back," I said. "Hey, we've gotta split...we haven't eaten yet."

"Get the fuck out of here before I jam one of these records up your ass. And don't go to Arby's—it tastes like rancid dog."

"See you later, Nick," Peter added.

We walked past the records and water bongs and back to the Rabbit.

Within moments, the VW rolled down McKinley, voyaging onward to University Park mall. The wind whipped through the open moonroof, providing some relief from the hot May temperature. The road held a great familiarity to me: Nick and I drove the same stretch almost every day during my tenure at IUSB last year, when we blew off classes and went to the mall to play video games.

"Is Nick acting weird or is he just pissed at me?" Peter said.

"He talked about fucking sluts and jamming stuff up people's asses—that's pretty normal," I said.

"I don't know—he's just..." Peter shifted in the seat, to look at me. "He's always acting like mister tough guy or something."

"Well, he hates his job, lives at home with a neurotic mom and an alcoholic dad, works a job he hates even though his family is rich, and is stuck in the armpit of the Midwest with nothing to do at night, on the rare chance he gets a night off because his boss works him constantly for almost minimum wage. He has reasons to be fucked up."

"Yeah I guess," Peter sighed. "It just seems like he could do something to escape. Both of us are busting our asses, to go to school and get the fuck out of here someday. Why isn't he?"

"I don't know. I wish I could get him to transfer to Bloomington, but he's so tied into his life now, his routine. I asked him once if he could transfer back, and he went into a giant speech about how he'd have to find a new place to buy his comic books. He always talks about how much he liked it at the Bloomington campus, but he never takes initiative to get down there again."

"He went to IU?"

"Fuck yeah, he went to Bloomington for a semester, in '89, the same semester I started there," I said. "He transferred back to IUSB because his dumb bitch girlfriend ran out of money. She dumped him a few months later, and he's been trapped in South Bend ever since. And now he's got all of these issues where all women are whores and objects and he has to demean them."

"What the fuck?" Peter asked. "Why didn't he just dump the bitch and stay?"

"He was so fucking whipped," I said. "When he wasn't in classes, he was at her dorm. She hated it there, and had no friends, probably because she was such a bitch. She kept him on a short leash, and had him walk two miles across campus every day to sit in her room and do nothing. When her funds ran out, she convinced him it was a horrible place and that they had to leave."

"That's too much," Peter said. "Why didn't you hit him in the head with a brick or something?"

"That's the fucked part—this bitch completely hated me. She never let Nick hang out with me, and I could never get ahold of him anyway since he was always at her dorm. He never visited or even called, and I stopped calling after a few months when I got the picture. I'm glad he returned after the breakup—I had completely written him off for life. I'm glad he finally got free from her."

We continued down Grape Road and its six-lane stretch of appliance stores, new car dealers and family restaurants. Some of our favorite old businesses remained, like Hot and Now Hamburgers, still selling the best burgers 39 cents could buy. The road crept upward, all six lanes passing over the Indiana Toll Road. Mini-malls with office supply stores, hardware stores, and big discount department stores loomed below us, hinting we were close to our destination.

We climbed the incline to its crest, and parking lots teeming with cars stretched from horizon to horizon, with small banks and drive-up ATM kiosks on each side. The view quickly filled with the large brick mall building, sprawling across the middle of the asphalt lake. Tall department stores with big names and all-glass storefronts capped the ends of the mall, and between them, long stretches of smaller stores built the body of the complex.

A large sign with the movie titles at the Cinema 6 marked the entrance to the mall's concourse. The VW banked hard as I swung the turn from the highway, sending my tape case and other assorted garbage from one side of the car to the other. Cars swept by the window as I navigated to the far parking area beyond the traffic of the shoppers, and shut down the engine.

"Hey man, can we just chill out for a second before we go in? I just want to talk for a while," I said.

"Yeah that's cool, what's up?" Peter asked.

"It's just this Tammy situation," I said. "I'm just completely fucked out over this."

"So what's the deal, you two split for the summer and you're getting back together in the fall?"

"That's what I thought, but I'm not sure if I should believe it. Didn't you get the same thing when Rebecca went in the Navy, right before she fucked like everyone in the state?"

"But Rebecca was screwed in the head. I couldn't trust her when we were together, let alone with her half a world away. I didn't expect her to fuck around on me, but everyone else did."

"When I really think about it, I don't know why Tammy wouldn't cheat on me. She's only eighteen, and she hasn't had that much experience in relationships. I'm not saying she's a whore, but a summer is like a lifetime to her. I doubt she'll even remember me in a month."

"Don't say shit like that, man. Give yourself some credit. You've had good times with her—it sounded like a sure deal. Maybe things will go okay and you'll continue in the fall, and maybe they won't. But you can go on with life."

"That's a pretty fucking broad simplification. I could barely function yesterday morning after having this shit ferment in my brain overnight and then having to say goodbye to her, not knowing if I'd ever see her again. If the last day's been this tough, keeping my life in limbo for three months will be impossible. I really don't know how the fuck to handle it. You know how I get about this shit."

"I know, I know. Look, maybe this time you should break the fucking cycle of destruction. You'll be down in Bloomington, with your own place, a car, no parents—you can hang out, date around, look at your options and keep in touch with Tammy. Do some comparison shopping, man. Maybe by fall, you'll find someone else, or find out you just want to stay single. Or maybe she'll come back and you'll be more in love than ever. Stranger shit has happened, man."

"I don't want to look for other women, I went through that shit for months, and I thought it was finally over..."

"Dude, you were looking for THE woman. Don't do that shit. If you follow this perfect picture of a woman, you'll never fucking find her. Just look for women to hang out with, spend time with. If they have an away boyfriend, don't want a relationship, so what? You could still go tip some beers with her, meet her friends, or maybe even fuck around with her, but you don't need to size her up for marriage the second you feel a stir in your pants. Just do what happens, and worry about other shit in life for a while."

"That sounds like a plan, but I don't know how to implement it. I need to clear my mind of a lot of emotional baggage first."

"Then clear away," he said. "As for remedies, loud music and cold brew come to mind. Some might say work and school, too. Hey, what are you doing about work, anyway?"

"I've got the computer job for a few hours here and there, and it looks like I have a job doing roofing and construction shit, pretty much a nine to five. Hopefully, I'll be able to get a few bills paid and deal with tuition. I'm taking a couple classes to make up for last semester."

"What do your parents think?"

"The usual. They think it will fail and I'll become a skid row alcoholic by next Tuesday. They want me to move home and play their game. I need some cash for summer session classes, hence this trip," I said. "What are your plans?"

"It looks like I'll be working the factory thing for most of the summer, but I'll be doing the Goshen summer theatre for a few weeks. I'm going to live at home for most of it, but on the tail end, I'll be babysitting someone's house for a month or so, just off campus."

"Sounds hip," I said. "Hey, let's go inside and see what's up with the mall poseur scene."

"Cool, we're there," he said. I cranked the moonroof shut, locked the VW and we headed inside.

University Park Mall prospered more than most malls in the Elkhart-South Bend-Mishawaka area, probably because of the large amount of traffic and shoppers from all over northern Indiana and Southern Michigan. Where the Concord Mall and others catered to local shoppers, the U.P. was the place to be for any serious consumer within thirty miles. Because of the vast quantity of people, the mall lent itself to the sport of peoplewatching quite well, and Peter and I were seasoned veterans of the game. We'd sometimes sit on a bench and stay stationary, but often we'd just walk the interior perimeter of the mall with no interest at all in the stores themselves, just the people.

Of course, one of the obvious checklist items were women of the finer quality, something U.P. had in great quantities. In high school, some of the most incredible women we'd ever seen in our lives walked the aisles of that mall, ones that were surely flown in from afar and recruited just for their incredible beauty. We never had the nerve to talk to any of them, but we always wanted to. And the other thing we often sought were abnormal people. The punk with the foot high hair, the lady who brought her dog to the mall, the guy yelling at his kids for stupid stuff outside the toy store, or the guy wearing Village People leather bondage gear. With so much volume, there were always truly unique specimens to be found.

After a quick stop for some Cokes, we found a bench and parked it, and casually chatted as the people walked by. The conversation went from past to future to present in a never-ending swirl of non sequiturs, as expeditions to the past sparked from the visions in the present, and what we saw in the present made us wonder about our future. The women walked by that we wished we could have, but we also had to talk about the issues with the women in our life that we couldn't figure out. Cute girls shopping for clothes and shoes piqued my interest and made my mind wander, but I still pulled back to the problems with Tammy and had to talk to Peter about the situation.

Peter's advice sounded good, but I didn't know how to forget Tammy and date casually. Leaving the pain behind me and continuing my dating life after such a perfect situation didn't seem like an easy thing to do, and I didn't think I'd be able to do something like that in a years' time, let alone the summer. Also, I didn't know the feasibility of an open dating life, especially since I had so much trouble getting a date or two a semester. It sounded fun, but unrealistic. I cherished any advice Peter gave me, but knew it wasn't the final word in my situation.

The chatting and staring and relaxation offered by the bench seat ceased as our hunger picked up, so we went back to the car and cruised the strip for some food. Grape Road's frontage flowed with all of the popular fast food joints, their large colored signs lighting the pathway. The Hot and Now drive through window finally tempted us, with a bright red and white sign shouting about its 39 cent burgers. We ordered a sackful of greasy fries, no-frills hamburgers and a couple of Cokes, for a grand total of less than five bucks. Hot and Now operated on the back-to-basics principal of having only a few items on the menu, and absolutely no frills whatsoever. Since they considered a big parking lot and dining room an extra, we had to park in a grocery store's half-empty lot across the street.

We snarfed the burgers and fries while listening to the tape player and talking through mouthfuls of food.

After the greasy feast, we cruised the area more, cruising past all of our old hangouts: Notre Dame, downtown South Bend, the porno stores on Michigan Street, the waterfront by Century Center. We talked, drove, and remembered the past well after the skies turned dark. The town held little for us after 9 PM, except the redneck bars and overpriced strip clubs, but we managed to keep busy for a few more hours, glad to be in a car and repeating the same routes that we traveled back in high school.

The night road continued to roll under the tires, humming and whirring. When the night wound down, we found US 20, and cruised back into Elkhart and Peter's neighborhood. I pulled into the alley behind his house, clicked off the lights, and shut down the engine.

"Here we are dude," I said.

"When are you taking off?"

"Tomorrow afternoon, I guess. About 15 seconds after that money talk with my mom, I'll get the fuck out of here."

"It sure is gonna be weird not having you around this summer."

"Yeah, I'm looking forward to some pretty bizarre experiences, though. I'll keep in touch, and let you know I'm surviving."

"Okay, hang in there. I'm sure all of this shit will settle down in the end. Just don't let it get to you too much. As Nick would say, 'Fuck some sluts.'"

"I'll try," I laughed. "I'm just so damn worried about how things will go. I've never cut it this close on so many things at once before. I don't have a backup plan for a lot of this shit."

"Don't worry. You're smarter than you think. And if things totally explode, you can always come up here and crash my place for the rest of the summer. I'll help you out as much as I can."

"Thanks, I appreciate it. I will be up here before the fall at least once, so we'll hook up somehow."

"Okay, cool."

"Well, I better get home. My fucking parents are going to wake me up in a couple of hours."

"Yeah, same here," he said, opening the car door and stepping out. "Well, give me a call when things happen, and I'll see you when I see you."

"Okay, take care man."

Peter closed the car door. "Green hell John, hang in there."

"Green hell!"

Green hell. Our salute to glory, stolen from a Metallica song, and they stole it from a Misfits song. It still meant the world—our battle cry of victory over the last five years. I fired up the engine as Peter walked to the back door of the house. Before I put the car in gear, he turned around and mockingly saluted me as he smiled. I tore off an exaggerated salute, put the car in first, and eased the car through the narrow alley, toward Main Street.

Back in my room, I nervously argued doing something I promised to do the last few times I visited. I quietly slipped out of my room, heart pounding, and tiptoed across the makeshift basement hallway and into a storage room.

The fluorescent lights ebbed, their green-white glow illuminating a room full of boxes, Christmas ornaments, tools, decades of National Geographic magazines, and long outgrown model airplanes and racecars. Trying not to make any noise, I carefully rummaged behind a burned-out console TV, trying to find something I left there years before. I pulled loose a parcel—a long, narrow nylon bag that smelled like an old Army uniform, molded with time. Regardless of its innocent exterior experience, my mouth instantly dried and heartbeat headed skyward with the kind of fear only reserved for those things diabolical and life-taking. In my hands, wrapped in the cloth case, I held a single-barrel 16-gauge shotgun.

I wiped the dust and cobwebs from the fabric sheath, and opened the top flap, exposing the wood butt. My uncle gave me the gun five or six years ago when we went deer hunting. We took a few trips to southern Michigan, where I woke up far too early and walked around in the freezing cold for hours, never even seeing a deer and being scared to death that we would. He showed me how to care for the gun, and how to load and fire it. I fearfully targeted some aluminum cans and trees after each failed deer mission. When I decided the hunter's life wasn't for me, I stashed the gun away and forgot about it.

But recently, I remembered it. I kept thinking about my spiraling moods, the course of my life, and everything else. And when I hit bottom and kept heading down, I often contemplated suicide. When I wanted a way out, I'd weigh my options and frustrate myself even further. No amount of pills would kill me; I'd either throw up, get caught and have my stomach pumped, or end up in a coma with brain and kidney damage. Knives were too painful, and I saw how much blood they drew during a blood donation and couldn't imagine having patience to repeat that several times before death would occur. There weren't many tall buildings in Bloomington, and I didn't have a garage to fill with car exhaust. My mind always circled back to the gun.

It felt important to have an insurance policy, a final way to get out if things got worse. I wasn't planning on killing myself in the near future, but I knew if suicide became mandatory, I'd regret not having a formidable method of death. It felt insane, but it felt right.

Pulling open the cloth case, I revealed the aged wooden stock and blue gunmetal of the hunting weapon. I opened the bolt and checked to make sure the gun was unloaded. On a shelf cluttered with nails, spray paint and wood stain, I found a small box containing four rounds of ammunition. Confident the gun wouldn't accidentally fire, I pulled the burlap back and tied shut the top flap. I dropped the shells in my pocket, and tried to conceal the awkward cargo under my jacket, the long barrel protruding against my leg. With the lights flicked off, I stealthfully moved upstairs, each heartbeat slamming in my eardrums louder than death.

Once I cleared the house, I would be home free. Peeking from the basement door, I made sure no lights were on in the rest of the house. The patio door audibly clicked when I opened its lock, but I stifled its sound as I pried it open and exited. I crossed the backyard to my car, lifted the hatchback, and pulled open the false floor, exposing the spare tire. The gun fit perfectly above the spare, the fastening hardware for the bumper jack holding the nylon case in place. I wedged the box of shells in the compartment, carefully replaced the false floor and snuck back into the house.

In my room, I tried to forget about the covert mission. The gun would be safe in the car until I got back to Bloomington, where I could safely move it to my room without incident. I slipped into bed and tried to sleep, eventually worrying about Tammy and summer classes and money instead of the gun.

"John, wake up! Mom wants to talk to you," my sister Natalie yelled, as she opened the bedroom door and flooded the room with light.

"Dammit, what time is it?" I asked her, quickly shielding my face with a pillow.

"Ten twenty-two," she replied in a snotty voice.

"AM or PM?"

"She's waiting in the kitchen!" She ran back upstairs, but left the door open and the basement lights on, shining in my eyes.

I crawled out of bed and slipped into a pair of dirty jeans and the t-shirt I wore the night before. In the bathroom, I quickly splashed some water on my hair, and tried to roughly arrange it with a comb.

"John, are you awake?" Natalie yelled downstairs.

"Yes! I'm in the bathroom! Jesus Christ, gimme a minute!"

When I stumbled upstairs, my mom sat at the kitchen table, reading the Sunday paper. I grabbed a Coke from the fridge, and cracked it open.

My mom launched into the expected money argument with the ferocity of a Blitzkrieg attack. I slumped in a chair at the kitchen table, staring at the floor, staring at the clock, listening to her lecture about how this all happened because I went away to college instead of staying at home. She argued with circular logic about how it would be better for me to stay home forever and go to a nowhere school and get a nowhere job and buy a house across the street and live an identical life to theirs with the only difference being that I would make more money. According to her rules, only money mattered, and there wasn't a qualitative aspect to education. I believed that everything you really learned from college took place outside the classroom: the struggle to stay alive, pay the bills, study for the tests, and meet some people on the side. But she never believed this, and continued to accuse me of partying, and deliberately wanting to waste my life and flunk out of school. She criticized my plans, my choices and what I wanted to do with my life.

In a move I learned from my pal Gandhi, passive resistance got me through the argument. I couldn't fight back, or defend myself with words or actions, since by default any of my actions, even those that they endorsed, were wrong. For a year, I moved back into her house and bought the car she wanted me to have and went to the school she wanted me to and dated the girl she wanted me to and took the drugs she made me take and went to the doctors she wanted me to go to. Instead of loosening the grip that was around me during my first year of college, the actions made the fist of her control tighten on me even more. Now I learned to let her spew venom and ignore it. The less I followed her advice, the more I could live my own life. She outlined a giant plan to "put me on the right track," while I stared across the room at the clock changing numbers and concentrated on the fact that I wouldn't follow step one of any plan—I'd go back to Bloomington and do what I needed to do to survive, and to break away from her control in the future.

One good thing came out of the session: she gave me a credit card and told me I could charge my classes and books for the summer with it. It was in my name, something I applied for while at school that got diverted to my "permanent address," but she would take care of the minimum payments until I got my act together. It was basically a loan at 21 percent—not exactly courteous, but it guaranteed me I could get my school paid in advance. The lecture tapered off, and I finally exited after about an hour to take a long shower, and sit in my room and rest before the trip. It felt good to know I could use the Visa for classes. One big worry was removed from my list, but the grating insults about the direction my life was going added to the deep wounds already present in my confidence.

Shampoo, brush, toothbrush, toothpaste—I repeated the procedure of searching for what was mine and cramming it in the gym bag. The room became alien again as my CDs and player went into the satchel also. After a second pass, I felt like everything was there, and went back to the car to load in everything for the trip.

As I opened the hatch and proceeded to drop in my luggage, my mom trailed behind. "Did you make sure you have everything?" she asked.

"Yeah, I'm okay. I checked the fluids, checked the tires, I have a quarter-tank left which will take me almost to Peru, but I'll stop in Elkhart before I hit the highway."

"Okay, as long as you don't forget anything."

"I'm fine."

"I'm going to worry about you. I hope everything works out. I think you should stay home, but if you think this will work..."

"Don't worry. Everything will be fine. I can take care of myself."

"Well I'm just worried that this job won't work out and then what?"

"Look, if the job doesn't work out, I'll get another one. It isn't like Elkhart is the only place in the world that has jobs."

"Well you could probably find something that pays more up here..."

"I think we've had this discussion enough times. It won't be productive to have it again. I'll be fine. If things don't work out, I'll find another job. If it totally doesn't work out, I'll come back."

"Okay, when are you going to visit again?"

"I don't know. Sometime. I'll keep in touch."

I fired up the car, swung my legs into the compartment and shut the door. "I'll give you a call in a week or two and let you know how the job and classes are going. I'll see you later."

I backed out of the driveway, and gunned the silver car down the road, past the manicured lawns and identical tri-levels, and toward the highway.

Every time I left Elkhart, it reminded me of when I left my parents after spending a year at home. After my torrid freshman year, I transferred to the IU branch campus at South Bend. I intended to move back home, commute every day, get good grades at the easier campus, save loads of money, and transfer back to Bloomington in style. However, everybody assumed that once you moved home and transferred, you never left and either finished school there and got a job locally, or dropped out of school to work at the factories.

At IUSB, I didn't get good grades, saved no money (the commute and car wear/tear probably cost more money than what I saved in rent,) drove myself into overwhelming depression due to the lack of friends and by being surrounded by incredibly conservative, vocational and middle-aged students, and I desperately had to fight to return to Bloomington. I finally managed to get my act together, save enough money to pay the deposits on the boarding house room, and get enough vital belongings in my car to head south for the fall semester. As I merged the car onto US 31 for my final ascent from a year of hell, I felt like I was truly returning home. Not the home where I grew up and went to high school, but the one that I made for myself in Bloomington, the one where I felt that I really belonged. That uplifting feeling kept with me every time Elkhart was in my rearview mirror and Bloomington loomed southbound on the road in front of me.

And the same feeling hit me again, as I continued down the road to my first summer away from Elkhart, away from my parents and away from the security they offered. School was no longer a nine month a year activity, which necessitated me to return "home" for the other three months. As I drove back, I closed the door that caused it to be a year-long fate. All official ties were severed, and from that point on, my home was Bloomington, Indiana.

I cranked the stereo, and continued home.

5

My alarm blared and knocked me from sleep at an hour I typically staggered home from a computer cluster. Rising from bed to disengage the electronic howling took a great amount of strength, an incredible level of unconsciousness tearing through my head. I stumbled through the room, trying to find a towel and my bathroom toiletries. With vision blurred, balance skewed and coherence distorted, my flailing arms knocked things from shelves and walls. I cursed and tried to pull myself from the far levels of ether. Job, I thought. Must go to job. Must show up for work.

After my sudden decision to stay for the summer, my brain spent most of its free cycles replaying a scenario where I wouldn't be able to keep a good job, causing me to run out of money, flunk out of school, and spontaneously develop some sort of aneurysm causing immediate death. During finals week, I made my first trip to the student employment center, and scoured its large pegboard wall full of job cards. They contained mostly jobs having to do with day care and summer camps, but I found the phone number of a construction place that did home renovations, like re-roofing, decks, add-on rooms and other home additions. I wanted to find a computer-related job where I could make six or seven bucks an hour installing DOS or doing data entry, but the idea of spending a summer working outside, getting a tan and working myself to Schwartzennegar-like proportions seemed fine. A little bullshit about my carpentry work in theatre got me the job, and the foreman assigned me to help re-roof a house. He gave me the address of the site and told me to show up that day, Monday, with comfortable clothes that I could get dirty.

After my quick shower, I arrived at the site, a small ranch house with a large dumpster full of dissected roof, and wooden pallets stacked with shingles. I couldn't find anyone there, but I was a few minutes early. Wandering around the yard, I wondered if I went to the wrong address, or if he had forgotten me.

Twenty minutes later, a late-model pickup with a toolbox on the bed pulled into the driveway. The foreman, a weathered man in his forties dressed in neatly pressed work clothes, climbed out of the cab with a clipboard.

"Morning! You John Conner?" he asked, in a slight southern accent, as he quickly checked the clipboard.

"Yessir," I said.

"Okay, here we got a basic roof job. This is a rental I own, so be neat about it but don't worry about putting on a show for the tenants," he said.

He let me to the side of the house, where a dumpster held large chunks of shingles, tarpaper, and rotting wood.

"All of your tools are over here." He pointed to a few crowbars, hammers, and other hand tools. "All I need you to do is scrape all the shit off the roof, pull the shingles, and make sure you get any odd nails out. Throw everything in here," he said, pointing to the dumpster. "And be careful while you are up there. Make sure you don't put your foot through some rot or fall off, because I'm leaving you alone all day. I'll be back at about four to see how it went."

The job sounded easy enough, and I had no fear of heights, so I scaled the ladder and started tearing the hell out of the roof. Within a half-hour, boredom kicked in, and I wished for a radio, walkman, or a coworker to shoot the shit with. I also never realized how fucking hot a roof gets when it absorbs the full power of the morning sun. By nine or ten, I felt like I spent the morning in a deep fat fryer; half of my body weight transferred to sweat and grime, now soaking through my clothes. I drank the Cokes I packed with my lunch, and started praying to gods of various mythologies for rain.

With the drudgery, my attention wandered, and I slipped into daydreams, extended self-soliloquy, and other mental games designed to pass time while repeating the same physical tasks for hours on end. At my last summer job as a punch press operator, I would put a piece of copper into a machine and hit a pedal, then repeat the cycle hundreds or thousands of times in an eight-hour shift. During those periods, with earplugs and guards blocking the rest of the world and a simple task preoccupying my body, I would enter an almost meditational state, planning my weekends, scheduling how I would finish college, daydreaming about women or money, or just rethinking current events and imagining other possible divergent realities that would have happened if things went differently. And when I really started to get involved with the internal mind games, I could forget about the repetitive tasks my hands were doing and let the clock advance at a seemingly faster rate.

Now the fantasy daydreams focused on Tammy. My first dream was to visit Pennsylvania and see her. A realistic fantasy, it seemed workable at first. I checked a map once and estimated we were about 400 miles apart—that's seven or eight hours on the road with traffic and stops. The Rabbit could do that on a tank of gas—the round trip would cost twenty bucks. If I could scrape together a couple hundred dollars, I could drive out on a Friday, pick up a room at a Motel 6, and stay the weekend...But the fantasy cut into worries about the long-term health of the Rabbit—the exhaust that needed some work, the fading brakes. And where would I get 200 bucks for a visit?

When the visit mind game fell apart, I went to plan B—bringing her to me. She hated her parents, and had no job or summer school keeping her there. What if I moved her back to Bloomington? We'd live in my closet of a room until we got a two-income situation going. Then we'd move into a new place, spend time together—she'd take music lessons and I'd go to summer school and then...This felt awesome to me, but if she left home, her parents would probably disown her, and she'd have to quit school. In wild versions of the scenario, I'd stumble into a job at a computer game company that paid me $50K a year to stay in Bloomington and hack at games. We'd buy a house, I'd put her through school and...It all seemed like a long shot. She didn't want to see me anymore, and I perpetuated the fantasy with these little games. Dreaming about crazy schemes to get her back made me fear that she wouldn't return in the fall. Would her parents make her transfer to a state school? Did she plan on seeing other people back home? Did I already screw things up beyond repair? Did she really love me?

Thinking about it made me feel worse, so I calculated how much money I could make ripping apart houses. I added hours, weeks, and months and subtracted car repairs, tuition, rent and deposits for next year. After every new total, I would always come to the conclusion that at best, I'd break even and I was sweating away my life for no reward. But then I would wipe the slate and try to recheck my math, hoping I forgot something essential like the number of weeks in the summer.

The numbers spun, the crowbar swung, the shingles fell from the roof to the dumpster below, and the dust and grime rose onto my clothes, into my hair and all over my skin. Rotting timbers started to show through the patches I removed, and the sun kept making the job more unbearable. Only a few more hours...

Those hours felt like days, but I finally made it home alive. I spent almost an hour showering and scrubbing pieces of tar, dirt and shingles from my body. My arms and neck glowed with a soft pink prelude to a serious sunburn, and my forehead and face were broken out in acne and blisters from the layer of grime I wore all day. Even after three or four passes with the shampoo, my scalp itched with the fury of a lice epidemic. I left the repugnant clothing outside my bedroom door for the time being, the pants almost completely black from the broken roof pieces that dragged across my legs, and the shirt reeking of sweat. After the cleanup attempt, I put on a pair of shorts and didn't bother getting dressed again that evening.

The first day felt like a week of work, the dirt and grime and sweat and the aches and pains from bending over all day and prying at shingles removed any glamour from the job. It felt like I was back at my high school job in an Italian restaurant washing dishes, ticking away the minutes and watching the clock and doing something I hated, just to make ends meet. But even after calculating and recalculating the paychecks and my bills, I wondered how I'd come anywhere near surviving the summer. There were a lot of ifs—if I could get more hours with UCS, if I could get my car's problems fixed for cheap, if I could get some other odd jobs. Too many variables—I really needed a better job.

After my cleanup, I collapsed in bed with a can of Coke and wrote Tammy a letter, a sappy "I miss you so much even though it's been only three days" sort of thing, probably the third letter I penned since she left. A good correspondence campaign might save some money on long distance, but I didn't know if she'd return my mail. In moments of clarity and pessimism, I didn't think I would make it through the summer without her. I didn't accuse her of it, but I almost knew she would find someone else and forget about me.

A knock on my half open door roused me back to reality. "Come in!" I yelled, not wanting to get out of the bed.

"Hey John!" It was Deon, enthusiastic about nothing in particular and wandering around the house. "How was that construction job?" He wandered into the room and sat down on my computer chair.

"It sucks," I moaned. "The money's good, but it's really fucking hard work. Plus I don't think he'll give me a straight forty a week," I said.

"That blows," he said. "Do you think you could keep at it, though? Jobs that pay more than minimum are hard to find in the summer."

"This is worse than any fast food work I've done. I could survive it, but he's got too much help, and not enough business. I really need to find a new job, something with computers."

"Yeah, that's more your deal. I'll keep an eye out if I hear about anything at the library," he said. Deon worked part-time in the geology library, watching the counter and checking out books for people. It was mindless, and he hated his fundamentalist christian boss, but it was air conditioned, and regular work.

"What's up with you anyway? What are you up to?" I asked.

"Not much, just waiting for classes to start tomorrow. You taking anything?"

"Yeah, I think. I have to skip a half day of work to register tomorrow," I said. "The bastard's probably going to fire me for it. I told him when I started, but he's sort of being a shithead about it."

"Well dude, I hope it works out," Deon said.

"Yeah me too. Hey, I think I'm gonna crash for a bit. I'm not used to this early morning shit."

"That's cool, I'll get outta here," he said. "Catch you later, man."

"Okay. Later, Deon."

I rolled over and stretched my aching legs, trying to find a comfortable position that didn't wear any of the sore spots on my body. Within five minutes, I fell into a deep sleep.

During my comatose state, my mind jumbled through vivid dreams that made no sense, pounding my brain with REM sleep to distract from my aching body. However, most of the images I remembered had to do with me hunched over, pulling shingles and throwing out my back. Instead of being on a roof, I would be downtown, pulling shingles from the sidewalk, or in the middle of my parents' back yard, pulling sod like it was shingles. The images weaved through a confusing cloth of distant and recent memories, but felt like it continued for hours and days.

After a cycle of thick dreams, I'd wake up, sweating and still sore all over. My mind would feel hazy and want to return to sleep, but my body couldn't endure the sticky summer heat and tender muscular damage on all sides. Tossing and turning, any position would either feel too hot or too painful on some damaged body part. The struggle would continue for what seemed like hours, and then the heavy dreams would begin again.

Finally, the alarm rang and I instinctively slammed the snooze. 7:56 AM, and I remembered looking at the clock at least once an hour since bedtime. At least I got to sleep a few hours later than the day before, due to my morning registration appointment. But the constant periods of sleeplessness and the lifelike dream state made it feel like I never really went to sleep. Even worse, every sore muscle from the day before became stiff and seared with pain. I wanted to go back to bed, but I was sure I'd sleep until noon and miss both class registration and beginning of work. This is going to be a long fucking day, I mumbled as I climbed from bed to get into the shower.

The fifteen-minute walk from my apartment to Franklin Hall soothed my nerves a good deal. The Indiana University campus at 9 AM on the first day of summer possessed such a relaxing aura that I couldn't help but feel good about starting classes again. The sun illuminated the limestone buildings, trees in full green rustled above me, and the fresh-cut grass and flowers in bloom lined the paths on either side of me. A campus built for thirty thousand, I now shared the acreage with less than six thousand people, at least in the first, shorter summer session. Even with my walkman blasting a soundtrack directly into my ears (Motörhead: *1916*— an album that strongly defined last summer's roadtrips to Bloomington and time-killing with Nick back in South Bend. I'd need to find this summer's definitive album, but 'don't fix what's broken' crossed my mind when I grabbed the tape that morning.) I felt the incredible feeling that I wasn't back in Elkhart, I wasn't on a factory floor, and I wasn't in my mom's basement.

Franklin Hall used to be the main library, back when IU consisted of only the half-dozen buildings arranged in a crescent shape on the west side of campus. Now the ivy-covered hall contained the bursar, registrar, and some other support-type departments, like parking and ID cards. It sat at the end of the crescent, at the mouth of Sample Gates, the symbolic portal that connected the campus to the city's main drag, Kirkland Avenue. I trailed down the brick path to the front door of the registrar, which already bustled with people trying to pick classes and arrange paperwork for registration.

I didn't even think about taking summer classes last spring, let alone register for them, so it took some bureaucratic bitch-slapping to get the proper paperwork in order. I stole a schedule of classes, sat on the tile floor outside the registrar's office. The building reminded me of some kind of Ivy League school, something out of Dead Poet's Society or John Knowles' *A Separate Peace*. Intricate woodwork, high ceilings, and narrow, multi-paned windows with leaded glasswork surrounded a sophisticated interior recently remodeled. I gazed in awe, and tore through the booklet and tried to find something I could pass without difficulty. I considered an English class that met the intensive writing requirement, but couldn't find anything in the short session that did the trick. There were also no computer classes worth taking that would help with the degree. Many time slots were during the nine to five zone, which I wanted to keep free for work. I found an intro political science class that met at night. Last summer, I took another hundred level polysci course and got a C, even though I only showed up four times. With more frequent appearances, this class might mean a better grade.

After some scantron sheet bubble-filling and a swipe of my new Visa card, I was the proud owner of a polysci class that met twice a week, for three hours a night. I shuffled out of the building, put Lemmy and the boys back on the walkman, and walked back to Aristotle's to buy the books.

Day two of the contracting job made day one look like a leisure activity people would pay money to do at a theme park. After my morning at the registrar, I spent the afternoon raking a back yard—basically doing the action of a roto-tiller but 500 times slower. The sun bore down with a fury, causing the pink medium-rare hue on my arms and neck to boil and sweat. I hunched over the rake, stressing my back the wrong way for hours and tearing apart my hands by holding the rake the same way and the wrong way for the whole ordeal. All of the dirt in the yard looked fucked up and broken apart, and I couldn't tell what he wanted me to rake, or how I could tell when it was sufficiently dug up. It felt like trying to paint white paint on top of white paint and being completely incapable of figuring out what spots weren't getting coverage. I kept wasting the day guessing, hoping I wouldn't get caught, throwing out my back, and scraping the flesh from my hands with the wooden handled rake.

The ritual cleanup followed the workday, tired arms scrubbing wearily, the sink filling several times over with flaked dirt and the mix of soap and sweat. I made a first pass at the basin, still wearing all of the soiled clothes except the dirt-filled shoes. Before I even walked in the door, I removed the hiking boots and dumped out what seemed like a metric ton of soil, kicked in by the day's raking festivities. Even after removing the boots and the white-turned-black socks, my feet seared with pain. The shower, which always contained the scum of a half dozen tenants, probably never saw the filth my body produced as I lathered on three or four coats of bar soap, and peeled at my scalp with fingernails and shampoo.

I made a wonderful footbath with a plastic dishpan normally used to hold my dirty drinking glasses and silverware. Filled with a gallon of cold water, it cooled my feet like a blacksmith submerging red-hot horseshoes into a trough. Sore pressure points covered my soles, but the immersion removed some of the pain from standing all day.

After a brief soak and a relaxing drink, I rummaged on top of the dresser for a folded piece of paper with a phone number. I hadn't called Tammy since she left, and even though I wanted to dial her after the first night apart, I waited for things to settle down. I grabbed the phone, and punched the eleven numbers on the slip. It picked up on the second ring, and I heard her familiar voice, the same voice I heard when I called her months ago in her dorm room.

"Hi, it's me," cheerful to hear her again, to be on the phone again.

"Hi," replied Tammy, nonplussed. Off to a bad start, I thought. Maybe she was mad because I didn't call earlier? Or maybe it was a problem with her parents, with living at home. The untold tension built, and I felt like a comedian facing a silent audience, ready to be booed and heckled.

"So how was the trip? How are things back home?" I asked

"It's okay I guess. The man my mother married is still being an asshole, the usual," she sighed.

"Is something up?" I asked. "You don't sound too excited to hear from me."

"Look John," she said. "We really need to talk."

The magic words no man wants to hear. All of my fears and paranoia cycling through my head during the last weekend were true. I was in the electric chair, and they were shaving my head for the electrodes...

"Okay, let's talk. What's on your mind?"

"Look, I think you're expecting too much out of me. I thought we figured things out before I left, but..."

"But what?" I snapped. "I thought we would..."

"John, we made a deal that things would be off for the summer. I don't know if I'm coming back to Indiana in the fall, and I don't know what will happen before then. Things are up in the air and I can't worry about keeping in touch with you or upsetting you. If there are other people you want to see, or if other things happen, I don't want you to be committed to someone that's a thousand miles away."

"Tammy, I don't want to date anyone else. I'll wait to see how things will work out."

"You're saying that now, but three months is a long time. We haven't even known each other that long. I need to go on with my life. I can't spend my summer expecting that we will get back together and then find out I have to go to state here next fall. I went through that last fall with my high school boyfriend and it almost killed me."

"Is that the real reason?" I asked carefully. "Is there someone else?"

"No, there isn't someone else!" she snapped. "But I do have a lot of guy friends that I spend time with, I hang out with a group of people, and I don't know what will happen over the summer. I don't want to hurt you if I do meet someone else and things get serious."

"So..." I paused. "Is this it?"

"I don't know, John. Maybe I will be back and maybe we will both be single in the fall and maybe the magic will still be there, but that's a lot of maybes. Neither of us can depend on that. I know I would be a nervous wreck if I tried to rely on that all summer, and I know you probably would have a lot of trouble too."

"Yeah, you're probably right. I've had a lot of trouble just making it this far. I guess my patience is low. I don't know..."

"John, you really are wonderful. I've never had a guy do as many nice things as you did. I'll always remember that."

"You know this has been the most perfect thing that has happened to me," I said. "I feel like I'm going to say that forever. Everything seemed perfect, everything except the end. There's always a catch."

"I know. I didn't want to think that either, but I know."

A pause came from the phone, a moment where neither of us wanted to be the person to end the call, but neither knew what to say next. I thought of a million last lines, last proposals, or things I really wanted to tell her, but each time I started, something stopped me. I didn't want to say anything I'd regret. I didn't want to burn any bridges, or look stupid trying to save the ones already burning down. Finally, she broke the silence.

"John, can you make me a promise?" she said.

"What?"

"Promise me you won't do anything? If you feel like you can't deal with this, don't hurt yourself. Go talk to Mike or Nick or Peter or somebody, or go to your doctor, or something, okay? I don't want you to get hurt."

"I can't promise you that."

"What do you mean?" she replied, alarmed. "Are you planning on doing something? I don't like it when you scare me like this."

"I'm not planning on anything," I said. "I just can't promise you anything, for the same reason you can't promise me anything. I don't know what will happen this summer. I've been depressed before I met you, and I'll be depressed after you're gone..."

"I wish you weren't like this."

"Me too. But it's something I have to face by myself."

"Well, just promise you'll go to the doctor, and that you'll take your medicine and stop drinking."

"I always keep up with the medicine, but no promises on the alcohol, either."

"John, I just worry that you'll do something and it will be my fault."

"You've never been responsible for my actions, and now that this is over, you definitely aren't. It's nobody's fault but my own at this point."

"Okay, well I've gotta go," she huffed, upset and trying to end the conversation.

This was my last chance to say anything, before she hung up. I remembered all of the times I hung up in the past, saying "I love you" and knowing she would reciprocate. I couldn't say "see you later" or "I'll write" or anything else. I wanted to say "you've meant everything to me" and "I've got a loaded gun under the bed and my brains will be on the ceiling three seconds after I put down the phone." But in the half-second pause, I realized nothing would work, and even if I spent the rest of my life torturing myself, I should just walk away and say nothing else.

"Bye, Tammy."

"Bye John."

The phone clicked, and returned me to the dial tone. I was, once again, truly alone.

6

The contracting boss didn't give me an assignment on Tuesday night after work, and the next morning, I rolled out of bed and saw a torrential downpour outside. In the early darkness, I could see the thickness of a heavy summer storm, washing away yardwork and making roofing impossible. I crawled back into bed, knowing there'd be no call for work that morning.

Even after worrying about the ramifications of missing a day of work, sleep came fast and engulfed me. The inverted, nocturnal schedule of last spring wasn't conquered yet, and I still felt a strong, biological need to stay in bed past noon. The sound of showers dancing on the rooftop tranquilized me further, and I faded in and out of sleep for hours.

Around lunchtime, I started the day with a long, relaxing shower, and shuffled through the house in a bathrobe, wondering what to do with my afternoon. Outside, the rain stopped, and the sun peeked through a gray sky to illuminate the trees and grass, a heavy green from the recent weather. In the kitchen, I stared at the tiny backyard's thick trees, and felt a weird chill through my body, like I was in a place I wasn't supposed to be. It was like playing hooky and driving three states away, then realizing you should be in class or at work instead of taking pictures from the top of the Sears Tower. I'd worked a steady job since I was 14, with no gaps of longer than a week in my employment record. The whole idea of working bits and pieces here and there would take some getting used to.

After putting on my usual uniform of jeans and a t-shirt, I spent a few minutes looking over my books for my polysci class, which would meet for the first time that night. In the stereo, a Carnival of Shame promo CD, courtesy of Nick, played in the background. The soft-cover polysci book read slightly more advanced than a high school text, and the chapters, on subjects like causes of war, international organizations, and imperialism looked easily digestible. He also assigned Orwell's *1984*, a book I'd read and enjoyed greatly during my Dalton Trumbo, *Johnny Got His Gun*, anti-war, anti-Reagan period in high school. Maybe this teacher wouldn't be too bad.

That evening, I armed myself for the first class session, assembling together pens, pencils, paper, books, backpack, and walkman. I downed two microwave burritos and a Coke, hefted the backpack on my shoulder, and hit the road for Woodburn Hall. In the trusty Aiwa walkman, the Virus 100 compilation blasted into the headphones. Nick was right about the tape; in commemoration of the 100th release on Jello Biafra's label, the label put together a collection of Dead Kennedys covers by bands including Napalm Death, Sepultura, Faith No More, and many others. The mix of heavy, weird and eclectic versions of the songs that first introduced me to punk sounded timely during my orientation to a new life on the campus in summer.

I arrived early, and circled the front of the building for a bit, to kill some time. Woodburn Hall, an odd, castle-looking structure, housed the political science department. Built in the early forties under one of the Depression-era government programs, it looked even more peculiar sitting across Seventh Street from the massive, Star Wars-like, I.M. Pei-designed art museum.

In the basement, bright orange and yellow walls showed that this building hadn't been remodeled in 20 years. I found the room, a small lecture hall with six rows of fifty-year-old theatre-type seats arranged on mesa-like steps. I grabbed a seat comfortably toward the back, and stared at the people slowly filing into the hot room. From first estimates, it looked like about 30 people were registered, a mix of fraternity/sorority types and middle-aged continuing studies students, with a token Marxist in all black, and a couple of hippie types in the mix. Not too bad, I thought. It seemed like a good crowd.

The teacher jumped into the classroom on time, and dumped his briefcase onto the desk. He looked like Woody Allen's younger brother—no glasses, but the same wiry, curly, out of control hair, a beanpole thin body with a button-down short sleeve, and a look that screamed Brooklyn to me.

He grabbed a stack of syllabi from the briefcase, and handed them to a person in the front row to pass around. "Okay. Nuclear physics? Just kidding. Introduction to World Politics Y109." I called it—he even had a New York accent thicker than the humidity in the basement classroom. "This is my first time teaching a class in the summer..." The thirty-some students gasped a silent, collective sigh of relief.

The teacher explained the class to us, as I wavered in and out of consciousness. Different political systems...two tests, two papers, some quizzes...readings from a paperback textbook, and Orwell's *1984*...The whole class slid slower into their chairs, the heat mesmerizing us. He began to lecture on what constitutes a government...

I stopped taking notes, and let my eyes wander around the room. Any cute women? Not really—there were a few that I'd start fantasizing about, once the oxygen level in the room dropped and the temperature rose. What did these people do once class got out? I wondered if the bars had an influx of people, coming in at nine to drink away what they learned in summer classes. No, these people, at least the ones my age, probably lived in houses with three or four other close friends, and led soap-opera lives with a rich cast of characters. I didn't get that sense of community living in my lowest-bidder apartment, when most of the other tenants were clinically insane or inciting riots over the disappearance of their last beer in the fridge. I wondered what would've happened to me if I'd lived in the dorms last year, instead of living at the house. For one thing, I'd be in Elkhart—the dorms close for the summer and rent the rooms to high school band camps and other summer conventions.

Thinking about the dorms made me think about Tammy. I still remember being at her place one evening, a beautiful April night when the cool air and clear sky made me think the world was built just for me, when everything I touched and smelled and saw was sensual. She had a double to herself, a stock Forest quad room with a wall of closets, a set of windows across the full length of the room, and stark white walls that ran up to a tall ceiling. It felt institutional, like a hotel room, but she had pictures and posters on the walls to add some sense of individualism. We listened to a Shadowfax CD, and she showed me her two saxophones, and pictures of famous musicians she met. I wrapped my arms around her, and we stood at the window, both looking in the darkness, at the cars passing stories below on Third Street. We smelled the fresh air of spring and looked at the trees and lamps of the circle drive in front of the buildings, the people going out and coming back from parties, and on the left, the ten-story tower of limestone and lights that made up Forest B. A month later, I could still smell the trees, feel her sweatshirt pressing into me—it was one of those moments that got burned into my mind forever.

I still felt like dialing 857-5604 every time I picked up a phone; I still thought she'd answer. I saw the evidence though—I was there the day the loft went back to the rental company, when the posters were pulled from the white cinderblock and her boxes went into the family wagon. It felt like that Twilight Zone where the guy woke up and kissed his wife and kid, and then a director yelled "cut!" and he found out he was on a movie set, and the kitchen was really built out of flat panels painted to look like cabinets and windows. A few weeks before, we were having the most beautiful moment of my life, and then—it's a wrap! Strike set!

"Okay, let's stop for now and take a fifteen minute break." The teacher snapped me from my daydream, and I knew the lecture would only get worse for the second half. I shoved my stuff into the backpack, shuffled out of the class, and headed for home. I had the reading assignment for the next day, so I wouldn't miss much. I needed to go back to my room, focus on this depression, and either break through it or let it consume me until I fell asleep for the evening.

The next morning, I stumbled through the house for a few minutes before my shower, to curse the rain that drizzled over the windows and kept the skies dark during the first completely free day of the summer. The evening before consisted of a great lead-weight depression, sending pathetic email to everyone I knew, and attempts at sleep intermixed with a couple of long walks and many depressing CDs. Since it was past noon, the mailman already visited, and left the residents' letters in the two metal boxes outside the house. As part of the daily mail ritual, somebody else had taken the letters and moved them to the mantle without a fireplace that stood in the main hallway, and arranged them on the ledge, sometimes even sorting them by recipient.

Mail. Great. I looked at the piles of paper and noticed a common letter in most stacks, one with the Indiana University seal on the return-address. I found mine along with a CD club past-due notice, and tore open the IU letter first, to see how bad I did.

Its contents were the ominous, single-page semester grade report. Luckily, I changed my permanent address to 414 S Mitchell #13, or my parents would be reading this—and they wouldn't like the results:

```
DESCRIPTIVE TITLE OF COURSE   DEPT.   COURSE   HOURS    GRADE    SECTION
DATA STRUCTURES               CSCI    C343     4.0      W        1751
CALCULUS II                   MATH    M216     5.0      W        3356
INTRO TO MACROECONOMICS       ECON    E202     3.0      W        2019
INTRODUCTORY PSYCHOLOGY I     PSY     P101     3.0      F        3710


UNDERGRADUATE GPA HRS 75.0   HRS PASS 64.0  POINTS 146.3 GPA 1.95
CREDIT POINTS THIS SEMESTER  .0      THIS SEMESTER GPA       .00
HOURS ATTEMPTED              3.0     GPA HOURS THIS SEMESTER     3.0
```

I should frame this one, I thought. This even beats my 0.37 GPA last spring. The report didn't surprise me, except for the psych grade. I'd bailed out of everything else, with the aid of a note from my shrink, to avoid adding 12 hours of F to my GPA, but I kept the psych class, because I thought I had a shot at a D. After spending hours at extra credit labs and all-night study sessions, I didn't make it.

My scholarship required me to finish 24 credits per calendar year, and attain a GPA above 2.0. In each of my first two years, I seriously fucked up the spring semester, and then took enough summer classes to pad my stats. I hoped that three credits of D would get me three credits closer to the magic 72 hour number, but it looked like I should have taken the W and lost a semester of tuition.

Now I needed eight credits, which meant passing this polysci class and taking two more classes in the second summer session. I'd need better than straight C's to get above the 2.0. It sounded simple, but many of my best semesters were straight C's. I'd need to work like hell to pull above the 2.0 line for this one, and that didn't mean leaving lectures halfway through.

The most ominous part of the report was the 1.95 GPA. I was already on academic probation last spring, and needed to pull back above a 2.0, which I didn't. I expected some sort of evil paperwork along with my report card, but maybe I'd get the notification later, in a separate letter. Maybe I'd get a phone call from my advisor. Or maybe one day, I'd try to log into my computer account and it wouldn't work. The wait began, and I got paranoid enough to start reading my polysci book on my day off.

Spending a weekend alone in Bloomington with no money was an art form I mastered over the years, and my first weekend that summer was no exception. I spent a big chunk of Friday night at Morgenstern's, my favorite bookstore, reading unix programming books. After a few hours of that, I returned to the random driving, the walks, staring at computer screens. Amidst the wandering around alone, I mentally budgeted my bank account and the change left in the ashtrays of my car to find how much I could spend on groceries for the month.

Even with the busy work, I still couldn't shake the thought of Tammy. With such picture-perfect images of her every time I walked the campus, I felt like I should give her a call, and try to talk through it. This alternated with moments of clarity when I realized I was a step away from becoming Mark Chapman, and I should never read *Catcher in the Rye*, buy a handgun, or fall for Jodi Foster. I'd catch myself obsessively opening and refolding the slip of paper with her number on it, tracing the loops in her handwriting with my finger, and thinking about how the paper was in her hand only a few days before. I'd dial the first ten digits of her number and then hang up. I even sent her a half-dozen carefully composed emails, knowing she wouldn't read them for three or four months, if at all. But the reflex of typing her name on the computer, typing my thoughts, and hitting Control-Z to send the message felt so good, so familiar.

I couldn't talk to her, I couldn't spend my money, and it was through. I needed to talk to someone else, and I didn't even know the full roster of friends on campus for summer session I. More people bailed town for the first, shorter session. But people would turn up from hiding, and a wave of students would arrive for the longer summer II session.

I spent Saturday doing my laundry at the campus laundromat. Even this made me think of her. It felt like destroying evidence—washing the same shirts and jeans that smelled like her, like her perfume. I forced myself to wash everything, to remove the association. While the clothes spun, I walked to the opposite end of the strip mall. I went into Morgenstern's, bought a magazine (some kind of conspiracy theory journal that talked about Gulf War Syndrome about four years before everyone heard about it) and went to the Chinese restaurant next door for some sweet and sour pork. This was a new tradition for me, but a comfortable one. I felt good about reading, eating some good food, and getting my clothes washed. But the Chinese food—the smell of soy sauce and texture of rice and sweet and sour made me think about when I cooked Chinese for Tammy...After finishing the clothes and the food, I spent the rest of the night alone, reading the magazine twice over and logging in every hour.

On Sunday night, the contractor called to tell me he wasn't getting many new jobs and that I should start to look for something else. He did promise to mail a check for two days' labor, which would buy me a cartload of groceries with a couple of bucks to spare. But, I seriously needed to think about some other work to get me through the summer. I vowed to get back to the job placement center and find something else, even if it did involve telemarketing.

Monday morning, or rather afternoon, promised smoother sailing for me, with a bright, sunny day waiting outside. I wandered to the mail ledge, spying today's bounty of envelope, sorted by tenant. My only mail—a letter from the recorder's office of the College of Arts and Sciences, ominous in its official look and lack of any other distinguishing markings. I tore it open, and read the single sheet of watermarked letterhead inside:

Dear Student:

As a result of your unsatisfactory academic performance last semester, you have been dismissed as a degree candidate in the College of Arts and Sciences. This action follows the policy regarding dismissal published in the Bulletin of the College of Arts and Sciences under the heading "Academic Standing of Students."

If you registered for fall classes during April computer registration, your registration will be canceled unless your Petition for Readmission has been approved by the Scholarship and Probation Committee. To be considered for readmission for the fall semester, you must submit a petition no later than June 20. You may request a petition from this office. If you are approved for readmission, your registration is valid. If not, your registration will be canceled. (You will be notified in writing concerning the outcome.)

If you wish to discuss your academic status further with an Assistant Dean, or have questions about the procedure you may write or call...

Fuck...I ran into the bedroom, and dialed the number. My pulse felt like it was at 300, and I hoped a human would pick up the phone. After a transfer, I found a person who knew what I was talking about. Almost unable to speak, I rattled off my student ID number, and she asked me for my question. I imagined that her computer screen would be flashing DISMISSED in giant red letters, but maybe not.

"I was recently dismissed and had a few questions. Will my summer courses be dropped?"

"No, registration won't be withdrawn for summer courses, but any registered classes for the fall will be dropped if you are dismissed from the College of Arts and Sciences. You can still register for the rest of the summer, or any other summer session with no problem."

"Okay, great. My second question—I am at a 1.95 GPA, and I'm taking a full load this summer. If I pull back to a 2.0, would I still have to petition for readmission?"

"You'll still have to petition for readmission, but if you have a 2.0 GPA when your petition is evaluated, you'll probably be automatically readmitted."

"Last question—I had a petition approved to drop some courses last spring on medical grounds, and COAS has some documentation from my doctor concerning my performance last semester. Do I still have to petition for readmission?"

"Yes, you do. But if you get above a 2.0 cumulative GPA and have the medical petition, you'd almost certainly be readmitted, and you wouldn't have to re-register for fall classes. It's still very important to document all of this in a letter and petition for readmission, though. Without a formal request, you'll be dismissed regardless of other documentation or improvements in your GPA."

I thanked her for her help, and hung up.

What a relief, I thought. I'd still have to come up with some bullshit for that letter, though. And I still worried that I'd fuck up my grades over the summer, or mess up something and end up kicked out of school. Another constant worry to haunt me for the summer...

Time passed, but I still thought of Tammy. A heavy weight passed through my chest and into my body, and I'd feel weak even when the slightest reminder of our past togetherness entered my mind. I couldn't snap out of the depression or make it go away any easier than a person could will away pneumonia and instantly return to being better. I knew it would take time, and I didn't know how much—I hoped in days or weeks, I'd return to the same old miserable John, out trying to find a date and spending too much time on the computer, coding some godawful project in VAX C. But this time, it would take longer. Walking away from something perfect isn't easy.

While trying to calculate my mean average downtime for breakups, I kept thinking about the first time I dumped someone, about two years ago—the first time I was on the other side of the knife. The girl in question degraded me, insulted me, demanded all of my time, and expected perfection. But, when I tried to dump her, she cried and pleaded and begged for me not to leave. I spent weeks and hundreds of bucks with a shrink who insisted that I sever all ties with this bitch. I got back from an therapy appointment, and before I could back down, I called her, said it was over, said I'd mail her stuff back, said I wasn't willing to negotiate at all, and hung up. It felt so righteous to be single again, on a campus full of women walking around in shorts, willing to talk to anyone who said hi, especially after months of psychic torture and abuse.

A few hours after I dumped her, I realized that life would be different. I sacrificed so much for her—friends, activities, music, routines—and I'd need to start over. There was nothing in my life, even with this great victory. And to rub it in even more, this was toward the end of the semester, when everyone was buried in their books, and I could barely find anyone to talk to about the whole situation. I went to the movies alone, feeling like a destitute, the last person alive. The uncertainty of not knowing the next step in my life hurt deep in my soul. When you're in a relationship, you take for granted the hugs, the kisses, the closeness, the holding hands and daily activities and phone calls and affirmation of your existence as a human. When that's suddenly removed, you realize how alone you can be.

Once again, I felt that every minute of the day, and I tried to find a plan to avoid it. I knew Tammy wouldn't return, and I knew I had to kick ass in my summer courses to stay in school. I also knew I had to figure out something to do about money. I still wanted to find another perfect woman again and start over, but I knew it wouldn't happen—women can smell desperation a mile away, and the only ones that enjoy it are the ones who will fuck you over even worse. Instead, I tried to think about passing this polysci class, reading the text and the Orwell book, and spending time in my little twin bed, learning enough about comparative politics to get a B. When the heaviness of it consumed me, I'd hit the computer like a junkie, checking new mail and scanning every second for someone new, someone to talk to. But during my time alone, I still felt like a part of me had been removed, like I could never live a normal life again.

No new mail on the computer, nothing happening. I sat at the console, picking for someone to dump my problems on, but it seemed everyone's distant early warning tipped them off to my typical desire for instant sympathy, and my friends were out having lives and stuff. It was a Tuesday night, which usually meant an empty house on the VAXes anyway.

Flashbacks of Tammy's phone call last week continued to haunt me, alternating my ambient mood between the depression of losing her and the anxiety of not knowing what to do. After giving up with the computer, I sat in bed with the phone in my lap, trying to think of who to call, who I could talk to and gain some perspective on the situation.

Under the mattress, a lump pressed into my back, something to remind me of my last option. I lifted the top mattress, and pulled out the shotgun.

With gun in hand, my mind wandered over the last part of the phone call. "Promise me you won't do anything?" Her words burned in my head, reminding me of what I did want to do. In depression, with her gone, the last person I thought could understand me had left. Depression coursing through my veins, the idea of just putting the shotgun in my mouth and ending everything appealed to me. The alternative seemed to be a life of bouncing from person to person, never finding love, never finding shelter, never finding a soulmate, but just showing up for work every day and never realizing the prime emotions that made life worth living.

The feeling wasn't unique, or new. My first flirtations with suicide came in high school, when moodshifts ran rampant and without treatment, alienating me and making me feel that nobody else on the planet knew I existed. When the other boys and girls turned into men and women, my social life never blossomed. I spent the weekends working in a department store, reading books, or hiding from the world with my one or two friends like Nick and Peter. And when that didn't work, I thought about ending things.

That never panned out. I didn't have a method, and eventually I started spending my Tuesday afternoons on a therapist's couch to drill out these thoughts and replace them with more positive ones. But on occasion, I still felt like things just weren't going to work out, like it was time to just give up fighting against something as overwhelming as clinical depression.

"Fuck!" I mumbled, the gun shaking in my hands. Now wasn't the time, this was all too stupid. Maybe there was a better way out of the situation. I could talk to someone, get out of the damn house, something...

A few possibilities flashed through my head, then I thought about calling my friend Susan. The gun went back under the bed and with some digging around, I found her new summer phone number on the back of an envelope. After a few deep breaths, I dialed and waited for an answer.

I met Susan last winter, from the computer. I felt drawn to her because of some sort of girl-next-door quality; she seemed very energetic in our conversations, like Tricia. I gave her a surprise phone call one night, and found her just as sweet on the phone, her voice cute yet seductive. I didn't ask any further, but always imagined that she was somewhat attractive.

Susan put considerable effort toward finding Mister Right and having fun while doing so. Every day, I got another update about who was in and who was out. Keeping up with her crushes, dates, interests, boy-toys and man-friends became more complicated than keeping up to date with the New York Stock Exchange. But, I also dumped my dating problems in her direction, and she always gave me a good female opinion on what I was doing right and wrong in the game of love. When our updates, which sounded like commodities exchange transactions, went across the line, we always had codenames or abbreviations for the people drifting out of our life. She'd fire me an email talking about the baseball player, the beta, the poet and the lawyer, and I'd tell her what happened with the freshman, the redhead, the Russian, and the cellist.

Right before my first date with Tammy, I told Susan I had a blind date with some other random girl, but didn't know what to wear. She asked me if I had any room on the plastic, and I did, so she offered to take me to the mall and pick out my clothes for the date.

When I went to her dorm and picked her up for the shopping trip, I couldn't keep my mouth off the floor. Even in a pair of old jeans and a sweatshirt, Susan put supermodels to shame. She had the best hair I've ever seen on a human being in my life, a light brown, curly, but long, almost halfway down her back. Everything about her looked perfect—her figure, her face—her eyes were a cutting emerald green color, and her skin had an incredible tone with a perfect tan. I had to think hard to keep the humorous and friendly conversations going like I did online, but within a few minutes, she didn't intimidate me. It was just like hanging out with any of my other friends. We bought clothes and wandered the mall and got me dressed and ready for romance.

That blind date didn't work out, but a few weeks later, I met Tammy, wearing the same shirt and cologne that Susan picked out for me. My e-mail reports to her and Tricia went from describing a field of dozens to just describing the details about Tammy. Both Susan and Tricia were happy to see me happy after so much depression and failure in the previous months. Now...well, I hoped Susan would be as understanding as she was during the previous low times.

The phone rang twice and picked up. "Hi!" answered a vibrant, bouncy female's voice.

"Susan? It's John Conner."

"John Conner!" said a familiar sexy and invigorating voice on the phone. "How's your summer going sofar?"

"Not good. It's Tammy," I said. "It's...it's over. I talked to her last week, she can't handle the away thing for the summer and she's not sure I can either, so she wanted out."

"Oh, John...I'm sorry," she said. "I don't know what to say—I thought things were really working out for you two."

"Yeah, me too. I don't know what to do."

"Look, don't blame yourself," she said, "I know you loved her, but if the distance killed this thing, there's nothing you could've done about it."

"I know, but I do blame myself. You know what my track record was before going into this thing. It took me so long to find someone that I thought was perfect, and then something that isn't my fault ends it. I don't know what to do next."

"You need to stop worrying about her and start worrying about yourself. Maybe you need to bury yourself in schoolwork or the computer, or hang out with friends for a while. But don't tear yourself apart over this. I know it sounds corny," she said. "But it's all you can do. You can't control it, you said so yourself. Work on the things you can control. And don't do anything sudden, okay?"

"It seems like everyone thinks I've got a gun to my head or something."

"Well, if you had one, would it be?"

Well, it was a second ago. "Good point," I said.

"John, I am really sorry. I know she means a lot to you."

"I know. I'll live I guess."

"I really worry about you sometimes," she said. "Last spring when you had so many problems, I wanted you to settle down with someone and get better."

"You and me both," I said.

"It'll happen again. I know you're sick of everyone saying that to you, but it will. You have potential. You just need to make sure not to blow it."

"I'll try. I've got to do good in school this summer, so maybe that'll take my mind off of things."

"That sounds like a plan. Hey, I've got to run, but send me email and let me know everything is okay. And feel free to call if you need to talk. But be warned, there's four girls here so the phone can be pretty random."

"Okay, thanks Susan..."

We said goodbye and hung up, and I rolled up in the bed and tried to think of what the hell would happen next.

7

Another sunny, enchanting day made for a pleasant walk to the job placement center, where the unbearable task of sponsoring my daily bread awaited me. The center, a small building that looked like a cottage from *The Sound of Music*, stood across the street from the campus health facility, a place I knew well from my psych appointments. The job center's cobblestone paths and giant awnings make it look different than any other campus facility, and more like a gift shop at Disneyland. Maybe it was an international student center in a previous life, or an academic fraternity.

At the reception desk inside, I signed in, and went to the job board, the room of hope. Four walls of screw-in peg hooks held paper cards with descriptions of job leads, segregated by job type and location. When I found something I liked, I had to write down a code number, and a person at the desk would give me a card with information on applying for the position.

The system sounded great, like there were jobs lying on the ground ready for anyone to pick them up. I heard about the center the day I decided to stay for the summer, and I thought I'd find plenty of menial labor jobs, making it trivial to get in at least 10 or 15 hours of minimum wage employment every week. In reality, the cards were horridly out of date, and the most current ones were for day care and kids' camps. Several more were for various multi-level marketing scams, or other college campus rip-offs, like handing out credit card applications or telemarketing. A few decent-sounding campus positions were open to work-study students, but I didn't get any need-based financial aid because of my scholarship. At this point, food service and telemarketing were my only options.

I scanned more cards, hoping to find a will-train position as VAX operator, but there weren't any postings in the computer section. I also browsed the national board, looking for any interesting openings around the country. I daydreamed about a job in California or even Chicago that didn't require a degree, maybe a suit-and-tie sales job, a Wall Street trading intern or a computer job that cared about coding and not academics. I'd give up Indiana and school in a second for a good opportunity, but it was obvious that I need to get school finished first.

School, school, school—I'd start next fall as a fourth year junior, no matter how much ass I kicked in the summer session. I'd hopefully fill some of the annoying prerequisites—my polysci class filled part of a Social and Behavioral prereq, but the wimpy general degree requirements didn't worry me. I faced a death march over the next couple of years: three semesters of Spanish, three semesters of calc, three more core courses and a computer science sequence, plus the start of another. With luck and hard work, I'd clear out a lot of those courses over the next school year and finish next spring with about a semester and a half of coursework left. I didn't know how I'd foot the extra year, but I'd been telling my parents "nobody graduates in four" ever since I was in high school.

Aside from the grades and the slippage, I often wondered why I was a CS major. Last year, I decided to slip from the more difficult Bachelor of Science program to a straight BA, and my lackluster performance in two core classes this year made me wonder if I had what it takes to code for a living. Business majors and non-coders filled my Data Structures class last spring, and I scoffed, thinking I'd be able to hack the C++ assignments better, faster, and easier than anybody else in the room. It turned out I had to struggle to get anything done, and the people who went to class and brown-nosed managed good grades. I always hoped to be a hotshot coder, but in reality, I was sloppy and probably not one of the best and brightest. I could code my way out of a paper bag, and I could talk the talk, but I didn't know if I could finish the degree with a C average, let alone pull in a job with a Fortune 500 company. But until they kicked me out and it stuck, I'd keep trying. And if they kicked me out, I found out about a joint Philosophy/CS program that required less calc.

I grabbed a half-dozen job cards for telemarketing gigs and one for a chemistry lab monitor position, and headed back to the main desk.

I walked down Tenth Street, gazing at the occasional jogger and thinking. Money, money, money—I thought of the energy it took to walk around campus, the amount of calories, groceries, meals, I'd spend to get seven leads on a job. My savings consisted of fifty-some dollars, an upcoming eighty hour paycheck, and the two days' pay from the construction gig. The balance of those three looked great in my checkbook, but that would be it. My next consulting check would be for a handful of hours, and no other money was coming in. By the end of May, I'd be selling my CDs and furniture.

Next to me loomed the psychology building. I walked to the entrance, and looked around for the experiment center. Last spring, I had to do three experiments for the psych class I flunked. The first was a waste of time—comparing the sizes of circles and squares on a computer screen. But someone in class told me the magic secret to signing up for the labs—find ones that were for males only. I got in with a group where we had to watch videotapes of men and women arguing, and then buzz in whether it was the man's fault or the woman's fault. Then, in a covert way to fuck with us, another guy came in between videos and administered random and fake math tests, while leaning over our shoulders, rushing us, and calling people in the group idiots, so they'd get pissed off and vote differently. I also had an experiment where they put me in a room alone and told me I'd have to meet a female participant and then complete a survey saying if I found her desirable or not. First, they made me read over all of her application surveys and comment in advance as to what kind of person she was. I didn't meet the woman, which was probably planned, but reading her opinions on school, religion, abortion, drugs, family and everything else was old hat to me after tabulating my own useless questionnaires after endless first dates.

Yehoshua told me he planned to sign up for psych experiments to get some occasional weed money. They paid $5 cash for each round of trials, and there were some experiments paying more, or with multiple sessions. Rumor had it there was even an alcohol studies group that paid you $7 an hour to come in and get fucked up three or four times while solving crossword puzzles. I'd always hoped for better fare—as a manic-depressive, I wished for a high-end study of depression that involved free psychiatry and a decent weekly paycheck. But this wasn't a clinical facility, and it didn't even offer an MSW program—mostly just rats, mazes, and a disproportionate amount of auditory research.

I entered the glass double doors and into the side atrium of the facility. It looked like it was built or remodeled in the 1970's, with too many browns offset by golden amber and carpeted walls. I expected Kiefer Sutherland to walk out, wearing a handlebar mustache and talking about Freud. This was the very first academic building I ever set foot in. The week before my freshman year, I had to go to the aircraft-hanger classroom down the hall to listen to an academic advisor talk about how much we should study every week and how we should get help if we had problems. In retrospect, I wish I had tattooed the advice to my arm. I spent most of the session trying to hook up with a beautiful blonde aspiring actress from New York City who I didn't see again for months, when I found her tripping acid in one of the dorm stairwells and asking me if mixing blotter and antibiotics would kill her. Fun times.

In the main hallway, I grabbed a form and hastily signed up for the experiment pool. I also asked about a slot in a study on, you guessed it, auditory response, and a secretary enclosed behind a glass window took my form and told me to show up at 2:00 for an experiment. They'd also call in when they needed people for experiments during the times I said I'd be available, which was pretty much any nine to five slot for me. I thanked the lady in the tomb of glass, and snuck around the corner to the computer cluster to check my mail.

Even with a gentle breeze in my hair and a royal blue sky over my head, I had to wonder why I was even walking across campus. With one night class, no job, and no friends to speak of, it was pointless for me to go anywhere or do anything during the day. My apartment, now turning into some kind of pottery kiln by eight in the morning, wasn't a place for me to hang out. And I could sit in the IMU computer lab for only so long before I ran out of things to do. Having too much spare time on my hands sounds like a cardinal sin, but it's even more impossible to deal on a dwindling bank account and no job.

Every day, I thought about calling people—something I'd do when Tammy wasn't around and I needed another person to talk to, or someone to grab a meal or a brew with while she was out with her female friends. Instead of a phone book or a day planner, I kept a folded sheet of typing paper in my wallet, and added new contacts to the sheet. Because the eighths of the page gradually creased, folded, and split away from each other, I'd start anew each semester. The lists, an exact history of my social life over the last few months, read like a chronological list of everyone I dated or met. But now, from the spring '92 list—almost filled with names on the front side—only a half-dozen still lived in town. The summer would require more new friends, but where would I meet them? The whole idea of meeting same-sex or neutral gender friends seemed paradoxical. Society favored the meeting of opposite sex couples in movies, films, bars, 1-900 hotlines, personals ads. But how does a guy meet a bunch of other guys to drink beer with?

Instead of friends or jobs, I missed a belonging. On the way home, I watched some skateboarders grind up and down the church parking lot on Mitchell, a block up from my house. It seemed so simple—if you had a board and some skill, you could walk up to a skatepark and have instant buddies. It's like a fraternity, except instead of kegs and pledges, they have skinned knees and cool music. Where did I fit in? What if I joined a band? Wrote a book? Had a fast car? Hung out at bars until I was a regular? Joined some sort of new-age church? Volunteered? Got into academics? I could think of thousands of activities that would keep me busy and maybe introduce me to a larger group of people, offering some sense of being. But most of them were idiotic, or something I'd never do. I'm going to have to stumble along something on my own, I thought. My life happiness isn't as simple as joining pep club.

I trucked home for a lunch of peanut butter sandwiches and Cokes, and tried to kill a few hours by sitting around the house. Deon came back from a class, and spent an hour and a half bitching about his ultra-religious boss at the library, which was monotonous yet somehow entertaining. I also fired off some emails, and checked for any computer shifts, but there weren't any.

Back at the psych building, I got set up in a tiny booth with a pair of 1960's era headphones, and went through a 45-minute regimen of pressing one of two buttons, depending on whether or not I heard a certain tone. I had no idea what the experiment had to do with, and after ten minutes of boredom, I had to struggle to keep with the series of beeps. I pulled through, and they autographed my paperwork, which I was able to turn in at the front desk for a crisp, new five-dollar bill. It wasn't much, but five bucks was five bucks.

The next day, I beat the odds on filling in for a sub shift at the Fine Arts Mac cluster. A handful of shifts were open to subs during a typical summer week, and the dozens of people hungry for more hours immediately snapped them up. This gig was a double stroke of luck—not only did I get four hours of paid work, doing not much of anything, but Fine Arts had incredible air conditioning, and the fastest Mac computers on campus, with dual-monitor setups, color laserprinters, and flatbed scanners. Every time I worked there, I'd bring along some demented project and claim to be learning PhotoShop to better help the customers.

When I arrived, my friend Chad Brecken sat at a Mac in the far corner of the lab, dicking with a scanner. Brecken was a big guy, with short, dark hair, and a babyish and too-honest face. He'd talk in cheerful, friendly way to anyone he was within ten feet of, which was somewhat pleasant, but also annoyed a lot of people. It wasn't the charismatic fratboy sort of thing—it was more like an Amway salesman without the Amway to sell. Although most people disagreed with me, he was a pretty good guy, and since I knew him for a few years, he was always fun to chat with. He went through radical ups and downs with money and life; he'd have a semi-decent job, a car, a girlfriend, and would be going to school, but then the job would give out and he would owe the school a few thousand dollars, the woman would split, he'd total the car, and he'd be living in a closet above a Chinese restaurant, desperately looking for employment and hitting everyone up for job leads or a couple bucks. But then, a few months later, he'd be on the high end of some multilevel marketing scheme, with a nice apartment in a condo complex and a decent car, throwing around cash at the bars and buying people food, dressing in nice clothes and offering everybody in on his newest scheme for money. My cycles, although not as dramatic, often mirrored his. Like some kind of synchronized menstrual cycle bullshit, our tragedies were paralleled, almost to the week sometimes. We both helped each other with favors or support whenever possible; there were many times I was down for the count when Brecken was the only friend to save me. My other friends would make fun of him or try to avoid him, but I'd always jump into the ring for him.

"Brecken! No porno in the labs!" I yelled.

He jumped up from the keyboard, and spun around. "Hey John," he said. "I'm glad it was you, I thought I was busted this time."

"Nah, I don't care. What are you working on? Still trying to remove Paulina's swimsuit?"

On his screen, he was manipulating an image of an Indianapolis street vendors' license. "I'm working on something for Bruce, my boss," he said. It's so we can sell glowsticks at the Indy 500.

Last summer, Brecken's get-rich ploy was selling glowsticks—clear plastic strings filled with some sort of phosphorescent chemical. When bent to snap open and activate the chemicals inside, they'd glow for a few hours, and they could be ringed around and worn as bracelets or necklaces of glowing green, pink and blue. He worked for a distributor in town, and drove to county fairs and fireworks shows to sell them. When it got dusk, he'd bust out a few hundred sticks and the little kiddies would bug the hell out of their parents until they would buy a few at two or three bucks a pop.

"See, these permits cost fifty bucks, so Bruce bought one. But a dozen of us are going up there, so..."

"So as long as you're not in the same place at the same time..."

"Exactly," he said. "The permits are just black on white, but you have to wear a bracelet too. If anyone gets caught without a bracelet, they can just play dumb."

"Sounds like a plan," I said.

"Hey, are you doing anything this weekend? You should come up with me a couple of nights. It's pretty wild, and it's good money."

"What the hell man, I could use a few bucks. How much did you make last year?"

"I went on Friday, Saturday and Sunday nights," he said. "Saturday was the best night—I think I cleared a hundred. The other nights were less, 50, 60 bucks."

"I could use a hundred bucks," I said. "Count me in."

He reached into a folder of bogus work permits and maps, and produced a business card. "Here's Bruce's number. Give him a call as soon as you can, so you can get over there and do your papers before Friday."

I took the card and looked at the logo: S&T Marketing. "Okay, I'll give him a ring as soon as I get done in here."

"Hey, I haven't seen you at the fountain yet. Did you know we're doing it again this summer?"

Last summer, a bunch of people from the computer started meeting at the Showalter fountain every midnight. A handful of regulars and a bunch of occasionals met every night to talk, meet new people, and match usernames to faces. On the weekends I visited Lauren, we'd go to the gatherings and have a great deal of fun, joking with others and enjoying the cool evening weather in the greenish light of the fountain. I didn't know the meetings continued, and thoughts of regular conversation, new friends, and maybe even a few women ran through my head.

"Shit, I didn't know you guys started it again! Count me in, I sleep in every morning anyway."

"Cool, maybe I'll see you there."

A customer approached my Mac, looking for help. "Gotta run, man—I'll catch you later." I helped the person with a scanner, thinking about how cool it'd be to hang out at the fountain again, and how much I could really use a hundred bucks.

After helping someone scan some vacation pictures, I returned to the consultant Mac. I fired up a telnet connection to Bronze, the ULTRIX machine where I read my mail and did the brunt of my messing around, another to the Rose VAX, and a third to the Aqua VAX, where I was logged in as UCSFA, the site's email account. So, I was using $5000 of hardware to do what a $100 secondhand terminal could do. I didn't bring any graphics work with me, although I wanted to think of some larger zine project that would exploit the equipment in the lab. Once, when Nick was visiting, we took a stock picture included in PhotoShop, an overhead shot of nine babies lying in their nursery beds, and altered it so the kids were brutally dismembered. We digitally removed one kids' head and made another one chewing on it; another kid was gangrenous, and the one next to him had a spear through his heart. It was fun, but I could never find any other worthwhile graphics projects to bide my time.

Instead of graphics, I did some trawling. The process of randomly meeting women on the computer started as a joke, and became an addiction I strongly denied. Before I met Tammy, I mastered the primitive technology of finding people on the computer to an unsurpassed level. I'd scan the list of users on VMS and check for process names, the 16-character label you could assign to yourself that would display next to your username. Process names were like custom license plates or bumper stickers—they ranged from the funny to the vain to the stupid. By default, mine was "Doctor X," an obscure reference to Queensrÿche's 1988 concept album *Operation: Mindcrime*, but I had a program that ran on startup so I could pick anything from "At Work" to a dozen different metal-related song titles.

Because they weren't easy to set, I knew anyone with a process name was more than a casual user of the VAXes. I'd scan the userlist, find people with procnames I thought were funny or cute, and then look them up in the online address book, to see if they had an interesting major, or to see if they filled in the comments field in their entry. If I found somebody interesting, I'd send an email and see if they'd respond. It was nothing intrusive, and more than half of the people would respond just out of the novelty of getting email.

Did I feel terrible for scamming over the VAX? Not really. I wasn't out for sex, and I wasn't as bad as others. At least one guy a semester would email every woman that used the computers and sexually harass them to the point of messy disciplinary action. I'd never even ask to meet a woman from the computer until we talked for a while and I was sure she wanted to meet me. I exchanged mail with many people I never met in person, and many of the meetings resulted in friendships that continued for a long time. A handful of my email contacts resulted in something more intimate, and there were some that I wanted to date or get serious with. But I never asserted myself well with women, and the only times romance came my way was when it fell into my lap. Until that happened again, I kept busy writing email and wasting time at work.

Was I addicted to scamming? Not only did I spend a great deal of time looking for people, I spent time making tools to look for people. After a VMS upgrade a year and a half ago, typing in SHOW USER/FULL would display a user's Internet Protocol number after their name. An IP number, a unique grouping of numbers like 129.79.1.15, gave away your location on campus. In fact, in clusters like the IMU and Library, it even gave away which seat you were in. My friend Sid and I quickly hacked together scripts to find the location of people, or do stuff like list all of the people logged in at Forest quad. Sid also ran a utilities program, a bunch of handy shortcuts and wizbang programs not supported by the university. I created a database system for users of Sid's program, a sort of alternate version of the university's stodgy online address book. I purposely made it easy to use, and let people fill out tons of custom information in their profile. Did I hit on women who filled the database with interesting or funny details? Hey, it was my program.

I passed through my wholist again, and relaxed in the air-conditioned lab. It was boring, but it was money.

On the walk home a few hours later, I thought more about the fountain and last summer. It felt strange imagining the love I felt for Lauren only a year before, after living through the fights and the horrible breakup that occurred after our mystical summer together. I remembered the hot nights in bed, naked, with no sheets or covers, just the moon's rays from the double windows in her second story bedroom. The drives down and back were quite a recollection, also. I'd leave the second shift at the factory around midnight, take a shower at home, and dart back to the car, with my bags packed and a full tank of gas waiting for the full-bore excursion down the center of the state. With Motörhead blaring, the moonroof open to a view of the stars, and nobody in front of me, I'd scythe down the center of Indianapolis and jump down to her house in Bloomington. Like clockwork, I'd run to her room, drop my bags, and wake her from sleep, ravaging her after weeks of celibacy. We'd tear at each other's clothes and fuck like our lives depended on it, then collapse in each other's arms as the orange sun's first summer rays broke across the horizon.

But the clearest moments that defined that summer were the midnight excursions to the fountain. The sense of community, of seeing Chad and all of the other regulars every time we went made me wish I could've spent last summer on campus. Knowing that another summer of these receptions would happen made me feel like the tide was turning.

Once home, I called the number on the glowstick business card, and Brecken answered. He told me to come right over and gave me directions to the house. I hopped in the car, dressed in a t-shirt and shorts, and took off across town. The interview wouldn't be like trying to get a job at IBM, if Chad, a shorts in December kind of guy, had a job there.

Brecken's directions led to a small box-house on the west side of town, past the border where Bloomington goes from the 1990s to the 1940s. I ditched the Rabbit in the driveway, and entered the front door. Inside, it looked pretty much like a regular house—couches, a TV, an entertainment center, and a fully stocked kitchen.

"Hey John, thanks for stopping by!" Enter Bruce: a bearded, thirties, Patrick Swayze wanna-be, with a wife that made some real money while he farted away most of his day with the glowstick business and drinking too-expensive bourbon straight from a coffee mug. He looked like the kind of guy that drifted from skydiving instructor to junk-bonds dealer to NASCAR financier to European sportscar importer, with nothing to show for it except a trail of divorces and maybe a good big-screen TV or an alligator-skin briefcase. He shook my hand, a firm grip that said he could've been a lumberjack, but he probably didn't even get out of the chair to answer the door if he could get his kids or Brecken to answer it for him.

"So Chad tells me you've got some kind of magazine business going on," he said, motioning me into his office, a small bedroom with a desk and an odd number of igloo coolers. I sat in a folding chair, and he sunk behind the desk.

"Yeah, I started my own zine, but I've been doing a lot of work for a friend's zine for the last few years. Sales, writing, computer help, going to shows for him—a jack of all trades thing."

"Those metal shows get pretty wild?" he asked.

"Some fights, the mosh pits are more organized than they look—I can hold my own there, unless there are skinheads out to mess with people, then you've gotta know when to back off. I've never been hurt, though."

"It sounds like you're what we're looking for. The 500 is a decent event, but it's not as tame as the kiddie fireworks shows. It's mostly people drunk off their gourd, trying to fuck with you. Nothing violent or anything, but you have to put up with some shit. I guess you heard about the permits?"

"Yeah, Chad was printing them out earlier today."

"You don't have to worry about that too much. They never ask about them, and there's a million people out there selling stuff. If someone asks, just play dumb and hand them my business card—I'll take care of the rest. That sound okay?"

"Sure, I can handle that." It sounded like some kind of Mafia operation, but I'd done riskier things before.

"I can trust you with cash, right?"

"Yeah, I'm cool."

"Okay. You're going to be with Chad most of the night anyway, but remember to be extra careful with money, so nobody grabs your shit and runs. We'll talk about that more the night of the gig. Let me get you some paperwork to fill out." He dug through some manila folders on his desk. "You'll be a contractor, which means I don't take taxes and you're responsible for paying them..." He produced some papers and a pen, and I filled away.

"Like I said, you'll be going up with Chad, on Saturday. I'm planning to send a half dozen people to work 38th Street the nights before the race, where the action happens. It'll be wall-to-wall drunks and cruisers, hopefully with fat wallets," he said. "Sounds gross, but it'll be easy to unload all of your product, make some cash, and grab a beer with the yokels on the strip before you take off."

I slid the paperwork across the desk to Bruce, and he scanned it quickly for errors. "Looks like you're good to go. Show up Saturday around six and we'll set you up with some product and give you a crash course."

I shook his hand again, told Brecken I was in, and then took off for home.

8

"Winston felt a need to act against the society that Orwell described," said the professor, pacing in front of the half-asleep class. "And because of these differences, he started writing in a diary, building up feelings against the government, thinking about sex, love, freedom, and even turning his back on the mandatory actions required of him by Big Brother." The teacher paced on the stage of the small, half-filled amphitheater lecture hall, trying to keep the class awake during the humid night lecture in the non-air-conditioned building. The dozen and a half students lazily doodled notes in their spirals, in a heat-induced trance, awaiting their escape to cooler climates.

George Orwell's *1984* was one of my favorite books of all time. By coincidence, this teacher thought everyone in his Intro to World Politics class should know what a worst-case scenario in government would look like, and assigned the novel. In between studying the political differences between Cuba and the Ivory Coast, we talked about the book and how its government affected the characters. I'd hide in the back of the class, seldom take notes, and try to keep cool by drinking the awful Coke dispensed from a machine in the basement of the lecture hall.

The professor continued, "Does anyone have any ideas why Winston acted differently than the rest of his comrades? John?"

"Maybe because of his childhood?" I stumbled, waking from my heat-stroke stupor. "Um, he talks about losing his parents early on. Just a guess, maybe without parents who were role models of the party, he developed feelings against the Orwellian society and felt a need to question authority."

"Good thought. It's possible Orwell might have been talking about conformity in society..." The instructor continued talking about Winston as I chewed on the small pieces of ice left from my drink, and flicked a pencil around the small, fold-out tabletop covered with decades of graffiti.

During the summer, most of the full professors left the university to the graduate students, who taught abbreviated syllabi in the short sessions. And because most students would rather be outside in the beautiful summer weather, the teachers would try to make their classes brief and interesting. Instead of spending weeks talking about every single detail about communist China, a summer prof might just say "Then there's China. They're Communists, but that won't be on the test. Now, moving on to Russia..."

Our teacher would lecture for a few minutes about some key points, and then turn the session into an open discussion, drawing in everyone to talk about what they thought was important. Also, he researched North African politics extensively, spending years overseas doing dissertation work and traveling on grants from various highbrow New York foundations. When people started falling asleep during lecture, he'd scrap his planned outline and tell stories about Niger for hours, about how he'd trade his American money on the black market in the back room of a Mercedes dealership, or how Guinness beer was so heavily promoted in poverty-stricken Africa that you would see Guinness signs on mud huts in the middle of the plains. Always good for a few laughs, his tales also kept the three-hour lecture much more bearable.

As the clock crept toward eight, the shuffling of books and rustling of folders being shoved into backpacks gradually drowned out the waning lecture. "Okay, let's quit for tonight," the prof yelled, raising his voice to be heard over the people packing their belongings and starting post-class chatter early. "Keep reading Orwell, you should be about halfway through, and don't forget to read the chapter in the text about

Nigeria—I'd like to discuss this next time. Any questions, I've got office hours tomorrow!"

The few remaining students shuffled out the classroom, leaving the teacher to answer the questions of brown-nosing stragglers while he wiped down the chalkboard. I followed the small crowd tramping through Woodburn Hall's wide corridors, and emerged to the evening outdoors. The thick humidity and greenhouse temperatures of daylight were slowly breaking as twilight danced among the trees and meadows of campus. A serene atmosphere dwelled over the limestone giants lined up on Seventh Street, ivy covered and forever resting in the relaxed peace of summer. Two months ago, the sidewalk between Ballantine and Woodlawn teemed with hundreds of pedestrians, walking, riding, running, skating, wheeling to classes. Now, I shared the acres of landscape with a few dozen other students, and enjoyed the tranquil show as night emerged.

During my walk home, I took pleasure in twenty or thirty minutes of pre-dark peace, absorbing the beauty of the gentle Jordan river. Trees bloomed on either side of the narrow trail, and soft hills carved the campus in the diminishing, available light of orange. With my walkman blaring, and backpack over one shoulder, I hiked the familiar path next to the timid creek, and crossed a wooden footbridge, leading out of the woods and onto Jordan Street. Listening to the pop-punk sound of Les Thugs covering the Dead Kennedys song "Moon Over Marin," I trudged south on the street, onward to my apartment.

"Hey man, we're going to Second Story for Zydeco-fusion night," Yehoshua blurted as I walk in the front door. "You wanna go? I think it costs like four bucks, but it's gonna be a really cool show."

"I'm broke," I said, checking the pile of mail by the door for anything new. "I'll probably hang out here tonight, maybe go to the fountain later," I replied. This was one of his little tricks to get someone to pay his cover. While the broke part wasn't a lie, I didn't want to get dragged away and trapped for ten hours, watching Yehoshua talk to his pothead friends while getting incredibly blitzed on scammed drinks, leaving me completely bored, broke and friendless.

"Whatever man, maybe some other time," he said. "You seen Deon?" he asked. "Deon!" he shouted to the back of the house. "You want to go to Second Story tonight? Its fusion-reggae night, or some shit." He disappeared for the other kitchen, leaving me to finish sifting through the pile of mail.

Like a fireman entering a burning house, a backdraft of heat hit my face and rolled into the hallway when I opened door 13. I clicked the light switch, and the overhead fluorescents started with a flicker and painted the room with a drab white-lime glow. The thick, accumulated air tasted dry and stale, like the smell of the cheap wood paneling and aging ceiling tiles. I fumbled with the knob on the dirt-encrusted box fan resting in the window. It hummed, started with a shake, and pulled the fresh outside air through the window screen with a hypnotizing whir.

I tossed my backpack onto a mosaic of magazines, papers, and computer printouts lining the floor. At the card table, I powered up the computer, and pushed aside books, tapes, and empty cans to find the keyboard. The monitor, an el-cheapo grayscale VGA with a disassembled case, flickered and awoke with the usual BIOS memory test. The drives grumbled and the tower case's little fan wheezed and spun. I leaned over to a bookcase holding stereo equipment, CDs and a few cheap novels and old textbooks, and clicked on the CD player. While both the stereo and computer started up, I went to the old fridge just outside the door and located a cold, unopened can of Coke.

Deon strolled down the hallway and appeared in my room, in his usual role of wandering around the house to see what everyone was up to. "Hey John, what's Yehoshua talking about with this Zydeco stuff? Is that a heavy metal group?" As Deon talked, he picked up and examined pieces of mail lying on my floor.

"No it's...Well, I don't exactly know what Zydeco is," I answered. "But it isn't heavy metal. It has washboards in it, I know that much." I cracked opened the aluminum can and tilted back a long swig from the Coke. "Don't fall for his tricks, he's just trying to find someone to pay his way."

"No shit, he's pulled that one on me before," he said. "Hey, how's your class going? What were you reading in there? *Brave New World?*"

"No, close. *1984*, Orwell," I said. "Same idea, different dead English guy."

"Cool," he said. "I guess I never saw the movie then. Hey, what are you doing tonight?"

I finished another swig of Coke and belched. "I'm going to the fountain at midnight."

"Showalter? What's going on there?"

"A bunch of us meet there every night at midnight, just to talk, fuck around." I said. "A couple of computer geeks started it last year. But people brought friends, and it just sort of went from there. You wanna check it out tonight?"

"Sure, I'm not doing anything," he said.

"Cool. I'm gonna get some stuff done," I said. "I'll stop over at your room around 11 or 11:30 and we'll head out then."

"Okay, catch you then."

Deon wandered back down the hall, leaving me to kill time with my favorite addiction. I punched up the newest Carcass album in the CD player, and started Procomm on the computer. With a quick Alt-D, I told the modem to dial the university. It replied, instantly seizing the phone line and hurling a series of beeps at an eager dial tone, starting the connection.

I used email since the beginning of my freshman year, at a time when few people even knew it existed. During my first week at college, someone told me that anyone could get time on the university's mainframes for free, and they had a lot of services like email and a BBS forum. I got an account, and struggled with the VAX mainframes, slowly trying to figure out how to send messages and read FORUM, a simple local BBS full of college-student arguments and discussions about politics, the existence of God, and how to use frozen food during sex. I'd walk to the library or the hardwired terminal in the dorm basement and clunk through the college's academic information menu system, looking up addresses and reading an endless stream of help pages for the mail system in an effort to learn the basics. After some initial frustration, I started returning to the old DEC terminals more frequently, and the commands became more familiar.

After treading water for a few weeks, I started to "meet" people online and talk to them frequently. This plunged me into a complete, developing virtual culture on the computer, consisting of FORUM "regulars" and people who kept up with their email correspondence on a daily basis. The ties to this group convinced me to spend more time between classes and in the evenings chatting with people, reading FORUM, and playing an online strategy called Nuke Em (I never won, but came close a few times,) until the new online community consumed more of my time than TV, real friends, or studying.

Soon, my VAX friends started carrying over into real life, when I found that a few of the regulars from FORUM also spent time in the same computer lab near my dorm. After meeting some of these cyber-celebrities, I realized that the computer would be a great way to not only meet friends, but to meet women. I always held a theory that if a woman didn't get turned off by my looks and I could manage to talk to her for more than a few minutes, she'd like me for my intelligence or sense of humor. With the computer, the looks stage would be skipped and I could immediately start talking and getting to know people.

The plan got tested, with mixed results. Sometimes it worked to an extent, and I could make a good friend, but most of the time it failed miserably. After I talked to a woman on the computer for a while, she'd eventually get to a stage where she'd want to meet me in person and see where her typing went. And I'd usually screw up the face-to-face meetings, or be incredibly shy in person after being very open over the computer. It usually went over worse than a catastrophic blind date, because after talking to someone for days or weeks over a computer, expectations became high, and the physical encounter distorted or shattered the image they'd have in their mind about you. Also, most people playing on email expected the person on the other end to look like a movie star or rock idol, when really they were just another pimple-faced college student. I never gave too much importance to physical looks, but I saw some bad email matches go down because of it. People can be cruel, I guess.

The squelch and garble of the modem stopped, and the computer beeped to signal that it was complete. I made a connection to Bronze, and typed in a username and password. Carcass continued their symphony of sickness as I bathed in semi-cool air from the humming box fan and clicked at the keyboard. The screen told me I had new messages, and once a prompt appeared, I quickly checked what email waited for me. Four new messages sat in the queue: three inter-office type letters from my UCS job that didn't pertain to me and another random message of no particular excitement. After deleting the three work mails, I checked to see what friends were currently logged on. My friend Bill was on in the Union, probably writing poetry and cruising for guys. I fired off a quick message to see if he would be at the fountain later, and started scoping the list of users online for people to mess with.

In the summer, anyone logged in after nine would probably be playing around, so my late nights became great for trawling. Occasionally, someone would reply to the communication, and we'd exchange mail a few times. These brief encounters were like flipping through channels at three in the morning, and watching 20 seconds of a show before moving on to find something else. On rare occasions, I'd meet someone who would put time or seriousness into their replies, and correspond on a daily or more-than-daily basis, but most mails went unanswered.

This evening's crops looked pretty lean, and after a few scans of the userlist, I bowed out and powered down the box. The CD continued to grind out songs of death and gore, while I wandered the heat and humidity of the small room. In boredom, I arranged and re-arranged the stuff on my dresser, putting spare change in a jar and tossing out old tissues and pieces of lint. I laid in the bed, shoes still on, and lazily flipped through an almost memorized, heavily worn, three month old Popular Science retrieved from the floor of junk and laundry, waiting for midnight.

The VW whirred and churned up the curving hill, passing the moonlit dorms and sororities of the south campus. Most of the buildings stood abandoned for the summer, with only service vehicles and minor construction occupying their empty grounds for the vacation months. Others, like the School of Music, stayed lit and fully visited by students year-round. Most of the campus still kept its scenic landscape lights burning, and the rows of streetlights on Jordan Avenue integrated the features with the night.

Deon played with his seatbelt, fidgeting in the passenger's seat of the car. "Hey man, do you know who's gonna be there?" he asked.

I shifted from third to fourth as we passed the vacant Sigma Kappa house. "You never know who's gonna show. That's why you've gotta go every night."

We turned on Seventh, running just south of the mammoth Main Library. Lights illuminated a pedestrian path of carefully carved stone slabs set in the side of a hill, surrounded by perfectly trimmed hedges and trees. On our other side, the back of the majestic Auditorium stood stoically, its hundred-year-old limestone covered with rampant ivy.

After driving past the Auditorium, the road opened to a large courtyard almost as big as a city block. The front pillars and steps of the giant theatre formed the east side of this plaza, with the art school's large limestone face making the north facade. On the south, the Lilly Library stood at arms, and the western bound flowed into the central road of the campus.

In the center square stood our destination: a large dais of ornately carved limestone jutted up from the ground, surrounded by stone benches, sidewalks and carefully manicured bushes. A platform raised from the middle of the small park to hold a large circular basin, full of churning water. Four stone dolphins swam forever in the surf, jetting water from their mouths into the night sky. In the middle of the artificial lake, the Goddess Venus lay outstretched on a large limestone seashell, with another fish behind her, also spitting high into the air. Underwater floodlights illuminated the small lake, reflecting the splashes and shadowing the stone characters. On the flat bench-like rim of the fountain, two men and a woman already gathered, chatting and waiting for the strike of twelve.

I drove around the fountain on the circular path, and pulled up to the steps in front of the auditorium to park. As we climbed out of the car, I waved over to the fountain to the three people and they waved back.

"Hey everybody, I'm here. We can start now," I jokingly said to the group, as we strutted to the gathering. "This is my roommate Deon," I said. "Deon, this is Bill, Linda and Joe." Each of the three returned the greeting, as Deon and I sat down on a set of steps going up to the fountain. Bill, with his long, dark hair in a ponytail and pair of thick Coke-bottle glasses, sat cross-legged on a stone park bench. Linda, a short but energetic woman with short, dark hair, was giving Joe a backrub while talking to the group. Bill's friend Joe towered over them, a few inches shy of seven feet tall with short blonde hair, ice blue eyes, squarish features and a body conditioned from regular mountain biking.

"Okay John," Linda said to me, while working on Bill's shoulders. "I'm glad you're here. We're talking about my fucking roommate, this is your forte. Anyway, when I got back from a seminar the weekend, ALL of the mayonnaise that I bought was gone, and there was an empty jar in the fridge! How the hell can a person eat only fishsticks for a whole damn weekend?"

We all laughed, then I yelled, "Plant Man! Tell them about Plant Man, Deon!" laughing at our inside joke.

"Yeah! Plant Man!" Deon yelled, laughing hysterically. "There's this dude we live with, we call him Plant Man. That's another story, but get this: all this dude eats, EVERY DAY, is macaroni and cheese and cream of mushroom soup!" he blurted.

I tagged in and continued, "He's this really big guy, a real Star Trek convention looking motherfucker, who sits in his room all day and plays dungeons and dragons through the mail and reads horrible sci-fi novels. Every FUCKING day, he gets back from his PhD librarian classes for lunch, and makes a box of Kraft Macaroni and Cheese, and a can of Cream of Mushroom soup. He inhales the shit, and goes back to jerking off and memorizing J.R.R. Tolkien or whatever the fuck he reads. EVERY FUCKING DAY! I've never seen him cook anything else, and his cabinet has like 400 boxes of Kraft and 1000 identical cans of soup."

We all laughed, and the conversation continued, slightly mutating to a different topic as each person spoke. The fountainside chats often continued like this for hours, with no real agenda or synopsis, but synergy in the laziness of the summer evening. Sometimes current events or news would dominate, whether it was a bad class, a difficult job, or some trouble on the dating front. It wasn't always a bitch session, the discussions would go to seriousness, or to reminiscence, but often to laughs. Everyone kept a good sense of humor and relaxed attitude, so we'd often get on a roll of telling old, funny stories of the past to entertain the group. Other nights, everyone would be unenergetic, too worried about projects or classes or life to really keep the momentum going. But even then, it still remained a decent break, a way to get out of the house for a while.

Because it was a weekday, nobody else showed. Our conversation still wound on for an hour and a half before we decided to break up for the night. Linda and Joe both drove, and Bill walked back to the 24-hour lab in Lindley, where he was working on his writing. Deon and I walked to the VW as everyone else went their own way, and cranked back to Jordan to head to the house.

"Hey man, is everybody always that cool?" Deon asked.

"Yeah, Bill and Linda and Joe are all pretty decent," I replied. "There are usually more people than that. It's slow on weeknights," I added.

The amber streetlights of Jordan flashed overhead through the open moonroof as we swung up the hill. "Man, I'm still pretty awake," Deon said. "What time do you have to get up tomorrow?"

"Umm, on Fridays I don't really have to get up." I answered.

"Man! You're lucky. I have to be at work by 10," he said.

"I'm going to be lucky and poor soon," I said. "I need to get another job pronto. I'll probably do another round at student employment tomorrow, maybe go through the want ads again."

We pulled into the driveway, and I turned off the lights and wound down the four-banger. After powering down, I cranked shut the moonroof and we headed into the dimly lit house.

"Hey man, I gotta crash," Deon said. "I'll catch you tomorrow after work."

"Sure, see you then," I said, heading down the hall to room

The period after the fountain and before sleep caused the greatest amount of loneliness and despair I'd experience in a day. With nobody awake at four in the morning, the isolation from humanity, the darkness of closed stores, people and the rest of civilization asleep, it forced me to think about myself and what was really going on, without distractions.

I took the walks as a masochistic reminder of my depression. It was the same theory as being depressed and pulling down old letters from your ex, that copy of Pink Floyd's *The Wall*, or a cheery Morrisey album. You KNOW it isn't going to make you better, it's a giant spoonful of dread to coat your horrendous mood and make the pain sear your nerves even more. The strolls on the dark pathways made me think of Tammy, and how on a bright and sunny day only a few months ago, I walked with her hand in mine. Now, the blue-gray sky, shadows of trees, and even more vacant summer campus magnified my aloneness.

But on this night, like many others, I put the stereo on low and sat in bed with the lights off. The only other sound, the churning fan, buzzed at the open window. I bathed in a mixture of hot summer air and self-pity, thinking about a woman I couldn't have. I drove myself out of school, I screwed up my financial situation, and I didn't know what I was going to do with my life anymore. And it was four in the morning and I was staring at a piece of paneling instead of interning for IBM or getting a 4.0 at MIT or making 20 bucks an hour running a third shift punch press so I could buy a new car and go to school with no debt.

    I clicked off the light and climbed into the bed, abandoning the covers because of the humid air. My mind burned with thoughts about jobs, Tammy and the idea of having a full-blown breakdown and becoming an alcoholic. My eyes stung with tears as I stared into the dark for what seemed like hours. And my body incinerated in the summer heat, as I rolled and fidgeted against the uncomfortable mattress, knowing that my bedroom back home had central air.

    I got to the IMU Mac cluster around lunch, and had no trouble finding a seat at a machine. My head was still groggy from my insomnia of the night before, but after a shower and a walk across campus in the sunlight, I felt 80% functional. I lugged copies of the Schedule of Classes, my medical petition from last spring, and the mail they sent me about my dismissal. Today's task: to start banging out the letter to the dean's office so I could get back in school.

    First, I logged onto Bronze, to check my mail. There were six UCS messages: three sub shift announcements, and three messages saying the shifts were filled, each pair of messages painfully close to each other. I should start hanging out at Lindley all day to pounce on those open shifts, I thought. Besides, it's air conditioned there.

    I also had a message from Abby Wagner, a woman I'd casually met last spring. She now stayed with her parents in New Albany, just across the river from Louisville, and spent most of her day bombarding me with constant email. Since I also had some free time, and we had a lot of fun joking around, this seemed like the perfect combination. The only problem was that she spent most of her morning online, while I burned away the late evening and some times in the afternoon. I'd always had mail from her when I woke up, and she always read my 3 AM ramblings when she woke up at 8 or 9, but we almost never caught each other to chat. Today's message was par for our email conversation:

Date: Thu, 21 May 92 08:19:57 EST
From: you're so pretty when you're faitful to me
<AWAGNER@ucs.indiana.edu>
Subject: nonvenomous snakes
To: JCONNER@ucs.indiana.edu
we used to own about 20 nonvenomous snakes and i've been thinking about them today. don't know why, i wasn't that fond of them. whenever i held on it always went to the bathroom on me which really irritated me, plus snake waste smells really bad for a really long time. i got the diaries of andy warhol today. he was a pretty cool guy. needless to say he was really fucked up, but most cool people are. kind of an exorbitant price for it. but then it is 800 pages and people will pay any amount to read that kind of bizzare trash (including me) i'm outta here. no one wants to play. best of luck to the hormone boy.

abby x

I earned the hormone boy nickname from my endless hours of scamming the VAXes and drooling over various supermodels. Also, the abby x thing was a poke at my process name of Doctor X. I logged onto Rose, to see if she was still around, and she wasn't. Maybe later, I'd answer the mail—right now I needed to fuck with that letter. I put in a disk, fired up WordPerfect, and started to fill in a business letter template with the info from my dismissal. Since I'd spent the last few days rehearsing the letter in my head, this wouldn't be too difficult. "I would like to petition for readmission to the College of Arts and Sciences" The words carved out the blank page, and I carefully stared at them, hoping I wouldn't fuck up a one page letter that meant life or death.

After typing a jumbled paragraph and a few more lines in the letter, I switched back to the Rose VAX and did another who to check for any new friends online. My list said that JPSMITH had just logged on, and she was in the IMU, but not in this cluster—in an office somewhere in the building. JPSMITH, June, was a new person, someone I'd talked to a few times in the last week. She seemed nice enough, and was a speech communication major, from Chicago, and my age. I fired off a quick "Hey!" and went back to my letter, waiting for a reply.

"Hey John! Are you on campus today?" flashed back, and I abandoned the letter again to talk to her.

"Yeah, I'm at the IMU," I said. "What about you?" The trick of determining location by IP number was a skill known only by wizards and stalkers, and I didn't want to blow my cover.

"I'm in the IMU, too. In the student government office," she said.

"Well, hello from IMU061," I said. "What are you up to today?"

"I'm supposed to be doing some work, but it's not going well. What about you?"

"I'm typing a letter," I said. "No laserprinters at home."

"Hey hormone boy. Are you awake?"

What? I looked at my screen twice, then saw that Abby had logged on, and was also bitnetting me.

"Hey Abby X. Can I play in a bit? I've got a babe on line one." I told her.

"Hmph. You and your women. I'll be here waiting," she said.

I got ready to send a message back to June, when she beat me to the punch. "Are you going to be down there for a while?"

"Maybe for an hour or so," I said. "It's too nice out to do any more work than that."

"Do you mind if I come down there to say hi?" she asked. Instantly, a strong fear gripped me. I was wearing cutoff jeans, a pair of boat shoes, no socks, and a faded Mercyful Fate t-shirt, plus I had on my glasses and I brushed out my hair in about two seconds and let it air-dry that morning. Oh well, it's now or never, I thought.

"That'd be great. I just woke up, but I'm coherent today."

"Where are you sitting?" she asked.

"On the left end, third row," I said.

"Okay, I'll be down in a minute."

She logged off, and I waited in nervousness. I checked my wholist, and Abby was still on, so I fired off a message to wake her up. "Harry Bellafonte started the civil war."

"How was the babe?" she replied. "You give her the time right there in the lab?"

"She's coming down in a second, so I've gotta split."

"If I showed up at the IMU, would I get your undivided attention?"

"If you were a babe, and I'm not saying you're not...Now scram..."

I watched the door, waiting to see who would appear. The Mac lab was at the end of a fifty-foot hallway, and only computer users walked down the corridor, which meant I'd see her for a few minutes before she saw me. I went back to the letter, and tried to do a little more work, while keeping an eye on the door.

Within a few minutes, I saw a shapely, sophisticated woman standing in the door. She had dark hair just off the shoulder, and a dark complexion, maybe part Italian, with sharp features, and was wearing a tight sundress that showed off her incredible figure. She stunned me at first glimpse, but I kept my eyes on the monitor, and let her have the first move.

She walked to my desk. "John?"

"June!" I said, in my best affirmative voice possible. She was a speech communications major, so I imagined she was analyzing everything I said and did to read the situation. "Nice to meet you," I offered my hand and she shook it, smiling.

"What are you working on?" she asked.

I suddenly remembered the dismissal letter. What if she was a model 4.0 student? Would she reject me for being an academic leper?

"Umm, I got kicked out last semester, and I'm petitioning to get back in."

"What a coincidence," she said. "I got dismissed a year ago. I petitioned and got in on contract. I think I'll finish it next semester." Returning on contract was an annoying provisionary measure where you promised to get certain grades and take dumb remedial classes about learning how to study and use the library in exchange for readmission even though you completely blew it GPA-wise.

"That's cool. If I pull through summer school, I'll start fall semester without a contract. Keep your fingers crossed."

She laughed. "Hey, I've got to get back upstairs, but maybe I'll catch you on email?"

"Sure, I'm not hard to find."

"I know, I see you and Sid on the computer every time I log on. What are you guys doing?"

"Saving the world," I said. "Saving the world, getting kicked out of school..."

"Well be careful. I'll catch you later."

"Bye June."

She walked to the door, waved goodbye and smiled again, and continued down the hall. I watched her walk to the Mezzanine elevators. Simply incredible, I thought.

"Wow," I bitnetted back to Abby. "That was easy on the eyes."

"If she was Princess Leia and you were Darth Vader, would you use the torture droid on her?"

"Abby, I don't even know the correct answer to that question," I said. I looked at the letter again, and thought more about how I could add some more to it, but my mind kept drifting back to June...

With the letter mostly done and fermenting on a floppy disk, my habit of hibernation in bed continued. All that the outside world offered was direct sunlight, more heat and stifling humidity. My window fan ran all day to suck some of the heat from the little studio shithole. But even with the metal blades jamming away at maximum output, sweat still covered my face, ran over my skin and drenched my clothes. Air conditioning became my mantra, and my insides continually boiled and melted back through my pores.

I pulled a piece of paper from my wallet, the well-folded slip with Tammy's phone number out east. Staring at the ten digits in her bubbly handwriting made me feel like a heroin addict, fondling an empty needle and wishing it could plunge back into a vein. It seemed so easy to call her, hear her voice again, talk to her like I used to, and make it all like it was before. My mind wanted me to believe she would be there, waiting, just like she waited for me every night at her dorm room phone, waiting for me to get done with work and spend the night with her in my arms again. But what would realistically happen? I'd screw up, I'd try to ask her back and infuriate her. She wouldn't want to hear from me, and she was probably sick of my spineless begging. Maybe she already found another relationship, and her life didn't require any input from me. She'd consider my calls a nuisance, a part of the past she wanted to forget. Even if I tried to be nice, she would interpret it as some sort of plan to get her back, which it would be. Making her feel sorry for me would make things worse and get her angry. No possible outcome would work; no matter how much I wanted to call, it was assured disaster.

I refolded the slip of paper and put it in the top drawer of my dresser. Maybe someday I'll call her, I thought. Someday when things were sorted out and troubles were behind me, when we both healed, I'd call her. She'd be happy, and I'd be happy.

Until then, I crawled back into bed to feel unhappy.

9

The next weekend promised to be my glowstick baptismal in blood. The Indianapolis 500, the largest event in motor racing history, ran that Monday, on Memorial Day. Speedway, Indiana would be a giant outdoor party zone for the three or four days leading up to the event. Bruce planned to send plenty of us troops to the front, trading glow-in-the-dark necklaces for cash. I would be one of the few and proud, wearing a money belt and toting a glowstick holster.

I spent Friday night by myself, playing on the computers at the library until midnight, when a mediocre fountain gathering got me more depressed than entertained. I kept thinking more about the dissolution with Tammy, and whether a phone call would make it all better. Deep inside, I knew it wouldn't, and the constant struggle disconnected me from everyone around me. The idea of dealing with humans that Saturday wasn't enticing, but I was willing to tolerate almost anything for the money. Maybe a million drunken fiends would cheer me up. Or even better, maybe unclothed, nubile women would parachute from the sky in search of me. Of course if they did, I'd be stuck with a bunch of fucking glowsticks and no free hands.

I pulled into Bruce's house/office on Saturday afternoon, and spied a few cars already in the driveway, including Chad's beat up Jetta. Chad sprawled across an old couch on the front porch, drinking a soda. "Hey man," he said. "Bruce's busy with Jim right now, but he'll be right out. You want a Coke?" he asked, pointing to a large ice chest.

"Sure, I could use one." I climbed the front steps, opened the cooler, and pulled a red can from amidst the beers in the fridge. I wondered if he didn't offer a beer because we were going to work in a bit, or if he'd witnessed too many of my drunken rampages. At one point last spring when I was certain I was an alcoholic, I gave him at least a hundred bucks' worth of hard liquor from my apartment and told him to get rid of it in any way possible, as long as I never saw it again. What are friends for?

"How you doing, man?" he asked me, as I sat down on a lawn chair and popped the top to the drink.

"I haven't been in the best of moods lately," I said. "This whole Tammy situation is still tearing at me."

"Are you still worried she won't come back?"

"Dude, things are over. Completely over. I blew it."

"Don't say that! Have you talked to her lately?" he said. "Are you reading too much into the situation?" he asked. "I mean maybe she's..."

"Look, she's gone. She said it's over, and it is."

"Well, maybe you have a chance..."

"No, you don't get it, man? When a woman says 'maybe someday, but not now,' it means forever. It means it's over, she doesn't want to see me and...and its over." I tried to hold back all of the pain this was bringing me, but it wasn't working.

"Well..." he hesitated, "Well, I'm sorry man. But hey," he picked up, in a cheerful voice. "We're going to the Indianapolis 500 tonight! You're going to have a lot of fun. You ever been up there?" he asked.

"No," I said. My closest experience to the race, aside from watching it on TV, was stopping for gas about 10 miles from the track.

"Well, we'll be working, and you'll get a chance to make a lot of money. Plus you'll get to talk to a lot of people," he added, jumping into his good-guy, telemarketer trance voice. "There will be beer everywhere, and topless drunk women all over the place. Just imagine, good looking women everywhere, everyone partying and having a good time. It gets totally insane there, it'll take your mind off things."

"I hope so," I sighed.

"Don't worry," he said. "After you're up there for a few hours, you won't be worrying about anything."

We heard talking from inside, and the front door opened. Jim stepped out, a forty-something man with a solid beer gut and clothes that made him look like a lawyer posing as a relaxed-type in leisurewear from a yuppie department store. He carried a money belt and a shoulder-slung contraption made with four long mailing tubes duct-taped to a sling. Bruce and Jim laughed, continuing their small talk as Jim walked out to his car and left.

"Come on in!" bellowed Bruce, sporting some rumpled shorts and a shirt unbuttoned in the front. "You want something to drink?" he asked, gesturing with a can of beer he held in his grip.

"No, I'm cool," I answered, lifting up the can of Coke I was still nursing.

"Step on in the office, let's get you set up," he said, turning to one of the bedroom/offices. Inside, paperwork and half-opened packages littered the small room. Bruce pulled a stack of papers from the chair at the desk. "Take a seat, men," he said, gesturing to the metal folding chairs across from him.

"Okay, we have two types of product," he said, juggling around manila folders and clipboards on the desktop. "There's the standard sticks and the frozen sticks." He pulled a clear plastic wand about a foot and a half long and about 1/8 inch thick from a mailing tube riding the sea of papers. "This is a standard stick. It has two types of chemical in it, and some kind of solid resin shit that keeps them apart. But, when you break it or snap it..." He bent the rod down its length, making a cracking sound like a ziploc bag being pulled open. "That shit breaks and the two chemicals mix, and in a minute, you have a glowing stick." Per his explanation, the juice inside the long straw turned a bright purple and glowed like an alien firefly.

"Important facts to remember," he said. "Once broken, these things glow for about four to six hours, depending on the temperature outside. If you throw one in the freezer, it'll slow down a little bit, but you can't get them to reverse or stop. Also, bending these things sets them off, so you have to be careful not to fuck with them or all of your product will be glowing and you won't be able to pace yourself for the evening."

"We carry these things in the shipping tubes they come in from the factory. But we've set up shoulder mounts, like this." He grabbed a parcel of four mailing tubes from behind the desk, the quartet wrapped together in a two by two arrangement with duct tape. A shoulder strap extended from one of the duct taped ends. "You can carry it on your side, set it on the ground, or even use it as a seat. Just make sure it doesn't get ripped off, and if it rains or you are around some puddles or something, try not to get these things wet. It won't hurt the product, but the tubes are just cardboard and it'll fuck them up."

"Now, these things are foil wrapped, fifty to a pack, a pack is all the same color. We try to dot each end of the pack with a marker so you know if it is red, green or blue, but if they aren't marked, you can open up one end and check. The important thing to remember, pull these things straight out of the tube. Don't bend them to the side or you'll break the shit in there and the stick will activate."

"When you get to the venue, the best thing to do is pull out about two or three of each color and activate them. String them on as necklaces, wrap them around your tubes, wave them in the air, whatever works. Chad, you can tell him about that shit when you get up there. The important thing to remember is that if you don't have the product out, nobody will want to buy it. But if you get too much of the product out, you'll waste the shit. You have to figure out what the balance is depending on how many people are out."

"Okay, here are your tubes." He hefted the four tubes by the shoulder strap and dropped them on the table in front of me. "Here's an inventory sheet. What I need you to do is sign out what you have in there. If your packs are unopened, you can assume there are fifty sticks in there. But if one is open, count 'em and make sure none of them are duds or broken. If you get any bad sticks out in the field, just put them aside and I'll mark them off. You won't be held responsible for them."

I checked out the tubes and counted off my supply, while Chad got his own stash. Bruce gave me 200 sticks; if I could ditch all of them, I'd make about 50 bucks. It wasn't the hundred bucks Chad made the year before, but it would be decent pay if I could unload them in two or three hours, especially since it was basically tax free.

Another team of four loaded up right after us. They'd go up in a separate car, but hit the same area. According to Bruce, there would be enough business for all six of us with no problems. We all met on the porch, and Chad, the leader for the caravan, announced the battle plan for heading up to Indianapolis. We would drive separately, stop to eat on the way, find some place to park a few blocks away and head to ground zero on foot.

Chad and I loaded our tubes in his car and wished everyone else good luck. The other team set up in a big four-door sedan, and headed out to SR 37 for the trip north. We tailed them, and within moments we were cruising the split four-lane road to the center of Indiana. About twenty miles up the road, we left them and stopped at a Taco Bell, ordering at the drive-through window and taking the bags of food on the road with us. Even though we were quick about it, the other team lost us, and vanished past the horizon. We kept heading north on our own, eating tacos and hoping we could find them when we got to Speedway.

With the food eaten and the garbage stashed away in the car's back seat, I relaxed and watched the scenery. Steep, rusty brown chasms in the hillside ran next to the road, which sat in the groove cleared by the explosives of roadway crews decades before. Now, ivy and small green bushes poked from the eroded faces of stone, and grass and larger trees grew above the cliffs and in the deep chasm of a meridian between the two strips of road. The plants bloomed with the beginning of summer, drinking the spring rains and basking in the May sun. Everything green seemed to be reaching skyward, and bulking outward, becoming invulnerable now that they conquered the forces that caused them to lie dormant or dead all winter.

"I can't stop thinking about her, Brecken," I said, interrupting the silence in the car.

"You were in love with her, man. It's never easy," he said.

"Things still off between you and that chick in Iowa?" I asked. Brecken did as much computer scamming as me, but always seemed to hook up with women six states away.

"Way off," he said. "I haven't talked to her since February, maybe. I've been whatevering with Diane Smith. You know her?"

Know her? I thought I had a good chance at her before I dated Tammy, but she was older, divorced, and had a kid. We talked on the computer a lot, and it's always nice to have an older woman who likes you, especially when you have as many self-esteem hang-ups as me.

"Yeah, I know her. We talked a lot last spring," I said. "You two an item?"

"We've been fooling around, but not much more than that. It's weird with the kid, and...I don't know. We fuck around, and I like her, but I don't think she's serious about it."

"Hey, as long as you're giving her the salami, you're a step ahead of me," I said. "I can't talk about this anymore. What are the tricks of the trade you're supposed to teach me before we get there?" I asked.

"Oh yeah," he said. "It's mostly common sense. Watch your money, and be careful when you're making change, so people don't see how much you're carrying. If you get more than a hundred or so in your belt, take some of it and put it in a front pocket. If you need change, ask a ticket scalper, they usually want to get rid of their small bills. There's not much else you need to know that you won't figure out within a few minutes..."

The red and white smokestack popped over the horizon, and told us that Indianapolis lay ahead. After a few more moments, the long loop of

I-465 became the horizon, and we sped to an on-ramp to climb the west side of the city to Speedway. Traffic didn't seem too heavy, but the loop sat deceptively far from the city. If an event clogged part of downtown, the congestion happened right at the I-465 exit and within the smaller arterials of the city.

Keeping up with the flow of traffic required pushing the little Jetta up to 85. The flocks of RV's and vans full of people predicted the upcoming frenzy at the track. A few moments later, we followed the signs and exited for Speedway, Indiana—home of the Indianapolis 500.

The exit from the highway sat a considerable distance from the track, and heavy traffic backup didn't happen for several miles. There was no official speedway parking, or if there was it probably filled days ago, so most people opened up vacant lots or their front yards and sold spaces for a few dollars. We opted to ditch the car about a mile and a half from the track, where parking was available in the single-digit price range. Chad paid an old man in a lawn chair for our spot, as I pulled the gear from the trunk, and we started the hike to the track.

The sky started the descent to twilight, but we decided not to open the tubes for another 15 or 20 minutes, when the darkness would help us sell. Even a mile from the track, crowds formed in the streets and yards of suburban Indianapolis. In front of every house, middle aged men with no shirts and big beer guts manned the charcoal fires, barbecuing weenies and bratwursts for the guests and kids. Their buddies and the ladies sat in folding lawn chairs, cans of beer in hand, laughing and waiting for the food. Most people didn't even care about the race. The weekend provided the people with a reason to get out, get together, drink a few beers, and have some fun in the beginning of summer.

The people on the street also used the race to run through the crowds and consume alcohol to the point of stupidity. Little red wagons with coolers of beer followed behind many of the Indiana cowboys, and the insurance salesman types wore their brand new Indy 500 t-shirts and dragged along kids with stuffed animals and toy cars bought at the vending booths near the track.

"Okay, it's showtime," Chad said. We opened our tubes and pulled out about three of each color stick. With a quick swipe and a cracking noise, I bent the clear strips, and the color quickly clouded and flowed through the capillaries, glowing in the dusk twilight. I looped a few of the strands around my neck and fastened them like a necklace, and clasped the others in my fist as we continued toward the track, now ten blocks away.

Kids and adults gazed at the neon glow of purple and lime around our necks and in our hands. The first kids started running up to us. "How much? how much!" they gleefully yelled, and Chad told them three dollars each in his nice sales voice which seemed to be a half octave higher and full of artificial cheer. Kids ran back to mom or dad to beg for the money, and a few came back with crumpled dollar bills in exchange for the products.

The occasional sales slowed our walk, but before long, we approached the final stretch to the track. About six or seven blocks from our destination, the streets were barricaded by police officers and traffic blockades, and the number of cops steadily grew in number. The foot patrol officers with radios, helmets, maglites and guns calmly showed their presence, but ignored most of the people drinking beer in the streets and throwing their cans on the ground. More cops were out in one place than I had ever seen in my life, probably more than were at some of the badass riots back in the sixties. With teargas, batons, tazers, and full riot gear, they definitely meant business.

The left side of the street went from houses to tall chain link fence, and the colossal track structure rose from the street level. From TV, the 500 looked tiny, like little cars rushing around a slot car track. In reality, the banked tracks stood several stories high, with the stands adding even more elevation to the structure. The infield itself probably took up more real estate than most golf courses or subdivisions, and the fenced perimeter easily outflanked small cities. Once I heard a factoid that all of Disneyland would fit inside the Indy 500 track—three times. The backside of the track filled the horizon, plastered with various race banners and signs telling which gate was where, and stretching out over the next mile of roadway.

The landscape quickly changed from a quiet Memorial day picnic to drunken anarchy. Little red beer wagons crisscrossed through the streets, where thousands of people either stood drinking brew and talking, or walking up and down the strip to see the sights. Square miles of asphalt became a tightly packed fraternity party where everyone was invited and you could bring in anything.

To the right, vendors set up shop on the curbs, with portable booths or card tables. Hundreds of bootleg Indy 500 t-shirts, from serious to deranged, lined the streets, and other high-impulse items and junk food trucks were out in full force. Watered-down Cokes, chilidogs, nachos, elephant ears, stuffed animals, belt buckles, cowboy hats, race programs, inflatable toy cars, and cotton candy changed hands for high prices, and the people in the crowds gleefully mass consumed. In the background, three or four cranes were set up, where people were bungee jumping for 40 bucks a pop.

"Okay," Chad said, "up ahead is the main split. These roads tee and go in either direction. The other road goes left and right from here, and it's open to traffic. We'll split up—just prowl up and down each part of the tee. If it works better for you, stay in one spot and continue selling there. But feel free to move around. We'll be able to find each other later. Keep at it, and I'll try to see how you're doing in an hour or two."

I continued to the intersection and broke left, as per Chad's instructions. The main road, open to traffic, held more cruisers than I'd ever seen in my life. Cars were backed to the horizon, and at least miles of vehicles were crawling at two miles an hour and listening to their stereos full blast. I continued down the length next to the track, walking across from another set of vendors with bright lights and fancy food carts.

People in cars started asking about the sticks, and I sold a few to passing motorists. I found that cars would line up at each red light, and I could walk up and down a block or so and quickly sell a half dozen sticks. The kids in hotrods and lowered trucks would buy them to wrap around their inside mirrors or steering wheels, illuminating the compartment with the chemical neon. Then when the light turned green, I'd walk back and start over again, this time with a new bunch of cars.

Between the spurts of happy customers, I walked back and forth in the desolation and shadow of the big track and continued to bathe in the hurt and self-pain of the whole dating situation. More than just Tammy, I gloomed in the entire situation of being in a sea of people but still standing alone, drowning in the sound of stereos and music and joy and laughter and still only hearing the sounds in my own head. The thought of this continuing forever haunted me, and I imagined a future where I would pull together my grades and get a degree and a decent job and spend my entire life after 5 PM watching the tube and eating frozen microwave dinners. This recurring theme knocked around my head over the last two years of fighting with my computer science classes and made me wonder if finishing a competitive degree meant anything except a death wish to my social life. Maybe I did need to make the last couple years in Bloomington count.

The event continued despite my gloom, and after a half hour, I saw the other four members of the glowstick team wandering the strip and working the crowds. I moved to the other side of the road, near the booths, and sold more of my merchandise while eyeing the food and the Harley-chicks with big hair and skimpy tops working at the t-shirt tents.

The people coming up to me were for the most part polite, asking the prices and how long the glow would last. Sometimes, a drunken redneck would argue about the $3 price tag or wonder what the hell a glowstick was, but I learned to ignore them. Also, the passing cars seemed to enjoy shooting squirt guns or spraying beer from their windows. Walking next to the street had me soaked within an hour.

After selling about half of my sticks, I stopped and ordered an expensive corn dog and Coke, and used the tubes as an impromptu stool to sit, eat and watch the crowd of people walk by. After the Coke, I had to take a leak, and found a vacant lot with a line of trees where at least three dozen men were lined up and pissing. I decided I could hold it a bit longer, and found the only six honey buckets for the entire event. They smelled like it too, and after getting inside, I thought maybe I'd be better with the treeline approach. I didn't miss the target, though—the glowsticks on my neck nicely illuminated the inside of the pitch-dark stall.

I continued to sell, and things kept busy several hours after dark. When all of the families with kids started leaving, sales slacked, but I still managed to sell a stick every couple of minutes. Most of my time was spent watching the people, and watching a group of guys yelling at every woman who passed by to take her top off. "Show us your tits" was the mantra of the Indy 500 for some, and remarkably, it worked about ten percent of the time. In the few minutes I watched the drunken group, three or four women parted with their shirts and bared all for the screaming fanatics. Another group set up their own bungee jump—they strung a web lawn chair from a fence with a foot-long bungee you'd use to tie something down in your trunk. Then a guy would shotgun a beer, poise himself by the chair, and as the crowd yelled "go! go! go!" he'd jump backwards, and land on the chair, knocking it onto the ground with the crowd's cheers.

Just after eleven, Chad and two of the other guys found me. Everyone else was drinking beer from cans, as opposed to the plastic cups from the beer tents. "Hey, we're totally out of sticks," he said, "You ready to get out of here?"

"I have about four left," I said. "But it doesn't look like I can sell them off that fast. Where did you guys get beer?"

"We traded off the last of our sticks," he said. "I got a couple of cans from the activated ones I was wearing. Just tell Bruce you gave away your old demo sticks—he won't care."

Heeding his advice, I chased down a few people with little red wagons, and managed to get rid of my half-dead sticks for two cans of Miller Lite. I popped open a can, chugged down half of it, and started on the way back.

The twenty-block hike to the car promised to be grueling, and we walked with the tubes slung low over our shoulders and beers in hand. We joked around, talking about the women we saw half-naked and how fun it would be to bungee jump while drinking a beer. Someone started wondering what it would be like if the tubes were really rocket launchers, and we could heft them over our shoulders and take out the houses and police cars in the distance. One of the other guys started quoting lines from *Platoon* and *Apocalypse Now*, and he was right—it did feel like a battle to me. But instead of the blood of enemies, I was soaked in beer.

Dark and thick clouds kept their promise, and within a few minutes, a chilling wind cut through the air, warning us that it would start to rain in a few moments. With no formidable cover for miles except for our cars in the distance, we had no choice but to rough it. It started to sprinkle, and then broke into a harder mist. The sweat, beer, water and grime on my clothes and skin slowly rinsed away with the cold rain of late spring, and my glasses coated with tiny droplets. I ditched the beer can, which was now almost full of water, and carefully removed the specs. I'd have to forage on with almost no eyesight, but my horrid vision sans glasses was better than trying to look through the soaked lenses.

With the combination of the beer, my earlier Cokes, and the cold, rainy weather, my bladder furiously demanded some release. By counting street signs, I determined we were only a few blocks away. The walk transformed from a leisurely stroll to a desperate journey, like in those disaster films when they send two of the crew members to swim to the other side of the wreckage to Thailand to get medical help or something. I kept putting one foot in front of the other, hungry, tired, soaked wet, and in desperate need of restroom facilities.

After what seemed like hours of fighting the rain, we closed in on the car lot. There was a Taco Bell on the same block, and Chad offered to order a bunch of food, while I found a bathroom. I told him what to get me, and ran to the side of the building, which was locked. Furtively searching for another option, I saw a large, wooded lot behind the restaurant. After walking in a safe distance, I found a tree and let things fly.

Back at the car, Chad already bought a bag of tacos, and materialized a few towels from the rear seat. "I knew it would probably rain, I'm glad I brought these," he said, drying his thick black hair as I toweled the droplets of moisture covering my face and hands.

"You're a saint, Brecken." I grabbed a towel and dried my face and arms before diving into the tacos.

We idled the car engine and ate while the heater started to wisp warm air into the compartment. After we got warm and somewhat dry, Chad pointed the car to the loop and headed south. I watched the rain-drenched landscape for a few minutes from my soaked passenger seat, then drifted asleep.

10

Another Friday night started as the sky outside my bedroom faded to twilight. With no plans, dates, or friends, I dropped in a pair of contacts, combed back my hair, put on a semi-nice polo shirt—the only thing I wore with a collar—and dabbed a few hits of cologne on my neck. The week went by like a ghost; I drifted through classes and went to fountain meetings, but didn't find a job, a woman, or anything else worth mentioning. Tonight, I needed something different. No particular plan for the evening ran through my mind, but I thought if I wandered around, I might run into someone I knew, or find two dozen drunken sorority babes who needed help with their computer. Or at the least I could check my email for a few hours and then stumble around campus in a daze until the fountain meeting at midnight. I hit the door, and went to the car, but decided it was nice enough out to wander campus on foot instead. I strolled down Mitchell, hoping a walk down Third Street would do me some good.

Twenty minutes later, I sat in front of a Macintosh in the IMU, writing long, depressing diatribes to people about how I no longer had any true friends, quoting *Stranger in a Strange Land* and Sillitoe's *Loneliness of the Long Distance Runner*. At this period in time, I didn't realize that writing to people and telling them they were lousy pieces of shit for never being good friends was a good way to lose the few acquaintances you had.

Few people used the labs on a Friday night. An occasional individual or small group of people would filter in to check email, but they usually left after five or ten minutes. They had other plans, other things to do with their evening. The IMU was a stop before the bars, before the clubs, before their dates, before the house parties or night on the town. But for me, the time spent basking in front of a CRT's pale fire in an abandoned lab was the evening's main event.

I saw a group of four or five people come in the lab to grab computers, and then I realized that one of them was June. I never really knew if she had a boyfriend or not, and when I saw her with the group, it hit me that maybe she did and my dream was crushed. She caught me across the lab, and headed over to my station. Before she could cross the room, I ditched a pathetic email and opened a VAX Pascal SMG$ header file that looked important, yet unreadable.

"Hey John! Wow, you look really different without glasses," she said. "What's up?" She smiled at me like she did the week before in her sundress.

"Not much, just the usual. Working on a program." I half-gestured to the bogus screen on the Mac.

"Hey, we're headed to the movies in a minute. Do you want to join us? I promise we won't talk about student government too much."

"Nah. Saving the world, you know..." I half-smiled. I probably should have gone, but I didn't want to deal with her friends, instead of a controllable, one-on-one situation. "No really, I'm supposed to meet up with someone in a bit," I lied. "Maybe I could take a raincheck?"

"Sure, sounds good," she said. "I've gotta go, but I'll talk to you later?"

"Yeah, I'll drop you a line," I said. The rest of her group gathered their things and they headed out the door. Well, maybe she didn't have a boyfriend, and they were just government friends, I thought. She still probably thinks I'm a loser for being here on a Friday night...

I shuffled through some old email, and a new message popped on the screen. A girl named Carrie told me she was having a party, in a short mail with jumbled and cut off text. While trying to decipher the countless spelling errors, she started paging me to chat interactively in the VAXphone.

Carrie was someone I went back and forth in email for a week or two, and hadn't exchanged much more information than name, rank and serial number. We hadn't met or talked in person yet, either. But, she seemed cool in her email, and meeting her at a party sounded okay, as long as it wasn't a drunken fraternity brawl or something else particularly alienating. At least I looked halfway presentable tonight.

I typed PHONE ANS at the VMS prompt, which started the VAXphone program. The screen split into two boxes, and each person could type away a conversation in one little rectangle, while the other person's typing magically appeared in the other half. The VAXphone painfully showed her dysfunctional typing; when she entered "Hey! I'm having a party, come over!" it took minutes and showed her backspacing and sloppiness.

After a pause, some faster and more coherent typing started on the screen. "Hey John, this is Carrie's friend Donna." Carrie had mentioned Donna before, that she was older and married, and a good friend of hers from geology classes. "Give us a call over here in a minute, we're having a party at Carrie's house." She gave me the number and told me to wait a minute so she could hang up the modem. An old black rotary phone sat on the consultant's desk (when we left the hi-tech touch-tone office phones in the late night computer labs, assholes would steal them,) and after stalling for a few moments, I spun the dial, clicking the phone number written on my hand.

A female answered. "Hey John, this is Donna," she said. "What's up at the IMU? Are you working?"

"Nope, I've got the night off. It's pretty dead here."

"We're having a little get-together here at Carrie's," she said. "We're making margaritas and shit and we've got a warchest of booze here. What are you doing in the IMU?" Her slight southern Indiana accent sounded slightly older, but friendly and inviting.

"Not a lot," I said. "Just hanging out on the computer, playing around."

"Well come over here then!" she said. "It's Friday, you shouldn't be on the damn computer. Look, we've got margaritas and some rum and vodka and shit too."

"Okay, okay," I said. "I'll stop over and see what's up." What the hell, I had a few hours to kill before anyone showed up at the fountain. I could at least see what Carrie was like in person, have a quick drink, and leave. "OK, where's her house?" I asked, as I grabbed a discarded printout and pen. I wrote down the directions and told her to give me a few minutes.

I left the Union and hiked the sidewalks in the cool night air. Darkness painted the campus an hour before, and broke the earlier sweltering temperature. A nice breeze stirred the humidity a bit and made the walk relaxing and tranquil. Without my walkman, I listened to the sounds of the evening. Donna's directions looked pretty simple. Carrie lived five or six blocks south of the IMU, in a little cinderblock ranch among similar dwellings just east of an older student ghetto. The place didn't look much like a student rental, especially with a well-groomed lawn, immaculate flowerbeds, expensive windows, and shipshape paint. I climbed the steps to her porch and rang the doorbell, expecting the worst.

"Hi John!" Carrie half-yelled, drunkenly slurring her speech. She was short, about 5' 6" and extremely thin, almost like a little girl. She still sported an impressive figure, and had long, perfectly straight, silky black hair like a European model from a Mademoiselle photo shoot. She wore jeans and a fashionable t-shirt, with bare feet and perfectly painted toenails. "How did you get here?" she asked in a puzzled voice.

"Umm, I walked." I entered the living room, and checked out the place. It looked like Carrie's roommates were either law students with rich parents, or independently wealthy. Esoteric thirtysomething art in cast aluminum frames spanned the walls in perfectly planned decoration, and matched leather chairs and sofas clustered around an expensive Sony TV. A VCR, all-out stereo, floor-to-ceiling rack of CDs, high-end cordless phone, plush carpet, and copies of GQ and the Wall Street Journal on the endtable finished the motif. The place looked like something out of a Bret Easton Ellis novel, but with even more blatant brand name placement.

"Don't mind her, she's a little trashed," said a voice from the kitchen. "I'm Donna," said the woman in her early thirties, as she walked into the living room with a man two paces behind. She looked like the average grad student: tall, slim, with short blonde hair, and wire-rim glasses. "This is Lee," she said, and the man politely nodded. He looked her age, and tall with bland features and short hair; he resembled either a realtor or an insurance salesman. "Can I get you something to drink?" she asked.

"Yeah! I can make you a margarita!" Carrie happily replied, bouncing around the living room.

"I'll hold off this round," I said, sitting on the leather couch. "Pretty nice digs you've got here," I said to Carrie.

"Oh, thanks!" she yelled. "I'm going to make another margarita!" she gleefully hollered, vanishing into the kitchen.

Donna and Lee came over and parked on the white leather furniture. "She's been drinking margaritas and laying in the sun all day," said Donna. "She's pretty fucked up, so just try to...well just don't expect much response from her."

We vaguely watched the tube, flipping through channels as the Lee and Donna nursed their drinks.

"So, you and Carrie always have parties like this?" I asked, reclining on the leather couch.

"Not always, just a few times," she said, looking over from the TV. "My husband works third trick in the coal mines down in Spencer, so I have the nights to do my own thing," she said. I didn't know Donna was married or that Lee wasn't her significant other, so it took a minute to sort out the details. "What about you?" she asked.

"Me? I'm usually in front of the computer," I said. "I'm sure Carrie's told you the stories. I'd be in front of a computer right now if you hadn't tracked me down."

"Yeah, you always seem to be on the VAX. I see your name in my wholist all the time. Did you write that program?"

Sid and I made a lot of new friends by making our names the default friend list in the who program. I also put my name in a copyright notice that appeared on everyone's screen when they logged in. Between those two things, at least 10,000 people knew my username on sight, which helped my odds immensely when scamming.

"No, I didn't write the program originally, but I wrote a lot of other stuff for Sid, and spent the last year optimizing his work."

"That shit sounds pretty cool. You're about set for a job once you get out of here."

"I wish I could get a job now," I said. "I'm working at UCS in the sites right now, but I'm lucky to get a shift a week during the summer."

"You should talk to my brother-in-law," she said. "He works down at Crane Naval Weapons Center. They've always got computer shit going on down there. They pay pretty good too, for those military contracts..."

"Could you drop me an email about that? I'd like to check it out." The thought of landing a contract and some good resume fodder made my mouth water, but I wondered if she didn't know shit about what her brother in law did, and he was really a janitor, several degrees removed from the computing staff. I told my parents I worked in the computer labs, and they thought I knew how to reprogram their garage door opener.

"Hey, what is there to drink in there?" I asked. I went into the kitchen and surveyed the damage. At least two or three dozen liquor bottles rested on top of the fridge, in the neon glow.

"Do you want me to make a margarita?" Carrie said, jumping toward her precious blender.

"No, I'm not drinking right now, do you have anything else?"

"Hey John," Donna yelled from the other room. "There's some Cokes in the fridge."

I grabbed a cold red and white can, and snapped it open. "Thanks, Donna," I yelled back. "How are the margaritas pouring, Carrie?"

"They're really good, you should try some," she said, dumping more ice into the blender.

"Maybe later," I said, moving back to the living room.

Donna kept the lazy conversation going, as I occasionally watched the flickering TV. She asked about my UCS job, what I studied, where I was from, and countered each with a long story about someone she knew, or a class she took, or something else relevant. Lee occasionally added a few words, but stayed pretty quiet, tending to his drink. And Carrie kept trying to make margaritas with the blender, which was emitting disaster-like noises from the kitchen. Although the Donna's company was decent, being the only non-drinker in such a small crowd bored me, and I spent a good deal of my mental time trying to figure out when I would politely leave.

Suddenly Donna rose from the couch. "Well hey, me and Lee are gonna have to hit the road," she said. "You gonna be okay Carrie?" she parentally asked.

"I'm fine!" she drunkenly said. "Are you guys okay to drive?" she asked, while wobbling around the room.

Both Lee and Donna laughed. "Don't worry," Donna chuckled, "we're both hard drinkers from way back. A couple of margaritas aren't going to do much to me. Are you sure you'll be okay?"

I was almost sure Donna was trying to ask Carrie in some secret female code if she would be okay alone with me. But it didn't seem like Carrie caught on.

"Yeah, I'm fine!" she repeated. "Are you sure you don't want stay for another drink?"

"No, Lee's gotta work tomorrow, and I have to get back." Donna turned to me and asked, "Can you make sure she is okay?"

"Sure, everything's cool," I said.

Donna and Lee made their departure. "Good to meet you John! Thanks for the drinks Carrie, I'll give you a call tomorrow!" Donna yelled as she walked to her car with her silent friend.

"Bye Donna! Bye Lee!" Carrie yelled back drunkenly.

Carrie shut the heavy front door as I sat on the couch, remote jockeying through the channels on the TV. "Hey, do you want a margarita?" she yelled, still talking in the louder drunken voice.

"No, I'm cool for now," I said. She walked into the kitchen, leaving me to look around the house a bit.

"Don't you drink?" she yelled back from the kitchen.

"I just don't like tequila," I said. "Bad experiences." I had a sudden flashback of drinking shots at the kitchen table with Deon and Yehoshua last spring. I wasn't into the rotting taste of the stuff, or the whole thing about the worm. I'd rather take a straight shot of rum or a cold beer any day.

"This place is huge," I yelled. "How many of you live here?"

She stuck her head out of the kitchen holding a bottle of Jose Cuervo. "There's three others. We all have our own rooms though," she said.

"Where is everybody? At the bars?" I felt a need to question this, not because I wanted to rape her, but because I was hoping someone would show up so I could split. I felt obligated to hang around long enough that she didn't hurt herself, because she was drunk enough that she really should not have been left alone. But, I wanted to get the hell out of there and make it to the fountain in time to catch the weekend crowd.

"Oh, they're all gone for the weekend," she replied back. "Nicki and Renee both went home, and Rachel goes to her boyfriend's in Kentucky every weekend."

"Oh, that's cool," I said, knowing I was fucked. "Hey, you got any rum?" I ask.

"Umm," she said, rummaging through the dozens of bottles on top of the fridge. "Do you drink Bacardi?"

I didn't drink much of anything at that point. Except for the occasional beer, I'd been dry since the spring. As the child of an alcoholic and someone with an addictive personality toward women, CDs, credit cards and computers, I tried to keep dry unless I needed to drink. And because of the situation, I felt I really NEEDED to drink.

"Yeah, that would hit the spot," I said. I grabbed the bottle from her as she teetered around the kitchen with it. "I'll mix it myself, if that's cool."

"Okay!" she yelled, and went back to her concoction in the blender. She randomly poured tequila and triple sec at the open container, occasionally getting some of the alcohol into the drink instead of on the counter. With a tall plastic glass from Pizza Express, I dumped in a can of Coke, a couple of cubes of ice, and then topped it off with the rum. From the before and after heights of fluid in the tumbler, I guestimated the alcohol content to be about 7 or 8 shots, enough alcohol to deal with the situation.

I watched Carrie, and felt attracted to her, and attracted to the situation, something that I felt guilty about. After suffering so much loneliness and rejection, and bitching for years about how life was unfair, here I was with a beautiful, drunk woman and the potential opportunity to do whatever I wanted with her. I felt like I just used an ATM machine to take the last five bucks out of my account and it told me I had a balance of $900,000 available for withdrawal. I wanted to go for it, but I knew I couldn't. I felt sorry for her and felt a need to take care of her more than I felt any sexual attraction. I guessed it was my codependent side taking over.

I went back to the couch with my drink, reclaiming the remote. I tilted back the concoction, downing a hearty gulp and trying to suck back the fumes of the rum. Hard drinking was never my forte (well, drinking in general wasn't,) but I always went to the rum and Coke, hoping that after the first few mouthfuls of the mix I would forget that it tasted like kerosene.

Carrie crashed on the couch too, passively watching the TV and downing what must have been her twentieth margarita. In the time it took me to sip a few swallows of my drink, she pounded down her entire drink and got up for another. Her drinking astonished me; for such a thin little woman, she had a catastrophic amount of alcohol in her system, but still functioned for the most part.

My drink did not go unnoticed. I figured that some alcohol in my system would lower my inhibitions enough to let me deal with this alternate reality. By the time the blender noise and spilling sounds in the kitchen stopped, I pulled down about half of my poison and felt the alcohol burn my senses, equalizing my worry with illusion.

When she got back, I felt silly enough to get into a bizarre, Seinfeld-esque monologue about Batman, and although she struggled to keep up with me, we both laughed and enjoyed the stupidity the alcohol gave us. We both finished our drinks and kept channel surfing for a bit.

Quite suddenly, the alcohol in Carrie's system rebelled, causing her body to declare martial law. She went from manic to miserable, mumbling that she didn't know if she was going to be sick or not. I tried to help her as much as I could, as I was still semi-sober. We went out to the porch for some fresh air, but it didn't help much. While we were outside, she mumbled about an ex-boyfriend and how "it wasn't fair." Oh boy, I thought, as I dragged her back inside and to a kneeling position in front of the porcelain pew to confess her alcohol sins.

She couldn't throw up, even after trying several times. The alcohol was there to stay, and her only real option was to sleep it off. Great, I thought, I'll just put her to bed and leave. I needed to take my drugs, I needed to take out my contacts, and I wondered if maybe there were still people at the fountain...

I dragged her to her bedroom and helped her climb into bed. She lay on top of the sheets, fully clothed, but that was close enough for my mission.

"Okay Carrie, are you going to be okay?" I asked. She just mumbled a bit and asked me not to leave.

What? I wasn't getting something here. I already decided nothing would happen. I just wanted her to go to sleep so I could get home. But then John Bonham-esque visions of her choking on her own vomit made me think I should stay for a while. I could clear a space on the floor, steal some pillows from a housemate's empty bed, and crash. It wouldn't be comfy, I'd miss a dose of lithium, and my contacts would quite possibly fuse in my eyes, but if she started to freak out, I would be there to help her out.

Cleaning a spot on the floor became a monumental task; for such a beautiful and in-order woman, the place was a pit. But I got a spot to camp out, made sure she was okay, and then turned out the lights.

As soon as I tried to relax, she started sobbing and freaking out. I went back to the bed. "What's wrong Carrie? Are you okay?"

"Don't go away," she cried. "Don't leave."

Great. I tried to figure something else out. "I'm not leaving. I'll lay next to you up here, and make sure you're okay. I'm leaving all my clothes on, and I'll just sleep up here so nothing will happen, okay?"

She mumbled in agreement. I turned off the lights and climbed into the narrow twin bed with her. This isn't as glamorous as I thought it would be, I thought, trying to get comfortable without groping her.

Within two minutes, she was out cold. I could barely move, scrunched against her. I rested one arm over her, trying to relax without doing anything that could be transferred as sexual, sensual or even comfortable.

"Sweet dreams, Carrie," I whisper to the comatose body, before closing my eyes and letting the rum's sleepiness wash over me.

Somehow, I woke up when it was still twilight out. Her bedside clock said 6:07, and I reached for my watch to confirm. The rum felt like it was out of my system, but my contacts were on fire and I needed more sleep. Carrie was out cold, sleeping ungracefully on her stomach. Thoughts of her waking up next to a stranger suddenly filled my head, and I didn't want her to think I stayed just to try something. Time to bolt.

I put on my shoes, went to the bathroom and splashed cold water on my face. I used some of her roommate's contact solution to rinse out my eyes, ran a wet hand through my hair, trying to mat down the stuck-out hair, and tried to reassure myself that she'd be okay.

On my way out, I dug around the kitchen table to find a writing utensil and a piece of paper. No paper advertised itself as being there for writing, so I took out the crumpled directions from last night and tore off a clean half of the sheet. After thinking for a moment, I scrawled out a note:

> Carrie:
> I left at around 6—I stayed to make sure everything was cool. I hope you're OK—give me a call when you wake up, and let me know if you need anything.
> John—333-2254
> p.s. Take about 6 aspirins, drink a bunch of water, and don't try eating anything today.

I left the house, as twilight started to break, and the sun's rays just began to arc through the dark sky. A ten block walk east though the rich student ghetto would deposit me a dozen feet south of my house, so I didn't have to worry about getting lost during the surreal episode. I stumbled down the road with only the slivers of morning light to guide me on my path. The cool morning air cleared out my head, and I had no trace of a hangover, although my mouth tasted like I was eating pencil erasers, and I kept thinking I should've stolen a Coke from her fridge before I left. I also worried that Carrie would be mad at me for some reason. I knew I had no chance at her, but she'd make a nice friend. It all seemed so weird, I thought. I was just going to the fountain...

At my house, I walked past my beautiful sleeping VW, covered in a blanket of dew. Inside, I pried out the contacts, and could feel the blood and oxygen returning to my corneas again. I took a double-doze of lithium with lots of water to clear out the mucilage taste in my mouth. My clothes hit the floor and I crashed, enjoying the feel of my own bed, my own sheets against my skin, and no inanimate body next to me.

The phone rang a few hours later, and I grabbed for it. "Go," I said, half asleep.

"John? It's Carrie. Did I wake you?"

"No. I mean, yeah, but I need to wake up anyway. How are you feeling?"

"Pretty miserable," she said. "But I took some aspirin, and drank a bunch of water. I'll be okay."

"Good," I said. "I was worried about you."

"Thanks for taking care of me last night," she said. "I'm glad you helped out."

"No problem, what are friends for?" I said.

"Hey, are you doing anything later?" she asked. "Do you want to go see the new Batman film?"

"Sure, that's be great. Let me take a shower and call you back, and we can hook up then," I said. We exchanged good-byes and hung up.

After a shower and another quick call, I went to grab a bite to eat before I went to see her, since she would be sans food for the day. I went to McDonald's for usual Quarter Pounder with cheese, no pickle meal, and found some very cool Batmobile happy meal toys, one for each of us. I sat in the restaurant, snarfed down the food, and thought about the strange whirlwind of events. It would be cool to have friends like Donna and Carrie.

11

Thick summer air drifted through the room, the windows wide open to the Sunday night's heat. Sprawled across the mottled carpet, I clutched the phone and chatted with Nick, an Entombed CD case idly opening and closing in my hands. The fountain that night had been a bust, with only Linda, Bill, and me in attendance. I got home and called Nick to beat the post-fountain depression and kill a few hours.

"So, what's up with Cursed?" I asked him, referring to his zine, Cursed Metal.

"I'm trying to get the next issue done," Nick bitched, "but I'm a couple hundred reviews behind, and the printing costs are getting so fucking high."

"That sucks. I'm still trying to figure out what to do about my magazine," I replied.

"The email thing?" he asked. I started a zine a few months before by reviewing a bunch of tapes and sending the text to a bunch of people on the computer. This was long before the "Information Superhighway" revolution, so the whole thing was very unheard of. I could "publish" with virtually no cost, and quickly send out information, but no record label thought of this as a zine, and it was hard to get albums to review.

"I still haven't heard from any of the labels I wrote, but that Pete the Freak guy wrote back and sent a bunch of fliers. I'm writing everyone he sent me ads for," I said. Pete the Freak was a friend of Nick's with a band, and heavily involved in the metal underground. I ordered a demo tape of his, and he stuffed the envelope with photocopied ads for other bands and zines, a customary action of most people selling zines or demos direct through the mail.

"Yeah, just write everyone you can. Maybe you can work out some trades or something, or help them sell demos in email. If you could get an issue with a lot of demo reviews and print it out, the labels might help you," he explained.

"I just want to get this thing rolling," I said. "I want to get to the point where I have zine-related mail every day."

"Shit, I wish I didn't get mail every day. I've probably got 300 letters I need to answer. Give it time, and you'll get stuff," he said. "Speaking of mail, I should get the fuck out of here and try to answer some," he said. "I wish you would've stayed here this summer so you could help me with this shit."

"Yeah, well...If I was home, you'd be helping me dig shallow graves for my family members," I said.

"Fine by me. Let me know if you get another issue of the zine done or you meet any hot chicks that have roommates or sisters."

"When the hell are you coming down here, anyway?" I asked.

"I'll try to figure out something with work. Maybe I can take a Friday off and come down for three days. You've got to promise you'll do a better job on lining up some sluts this time."

"I'll see what I can do."

"Okay psycho, I'll catch you later."

"Later Nick."

I hung up and looked at my watch—just past three. We'd been talking for about two hours, which was par for the course. I'd call Nick almost every Sunday night, and he'd call back using his mom's business calling card, so we could keep in sync and have the kind of long, pointless conversations that were the basis of our friendship over the last five years.

In the fridge outside my room, no more Cokes awaited me—just a pizza from the fall of 1989, and a half-eaten plastic container of tofu. I went to check the kitchen fridge and ran into Yehoshua sitting at the table, strumming chords on his beat-up acoustic guitar.

"Hey man, what's up?" I asked him, looking in the other fridge for a drink. No luck.

"Just chilling, man," he said. "You ever read the *Lord of the Rings?*" he asked.

"I've been out of my D&D and glue-sniffing phase for a while," I said. "But yeah, I read the trilogy. Sixth grade maybe?"

"You still have any of the books?"

"No, I went the bookmobile route on the fantasy and sci-fi stuff," I said. "I read them faster than my folks could buy them. Why?"

"I think Tolkien was really into the drug culture, man," he said. "All of those dwarves running around with pipes."

"And let me guess. The magicians..."

"Peyote folklore," he said.

"You're fucked man," I laughed. "Those books are like fifty years old..."

"I still think he was on shrooms or something. I'm going to find the books at the library this week, and write a paper on it."

"Hey man, do you want to go to the VP? I've got to get some Cokes."

"You need some coke?" he said. "Just kidding, man. Yeah, I'm up for the walk."

I grabbed some money, locked up my room, and we took off for the walk to the convenience store at Third and Jordan. Having a Village Pantry this close meant a constant drain on funds. Every time I got a little hungry in the middle of the night, I'd comb my room for change and grab a candy bar and root beer or Coke. The Kroger by the mall had better prices, but that was a ten-minute drive away. It also gave me a chance to say hello to the 24-hour cashiers, who I knew by name.

"You taking classes this session?" I asked.

"Not really," he said. "The music school doesn't offer anything first session, and I didn't have the money to take any general stuff, so I've been taking lessons on the side."

"You working, or just hanging out?"

"I might have a gig mowing lawns for the landlord, but I've mostly been playing out and partying. I need to get it together before second session, or I'll be broke."

I couldn't imagine Yehoshua any more broke than he was now. He scammed most of his food, washed his clothes annually, and owned little more than three guitars and an amp. His room had a strange yet cool minimalist approach, like someone completely focused on their work.

We passed into the alley between Aristotle's books and the strip of stores in the crossroads plaza, the dark and narrow pathway that made the rural area look almost urban.

"Hey man, have you heard from Tammy?" he asked. I often forgot, but Yehoshua knew Tammy longer than me—they were in a music theory class together. Yehoshua slept through the final for that class, and would have to re-take it next fall.

"No. We split things off a while ago, I haven't heard from her since."

"That's too bad," he said. "She was really good in music theory."

"What about you? Any new female prospects?"

"I'm workin' on this guitar-guru-hipcat thing, man."

"Does it work?"

"No, but I'm workin' on it."

The alley opened into Third Street, and we headed over to the glowing amber and green Village Pantry sign across the street. Bright panes of glass illuminated the front of the oasis, displaying signs for lottery tickets, prepaid phone cards, and refillable plastic fountain drink mugs.

We burst into the doors, and saw Mike, our favorite graveyard shift cashier. A pudgy guy with a timeless crewcut and the start of a goatee, he looked like some kind of amateur sumo wrestler. He slumped against the counter, reading a book. "Hey guys," he said, only briefly looking up from his reading.

"I wanna get some gum, man," Yehoshua said. "I really want something sweet." He started rifling through his jeans, looking for change.

"Why don't you get a candy bar or something?" I asked. "Gum seems like such a waste. You never get to eat it. It's like renting something sweet to eat and having to return it." I went to the coolers and picked up a two liter of Coke, then grabbed a bag of Combos.

We walked to the counter with our purchases. "How's your evening been, gentlemen?" Mike asked us.

"Have you ever read *The Lord of the Rings?*" Yehoshua asked.

"Oh shit, not this again," I said. "He thinks Tolkien's writing is full of drug references."

"I never got to read any of that stuff," Mike said. "My parents were Jehovah's Witnesses. They thought it would drive me to worship the devil. Now here's the question: if I worshiped the devil, would he make me wear this brown and orange jacket?"

Mike rang up our stuff, and I dug a pair of wrinkled ones from my wallet in exchange for the goods. We walked back to the house, and I poured a tall glass of Coke and sat at the computer to do a little more email for the evening.

During the days with no UCS shifts, I slept in and spent the late morning and early afternoon reading email. After my shower and email routine, I tried to find more work. I tiled my floor with the classified section I robbed from a broken paper machine at the VP, and attacked the job section with pen and careful eye.

Finding work wasn't easy in a college town. Bloomington had people with double PhD's in Chemistry and Thermonuclear Particle Physics washing dishes for $4.25 an hour because no other work was available. A few factories operated on the far side of town, but employers would rather hire a local with a house and family who would keep the job for 30 years than a smart-ass college student who would work for three months and then quit. Most of the jobs in the paper consisted of semi-skilled/skilled labor that I couldn't do, babysitting for like five hours a month for a dollar an hour, and the "Opportunities" section, filled with ads similar to this:

WANT TO BE YOUR OWN BOSS? Sick of working hard for no money? Would you like to earn up to $482,000 a minute? We have the opportunity for you! Call xxx-xxxx...

Certain rules applied to the filtering of the Ponzi ads. A job saying you could make "up to" a certain amount also meant you could earn "down to" zero dollars, and usually involved high-pressure sales. Something guaranteeing a lower wage was better, but if it involved sales, they might fire you after a day or two if you didn't perform. Anything with the mention of startup costs or investment got the axe, so did anything that sounded like door-to-door work. The field quickly thinned.

I saw an ad in that morning's paper that looked like the typical telemarketing job. Phone work didn't bum me out too much after I realized it was only temporary. It would suck for a couple evenings, and I'd get fired after that for low stats, but I'd get 40 or 50 bucks for groceries and walk away from it without destroying my career or my pride. I wrote down the address, combed back my hair and hit the deodorant, and went for a spin.

The address was 1248 North College #48, so I hit the strip and drove past the Denny's, McDonald's, and the other fast food joints on the north side. I kept thinking about the job; maybe I could stay there for a couple weeks, get enough money to stockpile for groceries and buy a few albums...

I passed the cutoff that went to the highway, and looked over at a liquor store. 1004 N. College—close, but stuff started to spread out a bit more. I was out of fast food country and into the executive offices made of space age mirrored glass with fake fountains and hundred-yard frontage. Maybe it was a big place, I thought, keeping my eyes peeled.

A house sat at the 1150 mark. Then a gas station. Then nothing, just a bunch of undeveloped property, and then an office building at 1320. What? I pulled into the office parking lot and tried to rethink things. A house, a gas station, a roofing place? Another little house, a hotel or something, a small body shop, the office. Oh shit—I realized what was going on, and turned back toward town.

I went south another block, and saw the Bloomington Hotel. I pulled into the front carport, parked the car, and calmly walked in.

"Excuse me miss," I said to the lady at the front counter, "what's the address here?"

"1248 North College, sir. Are you expecting incoming mail?" she asked politely, thinking I was a patron.

"No, no ma'am. Thanks," I mumbled as I walked back to the car. What the hell? Did they rent out an office suite somewhere here? Was the hotel doing telemarketing? Were they doing interviews at a suite here and then the job site was elsewhere?

I pulled the Rabbit into a spot and walked around the parking lot. The place had a main building, probably with an overpriced bar and a rinky-dink gift shop full of two-packs of Alka-Seltzer for a dollar; the rooms were in a half dozen two-story barracks buildings surrounding a pool.

I walked around the pool, trying to navigate a maze of fencing. A mother stood in the shallow end, as her children floated in the water and yelled and laughed and splashed each other. It reminded me of when I was twelve and my parents brought me and my sisters to Florida. We spent every day in the giant, lagoon-shaped pool in the middle of the Tampa Holiday Inn. But who vacations in Bloomington? Tampa may suck, but it has Busch Gardens, the Gulf of Mexico, and it's warm in the winter.

I rounded a corner to the last set of barracks, and found the scam. Room 48, overlooking the pool, had the front door propped open and the front shades removed. Inside, the two-bed hotel room had the furniture replaced with four rows of flat tables, each table with four or five phones and telemarketers mad at work. Even from the pool, I could hear the bloodletting, phone sharks selling coupon books to unsuspecting housewives. The piece of shit hotel room was wired with a PBX and rented by the month so they could run their boilerroom from the poolfront, and then vanish after their campaign was over.

I thought about the probability of working there for a week or two, and then coming in to get my check and finding a vacant room 48 with no forwarding address. Fuck it. I went back to the Rabbit, wound back home, and slept for the rest of the day.

The fountain water looked clean tonight, the underwater floodlights clearly shining through the turgid surf without illuminating large chunks of slime and dirt. I sat on the smooth lip of the basin, sifting my hand through the surface of the pool, feeling the cool water. Staring into the basin and listening to the splash of the five jets relaxed me with an almost hypnotic power. It combined staring at a goldfish bowl with the gentle, ambient sound of running water. Usually, my only two or three minutes of clarity a day would be my time alone at the fountain before the others arrived.

A familiar silver Jetta circled around the fountain drive in a sweeping arc, then rested at the base of the auditorium steps. The engine wound down, shaking the car with the vibrations of poor maintenance. The door swung open with a creak, releasing a handful of papers and fast food garbage onto the sidewalk. Then, the familiar, dark-haired, roly-poly man crawled from the heap of VW and slammed the door behind him.

"Hey John!" yelled Chad, waddling toward the fountain with a pair of flopping sandals and his trademark large, overly roomy shorts. Well, so much for an evening of clarity.

"Hey Brecken, how's life?"

"Same old, all work and absolutely no play. I've got some news for you, by the way."

"If you're going to tell me how you got laid..."

"No, no, and I haven't. This concerns an old flame of yours, someone who will be at the fountain tonight."

"If you somehow managed to get Lauren to show up, I'm going to..."

"No, you might actually be cool about this. I ran into Cindy today, she said she'd stop by."

"Cindy McKim, No shit?" I met Cindy during my first summer of VAXing from home. We talked frequently, ran up the long distance bills occasionally, but didn't actually meet until a year later, after she hooked up with Sid, my VAX hacking partner in crime. "What's she been up to?"

"She isn't with Sid anymore. She's getting her shit together, trying to finish school. She looks a lot different now. I mean, she's dressing better, her hair is different...Well, I guess she's doing okay. You'd probably like her now."

"What do you mean? I've always liked her."

"No, you know what I mean. She's single, you're single..."

"I don't think that would happen. I'm all fucked up right now. We'll see, but don't expect any magic."

"Boy, you're just mister optimism tonight. Why don't you chill out about this stuff?"

"Look man, you've crawled to me worse off than this more than a few times, and I didn't bitch. This breakup, all of these freak near misses—I'm about fucking ready to move to Montana and start fucking sheep."

"Well, I never thought about sheep, but I know what you mean. Maybe if..."

"Look, let's not have this discussion, okay? I'll get out of it when I get out of it, don't rush me."

"Okay, okay..."

A tall figure with a slouch hat and canvas backpack strolled up from the west. It was Bill, walking with a humble, slightly limping stride, carrying the years proudly on his tall frame.

"Hey guys," he said, climbing the steps to the dais. "What's up tonight?"

"Hey Bill," Chad replied. "Not much, just the usual. No money, no women, nothing to do."

Bill fumbled with the olive drab bag, looking for a pack of cigarettes. "I've learned to live without money or women over the years..."

"I don't think I'm ready to make the switch, Bill. You know how I am with women," I said.

"Yeah, it's a shame..." He found the pack of Camels, put one to his mouth, and fumbled with some matches. "If you ever change your mind, just let me know."

"Don't hold your breath," I laughed. "Hey, how's your writing going?"

He breathed from the now-lit cigarette, shaking out a smoldering match. "It's going. I'm working on a collection of poetry, a lot of stuff from over the years. Plus, I've been pecking away at a longer piece of fiction. I don't know where it's going, but it's definitely going."

"How can you write a book and not know what it's about?" asked Chad.

"It's easier than you think. I've got a whole idea, a montage of characters and scenes. I don't always know what's going to happen, but that doesn't stop me from writing and developing them. Usually along the way, I figure out what's going to happen."

"Well, at least we know what keeps you busy," Chad said. "How's life been otherwise?"

"The usual. A bunch of relationship stuff I don't want to get into, and I've been an insomniac lately. Plus they're tearing apart the roof on my house, which means I can't sleep in the day."

"Hey, at least you're getting a roof," I said. "I've still got that hole in my ceiling, where I have to play bucket brigade when it rains."

"Do you guys know anyone with a Celica?" Chad asked, looking over to the front of the auditorium.

I glanced over, and spotted the familiar car. "Oh yeah! That's Alex and Renee. I didn't know they'd be here."

Renee and Alex were regulars at last year's fountain gatherings; their relationship actually started during the midnight meetings. Renee was a business major who kept quiet in person but openly conversed on the computer, where I met her during my freshman year. Alex started as a legend, a friend of several friends (and ex of a few too) who I never met but always heard many stories about. We finally crossed paths a year ago when I crashed a party of his on Memorial Day, and we kept up to date on our scamming activities ever since.

Last summer, Lauren's birthday party became a pre-fountain event, with the usual gang of idiots converging on her house for cake, beer, food, and a few games of Ping-Pong in her basement before the regular gathering at Showalter. Renee and Alex met for the first time at the party, and by the end of the evening, the unlikely couple of scammer and puritan seemed very glued together. The next night, they appeared at the fountain together, and after they left, the remaining fountainheads started a betting pool on the duration of their tryst. Everyone lost; they were still together a year later.

Alex and Renee walked from the car. "John, Bill, Chad," said Alex. Renee said a slight hello, as the two strolled hand in hand to our gathering on the fountain edge.

After they arrived, a blue late-model Taurus foreign to me circled and parked with the others. From inside, a shapely young woman dressed nicely with chin-length blonde hair emerged, and strolled up to the fountain. Cindy. She looked so different from her alterna-punk appearance of the last few months, with dyed hair, torn flannel and bland features replaced with styled, golden hair, nice jeans and shirt, and carefully done makeup.

"Hi everybody! I'm here!" she said, waving to the group.

"Cindy! Wow, it's been forever," I said. "You really look...different." I stumbled, like a fuckup. "I mean, you look nice. Not that you..."

She sat next to me on the edge of the fountain. "You don't need to say it. I've been dressing like hell for the last year or so, for obvious reasons."

"Well, you look good. How have you been?"

"Things have been a little weird, I'm still getting used to being without Sid. But I've been feeling better, getting a lot better about things." she said. "What about you?"

"Things haven't been optimistic, but I'm still here." I said. "I sort of went through a bad breakup, and the usual money, grades, et cetera."

"Yeah, my GPA is still pretty damaged too," she replied. "You broke up with that girl you were dating last spring?"

"Not exactly, but...We separated for the summer, and then she decided it was a more permanent thing."

"I'm sorry. Are you doing any better?"

"No, I'm still really fucked up. I'll explain it all sometime..."

"Hey Conner, you going in the water tonight?" Brecken yelled at me. He straddled the lip of the basin, with one foot in the water, and one out.

"You've gotta be fucking nuts," I said. "That water's like 50 degrees." I moved from the lip to one of the stone park benches, to avoid any of Chad's stupid hijinks. Alex and Renee followed me, and Linda arrived with Doyle Martin in tow, another VAX regular. He spent all of his time online obsessing about vampires and role-playing games, but he quickly hit off a conversation with Cindy, and started talking about Monty Python or something.

"So what's the status with Cindy?" Alex asked. "Gonna go in for the full court press? Afraid of seconds after Sid?"

"Don't start," I said. "I'm not up to speed with the woman thing right now."

"That doesn't sound like the John Conner I know," he said. "I remember when your weekly hitlist looked like a copy of the Racing Form. Where's your sense of adventure, man?"

"Cindy knows too much about me," I said. "I need a stranger. And they're getting harder to find at these incestuous little get-togethers."

"Hey, you work any shifts lately?" Alex asked.

"I've got a 4-hour Business sub tomorrow," I said. "I don't have any regular hours. I'm about ready to sell my kidneys for food stamps."

"Have you heard about special projects?" Renee said. "They have to use all of the leftover fiscal year money by July 1, so they're paying people to write and test the fall training classes. I've got 10 hours a week for the rest of the month writing a Lotus macro class."

"I'll have to look into that," I said. "Maybe there's some Mac or unix stuff. I'd take anything I could get, though."

We talked more, and watched the others talk, for about an hour. Linda and Doyle both went to the Library cluster, and then Cindy took off, first stopping over to say goodbye. After Alex and Renee said their good-byes, Chad drove off, and Bill hiked back to Lindley Hall, which left me alone. I sat at the fountain for a few more minutes, and watched the water jet into the air and back down into the pool. After more rambling thoughts about Cindy, I left.

My empire of dust. My room at 3:37 in the morning.

Telling Cindy, telling anyone about how Tammy left me brought out the pain like torn stitches. Trying to explain the situation, even in a two second summary, made me replay all of it again, brought it to the foreground, and started the undying process of evaluating it, examining it, trying to look for an answer. Like an accident I could've avoided, it haunted me as I lay in bed. But instead of thinking "I could've turned the skidding car to the left and missed the pedestrians," it was "I could've been more considerate" or "I could've given her more room" or "I could've been less attached" or "I could've been less of an asshole."

The room's ghosts continued. When she was in the same bed. When her things were sitting on the same chair. When she used the same computer to check her mail. The room's demons tore at my soul, recycling this joyous past into a harrowful and tortuous present.

Cindy seemed to heal from Sid. She looked happy, beatific. Her appearance changed, the tone, the color in her voice seemed improved, healed from the horror she endured six months ago, the fights, the cheating, the lack of direction, the pain. Maybe her process of repair worked differently, she had it bad and was now getting better. I had it perfect, and was now spiraling down.

When I saw Cindy earlier, it felt like she'd transformed back into the person I first knew years before, and I could unlock the secrets I previously told her and keep going like we'd never spent any time apart. But I felt scared—I could barely tell her about Tammy, and I didn't want to tell her that I was suicidal, and at the end of my rope. What if she didn't care anymore? It would take time, more time.

I took my medicine, got into bed, and tried to sleep. The heat baked my flesh as this new paradox filled my head, and I knew slumber wouldn't hit for hours.

I rolled over and looked at my watch: 11:48 AM. The sun already heated the room more than the box fan could cool it, and it would be impossible for me to sleep any more. I'd have to work with less than six hours again, which had become par for the course lately.

Once the crud cleared from my head and I realized where I was, the depression took over again. The heavy feeling of pain reminded me that I didn't know which way was up these days. Hopelessness weighted my body like a sinking ship. If it wasn't so fucking hot, I would've gone back to sleep and stayed in bed all day.

Time for my William Tell routine. I got up, reached under the bed, and pulled out a shoebox and my 16 gauge. In the shoebox, along with the gun's magazine, was a folded note I wrote weeks earlier, which simply said, "This was my fault. I don't feel like explaining my reasons. Don't blame yourself." Back when I thought of suicide as a form of attention, I'd spend weeks writing elaborate notes whining about my problems. Now, the form letter would simply alert the authorities that this wasn't a gun cleaning accident. Plus, this routine was too mechanical a procedure for the personalization of a note. The thought of suicide was more of a medical procedure than an artistic cry of help.

The clip held three of my four rounds of ammunition. With the gun resting across my lap, I pushed in the cartridge with a resounding click. I had three rounds, but I'd only need one. I turned over the gun, and pulled the bolt back and up. With a live round in the chamber, I pushed the bolt forward and locked it in place.

Now the hard part. I moved to the edge of the bed, put my feet together, and put the butt of the gun between them, so the blast wouldn't knock the whole thing across the room and cause less than mortal wounds. Then I lowered the barrel and steadied the business end in front of my mouth with my left hand, took a deep breath, and put my right index and middle fingers on the trigger.

This was the point in my day when everything got shoved into perspective. A few pounds of pressure to the tiny piece of metal under my fingers, and it would be instantly over. All of the bad would vanish, but so would the good. What is the good, I thought? What if I was in a dark alley and the gun barrel in my face belonged to a criminal? What things would I want to see or do one more time? What could I do to change things? One good thought would cause me to put down the gun and start my day. Sometimes I thought for a long time about kicking ass in school, fighting for my scholarship and graduating, to get a real job that took me far away from Indiana. Sometimes I thought about friends like Nick and Peter, and the good times we had. Sometimes I thought about my newer friends and my roommates. But sometimes, I just thought about taking a long walk, going for a drive, or even checking my email.

Today, I remembered that I had to work a four-hour sub shift in the business building. Nobody would be there all day, and four hours isn't a full time job, but after taxes, it's about twenty bucks—enough for a few days of food.

I put down the gun, unchambered the shell, and put it back in the box. Today's going to be an okay day, I thought.

12

"Okay, count 'em up and put your John Hancock here, and you're ready." Bruce sat at his desk, kicking back a beer, and watching me check the tubes. I counted three sealed packs, fifty per pack; I also checked out the money belt, which held the usual $25 in ones and fives.

I ran my fingers over the space-age foil bundles, and detected no breaks in the vacuum seal. "All here," I said. "Now where is this place?"

"It's a fair, in Brownstone. I talked to the owners, so you're cool. You'll be by yourself, but I'm sending Brecken about an hour after you, or whenever he gets off his ass and comes over here. You have gas in your car?"

Miraculously, I had filled up the day before. "Yeah, I'm cool. Where's Brownstone."

"It's east, southeast—about a 45 minute drive, maybe an hour. Here's the map." He handed me a photocopied Indiana highway map with some penned scribbles and an address. "Give me a call on the 800 number if you have any problems."

I shuffled out of the house and to the Rabbit, glowstick case slung over my shoulder. I never heard of the town before, but it sounded like a fun ride. Back roads with no traffic, a good tape in the player, and the sun in my hair—I'd enjoy the drive. I threw my stuff in the hatch, cranked open the moonroof, and hit the road, feeling the Sunday afternoon's air in the cockpit. With Judas Priest's *Painkiller* album in the stereo, the road whirred by faster, and I got into the nice, Sunday drive through the Southern Indiana countryside.

The country roads curved and swept over hills, and I pushed the VW hard, feeling it swing and take the corners without a lot of difficulty. It was an econo-car, and a piece of shit, but it felt like something out of a Euro-Rally race. I wasn't even driving that fast, but it was wide open—hitting the gas during the turns, holding my shifts and revving the engine, and careening down the straights, while farms, fields, and the occasional house zipped past. Through the open moonroof, some clouds drifted on the blue background above my head, and the sky became a perfect backdrop for my outing.

I couldn't remember if I was depressed before I left, but I knew I wasn't now. A man and his car. I wished I could've driven like this every day. The car and I had such a history of long roadtrips, boring commutes, and carting through town, but she really felt at home tearing up the back roads—and with a diesel engine! The Germans couldn't win a war, but they built a hell of an automobile.

Just over 45 minutes into the trip, I approached town, and went into micro-navigation mode to find the fairgrounds. The skies were starting to fade into darkness fast, but it felt too early for sundown. When I got a chance to look at the sky, I saw the clouds darkening. Fucking great. I navigated through central Brownstone, which was a Main Street out of a western film, but with new paint and some more flowers—one of those Indiana farming towns that reeked of 4-H and general stores.

The fairgrounds were a few blocks from the downtown district, and I ditched the VW on a city street to avoid the $2 parking field. With the gear on my shoulder, I hustled to the entrance and jumped through the crowd, keeping everything stowed in case Bruce didn't really talk to any people.

The area looked small for a county fair—a football fields' worth of farm buildings containing animal stalls and a handful of food booths outside, plus a few acres of grassy field with a sparse collection of kiddie rides. The tilt-a-whirl and mini roller coaster, the type that had been trucked across the country from carny to carny, ran at low capacity. Only a few hundred people wandered the concourse, and it looked like over half of them were World War II vets.

Oh well, a gig is a gig, I thought. I went to the strip between the paved concourse and the grassy field and set up shop, only taking out three sticks. I made a necklace, and waved around the other sticks like benediction over the pathetic crowd. People listlessly shuffled past, a few glancing at me, but most ignoring my presence, like I was a homeless leper begging for change.

I wanted to find kids and parents willing to blow some cash on a fad item, but instead, the few children running around looked like they were from dirt-poor farming communities, single-parent families, or both. I saw more of the barefoot-and-pregnant types wander past than I could believe, and a few high school aged couples wandered the evening. Most of the people there were senior citizens who wouldn't buy a glass of water if they were dying of thirst. I couldn't blame them much, either—if I had kids and they wanted to buy a glowstick for three bucks, I'd drag them away kicking and screaming, too.

After an hour and no sales, Chad shuffled down the avenue, holding his head low, no equipment in hand.

"Hey Brecken, good to see you," I said. "I'm getting swamped here, I could use some help."

"Sell anything yet?" he asked.

"Dude, nobody's even asked me how much they cost."

"This is a shitty event," he said. "Last year we didn't do anything like this. It looks like it's going to rain before dark, too."

"So why'd you drive out here?" I asked. "Something up?"

He sighed. "It's over with me and Diane."

"I knew this was coming. Hey, hang on a second." A mom and her three kids wandered over, transfixed on the neon glow.

"How much are they?" the mom asked.

Before I could answer, Chad cut in. "Sell them for a dollar each," he said. "Let's get out of here."

She pulled three singles from her purse, exchanged them for the three sticks in my hand and around my neck, and melted back into the crowd.

"They were already activated," Brecken said. "You would've thrown them out anyway. Let's go get something to eat."

I unsnapped the money belt and folded it into thirds, to shove it in the glowstick rig. "I'll go, but I'm short on cash."

"Don't worry, I'll pay."

I hefted the tubes and dangled them under my arm with the shoulder strap. We headed over to the concession stands.

We found a wooden picnic table and assembled together some dinner. Brecken found a greasy cheesesteak sandwich with a pile of onions on the cardiologically unsound pile of beef. I took the slightly safer route with two corndogs, drowned in a half bottle of ketchup, and a paper bag of french fries. Although unhealthy, the mixture of starch, grease, and cholesterol, with a tall Coke on the side met some inner addiction, and almost made the 45-minute drive and public humiliation worthwhile.

"So what was her excuse?" I asked. "It's not you it's me?"

"No, she didn't think it was working out," he said.

"Another guy?"

"She wasn't dating anyone else. She just didn't think it had any long-term potential and didn't want to get involved."

"Shit, if I were you, that would be my salvation. I thought she had a kid, you didn't want to get involved?"

"I didn't but...you know, you spend time with a person, and then you're alone."

"I know what you mean, man. I think I was telling you the same story a month ago."

He chewed away on his sandwich for a minute, and I ate in silence. It felt solemn, and also weird—we were once again in sync, both in the dumps because women left us. I hoped for both of our sakes that the slumps didn't last long.

"Conner, do you believe in forever?" Chad asked.

"Shit man, I don't believe in tomorrow," I replied. "I know you're going to start asking me dopey questions about if I believe that you could love someone forever, and you already know the answers I'd give you." I took a hit of the Coke, and continued. "You're not going to help yourself by wondering if this was the one, especially if she was just someone you fucked for a month."

"So what do I do?" he asked.

"You get on the fucking computer and start trawling for women. Get some email going, and fuck the first thing you see. I'd mail you my cheat sheet for the summer, but it's a tightly guarded trade secret."

"And you think that's going to help? Out of the frying pan into another?"

"I never said it would help, but it's another kind of pain. I could've gone through this summer depressed about Tammy or playing hit and miss with a trail of a hundred women. I guess I'm doing both, but the chase helps."

I finished the last of my fries, and bunched up the paper and wax-wrapped garbage. "Let's head out, dude," I said. "I want to ride out that storm. You coming back to Bruce's?"

"No, I think I'm gonna go home."

"Well, hit the fountain at least. Try to act a little social. Hey, thanks for the food, by the way."

"No problem", he said. "I'll see you at midnight, if it isn't pouring rain."

"Later Chad, take care."

I dumped my trash, grabbed the gear, and headed back to my car. As I installed the gear into the hatch, lightning danced on the distant horizon. So much for a Monaco GP drive home, I thought.

By the time I wheeled back to Bruce's, I ran through some heavy, sudden rain—the kind of storm that drops blotches of water instead of drops, and jitters the road underneath you with each thunder strike. In Bloomington, the worst of the rain was over, and I pulled the equipment from the car with only a slight drizzle overhead.

Inside, Bruce tended a beer and watched some documentary on the Alaskan back-country on the big-screen TV. "You bust some sticks tonight?" he asked.

"A complete fucking wash," I said. "I sold the three I had in my hand for a buck each before we left. Brecken didn't even get out his stuff. Nobody was biting—it was a total podunk, redneck fair. Maybe on a good Friday you could unload a dozen or two, but most of these people hadn't even seen three bucks in their lives."

"Come on, let's sign you in." he got up and we went back to the office, where I dumped my tubes and exactly $28 on the desk. "That's too bad, man," he said. "I heard there would be a lot more people there, but these county fairs can be real hit or miss." He counted the money, looked at the sticks, and signed my papers. "Sometimes it's Disneyland, and other times it's two show pigs and a pony ride."

"This was like a fucking garage sale with a tilt-a-whirl."

"I feel bad about sending you. Here..." He opened the cash box and pulled out a twenty. "Here's for driving out there for me," he said, handing over the Jackson. "At least it was a good recon run—we know not to send anyone else out there." He looked at a schedule on the wall for a second. "Hey, what are you doing this week?"

"I've got classes Monday and Wednesday night. What's up?"

"A milk run—Fun Frolic is in town this week, and next weekend." Fun Frolic was an annual IU carnival, basically, set up in the stadium parking lot. I went last year, and it had a fair number of rides and concessions. Best of all—it was up on 17th Street—no driving. "Name your nights, and I'll give them to you," he said. "You can have first crack on the weekend shifts."

"How about I start with Friday, and if it goes well, I'll add Saturday?" I asked.

"Sounds good. I'll put you down. Sorry again about tonight."

"That's okay, win some lose some," I said. "I'm gonna run—I'll see you Friday."

Outside, the rain stopped, but the humidity cooked in the summer air, giving it a relaxing but eerie coolness. I drove back to the apartment, still thinking about where to spend the twenty.

Monday morning, I walked to the Monroe County Bank ATM booth at Third and Jordan to check my balance and figure out how fast I could spend the cash Bruce gave me the night before. The little glass house had full-blast air conditioning that felt 20 degrees cooler than the hot day outside. I wondered if I could get a sleeping bag and sleep in there from now on. The machine spit out a balance sheet, reporting the damage. In the bank: $38.65. In my hands: $22 and change. Next payday: a week from Friday, with maybe 30-some accumulated hours in the queue. I could afford to spend the $20 on a case of Coke, a real lunch at the MCL cafeteria, and another 18-pack of microwave burritos.

I judged prosperity by the number of cans and two liters in my fridge. A somewhat bogus statistic, mostly because of the frequent food theft problem, it still projected well because I had to drink Cokes every day. Being removed from caffeine was unspeakable, like a diabetic quitting insulin. So when money ran below the five-dollar mark and the cans in the fridge went below a six-pack, I started looking at which CDs I could sell.

I felt good about money right now, but as the calendar pulled through the month of June, I wondered when I'd get some solid money in the bank for bigger concerns than 24-packs. By mid-August, I'd need to scrape up the deposit on next year's rent. Even if I worked a full 80 hours in two weeks for UCS, which would be impossible, I'd barely clear enough to cover a lump like that. Plus, the Rabbit's brakes felt a little scratchy. And if I didn't make the scholarship, how would I fund next fall's tuition? I'd have to run things close to the vest for a while, but I didn't want it to ruin the summer.

On Thursday, I answered a telemarketer ad from the paper, and they told me to come on down Friday morning and start answering phones. Hot damn—at least a day's pay at minimum wage, I thought. I even cut out early at the fountain that night and got to bed at 2 so I could wake up at 7:30 and find the place.

That morning, running high on an almost complete night of sleep and a shotgunned Coke, I drove west on Third Street—way west, past the graveyard and out toward the airport and UPS. The instructions said to find a strip mall with a biker bar in it, just past where Third crosses over State Road 37. I found it with no difficulty, and pulled around the back side, where, next to the dumpsters, there were a line of numbered doors. I got out, and went to #3—locked. I knocked, no answer—checked my watch: 8:54. What the fuck?

A beat up Monte Carlo, spewing forth blue gas from its tailpipes pulled up next to the Rabbit, bellowing a song I recognized from one of the two new Guns N' Roses albums. A guy appeared who looked a lot like Phil "Philthy Animal" Taylor, the drummer from old, *Iron Fist* era Motörhead: he had semi-long, unkempt brown hair that jutted every way in some Keith Richards-esque style, the start of a beard, a cut-up half shirt, and a total speedfreak appearance. Behind him trailed a girl that exuded both pure sex and extreme rural upbringing. With a nice figure, tight clothes, and an obviously dyed hair job, she looked like she'd be a wild ride—if you had any meth to spare.

"Hey man, you lookin' for Ed?" he asked, while cracking open a pack of unfiltered Camels.

"He's with the phone job?" I asked.

"Yeah, him. He's right behind us. We drive in from Indy every day."

True to his word, Ed pulled up in a battered S10 pickup just a moment later. Ed looked like glowstick Bruce, minus the strong business ethic. If you dried out a biker in his late 40s, got him a haircut, and slapped on a polo shirt, that's Ed.

"Hi, you're..." he said, extending his hand.

I gave him a handshake. "John Conner. We talked yesterday."

"Okay John, let's get you started. You met Gary and Shelly?"

"Yeah, we just met," I said. We nodded a hello to each other while Ed unlocked the door.

I expected the place to be a dump, but the inside blew me away. The office was about the size of my tiny apartment bedroom, with a half dozen phones on card tables, and Ed's desk opposite the door. There was also a bathroom the size of an airplane lavatory.

"Okay John, let's go over what you need to know. Didn't you say you worked on phones before?" he asked.

"Yeah, IU telefund, a few years back."

"Great, this stuff should be no problem. We're selling garbage bags and American flags to help disabled veterans. There's a script at each phone, and you ask the folks if they'd like to help the disabled veterans, and buy some bags or flags. If they decide to help, we get their address and Gary drives over with the merchandise."

"Any paperwork I have to fill out before getting started?" I asked.

"No, not really....This is considered more of a volunteer effort than employment, tax purposes and all. I pay you minimum wage or your commission, whichever is higher, and it's paid in cash on the next working day. So today's work will be paid when you come in Monday. Fill out the sheet at the phone with your name and your sales and give it to me at the end of the day. And let me know if you have any questions."

I went to a phone, and looked at the tenth-generation-photocopied script—typical telemarketing drivel. I noticed the cleverness of their scam after reading to the end—the company's name was something like Veteran's Fund Worldwide, and people wrote their checks to the VFW. Then Ed could donate a dollar a year to the Veterans of Foreign Wars and say "A portion of profits go to the disabled veterans..." Another piece of paper had a block of phone numbers in it, like 323-0000 through 323-9999, and we'd blow through the numbers sequentially, checking it if nobody was home or didn't answer, crossing it out if we failed, and putting an F next to it if it was a fax, data line, or business.

I started blasting through the numbers, waiting for three rings or an answering machine before stepping to the next call on the list. I got caught by a bunch of answering machines, and wondered who the hell would be home at ten in the morning to buy some garbage bags.

A few numbers caught, and I rattled the script to unsuspecting housewives that usually hung up on me. Shelly worked the lines too, and I listened to her southern Indiana accent reading the script with a slow, monotonous tone. In the background, Ed made some calls too, in between some strange business dealings on the phone—it sounded like he had another office running the same scam in Indianapolis. Ed's calls sounded perfect—he didn't even use the script. He ran through the facts with a voice that sounded like Robert Duvall in *Apocalypse Now*, and at least half the people he hit were sales. I had absolutely no respect for this operation, but I had the utmost admiration for this guy's ability to work the phones.

I trudged on until noon, and kept at the keypad and receiver with no luck, but it didn't seem like anybody cared. At the telefund, statistics were tracked instantly—call percentages and average pledge amounts were your life and death. It felt like the only thing that stopped me from writing down fake orders was Gary the speedfreak waiting for something to deliver. A few times before noon, Ed handed over a list of orders. Gary pulled some flags and boxes of garbage bags from underneath a card table and headed out in his Monte Carlo for delivery.

We stopped for lunch—everyone chipped in a couple of bucks, and Gary ran to Arby's and got us some food. I thought about heading home and making some sandwiches, but I anted up the cash for some roast beef and fries, and we all ate in front of our phones before launching back into the calls.

After another hour, I finally hit a college student that went for the trash bags, and I handed over the receipt to Gary. It felt good to have a sale, but

I figured it would take at least three to be out of the hole for the day, and I didn't think I could hit two more that afternoon.

It felt stupid being in a tiny room with no windows, wasting eight hours of my day to sell one box of garbage bags. If I stick with it, I thought, I'd at least make minimum wage. It didn't seem like Ed would can me for selling low or pissing people off with a poorly read script, but it felt degrading. The summer before, I did much less work than this, putting brass fittings in cardboard boxes, but I got paid three times as much. And brass fittings aren't the lifeblood of America, but they were a saleable good used in houses, cars, boats, and other products. Telemarketing was more of an exploited opportunity, a scam. People didn't need overpriced American flags, and they could help veterans in better ways. What I was doing wasn't much more than extortion.

The phone numbers blindly increased, and I moved down the page without making any more hits. Minutes slowly crept by, and with no more sales or good attempts, I finished the day with one box of garbage bags out the door. Ed and the crew cleared out, and I stepped from the dark coffin of an office to a sunny, beautiful Friday afternoon.

"See you Monday, John!" he yelled, as the caravan took off for 37 to head back to Indianapolis. I got into the Rabbit, and headed back toward my apartment. Fuck this, I thought. I'd rather keep looking and starve than drain myself doing that every day. If he won't pay me unless I show up on Monday, then chalk the last eight hours up to experience. I cranked open the moonroof, bathed in the clean air, and scooted down Third Street toward campus, thinking about the weekend.

I wouldn't describe Fun Frolic as fun, but it was mostly painless. Brecken, now somewhat cheerier since starting his full-time babe conquest campaign, worked the circuit with me. The whole event was trucked in and bolted together in the stadium parking lot. Neon lights, rigged baseball-toss games, haunted houses, amusement park rides, and plenty of food turned the gravel lot into a miniature Coney Island for the week.

We busted sticks at a slow but steady rate, and I spent most of my time in one place, watching the professors, their kids, and the townies tearing up and down the pathways, spending their yellow tickets on food and fun. I ran into almost all of the fountain regulars, including Cindy, who was with her best friend Jenny. I felt stupid working as a carnival hawker when I saw people I knew, but all of them seemed overjoyed to run into someone they knew "behind the scenes."

As with most events, the dead spots became a good peoplewatching experience. I played a lot of "why is he dating her" and vice versa, and thought too much about the single women in the crowd. There was no way in hell I could pick up a woman with a handful of glowsticks and a Fun Frolic staff T-shirt (oh yeah, we had to wear their uniforms,) but it made me think about what I wanted in a woman. I watched the way they talked to their friends, how they acted, smiled as they passed, and walked. I imagined talking to them myself, somewhere else, where everything was perfect and I could make them laugh, smile. It's a dangerous game, and after playing it for a few hours, I felt like some kind of stalker. I imagined a lifetime of working carnys across the country, leering at the townie girls and trying to get a piece of ass. Six months ago, I thought, I was sitting in a preppie bar, hair slicked back, expensive cologne, ordering mixed drinks and feeling at home. Now, I just hoped this wouldn't last.

We cashed out at Bruce's just before midnight, and I pulled in about $40. We ditched the Fun Frolic jerseys, and drove straight to the fountain, smelling like sweat, horseshit, and elephant ears. I put my wallet on the dash, and before saying hello or breaking pace, dove into the Showalter, letting the freezing water rinse me of any residual Fun Frolic. When my head broke water, I saw Brecken dive in right after me.

On Monday, I unknowingly sat through one of the most classic Ponzi scheme initiations that a college student could find. For weeks, I kept seeing signs and ads in the paper saying "Summer Jobs: $10/hr Call xxx.xxxx." Out of curiosity, I gave them a ring that morning and found out it was a company called Planar Marketing, and they invited me to attend a group interview later that afternoon. I didn't have anything else going on, so I took down the address and planned to head over.

The company was located north of town in a big office building full of smaller suites. I signed in at the main desk, and got whisked through a high-tech lobby and into a waiting room with a few other people. As we waited, more people appeared and sat down, and I got the full impact of the number of people also looking for jobs in this town. During my interviews and searches, I never had to sit and look at the scores of other people trying to get the same position.

I looked around the room for incriminating evidence, but I could only find stock art from one of those motivational stores in the mall. I imagined that the job would entail putting up posters, handing out fliers, or maybe some telemarketing, based on the name of the company. Plus the only reason they'd be getting together a group of people for a hard sell would be to convince people to do something awful.

After the room filled with about thirty of us, a skinny guy with blonde hair cut in a spiked, Top Gun style walked in, herded us into a conference room, and offered us a drink from a cooler filled with cans of Coke and other drinks.

"Today, we're going to talk about motivation, and opportunities..." The Top Gun guy started with the cocky, gestured sales talk. Ho hum. I looked around the room a bit more, and focused on the framed pictures here. Oh shit...Within moments, I realized what this was all about. The pictures on the walls were of knives—cutlery, hunting knives, silverware. Cut-All knives.

Peter went through this same scam the summer before. Cut-All made knives—really good ones, too. They lasted forever, had a lifetime warranty, looked good, and could cut through cans and bones and all that jazz. They were expensive, but worth it. But they didn't sell them in stores. Instead, they got Planar Marketing to herd up college students and sell them from door to door.

Door to door sales in Bloomington seemed asinine to me. Students aren't going to drop a few hundred bucks on knives—they eat pizza from the box and drink beer from the can. And the townies, the people living west of town, don't make dirt. If a student came to the door, they'd—well, the film *Deliverance* sums it all up.

He finished the motivational voodoo and started with the knives. From a big leather sales case, he whipped out a bunch of fine stainless steel and did the whole show—cutting cans, cutting paper, and passing the knives around the room. When I hefted the piece of cutlery, I wondered if I could throw it across the room and hit a vital part of his body.

After the dog and pony show, he went into specifics, ones I already knew. You'd be required to visit people every week, show them the knives, and give the demo. Each demo took an hour, and paid ten bucks, hence the $10/hour signs and ads. I knew in reality, it'd be impossible to get anybody lined up for the sales calls. Also, Peter got canned for making a lot of calls without selling many knives.

Almost an hour into the talk, he announced the kicker—we'd have to buy the startup kit, and it cost about $200. Ours to keep, of course, but we had to front the money for the fine knives before we could sell them. Everyone in the room suddenly looked like their mothers were raped in front of their eyes—they hoped for a $10/hour job, and now they were being wrenched over to buy some knives. Maybe this company made their money selling the starter kits to students, I thought.

They ended the first part of the presentation, and said they'd start taking people individually for one-on-one interviews and to discuss the details. People lined up to talk more about it, and I slipped past and made a beeline for the door. Outside the office, I found a newspaper machine, jimmied open the lock, and grabbed the newest daily edition. What a crock, I thought, walking to the VW. Time to start again...

13

I didn't want to sit through another humid night of class, especially on a Monday, but it would be my last lecture, and it was a review of what we needed to know for the final on Wednesday. Aside from an overwhelming depression out of nowhere, I felt bad showing my face to the professor, because of my damn final paper. I blew it off until I overshot the due date, which was last Friday. I ran to office hours and begged for mercy, without any real excuse other than my own stupidity. He gave me until three on Thursday, the last possible chance he'd get to slap a grade on it and hand in the final tallies to the report card people before the end of the day.

Everybody got a handout that pretty much spelled out the entire test. The teacher walked through it, reviewing each item at an agonizingly slow pace. It amazed me that I actually knew most of the stuff. I'd read the books, and attended most of the classes, but I didn't do anything more painstaking than that. Yet I was a step ahead of him in the lecture, which made it that much more boring.

It wasn't hard to ignore the teacher, but this made it easier to slip into the low-level despair coursing through my system. Even on the way over to Woodburn, the mood started churning through me like a Black Sabbath album at 16 speed, for no reason. Well, there were reasons: this class, the final, the paper, and next summer session. In a few days, I'd have to go to the registrar and find two more classes and hope they would be easy enough to coast me past the GPA finish line.

And after finishing summer session, I'd need to make a housing deposit to renew my lease. That gave me only a few more weeks to scrape up nearly $400, with no job. More UCS shifts, plus a full-time, minimum wage job at night, plus some more glowstick events might set me straight, but it would be difficult to pull off any one of those, let alone all three. With no backup system, financial scenarios like this scared the hell out of me. Unless I came up with the money, I'd either be living in my car, or moving back home and giving up everything I fought for. My parents would hang the "you were wrong, we were right" over my head forever, as I lived in their basement, went to a commuter college, and ran a punch press for the rest of my life.

Once the downward spiral started, it was never long before I started thinking about women. Money and women went together like white and rice in my book, since you had to have some of the former to have some of the latter. The same recurring nightmare always ran though my head—I somehow ran into the perfect woman, maybe on the computer, maybe hanging out at the IMU. We met, we talked, everything clicked, and I...invited her to my boardinghouse room? Took her for a drive in my beat-up Rabbit? Dressed up in my best Megadeth t-shirt and ripped pair of jeans and took her to a romantic dinner at White Castle? Granted, some women in college would understand my plight, but even the most forgiving person couldn't put up with my diet of microwave burritos and frozen pizzas forever. I felt that if I had some cozy appointed job as a staff member, changing backup tapes and answering stupid Lotus 1-2-3 questions, I could have the suit-and-tie stability that would catch women into that sort of thing. And more women seemed to want stability than some weirdo Death Metal guy with long hair and no foreseeable future.

The teacher called time, and I grabbed my shit and ran for the door. With his mimeoed review sheet and the crap in my head, I'd be ready for the final without the second half of the lecture. I thought about going to the IMU to ruminate in the computer lab for a while, but I didn't feel like running into anybody. I took the long walk through the music school parking lot to cut back to Third and Jordan, and stewed in the dejection, trying to think of a release.

The backpack hit the floor of junk with a thud, like it did every night I returned home from class. It felt like an oven in the tiny room every time I left for more than an hour. Even though a cool breeze danced across my skin the whole way home, I felt the sweat dripping down my arms. As if a dozen things weren't already making me want to move to a one-room shack in Montana, the heat consumed me, and made me think I'd never make it through another night.

I checked my watch, did a quick count of my cash, and thought of my options. It's funny how when in the height of my depression, I always considered my best release was to make things worse. I knew it was my only medication, to drive the depression straight into the ground. I grabbed my walkman, dug around for a tape, and headed back out.

With a howling feedback, Type O Negative's first album stirred a heavy spoon in a cast iron pot filled with thick and unconsumable sonic hatred. My feet grew heavy against the sidewalk, the chorus of "gravity...crushing me..." a boat anchor pulling my emotions to a stop in the cold and black waters of nothingness. I paced down Third Street, and across the street, Tammy's old dorm, Forest Quad, loomed over me. Every thought and memory of walking there to meet her, picking her up for a date, staying the night illegally in her room, crushed me, and made me walk faster, as if I could escape for it.

Past the quadrangle's parking lot, I crossed Third and headed up Union Street. The eastern border of campus, the narrow roadway split between the backsides of the Forest and Willkie quadrangles, and the start of more small houses filled with students. I pushed for seven blocks in darkness, rising a small hill and battling misery with each step. I should have drove, I thought, but I needed the walk—I needed something to burn the growing energy inside me. I crossed Tenth Street and went into the Village Pantry.

The inside of the store intruded my dejection, the bright 24 hour lights and crowded, colorful displays raping the gray, barren, two-dimensional hell I constructed in my solitude. I didn't look at the faces of the people buying gas, cigarettes, Twinkies or potato chips, people on the inside who would instantly know I was on the outside. The same people who ignored me, fucked with me, cheated me, forgot me, and undersold me. All the same.

I grabbed a cold twelve-pack of Bud from a cooler, and went to the cashier. "How's you doin' tonight?" I didn't answer. "That'll be $8.44, you want a bag?" "Yeah." I pulled a ten from my wallet, slapped it on the counter. He gave me the brown bag and change, and I slid back into the darkness.

I didn't bother with the walkman on the way home. I pulled a beer loose from the cardboard box inside the bag, popped the top, and slammed it. The sick taste of wheaty hops and ferment went down my throat, something I hated until after the third or fourth can, when I stopped noticing it. The cool, rich fluid felt good running down my throat, and made me want more. I chugged the can before I was halfway down Union, and cracked open a second. Am I technically on campus? I wondered if I could get a ticket for public intox, but didn't care.

Two beers into the half-case, I got back to my apartment and fired up the computer. I put beer three next to the keyboard and stashed the rest in the fridge. When I sat, I felt the slight spin of the room and the light headed passage from sober to buzzed, and felt pessimistically good about it. I'd have to drink more to forget the bullshit, though—right now I didn't have the focus I did during my depressive rant in the polysci lecture, but I'd be there soon.

The modem caught a connection, and I logged onto Bronze to check my accumulation of mail. Six non-UCS messages waited in the queue. I chugged the next beer, sitting back in my wooden chair and thinking about what to do next. I answered four of them with one line, all-caps messages like "WE'RE ALL GOING TO DIE," and then got another beer. The other two, from Meg and Donna, got long-winded replies, detailing random negative situations like money, women, and all of the crap on my desk. My typing got more erratic and I bounced from topic to topic, but I fired off the haphazard emails. Between messages, I stumbled back to the bathroom to recycle the beer.

I lined up beers five and six on the card table, and logged onto Rose. I set my process to "Anheuser John." 15 seconds, some stranger bitnetted and asked if I was drinking. I answered back with the classic Charles Bukowski line "IVE BEEN DRINKING SINCE BEFORE YOU WERE BORN, AND ILL BE DRINKING AFTER YOURE DEAD."

Alex then found me online, and we had an exchange that looked something like this (the stuff with NTY398 is him, the other lines are me):

> ACOOPER(NTY398): What's happening? You on campus?
> ACOOPER: THIS IS THE FAMOUS JOHN CONNER. WE KNOW OF NO BITNET PRODUCED BY ANY OTHER WRITER WHICH CONTAINS SO MUCH BULLSHIT.
> ACOOPER(NTY398): I take it you've had a few. Are you going to the fountain?
> ACOOPER: HIS EXCLUSIVE TYPING PROCESS PRODUCES A TASTE, SHALLOWNESS
> ACOOPER(NTY398): Let me know if you need a ride, can't walk, etc.
> ACOOPER: AND READABILITY YOU WILL FIND IN NO OTHER PERSON ONLINE.

I continued the process with everyone I saw online, laughing my ass off and getting viler and more dependent on the sides of empty cans for my dialog. I signed an email message "Brewed by pure genius from the finest manic depression, loneliness, and microwave burritos," and convinced someone else I was a 47-year-old plumber.

The userlist wound down, and fewer people wandered the cluster. With a long swig, I slammed the rest of a Budweiser, and threw the seventh can on the desk. Nobody logged on. I laughed, knocked over the computer, and looked at my watch. 11:40. Time to go. I grabbed beer eight and hit the door.

Walk to the fountain and sit down, I thought. Just walk there, and sit for a few hours. Even with great effort, my feet didn't follow a straight line and I swayed and staggered with laughter. Empty streets and darkened paths let me wander the road, with no real direction or purpose, just walking because it seemed hysterical at the time. The journey to the fountain kept on my mind though, and I tried to stagger in that direction.

The stumbling across campus felt like a time last spring, during the last week with Tammy, when I got completely loaded and tried to walk across campus to Teter Quad. Once again, the sadness and despair baked and etched my mind, making me want to do something, anything to escape it other than the usual self-brooding and consuming isolation. I went to the liquor store with only a handful of ones and bought the most damage I could afford, a pint of Bacardi. The little flask, a miniature of the big bottles I usually bought, looked funny and held as much liquor as the tiny wax and cardboard milk cartons the gave us in grade school. But I drank it straight up and warm, chasing with some Coke from a can while sitting at the computer chair and trawling for action on the modem.

After consuming almost the entire baby bottle of rum, the tarnish and haze lifted, replaced by a tranquil stupidity. I swayed in the rickety wooden chair, laughing and spilling and knocking things over. I kept at the computer, and this female I knew over in the dorms started asking me if I was okay, how much I drank, if I needed to talk, the whole concerned thing. I logged out and she called, asked if I would be okay, if I had too much, if I was depressed, all this. She was a psych major, thought she could figure me out, psychoanalyze me, try to help and pry apart all of my problems or at least stop me from hurting myself worse. She invited me over, told me to stop by and I could watch a movie with some of her friends, get out of the house, and mellow out. I agreed, scrawled her instructions on my hand with a pen and out the door into the cool spring air I stumbled.

The roads always seemed to take on a different appearance when I was drunk. I'd always notice the small landmarks like dumpsters, bicycle racks, manhole covers, everything else I usually ignored. While I gazed with astonishment at this new world, I missed the more obvious things like streets, sidewalks, crosswalks, traffic lights, moving cars, and buildings. Within moments, I formulated a great new shortcut to her dorm, and couldn't figure out how I ever missed it before. Without sidewalks, my shoes covered with mud and dirt as I followed the ingenious new system, and the streetlights mysteriously stopped painting the night terrain with illumination. After more jolly stumbling, I saw more dirt roads, and absolutely no light or sidewalks to guide me. Then, bulldozers and massive holes in the ground appeared, and I realized that I had walked into a large construction site for the new education building. In every direction, I only saw dirt, bulldozers, cranes, construction shanties, and more mountains of soil.

It took me a half hour to walk four blocks and find the goddamn dorm, I sat on her floor with the mud on my shoes and the booze wearing off, watching the movie *Backdraft* and feeling the onset of my usual post-drinking depression. The film was about two brothers, and one was all fucked up, a gung-ho fireman, and got all postal and started drinking heavily. I think he eventually died, or got killed, or killed himself. I don't remember, but I do remember seeing this guy take the downward spiral, and everyone in the room was so moved over this—it was a Ron Howard film and had all the emotional hooks to really pull people in. I felt like I was watching myself, thirty or forty years old, losing a shit job and drinking every day because it was the only out I knew. Except I didn't fight fires and didn't have Ron Howard directing me, so nobody really gave a fuck if I became an alcoholic.

I stumbled to the Showalter, and saw the whole gang already there—Brecken, Alex, Renee, Cindy, Linda, Kyle, Bill, and a half dozen others. I walked up to Alex and said "I don't give a god damn about your war, soldier," and then almost fell over laughing.

"Jesus Christ, John, you smell like a brewery. Have you been drinking grain alcohol again?"

"I've been drinking the souls of the dead..."

"John, give me your wallet."

I handed it over. "My money says 'In God We Thrust.' I was drinking before you were born..."

"Hang onto this," he handed the wallet to Renee. "Brecken, give me a hand here..."

I didn't feel four hands grab me and pull me to the lip of the fountain, so I continued my yelling. The next thing I knew, I was being tipped backward into the water. I held my breath and went under the surface, gently touching bottom with my back before pushing upward again.

"Fuck! It's freezing in here!"

"Are you sober yet?" Alex asked.

"I've gotta take a piss. Is this water chlorinated?"

"They don't put limestone fish in your toilet...Come on out, we'll find you some facilities." He extended his hand toward me. "No wise guy stuff tonight," he said. "Don't try pulling me in."

I waded to the lip of the basin, and with his help, surfaced from the water. I shook my head like a wet dog, and wiped my glasses on Alex's shirt. Wringing my shirt, I pulled it halfway over my head and wobbled around in circles like a drunken Jim Morrison, singing: "Can you pigeon what will be, so limitless and free, desperately in weed...in a desperate lamb....Father? Yes son. I want to kill you..." I forgot the rest of the words and started laughing.

"Let's go see about that piss, John." He pulled me away from the fountain, and toward Woodburn.

"Ride the king's highway, baby..." I stumbled behind me. "Ride the highway west, baby..."

Alex couldn't find an open door leading to a restroom, so we stood beside Woodburn Hall, hidden behind a hillside. He watched guard about ten feet away, while I leaned against the building for dear life and pissed all over the limestone.

"The west, is the best..." I bellowed out. It felt so good to release the cans of beer pushing against my bladder. Now if I only had a can of Coke, and a nice couch in front of the fountain...

"You know John, I think alcohol is a depressant."

"Everything's a depressant, man. Alcohol evens the score. I don't even remember what I was depressed about."

"This probably doesn't make sense to you now, but I think you're drinking for the wrong reasons."

"I've got a whole list of wrong reasons, and I'm gonna keep drinking until they're gone. I've been drinking since before you were born..."

"I'm not new to this intervention thing—I don't remember if you met my roommates last year, the ones who stole an eight foot tall statue of the virgin mary."

"How do you flush this thing?" I said. "Oh shit, I thought we were inside." I laughed more, and zipped up.

"We'll continue this discussion when you're sober. Let's go back and see if you can sit in one place for a few minutes."

Alex dragged me back to the fountain, where I saw everyone talking, sitting, and socializing. He walked me to one of the stone benches, and sat me down, in front of a group of people sitting cross-legged, talking about a trip to Europe.

"Where's my wallet?" I asked Renee. She handed back my money; I whipped out a fiver and yelled "Bartender! I'll have another," then kicked my legs onto the slab bench and curled up in a ball. The fountain in front of me still spun up and down, but I could feel my buzz edging down.

Brecken came over and stood over me. "How are you feeling?" he asked.

"I'm feeling like the other half of the case in my fridge, if my fucking roommates haven't drank it yet."

"How many did you drink?"

"Only eight, since about 8:00."

"Hang onto that bench, you're going to sober up any time now."

He was right. The dehydration crept through my veins, and a foul taste built in my mouth. I watched Linda talk to Bill and Kyle about the winters in Rochester, New York. Cindy and Alex discussed something about Carmel, Indiana while Renee listened. I didn't talk anymore, but felt the alcohol distill in my blood, the once mighty buzz now a dying fizz. Plus, my clothes were still soaking wet, but slowly drying. I held my wallet in my hands, and waited.

People started to leave. "We need to do something with John," Alex said.

"Don't worry, I'll take care of him," Cindy replied.

"Come on, I think we need to go for a walk," she said, taking my hand. I sat up, waited for the ground to rush back into place horizontally, then weakly stood up.

"Let's go," she dragged me like a rag doll by my arm. "I'll drive you home when we get back."

The soft moonlight perfectly accented the careful landscape of the arboretum. Cindy walked slowly with me, holding my hand, a friendly, platonic gesture that also kept me from falling over. It felt good to have her next to me, a beautiful woman on my arm. Even more, she cared enough to talk me down. She carried an enchantment about her that I felt

I could never have in a lover, but that she could deliver to me without thinking twice.

"I feel like I ran a marathon," I said.

"The crash is the worst part, isn't it?"

"I never think about that when I start. I think about forgetting, having fun."

"So, why the episode? What's been up?"

"The usual," I said. "I think you can figure it out."

"Okay, the John Conner I know drinks when it involves women, either before or after. Which one?"

"Neither. Both. I'm trapped in time."

We walked to the gazebo at the top of the arboretum. "Let's sit down here," she said. "Tell me why you're trapped."

"I can only think about my past, like when I was with Tammy last spring. I never enjoy the present, and I can't see the future. I feel like I've fucked up all of my chances in life, and in five years I'll be delivering newspapers. I mean, I couldn't become a doctor if I wanted to, or an Air Force pilot. It's too late to be a famous musician or a movie star. All that's left is different variations of the same desk job: insurance salesman or car salesman."

"Do you think this has to do with your clinical depression?"

"I really don't know. I don't say that I hate the present because I'm depressed about it. I feel like my eyes are wide open and I can see all of the problems in front of me. Other people ignore the ground they walk on, maybe because of their goals or their problems or their hang-ups. I think everyone revises their past—this whole country has a cottage industry of 'hey, remember ten years ago?' products. People remember Woodstock, but not Vietnam. I hated living at home, but sometimes I miss it, because it was more comfortable than the present, or worrying about the future."

"I know what you mean about comfort," she said. "I think the main reason I didn't want to leave Sid was because it was easier to stay. I wasn't happy—he was cheating on me every week—but it felt better than the real world."

"Exactly. I mean, I wish I could bring my experiences from the present and go back to the past, so I could change things—study more, save every dime, pick up on women that I had chances with but was clueless about, all of that shit. But really, I just wish I was back for the sheer comfort it offered, the comfort of never having to really do anything on my own. I mean, I'm sure that right now, you would not go back to Sid even if you had the chance. But in five years, you might think about how much fun you had with him, and even if you hated him, you'd still have all of these strong, ambivalent feelings."

"I wouldn't try to relive my relationship with Sid though, and I think you are hoping for the chance to relive Tammy. If you went back, maybe you'd do the same thing again. Or maybe in five or ten years, it'll be a step worse."

"Who knows. It's confusing though. I feel like a new chapter is opening in my life, and I don't know what the first step should be."

"How are you holding up?"

"Better, but I could use some water and a long nap..."

"Come on, let's head back to my car," she said.

We hiked back to the fountain and found her car, next to the auditorium, and drove down Jordan toward my apartment.

"I really appreciate you helping me out tonight," I said. "Sorry my emotional disasters have been becoming a regular event lately."

"I'm glad to help, but I do hope things pull together for you soon."

"We'll see..."

We pulled up to my apartment, and she dropped me off. "Try to get some rest, John," she said. "I think you'll be okay."

"Okay. Yeah, I will. Thanks again."

She took off, and I got that glass of water. I took my medicine and fell into a heavy sleep.

I didn't feel much of a hangover the next afternoon—at this point in my life, I'd never had as much of a headache the day after a heavy drinking spell. I went to my favorite daytime hangout, the IMU, to try and finish my reinstatement letter. The four paragraph, one page letter looked done, but it didn't feel ready. I kept reading it, changing tiny details, hoping it would work. It was due on the 20th, and it was the 16th. I'd need to stop changing things soon.

"Hi John, how are you?"

I looked up from my Mac and saw June standing over me, smiling.

"Hey June. Still working on this letter. I think it's done, but I'm scared it's not perfect." I took another look at her—another sundress. "I haven't seen you in a while. Where have you been hiding?"

"Upstairs in the government office. We've got a bunch of stuff to wrap up by the end of the session. I saw you online and thought I'd stop down to say hi."

"It's good to see you. I thought you forgot about me or something."

"Nah, just been busy," she said. "Hey, I have a proposition for you. I need to learn a little bit about unix. Would you be willing to give me a quick lesson in exchange for dinner?"

"Sure, that sounds great."

"Here's my number," she wrote down her number on a piece of paper. "Give me a call and we can figure out a time when our schedules are synced. Call anytime, don't be a stranger..."

"Cool, thanks."

"I've got to get back upstairs. I'll talk to you later..."

I watched her walk down the hall. Because of her, the sundress became one of my top five favorite inventions of all time—it had class and hid a lot of the figure, but with the right cut, it didn't leave much to the imagination. If I had the choice between seeing June in a string bikini versus the sundress, I'd take the sundress any day of the week.

Shit, that was easy, I thought. I was getting all bent out of shape over asking her out, and it fell right in my damn lap. Now I could start a phone campaign and wear her down faster than I could via email. Although I could barely deal with face to face encounters, I could keep almost any woman on the phone for hours. And she knew me in person, so I didn't have to deal with the pressure of a blind date, like I did in most computer matchups. My odds looked good...

After my 200th proofreading scan, I hit print and waited for two copies of the letter to jet out of the laserprinter in the back of the lab. I folded a copy into thirds, and shoved it into an envelope addressed to the Dean. I'll get back into school yet, I thought.

14

The Mac keyboard clicked furiously for several minutes, then stopped dead as I stared at the screen and wondered if my sentences made any sense. The process had been repeating for the last two hours as I banged away a paper for my polysci class in the Student Building Mac cluster. We had to write about a non-centralized government, so I decided to write about the Internet, and try to explain its somewhat accidental governing policies.

Although I would've preferred basking in the beautiful day outside, the Student Building provided a decent atmosphere for work. Built in 1906, the building housed the campus clock tower and was a focal point of the crescent of oldest buildings on campus. During renovation in 1990, a fire destroyed everything but the limestone shell. Thanks to overwhelming alumni donations, they worked double-time and completely rebuilt and renovated the building in only nine months, so the chimes once again rang by the 1991 homecoming. The refurbishment also meant an incredible interior, with huge bay windows, intricate wood trim, and a perfect integration of modern features with original beauty. I could look through the giant windows and see the sunlight streaming onto the old quadrangle of campus, with trees flowing in the breeze and students lazily hiking across the red brick pathways. I could also turn to the interior walls, which had windows in their upper half, and see the high tech sprawl of fifty IBM computers, a lab of NeXT workstations, and a special print facility jammed with high-end Tektronix color imagers and high-definition laserprinters.

UCS had four state-of-the-art computer labs on the second floor. A Mac graphics lab rivaled the Fine Arts lab, with fast, RAM-laden machines, huge color monitors, and flatbed color scanners. The beautiful atmosphere and nice machines made working in the Student Building a joy—during the summer, at least. In the regular school year, the lab would have an hour-long waitlist, or be closed for an art class. I enjoyed it while I could, and fought with the polysci paper.

At least my final for the class was done. On Wednesday night, I took the bluebook test with little incident. My original plans of a weekend of cramming didn't pan out, but I must've retained at least some of the knowledge; my short-essay answers seemed to make sense, and I even finished early. Always a fan of the blue book, I hated the scantron tests and loved to bullshit through a good essay test. Maybe I had a good chance with this one.

During one of my periods of paperwriting blockage, I saw my friend Michael working in the cluster. Aside from being a fellow coworker and a regular fixture in the Sun lab at Lindley, Michael and I went back many years. We hung out together a lot outside of the computer scene, and I spent a lot of time at his communal apartment, along with the three other computer-geeks he lived with and whoever else happened to be hanging out there. We even shared an identical birthday. We weren't close like Nick; it was more of a group-social thing among a circle of friends, and I was often the most introverted within the pack. When things with Tammy fell apart, I don't even remember when I told Michael. But during the school year, we probably spent 80 hours a week together in the Sun lab, and I ate dinner with him and the other regulars more than I did with her.

Michael saw me through the glass walls and came over from the print facility room. "Hey Conner, what's up?" he said.

"Not much," I said. "Working on a fucking paper."

"Hey, I lost all of my accounts this morning."

"What the fuck? What did you do? Send death threats to somebody?" I asked.

"Do you remember Eric's message about creating new newsgroups?"

"Yeah, sure. He sent me a copy." This was heady stuff. Newsgroups are the "channels" you subscribe to in Usenet news, like alt.sex or comp.sys.mac. When you read a newsgroup, the articles are sent to your computer from a local Usenet server, which holds a bunch of articles for a bunch of newsgroups. It gets all of its new stuff by talking to a bunch of other news servers and asking for new articles it doesn't have, while sending along new stuff the other server doesn't have. That way, a new article posted at IU is propagated to many news servers globally within a few hops, without relying on a central news server; even if a server "downstream" from IU was dead, articles would eventually propagate through the other half dozen places IU grabbed new news. Usenet configuration details such as new newsgroup creation, was similarly propagated, and Eric Fournier managed to reverse-engineer the process and send the details to Bill and me.

"Well, I fucked around with it a little bit, and created alt.ed.gray.likes.it.up.the.ass this morning," he said.

"Holy shit!" Ed Gray was this hacking poseur that many hated. Michael taught him everything about coding, then he got a salary programming gig with UCS, and copped a major attitude with Michael ever since. "I assume it took?"

"It was on the UCS news server, but they bagged it already," he said. "But...."

"It propagated?"

"Yeah, it's already three or four hops downstream, and news servers that automatically add all new groups are picking it up. UCS didn't know about it until someone at Florida State wrote back and complained. That's three hops away."

"Holy shit! That rules!"

"I got called to the dean of computing's office today, and Ed was there. He was PISSED. I denied everything."

"So they're still letting you work?"

"For now, but this might be my last shift for a while. My accounts are frozen while they try to prove that I did it. I denied anything, so if anyone asks...Oh, I heard you and Fournier were on the shitlist too—I'm surprised you didn't get called in for coffee and donuts."

"Shit, that's all I need..."

"What time did you wake up today?"

"Maybe noon," I said.

"You're probably safe then. This happened around eight—they can check your account for activity."

"So are they firing you?"

"I don't know, probably not. There's no way they can 100% prove that I did it. It could've been somebody else with my password." This was true; almost everyone in the Sun cluster knew Michael's password. He had a strange communal streak to him, and told it to anyone who asked. "I'm skipping out for the rest of the summer and going back to Vincennes, so I might be suspended from work while I'm gone, and everything will be cool in the fall."

"Heavy stuff..." I said. "Hey, I have a question for you. Do you know of a good FTP archive for RFCs?"

"Sure, just go to rs.internic.net, I think they have them all there."

"Cool, thanks. I've gotta get back to this. Give me a buzz before you leave town."

"Okay. Have fun..." He vanished back to the center office filled with printers and consultants. I knew he wouldn't call before leaving, but that I'd see him in the Sun lab on the first day of fall classes.

Back to writing. "The Internet is governed by documents called RFCs, or Request For Comments..."

I slammed away at the paper, and got close to the point of a final draft, when my telnet window to the Rose VAX beeped, and I looked to see that Abby was bitnetting me.

"Did you bag the chick yet?"

I switched windows, and replied back, "Which chick?"

"Student government, IMU, the one that always interrupts our conversations?"

Nobody but Abby even knew I had a thing for June, but she did the work of everyone else in bothering me about it. "It's two in the afternoon. Shouldn't you be asleep or something?"

"Hormone boy in denial. No chick. I thought you were in?"

"I'm gradually finessing this one, I think...I'll get back to you in a week or so. She wants me to teach her unix..."

There was an uncomfortable pause, the type either caused by the person on the other end checking a new mail message, or the real-world uncomfortable pause, the kind where you waited for the other shoe to hit.

"I've been worried about you," she said.

"An intervention because I didn't pick up on a woman? What gives?" I asked, thinking it was a joke. Abby was 97% laughs and bullshit, so I knew the message meant something more ominous.

"No, the nightly depresso emails. Are you going over the edge about this girl problem?"

I could trust Abby, but I didn't want to lay all of this on the only person who could make me laugh every day. "It's more than just the broads. It's a more clinical problem. Grown-up stuff."

"Anything you can't handle?" she asked.

"I'm working on it," I said. "Worst case, I will move to Tangiers and rape the tourists on fixed card games."

"That's the spirit," she said. "Hey, what are you doing in the student building?"

"Finishing up a useless paper for polysci. What's up at mom and dad's?"

"The Empire Strikes Back is on at nine. I'm totally keyed up."

"Cool. Hey, I need to get back to it. Tell Luke and Leia I said hello."
"Later, Hormone boy."

I spellchecked the paper for the fifth time, printed a copy, and headed out.

I dropped the paper at Woodburn, and headed home with a jumbled monologue in my head and no walkman on my ears. Writing the paper felt good—chiseling the outline, digging around the library, filling each point with crafted paragraphs of information. Writing code for a computer class felt similar, the whole idea of solving the problem with an algorithm, an outline, and then plugging in the code to execute your solution. But hacking C programs felt so much more unforgiving—a certain exactness was needed to get past the compiler and see your results. Writing had more of a gray area. Aside from the spellcheck, you didn't get yes or no results. There was also a certain tactile enjoyment of looking up books, paging through magazines, and sitting in the library, looking important with a stack of materials. It made me think about the lives of professional students, grads who spent a career digging through tomes and chipping away at answers to questions that haven't been asked. Maybe I could do that, I thought.

Then I thought about grades, and money, and my failing academic health, and realized I'd never get into a grad school. If I got two years of straight A's, I wouldn't clear a 3.0 GPA. And would this paper get past the teacher? And how would I finish this course, or the next two? The worries consumed me, even with a solid paper and good test scores sofar.

What to do next in life became the eternal question. I found a shard of a gift in turning out papers, but it made me doubt my ability to pursue a computer science degree. What would I be doing in five years? Hacking C? Writing books? Living in Seattle, playing in a grunge band? Back on the factory floor? I hated myself for never focusing on a point in the distance, for bouncing from idea to idea, taking up a new hobby every week, pissing away my time. I wanted to enjoy myself, but I got no enjoyment out of anything I did. The darkness consumed me, no matter where I ran.

By the time I got to my house, I had to lay down on the bed, and try to think things through again. My heart beat a thousand times a minute, and I tried to remember something...anything...

Another boring Thursday night fountain meeting passed, where I showed up sober and said about 10 words to the people there, who were all talking about nothing. I felt a strong self-hatred that evening, and while Linda talked about her stupid roommate, I felt like telling everyone there that I was going to leave, go home, and shoot myself in the head, just to see the reaction. But the whole idea of pulling a "Love me, I want to kill myself" felt too junior high to me. I knew too well that only the popular could pull that off—I was destined to be one of the types that nobody suspected, sort of like a serial killer minus all of the charismatic personal traits. Even thinking about this made me half-laugh in disgust. When I hated myself this much, it was obvious I hated everyone else, too.

I should have stayed home, but I went in hopes of a new face, or maybe some more time with Cindy. Diane Smith also promised to stop by some night, but I still hadn't seen her face-to-face. I knew I had no chance with Cindy, and going seconds on Diane after Chad was something I wouldn't do out of respect for him. The hope of a few slivers of compassion or comfort from either of them kept me going every night, but it produced no results.

Pink Floyd's *The Final Cut* spun on the CD player, filling the room with Roger Waters' most brutally depressing holophonic soundscape. The most underrated 'Floyd album, I found it the most interesting, because it defined the disappointment in life and unfulfilled expectations, and how much they hurt later. Other Pink Floyd albums like *The Wall*, *Animals*, and *Momentary Lapse of Reason* defined my senior year of high school, and the epiphanous moment where I realized I was clinically depressed was in a hotel room in Ontario, listening to *Wish You Were Here*. But *The Final*

Cut came later, the summer after graduation, when the biological depression hit hard, and I had no support mechanism to help me through it. I worked a job silver-plating clarinet and sax keys where I had to be on the line at 6 AM, but I'd stay up until three or four some nights, listening to tracks like 'paranoid eyes' and the title track, and planning my suicide. On an average day of depression, I might just listen to a little 'Sabbath, but *The Final Cut* was my heavy ammunition. When I absolutely, positively needed to be fucked-up, on-the-floor-unable-to-move depressed halfway through the first track, this was the CD to do it.

And tonight, it was in the player. I avoided the good stuff all summer, hoping I wouldn't sink this low. Even with the gun to my head, I stuck with Depeche Mode and other more pedestrian yet depressing tapes when I needed a woeful soundtrack. But tonight I needed more—I needed Roger Waters himself to tell me how much my life sucked. I slumped over in bed in fetal position, unable to mess with the computer, unable to write my thoughts on paper, and barely able to hold the remote.

The final song, "two suns in the sunset" spooled out, and I thought more about what Waters tried to say in the title cut. Part of it had to do with baring his feelings to the world, or at least to one person, and having them turn away in revulsion—something I felt almost every day, and a reason I hid in my depression. I felt I had a dark side I couldn't admit to my closest friends—the clinical depression, the medicine, the daily self-destruction and hopelessness. Every one of my relationships had a turning point where I had to fess up to why I went to the doctor and took pills and had needle marks from blood tests. Sometimes, it went from turning point to turning away point. I tried to hide, but I never could.

Waters also talked about never having the nerve to make the final cut. I thought about all of the times I pointed the gun to my head and couldn't pull the trigger—all of the times I counted out every pill in the house, put them in front of me, but was unable to swallow them—the times I stood at the edge of a bridge, or held a blade in trembling hands. Maybe I couldn't follow through. But maybe I could.

I dug into the dark closet, pushed aside the nylon and quilted lining of a blue sleeping bag, and pushed my hand further, until I felt cold steel. Gripping the barrel, I pulled the shotgun from its hiding place underneath the winter clothes and boxes.

My heart quickened as I nervously sat on the bed, looking at the wood and metal hunting weapon. I slid back the bolt slowly, trying not to make any suspicious noise through the thin walls, then laughed, thinking of the sound a 16 gauge would make in the closet of a room. Light streamed into the barrel from the missing cartridge underneath. Reaching under the bed, I pulled out a shoebox, filled with cereal toys and forgotten computer disks. I rummaged through the contents, felt through the junk, and found it—a carefully hidden metal clip, holding three red 16-gauge shells. With a click, I snapped it into the underside of the gun.

In slow motion, I cycled the bolt, feeling the first plastic and brass round pop into the chamber. It moved forward snugly as I pushed the small handle forward and then up. With weapon complete, my hands usually trembled with fear, afraid of accidental discharge, or an unexpected knock on the door or car horn outside would cause me to fumble the weapon and kill somebody. But the procedure, now regular to me, contained no fear.

My hands turned the gun 180 degrees, carefully placing the wooden butt against the carpet in front of me. Propping the gun upright with my left hand, I moved it to my mouth, and stretched my right hand to the trigger. The tip of the barrel tasted of machined gunmetal, resting against my lips and aimed deep into the roof of my mouth. Two fingers rested on the gun's trip; it required a sizable push of the mechanism to fire. This gave me time to think.

This was it. The easy solution to all my problems, in my hands. Push my finger half an inch, and end the pain. No more loneliness, spending the nights alone, spending my life alone. No more poverty, wondering where my next paycheck would come from, how to pay for my education, car, clothes, bills, and life. No more school, flunking classes, academic probation, dismissals, struggles, tuition bills. No more psychiatrists, lithium, medication, tremors, blood tests, side effects, group therapy sessions where I felt insane and the rest of the fuckups alienated me further. No more depression, endless agony, blackness, fear of the world, being an alien, not being able to relate. Uncertainty filled my life—this would make it certain. The shaky, botched, and half-complete project called life would be complete. For the first time, I'd do something right.

During my daydreaming in classes, my mental wandering at work, or my long, depressive spells late at night, I never had any focus on my problems, or what to do. But with death resting in my hands, I gained a tremendous amount of clarity. My two choices were clearly outlined: end everything, or continue life. Both decisions had vagueness, and I tried to fairly evaluate both. I didn't know what, if anything was beyond death. And I could guess what it would do to my family, the people I knew, my housemates, or others. It felt greedy to impact so many lives based on my own personal problems, but it also seemed selfish that I went through so much torment on a daily basis with no help, while other people didn't. I could only start to postulate solutions for getting my money situation, depression, love life, personal life, and everything else fixed, but everyone else had the answers, and lived life right. On top of that, society rubbed it in that they were doing better than me every time I turned on a TV, or talked to someone, or watched a movie.

With gun in mouth, both sides of the argument continued, and settled down to one question: Why should I live? With a good answer, I'd put down the gun and try to continue. A good answer wasn't a lottery ticket or a blowjob from Cindy Crawford—a cold, unopened 12-pack of Coke in the fridge or an email from a cute lady would usually stop me. But with no short answer, I'd have to put myself through a longer test before deciding to light the shell and scoop the top of my head clear off my spine. Tonight, as with the tougher nights, my rationale contained three parts. If I could think about these three parts, I'd live another day.

First, death was too permanent a solution for me. If I decided to join the army, quit school, get a factory job, get married, get a tattoo, fuck guys, start smoking dope, or anything else, I could always turn back later. There were several conservative solutions to my problems, like getting more jobs, moving back home, quitting school for a year, following my shrink's advice, or putting up with the shit life gave me. There were also several stupid solutions, such as becoming a full-blown alcoholic, moving to India, joining a cult, selling Amway, or going back to Elkhart to work at a trailer factory forever. But with any decision, I would find out if it really worked, and if it failed, I could once again make a different decision. With death, I couldn't.

Second, I always felt that because I had so much shit dumped on me over the course of my life, that eventually something good would happen to me. This motto kept me alive in high school, when I had no friends, no activities, no plans, and lived an existence of working at a department store, jerking off, and listening to CDs by myself all weekend. I never saw the payoff of this karma, and after all the hurt, bogus relationships, and false starts of life during college, I thought my time would eventually come. If I died, I would never see this. But if I lived, I might meet the woman of my dreams, win the lottery, or at least find some kind of stable existence.

Third, I was too lazy to do anything remarkable with my life, let alone end it. I never went on vacations in foreign lands, talked to beautiful women, bought big-ticket items, went to sports bars, or did anything else involving a certain amount of spine and initiative. Just like the work I'd never do on my car, the exercise I never got, and the books I never read, I would never be able to get involved in a project as big as my own death.

I stewed these three things in my mind. On most days, I'd taste the metal of the barrel for a few moments before convincing myself to live. Tonight, my trigger fingers felt numb, and I sat for what felt like an hour, thinking, meditating over the problem. It didn't matter. With my luck, in a few years I'd be drowning in a pool of my own shit and piss, my scrotum flattened in some freak car accident. Why go on? Why fucking continue?

This was it. I pushed the trigger, feeling its force, expecting to hear the jolt of the explosion before my body became a carcass. It took a lot of force to cap that old gun, I remembered from my first hunting trips. Maybe 50 pounds of pressure, an inch of action. I felt the piece of metal slide, a millimeter, two, three...My heart raced faster.

What the fuck was I doing? I pulled my fingers from the gun. My heart still raced more—I could feel my eardrums pounding with blood. The room felt 200 degrees, and I felt sharp pains in my chest, heart attack-type sharp pains. I hiked the gun onto the bed, and dropped onto the carpet floor, trying to think of what to do.

15

I lay in fetal position on the floor amidst the dirty clothes and empty cassette cases, taking deep breaths faster and faster, and grabbing my rib cage. I'm not having a heart attack, I told myself. I'm not having a heart attack...The ploy wasn't working, because I didn't know if it was one or not. The pain was no stranger, though. Earlier that spring, during the height of my stress with money and classes, I had a few of the heart attack like symptoms and thought I wasn't going to live past 21. I never got to a doctor, but a friend who lost her dad to heart trouble told me that my pains probably weren't cardiological, but maybe some kind of stress disorder, or panic attack.

Heart attack or not, it felt like someone broke my ribs and knocked the wind out of me. I knew I was hyperventilating, and looked on the floor for a bag to breathe in. I found an Arby's sack, and cupped it over my mouth, trying to slow down my lungs. It worked, and within a few minutes, I calmed down, and breathed normally. Then I laughed, and thought if I would've gone to the ER. "Doctor, save my life! I started having a heart attack when I was trying to kill myself!"

I still didn't know what to do next. On some level, I knew I didn't want to die, but I didn't know the steps toward long-term survival. I wished they had a Suicide Anonymous support group, or something to stop my cycle of thought. After what seemed like an hour of clear-headed terror and confusion, I went to the computer and dialed the university. Even though it was three in the morning, I hoped to find someone online. If not, maybe I could write a few long letters to a couple of people, and think out my frustrations that way. Nobody's dime store psychology advice could help a person who just put a loaded gun to their head, but I needed human interaction to let me know this wasn't a game that involved only me. If I spilled my guts to someone, even a complete stranger or an inanimate object, it would force me to think, and maybe find my own answers.

The modem dialed. In the back of my head, I kept wondering if I should get the balls to go through with the plan, the gun. I stopped myself so many times in the past. Maybe I needed to stop thinking about it, the reasons, the panic attacks, and just pick it up and pull the trigger. Maybe everyone on the computer and in the house and in my family would give me the same bullshit answers, and I'd be as miserable tomorrow as I am today—maybe worse. When you've got a gun to your head, who wouldn't tell you to put it down? Think it over, tomorrow's another day, there's other fish in the sea, you can always file chapter 11, this is America—anyone can be anything. You just need to snap out of it. They'll put you on Prozac, and you can start all over. Anyone would tell you to put down the gun, but nobody could help solve your problems. Telling people to snap out of it is one of America's biggest cottage industries, from the workout tapes to religion to new cars. Nobody would ever give me a straight answer.

After years of therapy, drugs, relationships, alcohol, problems, friendships, and everything else, I wondered if I could change myself to the point of being happy, or even content. I wanted to change myself 100%—what I looked like, where I lived, what I did, economics, romance, every aspect of my life. Realistically, I knew wanting to be like some rock legend or movie star was a vain and petty pursuit, something better left to people suffering away in coalmines and iron factories who'd rather be Michael Jordan or Tom Cruise. But my list of goals involved changing at least a third of my attributes, and I wondered if any human could change more than ten percent in their lifetime. Was Einstein born a genius, or could anyone hit the books every day and become him? If you're over the age of 20 and you haven't practiced piano since the age of three, could you become as famous as Chopin? What happens to those of us who aren't born with an extraordinary talent? Are we supposed to settle into mediocrity and be happy? And what about those of us who are born with something potentially wrong? I once read that because of the high suicide rate in manic-depressives, people with severe coronary disease typically had a higher survival rate. One in five people diagnosed with manic depression kill themselves. Maybe there wasn't a way out. Maybe the gun was my destiny.

A host prompt appeared; I connected to the Rose VAX. If nobody's online, don't freak, I thought, while typing my username and password. I checked my wholist: just Bill, logged in from Lindley Hall and me.

"Hey Bill, you awake?" I typed at him.

A moment later, "Yeah, I'm here. What's up?" he replied.

"I'm in a situation here," I said. "I need some help. Are you busy?"

"What kind of help? What's up?"

"I've hit bottom. I need to talk through some stuff."

"I'm heading home in a bit. Can you stop by Lindley, maybe give me a ride back?"

"That sounds cool. I'll drive over."

"Okay, I'm in the basement, small PC lab."

"See you in five," I said. I logged out, and shut down the computer. I threw my comforter over the loaded shotgun on the bed, and triple-checked the lock on the door before I left.

My hands still shook on the wheel of the VW, as I drifted the quiet roads of campus, barren except for streetlights and sleeping buildings. Lithium, notorious for its side-effect tremors, never affected me unless I was nervous or thirsty, and I was both.

Bill was the perfect person to talk to about this stuff. His years in the program (both Alcoholics and Narcotics Anonymous) meant he was a great listener. Although he was gay and I was straight, I found that if we swapped pronouns, our stories were essentially the same: we both dated someone incredible who later hurt us and left, and we passively put up with their shit and let ourselves get hurt. Aside from that, I spent more time in the last few months listening to Bill's sorrows, so it was my turn to dump my problems on him.

I swung the Rabbit through the winding curves on the narrow access drive that went behind the IMU and past the Chemistry Building, then jerked the car into a spot behind Lindley Hall. Inside, the building felt dead—the wide hallways, painted a battleship gray with ornate trim and the cast-iron staircases with old oaken banisters always reminded me of something out of a Stanley Kubrick film—like Jack Nicholson would come stumbling down the center staircase drenched in blood, wielding an axe.

I found Bill in front of two computers, one running a telnet session to a VAX, and the other running the familiar blue screen of WordPerfect 5.1. This was before the days of Windows, when multitasking involved a Mac, or a second PC. "Hey John," he said, looking up from the word processor and adjusting his thick, Coke-bottle glasses. "Let me print this chapter and then we can take off." A Shift-F7 later, the piece of his novel was on its way to a laserprinter, and he shut down both PCs and stuffed a stack of printed paper and a clipboard in a leather attaché.

"You feel like a short walk before we head back to your place?" I asked.

"Sounds good. I could use the air."

"How's the writing going?" I asked.

"I've been trying to anthologize a collection of short stories, plays, and poetry that I've written over the last thirty years." He grabbed his wide-brimmed hat, which made him look like a detective, and we headed outside, turning down the backside of the crescent buildings, and toward Third Street. "It's been a bitch getting all of this old stuff from college into WordPerfect..."

"Are you thinking of publishing it as a book?"

"No, I'm trying to convince the head of the English department to sneak me into the MFA program, maybe with some funding. Disability will only pay for vocational training, and creative writing isn't vocational. I've been trying to get them to pay for the rest of a bachelor's degree in English, as a prerequisite to law school, but it isn't working. I'll find some way to stay in school forever..."

We walked past Rawles Hall, and sat on the stone wall that ran down Third Street, by the sidewalk. Few cars passed by us, with only the stone giants of Swain and Rawles Halls beside us.

"So, what's up?" he said.

"I'm going to tell you everything, and I'm hoping you don't lock me up or anything."

"You're safe with me, I think..."

"I've been thinking about suicide," I said. "I...I almost went through it tonight."

"Holy shit...Why?"

"The usual. Nothing I could answer in a sentence."

"What were you going to do?"

"16 gauge shotgun."

"Jesus Christ, John—you shouldn't be keeping a gun around..."

"I know. It's been an insurance policy lately. Something in case I fuck up."

"Sigh—is this about Tammy?"

"It started about her, but it's really about what I'm doing, and what I can do with life. I feel like I've only got a couple of choices, and I don't want to take any of them."

"So you're having trouble choosing between the white picket fence and the life of a starving artist."

"Yeah, and I can't tell if it's just me, or if everyone has to deal with this. Because it seems like everyone around me is having a much easier time at this bullshit."

"I think everyone is fucked in the head, in some way or another. That's why you gravitate toward people that are as fucked up as you are. I take that back—you seem to gravitate toward people that are the yin to your yang in dysfunction. Like I am more introverted, passive, and codependent, so I always draw to more dominant, controlling, fucked up people."

"I wish I knew the way to break the cycle..."

"Don't we all. I think you eventually luck into a relationship that is manageable. I remember when we first started hanging out and you were first Tammy, how you always talked about how it was the greatest thing in the world. At first, I thought it was the typical euphoric 'I found someone' thing, but as I got to know you better, I realized you had a lot of bad relationships and experiences, and this one was different. Do you think you'd still be dating her if her parents funded her and she stayed in town for summer?"

"It's hard to tell. I think we could've lasted beautifully for another three, six months. I don't think it was for forever. It still hurts me to say that, but I think it would've gotten old."

"Well, six months of happiness is better than none..."

"Yeah," I said. The wind picked up its pace, whipping the tree branches over our head into a frenzy. I felt a few cool droplets fall on my bare arms. "Hey, it looks like it's starting to rain."

"Let's head back to my place," he said.

"Yeah, that sounds cool. I'm parked right behind Lindley."

We rushed back to Lindley Hall, and got into my Rabbit. It cranked in a second, and I fired up the heater to pull away the storm's blanket of cold. I wound through the campus tributary, and out to Seventh. The rain pinged on the windshield, and Bill gave me directions even though I knew the way.

Bill's house was a huge and dilapidated two-story on the north side of campus. The house was divided into three apartments—he had the front half of the lower level, including the porch, filled with old couches, overflowing ashtrays, and his improvised writing table, for nice weather.

We walked inside, to the frontroom—a wood-floored, high ceilinged parlor that at first glance looked like a tightly packed garage sale. On further examination, the knickknacks, pictures, books, records, and glassware almost told the story of Bill's life, and one could spend days studying every square foot of his house. It was a real writer's retreat, filled with old, leather-bound classics, and piles of rough drafts and incomplete chapters laser-printed on campus. No computer, no TV, no VCR—Bill didn't even have a telephone. But every day, he'd grab his trusty clipboard and write pages of poetry or novel longhand, to be transcribed later in the computer lab.

"Do you want anything to drink? I think I just have water and iced tea," he asked.

"Tea's cool. Plenty of sugar," I said. I followed him into the kitchen, even kitschier than the frontroom. On a fixed income, he spent much of his time cooking intricate dinners with a limited budget. This meant racks of spices and supplies, and well-used dishes in a shallow 1920's sink. He opened the freezer and pulled out two frosted mason-jar glasses, and filled them both with tea from a pitcher in the fridge.

"So what else is up besides the women situation?" he asked. He went into the living room and grabbed a seat.

I cracked open a handful of McDonald's sugar packets and dumped them in my tea. "There's school, you know that whole story—nine hours, above a B, or I'm out. Then there's money—I'm not working much, and I have no savings." I followed him into the other room and crashed on the chair opposite his. I took a long drink, feeling the caffeine course through my veins. "But so much of it is this non-specific detachment, this feeling that I don't belong."

"I know what you mean. When I went sober, I felt like that for a while, like my old life had been stolen from me, and I didn't have a new one yet."

"What did you do?"

"I don't know. But after a while, I realized that it's more about finding the small things in life that you want to pursue and defend, and working on those a day at a time. Writing to me is a large part of my life, but I didn't wake up and decide I wanted to be a writer. I kept at it, and tried to write every day, and then I woke up and realized I was a writer. You have to think about what you want to do, and go after it."

"I've done that a little bit, but I feel so alone when I'm not going after something mainstream. If I was a business major, and really into stocks and bonds, it's like you inherit this whole community of people that are your friends. Being into accordion music or something makes you more of an outcast..."

"You're thinking too much of the nuclear family bullshit, John. The reason they have all of that extra baggage is that their lives essentially have no meaning. They marry token wives and raise kids and buy minivans because they have no creative outlet in life. You do—you're beyond that keeping up with the Joneses bullshit. Focus on the art, whether that's music or computers or just being yourself, and the rest will follow."

"And the women?"

"I don't know much about the women, but if you think the pretending game will attract the women you want, you're probably right. If you think it'll attract the women who want you, you're wrong."

"Good point," I said. I kicked back some more tea. "Off the subject—what do you think of meds?"

"Psychiatric? No opinion, I guess. You thinking of quitting or something?"

"No, I've been thinking about going on a second med, like Prozac or something. Just to tide me over for a while."

"I know some would say Prozac is handed out like candy, but if you've got a legitimate need, and you've thought it through..."

"I'm still thinking," I said. I tipped back the last of my iced tea. "Shit, I should get back home and get some sleep," I said.

"Are you going to be okay?"

"For now, yeah," I said. "I need to think all of this over."

"Don't expect any sudden answers," he said. "I've been shuffling the same stuff through my head for decades. It's a never-ending quest. But feel free to stop by any time you need to talk. Some night you'll have to come over for dinner."

"That sounds great. Hey, thanks for listening." I gave him a big hug as we stood by the front doorway.

"I owe you one," he said. "I think you've listened to more of my relationship bullshit lately than vice versa. I was afraid I'd scare you off."

"No, it's cool," I said. "I think our problems are more alike than we think."

"Will you be at the fountain tomorrow?"

"Yeah, I'll be there."

"Okay, see you then."

I walked to my car, thinking more about the wisdom Bill laid on me, and drove back home.

When I got back to my room and hit the lights, I remembered the gun, peeking from under the comforter in my bed. On the drive home, I thought more about what to do, and decided I needed to break this cycle somehow. I went to the bed and carefully lifted the loaded gun from my sleeping place and sat down. The cartridge snapped out with a tug, and I pulled back the bolt to remove the third round and put it back in the magazine. I grabbed the black nylon case from the closet, and stuffed the gun and the loose magazine in there, closing them up with a zipper.

I checked my watch: 4:37. Plenty of time. I hefted the gun over my shoulder, and snuck out to the car.

The VW whirred down Third Street, the wet pavement underneath misting from the tires and against the wheelwells. The Rabbit didn't have any fancy options, which meant the wipers had two speeds: too slow and too fast. I cycled the blades on and off manually when the droplets collected on the windshield. In the hatch, the shotgun rode along, bouncing with each jolt of the pavement.

I cruised past the shops, the restaurants, and the apartment buildings that defined the College Mall area, and continued out of town. This is nuts, I thought. I wasn't even sure of my mission, but I knew it was idiotic. But I kept at it, and drove in the darkness. The rain slowly eased up, leaving the wet roads but keeping my windshield dry.

I hung a right on 446, and drove further into nowhere. I knew the beaten road continued way the hell into Hoosier National Forest, but I'd never taken it more than ten miles in. Even with the rain and the darkness, it felt good to cruise with only open fields on either side of me. I opened the moonroof, and got a blast of residual water from the rain gutter at first, but then had a decent view of the clouds rolling away overhead, a blanket of gray twisting and moving like a demented screensaver.

After a few miles, the road went from a straight path, to a twisting piece of string wound through the foothills. In the darkness, fishing shops and boat marinas lay closed for the evening, and I spied an occasional condo hidden in the bluffs. The empty fields melted into many old trees, and some of the curves were etched into steeper elevation.

I edged the VW up what I knew was the last big hill, and at the top, I could see it: Lake Monroe. Officially known as Monroe Reservoir, it was built decades before, wrapping around the top edge of the national forest, with a five-mile channel that cut through the middle of the preserve. Although 15 miles across from the southwest to the northeast, it felt more like four interconnected lakes. From the top of the hill, 446 looked like it went right through it, and below me, all I could see was still, black waters on either side, and the narrow road that cut right through the middle on top of a quarter-mile levee.

I zipped down the road, feeling engulfed by the lake on either side of me. A hundred yards past the water, I hung a hard left onto a gravel road that continued in to a public boat launch. The road wound out to a set of parking lots, with no inhabitants. Good. An uncanny silence hung over the car, with the idling diesel engine making the only human sound in the area. I pulled the car to one of the loading ramps, a wide concrete road that drove straight into the lake.

The lake. I walked around the dock, letting the car ping back to its resting heart rate. The feeling of natural darkness enveloped me, and my eyes got used to the night. Off to the left, I could see 446, a strip of asphalt balanced on a big dam of dirt. It looked like my horizon in the distance, a roller coaster of a road with nobody on it. On all other sides, my boundaries were made with trees—huge Indiana oaks that ruled this world before the Army engineers or whoever the fuck turned the area into a lake. It felt so good to be standing in a spot where you couldn't see a building, or a person, and where the only thing you heard was your own heartbeat in your eardrums, plus the occasional crickets and fish.

The lake was my favorite scamming tool over the last couple of years. When I wanted to take a date to a quiet place to talk, this loading ramp made the perfect spot. It never worked as well as I'd liked—I never got lucky with a woman there, or even kissed one. But when I had someone on the hook and needed some intimate time to let things develop, I loved to take the drive and sit under the stars.

Women at the lake...I guess the girl that I dated the year I was home, we went to the lake on our first date, and look where that led...But it never happened like a Meg Ryan romance movie or something. If I had the right girl and the right moves, we'd probably get to the lake when a dozen people were getting their boats in the water at two in the morning.

My eyes felt more at home in the darkness, and I could get a good look at the clouds above. The thick puffiness cruised past, like the storm needed to get the hell out of Indiana by sunrise. The breeze made it a bit chilly, but the sound felt tranquil.

Maybe I should throw the gun off the bridge. Would the cops find it? Would they print it and implicate me into some random convenience store holdup that coincidentally happened tonight? Would the gun turn up missing at my mom's three years from now? I'd be forced to explain that I threw a few hundred bucks into the lake to avoid killing myself with it, even though I probably wasn't supposed to have it with me anyway. My mom would rather see me shoot myself than throw away a few hundred dollars.

Fuck. I went to the car and yanked open the hatch. I pulled the gun from the trunk, and unzipped the nylon case. The magazine fell out in my hand, and I slapped it into the gun. Then, I chamber a round, like I did every morning, every evening when I determine my fate. I need to get this over with, I thought. I needed to push every milligram of fear from my body, and do this before I changed my mind.

Standing on the loading ramp, looking into the water and the trees, I pushed the butt of the gun against my shoulder, aimed it at the middle of the lake, and pulled back on the trigger. I squeezed the piece of metal back as hard as I could, remembering all of the times I only pulled halfway, with the gunmetal in my mouth. BAM—the wooden butt kicked back into my shoulder, and a loud report echoed back from the treeline. Lead rained into the water, and my body filled with an energy like a 12 year old playing with fireworks. I hadn't fired a gun in more than five years, and I forgot the amount of adrenaline that went through your system when that device in your hands exploded death outward, away from me in this case.

I quickly cycled the bolt, dropping the empty shell onto the pavement with a clink and jamming a fresh round in its place. With the chamber open, the smell of gunpowder wafted back to me, the odor of capguns and model rockets and blackjacks from long ago. The thought of some park ranger or a landowner calling the police entered my mind, and I envisioned getting arrested for poaching. Fuck it, I need to finish.

BAM! The second round fired across the lake, and the gun punched me again. I cycled out and in faster this time, and with no hesitation, BAM! I removed the clip, inserted the final round, and BAM! With only a second to admire my work, I zipped the gun back in its case, closed the hatch, and pitched the empty shells as far as I could into the water.

Before I took off, I walked around the ramp one more time, looking into the water. A month and a half ago, Tammy left, and I started this escape, and I didn't feel like an ounce of change had happened in me. I devised long term plans, and I did a lot of posturing and metaphorical debate about what I'd do, but I didn't take any steps. For the first time, I felt like I was moving out of one chapter and into another. I had patterns to break, and short term goals to achieve. I wanted to find the perfect woman, but I needed to talk to women. I wanted to cure my depression, but I needed to deal with it. I wanted to make more money, but I needed to spend less money. It would take change, something I needed to do.

I got into the car and drove like hell to avoid getting caught. At home, I managed to sneak in the empty gun and get into bed as the sun came up. With a pillow in my face and the birds chirping outside my window, I thought more about what needed to happen in the near future, and I fell into a deep sleep.

By the time the sun warmed my small room like an oven and filled it with light, I felt like a hangover from the lack of sleep. After I got out of bed, the events pulled back to me like a dream: the lake, the visit to Bill's, and the attempt. Until I smelled the faint odor of gunpowder on my clothes from the night before, I didn't believe anything happened.

At least I felt somewhat better. After a shower and a change of clean clothes, I was ready for the last day of the summer session. I'd need to break out the Visa card and head to the registrar's to pick up classes for the second session. Although I knew this would be a long chore and eat up hours of my afternoon, the thought of picking out classes excited me.

I headed out, and an incredible day greeted me. Last night's rain had all but vanished from the ground, and the sun blazed through a clear sky. With my walkman over my ears and this beautiful weather above me, I needed to run an errand before the registrar's office. I headed in to campus, and walked toward Woodburn Hall to track down my final grade for the polysci class.

The entire way, I tried to think about what I'd do if things went wrong. If I pulled a B+ for the course, my cumulative GPA would come back to a 2.0, and I'd be saved. I'd still need to finish six hours of at least 2.0 in the second session, but I wouldn't pull myself in any further. On the other hand, if I scored a C or lower in the class, it would leave absolutely no margin of error in the second summer session. I hoped for the best, but it all depended on how much the teacher liked my paper, and how well I bullshitted on the final.

This would be the closest I've ever been on a grade, I thought. A B would make my life much easier, but a C would give me an ulcer for the rest of the summer. If I get a good grade, I thought, I'm going to try to keep the hammer down for the rest of the summer. I knew that my eleventh hour promises were total bullshit, but I hoped to get this summer of academic blunders behind me.

I got to Woodburn, my heart pounding in my chest. I ran to the second floor, where the teacher promised to post his grades by 10 AM. It was already going on 11:30, so I knew they would be there. Any later, and he wouldn't be able to turn them in to get them printed on the report cards. I ran down the hallway of teachers' offices, found his spot, and looked at the printout of student ID numbers and grade breakdowns. I traced down the list for my grade, found my number, traced across the column of scores for the final tally....

B+, enough to put me right at the 2.0 mark. I must have re-checked five times to make sure it was my grade, and it was. This is going to make the rest of my summer a bit easier, I thought.

Book Two

16

In the tomb of the library computer cluster, I etched away the desolate Saturday afternoon in front of a Zenith PC, hacking VAX C. On the summer weekends, the campus emptied, the students and faculty finding other pursuits with which to enjoy the summer. Even with the larger Summer Session II population, many people retreated home, or took weekend vacations to anywhere but Bloomington. Everyone else hit the clubs, drank all night and spent the daytime hours hung over, shacking up with new-found summer lovers, or otherwise vanishing from sight. A small minority of ABD graduate serfs and dubious students isolated themselves from the bright sun of summer by retreating to the inner dungeons of the Main Library, banging away on the cluster PCs, or filling rickety, cigarette-burned wooden desks with piles of yellowed books and half-torn reference material. Far from an academic, I shared their desolation by firing off email, screwing around on the VAX and trying to get a little programming done.

That morning, I thought about wandering around, taking a long walk, and exploring the vacant city. The emptiness felt like some *Omega Man* parody; on a campus built for 40 or 50 thousand people, there was just me and 12 Asian grad students.

It felt good to code again, though. For the first time since Tammy left, I hacked away at a project I started when we were together, when I was trying to turn my life around. It was a unix-like command shell called nsh. Originally a solution to the asinine command line editing in VMS, it became a way to develop my C skills. It didn't have much practical use—you couldn't spend all day in nsh and do your regular work. But it supported a meager list of commands, and I pecked away at adding new features, in whatever order came to me naturally. That afternoon, I messed with the date command, so I could type 'date' at the prompt and it would return "Sat Jul 27 13:22:09 1992." At that point, it would only return "Foo Bar 27 132209 92." And no, my code was not Year 2000 compliant—in seven and a half years, if there were still VAXes in the world (and I guessed there would be,) the code would start saying it was the year 1900. I kept chipping away at the bits and pieces, compiling and tweaking. This exercise was meant to increase my time with C, and get back in coding shape by the fall. But, I also kept doing a who every three minutes, and habitually checking my mail. And outside, it was Saturday, it was nice out, and I kept thinking about an escape.

I could've been working on homework, now that I had new classes. A week ago Friday, with credit card in hand, I went to Franklin Hall and nabbed two courses for second summer session. This time, I didn't have to fuck with people at a half dozen offices all over campus to get a "computer" registration ticket. Although the registration part was computerized with cream and crimson scantron sheets and little golf pencils to fill in the ovals, the actual class postings were done the old fashioned way. In a giant paneled room about the size of a regulation swimming pool, carrels covered with bulletin boards held up to the minute/second/hour/year sheets with listings of open class session. I went from department to department on the boards, with a schedule of classes in hand, and tried to find open sections that I needed, that were easy, and that were in a good time spot.

Once again, no computer classes worth a shit were open, and all of the fun and easy classes like human sexuality (IU was the home of the famed Kinsey Institute) and skeet shooting were closed. I couldn't find a good run of night courses that were open, either. I filled out three or four scantron sheets, all of them rejected because classes listed as open were filled (it also rejected a sheet because the fucking golf pencil wasn't dark enough; I got back a confirmation saying I was registered for M672 Numerical Treatment of Differential and Integral Equations II and M815 Individual

Readings in Rumanian Language and Literature, and it took me 20 minutes to drop them.) In desperation, I gave up on any sensical timeslots, figuring I'd never find a solid nine to five job this late in the summer anyway.

On my fifth attempt, my choices were golden. For class one, I'd make my third attempt at macroeconomics, on Mon-Wed-Fri from 9:45 to 11. For the other class, I snagged a 300-level advanced expository writing class. The topic was metaphor and simile, and it met the dreaded intensive writing requirement I had to fill. The problem: it met from 8:00 to 9:15 in the morning, four days a week. Because I never woke up before noon, this absolutely forced me to get my act together. I worried that this would mean the end of the summer, fountain gatherings, late nights on the computer, and everything else fun, but I knew I'd either skip class or go on two hours of sleep if it meant my freedom. The summer before, I worked second shift, got home after midnight, blew several hours talking to Lauren on the computer, and still managed to commute into South Bend for 9 AM classes. I reassured myself over and over that this would be the best thing to do.

Over the last week, I surprised myself with how well I was able to adapt to morning life. I didn't miss a class, and I made it to every fountain gathering that week. I'd get home after econ and crash for an hour or two, and manage to get five or six hours of sleep each night. The English class looked good—we were reading Susan Sontag's *Illness and Metaphor* and *AIDS and its Metaphors*, and had both creative and research writing in the future. My econ teacher looked and talked like a blonde Michael J. Fox, and dumbed down the class to incredible levels. It looked like straight C's or better would be an easy task.

The money situation improved slightly in the last week, too. I got in at the IU telefund again. They lost my record from my stint there three years before, and I pressed all of the right buttons on the interview. They sat me down in one office and called me from another, to see what my phone personality was like. When they asked me the typical questions about "what would you do if..." I gave almost verbatim answers from their own training manuals. They put me in the Varsity Club campaign, collecting gifts for sports scholarships. I knew absolutely nothing about sports, but because the basketball ticket waiting list went on a bizarre points schedule based on how much you donated every year, it meant I'd have some people willing to give anything to shave time off of the ten-plus year wait for tickets.

Aside from the new classes, I also went to three afternoon training sessions that week, to re-learn the art of phone solicitation. There were about a dozen new trainees, half of them female, and most of them cool to hang out with. A lot of the training was boring paperwork and procedures, like any other job. But it also involved a lot of simulated calls, role playing games and rapport building exercises, which were more fun than pushing pencils. We had to talk about ourselves a lot, where we were from, what we did, and who we were. It was like the first day of class, when the teacher went around the room and had everyone introduce themselves. And I learned more about the females in my class than I'd pry from the average first date. On top of that, I got paid. Starting Monday, I'd be working four nights a week. Plus, new shift assignments went out for UCS, and I got some regular hours. In a matter of time, the cupboards would no longer be bare.

In the middle of fixing the days of the week output in my program, a new message notification flashed on the screen on my session to the Bronze mainframe, where I read my mail. It came from Jenn Young, a new username to me. I did a quick who and her name appeared—I must've been trawling, and added her name to my list. I couldn't put the username to a face, and it was her first mail to me. The message was said little more than "thanks for writing/just got out of work/how is your day?" which didn't give me many clues.

I fired up the IU online address book. I should fucking automate this, I thought. Scam-bot 2000. Within seconds, I browsed her info: biology major, junior, off-campus phone number, and nothing else. A quick check showed her logged in at the IMU, but this still didn't give me any clues as to her identity.

Of all the labs on campus for her to be hiding in, IMU 061 was my trump card; I could drink two gallons of Finlandia Vodka and read off all of the IP numbers in that lab in under three seconds. If I knew she'd be parked there for ten minutes, I could easily sneak in the lab and figure out who she was. 129.79.110.1 was the far left desk of the front row, 129.79.110.2 was next to it, and so forth. If I was working and saw a cute girl in row three, two seats over, I'd check 129.79.110.18 and if she was using her email, I'd be in.

But would she be there a few minutes from now, by the time I ran across campus? Probably not—and I didn't want to give up my computer, trudge over to the lab, and then miss her. I wished I could've remembered her. I mailed so many messages while trawling that I had no way to keep track of the replies. Maybe I could merge a new version of the xinfo database into the Scam-bot 2000 to do that automatically...Anyway, her reply to my mail seemed simple and cheery, asking who I was and what was up—much better than the people who couldn't deal with an occasional social message, who fired back evil and scathing mail telling me to get a life. Based on her reply, I decided it would be safe to play.

"Hey, how are you?" I asked, firing off a one-line message to her on the computer.

"Hi! I just got your mail," she replied, a few seconds later. "Are you busy?"

"Not really, just messing around in the library," I said.

"I just got out of work at the IMU," she said. "Do you want to come over and meet?"

What the fuck? The first rule of the scammer's manifesto was to control the situation. I wanted to get in some emails, wear her down a bit, let her know I'm a nice guy before she sees me, and sneak a peek of her beforehand. Every department on the damn campus told you to do your research. You don't drop atomic bombs without checking out how they work first—why would this be any different? I guess that line of thinking was hypocritical for me; after all, I drove over to Tammy's dorm after only a few lines of bitnet and a few minutes on the phone, and I fell head over heels in love with her.

I thought about the promises I made to myself: The Summer of John. I needed to get out there, even if it meant getting rapped in the head a bit on first dates and stupid match-ups. She took a big step in asking first. And hey, maybe I saw her in the union when I was working. Maybe she's a babe. Maybe I'd do okay. It would be better than sitting inside all day.

"Sure, okay. I'll stop over," I said. "I'll be there in about five minutes. How will I find you?" I said. Better not tell her I know she's sitting in the last row, next to the printers, I thought. That kind of shit freaks people out.

"I'm in the very back, closest to the printers. Tall, brunette, and I'm wearing a white t-shirt."

"Okay, see you in a few," I said. I saved my work, and left the inner chamber of the library for a sunny trip to the Union.

My heart slammed in my chest as I walked down Seventh Street. I ran my hands through my hair, tucked in my shirt, wiped clean my glasses, and I tried to look sociable with only three minutes of lead-time. What if she was the Barbie doll type and got offended that I didn't own a Saab or have a doctor for a father? Or the too intellectual type and upsetted at the fact that I wasn't on the dean's list and didn't speak Latin and two other languages? Or what if the tables turned, and she annoyed me, and I couldn't find a method of escape? I climbed the steps to the Union, and the millions of possible problems hemorrhaged through my head, making me wonder if I should just pull a no-show.

No, I've got more balls than that, I thought. Summer of John. I walked down the long, empty hallway to the lab, knowing she had a perfect view of everybody coming in and out of the lab. But she didn't know my face—if she looked like Lemmy from Motörhead, I could duck out without a problem. I got to the end of the hallway, stood in the doorway, and scanned the almost empty lab for 129.79.110.20.

When I saw her hiding by the printers, I absolutely knew why I first dropped her a line when we were both in the lab. She looked about six feet tall, with a light tan, shoulder-length straight brown hair and mix of girl-next-door gentleness and the well-proportioned curves of a swimsuit model. Very easy on the eyes, I thought. I hoped I wouldn't tank this one in the first five minutes.

She saw me as I approached the printers and smiled. "Are you John?" she said in a soft and compelling voice.

"Yeah. You must be Jenn?" I stumbled, almost stunned by her beauty. "Umm, nice to meet you."

She giggled at my clumsiness. "So, do you want to go for a walk around campus? It looks nice out."

"That sounds great," I said. She logged out, and we headed for the door.

I couldn't have been given a better day for a get-to-know-you-better walk across campus, with the sun out and the air fresh and a little breezy. Even still, I struggled to think of anything to say to her. She looked incredible, but I knew nothing about her. We hiked up Woodlawn, toward Tenth and the north side of campus, and I tried to think of an ice-breaker.

"Hey check it out," I pointed to Collins. "That's where I lived in my freshman year."

"Really?" she said in a curious voice.

Oh shit, I already blew it, I thought. Everyone but Collins residents thought Collins was a freak zoo.

"Don't worry," I said. "I'm not a vampire, a heroin addict, or gay. Where did you live?"

"Over in Read," she said. "I'm going back next year, but I'm subletting this summer. What about you?"

"Off-campus," I said. "I'm in a boarding house, and it looks like I'll be there next year, too. Hey, where do you work in the IMU?"

"I work for the IMU caterers," she said. "I worked there last year, and it was okay, but I don't get many hours this summer. I worked at a wedding today, and I got a $20 tip, so that's cool. I've got two other jobs, too."

"Wow—where else?"

"I work at Steak and Shake in the evenings, and I work a few hours for the store that's in my apartment building. It sounds crazy to have three jobs, but I only work like 25 or 30 hours a week."

"I know what you mean, I've been doing everything to hold down the fort. I work at UCS, but I only get a few hours a week. I'm also starting at the telefund on Monday, I've been doing the training all week."

"I knew someone on my floor last year that worked there—they didn't have many good things to say about it."

"I know—I worked there my freshman year, and it sucked. But they pay for the training, and I can probably hang on for a few weeks, so that's a few checks in my pocket. It's not like I'm putting it on my resume or anything."

"Are you taking classes, too?"

"Yeah, I took a polysci class last session, and now I'm taking an English class and macro econ."

"What's your major?" she asked.

"Computer science. I might try to get a minor or another degree in English or Philosophy or something." I was always proud of this line—I didn't want to be just another heartless code-hacker. It's good to have a soft side, too. "What about you?"

"Biology. I'm getting a teacher's certification to fall back on, but I'm hoping to go pre-med."

"Pretty ambitious," I said. Don't discuss grades, I thought..."I thought maybe you were going to say music, because of Read."

"I do play sax," she said. "I was in the marching hundred, and I took a few classes, but I don't really study anymore—not enough time. I still play, though."

We reached the intersection and turned down the long stretch of Tenth Street bordering the north of campus. With the running fields next to us, we headed toward the library.

"Hey, what kind of sax do you have?"

"It's a Selmer, tenor."

"No way! The summer after I graduated high school, I plated keys for silver Selmer tenors, altos, and clarinet keys. I'll have to check yours out sometime..."

"So you're from Elkhart?"

"I lived there since the second grade. I consider myself from Bloomington now, I guess."

"I know what you mean, I like living here a lot more than I like my parents' place in Cincinnati."

"Yeah, I have the same problems with my mom," I said. "Money, money, money—you're paying out of state tuition, you know the drill."

"Yeah, that's exactly what I was thinking," she said.

"What can I say, I'm a mindreader," I laughed. "It's part of my job as a computer consultant."

We both laughed, and I felt a little more at ease with her. I never would've approached her in person—she looked too perfect. But she seemed more down to earth while we made small talk and headed across campus. Maybe...

"Hey, let's grab a seat in here," I said. We hiked to the middle of the arboretum, and sat at a wooden bridge that spanned a scenic, man-made stream. The arboretum was the site of the old Tenth Street stadium, where the huge bike race at the end of the movie *Breaking Away* took place. A few years after that film, they built a new stadium north of campus, and tore down all of the old one except for two of its corner posts, which now stood as monuments to the west side of the area. Then, they created a huge park, hundreds of acres of pedestrian campus with walkways, rolling hills, a gazebo, some fake ponds and rivers, and tons of trees, flowers, and green grass. It would remain untouched for development, a nature area that was displayed prominently on many postcards, promotional photos, and brochures about the university. And it served as a great shortcut when walking across campus. Instead of cutting through some parking lot, I would often get to walk with the trees around me, people rollerblading past, beautiful women getting tans or studying between classes.

I took a better look at her as we sat, the sun on her long, brown hair, and wondered if maybe she was the one. But it didn't feel like it—I wasn't sure that I was entirely into her, and it didn't feel like that Sunday morning when I first saw Tammy. But the novelty of talking to such a beautiful woman confused me enough that I couldn't really tell.

"So what brought you to Indiana anyway?" I asked.

"It's got a good pre-med program, and I knew someone from my church back home who was a music major. And it's a beautiful campus, a great place to spend four years."

"Or more," I said. "Where do you go to church?"

"Saint Charles, the Catholic church on Third."

"Yeah, I know where that is. I drive past it every time I go to the mall."

"What about you? Are you religious?"

"I used to be Catholic, but I stopped going when my parents split up. Maybe someday I'll go back when I settle down, but I'm on my own now." I picked up that this was the wrong answer, but I didn't want to throw her a bunch of lies, especially about this.

"My parents split up too, when I was about six," she said. "I had a lot of problems with my mom, so I've mostly lived with my dad and his new wife."

"Yeah, mine split when I was 13. I've always lived with my mom, though. My dad is okay, but I didn't want to move away from home. I guess it's worked out okay."

"I wish I could've stayed with my mom, but she pretty much went crazy. That's why I'm here this summer, and working three jobs."

"I know what you mean. I don't like to starve, but it's better than being under my mom's roof."

I kept the conversation going, and slid in a few questions to find out more about her. After some patient prying, I managed to find out that she was single, but that she was having some sort of ongoing problems with her ex-boyfriend back home in Ohio. I didn't try to ask any more about it, but the information made me wonder what my odds were. She seemed open and enthusiastic about a friendship. I liked our conversation so far, and I was very attracted to her. She was the type of woman I always thought about dating in college before I got into college: beautiful, intelligent, sophisticated and yet informal. My mind continued to explore the possibilities, and how I could pursue this further.

We kept talking, but it got to be like a game whose object was not to look at your watch the longest. And I lost total track of time while we were on the bridge. But she eventually noticed the time, and the spell was lifted.

"Wow, it's almost five," she said. "I've got to get home and get ready for work soon."

"Where are you heading? Maybe I can walk you part way there."

"I'm just south of campus, in a house right by Third and Jordan."

"Really?" I said. "I live right near there too, on Mitchell Street."

"Do you know where that boarding house is between Swain and Mitchell, on Atwater? It has a party store downstairs, and rooms upstairs?"

"I totally know where that is! I walk through that parking lot every day. I live just south of Atwater, maybe fifty yards from there."

"That's too weird," she said. "We're practically neighbors."

"Yeah, I guess we are. A day of coincidences," I said.

We hiked the usual route through the library parking lot and then down Jordan, but it felt weird to walk it with someone else. I knew I only had the next ten minutes or so before she reverted back to just an email name on the system, so I quickly tried to think of a plan.

The hike led us through my usual route home—down Jordan, to Third, behind the bookstore, and within minutes, we were at the big parking lot and two-story boarding house where she lived. Her place was much newer-looking from the outside, with square lines, light yellow siding, and faux wood shutters on each window. I always walked by and saw the signs for female-only boarders, and knew it would probably be a jackpot of Penthouse Forum proportions if I could ever get inside. But would I? I've got to do this, I thought. If I don't now, I will regret it for the rest of my life...

"Hey, could I give you a call sometime? Maybe we can catch dinner or hang out again sometime?" The words exploded from my mouth without thinking, but it was done. It was like pulling off a Band-Aid real fast—it only hurt for a second.

"Yeah, that sounds great. Hang on, let me get something to write with." She vanished into the house, leaving me on the porch, and quickly reappeared with a pen and paper. She scribbled down her number, tore off the paper, and handed it to me. "There, I'm kind of hard to get ahold of sometimes with the jobs, but I have a machine. Can I get your number, too?" she asked.

"Yeah, yeah sure." I took the pad and wrote down my number. "I've got my own line and a machine. I'm not too hard to get ahold of, feel free to call anytime. And there's always email."

"Okay great. Hey, I've gotta get to work in a bit, but it was really nice meeting you."

"Nice to meet you too. I'll talk to you later."

She went inside, and I hiked the last block home, wondering what would happen next.

"Hey man, where you been all day?" Deon stood in the front hallway, drinking Big-K grape soda, the cheapest brand on the face of the Earth, straight from a three-liter bottle. "You didn't get any mail today."

"Thanks for checking," I said. I went to my room, dropped my book bag, and grabbed a can of Coke. "If you must know, I was hanging out with a chick all afternoon."

"So what's the deal? Are you after her?"

"Eh, I don't know. She's cute, but religious."

"Religious? I thought you worshiped the devil?"

"Yeah, me too. I don't know. It's nice to be around someone and talk, but nobody's really home. You know what I mean?"

"Not entirely..."

"Look, I'll explain it later. I need to crash for a bit. What do you have going on tonight?"

"I'm supposed to go to a party out at the Villas later on, but it's probably going to be stupid. What about you?"

"Not much. Maybe the mall, then the fountain."

"Cool, I'll catch you later man."

"Later Deon." I went to my room, checked my email (none), and tried to think about whether I was ready to jump into yet another ambiguous chase.

17

10:30, Saturday night. Wholist, nobody on. A little Peter Gabriel bounced off the walls, one of my favorite non-metal musicians. None of that "In Your Eyes" bullshit, either—I cranked the *Security* album, the words to "The Rhythm of the Heat" possessing me, twisting with the almost-July air and weird mood to make me feel like something extra-sensory was looming on the horizon.

I called Cindy a few hours ago, after my McSupper, to tell her about the meeting with Jenn, and my feelings about it. The conversation probably sounded as confusing as the situation. I rambled on about how I talked to Jenn for hours in the arboretum, how she laughed at my jokes and seemed nice, and how we walked home and I got her number and she asked for mine. It seemed like the ideal, lazy summer fling, or maybe even the precursor to a longer situation.

But, she was religious, and that scared me. With my need for some kind of relaxed sexual relationship, and the piles of highly Satanic CDs and zines lying around the house, I wasn't sure I could keep up a false front for too long. And I wasn't sure it was a good match intellectually; she seemed like too much of an over-achiever, not the kind of slacker I needed. But, I had her number. And doing something with the imperfect match seemed better than sitting around by myself. Cindy seemed to ignore all of the negatives, and was overly excited for me. I guess she was an optimist when it came to these things, and she saw me struggle through many bad relationships and false starts. Maybe she was right, and this would be a fun thing for the rest of the summer. I had no choice but to pursue it until it failed.

Hours after the call to Cindy, I stared at the vacant monitor and wondered where Jenn was, and if she was thinking of me. I also wished I knew what was up between her and her ex, and what went down with their phone conversation. I didn't know much about their status, except that she said they broke it off at the beginning of summer, and he wouldn't stop calling. It sounded familiar, like my obsession with Tammy. It felt good to be on the other side of the equation, but I didn't have any wise advice to give her.

I hadn't emailed Jenn since our afternoon together, and I tried to plan my next move. I didn't want to creep her out by being overly anxious or possessive, especially given the problems with her former boyfriend. But I did want her to know that I liked her, and wanted to see more of her. Most of all, I wanted to find out more. I didn't have enough background information to see if I wanted to jump on her or back away, and I wouldn't be able to decide until I got more information from her. I considered asking a handful of carefully calculated questions in an email, but I didn't want to ask too much. The stupid mental game just caused more anxiety, and didn't help pass time any faster.

I logged off, dropped carrier and started looking for my shoes to begin the trek to the fountain. As I dug through the laundry and papers, the phone rang, and I jumped across the room to grab it. I half-expected a call from one of the fountain regulars, asking if I'd be there or if I was bringing anyone.

"Acapulco Pizza," I said, catching the phone mid-ring.

"John?" It was Jenn, sounding somewhat distraught.

"Yeah, what's up?"

"This is Jenn. I didn't wake you up, did I?"

"Are you kidding? I'm usually eating supper around now. What's up?"

"It's Gregory. He just called, and we got in this giant fight. I'm really upset about it. I don't know what to do about him."

"What's up? What did he do?"

"He keeps calling, and going on and on about how much he wants to be with me, and how I hurt him, and won't listen when I tell him I don't want to go back to dating him. It's like every time he calls, I have to break up with him all over again. He's driving me nuts."

"I think you'll be safe," I said. "He's not going to show up on your doorstep, is he? You can screen your calls, and..." I knew the situation all too well, from being on the other side of it.

"What if he does show up? I mean, it's like a four hour drive, but he says I mean the world to him, that I'm his life, we were meant to be together."

"Umm," I stalled, "I don't know. Maybe we can hide you in my closet or something. Look, seriously—you've got like 74 roommates in that house, and I'm only a block away. Even if he did show up, nothing would happen. I mean it would be an ugly scene, but it's not like you have to go back to him. This isn't medieval England or something."

"Yeah, I know," she sighed. "I don't want to think about him anymore. I left him because I felt I could never be myself. We dated since high school, and it was time to move on. Now he keeps pulling me back in. I feel so alone during the summer, but I've got this guy practically stalking me..."

I looked at my watch: 10:42. I didn't want to cut her off, but the fountain remained in my mind. But, I could afford to skip it this one time, especially if it helped me put my evil plans in motion.

"Hey, I hate to interrupt all of this, but I have a confession to make—I was going to leave in a few minutes and meet some friends at Showalter fountain."

"Oh, I'm sorry. I can talk to you tomorrow..."

"No, no—I still want to talk to you about this. I can skip out the fountain, but I was thinking we could go for a walk and talk about this. It's such a nice night out and everything..."

"I don't know. I don't really want to go out. I mean, I do, but..."

"Come on," I said. "The walk will do you some good. And I'd really like to talk to you some more. It's incredible out. I promise, no funny stuff."

"Okay," she said. "I would like someone to talk to about this."

"No problem. I'll stop over in about five minutes?"

"Sure, meet me outside the front door of my place. I'll see you in a bit."

We hung up and I tried to find my other shoe in the sea of dirty laundry.

The clear night sky teemed with bright stars, shining brightly against the dark velvet backdrop. During the short walk to Jenn's house, I swam in the cool midnight air, a nice change from the pounding June sun. With only the occasional car on the road, I easily walked across the one-way street usually packed with traffic, and cut through the parking lot to her building.

Jenn stood on the porch of her house, dressed casually in a pair of loose jeans and a baggy t-shirt. "Hey there," she said, smiling at my arrival. She came down the steps to meet me, like some choreographed 1950's date to the movies.

"Isn't it incredible out here?" I said. "This night is perfect for a midnight walk."

We headed toward campus, strolling across the route I took every day. "It is wonderful," she said. "It takes my mind off of things. I used to take a lot of walks with my roommate last year. It's hard to do by yourself, I mean, if you're a female."

"Yeah, I used to take a lot of late walks, too."

"I wish I could go alone, but I'm always scared. We used to go to the midnight movie a lot, with people from the dorm. Then we'd take our time on the way home and goof around."

"Man, I miss going to those midnight films," I said. "I guess they still play them and everything, but it's not the same when you don't get half of your dorm to go with you. We saw almost every one in my freshman year: *Holy Grail*, *Batman*, even *Rocky Horror*. That brings back memories."

We cut through to Third and Jordan, and continued down Third. "This reminds me of my trips to Lindley," I said. "When I didn't have a computer, I walked this walk almost every night. Stop me if I'm being too nostalgic."

We both laughed, and bumped into each other in an accidental but premeditated way. When the laugh was over, I was holding her hand in mine. It was so subtle and unplanned, yet I knew it was the same exact thing that happened with Tammy months before. And from the way she smiled at me as we walked hand in hand, I knew the first steps of a master plan were in place.

With the moon over our heads and the stars breaking the sky, walking with someone else through the quiet summer campus felt like a dream to me. After the dark, melancholic and drunken stumbles through the paths and around the ivory-covered halls of learning, it felt good to have another person to talk to. The bonus was that this person was a beautiful woman, who also seemed happy to talk to me.

I flashed back to the last stroll across campus I took, and mentally compared Tammy to Jenn. Using Tammy as a standard to judge other women made competition tough, but I wanted to really know if things were as magic as they were a few months before when I thought I had it all.

As a sex object, Jenn led the competition. With a tall, leggy frame, full and busty figure, nice tan, fit lines, and a model-like face, she edged out Tammy's plain and simple beauty. But she didn't have the cute, cuddly aspect that made Tammy so adorable in my eyes. Jenn got good grades and took tough courses, but Tammy studied music and the arts, something more commendable in my book than just trying to get a good GPA. The big strike against Jenn was her religious beliefs. As a puritan who seemed to practice moralism in almost every aspect of life, she didn't match Tammy's open-minded laissez-faire attitude about the world. And although Tammy did look sweet and innocent, she was far from a prude in the bedroom, a factor that could eventually ruin things with Jenn.

Because of these criteria, part of me said this was not IT like Tammy. Jenn was far from perfection despite her outward appearance, and I knew this early in the game. When searching for a woman, I wanted to find a close-to-perfect specimen and then commit to them, saving myself from any intermediate models. I didn't seriously think Jenn was the person I was waiting for.

I thought back to Peter's advice he gave me when I visited him before the summer began. I burned a lot of my time and energy trying to find someone perfect to be with. During that search, I turned away many decent women, people who could have helped me get past the loneliness and depression. Most people thought I was trying to find a beautiful but dumb girl for temporary sexual use, like most of the rest of the males on campus, but I really wanted something deeper than that. Maybe I should have coasted through several short-term relationships with various people to help me through my problems, spend the weekends with, talk to about everyday events, or walk around the campus just like this. Maybe my plans for a long-term partner in crime wouldn't happen, and I needed to hunt for more temporary situations to get through the summer.

Our walk continued for over an hour, and circled us back and forth across the campus several times. Finally, I suggested we find a place to sit and rest. Since we were near the old crescent of buildings, I suggested we go to the old wellhouse and sit for a while. I didn't know if this would get me slapped or not; the wellhouse was a traditional make-out spot for couples for the last hundred years, ever since IU first became a coed campus. Either she didn't know this or she secretly knew my motives.

From the wellhouse's hundred year old arches, a half-ring of historical buildings lined up like a wagon train on three sides. The illuminated face of the old clocktower sat above the Student Building. Floodlit cobblestone paths led to the tall monumental Sample Gates through perfectly manicured grass, and carefully placed floodlights added to the moonlight illumination. A postcard image for 360 degrees, the wellhouse easily sported the most romantic view on campus after dark.

As we sat and looked over the hundreds of years of history and beauty, I reached over and carefully took her hand. She looked back at me and smiled as I carefully caressed her soft hand and held it within mine.

A moment later, she moved closer to me, and we both sat in the awkward moment, wondering what to do next although we both knew what we wanted to do. Finally, I broke the code of silence.

"Umm, I'm really awkward with this stuff."

"I know what you mean," she said. Then she lightly pulled me toward her, and I awkwardly pulled her toward me, trying to make the whole thing seem like one fluid motion instead of an awkward bumping of lips. I slowly kissed her, and we pulled away.

Suddenly, the Russians had pushed the red button, there was no turning back, and the President could only die, or die. Our lips locked again in a slow passionate kiss, but the passion wasn't on my mind. I was trying to figure out how deep I was getting involved.

An hour later, we stood at the door of my apartment, as I fought with the lock to my bedroom and wondered how bad my room looked. Running out of things to do on campus, we defaulted to my place, since she shared a room and the other two girls were probably long asleep.

After the short tour, I put on some relaxing music, and because she was still sore from work, I laid her down on my bed and gave her a gentle backrub. This of course led to more involved kissing, but things kept very soft and intimate, without an overloading explosion of passion.

From the kissing, we just lay in the bed and held each other, enjoying the closeness we found.

"Umm, I'm going to have to get you home sometime," I told her.

"No you don't," she replied.

"Do you want to stay?"

"Sure, I would love to."

"Umm, I don't want anything to happen though."

"You don't have to worry about that," she said. "I'm waiting until I get married."

"Really? Wow, that's impressive."

"What about you?"

Suddenly, I felt ashamed of my past experiences. "Yes, I have and no, I'm not. I'm sorry. I hope you don't hate me."

"No, no I don't," she said. I could feel the disappointment and tension in her voice. I also felt disappointed in a sense, but I also felt scared that I bought into something I didn't want. It wasn't that she was a virgin, but just that her religious and moral background felt so different to me, that I didn't know if this would work out.

But, I had a beautiful woman in bed with me, and I was tired. I clicked off the light, and curled up next to her, to try and sleep with someone in my bed again.

The evening together was magical, or at least as magical as it could be with two six-foot tall people in a tiny twin bed. I held her close all night, and neither of us thrashed around too much to complicate things. But the room kept hot, and we were both fully clothed, which made it that much more rewarding to catch a shower. I cooked her some breakfast, and we went over to her place so she could take a quick shower.

"You've got a lot of band trophies," I said. She was doing the customary beginning-of-relationship ritual showing of old pictures and other goofy stuff. I didn't mind too much, though. It gave me a chance to hang out with her, and see another side of her that could only be explained with a closet full of yearbooks and knickknacks.

"Oh that reminds me," she said, "I've got my saxophone here." She went to a closet of the room and started digging through it. She shared a space about as big as a studio apartment with two other girls, who were watching a small TV and talking about a night of barhopping while we sat in Jenn's bed. Just as it got disturbing, they both turned off the television and left for brunch.

"It's a Selmer tenor. I got it in high school." Jenn produced a battered hard-shell case, and popped open the lid to reveal a shiny gold instrument disassembled on a plush red velour liner. The instrument wasn't that impressive to me, after spent a summer plating real gold keys for woodwind instruments. What knocked me back was that Tammy played alto, and when we just started dating, she did the same presentation on me. Although Jenn and Tammy were radically different women, the repressed memory brought back an entire range of emotion about the old relationship. I thought something new would stop those feelings, but now I knew otherwise.

"Hey, what are you doing for lunch?" I asked. "It's a little late, but we could catch brunch at the Wafflehouse or something."

"I hate to say this, but I'm going to have to get ready for work soon," she said. "I'll probably get there a little early and get some free food."

"That's cool," I said. "What are your plans tomorrow?"

"I'm working at the gift shop from nine to five, and then I have the evening off."

"How about I cook dinner? I work at the telefund until a little after nine. If you can wait until then, I can cook Chinese."

"That sounds great."

"Okay, I'll give you a call tomorrow then. We'll figure something out."

I gave her a hug and kiss, and she followed me out to the porch, where I kissed her again. The farewell was awkward, since there were no pet names and I didn't know my boundaries yet. It was the first time I had to tell her goodbye since this whole thing started the night before. The boyfriend thing was pretty easy to pick up after a sabbatical, but the small details made it awkward.

On the short walk home, I thought more about her and the strange night before. Most of my relationships began in a quick explosion, just like this one, so that didn't bother me too much. But I did think that maybe I should've done more research first. I'd have to spend more time with her, or think it over a bit more.

Fuck, I needed to think of what to do with my day. It was only 2:00 and I had plenty of time to kill until my telefund shift. I got to my room, logged on, and thought a little more about some brunch.

"Dump her! Dump her now, goddamn it, while you still can!" Nick screamed through the phone receiver. I started our Sunday night call by telling him about Jenn. "She worships god and she doesn't put out. Hang on, I'm getting my car keys so I can drive down there and hit you in the head with a fucking brick four hours from now."

"Calm down, it's not that bad. We just hang out, and it's romantic, and..."

"Did you tell her you love her?"

"What? No."

"Did you agree to any kind of boyfriend/girlfriend thing?"

"Well, it's all pretty vague..."

"Oh lord Satan, you are fucked. I hope you have a CD player in the apartment, because you're going to have to listen to the first Deicide album 12 times before I hit you in the head with a brick. Are there any nudie bars down there?"

"Fuck, this isn't a serious relationship, Nick."

"Let me tell you about isn't a serious relationship. First, you probably aren't listening to Pungent Stench and Dismember when you're around her. So you've gotta listen to Bruce Hornsby or PM Dawn or some shit like that. Next thing you know, you stop doing the zine to make her Christian ass happy. You stop buying albums to take her to the movies. She talks you into going to her church. And that's it—you're some kind of zombie formerly known as John, and I'm trying to cut your head off with a shovel. Don't you have any doubts about dating some bitch that's saving herself until marriage? Doesn't that seem selfish to you? I mean if you were some kind of Jesus-loving freak who was following all of their rules, maybe she'd be the catch of a lifetime. But you're not. Don't you have your doubts about this?"

"Look, I have a lot of doubts about this. She can be annoying, there's the whole music thing...But she's hot, probably the most beautiful woman I've ever dated. When you've got that lying in bed every night, how can you walk away?"

"You dumb shit, would you buy a car you could never drive? You're going to call me up in a few weeks crying and all upset because she's still a block of fucking ice."

"Maybe I could convert her?"

"Dude, you may be evil, but you're not evil enough to do that. Dammit, I'm stuck here, and you have full reign down there, and you're dating Christian virgins. You should be elbow deep in two bisexual sluts right now. DUMP HER and I expect your next call to be from a woman's dorm, during some kind of blowjob ceremony of the black mass."

"Dude, it's not that easy to find women down here."

"Compared to Elkhart, it's raining whores in Bloomington!"

"Yeah yeah. Look dude, I've gotta wake up for class in like 45 minutes, I've gotta crash."

"I'm telling you man, get rid of the bitch."

"I'll see what I can do. If she's still around the next time you're here, you have full permission to kick my ass."

"That's all I'm asking of you. Okay man, I'll catch you later."

"See you Nick."

I hung up, and wondered if he was right. Nick went overboard with some of his discussions, but I'd trust his judgment better than any other human being most of the time. I guess I'd wait for a sign, a convenient place to exit. If it happened soon, the whole thing would be painless. Or would it?

I went to bed thinking about the whole thing, and still thinking about Tammy. I didn't get much time though—I fell into a deep sleep quickly.

The alarm pulled me awake at seven, the kind of awake where I didn't know where I was, or even who I was, for several minutes. I drank half a Coke and scrambled for the shower, a one-two combination that could possibly knock me back into the land of the living. The hot water coated my body, and I started to think more about my day—two classes, a four-hour shift at Lindley, a shift at the telefund, and then the dinner with Jenn. The logistics bounced through my head—when I'd get lunch, where I'd take breaks, when I'd shop for groceries, how I'd get around the campus. It wasn't any more complicated than some of my busier days last spring or fall, when I actually went to classes and booked a heavy schedule often. But that was a while ago, and this would take getting used to, especially with the 7 AM wakeup.

While washing my hair, I started to think about Jenn again. It always felt weird to me at the beginning of a relationship, how I would wake up and not entirely remember I was dating someone—it usually hit me a few minutes later. I went from alone and depressed to having a girlfriend so fast—I still couldn't fathom the idea of having a relationship again. I questioned if I was going too fast, and I went just as fast with Tammy, but it felt better. Maybe it was the religious stuff, the ethics problems that would prevent anything else from happening in the relationship. Sex wasn't the most important thing, but it would be impossible with Jenn. It felt good to have someone, but it seemed retarded to have to go through this. I knew that something would have to give soon.

I got out of the shower, threw on a pair of jeans and a t-shirt, and ran through the rest of the morning routine as fast as possible. Within five minutes, I had a pair of headphones on my still-wet hair, and was trotting toward Ballantine to make my 8:00 class. The brisk walk, along with the last Carnivore album, helped to knock the remaining sleep out of my head. In a minute, I'd be in the quiet and serene environment of a writing class, and I needed to be as alert as possible. I had a great fear of being incoherent and using the fuck as every other word in my classroom discussion, especially with this group of people.

It always amazed me how much I could get into classes during the first few weeks of a semester, even though I knew it was inevitable that I would stop going and screw everything up in a few weeks. Maybe that's why summer sessions suited me so well—by the time I got apathetic and lazy, I'd already done two-thirds of the work. Today, I was still ahead of the curve, going to both classes without incident. I simply sat in my seat, in a daze, and thought about Jenn and the evening ahead.

By the end of econ, I hit the door like a horse out of the gate, and ran to my place for an early lunch of microwave burritos and Coke while picking at my email. My schedule allowed about an hour to eat, sit around, and then rush back to campus to work at Lindley. I also tried to clean the apartment as much as possible, and wash all of the dishes I'd need for the dinner later. With almost no time to spare, I finished everything and bolted over to Lindley for a four-hour shift.

Summer shifts were never a real killer, although sometimes I'd get saddled with one person's extended problems for a few hours. I headed out of Lindley by four, after spending most of the afternoon working with a guy, a huge dissertation in WordPerfect, and some really weird footnote problems. It was an agonizing task, involving a walk through 400 pages of cleaning up hidden codes until things figured themselves out.

I hustled down Third Street, still fueled by the adrenaline of the busy day and the anticipation of a big evening. Even with no sleep, I felt charged up to get my shopping done for the big dinner, work my telefund shift, and then cook for Jenn. I wanted to see her again, and figure out if this relationship was really a good idea. Part of me was excited to make dinner, hang out with her again, and maybe spend the night with her in my arms. But part of me knew that Nick was right.

Before going home, I stopped at the Chinese grocery store on Third, just up the street from my place. The store suddenly appeared a few months ago, in a building that used to be a frozen yogurt place. I went inside the tightly packed warehouse of food items, and wandered the aisles of brightly colored packages, labeled with mostly Chinese instructions and some broken English descriptions.

Kroger's had better prices on stuff like meat and Cokes, and fresh vegetables, but the small market stocked esoteric goods I'd never find at a grocery store. And even though I'd only shopped there a dozen times, the people behind the counter already knew me. It made me wish I had enough money and patience to cook Chinese food for dinner every day.

I already had chicken in the freezer, so I assembled together a collection of fresh veggies, canned stuff, and packets of powdered sauce until I had enough for a decent dinner. I hope this goes well, I thought. I walked home with the bag of food, and thought about how much cleaning I'd need to do before I left for the telefund.

18

I got to work early, and parked the Rabbit in the gravel parking lot, way the hell out on the bypass by the university golf course. Although the IU Foundation had a huge, new building with tons of glass, fountains, and chrome, the telefund itself was in a brick structure that looked like some kind of abandoned Army Engineers bunker from the 1940's. I let Ozzy's *Diary of a Madman* echo through the car for a few minutes before shutting down the power. Jenn's going to eventually find out about my music, I thought. Nick was right—at some point, the gig would be up.

Inside, the rows of phones lay silent, like a battlefield before the fight. Steve, the fratboy program manager, sat inside his office. With the door shut, I saw him through the glass window; he had his feet kicked back on the desk, talking on the phone, and tossing a mini football in the air and back.

I ran down the rows, looking for my seat for the evening. They mixed the seating assignments every night, to put newbies next to veteran callers. It meant I got to meet a lot of new people every night, but it also meant I'd eventually end up right by the Steve's office, scared shitless with each call as he overheard my poor technique. Tonight's neighbors were some new guy, and...Carmen. Ahhh, this could be fun. I wandered outside, and started thinking about how it would be to work next to her.

When I went inside, Carmen was already sitting at the phone next to mine, looking through her deck of cards. I sat down, and opened my folder, pulling out my various notes and cheat-sheets. I sat next to Carmen the week before, and we flirted enough to make me think I actually had a chance with her. She looked a couple of years older than me, with long, curly brunette hair, and a somewhat cute yet introverted appearance. I imagined scenarios where we went back to her place to hang out and split a bottle of wine sometime. But now, I had a girlfriend. I might as well be honest about it, I thought. At the least, it might make her more interested if she knew I was a taken man. And then when Jenn split—I'd have a backup plan.

"How's it going, John?" she said.

"It's going. I want tonight to go fast," I said.

"Got big plans after work?"

"Yeah," I said. "I'm cooking dinner for my girlfriend."

"Cooking dinner for her? I wish I could land a deal like that."

"Well, we just started dating. Maybe she'll hate my cooking, and I'll be a free agent again," I smiled.

"I'll keep my fingers crossed," she said.

We continued to mess with our paperwork, before Steve came out and started the evening.

I put the chicken pieces and cornstarch in a baggie, and boxed it around until the little cubes of meat were coated with white. The heated oil danced in my trusty frying pan, a nice aluminum beast that always cleaned like magic, something I stole from my mom's kitchen. I dropped the breaded chicken in the pool of oil, and watched the brown syrup pop and bubble. I chased it with a few spoonfuls of water and soy sauce, and let things simmer.

Even though I was tired as hell from a long day, the dinner made me manic with expectation. I went to the sink and chopped the green peppers on the cutting board, and cracked open a tin of water chestnuts and a can of pineapple, while the chicken browned. Another bowl full of sweet and sour sauce also awaited the mix.

While one part of my brain focused on the timing of the chicken and the sauce, another part dealt with a pot of boiling rice. The only art to this procedure was finishing both races at the same time. I'd already tried to clean the place as much as possible, and make the place as welcoming as possible. Now, with all of the food ready to roll, everything would fall into place in a few minutes.

I heard the front door open, but didn't leave the stove to check who it was. A second later, Jenn poked her head in the kitchen. "Hey!" She strolled into the kitchen, and sat down at the table, smiling at me while I kept stir-frying. "What's for dinner?"

"Oh, sweet and sour chicken," I told her. It'll be done in a bit."

I tried to gauge the situation while at the stove, and felt a heavy tension in her silence. It felt like I was back with the rugby groupie, or any of the other one-night dinner disasters last spring. This time, I wanted to get out of there just as much as the others did before me. The closer I got to finishing dinner, the more I wanted to drop everything, run to my car, drive 250 miles to Nick's house, and take my I-told-you-so beating to the head with a brick, while I still had the chance.

"Okay, we're about done here," I said. I scooped the food onto plastic plates, and got her a Diet Coke I'd bought earlier. The food looked as good as ever, but I knew it wouldn't be an incredible dinner. She looked on, but still acted like I'd fucked her mother or something.

"Is everything okay?" I asked.

"I can't keep doing this," she said. "This isn't right."

"What do you mean? Is it something I did? The dinner? What?"

"I just...I don't know," she replied.

"Look, something weird's going on here. Is there something you need to tell me about?"

"I don't know. I'm just...I just don't feel right about things. It's not you, it's just..."

"It's not you, it's me. How creative. Why don't you tell me what's really wrong?"

"John, this just isn't going to work out. I have just been so worried, we are so different."

"What? You mean because I'm not a virgin?"

"That, and a lot of other things. You don't have the same beliefs as me, you don't want to do the same things as me, and we are just on different paths in life. I think if we stayed together as anything more than friends, we would tear each other apart."

"I don't think...." my head raced. "I don't know, in a sense I agree with you. I don't know."

"I still want to be friends with you. You've just got to realize, I just got out of a serious relationship, I'm still messed up from Gregory and I just need time alone to be myself."

"I know the story, you don't need to tell me."

"Are you saying I'm lying about this?" she yelled at me.

"No, I'm just saying that I've heard it before."

"Thanks a lot! I'm getting out of here. Call me when you decide you can be civil about this!"

She jumped from her chair, tore out of the room and slammed the door behind her. On one hand, I wanted to chase her down, and do whatever it took to get back the companionship that I wanted. I couldn't sleep with her, and I couldn't be myself, but she was a warm body to hold while I was asleep. I wanted somebody, a somebody.

On the other hand, I knew everything would be fucked if I did stay with her. At least I could live my life in peace, instead of taking cold showers and hiding my Morbid Angel albums every time she came over. And I still had hot Chinese food waiting for me at the table. I'd be okay.

I spent Tuesday recovering, struggling through school and work like a zombie. I wouldn't miss Jenn, but I'd miss having a girlfriend. I got to the telefund early, and talked to Carmen for almost twenty minutes before our shift. We sat on the grass behind the cinderblock office, looking at the golf course and talking about everything and nothing. I told her about Jenn, and the stupid breakup. I got back the "I'd never dump a guy who cooked for me" line. Maybe someday I'd have my chance with her. Maybe this down cycle wouldn't be bad after all.

On Wednesday, I skipped econ and headed to the IMU to find a free computer. I'd need to get a bite to eat and run to a training session at Lindley Hall, so I wanted a few minutes on a Mac without waiting in the lines at Ballantine. I rushed in the lab, and saw many empty seats, and many beautiful women. Someone was looking out for me, I thought.

I sat down at a computer, and fired up connections to Rose and Bronze. Before I could even do a who on Rose, Abby bitnetted me a "hey hormone boy, are you sleepy today?" I bitnetted back "yeah—rough week on the woman front." Then I did a who—she was at IP 129.79.110.2, and my IP was 129.79.110.1.

What the fuck? I turned to my left, and there was Abby, laughing her ass off at me.

"Don't you remember what I look like?" she said.

"Like I said, rough week. Me and Jenn broke up."

"Is that the one you were dating for like 15 seconds? I left my hormone boy cheat sheet at home."

"Yeah, yeah..."

"So did you give her the time? Do the deed? Give the dog a bone? Please tell all, I have a bet with my brother riding on this."

"My path to first base was obscured by the entire Catholic church..."

"You mean John Conner, unholy servant of Satan was dating a religious girl? This is rich. I'm glad you got out when you did."

"Yeah, I guess I am too," I said. "Hey, do you want to go get something to eat? I've gotta get some lunch and then go play UCS consultant."

"Nah, I'm supposed to meet my cousin in a minute."

I took a quick look at Bronze—six sub requests, six sub request taken messages, and a message from Abby saying she was in the union.

"Hey, aren't you going to answer that mail?" she bitnetted me.

"Yeah, yeah. I'll get to it. So how's your hot romance with Gartman?" I asked. Gary Gartman was a guy stalking about half of the women on campus. Normally, I didn't care about shit like this, except he was harassing almost all of my female friends. Plus he gave VAX-scammers like me a bad name.

"I haven't shown you that mail yet?" she said. "Lemme forward it to you." She looked through her old received mail, and bounced a message to me. "This one is classic Gartman."

A second later, I got the message on Bronze, and checked it out:

> From: IUGATE::GGARTMAN 4-MAY-1992 17:24:56.67
> To: AWAGNER@ucs.indiana.edu
> CC:
> Subj:
> I saw you yesterday in Teter. I was disappnted with your looks and thought that your rude comments about me were excessive.
> You really pissed me off!!!!
> I followed you to collins with the blond haired consultant. I waited outside in my car until you came back out. I followed you to Willkie. Today I found out what room you live in and walked around on your floor. I really love women. I passed by your room and you were not home and someone said you were doing laundry. I was hoping to get to know you a little better. I really hope you are not dating that fucking consultant because I feel that it is our destiny to be together.
>
> Gary
>
> P.S. Maybe we could get together and talk about Star Trek.
> You look like a Trekkie ,and if your not I'm sure you will learn to appreciate Star Trek AND me!!!!!

"That's primo stuff," I said. "I think he really, really loves you. Hang onto this one."

"Yeah, I think I'm going to renounce all worldly possessions and join his harem."

"You're a gem, Abby. Hey, I'm gonna split. Thanks for the pop-in."

"No problem hormone boy. I hope you are up to full speed soon. You know I'm leaving for Montana on the 7th."

"Shit, I almost forgot about that." Abby told me about the summer excursion to a geology field camp, but I never remembered the date.

"I hope you can survive without me. I'll try to send a postcard or something."

"You're irreplaceable, but I'll hang in there. Catch you later Abby."

I left the IMU, and went to Kirkwood to grab a slice of pizza.

After a quick lunch, I went to Lindley with an hour to spare, in hopes of spending a few minutes at a SPARCstation before work. I wasn't really working—I was testing, sitting through training classes. Some of the senior consultants wrote orientation classes for the next fall's incoming consultant pool. This week, they were running through the classes in labs full of other consultants. Everyone would walk through the steps, make their comments and suggestions, and debug the training material. For our trouble, we'd get paid to sit through the 90-minute sessions. Today, I'd be sleeping through an advanced WordPerfect 5.1 class, and hoping for brownie points because I signed up with almost no notice.

I went down to the consultant's hole to see who was working. When I got there, I found Peg, the manager in charge of public facilities. She said, "John, do you have a second?" and motioned me to her small office.

"Sure, what's up?" I asked.

"I was wondering if you could help out with a project outside of public facilities," she said. "Mark Osborn is looking for people to test the new machine setups for System 7 and Windows 3.1 that will be rolled out in the labs soon. You'd need to go to different machines on campus, rebuild them with a new OS, and test applications on the server for problems. Does that sound like something you'd be interested in helping with?"

"Yeah, sure," I said. "What's the timeframe?"

"You'd need to start as soon as possible. It would involve 30 hours of testing before the 17th, and you set your hours."

"That's fine. I'll start today."

"Great. I was hoping to find something for you—I feel bad that you worked so hard last year, and we couldn't get you on the schedule during first session. How are your shifts doing?"

"Quiet. I've been keeping at the Macs in Fine Arts, and trying to learn more about PhotoShop."

"I'm hoping to put you in Lindley for most of your shifts next fall. I think you'd be a great addition here."

"I'd love to," I said. "This is my favorite place to work."

"Oh, here's the information for the beta testing." She wrote down a name, number and email on a piece of paper, and handed it to me. "Let me know how it goes," she said.

"Okay, thanks again."

8:00 PM. I waited in the IMU, trying to think of a way to kill four hours before the fountain. A lot of the regulars were all on the VAX tonight: Bill in Lindley, Alex and Renee in the B-school, Brecken at Woodburn, and even Abby popped in for a few minutes, back home in Jeffersonville. I fired off an occasional bitnet to Bill, but stuck to reading Usenet news and knocking around a few ideas for an English paper.

I got a message from Rick Thompson, a guy who Bill knew that had started writing me a few days before. I knew he was a scammer from way back, just like me—we even had some common targets.

"Hey man," he said. "How's the union tonight?"

"Same old shit," I said. "Just waiting for midnight."

"You gonna be there for a while? I'll stop over."

"Yeah, sure," I said. I had no idea what to expect of him, but thought the encounter could be interesting.

"Okay man, see you in a bit."

I got back to the boredom, and forgot that he was going to stop in. I hammered away at this paper on metaphors. It wasn't a real paper—you had to rewrite a series of paragraphs using metaphor, and again with simile. Some of them snapped right onto the screen, but I had to struggle with others. It felt good though, like solving a puzzle.

"Hey, Conner?" I looked up and saw Rick had sat down next to me. "I'm Rick, good to meet you." He extended his hand and I shook it. He was an inch or two taller than me, but way thinner and well-built, with a chiseled face and a short blonde crewcut. Between his looks and his North Carolina accent, he reminded me of one of those Navy test pilot guys in *The Right Stuff* or something.

"Good to meet you, man."

He fired off a connection to Jade, and did a who. "Hey, you eat supper yet?" he said. "I'm starving."

"Not really," I said. I'd eaten a burrito around four, but realized I'd be ravenous by midnight. "I could use some food, too."

"You want to go catch something to eat?"

"Yeah sure, let me save this shit, then we'll take off."

After logging out, we walked to his car, in the lot on the corner of Seventh and Woodlawn—a brown, two-door Rabbit, about the same year as mine but in much better shape.

"Nice car," I said. "That silver one over there is mine."

He laughed. "Yeah, you can beat the hell out of 'em, but don't pick up your date in it."

"I know what you mean," I said. "At least yours is a two-door. That's a minor step up."

He unlocked the car and we climbed in. "What are you in the mood for? Miami Subs sound cool?"

"Yeah, let's head out there."

He fired up the engine—gas, not diesel, and the tape player jumped to life with Rush's *Moving Pictures*.

"You into Rush?" he asked.

"Shit man, I've got all their albums. I saw them on the *Hold Your Fire* Tour in Chicago."

"That must've kicked some ass." He gunned the car out of the lot and down Seventh. "I've never seen them live."

"The sound was kind of fucked up in Rosemont Horizon, like it was inside a big oil drum. But they always put on a good show."

Rick navigated the car around Showalter fountain and kept going east, through the middle of the campus. The sub place was over near the mall, a few minutes away. They stayed open late enough for us to grab some food and a drink before the fountain.

"Hey, I heard you met Steph Davis," he said.

"Shit man," I said. "I met her all right." Steph was one of my failed dates from last spring. "Fuck! It was one of those deals where I was going to get dinner, and then she's there inviting herself along, so I pick the bitch up and she starts waffling about where to go. I know no matter where the fuck we go to get food, she's gonna bitch about it, so I dragged her to BW3 and got the hottest, greasiest, messiest chicken wings—the kind you have to eat with your hand and get shit all over. It was a real horrorshow."

"Shit man. I met her a couple of times. She was all over me, but that whole virgin Jewish princess virgin thing hits all the wrong buttons."

"You think she's really a virgin?"

"She's so clueless, she has to be."

"Can she suck the chrome off a trailerhitch and sit back with a beer? To me, that's a lady," I said. We both laughed at the Andrew Dice Clay quote.

"So you're into Dice too?"

"Yeah, from way back," I said. "I need to pick up his new one."

"So you got any other VAX babes going on?"

"Not really," I said. "Lots of emails, but I haven't hooked up with anyone since last spring."

"You know Erin Miller, EMILLER?"

"No. I think I've seen the name, but that's it."

"She's pretty cool," he said. "I've been talking to her a lot. She might be into your shit, you should drop her a line. I think she has a boyfriend, but she's always on the VAX, sending me weird shit."

"Cool, I'll write her later," I said.

We pulled into the parking lot of the new restaurant, which used to be a Rax, but was gutted and redone in some kind of corporate Miami white-and-pink flamingo bullshit. It looked like a homosexual White Castle, but the food was good, fast, and relatively cheap.

We shuffled inside, and ordered from the Hawaiian-shirt wearing crew. I got the gyros plate, and Rick got some kind of super-burger, with bacon and tons of other toppings. We rustled up a table to deposit our pink trays full of food and sit down.

"Man this food is really good, but I'm not sure about this place," he said.

"Yeah, I mean it's the most food I can get for six bucks anywhere in town, but it looks a little too happy. I miss the Rax."

"No shit," he said.

We both dug into our food, and he was right—the gyros were the best I'd ever eaten.

"So, no other prospects lately?" he asked.

"Shit man, I just went through the weirdest fucking relationship of my life, if you want to call it that. The whole thing only lasted a couple of days."

"What, one night stand? Several night stand?"

"Not even. Some chick I met off of the computer. I wasn't talking to her much, then we met, and the next thing you know, we're all attached and everything."

"That's fucked up man. Did you at least get any out of it?"

"No, this chick was really religious. It was a bad scene."

"Fuck, man, I'm sorry. How the hell did that happen?"

"I don't know. It just got below my radar. Luckily, it all went by fast. Met her on Saturday, broke up on Monday."

"That's cool. Was she cute?"

"That's the worst of it—she actually wasn't bad. Really tall, as tall as me, cute face, big tits. Waiting until she gets married."

"What a waste, man. At least you learned your lesson."

"Yeah, I'm gonna start asking more questions up front," I said.

I ravenously tore through my food, and got another refill on my Coke from the self-serve dispensers at the counter. Rick also finished his food quickly, and we sat in the almost-empty restaurant, trying to think of our next plan.

"Hey man, what time is it?" he asked.

"Almost ten," I said. "Two more hours."

"Shit, let's go back to the lab and see if we can bother anyone else."

"Sure thing man." I dumped my tray of garbage in the trash, and followed him out to the car. I didn't know where the evening would lead me, and I imagined it would be just as slow and boring as my own efforts to kill time. But at least it would be fun to hang out with Rick more. I regretted the fact that I didn't have more male friends on campus, but now I could talk to someone who knew about being single on the big campus as well as I did. This could work out handy, I thought.

The next day was computer testing day, and I spent most of it staring at PC monitors. A dot appeared on the screen every few seconds, telling me that the clunky box of a 386 was a moment closer to downloading all of the crap it needed from the network to start Windows 3.1. I didn't know how the hell they'd pull this off, especially when the network performance took a nose-dive during the school year. The performance of Windows didn't impress me—years on a Mac made the clunky Microsoft interface seem like a joke, and with the number of random DLL errors I logged during my simple tests, it also seemed way more unstable. Oh well, I thought, at least I'm getting paid to wait.

The claustrophobic Woodburn 211 lab looked as medieval as the rest of the castle-like building. I hid in the back row, with a wall of windows behind me, overlooking Seventh Street. On a second computer, my usual connections to Rose and Bronze sat idle inside Clarkson Telnet sessions. So much for Windows multitasking.

Windows booted, and I dug around the system for a minute, and then exited. I didn't need to test things in much detail—just that the applications were there and could find all of their files. After I quit Windows, I got kicked back to the familiar DOS menu that appeared on all of the PCs on campus. I went through the list, and booted the next application to check it for problems. While the computer churned and grunted, I checked for new mail on the other machine.

A few minutes later, I finished my checklist for this model of PC. From a manila envelope, I found my rebuild disk, slammed it in the drive, and gave the machine a three-finger salute of Control-Alt-Delete. The machine lobotomized itself, and reinstalled all of the software from a server while I finished my paperwork. My last test machines were ones not on campus yet—I'd have to go to the Wrubel Computing Center and try them at the network lab. I logged out, and walked home to get my car.

The Wrubel Computing Center sat at Tenth and the Bypass, vaguely near the mall. Once an elementary school, the building now housed the offices of many full-time UCS employees, along with a ludicrous amount of technology. All of the VAXcluster lived in a huge machine room, along with Bronze, Silver, and all of the other central systems machines. Miles of network cable terminated in the building, hooked up to millions of dollars of routers, switches, modems, and the campus network backbone. Almost all of the full-time code hackers, policy makers, administrators, and people in the know lived in a sea of cubicles within the walls of Wrubel.

I knew a few people inside UCS, and got to wander the halls a handful of other times. The machine room's white walls, halon fire extinguishers, raised floors, and humming equipment reminded me of the most high-tech sci-fi film set you could imagine—like the part of the ship in 2001 where they stored the spacesuits. Most people never understood that a

VAX login went across the wire to a big beige refrigerator box. Actually standing in front of the machine I used every day, looking at its flashing lights, and touching its metal panel felt like cracking open your own chest and looking at your own still-beating heart. My main electronic hangout, the DECstation computer that housed the Bronze node, was there, too— that DEC cabinet had one of those yellow diamond suction-cup signs on it, saying "Ultrix on Board."

I tried more than a few times to land a desk job after I started consulting for UCS. I wanted Ed Gray's old job, programming Mac stuff for the public facilities machines. I interviewed for it last spring, I hoped that I'd land the position and stay for the summer in style. I didn't know if it was Ed, or my involvement in Sid's politically tainted utilities program that blew my chances, but it still didn't feel good. I hoped someday to get a better job within UCS, instead of fighting on the front line of public facilities. Maybe someday, the projects and the brown-nosing would pay off. I showed up for all of my shifts, worked fast, didn't complain, and dealt with problems faster than many consultants could. Last semester at the library, they scheduled three consultants for the two labs every night for the slaughterhouse eight to midnight shift. Almost every night, without fail, I'd be the only consultant there for four hours, working like a soldier behind enemy lines with no weapon. At the Christmas party, the head of public facilities gave me an award for "Worst Shift of the Year" award, when I worked in the library alone on my third shift of my career, with a blown-out network connection, two dead printers, no toner cartridges, two dead VAXes, and two hour waitlists. Someday, putting up with that much shit would get me a good job.

I parked the Rabbit in the huge parking lot, and walked to the front of the building. The place looked more like a software company in Palo Alto or a set from a Star Wars movie than an educational facility, with long runs of glass and giant translucent portals at the front gate. I went in to a lobby where more chrome and black trim circled the waiting area, and the receptionist had a brand spanking new all-black NeXT slab at her station. I flashed my badge, said I was working in the network lab, and she pressed a button, popping open a door that led to an atrium.

It was almost like fucking Star Trek, how the doors worked in this place. Everything had a sensor, and if you were a full-timer, your photo badge had a tiny computer on the back, which triggered the sensors and let you into restricted areas. I didn't have a cardkey, since I was a peon and only worked in the labs. But I dreamed of a day when I could fire open the doors to the machine room and take a look at the VAX machines whenever I wanted.

The lobby door dumped me into a huge atrium with a high, domed ceiling and many loose tables and chairs, where people ate lunch or hashed out various computing problems informally. Right after I went inside, I ran into Steve Davis, the guy in charge of all of Public Facilities. A Randy Newman look-alike and overly communal and optimistic, he was very nice to me, which was a good sign in such a huge graduating class of consultants. He nodded a hello, and then vanished with a group of other high-end brass that I'd only seen on a stage during orientation day presentations. It made me feel like I'd just stumbled into a United Nations secret conference room.

My next task was to find the fucking lab. The whole building was originally made from an elementary school, so it had this weird, repeating fractal pattern. Then, most of the rooms were removed and replaced with a sea of cubicles. So I followed the right wall of the maze, and eventually found the lab.

The network lab was a collection of machines, routers, modems, phone gear, and other stuff that was constantly being torn apart and reassembled into test configurations, either to evaluate new equipment or find a new way to rearrange the old stuff. When I got there, two guys I didn't know were beating on a Xyplex terminal server and a bunch of rack-mounted modems, making them screech with a carrier connection and then drop back to dial tone again, over and over and over.

I found my objective: a PS/2 model that wasn't anywhere on campus except the dorms, which were closed for the summer. I put in my rebuild disk, and fired up the beige beast, while the two modem guys continued their quest and ignored me. After waiting forever (this PS/2 was the slowest and shittiest one in circulation at IU,) everything checked out. Easy money. I filled out the rest of my paperwork, sealed everything in an interoffice envelope, and left it there for Mark.

I wanted to find the VAXes again, but I was afraid of getting busted, or lost in the maze. Instead, I wandered back into the sunlight outside, cranked open the sunroof in the VW, and drove back home with a few hours to kill before supper.

19

The Fourth of July promised to be the glowstick jackpot according to Bruce and Chad. With the holiday on a Saturday that year, it looked like the virtual Christmas of the street vendor's life, and Bruce was prepared. Massive quantities of stock appeared at his office/house, which was now just an office; his family moved into a new place across town, leaving extra rooms for debriefing, storage and various staging areas. Because I suffered so much on previous sorties to virtually nonexistent county fairs, Bruce promised he would try to line me up with one of the top-notch runs somewhere in Indy, provided I could drive. He promised to pay for my expenses, and I even recruited Yehoshua to come along and work with me.

On Saturday afternoon, I fueled up the car and Yehoshua and I headed over to Bruce's, charged up with the idea of an exciting night and a decent cash reward. When we pulled in to the house, the driveway and street were overrun with cars. A huge crowd of people congregated on the porch and yard, overflowing from inside the house. The people ranged from college students to hippies to townies to make-money-fast types who responded to Bruce's ads in the paper. Chad was on the porch, herding in people. "Hey guys! Go on in, use the side door!" he yelled to us. "Bruce is in the back office!"

We snuck around to the side of the square bungalow and opened up the back door. Bruce had two Grateful Dead groupies filling out papers saying he wouldn't be responsible for any income tax they might have to pay from their profits. He had everyone sign forms saying they were independent contractors, so he wouldn't have to pay unemployment or Social Security.

"John! Come in!" he said. "I've gotta finish up with these guys, then I'll set you up," he said. "Go hang out to the living room and grab a beer, I'll be right out in a minute."

We shuffled out to the area that used to be a living room, which still had couches, chairs and a big-screen TV playing some unknown car race.

"Dude, where's the beer?" Yehoshua asked, slinking around the room looking for a brew.

"I think the cooler's on the porch. Get me a Coke if there's any left," I said. I sat down on a couch and passively watched the race, hoping for a wreck or a pit fire.

Yehoshua crashed on the couch next to me with a beer, and handed me a Pepsi. As we slurped from our condensation-covered drinks, I spied around at the gathering of people. Usually, there were only three or four of us at check-in, but today there were dozens of new faces wandering around cluelessly in the house. Bruce's wife tried to do some crowd control, seeing if new people had already done the correct paperwork. Chad and the other assistants herded people into groups in the yard, trying to explain how to handle the products and how to sell stuff and take money. I got up and saw Brecken showing a group how to keep the fives in one pocket of the apron and the ones in another pocket, and how to make change for a twenty. He was willing to give money and a bunch of a product to people who couldn't change a twenty without instructions. Incredible.

"John! Come on back!" Bruce yelled, as he poked his head out from the back room. "Is this your roommate?"

"Yeah," I answered. "Bruce, Yehoshua, Yehoshua, Bruce," I mumbled, getting out of the couch and walking back to the office.

"Nice to meet you, Yehoshua," he blankly said. "Come on back and we'll get you set up with some product and change."

We followed him to the back room, which was set up with card tables and tons of glowsticks. Hundreds of carpenter's aprons sat in a pile, and a large map of Indiana hung on the wall, marked with circled towns and scribbled notes. Two assistants also sat in the room, busily helping with the deployment of the army of glowstick salespeople.

"Rick, get two coolers of stuff from the basement and plenty of dry ice," Bruce said to one of the helpers, who quickly ran out of the room to follow the orders. "Okay John, since you've had all of these podunk runs lately, I'm going to try to set you up with something good. You guys know where Zionsville is?"

"Yeah, I used to live in Indy," Yehoshua replied. "Up on the north side."

I shrugged, "Never heard of it."

"Well, it's a suburb, and they're fucking rich up there, a real Mercedes and BMW kind of town, a bunch of doctors and lawyers. They have their own fireworks shoot, a real primo event. You'll have time to get a bite to eat and make it well before dusk."

"What's our clearance on this?" I asked.

"Somewhat unclear. The city didn't say anything against vending, but we didn't get permission for it. You'll probably be okay. If not, just do the usual procedure." He sat at the desk and pulled out two rolls of bills, and a clipboard. "Here's your starting change, here's the form saying I gave you the cash and the product. Sign on the line, men, and we'll get you on your way."

I looked at the form and saw we each had 200 sticks of each color, for a total of 1200 sticks. "1200? That's like at least 2400 bucks if we sell out, more like 3600 if we don't cut deals. Is that right?"

"You know it, baby. You'll probably run out. I'm giving you guys the cold stuff, just keep it on ice and you'll be fine until you get up there," he explained. The "cold stuff" meant that the sticks were not the type that you snapped and activated the chemicals, but were already pre-mixed and frozen in dry ice. After being removed from the sub-zero temps, they'd get warm in the July air and quickly light up. The disadvantage was that you had to cart them in dry ice. The advantage was that they were cheaper per unit. In big events, we used the "cold" sticks because we could sell them faster and not have to worry about holding time.

Rick the helper came up with two large Igloo coolers, slightly smoking in the summer air. "Here you are, there's 200 of each color in each cooler," he said, dropping the containers on the floor. "You guys handle dry ice before?" he asked.

"Yeah, I know the drill," I said. "Don't touch it, use a towel, don't let anyone fuck with your cooler. I can give Yehoshua the full glowstick 101 training on the drive up."

"You're the expert," he said. "Have fun with 'em. Hey guys," Bruce said, "if Zionsville doesn't work, here's a list of alternates you can try to hit." He handed me a small slip of paper. "If all else fails, try downtown. There's a big setup there, tons of people. We'll have other folks all over it, but there's enough for everyone. Now that's a city of Indianapolis venue, the whole street vendor license deal, you remember the game?" he asked.

"Yeah, I got it," I said. "I'll give you a call on the 800 number if we're going to head in there."

"Okay, good luck! I'll see you guys later tonight."

We thanked Bruce and ducked out the back door, dragging our big-ass coolers with the money belts in our back pockets. Chad had a group of five or six deadheads in the backyard and was showing them how you could make a pair of fake glasses with two glowsticks. "Hey John! Where are you headed?" he asked.

"Zionsville. Hopefully it will be good," I told him, struggling with the steaming plastic cooler.

"Yeah, you'll do okay. Give us a call if there are any problems."

"Sure," I grunted, pulling my merchandise to the VW. I opened the hatch, dropped in the gear, and hoped for a good evening.

With engine whining, the Rabbit chugged up 37, making the jump to Indianapolis. We already made our stop at the Taco Bell in Martinsville, and were well on our way north toward the 465 loop. At the copilot's station, Yehoshua fidgeted in the seat and compulsively shuffled and arranged the five tapes that he brought with him for the trip, spreading and stacking them on the dash. Jimi Hendrix currently wailed in the deck, playing a fitting piece with his rendition of the national anthem shelling and exploding over the speakers.

"So, do you know anything about Zionsville? Is that near where you used to live?"

"No way man, Zionsville is all rich Jewish doctors and lawyers and stuff," he replied.

"It's a Jewish neighborhood? I thought they only had those in New York and Chicago and shit."

"Well, it isn't really Jewish I guess. Maybe the people who started it were Jewish or something, I don't know. But it's all people who fuckin' play golf and drive Volvos and own a billion shares of IBM and shit like that. I used to live in the badlands man, we had a house in this slum that the police wouldn't even go into. It was great."

"Weren't you afraid of being killed?"

"I used to live in the middle east when I was a kid. Drive-bys and car bombs don't really scare me too much. Besides, we never had to worry about the pigs raiding the house for dope. I don't even think you could get the cops to drive into our neighborhood if you called 911."

We continued down the strip, the tall trees passing in a full-green glory. Since the last time I made the trip, the struggling late spring growth exploded with chlorophyll-induced rage, changing the postcard scenes to a new fashion.

"Hey, Bruce said something about a procedure if we have trouble selling. What does he mean?" Yehoshua asked.

"Oh yeah," I remembered. "Here's the deal. If a person asks you if you need a permit to sell glowsticks, be vague. Say something like 'in some towns you do' or even better if someone asks you what you have to do to sell them you said 'well my boss orders these from this warehouse, and I'm not sure about the rest...' Say that your boss does the paperwork and you just do the selling. If a cop or any kind of official asks you for a permit, you give them Bruce's card, which is in your money belt, and ask them to call him for details. If a cop absolutely tells you to stop, then stop. When he's gone, if you feel safe about it, start again. If they absolutely tell you to stop and threaten to take your shit, just say you'll stop and we will both get the fuck out and go somewhere else. But whatever you do, don't get arrested. And don't get your shit or your money taken. If we have to lose a bunch of sales or leave to prevent either of those, that's fine."

"That's not much of a procedure," Yehoshua exclaimed. "It sounds like we're selling pot or something."

"Yeah, well we aren't exactly Wall Street here," I said.

"Hey man, can we listen to some Dead? This is a car trip man, we're on the road. We need to break out some of the Dead."

"Look, I don't really like the Grateful Dead," I said.

"Have you ever listened to them?"

"No. But I don't like the culture, the whole drug thing and all of the mindless worship of Jerry Garcia seems like the Manson family with better marketing."

"Come on man, I didn't ask you to get in a van and follow them for two months, let's just listen to a few songs. It's good driving music."

"Okay, if it will shut you up, we'll listen to part of one tape. But then we go back to Hendrix."

Gleefully swapping tapes, Yehoshua took control of the deck and within moments we were listening to songs about trains and cocaine. The music was just a distraction to cover the exhaust of the car anyway, so I let him have his way for a while. I didn't really find great spiritual joy from the songs like he did. But it wasn't as bad as listening to country or rap.

With Yehoshua guiding the ship, we looped around on 465, trying to make good time before the sun began its descent and the show started. Our target sat on the far north side of Indianapolis, so we rode the loop to the maximum. Cutting through the city wasn't an option because of traffic, and we'd probably have to either go straight through the massive downtown festival, or take major detours on small roads and most likely get lost. We plugged away on 465, pegging the speedometer to make up for the extra miles.

Just before our exit, I managed to swap tapes and get some Black Sabbath going. We found the right offramp, and quickly went from the 85 mile-per-hour frenzy to a town full of one-story shops with intricate storefronts and old-fashioned signs framing the gently curving cobblestone roads. It felt like driving into a Disneyland exhibit on 19th century New England, except that hundreds of well-dressed thirtysomethings walked the streets with their kids, heading to a large, open field, where I guessed they would hold the fireworks shoot.

"Fuuuuck..." I said. "How the hell are we going to do this?"

"What do you mean?" Yehoshua asked cluelessly.

"I mean, look at us. Long hair, torn jeans, old t-shirts, how are we going to get into this thing without getting arrested?"

"Dude, we just have to act like we belong here, and if anyone asks questions, we will just fake it or something."

"I guess. We need to find a place to park first."

After circling around the main drag for a few passes, I found a spot that wasn't marked as parking, but wasn't clearly marked as being an illegal place to park, either. Convinced that nobody could get a tow truck in there in under an hour, I ditched the car and we carefully looked around before opening the hatch and pulling out the coolers.

"We shoulda got fucking permits," I mumbled as we walked in the crowd with the plastic igloo.

"Dude, they're just coolers. People think we have beer or something," he replied.

"Yeah, why is your beer smoking then?" I nodded down at the corner of his plastic container, which hissed out a gentle stream of the dry ice's white vapor.

"Far out. man! This shit's pretty cool!"

"Cold," I replied, "It's cold. And you better hope it stays cold until you sell all your sticks."

"You think it's okay? I hope I didn't break the thing."

"Yeah, you should be fine," I said. "Now let's figure out a battle plan here."

Still twilight, the walk with the crowd let us figure out where the action would unfold. A few paths crossed the field, with a couple of face-painting booths on either side, and a lot of open space for people with coolers and lawn chairs. I also tried to survey our crowd, mostly yuppied with kids. Married couples with the occasional Grandma and Grandpa made up the parental demographics, looking well-off and wearing expensive polo shirts on their days away from the office. The kids buzzed around, a good deal of them, and many already looking like they hit the face painting and balloon booths. The chemistry seemed just right, kids who wanted everything and parents who would buy it, and in a few minutes, a dark sky and nothing to do until the fireworks started.

"Dude, we're going to be fucking rich," I whispered to Yehoshua. "Okay, here's the plan. We'll split, each of us take half of the field. Don't get close to these little booths, but stay near the main fairways."

"Should I walk around?" he asked.

"No. You won't need to, they'll come to you, and you'll want to stay in one place so other people can find you. Once a few kids have them, others will ask where they got them. It's dense enough in here, you'll have no problem. I'll stay up here. If you run out or it tapers off, get back to me. I'll find you if I run out, so don't go too far. If it slacks, like less than a stick every few minutes, we'll get out of here right away. Bruce gave me some plan B's that aren't fireworks shows. This place will clear out fast, so if we get the fuck out before the bad traffic, we can catch a carnival or something. Another thing, sell all your sticks for $3 each. Don't go to $2 under any circumstances, and don't advertise 2 for 5 or any other deal, OK?"

"I thought we were supposed to."

"You do that at slower events, but you won't need to here. Besides, we are the only people here. We should both stick with the same prices. And if you sell everything for $3, you get more. Hell, we could almost sell for $4 here..."

"Okay, I'll stick to three bucks each. I'm gonna head out, I'll see you in a bit," Yehoshua said, hustling to the other end of the park.

"Good luck! And if all else fails, meet me here in an hour!" I yelled back to him.

Showtime. I quickly pulled the business from its stealth packaging: the money apron came out of my pants and went around my waist, and I cracked open the case full of product. A group of people watched curiously as the plastic lid popped loose and a cloud of white smoke rushed skyward. I quickly donned a pair of gloves in the lid, pulled a white chunk of dry ice, grabbed about a dozen of the worm-like plastic tubes, threw the ice back in the case and closed the lid. With a towel, also from the cooler, I wiped the flakes of frozen condensation from the sticks, and as their temperature rose, the phosphorescent color went from an inert clear to bright purple, red and green.

The sky was just starting to turn purple and red with sunset; perfect timing. I clipped three of the tubes into necklaces around my throat, and grabbed the other ones in hand. Like a multicolored torch, I swung the sticks overhead, waiting for business.

Within moments, kids and adults looked in my direction. The sticks glowed brightly with the setting sun, and immediately drew people like flies to a bug light. A small crowd gathered around me, and the cries of "I want one!" began. Fathers and mothers came to me with money in hand, not even asking the price until I handed back their change. The dozen sticks in my hand went out almost immediately, and I went to the cooler for a few dozen more.

At first, I sold in spurts, but the traffic at each hit was big. Families were buying two or three sticks for each of their kids. A bulge of ones and fives started to fill my apron, and things were going better than they had at any previous event. I still had enough time to look around a bit and check out the occasional hot lawyer's daughter that walked through the crowd.

Once the skies went from red to black, business picked up like a riot. When people realized they needed to get their glowsticks before the fireworks began, a circle of people five deep rushed toward me and my trusty cooler. "I want a red! I want a blue! I need two greens and three blues!" The requests rattled off as five or ten people all thrust money in my face at once. The cooler sat open, with scores of sticks in the open and a cube of dry ice resting under my towel on a patch of grass. I couldn't make change fast enough, but luckily I had fistfuls of one-dollar bills to quickly fire back to the people with fives and tens. My supply dwindled, but because of the sheer quantity we packed, I could keep up with demand.

The mob of people made me realize how Bruce could make enough money on his crazy enterprise, even though there were only a few decent months of carnivals and state fairs every year. I was selling the most useless product imaginable: a tube of glow-in-the-dark chemical that would dissipate in hours. But everyone there needed one. If I wasn't going nuts with the demand of people shoving money down my throat, I probably would've thought long and hard about how the country was falling apart because the people who had the most disposable income would start a riot over a glowing necklace. But I didn't have the time to think about anything except how to expedite orders and handle cash as fast as possible.

In the sky above, the first whoosh of a shell broke the crowd's murmuring, and wowed everyone as a gold explosion glittered the air. Everyone cheered for the first colorful explosion of the evening, and I tried to catch a glance, too. My huge crowd almost entirely vanished, but a few stragglers were still buying sticks. More shells burst, lighting the now-dark field with amber and crimson and indigo streaks overhead.

The rockets' red glare brought my sales down to a lull, and I knew they wouldn't pick up after the show. I dismantled my necklace and packed everything, including a bunch of dirt and grass, into the cooler. I removed my money belt, tightly folded it, and shoved it in the crotch of my pants. The giant bulge of ones and fives made me look like some sort of seventies gigolo, but everyone's gaze focused on the fireworks.

"Yehoshua!" I yelled, as I toted my plastic store in a box across the field. I saw him, still trying to sell a few sticks. "Come on, let's get out of here!" I yelled. "Pack up your shit, let's get to the car."

"Okay. Why are we leaving so early? I've still got some left." We sprinted up the hillside, and tried to find the car.

"This is a small show, the aerials will finish fast. When they do, people will leave and traffic will be backed up for months. We need to get the fuck out now. We'll sell the rest of the stuff at another show."

"Good idea," he said. "Where are we going next?"

"I'll figure that out in the car. You can read the map while I drive. Let's go!"

With the coolers in the trunk and the money in the cab, we tore out of the small village, with beautiful explosions of color visible through the open sunroof.

"Grab that map," I said, as I clicked on the dome light. "Are we near Lebanon?"

"Yeah, take 32 to 47 and we're there. Maybe 10 minutes." He turned off the light and folded the map. "What's in Lebanon?"

"There's some kind of outdoor public fair thing. The city sets up a bunch of shit, merry go rounds, ferris wheels, tilt-a-whirls. We supposedly have a go to sell there."

"We do? Don't we need permits?"

"Bruce's list says we're clear. He let the fair owner fuck his wife or something, I don't know." I navigated the car onto 32 and punched it. "How did you do out there?"

"Good I think. I sold maybe half my shit. I've got a lot of ones and fives, too many to carry," he said.

"Yeah, we'll hide a bunch of cash in the car when we get there. And I don't think we'll take in coolers, or maybe we can consolidate to just one. This will be a little slower than what we just saw. I think we can sell as many but it might take a couple of hours."

"Sounds cool. How did you do?"

"I think about 2/3 of mine are gone. Don't worry, if I run out, I'll help you get rid of yours."

Yehoshua quickly counted our cash with the glovebox light, trying to avoid mixing it together. "Okay, at $3 each, you've sold about 400 sticks, and I've done 350."

"That's 12, 105," I mumbled, doing that math. "Wait! You mean we have 2300 fucking dollars in ones and fives in this car?" I yelled.

"Umm, no it's like 2240 something. There's some twenties and tens in there, too."

"Lock the doors. Lock your fucking door," I yelled. "I don't think I've ever seen this much cash in my life."

"Man, it's no big deal," he said. "Back when my roommate was dealing..."

"Lock your fucking door!" I yelled. "This isn't our money to fuck with. Let's hope nobody's smart enough to break into this thing when we get there."

We made good time in the night air. Ahead, just off of 47, the neon lights of a large carnival burned in the night air. We got back into form, and exited the highway to the big event.

We parked in a huge vacant lot, which also seemed to serve as the restroom facilities. I skimmed all but fifty dollars from the belts and locked the remainder in the glovebox, along with a list of our sales totals scribbled on the back of a receipt.

"Okay, count up what you have left," I told him as he reached into the back seat for his cooler. We decided it would just be easier to each take a cooler and try to keep mobile with them, since the car was a decent hike from the fairgrounds.

On the walk in, we quickly sold the dozen sticks we each had in hand to some families who were going home for the night. The people weren't the same as Zionsville, though. The whole event seemed quite a bit more working class, which meant more work for us to unload the rest of our product.

Inside the fairgrounds, we split up to cover different territories. Yehoshua quickly decided it was best to hit people as they left for their cars, and I found a decent place to set up shop near the food stands. Business went slower, but it was still steady, and my supply slowly drained.

Just like any fair, there were a lot of teenagers walking around. I never understood who would bring a date to a fair, but this was the part of the country where it would get you laid every time. A few girls caught my attention, an occasional attractive woman showed up, but it only frustrated me because most women don't openly flirt with street vendors. The whole thing also depressed me because it made me miss Tammy, and the times where we wandered malls or shops or the streets of Bloomington, holding hands and gazing at the sights. It made me wish I could hit it off with some innocent, cute, redneck chick and have a girlfriend on my arm that adored me again. But I knew it would never happen while I was hawking glowsticks, so I tried to focus on the sell.

A trickle of buyers came up to me, and I made sales, usually one at a time. I walked back and forth, listening to Metallica's black album, which seemed to be the soundtrack of the evening; almost every amusement ride operator seemed to have a copy playing through their shitty PA speakers. Within a few hours, my supply finally ran out. I rejoined with Yehoshua and helped him work through the rest of his supply, but because the crowds were leaving, it took some more work. Finally, by about 11, we sold out, and got back to the car.

"Hey man, we finished a little early, do you think we could stop and see a couple of my friends?"

I wasn't so sure about this suggestion, but since we did work a decent night, I agreed. "Okay, show me the way. And let's lock up this money."

We lazily drove back to 465, but crossed the loop and went down to 31 and into the city. "Okay, we can take this almost right there. There won't be any traffic, because the downtown thing is farther down 31, and it's probably done by now," he assured me.

The car cruised down 31, past the well-lit mansions and riverfront property, set back from the highway by long driveways and much elegant landscape. After 20 minutes, Yehoshua went into navigator mode, barking directions that I followed.

Within a few turns, the stores vanished, and nice real estate turned to boarded up houses with high weeds and stripped out cars on the streets. The streetlights disappeared, and traffic thinned out considerably.

"Yehoshua, where the FUCK are we?" I asked.

"Oh, this is the neighborhood right by where I used to live."

"The neighborhood where the cops wouldn't go?"

"Yeah. Pretty trippy, huh? It looks like a warzone out there."

"YEHOSHUA?!? We have 3600 dollars in ones and fives and you're taking me through a fucking neighborhood like this????"

"Oh. Yeah. Well, we might want to lock up or something."

I frantically cranked the moonroof shut and locked the doors, certain I would be killed within the next five minutes. "Look, I'm not stopping at any red lights, I'm not stopping at any signs. If your friends live in this neighborhood, forget it, I'm not stopping. This is fucking homicidal!"

"Chill out man, they live up in Broadripple. It's way more cooled out. We can take the money in, we'll just be there a little bit."

"Look man, fuck this. We'll go see your friends when we don't have all of this money. I'm getting back on 31 and we are going straight back to Bruce's house. This isn't my money, this is a big fucking deal that I'm responsible for here. I hope you understand. We'll go back next weekend, you can spend more time with them and you'll have money to burn, too."

"Okay man," he sulked, "I guess you're right. Take a left up here, this goes on out to Meridian.

"I'm sorry I blew up, it's just this is a lot of money. Okay?"

"Okay that's cool man. We'll go another time."

Once we hit 37, I opened back up the moonroof and we zipped downstate in decent time, with stars above us in clear skies. Our check-in was just before midnight, one of the later returns but not as late as the people who went to Kokomo. After check-in and beer, we both cleared $150. As promised, we struck the glowstick jackpot with a vengeance.

20

"Shit, it's pouring out here," I said. Rain dropped like artillery from the midnight sky and pummeled the sidewalks and meadows outside the student union, with no sign of relief. Donna and I tried to find shelter, or an escape from the storm, with no luck. We slouched under the worn limestone archway in front of the building, safe from the attack of the late-night storm. The loud, percussive sound of so much rain slamming into concrete deafened me so much, I wasn't sure if Donna even heard me.

After a Monday night of studying and talking in the IMU, Donna and I were in the middle of one of our typical "What's wrong with John's life" discussions when the clock crept past the 12 AM mark and building security cleared us out of the building so they could lock up. Without umbrellas or any other raingear to keep from the downpour and our cars out of reach in the lot across the street, our only option was to wait for the storm to eventually pass.

"John, I wish you wouldn't get so down on yourself like this," she said, trying to continue the earlier conversation that I wanted to end a half-hour ago. I could now hear her over the rain, but I didn't want to. "Look, women are just evil. Look at me, I'm a woman, and I'm a bitch. Ask my husband, he'll tell you," she said. "Really, you shouldn't base your happiness on having a woman. Just live for yourself. You're one hell of a person, don't let someone else ruin that."

"If I'm such a great person, why do nice people like Jenn keep shitting on me?" I asked. "If I'm so great, don't I deserve someone to keep me at least moderately happy for some part of my life?"

We stopped the conversation as a stranger from inside the building made his way through the doorway. He opened an umbrella and made a Kamikaze dash for the parking lot across the street. The attempt failed, and we watched the heavy downpour tear around the nylon water shield long before he made it to the safety of his car.

"People like Jenn are immature. You get these girls that are straight off the farm who watch too much TV, of course they're gonna hurt you. There are a lot of other women on this campus who don't need fucking Beverly Hills 90210 to be happy. You just keep snagging these 19, 21 year old girls who don't know what they want out of life."

"I'm 21, and I know what I want."

"Well write it down, and in ten years, see how many items on your list are still important."

"I'm not talking about long-term goals," I said. "Well, maybe a little, but I really just want someone...someone who would sit in bed with me during storms like this, talking and joking and giggling. I mean, I want someone who really loves me, who respects me and puts up with my shit, but I really just want someone to be physically close to. Know what I mean?"

"So basically you want Tammy back?"

"After she left, I couldn't sleep. I physically couldn't sleep without her in bed with me, or at least knowing she was a block away in her dorm. The nights she was gone, I could still smell her perfume on the pillows, and see the clothes she left behind, and see her hair brush on the dresser and imagine that she was just in the bathroom and would crawl next to me in a few minutes. I've spent all summer telling myself she's not going to come back. She isn't. She's dating some other guy in Pennsylvania. Until now, I didn't think I could go on. I thought I would either spend my life as a hermit, or blow my head off."

"And now?"

"Even if I am desperate, and even if this whole dating thing hurts more than it helps, I think it's optimistic that I'm trying. I think its fair for me to look for someone else now."

"Yeah, it's fair for you to have someone," she said. "But just let things go at their own pace. Before you know it, someone will come along. You're gonna blow a gasket trying to find the perfect woman by the end of the week."

I looked down at my soaked shoes, and paused, struggling for the next word. After a deep breath, I continued.

"Look, I'm sorry I'm going off on you like this. I've been thinking about all of this way too much lately, and I think I'm just beyond the point where I can deal with this shit. My parents are right, I think I am too far gone to deal with life right now."

"What are you going to do?" she asked. "Let them lock you up?"

"No, if I'm doing this, it'll be on my own terms," I said. "I'm going to go to my doctor and see if I can get some more medicine, maybe talk to a therapist. I'm not missing any school or going home or anything. I'm hoping they can put me on some medicine to chill me out for the rest of the summer, so I can sort things out and start over."

"I don't even understand why you take medicine. Does it dope you up, or what?"

"It's more complicated than that," I said. "I was diagnosed with manic depression about two years ago. That means I go through cycles of mania—staying up all night, wild ideas, not being able to stay in one place at a time—and depression—total mind-numbing sadness and desolation. Sometimes it happens when bad things happen, and it makes them worse, like when I split with Tammy. Sometimes I get depressed for no reason, and then I think about everything wrong in my life, and magnify it until I'm miserable. With me so far?"

"Yeah. So how does the medicine work?"

"The manic depression is like a sine wave, the top half mania and the bottom depression. Lithium crushes the frequency of the sine wave, and removes more of the mania side than the depression. I never have serious manic attacks. It's like an aspirin—you take it for a headache, and it doesn't give you a buzz or knock you out, but before you notice it, your headache is gone. It has some side effects: I get thirsty, and sometimes my hands get a little shaky. But it's not like dropping Ritalin or thorazine or anything."

"So why do you want another medicine?"

"The lithium clips the mania, but doesn't do enough for the depression. I want to go on a straight antidepressant to pull back the depression, at least temporarily. I've tried Prozac and trazodone, and now I want to try something new."

"Well, just be careful. I don't like the idea that you're dealing with your problems by taking more medicine, it just doesn't sound right. I mean, I'm old-fashioned I guess, I don't really believe in it. But if you know what's going on, do what you have to do. Just don't hurt yourself."

"It's all I can really do. I don't have any other options right now."

The rain continued to pour down, glossing the terrain.

The next afternoon, someone went on vacation and I got a few extra shifts in the graphics lab, babysitting the big Macs and playing with the scanner. I got the lab early to check in and start my four-hour play session, and there was only one person hunched over one of the dual-monitor Macs, fidgeting with the scanner. I instantly recognized him, a twentysomething with short, greasy hair, a pair of torn up shorts filled with safety pins and covered with anarchy symbols scrawled in pen, and an old, never-washed WQAX t-shirt.

"Hey Sid!" I yelled. "You downloading porno, or just here for the air conditioning?"

He pulled his face from the monitor, looking up with a pair of Coke-bottle glasses that made his eyes look giant. "Hey Conner. I didn't know they let you work in the graphics lab. Can you get at the color printer?" he asked. His gaze returned to the document he was doctoring on the screen.

"No, they inventory that shit," I said. I sat at the consultant's station, took off my walkman and carefully rested it on the table. "Hey, what are you working on?"

"Some crap for the station," he answered without looking up from the screen. "I'm the acting General Manager until jerkoff gets back from vacation in September."

He referred to WQAX, a community cable radio station located in a small, dilapidated apartment downtown. I'd visited a few times, both to say hi to Sid, and to see a guy named Bill who used to do a six hour long Death Metal show twice a week. He let Nick and I visit once, and we got to select some songs and say hi on the air.

"Hey, you still into Death Metal?" he asked.

"Hell yeah! I'm still doing my zine, and I write for Cursed Metal too. I've had trouble getting decent CDs here, but I manage to find some stuff at CD Exchange."

"You want to do a show?" he asked. "Bill left, did you heard about that? He freaked out and became a Mormon or a Quaker or some shit, burned all his CDs and shirts and vinyl and everything and moved to Utah. I don't have any metal DJs except for these white trash freaks who do a glam fag metal show on Saturdays, and all of the cool metal labels are asking me why none of the unholy black Satanic metal is on the playlist. So what do you think?"

"Would I get to play anything?" I asked. "I mean, is there a required play list or anything like that?"

"Hell no. There are no other metal DJs except for those hillbillies and there's not even a metal program director. So you'd make up your own list, and play what you want. We get some new metal stuff, all of the new Earache and Century Media, Roadrunner, Black Mark, all that shit. You can play some of that, maybe do their scheduled publicity stuff, and play any demos or other stuff of your own."

"What about interviews?"

"Yeah, labels set up a few telephone interviews. We never get anyone in the studio, because we're so far off the fucking map, but you'd get to do some phone stuff. And if you can drag any local bands in the studio, that'd work too."

The gears in my head started churning. Full access to the latest Death Metal...I could review unreleased stuff for the magazine, pull in interviews, tape them, and then later transcribe them for the zine, plus work more with label reps and maybe get some free plugs for the zine.

"Shit man, how do I start?"

"Just show up," he said. "I'm filling in a lot of show time right now in the afternoons, and a lot of late-night spots are blank. We're running a skeleton crew because everyone is either gone or completely fucking apathetic. I can set you up with an eight to midnight once or twice a week. And I'll show you how to run everything in about an hour. Didn't you used to work at WIUS?" he asked.

He referred to the campus radio station WIUS, a more elaborate competitor to WQAX that basked in university money and student support. I DJed two or three graveyard shifts there before I realized nobody ever listened. "Yeah, I did a few shows there. I quit though, their metal director was sort of lame."

"Melanie? She's a real gash. I'm surprised she didn't make you play Skid Row every hour. Our equipment isn't as great as theirs, but you can do whatever the fuck you want."

"Sounds cool. I've got a lot of ideas. Do you get promo stuff before magazines?"

"Fuck yeah. We get advance CDs a month before zines get a copy, sometimes more," he said. "Hey, you doing anything Thursday night? Stop in and I'll show you everything. About eight o'clock. Wait, make it a little after eight, it takes a bit for me to get things going."

"Okay, cool. I'll be there."

"Hey, if you want, the hillbillies are looking for a sub for their Saturday show this week. If you get trained, would you be up for it?"

"Yeah probably, I never do anything on Saturdays. Let me think about it, and I'll let you know if it's cool."

"Okay, see you Thursday."

I went back to my desk, and excitedly emailed a few friends about the new deal. Forget the old, boring nights alone with nothing to do. My new life as a DJ had just begun.

"He said you could play anything?" Nick said. We were in another marathon late-night call, talking about WQAX. I sat in front of my powered-down computer, fidgeting with the case as we chatted.

"Yeah, anything. I don't have a playlist, and I can bring in whatever I want. He said they have stuff from all the labels—shit, you remember when we went there to see that guy Bill."

"Oh yeah, he was **awesome**! He had like every Nuclear Blast CD, but the GERMAN version of each one. And every UK Earache pressing, not the fucked up Relativity licensed copies."

"Yeah, and his **fucking** vinyl collection," I said. "He had more 7"'s than I have CDs."

"Shit, is he still around?"

"Get this—remember when we were talking about anally violating Amy Grant with a piece of furniture and he got all weird? Well, I guess his wife was religious or something, and he finally snapped."

"You mean he got all Christian or something?"

"Hardcore, dude. He sold all of his stuff for like a dollar and moved to Utah."

"FUCK! FUCK! FUCK! He had stuff I would've given my left nut for! He had Possessed demos! Pre-Metal Massacre stuff! FUCK!"

"I know man. But it means I'm in the driver's seat now. I'll be getting at new CDs before you will."

"Fuck man, I'm coming down then," he said. "What about this weekend? If I can get the day off Saturday, I could leave Thursday after work, and get down there at like midnight."

"You'd miss my Thursday show, but Sid said something about a cancellation on Saturday. We could do the show, hang out..."

"Fuck some sluts?" he asked.

"I'll work on it. You'll be sleeping on the floor again, so plan accordingly."

"I'll deal with the floor," he said. "The last time I slept on a floor it was with this crazy bitch I met at this bar, and my arm got completely fucked up."

"Yeah, I remember the drill. Wasn't she Catholic?"

"Yeah yeah. Okay, I work Thursday until seven. I could leave a little after that, and get there just after midnight. What else can we do?"

"Well, we could hang out a bit on Friday, go to Denny's for a midnight meal, and listen to some music back at my place. Then we'd sleep until noon on Saturday, do a four to eight time slot for the show, and then we can go to this place called Second Story, its a cool bar with live bands and shit. It isn't too bad."

"What kind of bands? Lame shit?"

"Actually, the band on Saturday will be the Dynamos. They're sort of a soul/funk band, they do a lot of James Brown and George Clinton and shit. They have this all-out brass section, and totally jam the shit out. The whole dance floor is usually shoulder to shoulder, with all kinds of hot, sweaty, drunk, half naked slutty chicks rubbing against you and jumping all around. I think you'd totally get into it."

"I'm not a big fan of soul music or anything, but as long as there will be chicks and alcohol, I'll go."

"Okay, cool. I've got to get out of here, but we'll plan for Thursday and go from there."

"Okay, catch you later psycho."

We hung up, and I logged on to send Sid an email about the Saturday DJ slot. I got a quick mail from Erin Miller, the woman Rick mentioned to me before. I dropped her a quick, stupid message earlier in the day, and she replied back with an even stranger message saying she had a position open for someone to be her slave boy, and I could apply. It involved unconditional loyalty, daily email, and occasional computer advice and bootblacking. I fired back an acceptance message, and added her name to my userlist, so I could start bugging her the next time I saw her. A quick glance at my watch showed 11:37—time to split. I powered everything down, and headed for the fountain.

On Wednesday night, I got out of the telefund, and drove straight over to the IMU, where I planned on meeting up with Donna and Carrie for a homework night. I didn't like studying with other people much, but I thought some group enforcement would make me get some more reading done. Besides, I wanted to hang out with the two of them, and they spent almost every night at the books. I pulled into the lot on the corner of Seventh and Woodlawn, and lugged my books up the stairs to the IMU.

I found Carrie and Donna sitting in the cafeteria, the huge area next to the bowling alley with partial wood paneling from the thirties, and a sea of small two- and three-person tables. I promised I'd stop by tonight after work, shoot the shit, and maybe study for a bit. Books and pads of paper already cluttered most of their desk, along with huge wax-paper cups of soda from the cookie shop around the corner. During the year, a deli and a faux Pizza Hut operated from the cafeteria during the lunch hour, but on a summer evening, it was just overpriced cookies and awful popcorn.

"Hey, sorry I'm late," I said. "What's your poison?"

"Calc III," Donna said. "Homework's due tomorrow."

"Is that required for geology?"

"Yeah. It sucks, but I could see why we need to know some of this shit. Geology's a lot more than digging up rocks."

Carrie scribbled across a piece of paper, then crumpled it into a ball. "God, I keep screwing up this problem. This is like my fourth try..."

"Hey, can you two watch my stuff? I've gotta go check my mail."

"You and your fucking mail," said Donna. "When's the last time you took a day off from that thing?"

"Christmas day, 1990," I said. "But that was a hardware problem. Be right back..."

A quick session at the computer didn't help me procrastinate much. My only new message was from this semi-anonymous girl who lived in a Jewish sorority house and teamed up with her roommate to send me all-uppercase bitnets and random mail messages at three in the morning. I could never tell if they were serious or just fucking with me, but I imagined them being very emotionally needy and turning to the computer when their entourage of rich boyfriends weren't there for them. Still, I played along—it gave me something to do.

Back at the table, Donna and Carrie were still churning away at their Calc problem sets.

"Anything worth mentioning?" Donna asked, without looking up from her book.

"Not really. These two Jewish sorority chicks keep bugging me, but that's it."

"You've gotta stop playing long shots like that. There are lots of other women in Bloomington, you know."

"Yeah, yeah..." I said. I pulled my Sontag book and notes from the backpack, and set up shop on the table. It felt impossible to read with so many people walking around me and making noise, but within a few minutes, I fell into a deep trance and started taking notes while Donna and Carrie kept scribbling away at their calc. A few minutes in, I checked my watch—still tons of time until midnight. Studying went slow, but at least it was constructive.

The next night was my first show at WQAX. Sid promised he would stay for about an hour to train me and make sure I could sweat all of the technical details. He scheduled me for Thursday nights from eight to midnight or whenever I got bored of it, and told me to decide on a show name. My choice, based on a Type O Negative song, was "Xero Tolerance."

I spent a considerable amount of time thinking about a playlist, and after dinner, I gathered my CD collection, demo tapes, and all of the fanzines I could find, and put them in a plastic milk carton crate. As I scoured my room for anything else I would need, thunder cracked in the distant sky, and a dance of large raindrops pelted the roof above. I quickly wrapped the carton with some plastic grocery bags from the kitchen, and loaded the car for my trip.

After a nervous and excited drive across town, I sprinted across Kirkwood from the parking lot to the studio building, and still got drenched by the heavy downpour. A slum apartment building housed the studio, a three-story tenement with a storefront dry-cleaner and solid stone walls. The interior of the building looked like an abandoned building from an action/adventure flick, like where Robocop's enemies held their secret cocaine factory. Spray painted graffiti covered the walls, which also sported kicked and punched in holes, and several stray cats wandered the halls. I quickly found the studio, just another door in a row of other rooms, except this one had a bunch of half-torn promo posters and large letters spelling out WQAX.

I opened the door, and the churning sound of the Misfits echoed from the studio. Inside the door, floor to ceiling shelves made of leftover wood held thousands of vinyl albums, which looked decades old. Past the vinyl warehouse, a large open area held two tape racks, and two large CD storage racks, containing newer media. In the middle of the setup stood a well-worn mixing board, surrounded by cablecast equipment, rack-mounted tape players and broken chairs. At the board, Sid flipped through a stack of 7-inch singles like a deck of cards, looking for some specific title, or maybe just something interesting.

"Hey, Conner," he yelled, looking up from the stack of vinyl. "Come on back, I'll show you how this shit works," he gestured.

Pulling up a chair to the board, I spied the equipment closer. A pair of turntables and some simple controls made up the main part of the console, with dual CD players and two tape decks resting on a shelf above. A large boom mic hung over Sid's general vicinity, and two handhelds on small stands sat facing opposite toward nonexistent in-studio guests.

"Okay, you worked at WIUS—our setup is similar except everything is a total piece of shit. Two tapes, two CDs, two tables, one mic. Ignore those piece of shit mics, I don't think they work or they don't work well anyway. You've basically got two ins, and you can punch the table, disc or tape on either side for the A or B in. Then you can use this fader to go from A to B. You've also got a punch in on the mic, and you can fade that. Plus this is a mic swap, you can go from boom to the telephone or both. There are in-studio monitors, you control those here, or you can go to just headphones, or either. And behind you is a receiver that picks up the real signal that the outside world's getting, in case you want to listen for clipping or any of that shit. Oh yeah, the tape player on top of it, you can use it to tape your show or whatever. I usually use it to cue tapes when I've got shit going in the other two. Got it? Course not. Just watch me for a bit, you'll figure it out."

Yeah. I studied the controls, trying to make a logical model of how it would work and what I needed to ask about to figure it out. I was sure I'd forget everything and blow up the transformer when I went on for the first time. Even though the equipment looked like it was from the early 60s, the setup looked much more usable than WIUS. When I worked there, they were an all-vinyl shop, with one high-end CD player and almost no discs. Sid worked hard to go all-digital media at QAX—there were dual CD players and a good number of titles available.

"Okay, here's a change," he said, grabbing some headphones. "I'm gonna do an announce too. Hang on..."

He quickly faded down the CD1 and clicked the mic back up. "Okay, that was some Misfits for you, hope you got into that. Hey, I've got Psycho John in the studio with me, from now on he's going to be right after me with his show 'Xero Tolerance', four hours of pulverizing, brutal, Satan-worshiping, corpse-fucking Death Metal. We gotta pay some bills, so I'll be right back. You're listening to The Beat House with Sid, on WQAX 103.7 FM cable stereo..." He clicked in tape2, clicked off the mic and unpaused the tape to play a commercial.

"Here's the Add Sheet commercial," he said, referring to a free newspaper of coupons that was carpetbombed on campus every Wednesday. "Sucks, dumb, stupid, bullshit, and required. We have to play it every hour or so. There's four different ones, the dumb mom, the queer guy, the slut and the old fart. Do what you need to survive them, make fun of them, satire them, sing along with them, play them right before Cannibal Corpse, but make sure you play them every hour."

After the change, I felt a bit more comfortable with what he did. We whipped through the station procedure as fast as possible, the logbook, the CD ordering scheme, the station ID tapes, the closing announcements, the public service announcements, and every other hint and trick. I' also carefully watched during his changes to see how things worked in practice, and tried to note proper etiquette and form. I knew I'd fuck up during my first hour on the air, but I tried to memorize enough so that it wouldn't be anything fatal, or noticeable.

"Okay, I'm going to close up my show, and then we'll get you started. I'll stay to watch your changes, then I've gotta get home before the old lady starts bitching." He already laid out a fresh logsheet, and a set of post-it notes outlined my closing procedure.

"Okay, that was some Ministry for you, from the 'Jesus Built My Hotrod' single. Hey, it's eight and I've gotta get out of here, so I'm going to hand you over to John Conner. I'll be back here tomorrow at noon for People's Choice. Lemme play some commercials, and I'm outta here..."

He clicked the mic and did a change to an Add Sheet commercial (The old fart, who whined about how he always loved pinching pennies for a great deal.) "Okay, it's yours," he said, pulling off the headphones and getting out of the chair.

Sitting down felt like climbing into an F-15 for a first solo flight. I obsessively adjusted and re-adjusted the phones and fidgeted with the mic stand to get it close but not too close to my face. Sid reached over my shoulder and clicked from tape1 to tape2, starting a station ID and promo, which gave me time to preload two CDs and nervously think of something to say. I tried to prepare my radio voice, tried to think of how to launch the first CD, then realized there were only a few seconds left before I went live. I took a deep breath and mentally repeated my cable radio mantra: don't worry, nobody's listening.

The promo tape jumped to life, with the voice of Jello Biafra: "Hi, this is Jello Biafra and you're listening to WQAX 103.7 FM. Why?"

Sid clicked over my mic, and I went live.

"Hey this is John Conner and you're listening to Xero Tolerance, the only underground Death Metal radio show in Bloomington. From now on, I'll be coming at you every Thursday at eight with the latest in underground demos, new imports, rare releases and some old favorites in the Death Metal and Thrash world. I'm gonna start off with a personal favorite of mine, this is a band called Nuclear Winter, from Elkhart, Indiana. This is from their 1988 demo, and it's called 'Asshole', on WQAX 103.7 FM cable."

Click from the mic, click to the CD, and I'm clear.

"Hey, that sounded okay," Sid said. "I'm sure you'll do fine. Hey, what the fuck is this band? Turn up the monitors."

"Oh, this is a band I was in back in High School with my friend Nick. Here check this out," I said.

I cranked the monitors, opening up the screamed lyrics by Lars:

> Anti, you don't like this
> Anti, you don't like that
> Die! Die! Die!
> Fuck you!
> Fuck you!

You're a fucking pig cock!
Fuck you asshole, get the hell out of my way!

"Pretty original stuff," he said. "Hey, I need to go, if you have any problems, just give me a call at home. Drop me an email and let me know how it went."

"Okay, that's cool. I'll talk to you later."

He left the studio, dragging a canvas bag full of records behind him, and I sat at the console, hypnotized by the pegging VU meters at the board. All alone, my show began.

After the Nuclear Winter tape, I dropped in my copy of Type O Negative's *Slow, Deep and Hard*, and faded into the show's namesake song. Then I went to the rack of CDs, to the right of the board. It stood about eight feet high, and must've held about 2000 discs. I scanned through the titles, and pulled things that I recognized: Dismember—*Like an Everflowing Stream*; Vio-lence—*Torture Tactics*; Immolation—*Dawn of Possession*; Massacre—*From Beyond*; Grave—*Into the Grave*; Deceased—*Luck of the Corpse*; Pungent Stench—*Been Caught Buttering*; Gwar—*America Must Be Destroyed*; Haunted Garage—the *976-KILL* single; Deicide—*Legion*. Fuck, they had everything! I didn't get halfway through the shelves before my song was up and I had to jump to the board, talk for a second, and cue up some Carcass. If I got paid for this, I thought, my life would be complete...

"Okay, that was Type O Negative, 'Xero Tolerance' from their first album. Still waiting to hear more about their sophomore effort, although they've just released a live album, which I'll hopefully get to later in the show. I'm John Conner, and you're listening to WQAX 103.7 FM cable stereo. Let's go to one of my favorite CDs of the year, and play some Carcass. This is 'Impropagation' from their latest, *Necroticism—Descanting the Insalubrious*, on WQAX 103.7." I cued up the disc while I was talking, and made the change like a pro. As the smooth, evil, Colin

Richardson-produced UK metal legends crept onward with their Grey's Anatomy-inspired lyrics, it bought me 6:19 to catch up the log and cue up the new Entombed album in the next player.

With the paperwork caught up, I had a second to really think about what was going on. I was running a radio station! During the rush of filling out things and stacking up CDs and getting it all ready to go, I was nervous as hell, but during the downtime, I got to check out the posters and equipment and CDs a bit more.

After the Carcass CD spun out, I got on the controls, and punched up the Entombed CD, *Clandestine*, on track three, "Evilyn." It started with a slow attack, which got progressively heavier after the first verse. The wooden floor vibrated with the pounding of Nicke Andersson's drums, and I wished I could do this every night. I looked out the window at the rain streaking through the downtown, glossing the asphalt roads, and thought there was no other way to listen to such great music, and send it out to others. The rain continued to sprinkle, and I watched it and let the CD play through to the next track.

21

I rushed back to my apartment after the radio show, with fears that my answering machine would be full of frantic messages from Nick, lost somewhere in the darkness of Southern Indiana. At home, I found nothing on the machine, so I launched into cleaning mode, and tried to burrow out a spot on the floor big enough for an unfurled sleeping bag and some luggage. Once there was enough room for a second person, I answered some paper mail for the magazine, and kept the phone free for any emergency calls.

This wouldn't be the first time Nick and I shared the tiny apartment for a weekend. Last fall, he came down for a few days, and got in a huge fight with Lauren in the mall parking lot about an MC Hammer album. And last spring, over Valentine's Day weekend, he rescued me from a deep depression from some transient relationship that fell apart right before the 14th. He snapped me out of it by taking me to see Prong play at a small club in Bloomington. After three or four hours of drinking rum, slam-dancing, listening to loud music, and checking out the women at the bar, I totally forgot about the other chick. It was also that weekend that, with Nick's help, I started the first issue of my zine. Cool things always happened when he was in town, and I hoped that this weekend would be no different. I told the telefund I'd be out on Friday, and I didn't have any UCS shifts, so we'd have the next four days to fuck around and cause extreme terror.

Nick said he'd hit town just after midnight, but I didn't hear anything from him at all. Although Nick harassed me for a lack of directional ability, I couldn't count the number of times he messed up fairly simple directions. Almost certain he was circling Atlanta by now, I patiently waited for his call. At close to one o'clock, the phone rang, and I dived for it.

"976-KILL," I quoted from Haunted Garage. "Two dollars plus toll, if any."

"My name is Dukey, and you don't know me..." Nick answered. I heard traffic in the background, like he was at a gas station payphone, or just off the freeway.

"Fuck man, you better not be in Elkhart."

"I'm in fucking Indy, on the south side by the big fucking McDonald's. I got a late start, and my parents gave me a colossal amount of shit. Anyway, I'm leaving here, just like the Motörhead song, and I'll be there in like an hour."

"Okay, see you then." I hung up, and went to the computer. I knew he'd be late—his parents were worse than mine, especially when he was in a hurry. I dialed up and checked my mail fast, then dropped carrier and waited.

Forty-five minutes later, Nick appeared at the front door, holding plastic grocery bags of junk food, clothes and CDs. "Fuck! I didn't think I'd make it. Help me with this shit, I'll tell you the story in a minute," he yelled from the front yard. We dragged two loads of stuff into the house, including his bass guitar, some issues of *Cursed Metal*, and plenty of compact discs.

Once inside, he scanned the room, threw down his last armful of CDs, and collapsed on the rickety computer chair. It looked like he just finished driving 20 hours, but I knew he had to work and put up with customers all day before he even hit the road.

I brought him a Pepsi I purchased earlier. "Thank Satan!" he said, quickly popping the top and downing half the can at once.

"So, what happened?" I asked, moving around his luggage to sit on the bed.

"The drive was easy," he paused to suck down more Pepsi, then belched. "I listened to about 40 Henry Rollins spoken word tapes back to back so it would go fast. The bitch was my fucking parents. My mom asked me 400,000 questions when I tried to leave, and then insisted on fixing me dinner. Since my dad was there, it took like four hours to eat, with fatboy sucking down beers and asking me when I would cut my hair and get a real job. I didn't remind him that he didn't have a job and probably only worked ten days in his entire life, and that was the grand total amount of time he's spent pushing shopping carts full of beer and three of everything. What the fuck's the deal with the stereo? Don't you have any Entombed?"

He knocked back the rest of the Pepsi, and I dug in the bedsheets for the remote and pressed play. In the deck sat *Clandestine*, the newest Entombed CD and the only album to ever get a perfect ten when reviewed in Cursed Metal. The tearing guitars crushed outward, filling our souls with the Satanic hate necessary to survive the world of darkness and go to Denny's for food.

"Okay," he said, dropping the can on the floor. "That's better. Some fucking Pepsi, some Entombed, no parents around, this is pretty nice. Now all we need to do is get some fucking sluts in here, and we'll be all set."

"The slut market has been pretty hit and miss, dude. I mean, I've been talking to a few women here and there, and they seem a little friendlier in the summer, but not much action lately."

"But you have friends that are girls, right? Can't you get them over here? If you can get them in the house, I can take care of the rest."

"Umm..."

"Come on, don't be such a pussy about it. What about food? My mom fixed about 19 pounds of meatloaf, but I missed lunch, so I'm still behind like two meals. Can we go to Denny's or do they just have an evil Denny's here?" Nick referred to any branch of a restaurant with poor cleanliness, food or clientele as the "evil" one. For example, if we would go to a hamburger place that wasn't very clean, was filled with screaming junior high kids, and had poorly cooked food, it would forever be considered the "evil" hamburger place and we could never eat there again. If a psychiatrist ever wanted to write an extended dissertation on Nick's disorders, they could start with his good and evil Subway list.

"No, this is a good Denny's, as long as you don't get there during the real bad post-bar traffic on Saturday. It can get a little weird then, but it should be pretty quiet tonight."

"Okay, let's get the fuck out of here then."

I stopped the CD player and we marched out to the car, to depart on a late-night mission of overly fried food and free refills on soft drinks.

Denny's didn't pull in much a Thursday night crowd, especially after midnight in the summer, so we walked in and got a booth in the front of the store with absolutely no wait. Our booth overlooked the giant wall of glass that made up the front of the store. It looked into a darkness painted by streetlights where the 45/46 bypass crossed over Walnut and College, the north/south roads through campus. The 24-hour mesa sat on top of a huge hill in the same territory as a bunch of hotels, motels, restaurants, and gas stations that served as the gateway to State Road 37. I think the Denny's corporation was too scared to put a restaurant right next to campus, or maybe downtown real estate cost too much. Either way, it served to isolate a small percentage of the weirdos, although every Denny's in the free world is a freak magnet, no matter how inaccessible it is.

A waitress dropped some menus on the table, and asked if we wanted anything to drink. "Do you have Pepsi?" Nick asked.

"Is Coke okay?" she asked.

"God damn it John, I didn't know Denny's only had fucking Coke. Okay, a Coke, with no motherfucking ice."

"I'll have the same," I said.

"No ice?" she asked.

"Whatever comes naturally," I said.

We opened our menus and started looking at the food. "So, is this Christian chick still around?" he asked.

"No, I told you she's gone," I said. "I raped her corpse and buried the pieces in the desert."

"She better be gone, man," he said. "I don't want you to be pulling any good-guy shit on me when some sluts appear. You need to be like one of those smart bombs they had in the Gulf War. When we're on slut alert, you need to be able to home in on a target twelve fucking miles away or some shit. A slut smart bomb."

"Yeah, yeah, just figure out what you want to eat..."

The waitress came back with the two Cokes. "Have you decided yet?"

"Yeah," I said. "I'll have the grilled cheese, regular fries."

"Okay, and you sir?"

"I think I'll have the steak dinner, rare, with a baked potato and a roll."

The waitress took the menus and vanished, leaving us at our giant table and control tower-like view. Every visit to Denny's reminded me of every other visit I'd made there in the last few years, and each table brought back memories of the previous times I'd sat there. This table reminded me of late-night study binges and meetings with other VAX junkies, late night meetings and Sunday afternoon brunches. And now, another strange memory of Nick and Denny's.

"So did you bring some demos for the show Saturday?" I asked.

He pulled back half of his drink in one hit. "Fuck yeah, I've got a lot of new stuff we can play. I really want to see what they have there, too. Do they have any way of dubbing CDs?"

"Yeah, I think so," I said. "We probably won't have time though. If there's something cool that you don't have, I can probably borrow it for the rest of the weekend and we can dupe it at my place. Nobody else plays Death Metal there. Well, sometimes Sid plays Type O Negative or Napalm Death, but that's about it."

"Did you know Type O Negative is releasing a live EP?" he said.

"Yeah, we've got it at the station," I said. "Sid was talking about playing it enough times to make sure the station reports it to CMJ as the number one metal song."

"Holy shit! That kicks ass. Is it any good?"

"I've only heard some of it once, but it's pretty cool. It wasn't really recorded live, though. And it's got a close-up picture of Pete Steele's ass on the cover. Other than that, it rules."

"Yeah, supposedly it was recorded in a warehouse and they added the crowd noises. I haven't heard it, but it's supposed to have a Carnivore cover on it."

"It doesn't, just a Hendrix cover, of 'Hey Joe'. Is Type O Negative playing a Carnivore song technically a cover? I mean, they're the same fucking band, just a different name."

"I was wondering that myself. I guess we can play it on Saturday."

The food showed up, and we ate like fiends, and kept at the waitress to bring round after round of Cokes to the table. While we ate, we kept talking about new demo bands, old stories, theories on time travel based on half-baked ideas from Omni magazine, the flying monkeys from the Wizard of Oz (Nick's favorite movie and book of all time, but not for the usual reasons—he had some insane theory that Edgar Alan Poe wrote the story under a pseudonym and it really had to do with some Satanic morality tale) and how you could fuck a girl inside a duffel bag. After a few hours of this, Nick paid the check—he paid for anything with a receipt, because his mom would reimburse him and file it as a business expense—and we headed back to my place by about 5 AM, getting to bed just before sunrise.

On Friday, we slept well into in the afternoon. I woke at 7:30 in a panic, and then drifted in and out of sleep for a few more hours. Nick slept like a log well after noon, but I had to get up and take a shower before then, because the heat and claustrophobia made any further napping impossible.

When I started to notice Nick stirring around a bit more, I headed for the computer. "Hey man, are you up?" I asked. "I'm going to turn on the modem. You want to take a shower soon?"

Nick appeared from under his sleeping bag. "Yeah, maybe a shower will fucking cool me off. This place is a motherfucking sauna."

"I never guaranteed AC, but the shower does help. There's towels over here, and you can use the shampoo and stuff in this bucket."

He rummaged through my toiletries while I dialed up on the modem, then stumbled into the bathroom. Ten seconds later, I heard a horrific scream, and Nick ran back into the room.

"What the fuck is wrong with your shower?" he yelled. "It looks like some kind of slime mold experiment. Am I supposed to stand barefoot in that?"

"Calm the fuck down," I said. "Just turn the water on real hot and don't touch anything. Didn't you take a shower at the gym with powdered hand soap and paper towels once?"

"Well...oh, that's right. Okay, if I'm not back in 20 minutes, just sell my car and tell everyone I died in combat."

"Sure thing dude. I'll be on the computer."

I went back to the bedroom while he took a shower. I knew I had a lot of time, since Nick typically spent an hour and a half washing his hair. On the computer, not much was happening, except for the usual sub requests and retractions. I also picked around on the Rose VAX, but absolutely nobody was logged on.

"I guess I survived." Nick appeared, drying his hair with a towel. "I don't see how you can endure this every day."

"$177 a month, and no parents," I said. "It's horrible, but I survive."

"What are we doing today?"

"After you're ready, we'll go catch some lunch, and check out the record stores, and maybe hit the computer labs for a while."

"Okay, gimme a minute, and we'll head out."

I logged out, Nick got dressed, and we hit the road to find a decent lunch.

That afternoon, we shopped for CDs and comics, drove around looking for women, and realized that except for the teenage skatepunks, Bloomington was pretty dead on a summer Friday. But things were still cool; I had the day off, we played on computers, wandered the campus, drove around and listened to large amounts of Death Metal. And I got to spend time with Nick, driving around in his Escort, just like we did every day when I was back at IUSB. We couldn't find anything to do that Friday night, but spent time talking about how the show would happen, and what we would play. The driving and searching and music and visiting of 24-hour joints continued almost until the morning, and then we crashed back at my room.

Saturday afternoon, we packed up our combined gear and headed to the station. When we woke up at two in the afternoon, rain already thundered from the sky, so I had to show Nick the little trick about wrapping up CDs and zines in two plastic bags. Between both of us, we carried almost 100 CDs and just as many tapes, so we took his car and went to the station.

Nobody was there when I unlocked the front door, which made things much easier to load in. I immediately powered up the board and monitors, and plugged in a Dismember CD through the studio speakers as we unwrapped the plastic bags and set up the CDs we wanted to play. The outbound rig remained powered down, and nothing was broadcast of the studio, but we got the place shaking with Death Metal while we took our time and joked around.

"Hey man, can we play any of these CDs on the wall?" Nick asked.

"Shit man, pull any of them you want to hear. We'll play all of them. What the shit, man."

Nick hurriedly scanned the rack, alternatively pulling Death Metal CDs and making fun of all others. "Hey, are they gonna know what we played?" he asked.

"No. I'm not logging it," I said. "Who gives a fuck? We aren't on the schedule, the hillbillies are. We can do whatever the fuck we want for 4 or 6 hours and not write it down."

"Cool. Oh FUCK! New Paradise Lost! We're fuckin' playing this!" He slapped the plastic jewel box onto his stack on the floor.

"Yeah, definitely—we have to play the last track, 'As I Die.'" I finished cueing a cassette, and stopped to think about how I'd load things for the start of the show. "Okay, let's try to figure this out. We only have one boom mic, so when we announce, we'll take turns. Later, if we fuck around with any in-studio stuff, we can use a handheld, but they're shit," I said.

"Okay, I've got what I want to play," he said. "Time to die."

"After the first CD or two is playing, we can talk about what to play next," I said. I'd never DJed with another person before, and was used to making the song-to-song decisions in my head. Making the playlist a group decision would be a new experience for me.

I ran down the yellowed instruction sheet that explained how to start the station after a shutdown, and clicked the large switches on the heavy equipment. The outbound gear surged with power, and the board lit to life. I felt like Han Solo firing up the Millennium Falcon, and I jumped in the pilot's seat, ready to hit lightspeed.

"Okay," I said. "We're transmitting dead air right now. Normally, I do a station announcement, then an ID, then a commercial, then we go. But let's do what we talked about last night," I said.

"Won't we get in trouble?" Nick asked.

"Fuck it. It's not our show, remember? Just get ready. On one," I said. I cued a CD, held it in pause, then hovered over the controls. Nick grabbed the boom mic and swung it right in front of his face. I raised one hand, with the other on the mic switch.

"Three, two, one..." I pointed at Nick and nodded, while clicking in his mic.

"AAAAAAAAAA MOTHER FUCKERRRRRRRRRRRRRRR!!!!!!!!!!!!"

I slammed the CD to play, cut the mic, cranked the fade to max and felt the concussive attack of the Dismember CD rip the walls off the studio. The entire room shook from the monitors, the VU needles slamming into the red.

"Now that's a way to start a fucking show!" I yelled over the bloodtearing guitar attack, both of us laughing.

The show plunged into chaos with more extreme metal from Nick's CD collection. Between tracks, we joked, did fake commercials, and changed our names constantly. We did a fake interview where Nick impersonated both Ice-T and the gangsta terrorist that broke into the studio to kill him. The two of us impersonated many more celebrities. With me as Anton LaVey, praising Satan and telling people to send in their virgin children and Nick pretending to be Jon Bon Jovi, telling the world that he really liked little boys, we did some seriously defaming activities. Plus, we played no commercials, and did IDs like "WQAX, Bloomington's only radio station in full support of state-run genocide" and "WQAX, we fuck the corpses of the dead."

After four hours, the game bored us and we wanted to get out to the bars to see some bands, and hopefully some women. We tore the station from the air without a signoff, packed up our CDs and went back to the rain and the car.

A few hours later, we sat at the bar in Second Story, my favorite small club. The place was right above the big gay bar in Bloomington, but it was more of an alternative-scene place, with a lot of grunge bands, or weird stuff like Latin, Salsa, Irish music, and anything that didn't fit in the mainstream places. The people there were much cooler than those at the typical college-town sports bars, and it didn't feel like as much of a meat market, which meant the women there were much more comfortable talking to you. Many of the regulars were people I knew from my old dorm a few years ago, and I regularly ran into people I hadn't seen for years, something that never happened at the big fraternity-type hangouts.

We sat by the bar, and I nursed a bottle of beer while Nick dumped back a Pepsi from a clear plastic cup. The band was setting up cables and amps and getting ready for a set, while people filtered in and started lining up by the stage or situating at the dozen or so tables in the far end of the club.

"This place doesn't seem too bad," Nick said. "Lots of chicks, at least."

"I told you, it's pretty laid back. But once these guys start playing, it'll get pretty wild," I said.

We both scanned the crowd, and I spotted a decent crop of females there, dressed in shorts and tight tanktops. I liked the tanktops—they left the neck and the arms bare, showing a little bit of the back while hugging the figure tight. The temperatures in Second Story got hot most nights, and the crowds dressed accordingly—a plus.

Soon, roadies and a few members of the band came out, plugged in their gear, and started with the initiation rite of pounding the drums one by one and checking each guitar and mic. After a few minutes of soundcheck, everyone filed on stage and a mix of applause and cheers started from the few dozen people on the dance floor.

The Dynamos had an ever-changing cast of members, but tonight there seemed to be a drummer, two guitar players, a bass player, a piano player, a percussionist, the singer and five people with horns of various sizes. They all climbed to their places on the small stage, took a bow, and then jumped right in with a fast funk chart, pounding out some cool rhythms. The drums kept up a beat as the percussion player, a freaky guy with long hair, no shirt and a stoned look on his face, shook around some maracas. The bass player, a hip black cat with a bald head and sunglasses, jumped around, slapping and popping his five string all over the arrangement and smiling back to the crowd. The two guitar guys, a younger Van Halen type kid and an older white blues guy, traded back and forth, filling the holes with speedy soloing and solid blues-box foundations. In the meantime, the wall of brass pounded out over the dance floor, hammering the chart in unison like a quartet of steelworkers firing out raw ore.

The crowd all but abandoned their tables and rushed the dance floor, all kinds of people jumping around, hands in the air, beers spilling, feet all over the place, one big human mass.

"Come on man, finish your drink! We gotta get the fuck out there!" I said, slamming back the rest of my second beer.

"Okay, okay," Nick said, pitching the plastic cup.

By the time we pushed through the crowd, the first number finished and the singer came up to the mic, an older cool black cat dressed in a slick zoot suit. "All right, Second Story, let's get rollin' with something you all know from my friend Wilson. One two three!" The band tore into a funked up chart I recognized immediately, Wilson Picket's "Land of a Thousand Dances."

We slammed onto the floor to do the alligator, or at least try. Within moments the cat needed someone to say it one more time, and we all sung along. The sax player tore through the solo at light speed, then broke off to leave the drums, the singer, and a bunch of people on the dance floor singing.

The temperature rose, the alcohol flowed, and the place moved. From "Cool Jerk" to "Soul Finger" and back to "Funky Broadway," these guys tore out some really heavy Motown. Both Nick and I kept on the dance floor, although after a few songs, I had to go back to the bar and keep the beer going.

We kept on the floor, even after everyone was covered with sweat and beer and water and smoke. The band slammed out two sets, and we kept with it. After an hour, we saw Yehoshua and a few of his friends, and they pulled out on the floor with us. The band went to some newer songs and we all kept hopping all over. They went into a Red Hot Chili Peppers song, and we did a bit of slamdancing when tempo permitted. After the band died down, we all sat around and talked, and Yehoshua introduced us to some music school people. I kept at the beer, but Nick kept sober. Before we knew it, they announced final call, and as they swept off tables and folded chairs, Nick and I stumbled out and looked for the car.

When the bars in Bloomington closed at three, the town rolled up the streets, almost every business shutting its eyes and turning off the lights. Nick and I got back to the car and headed for home, still laughing, full of adrenaline, alcohol and smelling like sweat and cigarettes. We didn't meet any women, but both of us bumped into a lot of them. Although every outing with Nick was centered around finding sluts, we always ended up empty handed by final call. But the fun of the chase usually made it a good evening anyway.

"Hey man, let's stop at the VP. I need some orange juice or something," I told him, pointing to the corner store ahead.

We parked, and both walked into the 24-hour home of caffeine, junk food and overpriced juices. Nick immediately went to the Pepsi cooler, and as I cleared the door and nodded to the cashier, I saw Jenn the Christian sitting at the front counter, chatting and joking with two other people who seemed to know the cashier.

"Hey Jenn, what's up?" I asked, in a somewhat drunken slur. I felt stupid, the wounds from the breakup were not yet healed, and I didn't really want to talk to her. Plus, she never drank, and I was sure my alcohol haze angered her.

"Hi John, how have you been?" she asked slowly, pre-measuring her words to avoid any sort of conflict or emotion.

I continued back to the orange juice cooler and grabbed a container. "Oh, I'm doing good. Just got back from Second Story, had a great time."

By this time Nick paid, and started to head for the car. "I'll be in the car, John," he said.

"Okay, cool man!" I yelled to him as he went out the door. "That's my friend Nick," I told Jenn.

She nodded, uninvolved in the conversation. I paid for my juice, said my good-byes, and went back to the car.

Nick pulled the car in the driveway and shut down the ignition. We shuffled back to the room, dragging in some of the gear along with our drinks. I crashed on the bed and started removing my shoes while Nick messed with all of his stuff on the floor. "So what was the deal with the pig?" he asked.

"She was the one you told me to dump, the Christian."

"You did dump her, right? I've got the brick with me, I'm prepared to hit you in the fucking head with it."

"Don't worry, it ended a day or two after I told you about her. I didn't dump her, it sort of fell apart at operating speed."

"Sort of like your last car."

"That was an engine explosion. Completely different."

"So I guess she doesn't have any friends that put out."

"Dude, I don't know if she has any friends, period. And I know she doesn't put out."

"How do you get involved in bullshit like this?"

"How does anyone get involved in any bullshit with women? It just happened. I just met her, and the next thing you know, she's all in love with me. And you know, any port in a storm."

"So now are you all fucked up because you saw her?"

"I don't know. You ever break up with a chick, and you see her months later and she's doing all great and you are doing all shitty?"

"Yeah, I went through all of that shit with Vanessa," he said. She got involved with some guy, and they got married right away, and I'm still dateless and working at a fucking record store."

"I know what you mean—I'm still not over the thing with Tammy. And I didn't have anything to get over with Jenn, but I still feel fucked up about it, like I didn't have the upper hand and I lost. And I don't know where things are going."

"What do you mean?"

"I mean, it was at the point where just thinking about dating made me hit rock bottom. I would think of women and my dating life and I would get so depressed that only going to sleep or drinking until I blacked out would stop it. I feel better about the dating, but I can't find anyone worth dating."

"That's the story of my fucking life. I don't know what to say. I mean I can tell you that the only reason I have survived without dating and in living in such an isolated area has been the zine. I mean, it sometimes feels sort of stupid, but I'm always spending my weekends answering mail and trying to write stuff for the next issue. Maybe if you were constantly immersed in work like that, things would get better for you."

"That's one of my options right now. I'd like to get more involved with the radio station, but they are saying that it will probably go bankrupt by fall, and nobody fucking listens to it anyway. But I am trying to get things going with the zine, maybe I can even get a slick printed version out in addition to the email version."

"Is there some kind of tool that will let you do an email version with all the graphics?"

"There is this thing out called the world wide web. It's supposedly this way you can set up pages and then people at other sites can pull them up and look at them. But it is a hacker's toy, I doubt any real users will ever get into it."

"Oh well, maybe you can figure out something else."

We kept babbling for a few more minutes, in a slow spiral, before we both fell asleep in the hot room.

After we woke on Sunday afternoon, I washed the grime and smoke away with a long shower, while Nick shoveled his equipment back to his car. While he took his shower, I cleaned, put away the sleeping gear, and picked through the rubble to make sure he wouldn't forget anything. I checked my email and made sure he got everything strapped down during his long hair-drying routine. By the time he was dressed, just about everything was ready to roll.

I knew the feeling Nick probably had as he packed his bags and left IU for home. I felt the same way the year before, when I finished my frequent trips to Bloomington and headed back to the misery of Elkhart. I enjoyed every second of Bloomington, and the short vacations and long weekends gave me a temporary release to a dreamland, a small pocket of culture where things were better, people were nicer and the I ran with the grain instead of against it. When I returned to Elkhart, a sunken feeling always diluted me and I wished I could stay in Bloomington full-time. I could imagine Nick felt the same way as he went back to his parents' house, branch campus and dreary job.

We went out to the car and checked the last of everything before Nick settled down for the drive back. There wasn't as much fanfare with his departures, but he was the kind of person who took 45 minutes to finish a phone call, so the end of a long weekend sometimes took a while.

"Well psycho, it's been pretty cool. I wish I could hang out here longer."

"Just get the hell out of here," I said. "Don't go all pansy on me. I'm gonna be up there before too long."

"When do you think you're coming to Elkhart again?"

"I'm sure I'll be there in August, begging my parents for tuition money."

"You know where to find me. Let me know if you get any more cool shit at the station."

"No problem. Gimme a call in a couple of days, and I'll let you know what's up."

Nick closed the car and started the engine. "Thanks again psycho, for letting me hang out here. I'm gonna have to come back again soon, maybe when school starts and there's whores everywhere."

"Sounds like a plan. Have a good trip back, and don't forget to listen to some Motörhead."

"You know it. See you later psycho."

"Later Nick."

I watched him back out of the driveway and taxi up Mitchell Street before turning onto Third and vanishing into the great unknown. What a weekend. I didn't have to return to parents or a closed-minded community, but my stomach still felt like shit and the weekend really drained the coffers. At least I had a few UCS shifts the next week, and no homework was due for class on Monday. It was time to play on the computer.

22

I cut through to the backside of Ballantine Hall and up the hill where the parking garage jutted out next to the eleven-story classroom building. 7:56. I'd make it to class barely in time today; most days I was lucky to stumble in by 8:15. Wednesday morning, almost three days since Ray left, my sleep schedule had almost reverted back to the 8 AM torture. He wasn't entirely to blame for knocking my internal clock upside down; I spent most of the spring semester going to bed when the sun rose and staying comatose for ten hours a day. Now, the most I could hope for was a two-hour nap after lunch on my days off.

My walkman echoed the new Deicide album through my earphones, the only thing that could keep me awake and propel me across campus. Glenn Benton growled away about killing God, and I slipped in the door, rushed down the hall, and climbed the stairs to the third floor. I broke into the classroom and found my seat before the teacher even got there. The act of simultaneously dropping my backpack, turning off the walkman, and removing the headphones caused a little dance to get everything undone and situated.

The class was small, maybe 20 people, and had only three guys in it, myself included. I spent a lot of each lecture gazing around the room and daydreaming. Most of the women were English majors, and all of them were incredible and far beyond my means. It wasn't a kind of slutty beauty like you'd see at a bar or in a Penthouse photo spread; these women all had an incredible, natural, almost eugenic beauty highlighted by years of obsessive-compulsive care and hard work. The lowest IQ in the room must've been 165, and although a lot of them seemed too sheltered, I knew there were at least a few that I would've enjoyed talking to for hours about books, philosophy, art, comedy, or whatever. But they all had it together, maybe too much. I imagined they had lengthy screening exams before they dated people, and they wouldn't be into hanging out with someone who came from a broken home, drank too much, flunked out of school, and didn't have their entire life planned already. I'd have better chances at getting into NASA and flying the space shuttle than getting into the panties in this room.

The teacher arrived, and started by going into Susan Sontag's book *Illness as Metaphor*, which would be an awesome name for a Napalm Death b-side or maybe an industrial noise metal band. The book talked about how tuberculosis was not only a killer disease at the turn of the century, but a popular metaphor for the devastating poverty of the lower class, and destruction in general. After World War II, cancer became the next big thing, and whether you wanted to explain the grow of Communism, or the rust eating away the fender on your car, you could use a cancer metaphor. Sontag also wrote second book, which we'd be reading next, about AIDS and how people perceived it as a "poor man's disease" or a "gay man's disease" or a "death sentence" or whatever.

I'd read about half of the first book, which was a little ahead of the curve, but I found the lecture boring. I thought about another extension to the whole Sontag deal, where you could talk about mental illness, specifically depression, in the same metaphorical terms, and the fact that every third person on the planet was depressed, and erasing the stigma behind it. When I started Prozac in 1989, the only person that anyone else knew on psychiatric drugs was Jack Nicholson in *One Flew Over the Cuckoo's Nest*. Three years later, it wouldn't surprise me if IU added it to the water supply.

Christ, with such a boring lecture, and this many women wearing short shorts with nice tanned legs...Every pair of female legs in the room looked like plastic, like they never grew hair at all. They must wake up at three in the morning to get ready for class. Even if I had to evenly divide the women among the men in class, I'd have a new one each day through next weekend. And since one of the guys looked a little on the effeminate side, it might be even more. And it wasn't just an endless staring match, like a business school class. On the days when I managed to stumble in and find a seat before eight, some of the women would make small talk, and ask me how I was doing or about my weekend, like I was their ragtag mascot or something. I should major in English, I thought, and finish my degree with early morning classes. I'd memorize 12 lines of Keats and fake my way into a different set of pants every week.

After an hour of delirium, class got out, and I took a second to say hi to the girls sitting near me and to the teacher on the way out the door. I wanted to run the mental illness theory past the prof, but I didn't want to 'out' myself, and I could save it for some later paper and kill two birds with one stone. Econ class waited for me upstairs, but ever since I found out that Alex P. Keaton was teaching straight from the book and running a massive curve on the tests, I stopped going. Also, I found out during one of his forgettable lectures that he used to be in the Army or Marines or something, so now instead of Alex P. Keaton, he became the character from *Casualties of War*, the bad Vietnam movie with Sean Penn. This made it even harder to keep from laughing while he was at the chalkboard, so I decided to bag every class that didn't have quizzes or tests.

The Ballantine post-classroom crowds were pretty mellow in the summer session. During the school year, people crammed the stairwells like the '68 riots or something. People would sit in front of the rooms, studying and waiting for a class to dismiss, and hordes of people would trip over them, step on their legs, and clog the hallways while navigating around them. Now, I could drive my car through the hallways without hurting anyone, not that there's anything wrong with that.

I hiked from one spoke of the building to another—there were two wings that both joined a central hub, like a demented space station, except the pieces were eleven stories tall. In the other piece, I went to rooms 307 and 308—the UCS computer labs. There were a slew of labs on the first floor, but they belonged to the language labs. That meant they were only open to the public on an erratic schedule, and you always ran the risk of sitting down at a Mac that was configured for Japanese or Korean. I poked my head in 307, and saw empty seats among the cramped room of Zenith PCs. I went in, grabbed a chair, and fired up telnet.

On Bronze, I got email from Cindy, addressed to damn near the entire free world, about a party at her place that Friday. A few idiots RSVP'ed by replying to the entire list, so I knew that at least a dozen people would be there. The invite promised plenty of food, plenty of booze, and free reign on her parents' swimming pool and hot tub. Spending time with Cindy would be great, but I knew if a tenth of the names she invited showed up, it would be a clusterfuck of people, and I'd get to talk to her for all of four seconds. But, aside from my own jealous needs, I knew it would be the huge VAX social event of the summer. I filed away the mail for future consideration, and went to the routine task of deleting the UCS sub messages.

"Hey John." I turned around from the screen, and June was standing right behind me, smiling. "What's up?" She wore a flattering top, and a pair of cutoff shorts. I saw just a hint of midriff, and her legs looked even nicer than my best fantasies—tanned, smooth...

"Holy shit, you scared the fuck out of me," I said.

"Sorry," she said. "I was down on the first floor and saw you log in up here. What's up?"

"Not much, just got out of class, checking my mail. You?"

"Same thing. Hey, I was going to ask you—I'm having a party this Friday. It's not a big deal, just a few friends, but I was wondering if you'd want to go."

"What kind of crowd?"

"Mostly student government people, and friends from when I lived in Foster."

"Sounds cool," I said. It didn't sound cool, except the part about her being there. "Tell me where and when, and I'll be there."

"Let me make you a map," she said. She grabbed a piece of paper, and scribbled some quick directions. "It's easy to find, it's just off of Third, but here's my number in case you have trouble."

"Okay great, I'll be there."

"I'll see you then." She smiled, and my eyes followed her out of the room while I thought about finally spending some time in person with her.

I walked home while the second round of people trickled onto campus. I hated every aspect of morning classes, except for the peaceful feeling of being done early and having the rest of the day to fuck around. But with no plans or projects, a slow depression filtered in, an emptiness I wished I could feel. It vanished during the high points, like Nick's visit, but now it creeped back to haunt me. Even with the prospect of seeing June again, the lack of anything better going on made me wish I could go to a pharmacist and steal a vat of Demerol and inject it right into my heart. Instead, I'd probably end up reading Usenet all afternoon.

I cut through the long strip of a parking lot behind the music school, with Queensrÿche's *Empire* in the walkman. The songs felt so out of place in the summer of '92, on the Bloomington campus. I bought my first copy of the tape in the fall of '90, and wore out three copies while commuting to and from IUSB every morning. Songs like "The Thin Line," "Jet City Woman," and "One and Only" reminded me so much of buying Spiderman comics at Miami Street, cashing my Friday checks at the Nortel bank, going to Scottsdale Mall to blow my money, reading dot-matrix printouts of Phrack magazine, buying Quarter Pounders at the Lincolnway McDonald's and eating them during my Friday shift, and racing the trains on US 33 for miles, sometimes dozens of miles, to get across the tracks from south to north. It depressed me even more to know that I almost missed those times a year before, even though I vividly remembered hating every minute of it. Every word, every note pulled forth hours and days of memories, things that happened a year ago that now seemed like they happened decades before, continents away. Would this happen every year for the rest of my life?

I shuffled back home by ten, too early for the mailman, too hot to sleep. I circled through the house, trying to find something productive to do that didn't involve money. But nobody was home, and I couldn't find any projects screaming for my attention, except for schoolwork which didn't count. I poured a tall Coke, put the new Obituary album in the stereo, and sat at the computer.

Why didn't I just stay in Ballantine? The temperature was probably 30 degrees cooler than my hothouse room, and the network connections were ten times faster. I guess I didn't need to check my mail anyway; I just read my messages ten minutes before. I logged on anyway, nursed the tumbler of Coke, and found nothing, as predicted. Instead of compulsively checking my wholist every five seconds for the next 14 hours, I logged out, kicked off my shoes, and sat in bed. Either I'd "meditate" in the rack and think about how horrible things were, or I'd somehow fall asleep in the hundred degree heat and make up for the paltry six hours of rest I scraped together the night before. Neither option would win me a Nobel prize, but I found an old copy of Omni, and stretched out on my tiny twin mattress.

While sitting in bed, reading about the helicopters of the future, I remembered something I'd been putting off for too long: the doctor. I'd been kicking around the idea of going to the shrink and getting some new medicine to help pull me from the pit of hell depressions that were plaguing me lately. I avoided the call because I didn't want to admit that I was dependent on a pill, and I didn't want to be plummeted into a sea of side effects. But I really wanted the crutch, the help in getting out of the darkness.

I picked up the phone, and dialed the numbers. "Hi, I need to make an appointment...yes, I've seen him before. Mornings are fine. Tuesday the

28th, that's great." I scrawled down the date and time on a piece of paper, and taped it to the edge of my computer monitor. The 28th was two weeks away, but I'd be able to make it until then. It would be no problem getting the medicine, but it still worried me. Two weeks seemed like a lifetime, especially at the syrup-like pace things were flowing now.

I wandered around Kirkwood that afternoon, and watched the people rollerblading down the strip, hanging out in the sun, and wandering the college-town hangouts up and down the street. Spending the day rambling down the street made me feel relaxed, like a sunny afternoon at a farmer's market. When I was a freshman, Kirkwood was the place to go for anything, from pencils to CDs to a slice of pizza or some Chinese food. Every time I walked the sidewalks of the Ave, it brought me back to the beginning of my long-running obsession with Bloomington, back to a day when my GPA was unmarked and any one of a million possible futures awaited me. After three years of fuckups, I didn't have such a rosy potential, but I still didn't know what the future held, and nostalgic excursions like this one made me hope that I still had a chance.

I ducked into the Dunnkirk Plaza, a cluster of tiny stores that looked like some kind of Asian city that grew and then grew on top of itself, three or four times over. A Chinese restaurant perched above a tiny bank, and coffee shops, bead merchants, t-shirt vendors, an Afghanastani restaurant, and a bunch of other shops clustered within the maze. I walked through its passages and headed toward the back, to my favorite place to buy music, CD Exchange.

I entered the glass door of the place. CDX wasn't much bigger than a small dorm room, but the wall to ceiling collection of CDs was the best in the city. I saw Tom at the counter, a cool ex-hippie type with a brush cut and John Lennon glasses who worked there almost every time I went in. He was listening to an Adrian Legg acoustic guitar CD that I had a copy of at home.

"Hey John, how's it going?" he asked. "How's the new show—you on tonight?"

"No, just Thursdays," I said. Tom hung out with a bunch of QAX DJs and helped them track down obscure stuff for their playlists, giving him this sort of fifth-Beatle peripheral involvement with a bunch of other shows. "Any new metal for me today?"

"Yeah, I got one of your orders in. Hang on," he said, digging through a divider box full of discs and paperwork. He pulled out a CD, wrapped in an order slip and rubber band. "Okay, it's Edge of Sanity—*Unorthodox*."

"Damn, man—I just ordered that Friday. Wasn't that a German import?"

"No, I can get the Black Mark stuff domestically now. Do you want to pick this up today?"

"How much is it?"

"For you—$11.99."

"Yeah, I'll take it. Let me look around first."

Tom always cut me deals on stuff, because any time I had a spare $20, I'd shove it his way for more new discs. He gave me good prices on trade-ins and cash sales, too. Plus he always kept an eye out for used Death Metal, and wasn't afraid to stock the coolest, sickest, and most Satanic stuff in town.

I wandered the wall of new CDs, and saw at least a dozen things that I wanted. A lot of them were titles that we had at the station, so I didn't bother buying them. At some point, I'd show up on a day off and dub them to tape for free. But if I had the cash, I'd be blowing $200 a month on CDs.

The used bins were my favorite place to look, and there were at least a dozen good Death or Thrash Metal titles in the racks at any point in time. I habitually went from A to Z, looking for some ultra-rare CD that I wouldn't find again. I saw several things I wanted, but I knew I had to keep tight with my cash for now.

I strolled up to the counter. "Find anything?" Tom asked.

"Everything but the money," I said. "Go ahead and ring me up on the Edge of Sanity."

I always spent my last few bucks on CDs, like some kind of addiction. I only had about $25 to my name, but I'd get paid on Friday. That meant it would be cool in my book to drop half of it on a CD and spend the rest on a couple of Burger King runs. Even though I had no idea where that fucking deposit was going to come from, I still wanted to play that CD on the air on Thursday. And I needed hundreds of dollars for the deposit, so in some strange way, $12 wouldn't make or break me.

Tom wrote out a receipt longhand; there was no fancy cash register, just a generic carbon pad and a wooden lock box. "I checked with this supplier, and they can get any of the Black Mark, Relativity, Roadrunner, and Nuclear Blast stuff just as fast," he said.

"That's all I need to hear," I said. I pulled out a twenty, and he handed over some change. "I've got an apartment deposit to scrape together, but I'll probably still order some stuff next payday. Hey, you talk to Doug about taking out an ad yet?" Sid and I had been scrambling to find any business to take out ads so we could keep the station running for a few more months.

"I talked to him, he's waffling on it. Maybe I can get him to change his mind."

"Well, I'm telling people to come here anyway. You're the only one selling half the shit I play."

"I appreciate it. We'll keep selling it if you keep listening to it."

"Thanks Tom, catch you later."

"Later, John."

I walked out with the CD and headed back home, trying to think of another scheme to kill time until dinner.

The heavy sigh is the mantra of the clinically depressed. And aside from deeply exhaling for no reason, the week carried no further substance. Although an empty schedule and nothing to do seemed much simpler than a jumble of complicated planning, I counted the days until Friday, when I had too many things to do and not enough time. I managed to kill Monday and Tuesday with studying and nothingness. Now, I wondered if I could do the same thing with Wednesday night.

I stared at the bedroom ceiling, trying not to move and produce any heat. The walk to Kirkwood ate up part of my day, and I listened to the Edge of Sanity album twice and made a Burger King run, but now that it was dark, it meant I had nothing to do until midnight. In the silent meditation of my room, the confusion of what to do on Friday ate at my brain. The easy answer was to go to both parties, eat as much free food as possible, try to fuck both women and any others that made themselves available, and see what ended up on my plate by the end of the evening. But my emotions made it a more difficult situation, like I was deciding between the well-established Cindy and the new contender June.

Fuck this, I thought. I needed to get out of the house. I grabbed my wallet, fished out the sheet of paper I used for a phone book, and scanned the list of scribbled numbers. After trying to remember who the hell was even around during the summer, I dialed a number, and waited for an answer.

"Shannon? This is John Conner. What the hell are you up to tonight?" I dialed Shannon, another VAX regular who I vaguely knew from various IMU encounters, but could trust for some kind of adventure.

"Not much," she said. "My little sister's got some of her bratty little friends here raising high hell, and I'm caught in the crossfire."

"Want to do something? Maybe get some ice cream, go on a small road-trip, drink a few quarts of rum and fuck shit up?"

"You're my fucking savior. I'll drive, just gimme directions."

I explained how to get to my house, and she said she'd be over in 15 or 20 minutes. After we hung up, I changed clothes, scraped together the last of my money, and wondered what the evening would hold for me.

The Shannon story was strange, at least in the beginning. Her 14-year-old sister used her VAX account frequently, and started bothering me a few weeks back. She'd write me vaguely suggestive messages, either in an effort to feel more grown up or in a covert plan to fuck with my head. Either way, I didn't respond to her much—I thought she might be an undercover cop involved in a pedophilia sting operation. But then Shannon stopped letting her sister use the account and started writing me and swinging by the IMU when I was there.

Shannon was a local, a resident of Bloomington who spent her first year out of high school living in the dorms, taking classes, partying, and playing with the computers. That summer, she lived at home, and worked in the mall at a department store. She flunked most of her classes last year, and her dirt-poor family couldn't afford to give her a second chance at it. Her conversations were almost always about parties or people she knew from high school, and I didn't feel too drawn to her. In person, I found her vaguely attractive—short, blonde, and a little too stocky, but a mix of sultriness and lack of a prudish aura made her interesting nonetheless. She always talked about sex, and looked like a better ride than most of the women on campus. I never really expected anything to happen with her, but I had a few weird and very sexual late-night phone conversations with her. Either way...

A few minutes later, a beat-up white EXP pulled into the driveway, with Shannon at the wheel. "Hey John! Hop in, let's figure out where we're going," she said. I walked around to the passenger side and crawled into the two-seat Escort. Shannon was dressed in jeans and a t-shirt, nothing special. I didn't feel drawn toward her, but I knew if we were wandering through the darkness of a park at night and she offered to fuck my brains out, I'd definitely accept.

"Glad to see you found the place," I said. "Where to?"

"I know it sounds high school, but are you up for some Dairy Queen?"

"Sounds like a start," I said. "Where the hell is the Dairy Queen anyway?"

"I'll show you," she said. She gunned the car in reverse and tore down Mitchell Street, aiming the car southward. "I hope you don't mind my driving. It scares the shit out of most people. I've only had one wreck though, and it wasn't my fault."

"Don't worry, my driving's worse," I said. "No wrecks, but a lot of close calls. Speaking of accidents, how's your sister?"

"I swear you're gonna see me in the fucking newspaper one of these days, after cutting her up with an axe," she yelled. "Does that sound fucked up to you or what?"

"It sort of reminds me of an old Pink Floyd song," I said. "At least she isn't sending me her little pricktease email anymore. That shit was really freaking me out."

"Yeah, I can handle sending you the pricktease emails," she said, laughing.

"I don't think your little games are very funny," I said.

"Yeah, well, I do."

The car hurtled down Walnut, toward the south side of town, until I saw the familiar red DQ sign. "Hey, there it is," I said.

"I just hope this one bitch from my high school isn't working there," she said. She swept the car into the gravel parking lot, and found a spot among the few high school cars. This wasn't the big restaurant version of Dairy Queen; it was old school, a small cinderblock building with a front counter, and a handful of picnic tables out front. A bunch of junior high kids sat around the store, and the whole arrangement reminded me of when I played peewee-league baseball several eons ago, and the coach would bring us to a similar place after each game—a bunch of second graders, in orange AstroBowl Astros shirts, buzzed out on intense sugar highs from peanut buster parfaits. Now I felt like a townie, hanging out at the only non-college joint on the strip, with Shannon the local.

I got the peanut buster parfait, just for old time's sake. Shannon got a vanilla cone that seemed to defy gravity with wafts of soft-serve ice cream that were twice as high as the cone. She didn't order one of those chocolate-covered banana things to further taunt me about her oral abilities, although I secretly wished she would. I was never entirely into the casual sex thing, but Shannon seemed like the kind of person who could blow you in the car, wipe off her chin, and go right back to being your pal without missing a beat. Or maybe I was hallucinating.

We hopped back in the car, and Shannon started in on her already-melting ice cream. "You're going to have to help me hold this thing," she said.

"I was about to tell you the same thing," I said.

"Very funny."

I looked around the EXP for the first time under the lights of the ice cream stand. "Hey, where's the back seat in this thing?"

"It doesn't have one. I figure we'd go somewhere and fuck later."

"Don't try to get me started," I said. "I'm onto your little tricks. Besides, you wouldn't be able to handle me."

"You shouldn't say stuff like that. Someday we might end up drunk together, and I'll make you regret it."

I laughed, but the kind of laugh where I secretly knew I wouldn't mind getting loaded and fooling around with her. She wasn't smart, sophisticated, or beautiful—but a good semi-anonymous one-night stand would hit the spot like the cool ice cream sundae I was eating on a hot summer night.

"Okay, let's hit the road," she said, her ice cream gnawed down to a more realistic scoop-height. She fired up the car, and we continued south.

"So you never told me your deal," she said. "You got a girlfriend or anything? Boyfriend? Dog friend?"

"No relationships, but I fuck a few sheep on the side," I said. "Seriously, I split with a girl last spring, haven't been able to get moving lately. I just got out of a fucked up thing with this religious chick."

"Fuck, don't get me started on those bible banners," she said. "Half of my high school was like that—holier than holy, but fucking everything left and right behind closed doors. They're all a bunch of fucking hypocrites. If you're that desperate for a woman, wait until August. If I'm not kicked out of school, I'm working as an orientation assistant. Maybe I can set you up with some new freshman chick that isn't completely insane. You deserve something better than some religious mind-job."

"Dabbling in the flesh trade now?" I asked.

"Hey, it's better than my current job selling women's clothing at the mall..."

"Hey, speaking of dream dates, you have a run-in with GGARTMAN yet?"

She laughed. "Oh shit, this is so fucking funny. You know how he's always hitting on women, right?"

"Yeah, that's why I asked."

"Okay, he started with his shit one night when he was at Eigenmann and I was in the library—all of this 'hey come over and we'll fuck' kind of stuff, really straight up. I could see why that would freak out most women, but not me. I came right back at him, with the most perverse shit you could think of. If he bitnetted saying he wanted to eat me out, I'd bitnet him for five minutes straight talking about blowjobs. I totally had him going, and then after like twenty minutes, I said I was coming over to his room right then to give him what he wanted."

"What'd you do, pull a no-show?"

"Hell no—I went over there. His address was in his profile, so I showed up at Eigenmann, went to his room, and said 'okay bud, let's get started.' He totally fucking freaked out! I thought he was gonna start crying. I mean, I wasn't going to fuck him, but I was prepared to do everything up to the point where I was holding his dick right up to my mouth before I told him it was a scam, and all I had to do was show up and he went completely nuts. It was the most hilarious thing I've ever seen."

"That's awesome. It's good to hear he got a taste of his own medicine," I said.

I watched the terrain outside as we whipped south, and into Hoosier National Forest. We continued to talk about the strangeness and nothingness of our suppers, the houses and shops on either side of the road vanishing into thick walls of trees that stretched for hundreds of acres. Shannon laid some great stories on me, and after a few miles, she started telling the kind of weird ghost stories that involved turning off the headlights and driving in the darkness while shitting your pants in fear. I liked it, and she turned out to be a surprisingly cool person to hang out with. But I couldn't help but wander back into thinking about Cindy, June, and the other hotter irons in the fire. Maybe I'd get drunk with Shannon someday, but I pretty much knew she'd just be an occasional curiosity.

We drove and talked for another hour or so, and then she brought me back to town so I could make the fountain at midnight (she didn't want to go—she had a fear of running into Gartman or some other person she regularly antagonized.) She waved bye, and I went from the white EXP back to the boardinghouse room, to mull over the conversation and get ready for midnight.

23

Even the heavy-duty air conditioning of Ballantine Hall couldn't keep me awake for an 8:00 AM class. I managed to stumble to English after a late night of the fountain and a long-distance Death Metal gossip session with Nick. The teacher's mandatory attendance policy got me through the door, but it couldn't keep me conscious past roll call. While the prof lectured on the important parts of a good essay, I fought the urge to pass out on the floor. I stared at the chalkboard and felt my head grow heavy and drop, only to be snapped upward by involuntarily reaction when my body realized it would fall out of my chair if I dozed off. My only tools for survival in the hour-long death march were my depraved sexual fantasies about each woman in the room, and various combinations thereof.

After dragging through the lecture, I knew no amount of the watered-down and vaguely caffienated fountain drinks from the basement lounge could keep me awake for a monotonous econ lecture with Marty McFly. Instead, I followed the flow of students through the hallways and headed to the cluster in 308 to check my email for the first time that morning. After a two-minute wait, I snagged a PC, and fired up two telnet sessions. On Bronze, it looked like I got a tug from some bait I threw the day before:

> From ARBERGST@ucs.indiana.edu Thu, 16 Jul 92 8:36:16 EST
> From: "plus ca change, plus c'est la meme chose"
> <ARBERGST@ucs.indiana.edu>
> To: JCONNER@ucs.indiana.edu

Subject: Re: your mail
Date: Thu, 16 Jul 92 8:36:16 EST

Is this the infamous John Conner, aka Doctor X? I'm assuming you're a Queensryche fan, right? I always see you logged on in the middle of the night—are you programming for the utils, or taking classes this summer? I do maintenance on computers in the Main Library, but it's mostly plugging in cables or spraying the dust out of the cases. It's not glamorous, but they pay me.
Speaking of which, I've got to get back to work, but feel free to write any time.

-Amy

   I couldn't remember why I wrote her, so I looked her up in the usual sources. There were two listings for Amy Renee Bergstrom in the online address book: staff (Library) and student (Honors English, French minor.) I smiled when I saw that she filled out a profile in my xinfo database—which put her on the high end of the bell curve of computer literacy, at least in my book. I read her mail twice more, and carefully crafted a reply.

To: arbergst@ucs.indiana.edu
Subject: ...I don't know why but, suddenly, I want to discuss declining I.Q. LEVELS with a blue ribbon SENATE SUB-COMMITTEE!
—text follows this line—

Hey Amy, Thanks for the reply. Yes, it's me, John, aka Doctor X. I haven't been doing much programming for the utils lately, just my own stuff. I'm taking classes this summer, but no csci—just an English class, and macro-econ.
How is the Library treating you? Did you get work this summer? I'm a UCS as consultant, but I'm not getting any hours this summer. I used to work in Lib102, but it will probably be Lindley this fall.

I gotta split—I do a radio show at WQAX and I have to get everything ready. What kind of music do you like? Talk to you later.

-J

I re-read the message a dozen times before hitting C-c C-c to send it. On my VAX account, I added her username to my wholist, so I could see when she logged on. She wasn't online, but I saw she just logged out a few minutes ago.

A woman who knew about Queensrÿche, worked with computers, and already knew my username sounded like an interesting prospect. All I needed to do was wait for her reply, keep the conversation going, and try to find more about her. It would all be easy work, except for the waiting part.

A quick nap before lunch sounded like the best plan for the day, so I snuck down the massive central staircase and headed towards home. During the stroll home, clouds rolled across the sky, and the scent of rain filled the air. Why did it rain every fucking time I had to do a show? After a fifteen-minute hike in the rapidly vanishing sunlight, I collapsed in bed, dead asleep before the raindrops started pelting the roof above me.

My pre-lunch nap extended past noon and well into the afternoon before I regained consciousness with a stomach rumbling like the skies above me. I wiped the drool from my face, found my glasses, and started thinking about some lunch. I pulled two microwave burritos from my cache in the freezer, nuked them, and transported my usual entourage of burritos, silverware, hot sauce, and a Coke to the clutter of my computer desk.

I got halfway through the first burrito while the computer spun up from its sleep and dialed the university. Procomm beeped three times to indicate a connection, and I licked the sauce from my fingers and logged in to Bronze. There was only one message, from my new pal:

From ARBERGST@ucs.indiana.edu Thu, 16 Jul 92 12:03:22 EST
From: "plus ca change, plus c'est la meme chose"
<ARBERGST@ucs.indiana.edu>
To: JCONNER@ucs.indiana.edu
Subject: Re: ...I don't know why but, suddenly, I want to discuss declining I.Q. LEVELS with a blue ribbon SENATE SUB-COMMITTEE!
Date: Thu, 16 Jul 92 12:03:22 EST

I will try not to be overwhelmed by email from a genuine VAX celebrity. I hate to admit that I know people who think Sid Savage is a fictional character, like Uncle Sam or Ronald Reagan.

Yes, the library did give me hours this summer—20 or 30 a week. Fortunately, they did not also give me much work, so it's more like a subsidized study hall. I'm taking L390 Children's Lit and Y109 Introduction to World Politics this session. I'm an English Major, but I've got to finish one Social and Behavioral class to graduate in August. Then, grad school—I'm not ready to face the real world yet. What English class are you taking? Are you minoring? Do you write?

You asked about music, and I'm probably not as fanatic about it as you are, so bear with me. I guess lately, I've been listening to the new U2 album, the new Pearl Jam album, and some older stuff–Peter Gabriel, Pink Floyd, and you already know about Queensrÿche. Don't worry—no showtunes, no Depeche Mode. And you? How does one listen to WQAX?

I just read your bio, with the nifty bio program you wrote for the utils. It seems very sparse and out of date. Does this mean I get to pick at your brain and send you a barrage of invasive personal questions? I'm sorry if I'm being too nosy, but I'm curious. And the arrangement would be mutual, of course.

It's lunchtime, so I've off to the cafeteria downstairs for a rubbery pizza and some water the color of a Coke. Have a good one!

-Amy

I read the message two or three times, soaking in every word. The intellectual part of me knew she was an interesting person, someone with broad interests who I could learn to like. The scamming part of me knew I had her hooked. I thought about a reply, but realized it was going on 3:00 and I had to run to the CD store and get some dinner before the show. I'd rather craft a more extensive reply later at two in the morning than rush through something less substantial. I logged out, powered down the computer, and started digging through piles of unlabeled tapes to get ready for my show.

After four hours on the air, I pulled my gear back to the VW, and made a beeline for Showalter. Even though I was a half-hour late, there were only three people there: Alex, Renee, and Brecken. I ditched my car, and headed toward the fountain.

"Hey Conner, how was the radio show?" Brecken asked.

I walked up to the bench where the three were sitting. "Pretty good. More new demo tapes are coming in, and I'm getting a lot of new CDs at the station. If the place wasn't going bankrupt within a month, it would be awesome."

An unfamiliar car circled, and parked in front of the fountain, a dark four-door Saturn, with dealer plates. The door opened, and out stepped Eric Fournier.

"Hey all, like my new wheels?" he yelled, walking over to the fountain.

"What the hell?" I said. "Where'd you steal the car?"

"My Disneyland is over, kiddos," he said.

"You've been saying that all summer. Shit or get off the pot."

"Well, I got a job with Andersen Consulting in Chicago. I'm moving up there in a week. Hence, the new ride."

"Fuck, man," I said. "It was that easy?"

"No professional programming experience, no computer science coursework," he said. "Of course, the finance degree helped. Get this—I have to go to a six-week COBOL class when I get up there."

"You're doomed. You know COBOL doesn't have pointers, right?"

"Hey, it's money. I'll buy a sweet PC for home, install unix on it, and hack all night."

"Well don't let them suck you in," I said. "I'd hate to see you with a wife, four kids and a mortgage, shuffling dBase records or some bullshit."

"I'll be careful," he said. "Hey, any of you guys going to Cindy's party tomorrow?"

"I am!" Brecken said. "She has a swimming pool and a hot tub. Everybody's going."

"I think we're going too," Alex said. "I've gotta see her folks' place. What about you, Conner?"

"Not sure. I've got something going on," I said.

"What's her name?" Brecken asked.

"I'm not going to jinx this one. No discussion of works in progress. I might stop by Cindy's later, we'll see."

"You mean it depends on if you get lucky," Chad said.

"No discussion of works in progress..."

By the time I stumbled home from the fountain, I knew I had about eight more minutes of consciousness, unless I caught a second wind that would keep me up all night. I wanted to run strong for another half-hour and then go comatose, but I knew I'd miss that narrow window and spend the night tossing and turning.

The computer's beastly whining and churning filled the room, the soundtrack for my nightly closing procedure. I swallowed my pills, took off my clothes, and sat down at the card table of antique equipment to see if anyone wrote me. They didn't, but I still owed Amy a message. I fired up emacs, the all-purpose editor I used to compose my mail, and started a message.

> To: arbergst@prism
> Subject: ...ich bin in einem dusenjet ins jahr 53 vor chr...ich lande im antiken Rom...einige gladiatoren spielen scrabble...ich rieche PIZZA...

—text follows this line—

Amy:
It sounds like your library job is exactly what I wanted to find at the beginning of this summer, but it didn't work out that way. I originally planned to go back to the dreaded factories of Elkhart, IN, but decided to stay in town at the very last second. It's a long and monotonous story that has caused me to work some of the most demeaning jobs of my life since last May.

English classes—I am taking W350 right now, advanced expository writing. The topic is metaphor and simile, and i guess i'm doing good with it right now. writing is a lot like computer programming to me, in some weird way, and i seem to do okay with it (except that this class is at 8 in the morning.) i haven't thought about minoring, because i'm afraid the medieval lit stuff would kill me. as for being a writer, i guess i have a secret desire to write a book someday. i publish a music zine, and write for a friend's zine, so i guess in that sense i'm a writer. and i write email—does that count?

WQAX is a cable radio station, meaning that about seven people actually listen. you need to have cable tv, and a special hookup for your stereo to get it to work. my show is mostly death metal stuff, although i listen to a lot of other kinds of music, and i am not a stereotypical heavy metal fan. i'm also into pink floyd and peter gabriel.

i would appreciate it if you asked me several dozen nosy and intrusive questions, as long as i can do the same. i will promise to tell the truth, unless i will impress you more by lying. you go first, and i'll send my questions next. i feel that i should get to ask twice as many questions since you didn't utilize my easy-to-operate utilities for posting a bio.

all of this assumes you survived your lunch in the library cafeteria. i used to "eat" there when i had regular shifts in 102a last fall. and you eat there every day? poor thing.

gotta sleep now. looking forward to your questions. catch you later.

-J

I did a quick check of who was on the VAX cluster (nobody,) then powered down everything before I found other excuses to stay up later. With the lights off and the fan humming away in the darkness, I sat in bed and thought about Amy. She seemed together enough to be interesting, but I didn't even know if she was single. June was a bigger priority—I seemed to already have my foot in her door, but Amy could be a decent contingency plan.

I stretched out on my blanket-less bed and waited for that six-hour coma I was hoping for earlier. It never arrived, and I wavered in and out of a heat-nauseated consciousness until I fell fast asleep, about three minutes before my alarm went off.

I barely remembered my morning bed to shower to class routine, except that I found it fitting to put Motörhead's *No Remorse* tape in the walkman and fast forward to the song "(We Are) The Road Crew." Lemmy's bottle-of-Scotch-a-day voice sandpapered over the fast, biker-metal beat, the only thing that could get my body moving on a Friday morning. I sat through English class, reciting the words over and over, thinking about how much I needed to have some fun this weekend and break out the class-work-show routine. Maybe some of my plans would work out. Maybe I'd get lucky with June. Maybe I'd get drunk and prank phone call ex-girlfriends. Something had to happen.

Econ class wasn't an option on a Friday morning. And it was even a payday, with a halfway functional check waiting for me. I went to one of the computer labs in Ballantine, and found email from this mysterious Amy woman:

From ARBERGST@ucs.indiana.edu Fri, 17 Jul 92 8:23:12 EST
From: "plus ca change, plus c'est la meme chose"
<ARBERGST@ucs.indiana.edu>
To: JCONNER@ucs.indiana.edu
Subject: Re: ich bin in einem dusenjet ins jahr 53 vor chr ich lande im antiken Rom...einige gladiatoren spielen scrabble...ich rieche PIZZA...
Date: Fri, 17 Jul 92 8:23:12 EST

Well, it's refreshing to actually find someone that answers their email in a timely fashion. It seems like all of my friends are scattered across the globe and respond to their mail on a quarterly basis. it's nice to have someone to play with who's on the computer pretty much all the time (except right now.)

The library job isn't bad, but you probably wouldn't want it. It pays less than UCS and is considerably more disorganized, if you can believe that. They're pretty flexible with my hours during the year, which is good because I'm always trying to balance 20 credit hours and honors seminars and all of that other junk.

Okay, about these questions—I guess I thought of a bunch of them while I was at work, but I don't want to bombard you like a bad job interview. Here's my pathetic list:

1) Favorite book/author?
2) Favorite movie?
3) Favorite album?
4) Favorite restaurant?
5) Where do you want to live after school?
6) Were you always from Indiana?
7) Have you ever been overseas?
8) What language do/did you take?
9) Single? Married? Dating? Involved? Monk? Asexual?
10) Any tattoos or other incriminating marks or scars?
11) Do you call it soda, pop, or coke?

12) I guess I can't do this without asking what you look like, although it sounds shallow. at least i didn't ask about religion or politics.

I'll stop there, since this is turning into a bad episode of the dating game. Turnabout is fair play, so feel free to ask me a bunch of third-grade questions also. I'll be patiently awaiting your reply.

How was your radio show? Do you rush right home and go to bed for your 8:00, or do you sleep during the day? I know almost nothing about death metal or anything heavier than, say, Danzig. I guess I hang out with a lot of boring people.

Well, I have a fun day of work ahead of me, then I'm going home for the weekend. Do you have any big weekend plans?

Talk to you later,

-Amy

Her letter was impressive, and got me thinking I definitely had her on the hook. When it came to answering questions, I could bullshit the most impressive persona without even altering the truth too much (errors of omission are a beautiful thing.) But, I had a paycheck waiting across campus, a noon to four shift at Lindley, and some lunch somewhere between the two. I fired her off a quick reply:

To: arbergst@prism
Subject:—I can do ANYTHING...I can even...SHOPLIFT!!
—text follows this line—

Hey Amy,

This is going to be a quick one, because I have to go to your stomping ground of the Library, pick up my paycheck (really, I'm not stalking you) and get some lunch before my shift starts at Lindley at noon. All of this on about 16 minutes of sleep. No, I don't sleep much during the day, I have been perpetually running on less than 5 hours a night for the last month or so. I'm hoping to sleep straight through the fall semester to get caught up.

I'm eagerly anticipating answering your questions, although I'm going to have to do it sometime this weekend (and send you a list, too.) Where is home? Can I give you some dirty laundry to take with you? I told two different people I would go to their parties tonight, but this is unusual—most Friday nights, I'm obsessively cataloging my extensive Hummel collection in dBase.

Okay, I gotta split. Have a good weekend, and I'll talk to you...Monday?

-J

I shut down the PC and headed back home for a nap.

Friday night, and I finally had something to do. After so many weekend beginnings alone, with no plans, I'd be double-booked. The thing was, I didn't want to go to either party. I liked June and wanted to see her again, but I knew it would mean hanging around with a bunch of dorky student government people. And I wanted to spend time with Cindy, but I knew she'd be busy with a hundred guests, and I'd feel jealous and alone. Neither of the situations were comfortable to me, but I needed to leave the house, fake a good time, and hope that something cool would drop in my lap.

I went through the regular drill—nice polo shirt, button-fly jeans, contact lenses, cologne, and checked everything twice. I looked as okay as I'd look. I took a deep breath, exhaled, and hit the door.

June's apartment looked simple from the outside—the top half of a huge box that sat behind a Chinese restaurant. It looked like a build-it-yourself storage building, with a thin wooden staircase leading to the second floor doorway. I wondered how she could put up with such a place—even my boarding house had more charm. I parked on the steep driveway; the Rabbit didn't have a parking brake, so I left it in gear and hoped it wouldn't slip.

I knocked on the door, and she answered. "Hi, come on in! Nobody's here yet." Right on. I entered and was blown away by the interior. The place looked like an all-out playboy pad. The living room was huge, with thick wall to wall carpet, a huge sectional leather couch, expensive indoor trees, a big-screen TV, and a fifty-gallon fishtank—with water, but no fish—against the wall. The kitchen was part of the big room, with a bar separating the two. A few barstools and a dozen bottles of booze sat at the counter, where she was setting out plastic tumblers and bowls of chips.

"This place is awesome," I said. "Did you have it last year?"

"No," she said, "I'm just subletting. I don't think I'd spend money on a leather couch, but they're renting me the place furnished for cheap. I like the novelty of it, but I'm going back to a nice, girly place next year. Hey, can I get you a drink? I bought some Cokes for you, I know you don't drink alcohol."

"Hey thanks," I said. "Yeah, I'll take a Coke."

She went to the fridge and opened it—cases of beer took up most of the compartment. "I have those Andrew Dice Clay tapes you wanted to borrow. Let me find them." We talked about the Diceman once, and she said she loved *The Day the Laughter Died* and I should check it out. I'd never met a woman that liked Dice before, but I considered it a good omen.

"Thanks, I'll give these a listen." She handed over the tapes and Coke, and I glanced at the homemade dubs, labeled in her immaculate handwriting. "So how many people are coming over tonight?" I said.

"I don't know, maybe a dozen." She went back to the fridge, and grabbed a bottle of Corona. "It's all student government people, but you'll like them. Unless it's the middle of election, they're pretty low-key."

"And during election?"

"Be glad it's July."

I went over to the couch, and sank into the leather. The TV, on mute, flashed pieces of videos from MTV. It had been so long since I owned a

TV and a cable connection, that the whole idea of sitting down for hours and watching pictures seemed almost ludicrous. But all of the cliche commercials and emotional hooks were brand new to me, and it was like drinking one beer after being dry for months—it knocked me flat on my ass.

June stood at the fridge, pulling out cans from cases and balancing the twelve packs and bottles so people could get a single beer without a crowbar. "Is anything on TV?" she yelled. "Maybe I should get some music."

She closed the fridge, which took a few tries, and then came back to the TV area. "Just put in a video on mute," she said. "People will figure it out when they get here." She put in a cassette, grabbed the remote and her beer, and plopped down next to me on the couch—RIGHT next to me. I didn't know if it was the shiftiness of the cushions, or an intentional move, but I liked it as much as I disliked that people would be showing up soon.

She pushed the remote button, and Kevin Costner and James Earl Jones appeared. "Oh, it's that one baseball movie," she said.

"*Field of Dreams*, I think."

"Do you like baseball?"

"You know," I said, "it's odd—I don't like sports at all, but I love sports movies. Watching a football or a baseball game is torture to me, but I'd pay money to sit through a four-hour biography on Babe Ruth. I guess I just like the best parts, all put together with a plot."

"I know what you mean," she said. "I spent a whole class studying news broadcasts, figuring out what kept people's attentions and what didn't. Pretty weird stuff..."

Silence. I knew someone was going to knock on the front door any second. If this was a quiet Tuesday night at home, I'd be at her in 38 seconds flat, I thought. Just feeling her sit next to me, her thigh next to my thigh, felt more sensual than anything I could've imagined...

There was a knock on the door. I can predict the future, I thought. She set down her beer, and ran to answer it.

"Hi!" a national-honor-society-looking couple appeared, and came in the room. "We've got plenty of beer, and mixed drinks..." June said.

The guy produced a bottle of Jose Cuervo. "Margaritas?"

"I've got plenty of tequila, but I'm not going to turn down more," June said. "Here, I'll set up the blender."

We sat around the TV, tightly packed on the sectional couch—maybe a dozen people, dressed like they were going to church, not to a party. I loved the couch, but it meant I couldn't sit anywhere without being directly across from someone else. Either this is going to crawl along for hours, I thought, or something's going to happen...

Then, all of a sudden, this tall, dorky guy started it: "Hey...aren't you JCONNER from the computer?"

Oh shit. "Yeah, that's me." I never knew how to react to the computer celebrity thing. Sid led a legion of whores, strippers, and yes-men with his fame, and Eric never acknowledged his work, except to other hackers with code samples. I was somewhere in the middle of the two. In mixed company and in the flesh it bothered me, but I didn't hesitate to use my celebrity status to help pull in and land the occasional cyber-babe.

"Does the university pay you to work on the utils, or is it for class credit?" a girl asked. Someone by the bar was erroneously explaining to another partygoer what the utils were and why I was "famous," the kind of explanation that made me want to beat someone to death with my shoes—like when your mom tries to explain satellite TV to your aunt, and it involves little men running through the powerlines, or something equally asinine.

"No pay or credit," I said. "In fact, we've had our share of run-ins with UCS, but we've played nice for most of last year. I do it for fun, in my spare time."

"Do you know Sid?" another girl asked. "Is he really weird in person?"

"Yeah, I heard he has a foot-high mohawk," said a guy.

"I heard he was blind," said another.

"I know Sid pretty well. In fact, I'm working for him at WQAX as a DJ now. He's not blind, but he's got Coke-bottle glasses. And he doesn't have a mohawk now, but he used to."

"Hey," said the dork, "remember when Sid lost all of his accounts last year?"

"Yeah, I was there," I said. "I thought I was going to lose my accounts and my job."

"Hey, I heard that Sid died," he said, "because everyone changed their nicknames to 'Sid lives.'"

"I'm pretty sure he didn't die," I said.

"Hey, how do I change my the quote next to my mail name?" he asked.

"Jerry, let's not ask John any more questions," chimed in June. My hero. "I'm sure he gets enough of those at work."

"Here, let me write it down for you," I said. I scrawled down the VMS mail instructions and handed them over. "If you have any more problems, stop by Lindley or the IMU when I'm working and I'll help you out."

"Thanks, thanks a lot," he said. He stared, perplexed, at the strip of paper, like I had just written down the recipe for a room-temperature superconductor that would solve the world's energy problems.

I got up, pitched the Coke can, and grabbed another from the fridge of beer. June followed me over and leaned right next to me, putting her arm around me, across the small of my back. "Hey, I'm sorry about Jerry," she half-whispered. "He can be a bit of a dork."

"Hey, that's okay—it happens to me a lot."

"So other than him, are my friends okay?"

"Yeah...I'm gonna have to split in a minute though," I said. "I've got another party to go to, and a friend that's leaving town this weekend is there..."

"Oh..." she frowned. "Are you sure you don't want to stay for a while?"

I wondered if she meant "stay until everyone else left," but I didn't want to spend six hours playing scrabble with Jerry while she drifted to sleep.

"No, I've really got to split. I've gotta catch my friend Eric before he leaves town. But maybe we can get together soon, for the unix thing?"

"Are you sure you still want to do that? I feel bad asking you computer questions on your time off."

"How about I get you some training pamphlets and set up your account, and you take care of dinner. Sound fair?"

"That sounds nice," she said.

"How about Friday?"

"Sure, I'm free. We can talk later and figure out a time and place."

"Okay, I've got to split. Thanks for the Coke, and the tapes."

"No problem, John." She leaned over and gave me a hug. I didn't know if it was intentional or a drunken gesture of friendship, but feeling her body against mine was my most erotic moment of the year. "Thanks for coming over," she said.

"Thanks for having me," I said. "Hey, I've gotta split," I said to the crowd. "It was good meeting all of you."

"Bye! Bye JCONNER!"

I went outside, and crawled back down the porch stairs. The Rabbit drifted about eight feet from its original space on the hill, but didn't hit anything. It fired up on the first crank, and I took off, wondering if leaving was a bad idea. All I could think about was sitting next to her on the couch, her arm around me in the kitchen, hugging her...Maybe if I would've joked around and grabbed her hand, threw an arm around her like I was being a pal, I could've seen her reaction. I wasn't turning on the charm or even trying and she reacted back—it felt like she was faking me out, but it felt good...

I drove to a payphone just north of the intersection of Kirkwood and Indiana, and left the Rabbit in the right lane of the busy street, blinkers flashing. In Bloomington, if you parked on top of a police officer with your rear tires on his spine, you could turn on your blinkers and not get a ticket.

One ring, two. "Hello?" a male voice answered, with lots of crowd noises and splashing in the background.
"Yeah, is Cindy there?"
"Hey is this Conner? It's Brecken. Where the hell are you?"
"Scamming," I said. "It sort of fell through for the evening."
"Anyone I know?"
"No, I checked."
"You should be here man. Everyone is here."
"Is Eric there?"
"Yeah, he's in the pool right now. Everyone is here, man. Even Gartman showed up. You gotta come out here."
"Okay, give me directions. I've got a pen."
I scribbled down a map from Brecken's instructions, and took off.

Cindy's folks lived in Elletsville, way the hell northwest on SR 46. I drove, with the Diceman in the player. *The Day the Laughter Died* wasn't his usual stadium act with the mother goose lines and written material. On this double album, he worked a small club, talking to the people, making stuff up, and doing all new material. It wasn't joke-a-second stuff, but more of a laid-back feel—the ambient comedy album. I dug it, especially for the drive alone.

I ducked off the highway and onto a twisty subdivision full of showcase homes. Cindy's dad was the dean of students—a prestigious title, with a home to match. I skimmed the cul-de-sac roads, and found a corner house with a few dozen cars in the drive and on the street. I ditched the Rabbit around the corner, and hiked in.

The house looked brand new from the outside, one of those eclectic designs that almost randomly combined arched ceilings, staircases, odd corners, and sunken floors so it didn't look anything like a cookie-cutter ranch or tri-level, even if it did sacrifice some practicality. On the side was a pool, glowing from the underwater lights, and a hot tub. Dozens of people were walking around with towels over their shoulders, jumping in, and bobbing around the water.

"Hey Conner, you made it!" I heard Brecken's voice yelling from the hot tub. "You bring a suit?"

"Just the one I was born in," I yelled back. I went to the patio, and saw at least a dozen faces I knew wandering in and out of the house. Brecken was right: I saw Bill, Alex, Renee, Eric, Rick, Linda, Joe, and many new people, too.

Bill stood over a gas grill, turning bratwursts and hot dogs over the blue jets of flame.

"Hey, this isn't part of some display, like the banana trick," I asked. Bill had a habit of showing people at the fountain that he could put a whole peeled banana in his mouth.

"No, these are too short," he said. "You want anything to eat?"

"Yeah, gimme two hot dogs."

He grabbed two franks from the grill with some tongs, dropped them in some buns on a paper plate, and handed them over. "Heard you had some kind of date tonight."

"Brecken should work for Western fucking Union. It wasn't a date, I just went to someone's party." I grabbed some catsup and mustard and did up the 'dogs.

"At least you're getting out of the house," he said. "I know I'm not one to talk, but this stuff helps."

"Yeah, I know. Still a lot of confusion, though. I'll have to explain it sometime."

"I'm all ears..."

"Thanks, Bill. Hey, I'm gonna go inside, and try to find Cindy. I'll catch up with you later."

Inside, the house looked even more incredible. The deck opened to a huge island kitchen with the latest in appliances and colors. I took a right into the living room, which had a cathedral ceiling and overlooking loft, a sunken floor, and stone fireplace spanning an entire wall. Some UCS people must've been there—a Monty Python movie was playing on the TV, and three or four people were repeating every line.

I saw a diva-looking woman with long, flowing black hair sitting on the sofa alone, nursing a drink. I went and sat next to her. "Hey, aren't you Jenny?" I asked.

"Yeah, I am. Shit, how did you know?"

"You don't look like a computer person, and I think I saw you with Cindy at Fun Frolic."

"Oh, yeah! You were selling glowsticks. What's your name?"

"John Conner. Cindy's told me a little about you over the years."

"Yeah, Cindy's mentioned you before, too. You used to live in South Bend, right?"

"Elkhart, but I went to IUSB. Total fucking nightmare."

"So you're a computer person?"

"I guess. Sometimes I wish I wasn't. I just went to this other party, and everyone there started asking me computer questions. I should've charged at the door or something."

"I don't know a single thing about computers. I'll be doomed when I try to get a job."

"You'd be surprised at how many people out there don't know shit."

Cindy appeared from upstairs. "John, you made it! How was your date?"

"God damn it, I'm never telling Brecken anything anymore. It wasn't a date, I just went to this chick's party, the one that asked me out a little bit ago." I bit into the now-cooling hotdog and got a mouthful of catsup and carbon-burned frank.

"And? Anything happen?"

"No," I said, my mouth full. "Well, maybe. I don't know. I can't understand women at all. We're going out on Friday, ask me after that."

"Hey, I've got to circulate. I'll be back in a bit." She vanished into the kitchen.

When I turned, Jenny was gone, too, which left me with the Monty Python freaks. I wandered around until I saw Rick running downstairs from the loft. "Hey bud, you just get here?" he asked.

"Yeah, I had this chick thing going on," I said.

"I heard. Did you buy the bitch pizza?"

"What?"

"Dice man, *Day the Laughter Died.* You gotta get that fucking album, man."

"I just did—I borrowed it from the chick. I'm still on side one. The Divider."

"Well memorize it. Hey, I gotta get another brew. Do you know if there's any left?"

"Dunno, I haven't checked."

"Okay, I'll be back. Hey, did you see Gartman?"

"No, where is he?"

"In the pool, I think. He looks like a little kid, short and bald. Like a chemo patient or something."

"Weird. I'll keep an eye out."

Rick vanished, and I went back to the porch, where Brecken was dripping wet on a lawn chair, chowing down on bratwursts and sauerkraut. I checked the chair next to him for dryness, and sat down.

"Good brats?"

"Yeah man," he said, with a mouthful of food. "Swimming makes you so hungry. You get anything yet?"

"I had a couple of dogs earlier," I said. "Hey, did you hand out fliers about me being on a date or what?"

"Sorry man, everyone kept asking me why you weren't here. How did it go?"

"Mixed, I guess. She was busy being hostess, but the few times we were alone went great."

"And..."

"Shit man, I can't call these. I've got a real date with her next week, or as real as the Conner first date gets. We'll see then."

"So you're going to spend the next week pissing and moaning about how you don't understand women and mixed signals."

"You got it."

"Well I hope it goes okay for our sake, then." He took another huge bite from the bratwurst. "Hey, you going swimming?" he asked.

"I don't think so. I think I'm gonna split. If you see Cindy, tell her thanks and that I took off."

"Why don't you go find her? She's around somewhere."

"No, she's probably busy. I'll talk to her later."

I went back to the cul-de-sac to find my car, and tried not to think twice about leaving so early.

"Hey Conner!" someone yelled behind me. I turned, and it was Eric.

"Eric! Shit, I almost forgot about you." He caught up with me on the road, a few dozen yards from the house.

"I just wanted to say hey before I took off," he said. "I'm driving up to Chicago tomorrow, and reporting to COBOL training Monday."

"Shit man, you find a place yet?"

"I'm staying with some family until the money comes in and things settle down."

"It's been one hell of a year," I said. "A year ago, Sid's lost his accounts and I thought I'd have to rewrite the whole damn util by hand. We sure got a lot done."

"Yeah, a year ago I didn't know shit about computers. I thought I'd be pushing car loans at a credit union or something."

"Pretty wild..."

"So what are you going to do next year, with the utils?" he said.

"I don't know, fight the good fight, while I can. I haven't told Sid, but I'm sure I'll be stepping out soon. I've got to get my act together with school, get buried in some classes that matter. I'm going to take

Weissman's C490 UI class and learn Motif, and get into more hardcore unix stuff, instead of this VMS shit."

"I don't blame you. But, love the one you're with."

"I guess so."

"Hey, I better get back. I just wanted to talk to you before I left. I'll drop a line once I get set up at work."

"Okay, cool. Catch you later Eric."

"Later, Doctor X. Happy hacking!"

I walked back to the car, fired up the engine, and flew back down 46, with Diceman still in the stereo. I thought about how much the whole VAX mafia was crumbling, and how much longer I'd still be involved. New people showed up every fall, but who would still be interested in hacking the old iron? I needed Obi Wan to show up and say "No John, there is another..." Instead, I got Dice saying "Ass eating? An art form?"

24

In the darkness of the heat-soaked room, my mind wandered, awake and unable to sleep. Drenched in sweat, the sheets wrapped around my body and over the worn and lumpy mattress. The thoughts and problems of the day clung to my mind. I should've stayed at June's party. I never should have left...

The fan tore apart air, but I couldn't get a breeze going with the horrible ventilation in the room. To keep cool, I cycled positions in bed, shifting from back to side to stomach. Each move interrupted the stream of thoughts, requiring a reluctant summoning of energy to push my aching body to a new position. It gave me temporary relief but it kept drifting back to the party, the few minutes before when she sat next to me on the couch.

I'd get up and turn on the lights, re-adjust the covers, and consider reading or playing on the computer for another hour. In the wash of fluorescent, my eyes felt heavy with sleep, and I'd crawl back into bed, ready to pass out. But, when the lights clicked off, the burning piss and vinegar of insomnia ran through me again.

As I tried to drift from the real world into sleep, my mind exploded through the gateways of depression, randomly focusing on all of the pressure points of my feeble life. It felt like a two-front war in my head. I felt jealous about Cindy, like I wanted to talk to her, spend time with her, but I never would. I could dismiss it if she was a consistent friend and not such an occasional appearance in my life. But I knew I couldn't rely on her—that she'd vanish after the summer, without reappearing for another few years. I knew I had to accept her varying availability as a friend, but it hurt because we connected so well. There were things that Cindy recognized at a core level that nobody else had. Maybe it was because I'd confided in her about my depression so much. Or maybe there was something more special about her? I needed to stop thinking about her.

And what about June? I wondered if she wanted something to happen tonight, if I was supposed to stay late. It would've been incredible if the same vibe I felt had continued afterward. If there wouldn't have been a room of her friends there when we were in the kitchen, I would've tested the waters, or more. Maybe she liked more aggressive men? Maybe it was like a test, and I failed. I hated the ambiguity at the start of a relationship, and I always took it too slow, but pushed things too fast once I got hooked. I know if I would've made it to the point of a first kiss, the push toward love and sex would've happened way too fast for her to handle. I always wanted to balance this, but it never felt right. My neurosis propelled things at such a disproportionate speed.

In the background of everything else, I thought about Amy. Even though we never met, she possessed so many qualities I wanted in a woman. I couldn't judge her just from the few emails we traded, but she really seemed to have her shit together in all the right ways. It hurt me that I had to take things at a crawl, and wait for her next move. If I was in charge of everything, I'd step up the schedule tremendously. But maybe that's why I kept derailing these things.

Fuck! A few hours ago, I felt so happy about June, and now I didn't think I'd be able to see her again. I kept thrashing at the sheets, and tried to focus on anything but her, so I could get a few hours of sleep before daybreak.

The Saturday morning's sunlight made it impossible to sleep past 11:00, but I felt wide awake anyway. After a Coke and a shower, I'd be ready for...nothing. Another day to kill.

I crawled out of bed, and fired up the computer and stereo. No email awaited me, but I still had questions from Amy to answer, so I got started.

To: arbergst@ucs.indiana.edu
Subject: Didn't KIERKEGAARD wear out his TIRES in VIENNA during a SNOWSTORM of FREUD's unpaid DENTAL BILLS?
—text follows this line—

Hey, I'm guessing you're away for the weekend, basking in air conditioning and running up a massive tab at a parent's expense, while I'm sweating to death in B'town. Anyway, I've got all day to sit in front of the computer, so I figured I should answer your questions and think of some more. Here goes:

1) My favorite book is probably a tie between Dalton Trumbo's Johnny Got His Gun and Orwell's 1984. (It's really The Bible, aka Kernighan and Ritchie's The C Programming Language, Second Edition, but I didn't want to sound like a total geek.)

2) I'm not sure I have a favorite movie. Maybe the Star Wars trilogy, or UHF. I don't have a TV, so I don't rent a lot of movies-just the theatres.

3) A favorite album is tough, since I listen to so much stuff. The CD of the summer sofar has been Chick Corea—Beneath the Mask. Last year it was Queensryche—Empire. (but not because of Silent Lucidity!)

4) I love Garcia's. Also Macri's. I spend a lot of time at Subway and Burger King too, though—I'm not a food critic.

5) I have thoughts about Chicago after school, or maybe California or somewhere else. I'm tired of Indiana, but Bloomington's not bad.

6) I was born at Grand Forks AFB, North Dakota and moved to Edwardsburg, Michigan before I was 1. Lived there until I was 7, then I was in Elkhart until I got down here.

7) The closest I've been to being overseas is going to the Stratford festival in Ontario. But after talking to all of these death metal people from Sweden, it makes me wish I could pack up my suitcase, put in a babelfish, and take off.

8) I took just enough Spanish to confuse myself. I need to get on the ball with it—I think I registered for more of it this fall.

9) I'm single. I split up with someone at the end of the school year-another long story. Not involved, and not asexual, the last time I checked.

10) No tattoos, although I've got the usual assortment of knee gouges that come with years of BMX bikes and climbing up trees. I also have a scar on my right hand where I accidentally fell on a nail. It's not as Jesus-like as you would think, however.

11) I call the Coca-Cola brand soft drink Coke, and Pepsi is Pepsi. I always say Coke because I prefer it, not because of any regional slang. (I do warsh my clothes at the crick, though.)

12) Looks—well, I'm about six feet tall, weigh maybe 175 or so. I have reddish-blonde hair, a little bit long but not really long, light complexion, freckles on my arms, glasses and sometimes contacts, blue eyes. I'm very much a jeans, t-shirt, and high-top type of person. I think that's as vague of an answer as I can get away with.

And the religious and political question is easy to answer, since I'm neither. Actually, I'm a recovering catholic and somewhat politically left-leaning, but don't let that discourage you.

Okay, now it's my turn. I'll keep all of my questions nice and generic also:

1) I'll ask you about looks first, so you'll think I'm as vein and shallow as everyone else on campus.

2) Why English with a French minor?

3) Where are you from?

4) Do you think Darth Vader was gay? Explain.

5) Favorite book/author?

6) Where's the coolest place you've traveled?

7) Single? Dating? Married? Scarred for life? Making someone's life hell?

8) What kind of car do you have? If you could have any, what would you have? (Don't be shy, I drive a beat-up VW Rabbit.)

9) Last movie you saw?

10) Your eventual goal in life in 5000 words or less, or alternately, what you wanted for christmas when you were 6.

That should keep you busy for now. I've got to go blow my paycheck now. I'll talk to you later.

-J

I logged onto the Rose VAX, and did a quick wholist to see who was among the usual gang of idiots today. I saw Erin logged on, with the username "KHARDER=slut", so I decided it would be worth an ask.

"Hey master," I bitnetted, "who's KHARDER and are you pimping her out or something?"

There was a long delay, and then she answered back. "Hello slave boy. KHARDER=my roommate Kate. She doesn't have any friends, so I'm trying to get weirdos like you to write her. Send her something tasty if you get a chance."

"Yes master. I'm going to take a shower now, but I will do your bidding later."

"Goodbye, slaveboy. Try to be good so I don't have to beat you."

I added KHARDER to my userlist, and made a mental note to write her some kind of scary email that implicated Erin somehow. I powered down the computer, got that shower and Coke, and started the day.

Saturdays with nothing to do were a long-standing tradition for me, going back to when I first lived in the dorms. It seemed like 80% of my floor would drive home to mommy and daddy for the weekend, and I'd be left alone, to catch up on the FORUM BBS online, and avoid homework. Even worse were the weekends of a home football game, where I couldn't walk around in peace without running into a drunken geriatric case wearing cream and crimson from head to toe, or some overly concerned parent who eyed me like I was the reason the whole world was on drugs. That meant hiding in the computer labs became almost mandatory. When that got boring, I'd try to wander the more remote areas of campus, walking circles, heading to the mall on foot or with my E bus pass, and do anything but sit in my bed all day.

That Saturday, I used the same methodology to kill time. I went to College Mall, and ate two hot dogs, some fries and a rootbeer at the nasty A&W. One time, me and Lars were in Chicago, at the huge mall near the airport, and we ate at an A&W that must've had 200 people sitting inside. I had the best hotdogs I ever had in my life, awesome french fries, and a rootbeer in a frosty glass mug just like the full-color poster in the store, not in a cheap paper cup with a plastic top. And it was the most incredible rootbeer, like drinking a quart of pure sugar water after eating a pound of sand. I kept going back to the A&W in College Mall, hoping to get the same combination, the immaculate grill worker that didn't fuck things up, but I kept getting the same generic shit.

I wandered the mall concourses, walking by the same shops I always saw, the glossy clothing stores with mirrored entrances I never entered. All of my friends hated the mall on some deep, philosophical level, and could never understand why I went every weekend. I never shopped—I only liked three or four stores—computers, music, and books, and I made all of my primary purchases along those lines at other places or from catalogs. But it felt like a drug to me—the mall calmed me. I watched the people, walked around, and meditated on my latest daydream, thought or problem.

After the mall got boring, I went across the parking lot to Target and did the same thing—stumble up and down the aisles, stopping in the electronics department to play a dozen games of Tetris on the demonstration GameBoy chained to the counter. In the fall, Target swarmed with good-looking women, but in the summer, nothing grabbed my eye. I headed across the road to Morgenstern's, thinking there would be lots of books and magazines I'd want to read for free. But a few minutes into an

O'Reilly book on unix, the sun caught me through the glass doors and made me feel like an idiot for reading books on such a nice day.

I gave up on the shopping and got back to the VW. I cracked open the moonroof, turned up Yngwie Malmsteen's first album on the tape player, and hit the road. Most people dismiss Malmsteen's fast-scale, guitar hero masturbatory playing as bullshit, but I thought his first album's neoclassical songs sounded awesome. It was the kind of music I'd only listen to alone in my car, which made me enjoy it even more.

I had cash in my pocket, and could've blown a wad on CDs or taken in a solo movie, but it felt like a bad move. Blowing the whole day on nothing was an art form, and I knew from past experience that shopping, or rather spending money would make the day go longer. I'd drop $40 on a few CDs, rush home, listen to them, and...it would be 2:30 in the afternoon, I'd be out of money, and just as bored. If I kept the money until later in the evening, something cool might come up that required cash, and I'd be set. It never did, but still...

I drove the Rabbit in the loops I used to walk—down the middle of campus, through the strip downtown, west of town in the boonies, way south of town, and in all of the funky subdivisions popping up just south of Bloomington. Bloomington was big enough to have a half-dozen McDonald's restaurants, but small enough that you could drive past all of them in 15 minutes. It made me wish I lived in Chicago, where every day could be another Ferris Bueller scenario. There weren't any hidden secrets, any cool spots anywhere on campus. I tried to find them—once I found that you could go spelunking under Seventh Street by crawling in a drainage ditch by the Jordan River, right by Seventh and Walnut. I brought a chick under there once, and found that you couldn't go much further than a block—not like those secret underground tunnel urban legends. It lost its fizz, and after I ended up dating the chick for a year, I couldn't bring anyone else there anymore. But I wish I had other things like that, a whole repertoire of them, so I could bring women to someplace other than Lake Monroe, and so I'd have something to do on my own.

The driving turned to walking, then more computer time, and Saturday afternoon melted into another Saturday night, with everyone else having plans that didn't involve me. The endless travel started to freak me out a bit, the feeling when you haven't said a word to another human being for 24 hours, and the only cure is loud, obnoxious, frightening metal at a dangerous level. Full of humid, stale air, my little prison cell echoed with a demo by a German band named Gut, who sampled porno films and the movie *Bloodsucking Freaks*, and played it back over Jabba the Hut's parlor band with chainsaw sounds and gargly-sounding vocals. The macabre yet silly songs like "Grotesque Deformities" and "Disgusting Corpse Dissection" served as a perfect soundtrack for my bored and randomly pissed off mood. With the fluorescent green etching my skin, I slumped over the computer, clicking away the keys and unsuccessfully trolling for people to talk to. Even the freaks in the house vanished, probably at some dope party in the student ghettos or something.

I kept at the computer, doing the obsessive-compulsive wholists, killing time until midnight. Absolutely nobody was on tonight, not even the regulars that spent as much time as me at their favorite VAX. I dug around my Bronze account, thinking about a bit of programming or something, but I couldn't get into hacking code. When I had free time to burn, I never had ideas for new projects or the motivation to continue with old ones. I also thought about reviewing some albums for the zine, but I didn't feel like writing. I didn't FEEL. And I had four hours to kill.

My stomach grumbled like I ate those A&W hot dogs weeks ago, so I figured I could get some good food for dinner and kill another hour. I logged out and dropped carrier to focus on making some sort of dinner plan. My wallet held two twenties, a ten, a five and a couple of ones, some of the remains of the last glowstick run. I also still had almost the same amount in the bank, which gave me full clearance to blow some cash on dinner. Part of me wanted to round up someone else like Brecken or Deon for some real sit-down food, but I didn't want to let myself down even more by confirming that every other person in town had plans but me. I dug through the clothes on the floor, found a pair of shoes, and checked my double in the mirror. With a three-day stubble, sleepless fatigue worn in my face, wrinkled, dirty clothes, and messy, random hair, I looked like one of the zombie extras from *Day of the Dead*. Oh well, I thought, quickly running a brush across my scalp to bring some sort of order to my appearance. I grabbed my keys, clicked off the lights and headed out the front door.

The night air felt cooler than the apartment, and in the darkness, the moon and stars etched their signatures above. A block and a half past my house, a strip of cheap pizza joints formed the southern boundary of campus, along with my favorite 24-hour haunt, the Village Pantry convenience mart. Cutting between the buildings, the lucid illumination softly painting the alleys in the night and the crunch of my shoes on gravel and dirt echoed through my mind in the silence. The walk still freaked me out, because it involved walking right next to Jenn's apartment. Every day, on the way to class, the labs, or the fountain, I hoped she wouldn't appear from the building and give me some huge Christian guilt trip or something. I tried not to think of it as I walked with my hands in pockets, craving food instead.

At the corner of Third and Jordan, the large neon signs and bright storefront at Mother Bear's Pizza contrasted starkly with the dark, empty night. It wasn't the kind of place I had in mind for tonight. There, they took your order, you sat down in a booth with all of your friends, drank pitchers of beer, and listened to music on the jukebox. Inside, I saw the men and women in red shirts and dusty white aprons, throwing dough in the air, pounding it into circles, ladling thick, red sauce into the pies and then scooping cheese and toppings over the paste. From the plate glass windows outside, their mechanical skills at pizza assembly were apparent, as they methodically slapped the pizzas to order and into the conveyor belt oven. It looked good, but I needed something faster, more convenient.

I kept walking, and went to Papa John's Pizza, a few doors down. Nobody could hold a monopoly on pizza in a college town, but Papa John's pizza was one of about three places that tried. To their credit, the pies were cheap, fast, and consistent. And with a store just around the corner from me, I ate there whenever I had a ten-spot to spare.

I walked into the store, a place with a front counter, a bunch of pizza ovens, and not much else. I already knew what I wanted—I always ordered the same thing. But, I still felt the urge to check the menu on the counter to see if something new could grab my interest.

"Hi! Welcome to Papa John's. What can I get for you tonight?" asked a lady at the red counter, her hands covered with flour.

After glancing at the menu one more time, I said "Gimme a 12 inch, pepperoni, some breadsticks, and a couple Cokes."

"Okay," she scrawled the order on a generic green and white pad, "that'll be $12.64," she said. I handed her the wrinkled bills from my wallet, and scooped up my change. "It'll be about 15 minutes. Do you want to wait here?" she asked.

"Sure, I'll be over at the games," I said.

While my pizza got constructed, Henry Ford style, I went to the far end of the lobby, where a handful of old upright video games beckoned. Spy Hunter, Galaga, Asteroids, and Tetris all stood at attention, flashing their teaser screens and high scores through their burned-in screens. Each game compelled me, but Tetris was the strongest addiction. In my freshman year, I spent serious amounts of time and money mastering the Russian revenge, to the point where I dreamed of the falling blocks in my sleep. A game or two would burn the time until the pizza was done.

Two games buzzed past, and the lady in the apron and red called up my order. The white and red Papa Bear's box steamed with the contents, and I carried the paper bag of breadsticks and two Cokes on top of the corrugated cardboard container. Hot in my hands, the box seeped the delicious smell of pepperoni, cheese, and fresh baked crust. I hurried back through the dark alley, still humming the Russian song and dance and trying to avoid opening the box in the parking lot to steal a piece or two.

Once home, I pushed aside the laundry and set up camp in the middle of my floor. With the box propped open on the carpet, I sat with my back against the dresser, scooping up pieces of the greasy pizza and shoveling them to my mouth. The crust crunchy, the cheese melting, the toppings spicy, everything hit my empty stomach with gusto. As a Chick Corea CD filled the room with heavy-duty modern jazz, I devoured the pie, interspersed with the garlic breadsticks and Coke from the can.

Most people might feel like some kind of loser if they were sitting at home on a Saturday, shoveling most of a pizza into their face. But to me, this was pure bliss. The few times I got to eat "real" food, something that was hot, fresh, greasy, and not from a wrapper or a can, felt great. The aroma filled the room and changed the bleak and stuffy cell into the kind of place that had a kitchen of food cooking, an oven baking. I worked through the pizza slowly, and after a half dozen slices and some sticks, I put the rest in the fridge and got back to the computer.

After seeing virtually nobody online for what seemed like hours, a roommate of an old prospect hopped on and immediately asked me if I could do her a favor. Seeing as it was really too late in the night for me to help her with her computer, I automatically knew she wanted me to buy her booze. I hated it when beautiful women asked me for favors based on my natural skills with computers or ability to legally buy alcohol—after all, I never asked them for favors on their natural skill of being a fuck toy. But as usual, I caved in and said fine, thinking that I could probably scam enough "personal excise" to buy myself a bottle. I told the girl I'd meet her over in front of the Village Pantry in ten minutes.

Another walk over to the corner of Third and Jordan; I spent two minutes trying to straighten out my clothes and brush my hair in the remote chance that one of her friends might want to fuck me or something. I didn't really know the girl; I chased her roommate last spring, but not that seriously. After three or four emails, I figured out the roommate was only into the rugby-playing type, and I gave up. I still talked to her on and off, and she sort of became a friend, but a very sporadic one. She frequently offered sympathy and pity, but not much else happened. I was hoping that since she had a million female friends and lived in an all-female dorm, she'd at least cast me out with someone on the B-list. But it never happened, and I didn't hear from here all summer—until now, when her roommate appeared, looking for a personal liquor shopper.

The girl pulled up in her daddy's car (an Audi 5000, incredibly expensive and stodgy,) with another female friend riding shotgun. I hopped in the back seat, and checked it out. They were both cute, but very cliquish, and typical freshwomen from some podunk town where everyone from the same high school went to the same parties and fucked each other. I rode in the back like a spare tire, listening to them gossip about various people I didn't know. During the ten-block ride to Big Red liquor, I think I got about 7 words in edgewise.

"Okay, here's our list and some money. You can have what's left over for your own stuff. We'll wait out here for you." I grabbed the list, and headed inside.

The Big Red on Third looked like a big barn, with a high ceiling, long racks of liquor, and a wall to wall fridge that could hold rain cold beer for 40 days and 40 nights. Once I got in the door, I looked at their list. It consisted of incredibly stupid and childlike stuff, like wine coolers, spiced rum, and pre-mixed margaritas. This was a store where farmers probably came in and bought big jugs of hooch with XOXO on them, like in the Beverly Hillbillies, and I would have to buy a combination of stuff that even the most retarded excise cop in the world would spot as a purchase for some dumb teenagers. I grabbed their stuff, and realized that they did pay me handsomely for the task—I used the skimmed cash plus a couple bucks of my own to buy a fifth of Bacardi black rum and a six pack of Corona.

I checked the parking lot about 900 times for undercover excise cops, then went back to the car with the large paper bag. "Okay, you're all set," I said. "Let's not look in the bag until we're out of harm's way." They pulled to the gas station across the intersection to fill up the car and get some pop, and I split the bounty among us. On the way home, they were both all smiles, and I managed to get about 30 words in this time, but I was still continents away from getting into their pants. They whisked me back to my apartment, said their fake good-byes, and dropped me off like used tissue.

At least I had the booze—cold Corona in one hand; warm, black Bacardi in the other. I wasn't planning on a binge that night, but the day of solitude and the few minutes of torture with them made me seriously think about a pre-fountain blitz. I still had a few hours, I had the tools, and I had some ice. What the fuck.

I dropped the stuff off in the fridge, and got back to my room. There was a message on the machine, a slurred, rapid message that wasn't done justice by the tiny microcassette's poor audio quality. It sounded like "Hi, this is Jen just calling to say hi, bye." I played and replayed the tape in the machine, but couldn't make out the name. Jen? June? It couldn't be Carrie; it was definitely one syllable. I knew at least two or three Jens, including the Christian one that just broke up with me a few days ago. She probably wouldn't be calling, though. Or would she?

Fuck it. I dropped the six of Corona on the piles of printouts and scrap paper on the computer table, put the tall bottle of rum next to my keyboard, logged back in and began the fun. I poured my first hit of the black Bacardi in my only shot glass, and held the liquor up to the light to check out its color. I never drank a full-bodied rum before, just the light stuff they used at bars when mixing rum and Coke. Only a few months before,

I'd never had rum at all, but last spring it became my default drink, especially when depressed. After I learned to love the highball, I dropped the Coke and graduated to straight shots of rum. And now, I braced myself for the first of the evening.

I kicked back the glass, and felt the dark rum burn my throat all the way down. Light or dark, it still tasted like slamming two ounces of pure jet fuel. I couldn't stand the fire in my mouth, and grabbed for one of the tall, cool beers in the cardboard carrier. I twisted it open and hiked back half of the bottle, the clear Mexican brew washing back the rum. I couldn't remember the beer after liquor rhyme, so I said fuck it, and kept at the Corona.

Nobody online. I felt stupid, logged on, by myself, pounding beers and shots, and I barely said 30 words to another human being all day. I liked to drink to get silly with my friends, at bars, at shows, just like anyone else. But when I was alone, I needed to drink, to try to mask things. It depressed me, it cost money, and sometimes it pissed off other people. But when I got this depressed last spring, before Tammy, or when she was about to leave, drinking seemed like the most natural thing to do. And here I was.

Fuck. I poured another shot, and slammed it down again. It still tasted like kerosene, but not as bad as the first time. I finished my beer, and got another one. Who the fuck called me, anyway? It had to have been Jenn, the Christian. She sent me an email at some point saying that maybe we could be friends eventually, but she'd need a while to herself, and she'd get in touch. I figured she was writing me off, but maybe she was ready to talk again. Or maybe something bad was going down with her? Should I call? Jenn drank as much as she fucked, which was never, and calling her with a few drinks in me might not be the best idea in the world. But what the hell, I was feeling brave. I took a good hit from my beer, dropped carrier, and fished for the phone.

I hung up the phone, went to the table, and poured another shot of rum. I bolted this one down without flinching, finished off my beer, and started another. Fuck, that was a bad idea, I thought. Maybe it would be one of those things I'd laugh at years later in my life, but right now, trying to call Jenn the Christian was idiotic. But I did, and I quickly found out she wasn't the mystery caller. She could totally tell I was half-loaded, and I expected her to run for a bible and a vial of holy water to protect herself. I was slurring, asking stupid questions, and telling tales like a senile old grandfather, which had her thinking I was the antichrist. I went on to say some of the truth I wanted to hide, like that I wasn't really mad at her, that I was really lonely and still thought about her even though we were totally wrong for each other. She gave me a bunch of typical, Christian, Reader's Digest advice, like that I should lay down and stop with the booze, and after I said I'd call and apologize when I was sober, we hung up.

Fuck, that stupid move made me even more depressed. The clock read 10:49—I still had an hour to work on my buzz and wait until the fountain. I finished my beer, staring at the blank computer monitor. June? I thought it was Jenn, but maybe it was June. I dug my phone numbers out of my pocket, and grabbed the phone again.

I somehow dialed the number to June's house, and she answered. She was watching a film with a few friends when I called. No, she wasn't the mystery caller either, but she was wondering what the hell was going on because she typically knew me as a non-drinker and a consumer of antidepressants, and I had a blood alcohol level so high that I should be legally dead in 37 states. I don't remember much of the call except that I was very out of character and that I kept going on and on about being depressed even though I was bouncing off the walls. June needed to get back to her company, but kept asking if I would be okay, and told me to call back if I got worse and she would stop over to make sure I was all right.

After this point, things got really vague. Only brief cuts and images from the experience remain, as my brain was preparing to black out. Even the next day, with the entire experience in my head, it felt like trying to piece together a twenty-year-old event, with just snippets and large gaps in between. I remember drinking more, spilling some rum and making it to bottle six of the beer, while constantly bitching about not having lime for the Corona (not that it mattered.) I also remember running through the house, knocking on doors and looking to see who was home because I had forgotten. Deon said I ran into his room yelling "Hey man! I'm fucked up!" and then ran back to my room.

I made drunk call number three, but I don't even remember dialing. It was to Carrie, and by this point, my stomach was revolted that I hadn't remember the age-old "beer after liquor" adage. I had never been sick before from alcohol, but found there was a first time for everything. I left her on hold as I ran to the bathroom and vomited, running back with a psychotic monologue about how I was afraid the landlord was going to show up in the middle of the night and evict me for puking. I ran back to the bathroom a second time, and Deon was there, not knowing whether to laugh or be concerned at my antics. I later found out that Deon mopped up my mess from the tile floor. What a guy.

Morning. I don't remember getting off the phone with Carrie, or falling asleep. I guess I didn't make it to the fountain either. I didn't even make it to bed—I was half-sitting, half laying at the foot of my bed, fully clothed, with the lights, computer and stereo still turned on. Patches of vomit that smelled strongly of pizza and rum splotched the floor. Six empties and a 2/3 empty bottle of rum still sat on the computer table. My first thought was that I needed to puke again, but I knew I couldn't. I felt dizzy, nauseous, and dehydrated. So this is a hangover, I thought. My first one. I wondered how long they lasted. I stumbled to the kitchen, filled a tall glass with water, and drank away. Within moments, Deon came in the kitchen laughing. He filled me in on the details I couldn't remember.

I spent my Sunday in pain, trying to get some shopping, laundry and cleaning done. Both Carrie and June called to check if I was still alive, and I got some replies to the weird email I sent out while blasted. I took June's advice and only ate white bagels and clear liquid all day and I fought back the sickness enough to finish cleaning my room before nightfall.

And while I cleaned the room and tried to rest, I got a call from Jen— Jen Taylor, a friend of mine from last year who was in town for the weekend. I changed my outgoing message to tell people to clearly leave their first and last names from now on.

25

With the aid of a solid ten hours of sleep, the last of my hangover filtered out my system by Monday morning, leaving me only with the usual dread of knowing it would be five days before the weekend. I made it to English class without any problems, but because of a fear of another GNP lecture, I skipped out on econ to head home for a nap. First, I wandered down the hall and got a Mac in one of the Ballantine labs to check for anything interesting in my email inbox. Aside from the usual work junk mail, a reply from Amy awaited me.

> From ARBERGST@ucs.indiana.edu Mon, 20 Jul 92 8:34:36 EST
> From: "plus ca change, plus c'est la meme chose" <ARBERGST@ucs.indiana.edu>
> To: JCONNER@ucs.indiana.edu
> Subject: RE: Didn't KIERKEGAARD wear out his TIRES in VIENNA during a SNOWSTORM of FREUD's unpaid DENTAL BILLS?
> Date: Mon, 20 Jul 92 8:34:36 EST
>
> What a pleasant feeling to return and find all of your answers and some questions for me. By the way, how did it work out with your multiple party plans? My weekend was okay. my sister and nephew showed up, which is a long story. I'm sorry I didn't get a chance to stop by and sneak some of your laundry in with mine. I think my

mom would be suspicious if she would've found Megadeth t-shirts mixed in with my clothes.

Okay, it looks like I have questions to answer, so here goes:

1) Thank you for being vein—now I definitely want to sleep with you. Anyway, I'm about 5'10", medium frame, relatively well-proportioned (never ask a woman her weight,) with shoulder-length, auburn hair, reddish-blonde highlights, wavy and usually up or in some kind of ponytail. Blue eyes, slightly myopic with contacts and the occasional glasses. I guess I'm part Irish, part some strange French-Italian-Polish mishmash of European ancestry. No scars or missing limbs, but I do have my ears pierced.

2) I got into honors English way back in high school, and found that I liked it. I like writing more than lit, but I'm good at both. I took French in high school and visited before my freshman year, so the minor happened naturally.

3) Born and raised in Indianapolis, if you can believe it.

4) I never thought about Darth Vader being gay, but I guess the all-black bondage getup and cape are a giveaway.

5) I don't know what one book or author I like most. I'm currently re-reading Orwell's Down and Out in Paris and London (and you should check it out, because I think you'd like it.)

6) Like I said above, I went to Paris on a school thing for two weeks. I want to go back!

7) I also got out the typical high-school sweetheart relationship this spring. I wouldn't say I'm scarred for life, but I'm trying to avoid a relapse. However, if you want someone to make your life hell, I think we could work out some sort of arrangement.

8) I have a nice, pretty, white Toyota Corolla that I've had since I was 16. I know, it's the typical chick car, but it gets the job done. She's starting to show her age though, and I wouldn't mind eventually trading up to a nice Jaguar or Mercedes, so I can be like all of the other girls on campus.

9) The Commitments, which was better for the music than the actual film, but it was worth the $5.

10) I want world domination, and when I was six I wanted the Donnie and Marie dolls that had a little motorized stage that pulled them around in various runway model maneuvers. It's amazing how priorities change over time.

Well, do you know feel you know every subtle detail about Amy Bergstrom? Do you need another round of questions? Maybe I should just sit down some night and write a bio with your brainchild program. For now, work awaits. Catch you later.

-Amy

Good answers, I thought. I read over the mail twice, trying to catch anything that sounded like a second shoe dropping, but I liked everything I saw. I logged onto Rose and did a quick who to see if Amy was still around. No dice, although I did see June hanging out in one of the other clusters in Ballantine. I went back to Bronze and replied to Amy's mail.

To: arbergst@ucs.indiana.edu
Subject: I want you to MEMORIZE the collected poems of EDNA ST VINCENT MILLAY...BACKWARDS!!
—text follows this line—

Hello and welcome to the Monday that never ends. I ended up going to both parties Friday, neither were incredibly interesting (no National Guard troops called, no cars driven into swimming pools, no stomachs pumped.) I went on a bit of a bender Saturday, the kind where you wonder why you woke up naked in a Presbyterian church on the south side of Louisville. I'm not much of a drinker, but it's important to know your limits. And hopefully, I'll be back on solids by this evening.

I was very impressed by your answers. It sounds like you're a beautiful, intelligent and interesting woman who could really make my life hell. If you'd like to start soon, give me a call at 5 in the morning tomorrow and accuse me of cheating on you. My number's in the book.

My sister had the Donny and Marie dolls. From what I remember, they both had holes in their hands to attach a toy microphone, and they vaguely resembled stigmata. I don't think I knew this at the time, though.

I need to go sleep another 4 or 5 hours to get my head on straight. I hope your day in the library goes well. I'll talk to you later!

-J

Another mail, another wait for a reply—I wished I could just go to the library and chat her up this afternoon, instead of the long, drawn out procedure. I didn't even know if she was dating, looking, or devastated from her last breakup, but I knew if I had five minutes alone with her to focus every atom of charm and determination in her direction, I could find out. I did a few more compulsive checks of my wholist to see if she'd reappear, then logged out and headed back to my hole in the wall apartment.

After a groggy nap, I pulled myself awake and tried to think about dinner. I wasted an afternoon doing nothing, driving south of town and listening to the new Carcass album. I sat down at the computer, dialed up, and found a new message from Amy:

> From ARBERGST@ucs.indiana.edu Mon, 20 Jul 92 2:14:23 EST
> From: "plus ca change, plus c'est la meme chose"
> <ARBERGST@ucs.indiana.edu>
> To: JCONNER@ucs.indiana.edu
> Subject:RE: I want you to MEMORIZE the collected poems of EDNA ST VINCENT MILLAY...BACKWARDS!!
> Date: Mon, 20 Jul 92 2:14:23 EST

I'm honored to know someone who actually went on a bender last weekend. I'm not much of a drinker myself, and all of my prissy honors-student friends were heavy teetotalers, so it's rare for me to run into those who imbibe. I hope I'm not offending you by saying that, it's just I take a certain comfort in knowing that I can live vicariously through you. And I hope you made it back on solids, you poor thing.

Yes, I am a beautiful, intelligent, and interesting woman, and since you are the first man who has fully realized that, I will be more than glad to make your life hell. How about I come over later and ask for all of my records back?

Likewise, I was very impressed by your answers. I just re-read them a second ago to see if I could add any snappy comments to them in response. I'm also a big fan of Garcia's, a recovering catholic, politically left, and I've seen Star Wars too many times to count (although Empire is the best of the three.) Small world, eh?

I'm about ready to get out of here for the evening—my roommate promised we'd order pizza and watch TV tonight. Hope your 4 or 5 hours of sleep went well, and I will talk to you later...

-Amy

I read Amy's message over a frozen potpie, killing time until a shift at the telefund. I couldn't shake my mental image of this beautiful woman, with long, flowing hair, an incredible smile, and the ability to make me laugh. Of course, I didn't know her at all—she could be an epileptic, smack-shooting behemoth with a clubfoot and a friend who helped her bathe, use the toilet, and compose such compelling email. But in my desperation, I hoped for the best. Even without seeing her, I constructed grandiose daydreams that revolved around meeting her, spending the rest of the summer with her, talking, driving, walking through fields and joking and everything else. I knew within three minutes of meeting her, I'd start the entire Conner routine of cooking dinner, taking midnight strolls, and convincing her I was the most unique thing she'd find on campus.

But not now—I had to get to my fucking job. I wolfed down the last of my pizza, grabbed another Coke for the road, and headed for my night shift at the telephone intimidation center.

The job inched past like detention in a slave camp. I never liked putting on a happy face and plodding through hours of work when I was depressed, and I couldn't concentrate on my phone rapport when daydreaming about Amy. The night was an ebb and flow of both emotions, the peaks when my fantasies consumed me, and the valleys where I wasn't sure why I was chasing her.

The strange obsession made me eye all of the women at work curiously. More than half of my female coworkers were from sororities, and all of them looked stunning. I sized up every woman I talked to or saw, wondering if she could be anything like Amy. Anyone with long, dark hair came into scrutiny, and I quickly tried to find differences based on the few things I knew about Amy. And I looked at the blondes too, sizing up their height, frame size, style of dress, figure, and features—anything that might match Amy's. It was like some sick version of an automated police description system that jogs through hundreds of sets of eyes, ears, noses, and hairlines to create a composite sketch of a criminal. None of the women at work looked anything like Amy, but the exercise kept me continually busy.

I kept at the phones, and earned $15 in bonuses by getting some poor sod in Arizona to donate $800 to the Varsity club. After my shift, the cliques of people talked about parties and friends while I wandered back to my car alone. I opened the moonroof, put some Dismember in the tape player, and headed back to my house.

It's hard to describe a day with any enthusiasm when the morning is spent asleep, trying to comprehend a teacher's lecture, the afternoon is spent in extreme fear about money, women, and psychological health in general, and the evening consists of drilling numbers into a phone from a sweatshop and asking people to send bail money to IU's overprivildged basketball team. Sometimes, during brief interludes during the day when I didn't know what I was supposed to be doing, I'd wander the campus with Ozzy blaring in the walkman and wonder if any of it was really real, or if Yehoshua sold my lithium on the black market and replaced it with psilocybin. I felt like I should be doing something great—getting my zine onto news stands across the world, creating some great new technology for the computer, writing the next great American novel. But in the end, each day seemed too similar for progress, too routine.

After another night of phone terrorism at the telefund, I returned to my closet of a room, drank a Coke, and stuck my head in the sink for a few minutes to wash away the summer heat. The thought of sitting in a kiln for the few hours before midnight didn't raise my skirt, so I thought about a trip to the IMU for a more networked and air-conditioned environ. Back in the VW, I zipped over to the Union building and found a space just a few hundred feet from the front door. I crawled up the long flight of steps, and headed down the long Mezzanine hallway into the Mac lab.

Inside, I saw Rick among the half-dozen people tapping away at Mac computers. He half-nodded a hello, and I grabbed the empty next to him.

"Hey bro, what's going on?" he said. He was telnetted to the Amber VAX, engrossed in a VAXphone conversation.

"Not much. Just got out of work, killing a few hours until the fountain."

"Yeah, I'm waiting for midnight too," he said. "I'll head over to Showalter with you later on."

"That's cool," I said. I fired up two telnet connections, and settled in for some involved time killing. "So who's STLSMITH?"

"Aw, just some chick I know from home," he said. "Hey man, Erin's over in Lindley," he said.

"You talk to her already?"

"No, not yet. I'll bother her when I get done with this."

On Rose, I saw that both Erin and her roommate Kate were logged in from Lindley, and engaged in a process name war. Erin had her usual "KHARDER=slut" and Kate changed hers to "EMILLER=bitch." Just for fun, I changed my name to "EMILLER=master" to earn any possible bonus points.

"Hey man," I said to Rick, "you wanna head over to Lindley and give Erin a scare?"

"Sure, what the hell. I'm just fucking around—I can do that over there too. Lemme wrap this up, and then we'll head on over."

"You met Erin yet?" I asked Rick. We walked behind the union, toward the labs in the basement of Lindley. It was a perfect night to hang out— cool temperatures, and a clear, black sky overhead.

"No, I haven't seen her at all," he said. "I haven't even told her what I look like, just that I used to live down in New Albany. I guess she's from the area, too."

"Shit man, everyone's from down there," I said. That summer, I met a disproportionate number of people from the Falls City area of Louisville, Kentucky, and the Indiana cities right across the Ohio River, like Jeffersonville, Clarksville, and New Albany. The list included Brecken, Rick, Erin, Kate, Abby, and my old friend Jen Taylor. There were probably more that weren't clicking in my head, too.

"Hey man, wouldn't it be funny if we switched identities once we got there?" he said. "I mean, if I told Erin that I was JCONNER and you said you were me?"

I laughed. "That would be fucked up. I don't know how long we could pull it off, though. We'd have to use each other's accounts. And she would probably figure it out pretty fast. It would fuck with her head though."

"Yeah, especially if we logged out and switched back to our real accounts without getting up. That would throw her off even more."

It still felt odd to hang out with Rick. It wasn't uncomfortable in any way; in fact, things were very relaxed with him, and it was just like hanging with Peter or Nick or any of my other old buddies. But he was the kind of guy who could start conversations with total strangers and wear a suit off the rack and make it look good, more like a movie star than the computer hackers I usually hung out with. I wondered how long the novelty would last, but I also enjoyed it while it unfolded.

Once at Lindley, we descended the half-flight of stairs and scanned the basement hallway of computer labs for our prey.

"How are we going to know where they are?" he asked.

"They're in the small PC lab. I checked their IP numbers before we left."

"Damn," he said, "you've gotta teach me how to do that some time."

We crept up the lab, and saw only three people inside. Erin sat at the end of a row, and Kate was next to her. We didn't announce our visit, so they didn't know the two strangers who entered the room were us. I sat down next to Kate, and Rick took the computer across from me. I logged on, and waited for Rick's username to appear on my list.

"What next?" he bitnetted me, giving me a quizzical but silent look from across the row of PCs.

"Hang on, I'll get things started," I bitnetted back.

I checked on Erin, and saw she was in the middle of a VAX Phone conversation. Perfect—I fired off a "Hello, master!" bitnet message to her, knowing she's probably blow me off, or at least not check on my location.

I got a chance to get a good look at both of them, while still pretending to be a stranger. I earlier imagined Erin as being some kind of geologist hippie Amazon woman into ultimate Frisbee, tattoos and the Red Hot Chili Peppers. In reality, she was a timid-looking, plain woman with a petite figure, straight hair, and glasses. It looked like she could've been a PTA mom or schoolteacher, although I knew from her mail that she had both naughty and nice in her system. Kate looked even more like the awkward librarian type, in a cute way. She had thick glasses, curly red hair up in a ponytail, and a pale, stick-thin figure. In comparison, Erin was much more athletic and mainstream, but both of them seemed much more reclusive than their VAX personae.

I set my procname to "I had EMILLER" and then fired up bitnet again, this time with "Master, that's a nice blue shirt you're wearing tonight." Two seconds later, I got a nervous reply of "where are you????" and I started laughing.

"So there you are, slave." she said, looking over from her PC.

"Hey Erin," said Rick, from behind his monitor. It turned out he was also pestering her while hiding his location.

"And I'm guessing you're Kate?" I said to the woman next to me.

"Yeah, and that's our other roommate Candy," Kate said, pointing to another similar-looking girl at the computer opposite Erin.

"Man, we've got a whole party in here tonight," I said.

"What is with your process name, slave boy?" Erin said.

I tried not to laugh, and then did another who. Erin was logged on twice, and the second process name was "JCONNER=MySlave." I started a second session, with the procname "whip me EMILLER" and a third with "1-900-EMILLER." Meanwhile, Rick already had "4goodtme=EMILLER" and "IAlsoHadEMILLER." Before I could do my next who, Erin also added "JCONNER=freak" and "RTHOMPSO=homo" to new sessions. My who list, which previously had about 5 matches, now had about twenty, making it look less like a summertime who and more like a list of people during the peak of the school year.

The lab filled with laughter, especially since nobody else was there but us. We all had anywhere from four to a dozen different VAX sessions going, and Rick started a multi-user VAXphone call between me, him, Erin and Kate. We were typing in one conversation full of nonsense, while laughing our asses off and talking about something else. Candy steered clear of the whole thing, but Kate reluctantly kept up with the rest of us, even changing her process names to anti-EMILLER epitaphs.

Every time a friend of mine logged on, I'd get another worried email, asking who the hell EMILLER was and why a dozen of her process names said bad things about me. Bill mailed me from the IMU, wondering who she was and what I was doing until midnight. I told him I was hanging out in Lind with Rick, and told him to come over and say hey. Bill and Rick knew each other, and even though Bill was head over heels with Rick's handsome rugged lines, he stayed neutral and a good friend. Rick was a jock, but he was also an English minor and knew more about literature and writing than I did. After a quick bitnet conversation, Bill packed up and headed over.

The five of us kept changing process names and firing off bitnets while giggling like schoolgirls. I kept talking to Kate and bugging her, and although receptive to me, she was also very quiet. In some strange way, I detected some kind of chemistry between us, although I'd already had one fatal accident with a too-virginal, too-establishment woman, and I didn't want to repeat it. But I kept flirting, when I wasn't bothering Erin.

Bill arrived just before midnight, with his trademark briefcase full of printouts and notebooks of poetry. By the time he got there, it was a quarter till, and the fun was winding down. Rick and I decided to leave our cars behind and hike with Bill to the fountain. After a last round of harassment and good-byes, we logged off of our many VAX sessions and headed out.

The idea of 8:00 classes might sound tolerable on fine print during registration, but after pulling in at two in the morning after fountain sessions every night, the novelty was wearing thin. I still managed to stumble into Ballantine around eight the next morning, and sit through an hour-long lecture on a topic I couldn't comprehend due to my dementia. I didn't even remember what went on that morning in class. Every single woman there was wearing shorts, and they all had such perfect legs. I thought I was trapped in some demented Nair commercial. There were many times I thought I had the testosterone levels of a habitual sex offender, and wondered if there was something I could add to my food to control it. By the time class was over, I was not only hornier than hell, but wide-awake. I decided to forego the usual computer lab session, and headed home.

Back in my little cube, I dropped my books on the floor, fired up the computer, and went to get a Coke. In the kitchen, something looked wrong, like someone had robbed the place. I suddenly realized that the microwave next to the sink was gone. The oven actually belonged to Marcy, my old next-door-neighbor who abandoned her room and stayed at a friend's place with AC. She left behind a bunch of her stuff, but must have come back that morning and grabbed all of it, including the microwave.

Fuck, I needed that microwave to survive! I had a freezer full of microwave burritos, and barely knew how to cook anything on a regular stove. The other kitchen didn't have a microwave, and neither did any of the people in the house. To make it worse, I HAD a microwave in the basement of my mom's house, gathering dust. I didn't bring it down last fall because Marcy brought hers.

After a few minutes of very concentrated hate and rage, I tried to think of a solution. I didn't have cash to buy a new oven, or even a used one, and I didn't have room on my Visa or MasterCard. But I had the L.S. Ayres card, and they had a housewares section, with small appliances. I did a quick calculation in my head, and decided I could handle a hike in the minimum payment until I started getting serious paychecks again in the fall. I grabbed my wallet, locked up, and headed to the mall.

Once inside the posh department store, I wandered through ladies' fashions and past the perfume counters, trying to remember where they kept the housewares. I felt stupid, walking through a place where socks cost $20, wearing an Anthrax t-shirt and tattered cut-off jeans. But, I had a credit card, and mission.

On the upper floor, past the expensive crystal goblets and wedding china, I found the kitchen department. They had shelves of juice makers, food processors, bread bakers, salad destroyers and every other useless appliance I didn't need. After much anguish, I found a shelf of broilers, toaster ovens, and a few small microwaves. After reading the features, I found a disposable $100 model that looked like it could handle burritos and TV dinners with no problem. I picked up the box, and hiked it to the counter.

On the way, I saw a clearance table of various items from the now-defunct electronics department, like cordless phones and fax machines. In the debris, I spotted a black box with the Kenwood logo. My home stereo was a Kenwood, and I had incredible brand loyalty for their stuff. I checked out the package, and it was a gray-market portable CD player. This was pretty heady stuff back then—Sony had a few CD Walkman models, but they weren't disposable consumer items, just audiophile gear. Like most Kenwood stuff, it looked two generations beyond current technology. It had a $229 price tag, but it was also 30% off. What the hell, I thought, I've got the room. I grabbed the player, along with the oven, and found a cashier.

At home, I set up the oven in the kitchen. Deon wandered in and started boiling cups of water. In my room, I cracked open the Kenwood box to examine my latest toy.

Although the box was a simple matte black with white letters, the player inside looked completely high-tech. About as big as three CD jewel boxes, it had sweeping, contoured lines like a futuristic car, and a clear window where you could see the disc spinning. The nose had a LCD display, and when I plugged in the AC adapter, I found that the display was backlit green. The four buttons also had small green indicator lights—the stop button had a rectangle, the play had a triangle, and so forth. It came with four nicad batteries—it took AA's, and I found that it had a built-in charger; you pushed a button and it counted down six hours on the LCD display while it juiced up the batteries. I also got a car adapter, a faux-cassette with a cord hanging off of it so I could use it on my next roadtrip.

Best of all—it came with a credit card sized remote. A CD player you could hold in your hand, with a remote! I loved it.

I loaded four batteries into the backside of the player, grabbed the adapter and a couple of CDs, and headed for the Rabbit. Within moments, I was listening to clean, clear sound of the new Chick Corea album, and zipping through the tracks with the remote. The player sat on the passenger side, and skipped a bit here and there, but sounded great. I wasn't this excited when I got my first player back in 1987. This would mean a new era in toting CDs all over campus, and having an even wider range of music as my soundtrack. I packed up everything, put the player on the recharger, and tried to find some kind of bag or backpack to conveniently haul the gear with me.

The Carcass *Tools of the Trade* EP echoed in my ears, the CD walkman resting next to my Mac keyboard in the IMU. The UK grindcore band's trademark sick vocals about medical terminology and rotting bodies kept me riveted to my own work. I hunched over the computer, editing the second issue of my unnamed fanzine, mostly just a list of my opinions on various albums and where to order a few underground zines and demos. I'd been at it all night, chopping down text and trying to polish the writing in my record reviews so it made sense. Most of this issue came from stuff I heard at the station, but long discussions with Nick about various industry news also helped.

The issue looked rough, but I liked it. It contained good information about a dozen albums, some of them previews that weren't even in stores yet. That felt awesome—I could review albums the second WQAX got a copy, and email it straight to the readers, instead of having a big delay while I dealt with printing and distribution.

I spellchecked the file for the fourth time, scanned it again for obvious errors, and crossed my fingers. Then I pulled up my electronic mailing list of Death Metal freaks all over the Internet, which now contained about 50 names, and fired the text file around the world. A total rush of nervousness and excitement ran through me as the computer chugged away and shot the zine to each name on the list. When it finished, I sat at the awaiting MAIL> prompt, and vowed to put in twice as much stuff next time. I powered down the PC, knowing that the next time I logged on, my mailbox would be full of replies of argument, rumor, news, thanks, and praise.

26

Another Friday night was going down at 414 South Mitchell, room 13. This time, I stumbled and rushed through The Ritual, the magical dance of preparation that occurred before a female visitor's first arrival to my place. I made another cursory check of the apartment for pornography, Satanic literature, serial killer novels, or anything else that might offend the average female, as if my piece of shit apartment didn't insult everyone but me. I spent the afternoon cleaning the place like I never would otherwise, and then suited up in my semi-nice preppie uniform: contact lenses, carefully styled hair, and Obsession cologne.

It was a rare occasion when a woman would come over, and it wasn't just any woman—it was June. I dwelled over every detail of her party the Friday before, how I may have had a window of opportunity, why I should have stayed until all of the other guests left. I hoped tonight would offer an even better chance for me, and I also hoped I wouldn't screw it up this time. This wasn't really a date per se, but an exchange of computer knowledge for food. I offered to help her get started with her silver account, the basics of unix. After that got boring, we'd go to dinner. Beyond that, anything could happen.

We made the plans in a game of email tag during the week, and I zapped her a set of directions to my place that afternoon. She called just a few minutes before to tell me she was on her way over. I hated being on the other end of the waiting game, checking the mirror, the room obsessively in the seconds before the other person's arrival. I nervously tucked away everything in the room that was the least bit questionable, and wished for a living room or even some space for a nice couch and table. I really needed to graduate to a bigger place some time in the future.

A car's tires crunched through the gravel spot out front, and I did one last glance around the room before heading to the front door. June emerged from her maroon Buick, and walked through the darkness to the front door. The front porch light worked for about three days of the year, until someone stole the bulb or rain shorted the fixture. Today wasn't one of those three days.

"Hey, come on in," I said. "Careful of the steps here." She walked through the door and into the brightly-lit front hall, where I got my first good look at her. She wore a laid-back outfit, jeans and a top that was tight enough to show off her curves, but nothing revealing. That and her perfume were more than someone would wear to a night at the study table, but still casual enough to imply that we were just friends. She was all smiles, and the crossed signals made me feel as excited and confused as ever.

"Don't mind the place—it's a dump," I said. We stood in the alcove, by the old mantelpiece and piles of unopened mail. "Let's see how much unix I can teach you before you get freaked out. I can get you logged in and teach you a few basic commands, and we'll see how things go from there."

I led her down the hall and into the carefully staged room, which looked like a disaster with the worst bits shoved in the closet or under the bed. "Have a seat at the computer," I said. There weren't two chairs, which didn't leave many options.

She sat down, and stared at the pile of junk wired together on the card table in front of her. "This is quite a setup," she said.

"I built it myself," I said. "Mostly spare parts. I needed something for when the weather's bad and I can't make the walk to Lindley." I dug out the pile of unix pamphlets I stole from work, along with some printouts of various cheat-sheets I wrote for friends new to unix. "Here, I got you some reading material. Some of this may be way out there, but this top one is a list of common commands and that sort of thing."

"Thanks," she said, eyeing through the stack of paper. "Oh, I have the card with my username and password." She dug through her purse for the small piece of paper.

"Great," I said. "Let's get you logged in." I turned on the monitor and hit Alt-D to dial out to campus.

She looked around at the panorama of cheap paneling, decades-old carpet, and layers of paint. "Is this a sublet?" she asked.

"No, believe it or not, I lived here last year. It's a hellhole, but it's the cheapest thing I could find that was close to campus." I paced back and forth as the modem dialed. "It's sorta like those Japanese hotels where they put you in dresser drawers. But it's cheap, and I'm always on campus anyway. It's just a place to sleep, mostly." The computer finished its squealing and connected to the university.

I looked over her shoulder, and smelled her perfume again. I got her logged in, and we changed her password so it wasn't a random string of letters and numbers.

"Let me copy a few files from my account into yours. They'll give you some abbreviations for commands, and make it easier to use the editor. Lemme drive for a second," I said, reaching over for the keyboard.

"Sure," she said, moving over so I could type. "So is this sort of like what the utils do?"

"Not entirely. The utils have a lot of programs—I'm just copying over some abbreviations and aliases to make a few things friendlier." I copied over the startup files from my silver account, and made sure everything would work in her account. "Okay, I think I'm all set here. So what do you want to learn? I mean, what do you want to do with your account."

"I just wanted to get logged in, and get some more information. It's hard to tell how to get started with this stuff."

"I know what you mean. There isn't much documentation available, but this stuff will get you started. And if you need help, you know where to find me."

"You're going to regret you said that," she said. "I ask a lot of questions."

"Don't worry, I answer my email pretty much constantly. You know where to find me."

"Okay, thanks," she said. "So, are you hungry? Do you have any ideas for dinner?"

"Yeah, I'm starving. You ever go to Macri's?"

"Once or twice—that sounds great," she said.

"Macri's it is, then." I shut down the computer and we headed out.

We got into June's car and she drove. It felt just as weird to be chauffeured by my date as it did riding in her grandpa-mobile. She actually had one of the sportier Buicks, a two-door with curvy lines, a lower front nose, and bucket seats. It looked almost brand new, and smelled showroom fresh. I glanced over at the all-digital dash and saw it only had about 16,000 miles, clearly the mark of a sweet-sixteen present that was only casually driven. We cruised down Third Street to the College Mall Road, and then past the mall and other fast food shops to a strip mall with a giant 24-hour Kroger. We parked a few doors down, in front of the restaurant, and walked in.

Macri's was a pseudo-Italian deli place, the kind of joint where you'd order a meatball sandwich and a dozen beers and watch the game with your buddies. It was all wood: a big teak bar, mahogany trim everywhere, and solid wood booths, tables, and benches with high dividers absorbing the loud conversations. Long banquet tables stretched across a front room where parties sat like Vikings, drinking brew from tall mugs, passing around appetizer trays with chips and all kinds of fried objects, and watching the TVs hung in the corners. And she didn't know it, but Macri's was my old scamming hangout. Although I also went there with a few of my computer science buddies for Saturday night dinners, I frequently used the place as a first date test area.

The Friday night crowd filled the restaurant, but after a two-minute wait, a server walked us to the back room through the maze of cubicle-like tables and sat us in a booth.

We took a quick glance at the menus, then June looked up and smiled at me. "Do you eat here a lot?"

"Every once in a while. My friend Michael likes it here a lot for some reason. I wish they had better pizza though."

"Have you ever been to Gino's East? In Chicago?"

"Is that the one where you can write on the walls? Or is that Uno's?"

"No, that's Gino's."

"I went there once, summer after high school. It was pretty good, but I couldn't find a blank spot on the wall." I looked at my menu for a second. "Shit, they should let us write on the walls here."

June laughed, and kept her eyes on me the whole time I tried to make her laugh. I knew if I kept calm and kept the jokes rolling, things would be okay by the end of dinner. Or at least that's what I hoped.

Our server showed up, and I ordered my usual, the reuben. June got the turkey deli, we both got Cokes, and the wait for food began. Around us, we could hear other muffled conversations, but no loud parties like during Big Ten football weekends in the fall.

"This is nice," she said. "It's weird to see a restaurant with this kind of atmosphere in a strip mall."

"I know, it looks like there would only be Subway shops and Pizza Hut delivery stores here."

"There's a really good Chinese place right next to Kroger," she said. "It's one of my favorite. It's got the whole Chinese decorating thing going on, with the pillars and paper windows and everything."

"I know, I've been there a couple of times," I said. "They're the only place in town that has really good crab rangoon. You should check it out the next time you're there."

The server came back with our drinks and June and I sipped them in an uncomfortable silence. She still gazed at me with her dark brown eyes, like she was hypnotizing me. Anyone else would've laughed or joked around about such continuous eye contact, but she didn't say anything.

"So, do you really use unix all the time?" she said. "I hate to sound like a geek, I'm just curious what you do on the computer all the time."

"Don't worry, it's a pretty common question these days. I'm on Bronze a lot, which runs unix. It's mostly a research machine, but I use it for email and programming."

"You mean programming for UCS or for the utils?"

"Neither, really. I don't program for UCS, and I work on the util stuff on the VMS machines. I taught myself to program in C on Bronze, and messed around with writing a chess game last year."

"Is this what you want to do when you get out of school?" she asked. "I mean, write games?"

"Sometimes I think that all I want to do is finish a CS degree, move to Chicago, and get the first job that pays me a decent salary. But sometimes I think I should quit now and start my own company or something. I think there's something waiting for me, beyond working in a cubicle, but I can't figure out what it is. And school has been kicking my ass lately. My transcript looks like hell right now."

"I know what you mean," she said. "I got kicked out in my freshman year, and then spent last year on contract. They have this weird points system where you get so much for an A or a B, and you have to earn so many points to dig yourself out. I just finished my contract first summer session. I've got to keep on the straight and narrow from now on."

"I'm not on contract, but I'm right at a 2.0 right now. I've got a scholarship riding on my summer grades, so I haven't been sleeping much these days."

The server came up with a heaping platter of food. "Who had the reuben?" I nodded, and she set down our sandwiches. Mine looked great—toasty bread, tons of corned beef, sauerkraut, and plenty of melted cheese and thousand island dressing. We also got baskets of homemade thick-sliced potato chips, fresh out of the oven and drenched in salt.

We dug in, and my thick sandwich tasted as incredible as ever. I could almost never finish a whole reuben at Macri's, but after a long day with only a slice of pizza for lunch, I tore through the first half before even thinking about it.

"How's your food?" I asked.

"Great," she said. "I should come here more often. This sure beats eating at Subway."

She looked so beautiful across the booth from me. The low lights and earth tones of the wooden surroundings brought out the brown in her eyes, and made her gaze even more vibrant. While I ate and looked back at her, I tried to pinpoint the unique combination of traits in her personality, the things I couldn't pick up in email. In one sense, she was a tomboy; she wasn't the salad-eating type, she liked a good beer, and she seemed very self-confident. But, she had very strong feminine features: her looks, her hair, her perfume, the way she moved. Just watching her amazed me.

We finished eating, and eventually the server brought the check, which June covered. We walked out of the bustling restaurant to a quiet and peaceful parking lot. It was only about 10:00, and clear enough to see stars in the nightfall. I didn't want to end the evening, but I wasn't sure how to invite her back to my house without making my plans obvious.

"Hey, do you want to go for a drive for a while?" she said.

"Yeah, that sounds cool." We got into her car, and I watched the dashboard burst to life with glowing orange lights and gauges. She pushed a button and the power moonroof's metal shield purred open, displaying the clear night through the tinted glass window.

We drove the same lazy circuits I drove when I was alone and bored—Third to Indiana to Tenth to Fee to 17th to Jordan and back again. I didn't pay attention to the route, but to her. We talked more, but it trailed off into a comfortable yet uncomfortable silence. I could visualize everything about her, everything I wanted to happen. I could taste her skin, feel her body pressed against me. I was so scared it wouldn't happen, but I kept asking myself if it was as sure as I wanted it to be. The way she looked at me, talked to me—her major was speech communications, she studied speech, non-verbal communication, persuasion. I knew it wasn't an accident. But it was just like her wanting to learn unix, but neither of us knew why. Was it all a fluke?

I knew I had to do something. While she slowly circled the campus again, I reached over, and held her hand. It felt awkward and sophomoric at first, but she smiled back at me, and held my hand as she drove. Her palm felt soft and sensual in mine, and her fingers wrapped around mine in a way that made me feel that all of my feelings were reciprocal. Since the time she sat next to me on the couch before her party, I dreamed of touching her again—hugging her, joking around, something. It felt incredible, and made my visions of us together even more realistic.

The drive continued for another lap of campus, but then she headed back for my place. It was only eleven, but she had stuff to do the next day, and had to get back early. We got back to my place, and I wanted to invite her back in, or give her a quick kiss, but I chickened out. I figured she'd keep for the weekend, and I could devise some better plan of attack next week. I thanked her for dinner, and she drove off, leaving me happy, a bit confused, and wondering what I'd do next.

Inside, Deon and Yehoshua were fucking around with a near-empty bottle of Jagermeister and some plastic cups. "John!" Yehoshua yelled. "Who's the chick?"

"She's just a...well it's a long story."

"She looked pretty good," Deon yelled. "Hey man, we're almost out of Jagermeister, or I'd give you a shot."

"That's okay man, I don't see how you can drink that shit warm. It has to be at absolute zero for me to get it down."

"Hey man, will you drive us to the liquor store?" Yehoshua said. "We want to get some tequila. And one of those little fucking bottles of whiskey."

"Yeah man, bring us to Jerry's," Deon said.

"I just walked in the door, man," I said. "Ask me later—I've gotta crash for a second."

I left them in the front hall to finish their Jagermeister, and went back to my room. It felt odd seeing the computer setup where June sat only a little bit ago. I took off my shoes, went to the bed, and stared at the ceiling, wondering what would happen next.

Seven minutes later, I heard a knock on the door, and Yehoshua opened it and came in. "Dude, will you take us to the liquor store now? You don't have to drink any of the tequila, just drive us there and back."

"Fuck, man." I didn't want to be their personal errand boy, but it would be good to hang out with the guys instead of replaying the whole evening over and over in my head. I took a look at my watch: 11:36. "I'll make you guys a deal. If I drive you to Jerry's right now, we go to the fountain and hang out for a little while."

Deon instantly appeared out of the hallway. "We're going to Jerry's? When?"

"Dude, he wants us all to go to the fountain with him, though."

"That's cool man. We'll buy a couple of cans of Coke, and then put the whiskey in that."

"Let me get my shoes on and we'll leave," I said. I got out of bed and got moving.

At about two, I got back to the house, depositing my half-loaded roommates in the kitchen with the remainder of their Jose Cuervo and Wild Turkey. The fountain wasn't bad, and nobody except Brecken asked me about my latest schemes. Yehoshua hung out with Bill, and didn't realize Bill was hitting on him the whole time—he just thought he was a really nice guy who gave him bananas that just happened to be in his backpack. And Deon and Chad got in a huge discussion about the virtues of various big and tall clothes stores. So I didn't feel bad for dragging them along.

I couldn't stop thinking about her. Was I too forward? It seemed like I'd be in or out on the first date, not in such a precarious position. The pessimist in me said I fucked it all up, and she just wanted to be friends, and I'd be getting The Lecture soon. But part of me held on the odd fantasy I had going on my head. I checked my mail before bed, and then turned in early, trying to think of how I'd play this next.

I woke up early the next morning, somehow thinking I had to get to class. I tried to go back to sleep, but by 8:00, I knew the heat would prevent any more rest, so I jumped in the shower and started another lazy day.

I still felt good about the night before, optimistic. It was the kind of feeling that made me think I could go out and start coding and working and cleaning and getting other things done I usually ignored. It reminded me of what I felt when I first dated Tammy. It wasn't as strong—June wasn't as sure of a situation. But it still felt better than a kick in the head.

While in the shower, I thought about seeing her again, maybe calling her. She had to go out of town for the weekend for a concert, but maybe on Monday I could give her a ring. I didn't send any email, because I wanted to be careful, and avoid smothering. It all seemed too orchestrated, but I knew if I gave it time and didn't push anything, I wouldn't screw it up. At least that's what I hoped.

I got dressed, grabbed my walkman, and headed for the IMU, thinking I could catch the breakfast buffet in the cafeteria. For only a few bucks, you could get a pretty kick-ass meal with lots of eggs, pancakes, hash browns, and the whole deal. I wanted to make it a regular ritual on Saturdays, but I never woke up early enough, and I never had the coin to afford an $8 breakfast every week.

On the way in to the IMU, I saw June's car parked with the blinkers on, by the backside, near the entrance by the computer labs and bowling alley. I walked up to her car, and as I did, she walked out of the union with a file box full of stuff.

"Hey June!" I said. "What's up?"

Before she said word one, I could tell something was severely wrong with the situation. Everything I loved from last night—the eye contact, the communication, her attentiveness—was gone. "Look, I'm sorry John. I didn't tell you this, but I decided to go home for the rest of the summer. Things haven't been working out here, and I need some time off to recharge. I've been thinking about this all session, but I need to get out of here. I'm sorry if I've misled you."

"No, it's just...I don't know."

She put the box in her trunk, and closed it. "Look, I've got to get out of here. I'll talk to you when I get back."

She got in the car and took off without saying goodbye. This is a new one, I thought. No longer in the mood for breakfast, I turned around and headed home.

The slow walk down the campus road behind the IMU immersed me in beauty and sunlight when darkness and despair saturated my mind. I knew nothing awaited me back at my apartment, and I could always catch some air conditioning and a fast net connection in a computer lab. Instead of turning around and going back to the IMU, I hiked into Ballantine, and found a PC lab on the first floor where I could drown my stories in telnet connections.

I logged in, checked for new mail on Bronze (none,) and got ready to begin the usual floundering on Rose, when Amy bitnetted me.

"Hey, what's up?" she said. "How's your Saturday?"

"Saturday is not optimal," I said. I did a quick check on her location—Library, PC cluster.

"What's wrong? Everything OK?"

"Umm, girl trouble, sort of." I said. I didn't want to admit that I had other irons in the fire, but what the hell—maybe it would make her jealous.

"I didn't think you had a girlfriend."

"I don't. And it looks like I still don't. Long story."

"Sorry to hear things aren't working out for you," she said. "And someday I hope I get to hear a few of these long stories."

"Don't worry, you will. So what's up in the Library?"

"I love how you always know where I am," she said. "I checked to see if a server at work made it through the night, and now I'm wasting time. You doing anything for lunch?"

"I don't know," I said. "I think I'm going to mope around, listen to loud music, read *Catcher in the Rye*, I dunno."

"Well, you're welcome to come to Garcia's with me, but if you need to mope, I understand."

"I'm sorry," I said. "Raincheck?"

"Of course," she said. "I'm going to split. Feel better—lots of fish in the sea, etc."

"Okay, I'll go home and make some lemonade with all of these lemons. Catch you later."

I logged out and hiked home, thinking about a nap for an hour or two. Instead, I stared at the ceiling, then began the dance of wandering campus alone for twelve hours until the fountain.

I straggled back to Mitchell Street just after two in the morning. There wasn't a bad crowd at the fountain that evening, which almost made up for a full day of mind-numbing depression. After unloading my stuff, and getting a drink, I got on the computer and checked my mail, not expecting to find anything. When I got to Bronze, there was one message, from Amy.

> From ARBERGST@ucs.indiana.edu Sat, 25 Jul 92 23:49:33 EST
> From: "plus ca change, plus c'est la meme chose"
> <ARBERGST@ucs.indiana.edu>

To: JCONNER@ucs.indiana.edu
Subject: A steaming bundle of self-promotion
Date: Sat, 25 Jul 92 23:49:33 EST

Hello there. I'm assuming you're at the fountain. I'm in a highly caffienated mood, and almost thought about dropping in there to findyou, but I figured I'd scare you. And I guess I can't call you at home and start making your life hell, as I had promised. But I thought you needed some kind of cheering up, given our conversation earlier today. I figured as a treat to you, I would sit down and write a bio. I already read yours with the BIO command, which gives me an unfair advantage. I didn't want to publish my info to the world like you, so I'm just sending you the sorid details. Here goes.
I was born on February 12th, 1970 in Indianapolis. I've got an older sister, born in 1967, named Tracy. My dad's a pediatrician, and my mom has a BA in psychology, and spent most of my childhood working assorted administrative jobs at various mental health care facilities, or staying home with us two. I'm the only person in the world who has parents who are still married, which can be slightly alienating–all of my friends get two Christmases and have twice as many grandparents. Oh well.
We grew up close to Broadripple, but moved to the stereotypical tri-level in Lawrence right before I started school. It was aluminum siding, a split-rail fence, two cars in the garage, a paneled basement, and everything else you'd expect from suburbia.
I learned to read at an early age, did well in school, and signed up for almost every activity thrown at me. I guess I felt a need to excel, so I tried to get every girl scout badge in the book, and read through most of the grade school library. I got into ballet, the clarinet, and spelling bees before I even knew I was a geek. My parents loved it, especially since Tracy wasn't exactly a model student. For every A+I brought

home, Tracy was getting into some sort of trouble at school. We didn't get along, and fought like most sisters probably did.

By the time I was in junior high, Tracy pretty much went off the deep end. Smoking, alcohol, pot, older guys, you name it and she was into it. Pretty soon, she was getting in trouble with the law, underage drinking and curfew violations. My folks grounded her, threatened her with therapy, lockup, and it just made things worse. She skipped school more than she went, and before too long, she dropped out and took off. My parents spent months trying to find her, until she reappeared, out of cash and strung out on dope. She spent some time in juvenile, and in an in-patient facility, but kept wandering. She'd stay straight for a few months, get a job, and then vanish. Now she's got a kid, and she shows up every few months to bum money off of my folks (hence her recent visit.)

In junior high, I met a few friends who weren't in the prep clique, and we kept together through high school. (One of them, Karen, was even my roommate here in Bloomington.) High school was a blur of honors English, AP math, honor society, and a part-time job at a Waldenbooks.

During my sophomore year, I met Dave, the high-school sweetheart I mentioned before. I'll spare you the sappy details, but this was the default high school relationship that everyone thought would turn into a marriage and a few kids. We were in love, went to proms and dances, met each others' parents, and all of that.

I liked reading, loved writing, and decided to try being an English major, with the eventual hopes of a PhD and a college teaching spot, or a BA and teaching credentials for high school. I applied to other schools, with vague thoughts about running away to Columbia or Stanford or Berkeley. But Dave wanted to go to Bloomington for business school, I wanted to be with him, and both of our parents seemed to be into the idea of us staying together.

I went to Paris the summer before my freshman year, as part of an extended tour group. It wasn't academic, but I learned a lot more about the language than I did in four years of French classes. I stayed for two weeks, and loved every minute of it. I don't know how I'll swing it, but I want to go back someday—maybe for a semester of grad studies, or just another vacation.

In my freshman and sophomore years, I lived in Willkie with my friend Karen, on the academic floor. It was a tight-knit group, with everyone pulling 4.0's and fairly naive about life. I have a lot of good memories of Sunday dinners, outings to plays, and the endless gossip between us. I'm still in good touch with most of the women from my floor, and we still hang out whenever we can.

Well, I'm running out of steam here, and the rest of the story writes itself. Things drifted with Dave after his last year of b-school, and at the end of the school year, we parted ways. He's in Chicago now, working for an accounting firm. I saw it coming, but it still hurt. I don't think I need to explain that whole ordeal any more.

So, that's the drill. Hope I didn't freak you out or anything. I've gotta split, so I'll catch you later.

-me

I read through it twice, and everything about her made more sense. I always thought she was a kind and caring person with an inexplicable interest in what I had to say. Now I saw that she was similar to me in many respects. It made me that much more hopeful that a bond would develop between us when she arrived.

I powered down the computer, and tried to imagine what she was like in person. I crawled into bed, and passed out within minutes.

27

By Monday morning, the depression over June made me feel like Iron Man from the Black Sabbath song, my boots made of lead and dragging across campus. I was so fucked up, I accidentally went to both of my classes, and even took notes. After that, I moped home to catch lunch before a shift at Lindley. During my usual ration of microwave burrito, I fired up the PC, and found a message from Amy:

> From ARBERGST@ucs.indiana.edu Mon, 27 Jul 92 9:39:22 EST
> From: "plus ca change, plus c'est la meme chose"
> <ARBERGST@ucs.indiana.edu>
> To: JCONNER@ucs.indiana.edu
> Subject: Re: All of life is a blur of Republicans and meat!
> Date: Mon, 27 Jul 92 9:39:22 EST
>
> Hey! I tried to log on and catch you after your class. Did you actually go to both of them today?
> How was the weekend? I didn't do much—got caught up on homework, rented JFK (opinions?) bought a new phone at Target. I hope you caught more excitement than me.
> Don't take this in a Mark Chapman sort of way, but I had a dream about you last night. I know I don't know what you look like, but I somehow knew it was you. I was at a party and you were in the band. The songs were all strange, Zappa-esque. I think you played guitar and sang.

OK, I guess you're not around. Let me know how the winds are blowing.

-Amy

The message from Amy lifted the depression enough for me to smile and half-laugh. Dreams about me...it made me wonder if I had a chance in hell with her. After June, I felt like vowing away woman for at least a three-month probation, until I could get my head on straight. But toying with Amy wouldn't hurt. While gulping down my processed lunch, I fired off a reply:

To: arbergst@ucs.indiana.edu
Subject: MY income is ALL disposable!
—text follows this line—

Hello you.
Believe it or not, I went to econ class. I can't say I remember any of it, and I can't read my own notes, so you'll have to trust me on this one.
My weekend was depressing. No, demoralizing. Maybe both. I guess I can trust you, so I will give you the synopsis. I've been vaguely interested in this woman for part of the summer. We went out on Friday night, and it looked like things were going well, but when I saw her on Saturday, the CIA's MK-ULTRA agents had injected her with LSD and some other mind-bending agents so she would fail to see any further interest in me.
That's the summary. I could go into more detail if my exploits humor you.
Blah—at least I am busy today. I've got a 12-4 in a minute at Lindley, and the telefund tonight. Speaking of which, I've gotta bolt. Catch you later!
-Jon
P.S. Oswald acted alone.

By the end of the message, my food was gone and I was running late. I dropped my dishes in the sink, turned off the computer, and grabbed my walkman. 11:47. I needed to get to Lindley by noon, and it was a fifteen-minute walk, ten if I really kicked ass. The adrenaline flowed as I got the headphones over my ears and ran out the door.

Amy's email spiked the happiness level of my day just a bit, like a quick shot of nitrous into a racing engine. But during the walk, it dissipated, and anxiety started eroding into me again. It wasn't just the fear of being late for a shift at work, but an all-encompassing feeling that something greater was playing with me, preventing me from working at full capacity. The jumble of what happened with June, with every woman that year made me wonder if Amy was nothing more than a cruel joke. I wanted to act cool, wait things out, and let it take its course. But it also felt like I couldn't deal with it, like I was signing myself up for something I couldn't handle.

The feelings surged through my system like a bad drug, eating at me like cheap speed. Each breath became heavier, more labored, like I had to sigh deeply each time I exhaled. Part of me knew none of this had to do with Amy, or me, or anything else. But with the sickness so directly wired to my emotions, I couldn't help thinking that my world was raining down on me. My only solace was that I had a doctor's appointment the next day. Maybe he could put me on some more medicine to stabilize things.

11:54. Lindley Hall was in sight, and I'd make it with time to spare. I relaxed my pace and tried to get myself ready for the next four hours of theatrics.

Although masking my mental stability from casual observers was a skill I'd mastered over the years, working while depressed was my forte. Even during the most homicidal arguments with Lauren last year, the kind of thing that made me want to jump off of Ballantine Hall after setting myself on fire, I managed to pull myself through many four-hour consulting shifts with virtually no suspicion.

And that afternoon was no different. Right after checking in, I put on my happy face and helped a customer with a twenty-minute WordPerfect problem, and then wrestled with a sick and jammed laserprinter for a few more minutes. Almost an hour into my shift, I finally got to sit down at a consultant's PC and log in. When I got onto the Rose VAX, I saw Amy logged on from the Library PC cluster.

"Working hard?" she bitnetted me.

"Yes, surprisingly," I said. "I thought it was the fall semester for a second."

"I'm done for the day here," she said. "I think I'm going to the mall now. Need anything?"

"See if they have a sensory deprivation chamber there. I'll pay you back."

"Does this have to do with your weekend?" she said.

"If I tell you it's a long story, do I get off the hook from telling you about it?"

"Only temporarily. I hope things straighten up for you."

"We'll see how it goes. Hey, I'm gonna have to get back to work."

"Okay, I'll talk to you later," she said.

I wandered the computer clusters, reloading printers with paper and answering stupid questions, but mostly fighting with the feelings inside my head. I wanted to talk to Amy about everything, including the depression. But I knew it would scare her away like garlic to a vampire, especially considering everything she'd been through with her sister's psychiatric problems. Maybe she'd understand because of that. But more likely, it would freak her out even more. I didn't want to live a double life around her, like I did among the anonymous computer users that asked me for help in the labs. But I didn't want to screw it up, either.

By the time I reached home, I wanted to take a long nap and wallow in my depression for the evening. But instead, I needed to catch a quick supper and go work at the telefund. I scooped up my mail, unlocked the apartment, and threw everything on the floor, to be processed later. I crashed in front of the computer, and saw the little red light on the answering machine. I hit the bar to play my messages.

"John, this is Carolyn from the telefund. I just back from vacation, and saw your calling stats. I'm afraid your percentages are too low, we're going to have to let you go. You can stop in next week for your last check."

Fuck! The machine beeped and resetted, and I sank into the computer chair, and tried to sort through what this would mean. I knew I promised myself the gig would be temporary, and I hated every minute of it, but I really got used to the extra paycheck, and I hadn't saved a penny of the money. Within moments, my brain was tightly deadlocked with the various arguments of money—scholarship—deposits—fall semester bills—car—everything else. I went across the room to the bed, crashed, and tried to sort through this one thing at a time.

First—the apartment. I hated the boarding house, and wanted to move to a real place, but the most Bloomington fall lease signings really started last January, and finding a place late in the summer would involve slapping down some heavy cash deposits up front. Also, I wouldn't be able to afford a single, and finding the ideal roommate in July would be nearly impossible. Aside from various fantasies about sleeping in my car for a semester and banking the rent checks from my parents (hey, Sid did it for most of his freshman year,) my only clear option would be another year at 414 Mitchell. That meant renewing the lease, and paying a $400 deposit.

I'd probably be able to pay the deposit, along with my fall semester, using my scholarship money. They paid me with a check made out to my name, so I could buy Nintendo games for all they knew. The big question was whether or not I'd get the scholarship, and if the review process would push it past the date when the landlord needed the cash.

At the beginning of summer, I thought that my posh roofing job would take care of the deposit, plus various repairs on the Rabbit, a trip or two to see Tammy, and maybe even some extra savings. But with the slim UCS hours and now-gone telefund job, I had zero in the bank and not much more coming in the door. And I couldn't easily call home and beg for

$400, because my mom was trying to find reasons to drag me back home and play by her rules again.

I kept spinning the numbers in my head, trying to figure out if saving every dime of my UCS checks would clear $400 before mid-August. Even if I assumed I could accumulate mass hours, the numbers didn't work out. I'd have to find some other work fast—a temp job, more telemarketing, some good glowstick gigs—or I'd be screwed.

At least the firing meant I got the night off. I could take a nap and get el depresso with some Pink Floyd in the CD player for the rest of the evening instead of rushing to get to work in an hour. I tried to push the mess out of my head and catch a few minutes of sleep before dinner.

By 11:00, I didn't think I'd make it to the fountain. I thought about doing my usual, long, depressing walk around campus at night, but I didn't think that would do much either. Until then, I sat at the computer, checking to see who was on every 30 seconds, and finding nothing.

I couldn't deal with it anymore. Within the wavering of my manic depression, I came to the realization that I needed to tell Amy everything. I knew I'd back down later, and this would be my only chance. I typically wrote a giant message at night while she was asleep, and she responded in the morning while I was still in class. In conjunction with our on and off one-liners during the day, it meant I got to dump a lot of stuff in her direction. But I kept it pretty sanitized and rehearsed for the most part—I was still playing the game, hoping I'd win her over.

That night, I didn't care. I opened a mail buffer, and thought about how I'd write this psycho manifesto. After composing some stuff in my head, I let it fly:

> To: arbergst@ucs.indiana.edu
> Subject: How's the wife? Is she at home enjoying capitalism?
> —text follows this line—

hey, it's me, hacking out one of those late night confessional-type emails. i feel like shit tonight, so i guess it's a good time for me to fess up and explain myself. i've been trying to be honest with you about everything, and i have, but there's a major error of omission i'd like to get off my chest. the truth is, i've been suffering from manic depression for the last few years, since high school at least. i'm in treatment, taking lithium and i see a counselor here and there. i guess it's never been seriously bad—i've never been in in-patient therapy or anything, but it's really been fucking with things this summer. i've been in an emotional rollercoaster with my relationships, my direction. i hit bottom last spring, and i've spent all summer trying to stand up again. i'm not suicidal, and i'm not destructive, but sometimes i feel very alone and emotionally hollow. lately, i spend about 70% of my time okay, and the other 30% i crash (like now). i dunno, maybe i should've went back to the factories instead of scraping by in an empty college town. i think if i make it to the fall semester, things will iron themselves out. i'm going to see my doctor tomorrow, to see if he can monkey with my lithium level and/or put me on some additional drugs to see if i can course-correct for the short term.

anyway, i don't know what else to say. i've waited to tell you this, because i don't advertise it to the world or tell anyone except those i'm close to. when i'm at work or in classes or whatever, i put up a fake front and don't let casual acquaintances see any of this. i think that you deserve to know the truth, and i don't want to feel like i am leading a dual life with you. i am hoping you will understand, i mean with your experiences with your sister. i'm also hoping you don't judge me for the same reason. from what i've seen sofar, you are an understanding and intelligent person, so hopefully this won't throw you too much.

well...i dunno i feel stupid typing email, no emotion, no feedback. it scares the hell out of me to tell you this, send it off, and then wait hours/days for a reply. i hope what i said doesnt freak you out. if it does, i understand. and if you want to talk about any of this more, you know where to find me.

-me

Fuck it. She'll read it tomorrow, and either she'll understand or she won't. I powered down the computer, grabbed my walkman and Type O Negative's first album, and hit the dark streets of Bloomington.

I don't know how I managed to get out of bed for the morning shrink appointment, especially after hours of wandering the campus in depression the night before. But I did manage a quick shower, a morning Coke, and a fifteen-minute hike uphill to the squat, nondescript health center building.

The bowels of the seventies-style health clinic building, looked like the interiors of most hospitals, filled with carts of linens, air conditioning ducts, plenums of metal, and extra-wide elevators with doors on either side. I walked through the semi-gloss covered cinderblock tunnels, looking for the lone Coke machine of the building. I found the glowing red machine, dropped in two quarters, and bought me something to do while I waited for the doctor.

A service elevator whisked to the fourth floor. Luckily, nobody else was in the lift, since everybody knew that the 4 button was for the terminally insane like me. Women visiting the clinic for birth control pills and pap smears hit the 3 button, and the armies of winter cold, flu, and respiratory infection casualties went to the second floor. I didn't like the main elevators, because I always feared pressing the 4 button in front of others. The freight elevator worked just fine.

The zombie at the reception desk on the fourth floor gave me a green and white form with my information on it and a checklist with every conceivable medical procedure written in an odd pseudocode only decipherable by health care professionals. My form had an X next to something like "Psy/ClDrEv 15m," whatever that meant. An eerie feeling of alienation passed through me as I walked down the hallway decorated with Nixon-era textured wallpaper and carpet borders on the wall that could have only been designed by an elementary school contractor on mescaline.

The magazines on the end table were all several years out of date. I started to read a Newsspeak filled with year-old Gulf War propaganda. After that got boring, I just read the green sheet. The rows of procedures like lice removal and boil lancing intrigued me in a morbid way. A menu of sickness. Maybe this was how bands like Carcass came up with song titles.

The heavy door at the end of the hall opened, and a distinguished Indian man in his late forties walked out, holding a clipboard and some charts. "John, come in," he said, in a heavy accent. Actually, I never knew if he was from India, Pakistan or somewhere else, and I never really had the courage to ask. All I cared about was getting my prescriptions and getting the hell out.

His office was dimly lit, and looked like an absent-minded professor's haven. Piles of papers, folders, charts, and pamphlets buried the desk, and the walls were covered with tall bookshelves, sagging with hard-core psychology books, thousands of pages thick. I sat in a deep chair and carefully rested my Coke can and green menu-form on the endtable.

He lowered himself into his thick leather chair, and flipped through a red folder full of transcripts and drug prescription charts. "How can I help you today, John?" he asked in his thick voice. "Do you need more prescriptions?"

"Yeah. But, I've been depressed lately. I mean more depressed than usual."

"Oh?" he looked up from the folder. "Can you explain?"

"I don't know. It's just that sometimes when situational stuff happens. I crash, I can't do much and I just want to sleep. And sometimes it isn't even caused by anything."

"Situational? What exactly?"

"Just the usual downward spiral. Thinking about women, dating problems, worrying about school, the future. Nothing specific. Just everything."

"Any problems with alcohol? Other drugs?" he asked.

"No, not really." I didn't want to tell him about my occasional drinking binges. What he didn't know wouldn't hurt him. Besides, I wasn't really an alcoholic, I just drank very occasionally to mask the depression I already faced.

"Are you taking any other medications?" he asked as he flipped through the charts again.

"No, nothing else." Dumbfuck. He had my charts in front of me, he should've known already. Maybe he was just checking if I was filling fake scripts or borrowing someone else's Darvon.

"Well, what we usually do with people who are taking Lithium but are still having this depression is use second medication, antidepressant, to help with these, how you say, 'crashes.' Have you taken Prozac before?"

"Yeah, about three years ago. It didn't work out," I mumbled. What an idiot, not only was that right at the top of my chart, but he was the doctor that prescribed it to me. I could see them forgetting around this place, though—they handed out Prozac to almost everyone who walked in.

"Side effects, what problems did you have?"

"Nausea, a little insomnia," I said, recalling my episode with the drug in my freshman year. "It bothered me more than it helped."

He paused, scanning one of the dozens of open books on his desk. "There is a new drug called Zoloft, much like Prozac, a selective serotonin reuptake inhibitor. It is different manufacturer, many people have better luck with it. I think the Zoloft you could take it," he said.

"Are there any side effects?" I asked, suddenly thinking of a Carnivore song with the lyric "every hole in my body drips blood..."

"Every drug has side effect. Maybe nausea, sleeplessness, maybe dry of mouth. Depends on person. But less side effect than Prozac. I have samples..." he rummaged the desk, searching under the folders and prescription pads for something.

"Okay, I'll try it," I said.

"Here, here it is." He pulled out a small cardboard box and handed it to me. A racy Zoloft logo flowed across the package. "That's a week of tablet, I give you prescription for the month, and for more of the lithium. They have pamphlets downstairs," he mumbled, scribbling on a prescription pad. "You read it, it has more instructions. Here are your prescriptions," he said, tearing the small white sheet from its pad. "If you have problems, call me."

"Sure, thanks," I said, leaving him behind in his desk of shit.

I dropped off the prescriptions downstairs at the drug counter and sat at the waiting area, studying the people filling their scripts. Since 95% of the prescriptions filled here were for birth control pills or Prozac, I loved waiting by the counter and mentally speculating which women were getting which pill.

The pharmacist, a white-haired guy with a starched lab coat who looked exactly like you'd see in a cliched Walgreen's commercial, handed over two white bags, stapled shut, with computer-printed slips on each seam. "Have you taken this before?" he asked.

"The lithium, but not the other one. Do you have instructions for it?"

"Sure, hang on a second..."

He vanished behind the counter for a second, and came back with a small pamphlet that reminded me of some kind of religious comic that a born-again would leave on a bus or in a phone booth. I put the drugs and the visit on my account—the health center would pass the charges on to the bursar in 60 or 90 days, and then my parents would battle over which one of them would have to cover my medical expenses. This arrangement meant I couldn't switch to a private doctor, but at least I got my medicine without insurance. I got dropped from my dad's policy long ago, and wouldn't be able to afford my own until I got a real job that supported it.

I grabbed my parcels, took a last look at the couple of beautiful women waiting on their pills, then hiked back home while listening to the new Cathedral EP.

At home, I dumped the white paper bags on my computer desk, and fished around the fridge for something to drink. The cardboard box around the starter kit of pills added a sense of elegance, like they were some kind of upscale French chocolates in a sophisticated, modern package. I looked at the little bluish tablets encased in foil and plastic, and shook them around inside their airtight blister pack. Would they make me happy? Insane? Sick? After I opened the precautions pamphlet, printed on thin bible paper with two point type, I found that even if it didn't make me happy, it would make me nauseated, sleepy, dry-mouthed, and if I was lucky, it would cause blood pressure shift, dizziness, ambivalence, trouble urinating, sexual dysfunction, spontaneous combustion and/or homicidal tendencies. I hoped it would just make me sleepy and lower my appetite so I would have to buy less groceries.

I punched two of the blue tablets through the foil backing, and knocked them back with a hit of my Coke. No change. 15 seconds later, no change. I was still thinking about it a minute later, but realized it was asinine and purely symbolic—it would take days, maybe a week for the stuff to build up in my blood and take effect. Nothing to wait for. I went to the computer, powered it up, and logged on.

From ARBERGST@ucs.indiana.edu Tue, 27 Jul 92 8:16:21 EST
From: "plus ca change, plus c'est la meme chose"
<ARBERGST@ucs.indiana.edu>
To: JCONNER@ucs.indiana.edu Subject:
Re: How's the wife? Is she at home enjoying capitalism?
Date: Tue, 27 Jul 92 8:16:21 EST

John:

I'm still not sure what to say about your message. I don't mean that in a bad way—it's just that you seem like such a humorous, outgoing, and energetic person, that it's hard to believe that you suffer from depression. But I also know that depression can strike anyone, and appearances can be deceiving.

I'm glad that you've chosen to talk to me about this. You don't need to worry about me running away because of your condition. I know you've had a lot of problems in the past, and you're correct that I can see beyond this because of my experiences with my sister. I've experienced some depression myself in the past, but I know it's much different to deal with the medications, doctors, and everything else.

I can't promise to be everything for you, and as you can see with my sister, I do have a breaking point. But I am your friend, and I'm here for you. I know that's a corny thing to say, but it's true. I want to be able to talk to you about anything, and this is a good step in the right direction.

Well, now that we have all of that off of our collective chests, there's not much interesting going on here in the Library, unless you think twisted-pair wiring is interesting (and maybe you do.) Let me know what goes on with your doctor's appointment—I hope it went well. No Norman Vincent Peale advice for you—I just hope you're feeling better today, so I get more messages from my favorite email correspondent. Anyway, I will talk to you later.

hug

-Amy

After reading her mail a few more times, I knew things would be okay. At least I didn't blow this one before I even met her. Now I just needed to actually meet her.

I spent the afternoon reading the classifieds in a newspaper stolen from the machines at Third and Jordan, trying to find anything even remotely interesting. I'd work anything to get that apartment deposit together—telemarketing, dishwashing, heavy labor—I'd even baby-sit if they'd let me. The only ad was a place I was reserving for a last resort; a place I knew I'd be able to go and get a week or two of work with no skills, no training, and no long wait:

Dial America.

I reserved this bottom-barrel telemarketing firm as my ace in the hole all summer, as a total, all-out emergency reserve in case I was dying of dehydration and needed to buy some water. Dial America ran the classic, low-quality outfit: high pressure sales pitches read straight from scripts, with a hard-to-win commission setup, asshole managers and an average employee lifespan measured in minutes, if you didn't average in the people who quit during the training session. But, they were always hiring, and I heard if you had prior telemarketing experience and could walk the walk, they would expect you to become hot shit and wouldn't be as mean. I hoped that I could sign on and duke it out for a few weeks, pulling in a couple of paychecks before they'd find out I wasn't pulling my weight.

I called the number in the paper, and they told me to come over later that afternoon for an interview. I knew this wasn't as much of a formal interview as it was a whitewash session where they convinced me that I could make millions by calling people during their dinner and begging them to buy the AssMaster-2000 or something. I'd have no problem getting a spot there; I just needed to keep a clear head about it.

Some back-of-an-envelope calculations told me that if I could stay at Dial America for two or three weeks, and pull in a decent UCS check or two, I'd be able to scrape by on the rent deposit. If that didn't work, there was the scholarship, which still wasn't 100%. And then I'd need to start begging.

After a quick shower and a change into some clothes without Satanic heavy metal slogans all over them, I headed over to Dial America for my interview. Their generic business office reeked of prefab modular furniture and motivational posters, even moreso than the telefund. A secretary handed me a clipboard with an application, and I doodled away my answers quickly. If I learned anything that summer, it was how to fill out a generic job application in under two minutes.

I waited for a few minutes, and then a manager escorted me to a private room for the 'interview'. He looked like the typical make-money-fast zombie, a strange look usually reserved for feral Christian televangelists. After I revealed my prior experience at the telefund, he quickly started explaining how much easier Dial America would be because there weren't such strict rules about the 'donation ladder' and the calls were supposedly much faster, making it easier to rack up multiple commissions. I didn't have to sell myself at all, but he went on about how great the program was and how they would be glad to have me.

So, I accepted. It all sounded like a scam, but as long as I could get a few bucks out of it, what the hell. We shook hands, and I agreed to start the next evening.

28

"How can you keep VAXing so late at night and still show up for morning classes?" Amy bitnetted me, while I sat at a Macintosh in the chilly Ballantine 308 lab. The climate control whirred overhead with an ominous Bespin Cloud City tone, and the seventies high-tech ceilings and decorations made the place look like a post-apocalyptic vision from one of the *Planet of the Apes* movies or something.

"I take a lot of naps in the day, while you're pretending to look busy at work," I said. "Plus I drink all of the Coke I can get my hands on." I typed in one window on the Mac while I ran a Bronze session in the other, mulling over my email.

"Any news on our new wonder drug today?"

"I'm still taking it—no problems as of yet." I kept wondering when it would kick in, and what my side effects would be. With most of these new anti-depressants, it's like they put a bunch of side effects in a hat, and make you pick two or three of them at random. I was hoping I would manage to pick x-ray vision, superhuman strength, and increased sexual function, but I almost knew I'd start losing sleep and appetite within a few days.

"Hey, speaking of naps, I think I'm going to head home and catch a few minutes of sleep," I said. "I've got this new job tonight."

"Good luck with it," she said. "I'll catch you later."

"Bye Amy." I did a quick who, checked out the people in the lab, and headed for the door.

Another walk home from Ballantine—I listened to Chick Corea and walked slow, with nothing to do for the rest of the day. The brief moment of clarity passed as I started to worry about my first day at Dial America. Even though I spent a fair amount of time on the phones at the telefund, I still felt nervous about getting on the line and asking random people to buy stupid products. It takes an incredible amount of self-confidence to pitch the impossible to a stranger without stopping to think "nobody really wants to buy this shit." Some people were good at it—the car, insurance, and home electronics industries depended on them. I was not one of them, though. I could stumble through the scripts better than most, but I knew I couldn't do it for long.

It's just for a few weeks, I thought. Just enough to make the rent deposit. I didn't want to depend on the scholarship, because I knew that even if it did show up, it would be late. I already sent photocopies of my last report card to BrassCo, and I hoped that would do it. But I needed the money soon, and I couldn't just ask my mom or dad for it. A couple of weeks at Dial America would pull me just over the line, though. I'd somehow make it.

I made it home a few minutes later—no mail yet, and nothing else going on in the house. I threw my bookbag on the floor, dug it open, and pulled out the Sontag book I was supposed to be reading. My brain chanted "scholarship...scholarship..." so I sat in bed and forced myself to at least get a few pages down. I started reading about Wilhelm Reich's bizarre theories about cancers of the biosphere and how it all related to TB and cancer in humans. Within two pages, I was unconscious, my legs still dangling off the edge of the mattress.

I woke a little after noon, feeling nauseated from the heat of the greenhouse room. It felt even heavier than the usual post-nap disorientation, but the room felt a little hotter than usual. My head also felt achey, a low-level pain that felt closer to my scalp than the center of my brain. I thought about lunch, and checked my wallet to gauge my money situation. I still had a few bucks, and wanted to eat a decent meal, so I combed my hair, found my shoes, and drove over to Burger King.

The Burger King on College Mall Road was my salvation. Although more of a McDonald's man, I found out that BK had a special on their bacon cheeseburger meal for only $2.49. For a while, they sold the meal and a kick-ass Coke glass for only $2.99, and now the $2.99 included a two-liter bottle of Coke. That meant I'd get more of the precious liquid for my stores.

I went through the drive-in with the Rabbit, got my food, and headed back home. They didn't have any 2-liters left, so they gave me another one of the Coke glasses instead. I hoped to have a full set by the end of summer. I still felt shitty by the time I returned home, but when I got to my room and unwrapped the bacon-covered beef and started in on the fries, my stomach felt fine. I devoured the food, my first meal of the day, and logged in to catch up on email.

That evening, I dressed in a semi-normal t-shirt and jeans, and tried to calm down before I went in to work. I felt a little bit nauseous as I got ready for work, probably from eating at BK and then falling asleep in the hot room. I ate my typical microwave burrito dinner, but that didn't sit well either. I finished eating long before I had to leave the house, so I habitually checked my email, tried to listen to a Shadowfax CD for a few minutes, and then headed out.

The Rabbit wound up Jordan, towards the library, and then right at Tenth. This place was at Tenth and the Bypass, a shopping center across the street from Wrubel. I swung the VW through the viaduct by Eigenmann Hall, under a concrete train trestle covered thick with hundreds of layers of Greek-related graffiti. The road wound uphill until I got to a massive intersection where the 45/46 bypass curved down and collided with the college mall area in a giant mess of concrete and traffic lights.

I parked in the lot of the large L-shaped strip mall, a collection of travel agents, pizza joints, insurance companies, and other small businesses. Dial America sat in an office space above a giant pet store. Since I was a few minutes early, I went in the store and checked out a huge display of kittens running around and crawling on a giant carpeted perch, and the giant tanks of fish surrounding a waterfall diorama near the front of the store. Wandering the aisles and looking at all of the toys and animals calmed me down a bit, and killed a few minutes until I had to go upstairs.

Inside, I saw the huge calling area vacant—the calm before the storm. Lines of tables and phones ran through the sterile white room. With nobody there yet, almost no sound echoed through the cavern-like area, but I knew in an hour, it would be almost deafening.

I got there a half-hour early, to get the quickie trial-by-fire training session. The receptionist at the front desk herded me into a small office along one wall, where a handful of other trainees, were also waiting, including...my old telefund boss Steve?

I sat down next to him. "What the hell are you doing here?" I asked. "You get fired or something?"

"I'm doing this on my nights off, trying to get some money together for a car down payment. Strictly temporary stuff."

"So you're still at the telefund?"

"Yeah, but I'm trying to get a full-time position at the Foundation. Don't let anyone here know that."

"Don't worry, I'm cool with it."

"Thanks. So what's up with you? I heard Carolyn finally caught up with you. Didn't you have something going at UCS?"

"Yeah, but I don't have the hours in the summer," I replied. "I'm trying to find something more permanent there, but right now I need an apartment deposit."

"Well, I've heard a little about this place," he said. "I think we can do okay on this if we're fast. The calls are completely scripted, it is just a yes/no thing with the legal three asks on the product. If you race through your dialing and act totally affirmative with the people on the other end, you can probably make okay money. Just don't spend all of your time with rapport like you did on the Varsity club stuff. It isn't big dollars, but volume."

"You think it's that easy? I was just going to collect the minimum until they fired me," I said. "That's still a couple hundred a week."

"That would work, but I think the best thing you could do is hit the ground running and pull in rapid commission until you get fired for pissing off a customer or conning people into false orders. Besides, by then you will be long gone, right?"

"Yeah, this isn't a career thing."

"Their program sucks, the calls will suck, and you'll be totally in the dark, asking questions from a photocopy. The job will totally blow and you'll be gone in a week. You might as well make as much commission as possible. They won't fire a rude person with incredible stats. You'll get your deposit with no problem..."

"Okay, are we ready to make some money?" Brian, the manager walked in and closed the door behind us. He looked like a cheesy 80's marketing executive who was brought back from the dead and forced to work in telemarketing by Lucifer. The six people all mumbled something resembling a yes in response to his question, and we got started on training.

Brian went to work, running through a bunch of posterboard displays showing the company's structure, how important phone solicitation was, why people buy stuff over the phone, common objections, and all of the usual bullshit. Instead of paying attention, I noticed how Brian's approach had the same strange, faux-marketing tone as many of the other scam businesses I investigated that summer. It was slick, but nowhere near perfect.

And what was Brian's story? He looked like he was in his early thirties, tried to dress sharp in clothes from JC Penny, and was trapped in a job that probably didn't pay dick, but promised more than 95% of the work in this city. They probably promised him a hundred grand a year if he worked 100 hours a week and met impossible stats. Maybe a good chunk of his pay was performance based. It would force him to work people to death for minimum wage, and convince everyone around him that he could turn water into wine. Brian was the perfect posterboy for everything that I didn't want to be in ten years, and made me think even more about how I'd be fired or gone within the first pay period of this hellhole.

Brian lectured everyone on how to make calls and talk to people on the phone. Or rather, Brian talked to everyone but me and Steve. It was intolerable for me to get babied through how to do this, but I couldn't imagine what was going on inside Steve's head. At the telefund, he coached people, listened in on calls, and hired and fired based on people's abilities to talk on the phone. Now, he sat there next to me, listening to some idiot talk about how to read from a script. At least we had fun answering all of Brian's theoretical "so, how do you..." questions perfectly, while the other four people sat there like deer staring into the headlights.

After twenty minutes of indoctrination, Brian left us there for a few minutes before the shift started. One of the other four, a mousy girl who looked like she was about 19, said "I can't take this!" and bolted out of the room, which made the morale of the other three newbies even worse. Both me and Steve got a chuckle out of it though. I didn't exactly want to be there, but I wanted to see how many hits I could crank out with my telefund skills. And I really wanted to see how Steve would totally slay everyone and make the management think he was some kind of telemarketing prodigy.

Twenty minutes later, I sat at a table divided into four workspaces with cardboard dividers, in a sea of similar tables with a hundred callers all talking to people from around the country. To the naked ear, the sounds of phone receivers dropped in and out of cradles, tapping pencils, shuffling papers, and dozens of voices reading from cards overwhelmed into one cacophony of noise. I tried to focus on my phone, my cards, and my papers to block everything outside of me in a trance.

I pulled through the cards, mostly east coast numbers, and started dialing. After a slew of busy signals, answering machines, and no-answers, an old lady answered.

"Hi, I'm calling on behalf of Time-Life books and I'd like to tell you about our new line of books about the African wildlife. Each book is about a new animal, displayed in full, living color with educational information and stories. Tonight, I'd like to offer you the first book. We'll send it free of charge. And if you like it, we'll send you more books for the next 80 years."

Within ten seconds the lady hung up. I knew my biggest battle would be keeping the people on line long enough to hook them. Also, even though the deal sounded vaguely interesting, the truth was that the people would have to pay postage to return the book if they didn't like it, so it wasn't really free.

Following Steve's advice, I ran it like a marathon, marked the card, went to the next. Called, nobody home. Third, busy. Fourth, machine. Fifth, nobody home. Sixth, no kids. No grandkids, no nephews or nieces or illiterate brothers and sisters who would want kiddie books. Seventh, they only spoke Spanish. I knew this would be a long night.

By my tenth call, I hooked a live one. I was pretty sure they agreed to take the first book just to get rid of me, and I didn't explain the catch about returning the thing, but that didn't matter. With the name and address verified, I was cool. I had to get two more, then they would pay me five bucks per person instead of my hourly salary of $5/hour.

Managers hovered over Steve's phone. He was already four for six, which was like walking on water or making the blind see. My one for ten was close to the average for a seasoned vet; the average person off the street would probably do one for twenty or worse. After my verification, I kept pounding the phone.

Within the first hour, I snagged my quota of three, but had to dial dozens of numbers rapidly to do so. When one of the managers saw me flipping through cards at such a phenomenal rate, he told me to pace myself and go get a Coke or something. I said okay, but ignored him. They paid money for every name on the list and didn't want me to burn through stacks of them in a night, which I was going to do anyway. I kept cranking.

Halfway through, I needed to stop and see the light of day for a bit. Although the shifts were too short for a dinner break, we got about 15 minutes to hang out in the parking lot, talk to others, and maybe get a quick snack. I found a Coke machine, got a drink, and headed outside.

It felt good to look at something other than my script and pile of numbers—the quickly setting sun and non-office air regenerated me a bit. While I sucked down a Coke, I wished I could be out in the beautiful summer evening, doing anything but making unsolicited phone calls. But duty called—I needed the cash.

I kicked back the rest of my Coke, and headed inside.

Walking back inside and sitting at my phone again drained me of any energy the 15-minute break gave me. I wanted to be outside, driving around, enjoying the summer evening. I knew if I didn't have the job, I'd probably be depressed and sitting in a computer cluster doing absolutely nothing. But that beat calling a bunch of unsuspecting strangers and launching this free book crap on them.

A new stack of cards sat on the desk, probably stuff in a new time zone. It seemed like "scientific" telemarketing places like this timed everything so you always called people during dinner. I'd be more willing to buy a book or a record over the phone at seven or eight at night, but either there was some law against that, or their endless statistics showed that I wasn't the norm.

I fired through the new stack of cards, with close to the same success as before. Hang-up, hang-up, busy, machine, machine, machine, busy, hang-up. I never expected ten kills a night like Steve, but I knew I could probably bag at least three with some luck. I watched the sky grow dark, and kept at it.

Halfway through the evening, I hit the wall. My stats were now four and 26. The four wasn't bad, but I was dialing way too fast, and the 26 showed it. I felt so demoralized and panicked, the thought of another week or two of this torture echoing through my head. I needed the money, I needed to hang in. But even shingling a hot roof was more satisfying than this.

Finally, closing time came up for the three-hour shift. The overwhelming noise came to a halt, and everyone gathered together their old cards and sheets and notes. People turned in their stats and receipts on the way out of the door, some getting praise from the floor manager.

"Hey man, how did you do?" Steve came up behind me, dragging his paperwork.

"10 hits, 10 for 45."

"Man, that's an awful percentage. You should've whittled it down or something. I don't think they'll check."

"Yeah, I thought about that," I said. "Hey, it's fifty bucks though. For three hours of work, that's okay. How did you do?"

"18 for 40. It was probably 18 for 100, but they don't need to know that."

"Holy shit, you better hope they don't hire you to be a floor manager here, too."

On the way out, I saw the marketers swarm over Steve's paperwork, slapping him on the back and welcoming him on the team. I tried not to laugh about his little secret, and headed out.

On the short drive home with the sunroof open, I got to enjoy a little bit of the evening air, whipping through the tiny car and waking me up after hours in the recycled office environment. There were no plans that night, and I didn't really feel like much beyond my email and maybe some

Usenet. The slight disorientation that I had before lunch still ran through my head, a slight nausea that made me feel like when I kept inside my kiln-like apartment too long. I hated the job, but maybe it wasn't that.

I thought back to the beginnings of other pharmaceutical experiments, and what happened then. Lithium, despite its bad rap, didn't give me many problems. I did gain some weight, and it made me thirsty. But after a few years, I didn't notice its problems anymore. Prozac was more similar to the Zoloft, and that did make me eat less. No food seemed to interest me anymore. It wasn't a gastrological thing, like a bad stomach or nausea, but something more complex. I lost a lot of weight on Prozac, but never threw up or got sick. Maybe this was a side effect, or maybe it was something I ate. Either way, I didn't feel 100% from it.

Once home, I took the next little blue tablet with a Coke, and got started on my email. I hoped for a huge wave of euphoria within the next week or two, just like I had with Prozac. I knew the feeling wouldn't last for more than a month or two, but that would get me past the summer and well into the next semester. Then I could try something else.

The walk to the fountain cleared my head a bit more, and made me think less about money and medicine and more about how much I enjoyed July in Bloomington. I even made the hike without a walkman, just to enjoy things a bit. The long walk uphill on Jordan, past the abandoned and massive Read quadrangle, wasn't the most exciting part of my trip, but the clear sky and quiet night made the whole trip worthwhile.

12:07. The only person at the fountain was Doyle, sitting on the edge and reading a paperback. "Hey man, am I late?" I said.

"John, good to see you. Where's your walkman?"

"I gave it the night off. It's too nice outside to listen to Dismember at full volume. Actually, it's not, but you know what I mean."

"So what have you been up to tonight?" he said.

"I worked my first shift at Dial America."

"Ugh, I didn't know you were that desperate for a job."

"Money's tight. It wasn't too horrible, though. I made fifty bucks in three hours."

"I used to make fifty bucks in a half hour, servicing computers."

"In Bloomington?"

"No, this was when I lived in New Orleans. I wish I could make that money here."

"Yeah, me too. I miss the good old days of 80-hour UCS checks," I said. "Hey, anyone else here already?"

"No, not really. Bill said he might stop by later, but he was in the middle of something in Lindley."

"Probably cruising," I said.

"Probably. I haven't heard from anyone else tonight."

"Shit, I think I'm gonna head back. I've got an 8:00 tomorrow."

"Me too, but I might as well work on the reading here. It's nicer than home."

"Yeah, but there's not a fridge full of drinks here, or a computer. I'll catch you later Doyle."

"Later man." He picked up his book, and got back to work. I hiked back around the auditorium and to my house, for an hour or two of email trawling and other assorted non-activity.

29

5:07 AM. I held my watch close to my face and pressed the button that backlit the tiny LCD and burned the digits into my eyes. 5:08 AM. I compulsively checked the watch every hour of the night. Did I ever fall sleep? I remembered some lucid nightmares, the kind where the dream continues after consciousness. I also remembered the throbbing pain in my head, the kind that would elude aspirin, even if I wasn't allergic to aspirin. It didn't feel like I slept more than five consecutive minutes. Fucking Zoloft.

A horrific nausea pulled through my system, a churning deep in my gut that reverberated through my entire nervous system. A heaving ran from my stomach to my mouth, like my digestive system wanted to turn itself inside out. Breathing deeply made it calm down, but I still wandered the line between nausea and vomiting. I kicked back the sweat-drenched sheet, and switched positions in the tiny bed, hoping to fall back asleep for a few more minutes.

I never felt such a queasiness that wasn't related to a stomach flu or drinking binge. The doctor mumbled something about "some slight nausea," and I read about along with the 10,000 other possible side effects in the drug instructions, but didn't know what would really hit me. The taste of bile increased at the back of my throat, and I sat up quickly, trying to fight it. After my last experience with black rum, one puking binge that summer would be enough.

I threw on a pair of shorts and stumbled in pain to the bathroom. I leaned against the wall, my legs weak and rubbery from a lack of sleep.

With the toilet in front of me, I retched and spasmed, but couldn't actually vomit. The torture of being so close to puking but not being able to get it over with frustrated me even more. After a dozen false starts, I drank some water and crawled back to my bed and stayed in the fetal position, hoping it would stop and wondering what to do.

Hours passed, and I repeated the cycle many times: try to sleep, try to puke. My stomach started rumbling from hunger, but I couldn't imagine eating anything with such queasiness. I tried a few stale crackers with no luck, and even the drinks of water started to bother me. I swished some water around in my mouth the clear the taste, and spit it back in the sink. For the last four hours, I alternated between lying in bed and kneeling at the toilet, wishing one of the two would feel comfortable and wondering if it would calm down enough for me to start my day. I also wondered if this meant that Zoloft was a dud for me, or if this would all go away in a few days.

Back in the bedroom, I dug up the phone and called the health center, asking for my psychiatrist. They said he was in mid-appointment, but that he'd call me back in a minute. I waited in bed, and about fifteen minutes, he called and told me that all I could do is cut back to a half pill if it got any worse, and hope things would clear in a day or two. He assured me that the nausea and headache was temporary, and after my body adjusted, I would be fine. If it got bad after three or four days, I could stop taking it, but the basic idea was that I should just ride things out.

I thought a shower might help calm me down, so I grabbed some clean clothes and a towel, and went back to the bathroom. An almost fatal mistake was brushing my teeth; the sweet, minty taste of toothpaste made me retch and gag. Abandoning the toothpaste, I briefly scrubbed my teeth with cold water, spitting out more of the foul taste within. I took a long shower, where the soap was almost a secondary feature and it was mostly about being hypnotized by the water cascading over my water and massaging my skin. After staring at the shower floor for a half-hour, I felt a lot more calm about some of the repulsive feelings the stomach pains were giving me, and I got dressed in the clothes to look somewhat more human.

Right after I got dressed, I rushed back to the bathroom for my first of many rounds of Zoloft-induced Montezuma's revenge. It's hard to describe with any dignity this part of the sickness, but I can say that it felt much more inhuman than any previous experiences similar to it. After my third or fourth rushed trip to the bathroom, I was pretty much passing pure water, and my gut felt like I'd had a battery acid high colonic. Back in high school world history class, the teacher taught us that back in the middle ages, the leading cause of death was dysentery. It was the only thought I could put through my head, as I thought of forcing my dehydrating body through more rounds of this torture. With no food or sleep and little water, my system wavered just above the total shutdown level, and I wasn't sure how I could fix any of these problems.

A quick hobble to the Village Pantry scored me some different crackers—those wheat cracker sandwiches with some kind of spackle-like cheese between the crackers that come three to a cellophane pack—and a plastic jug of Gatorade, the drink of champions and violent hangovers. If I would truly be sick for three or four days, I guessed I could live on just Gatorade and crackers. If junkies could live on sport drinks and heroin, I could survive with Gatorade and Zoloft.

A noon to four shift for UCS seemed an impossibility, so I quickly called in sick, even though it meant the loss of twenty-some dollars. I tried a few sips of the Gatorade, then crawled back to bed for another attempt at sleep. My stomach kept calm, and despite the heat and invisible weight pressing into my skull, I drifted off into a light, neurotic sleep.

At one in the afternoon, I got out of bed and still felt traumatic pain in my entire digestive system. I didn't want to cop out of both jobs and have a total loss of income, especially with thoughts of the apartment deposit in my head. But after two more trips to the bathroom, I decided to call Dial

America and tell them that I couldn't make it in that night. I didn't want to risk losing the money I already made, but I knew I couldn't sit through an entire shift with my current list of problems. I found the phone, and dialed the number.

"Dial America," answered a plastic secretary with a slightly bitchy phone voice.

"Hi, I'm John Conner, a new trainee and I'm going to be sick tonight."

"Hang on, I'll get a floor manager."

I got some fake Muzak that was actually playing last year's big REM hit, the losing my religion thing. I knew that if she had to get a manager, I'd be in trouble.

The Muzak clicked off. "Hi, this is Doug," said one of the many fake marketer voices.

"Doug, this is John Conner, I'm one of the new trainees that started last night, and I'm going to be sick tonight."

"We don't do sick days on new employees. If you want the job, come in. Otherwise, don't."

"Can I still get my check for last night?" I asked.

"Sure, come in a week from Friday, they'll have it at the front desk."

The receiver was dead before my "Okay, thanks." What a fucking jerkoff. I dropped the phone back to the floor and crawled into bed, to clutch my stomach more and try not to worry about all the money I was losing.

The hot room felt even more horrible than usual, but after I stripped off my clothes, I managed to drift in and out of sleep for a few hours. Each time I went under, intense dreams bombarded me, on the nightmare level, but about the most unrelated things. I went to a party with a bunch of VAX people that I'd never met before in real life, their faces and personalities built out of caricatures and opinions instead of pictures and facts. I met Amy—she looked like a derivative of someone I met while visiting Peter at Goshen college. She acted nonplussed when I met her, and then vanished. Later in the dream, I was working at the station, doing a live performance with the band Haunted Garage, and they had their whole GWAR-like stage show on the road and in the studio, littering the place with costumes, fake blood, wrecked cars, smoke machines, and inflatable dolls. The lead singer, Dukey Flyswatter, brought a giant CD case that held like 240 CDs, all of them unreleased Haunted Garage singles and live performances. While I started going apeshit trying to figure out a way to dub some copies of this stuff, I got a phone call from Amy, saying "I thought we had something together." Everything felt so vivid, the kind of dream where you wake up and the images still cycle through your head, more colorful than the surroundings around you. When thrown out of the dream with Amy, I thought for a half-hour that we really did date, that the call was real, and that there really were 240 CDs worth of bootleg Haunted Garage material.

I went in and out of the dreams, and felt nervous each time I woke back up. The nervousness melted and turned into nausea. It helped to keep me in bed and asleep, so I kept at it and slept through most of the day.

By evening, my guts weren't churning and I didn't feel like heaving on a continual basis. I managed to eat the packets of crackers and cheese with no problem, and drink enough Gatorade so dehydration wasn't an immediate concern anymore. I still felt like the living dead, but felt a need to get out of the house and do something. I went to the IMU to maybe answer a few letters for the zine. I decided that if I could survive an hour or two on campus, I would show up for my 8:00 radio show. I was going to show up late anyway, because of the job, so it didn't matter too much if I pulled a no-show.

I wandered through the halls of the Union, which felt like a ocean cruiser because of the slight swaying in my head, and saw Bill walking out of the computer cluster, hauling a bag probably full of fresh printouts.

"Hey John, what's up?"

"Not much," I said. We wandered through the empty Mezzanine floor of the union, with no real destination. "I've been really fucked up all day today, didn't leave the house and had to call in to work."

"I was going to say, you look a little pale," he said. "You want to sit down somewhere and talk? I'm just killing time until midnight."

"Sure, let's go out back," I said.

We climbed the stairs to the south side of the IMU, where a low stone wall ran next to the sidewalk. We sat down on the wall, a frequent spot of many of my long talks with Bill.

"They have me on this new medicine, a new antidepressant called Zoloft. I've really fucking sick all day. Nausea, vomiting, headache, dizziness, the whole nine yards."

"Shit, is there any way you can go off of it?"

"I've been thinking about it. The doctor said to break the tablets in half if it gets bad, but I'm trying to ride it out and see what happens. I really want this medicine to work. I know it's stupid to think a pill could cure me, but I just want the extra support right now."

"I know what you mean. If I had the funding, I'd probably try it myself," he said. "So did you manage to eat anything?"

"Not really. I feel a little better now, so I might try something when I get home."

"So what happened with the job today? You pull a no-show?"

"I don't know what's up. I called in to both places, but I lost the Dial America job, and I have no fucking idea how I'm going to get this apartment deposit."

"Any chance you could hit up the parents, or have you already burned that bridge?"

"I don't know if they'd front it to me. It's the conditionality I'm trying to avoid. I'll figure something out."

"How about the woman situation? Have things calmed down lately?"

"I've got one on the line right now. I mean, she wants to meet me, she seems cool and everything, but I'm not sure if I want to meet her yet. I'd rather string it out for a while, until I can really figure out her intentions. Other than her, not much is happening."

"Well, don't wait forever. I mean, it's just a meeting, right?"

"Yeah, but you know how fucked up I get over these things."

"Hey, you coming to the fountain tonight? I'm going over to Lindley for a while to make some more printouts."

"No, thanks—I'm gonna check my mail, and then see if I can make my radio show. If I'm still alive after that, I might stop in."

"Okay, sounds cool. Let me know if you need any help or anything."

"I should be okay once this stomach thing clears."

"Okay, well good luck with it." Bill gave me a hug, and then headed off to Lindley. I sat behind the IMU for a few more minutes, and enjoyed the summer air.

After Bill left, I went back inside to grab a computer, and maybe kill some time while my stomach remained calm. Being in a public place instead of doubled over in my room made me feel somewhat more in control over the medicine. But, weakness still pulled at my body, and I hoped I wouldn't get sick or have some kind of attack while surrounded by strangers.

I hunched behind a Mac, and logged onto Bronze and Rose. My wholist showed Amy logged on at Lindley Hall, and almost immediately, I got a bitnet from her.

"Hey, what's up?" she said. "Aren't you working tonight?"

"Not tonight, just killing time until my show. I missed work at Dial America and UCS today."

"Because of meds? How are you feeling now?"

"Still pretty sick. I haven't eaten anything today. But I'm going to try to make my 8:00 show, or at least the first half. What are you up to?"

"I couldn't find a computer at Ballantine, and I wanted to check my email, so here I am. I guess you know I'm at Lindley."

"Yeah, I saw that. Sixth sense."

"So," she said. "Are you interested in stopping over here? I'd like to say hello to the legendary JCONNER."

Oh shit, I didn't expect this to happen. I wanted to meet her, but I wanted a controlled environment, on my own terms. I felt like they just dug me out of my grave this afternoon, and looked like it too. I didn't want this to be my first impression on her.

"Umm..." How would I do this? I did want to meet her, just not that evening.

"Come on, are you sure? I just want to put a face to the email."

"I'm not in the best of shape tonight," I said. "I haven't slept in a while, and I'm still pretty sick from this meds."

"Okay, I understand."

"No really, I really do want to meet you. But I look like hell. I don't want to freak you out or anything. I'm sorry."

"Okay, it's not a problem. How about a raincheck?"

"Yes, definitely. I do want to meet you. Maybe when this drug stuff blows over, and I'm back on solids."

"Well, don't think I'll forget," she said. "Hey, I think I'm going to head out of here. It's getting close to my bedtime."

"Yeah, I've got to get to the station if I'm really going to do this show."

"Well be careful. Let me know how things are going."

"Okay. Sorry again—I really am. I'll talk to you tomorrow."

She said her goodbye and logged off. Just to be safe, I dropped my connections and headed out. I didn't think she was sneaky enough to hunt me down in the IMU, but I couldn't be sure.

On the drive to the station, I felt somewhat less nauseated, even though my muscles were weakened and atrophied. One bad thing about lithium is that it's easy to get dehydrated and royally screw up your medicine levels, and after a day of no food, it felt like that was happening. But I figured that sitting around the station by myself and playing records wasn't much different than sitting around my apartment myself and playing records.

The station door was unlocked, and from within, I heard the Sloppy Seconds song "Blackmail" echoing from the studio. The Misfits/Ramones-esque band from Indy sang the humorous song from the studio monitors.

"Punk rock!" I yelled back to the board. Sid was flipping through an endless pile of Indie seven-inch wax with DIY photocopied liners. "Hey, didn't CDs make those things obsolete?" I asked.

"I wish," he said. "I like how cheap it is to press vinyl, but other than that, I'll take digital any day. So what's up?"

"I just got fired from my fucking job at Dial America," I said. "I've gotta scramble for something else to get an apartment deposit together."

"Can you sell your blood with the lithium?" he asked.

"Nope. No plasma either. I haven't tried donating sperm, but I hear there's a screening test or something."

"It doesn't pay for shit. Besides, I'd hate to see a bunch of John Conner Juniors on the run. Hey, now that your evenings are free, what do you think about taking the Tuesday night slot?"

"You mean moving from Thursdays?"

"No, do Tuesday and Thursday. You could do a Thrash show, then a Death Metal show. Or a metal show, then an all-ABBA show. I don't give a fuck."

"That sounds cool. Maybe I could play all demos on Tuesday, and signed stuff on Thursday."

"Whatever lubes your tube. I don't care, I just need to fill up the blank spots on the schedule."

"Sure, I could do that. I'll try to think up of some stuff over the weekend, and start next week."

"Hang on a second..." The track was ready to play out, so he grabbed the headphones and manned the board. "Okay, that was Sloppy Seconds with 'Blackmail.' John Conner is in the studio and he's getting ready to take over for the evening. But first, here's your favorite role model, GG Allin, playing his wonderful lullaby called 'I Wanna Kill You.' WQAX."

He slammed to the B turntable and spun an already-cued record, pounding the studio with more punk.

"Hey man, you look a little green," he said. "Bad acid or something?"

"No, I'm taking this new antidepressant, it's got me fucked up. I'm not sure I'll make it through the show."

"Fuck it man," he said. "Nobody's listening. Go home if you need to."

"I'll stick it out until it gets real bad. I haven't eaten all day, and that's the worst of it. I at least want to play this new Edge of Sanity."

"Where are you getting your new stuff? Labels?"

"No, I got this at CD Exchange, from Tom."

"He kicks ass. I do a lot of business with him. Hey, how long you need to get ready?"

"I'm going right to a CD, but let me pull some stuff."

"Okay, GG is almost done. I'll cue up this Split Lip, and then it's yours."

I went to the racks, and pulled my usual arsenal of Deicide, Entombed, Carcass, Malevolent Creation, Pungent Stench, Bolt Thrower, Gwar, Haunted Garage, and a few others I could use to line up the first hour of the show. The GG Allin song spun out, and I heard "Animal Liberation" from the local band Split Lip. While Sid piled his records into a big crate, I reached above him and stacked jewel cases on top of the left CD player, juggling them in order. I also popped in the Edge of Sanity CD, and cued it for the first track.

"Hey, did you see this weeks' stats?" Sid asked.

"No, did I get the Massacre EP in the top ten?"

"Not this time. But not only did Type O Negative end up in the top ten metal and alternative, but it was the station's #1 single last week. So CMJ's going to get a big surprise when we report our numbers."

"Looks like our little ruse worked," I said.

"Yeah, maybe we can get them to fly out for a free homecoming dance or something."

Sid reached back to the cart rack, a wire spinner that held a bunch of aging rectangular cartridges used to hold commercials, public service announcements, and station ID spots. He grabbed a station ID cart and then asked "Hey, do you need the mature audience warning cart?"

"What the fuck do you think? I think my third song in is from the new Cannibal Corpse album."

"Okay, I'll play it. Get ready." The Split Lip tape ended, and Sid grabbed the mic. "Okay, that was Split Lip, and that is it for me. I'm Sid, and I'll be back tomorrow at noon. Now, here's John Conner with all-new, all-gore show called 'What To Do With Your Girlfriend's Corpse.' See ya." He clicked out the mic, and slammed in the station ID cart. A Christmas jingle played while someone said, "Happy Holidays from WQAX." While he got up and I crawled into the chair, he slapped in the warning cart, which gave the generic "this program may offend some audiences..." message. While that played, I slapped a cassette into one of the players, cued it, and right after the last word of the message, I let it fly. Vincent Price's evil, manic voice tore through the board, saying "There is no other god—Satan killed him! SATAN!"

Right on that, I released pause on the CD player, and started the show with the pounding drums and guitar of Edge of Sanity. A growling Death Metal voice started in, but thirty seconds later, the song suddenly stopped and pulled into a counterpart with only a pipe organ and a clean, operatic voice, telling another part of the story. The clean part totally showcased the incredible production of the Swedish band's album. And before things settled down, it launched right back into an even heavier, speedier Death Metal run that, when butted against the slower part, tore things apart even more. Instead of following the usual Death Metal formula of straightforward energy, this used much more complex arrangement, and made for a great way to begin the show.

The evening continued through the stock list of records I always played to open the show. But I wasn't into the dramatics, or the announcing. I simply dumped CDs into the players, and sat in the window, the cool air from outside swirling past, with the charged energy of an electrical storm about to happen. My heaving stomach and the back-of-throat gagging feeling subsided more when I sat on the ledge and breathed the air outside.

About an hour into the show, the rain started, which gave me something else to stare at while I looked outside. I gave up on any announcements, ads, or anything else. I knew I wouldn't puke, but I couldn't pay attention to all of the machinery, the rewinding of tapes and reading of PSAs. I wanted to leave.

And halfway through my show, I did. I quickly read the shutdown script, and powered off the machinery. It only took me a few minutes to refile my CDs, and put away the few items I brought to the studio. I knew Sid wouldn't care if I left, but it still felt weird. All I could think about was lying in bed again, and maybe catching some sleep.

Things progressed almost robotically from there: the drive home in the rain, the checking of email, the changing out of clothes. I took my nightly medicine, and stuck with the full dose of Zoloft. Even though my head was killing me, I fell into a deep sleep, hypnotized by the pounding rain on my roof.

30

The Friday morning sunlight streamed around the window blinds, inviting me to leave the house and start my day. I looked at my watch: only 8:00, another hour until my alarm clock would begin complaining for me to wake. Grogginess still filled my head after six hours of sleep, but I didn't feel like dozing off. Minutes after crawling into bed last night, I dropped straight into heavy REM-induced dreams minutes, probably for the first time all summer. I shut off the alarm, and sat in bed for a minute before starting my day.

The first thing that entered my head when I woke was the paycheck waiting for me at the library. I ran through some vague plans for the day, like where I'd spend it, where I'd eat lunch, and what I'd do over the weekend. While thinking about a good slice of pizza from Garcia's, I realized the nausea and sickness that racked my body for the last few days all but vanished. The heavy, drug-addled stupor had lifted from me like a bad 24-hour flu.

I found my glasses, got out of bed, and opened the shades to paint the room with sunlight. I washed back my medicine with a morning Coke, and ate some stale Doritos to test out my gut. My digestive system felt solid; I'd be back to pizza and hamburgers in time for the weekend. But first, I'd need to nab that paycheck, then work a 12-4 shift at Lindley Hall and make some more cash. I considered driving to the library, but with my body at functional capacity again, it would be better to walk it and enjoy the weather.

Everything felt good. I knew the beginning of my Zoloft euphoria started already, the uphill spike of all the right chemicals in my brain, firing off the right receptors and making me feel better. The phenomenon reminded me of when I have a canker sore in your mouth that bugs the hell out of me, and I spend a few days running my tongue over it, wondering when it will go away. And then I wake up one morning, and realize that it's gone, and that sore spot inside my mouth is once again smooth. When I took Prozac in my freshman year of college, the same euphoria pulled me from the deepest pit of hell and got my life started again. I looked forward to a little of that magic to help me punch through the rest of the summer.

Kick ass. It was all happening again. I finished the rest of my Coke, and hit the shower.

During the hypnotic uphill stroll to the library, I could feel my newfound energy pulse through my system. Even with the sun beating on the pavement, and heating the morning into afternoon, I enjoyed hiking with a Sepultura tape in the walkman, watching the gentle flow of people on Jordan Street, stepping closer and closer to a paycheck, some money, and a decent lunch as a reward for all of those microwave burritos. I crossed the parking lot and climbed the long row of steps that passed to the library lobby.

Inside, I found a UCS contingency set up at some of the study tables. Peg and a few of the lead consultants sat down, handing out checks in exchange for timesheets. My poor penmanship and bad memory of my sporadic sub schedule made filling out the pink forms in ink a major chore. Every payday, I asked if I could somehow electronically create my timesheet, but always got the same lame answer about how the whole process would be automated, "in a semester or two." Until then, I carefully inscribed my time worked in the grid of boxes and tallied the hours. Each pay period that summer looked better than the last. Maybe before fall, I'd pull in some fat checks like last spring.

I handed over the slip to Peg, and she dug through a box and handed me an envelope. I tore it open, and took a quick look at the cream and crimson paycheck. The total looked good, and I'd have a little extra money to buy some groceries more esoteric than one kind of frozen pizza. But the figure was nowhere near what I needed to put a dent in the apartment deposit I'd need to pay in a few weeks.

I ducked into Lib102a and grabbed a PC to check my mail before my walk downtown for lunch. The Zenith zapped to life with telnet sessions to Rose and Bronze, and I scanned the summaries of the seven new messages in my mailbox. After deleting the sub request/sub filled pairings, I homed in on the one I wanted to read first, one that just hit my account a few minutes before:

> From ARBERGST@ucs.indiana.edu Fri, 31 Jul 92 10:18:19 EST
> Date: Fri, 31 Jul 92 10:18:19 EST
> From: "plus ca change, plus c'est la meme chose"
> <ARBERGST@ucs.indiana.edu>
> Subject: blah
> To: JCONNER@ucs.indiana.edu
>
> It's Friday. It's sunny. It's payday. And I'm imprisoned within the walls of the Library until five. I'm going home for my mom's birthday later tonight. It's not much of an excuse, but hey—free laundry.
> How is your day? Did you pick up your paycheck? Just think—we'll be in the same building for a few minutes. But while you're getting money, I'm up to my arms in backup tapes. Sigh.
> see you,
> me

The message was short, but like all of her messages from work, it reminded me that she thought of me during the day. Possible alternate scenarios of the other night kept running through my head, when I had the chance to meet her. I wanted to see what she looked like, and thought about running to Lindley to get a quick look, while I had an IP number to match the name. But I didn't. In the height of my Zoloft sickness, I had nowhere near enough confidence to deal with the introduction, even if she really did want to see me.

The meeting...I wanted it to happen just like Tammy, like a perfect movie moment where I saw her face for the first time and I knew I would fall in love with her. But maybe I wouldn't. Every time I read her messages and thought about how I might interest her, I thought about her ex-boyfriend, her spotless academic record, her totally controlled life, and wondered how she would deal with a 21 year old with long hair in a Rotting Christ t-shirt and some ripped jeans. Maybe if I strung her along for a few more weeks, months...I'd know any sudden movements from her wouldn't be mixed signals. But she wanted to meet me the other night, so that was a good start.

"Hey, you're up early." The message from Amy popped up in my Rose session window. I switched over, did a quick wholist, and saw her logged on from some unknown IP number deep within the Library.

"Hey you," I said. "We're in the same building."

"I feel a great disturbance in the Force," she said.

"Aw, I wanted to be Darth Vader this time."

"I was hoping to hear from you," she said. "It's been one of those Fridays. I've been babysitting a backup for hours. And I hope you're not upset about last night."

"I'm not upset. I feel dumb that I didn't come over—I really wanted to meet you."

"Well, I did give you a raincheck."

"And I fully intend to use it. But now, I've got money burning a hole in my pocket."

"If getting rid of money is a problem, I'm just the girl for you."

"I know, I know. I've got to work at noon, and I need to bank and eat before then."

"That's fine. I'm going to eat lunch, too. I'll be on and off for the rest of the day, though."

"Okay, if I don't catch you, I'll email. Talk to you soon."

I closed my connections, and headed for the door. I looked at my watch—I had about 90 minutes to cross campus, get cash, get food, and get to work. I put in Judas Priest's *Painkiller* tape and hit the sidewalk.

The whole Friday Cashing of the Check routine went down like clockwork, something that I'd done every other Friday for the last four or five years. I darted across campus and toward Sample Gates, bathing in an absolutely perfect day. With a blue sky above me, the sun in my hair, and that invaluable slip of cream and crimson watermarked paper in my back pocket, I spied all of the gorgeous women in shorts, with some Judas Priest filling my ears. This is what summer on campus was all about to me. Every time I visited Bloomington during the off-season, the same feeling dominated me—the total carefree spirit roaming through a perfect diorama of beautiful landscape and old limestone halls. If every day of my life could be that perfect, I wouldn't need Zoloft.

I crossed through Sample Gates and a few blocks down Kirkwood, toward the Monroe County Bank walkup window. Before noon, only a handful of pedestrians and traffic flowed down the off-campus main drag, and all of my favorite hangouts, like the CD shops, weren't even open yet. But a few people wandered the drag, including all of the teenage skatepunks and anarchy wannabes, who reclaimed the Ave each summer when the college kids were mostly gone. I did see a few collegiates wandering around, and more babes in shorts, but it didn't look like the same Kirkwood as the one I usually knew.

I went to the drive-up bank, and got my business past a teller in a small cubicle of bulletproof glass. I left with a few twenties in my wallet, and even more in my checking account. That would mean I could follow my usual ritual of buying some fatty, greasy, empty-calorie food for lunch, my reward after way too many cheap and horrible microwave burritos. I hiked back toward campus, hung a right on Indiana, and headed for my favorite pizza place, Garcia's.

Garcia's was a famed VAXgeek hangout right across Indiana Ave. from campus, literally a stone's throw from the Sample Gates. I walked in the two-story brick building and entered a maze of indoor wooden decks, with multiple levels, sitting areas, big TVs trained to the sports channels, and plenty of places to either hide or gather. Although it looked almost like a sports bar, Garcia's was home of some of the most righteous computer hacker gatherings I ever witnessed. Once Sid emailed everyone on the util list (maybe 2000 people at the time) and told all of them to meet there at noon on a paycheck Friday for pizza and beer. It was like we were nobles among a mass of peasants—so many people were buying us drinks and asking us questions, I didn't think we'd make it out alive. There were many memories of many gatherings, so even showing up alone for a brew and a slice made it much more fun than the average generic meal at McD's.

Today's small crowd was much more sedate, with only a few people nursing beers or eating slices. I went to the front counter and ordered the usual: a cheese slice, some breadsticks with garlic butter, and a Coke. The place wasn't really known for their accuracy, quality, or value of their meals—it was slightly above average, if that. But it was quick, and only two minutes from Lindley Hall. I grabbed the food, found a small wooden table near the window, and ate while watching the people walk by on Indiana Ave.

Even with the great thoughts of Friday on my mind, I couldn't shake last night's events with Amy on my mind. I knew I wanted to see her. And I knew based on our brief bitnet conversation earlier, didn't shake her. I wished she would be around for the weekend, so I could invite her to lunch, or to go malling, or something else sedate and non-threatening. I knew I had to meet her, but I didn't want to be the one to initiate it.

With the beginning of my Zoloft mojo rising, I had enough introspective ability to pry apart the whole situation. I didn't want to meet

Amy because part of me didn't think she'd like me. And I didn't want to throw away the great email relationship we had just because I wanted to (allegedly) bed her. Was I afraid of what she looked like? Not really—I'd be willing to bet any amount of money on this human lottery. Based on what she'd told me and her basic email persona, it would be almost impossible for her to be a horrendous elephant woman-like crack whore who was staging such an incredible farce just to somehow back me into a corner. Worse things had happened, but I had some essential trust that she would be a clean, average honor student-looking woman with enough sexual attraction to lead me around like a dog on a chain (which wasn't much by this point.) But, would she like me?

Sometimes her emails made me feel like my appearance wasn't that important with her, like she appreciated my thoughts and ideas and wanted to meet me because of that. But, I couldn't completely trust her yet. Part of me wanted to take the ripping-off-a-band-aid approach, meet her under any circumstance, and find out if we were a match. But, last spring's long series of disastrous blind dates conditioned me to never trust that instinct. I invested too much time in her already, in building my persona in her mind with the computer. I could easily meet a person I've VAXed for an hour with no lead-time, but not a month. Maybe the perfect opportunity would come up, but now I needed to cover my tracks and reassure her that last night's gaff was just because of the medicine. I didn't want her thinking I was disinterested. It seemed all too complicated. I should've met her last night. No, I should go over to the library right now and find her. Or maybe I should go into hiding, and stop putting myself into these stupid situations.

I kept at the pizza, watched the people outside, and then hiked to Lindley for my noon shift.

Not much happened at work. I read the Death Metal newsgroup on Usenet for a while, and had a discussion with a business major that got a job offer in Kuwait that paid a six figure salary plus every benefit imaginable for basically what we did for just under seven bucks an hour. Amy popped on and off the computer a few times, but was too distracted with her end of the month backups and data shuffling to keep a conversation going. When my shift ended at four, I checked out and walked to the IMU. Campus seemed even more dead than usual, but it was a Friday—everyone was probably at the liquor store stocking up for their parties, or driving at full speed to opposite ends of the state to hang out with their high school buddies for the weekend.

At the union, it looked like a Star Trek convention—a bunch of people were wandering around with tweed suits and pin-on nametags. Must be a Library Sciences convention, I thought. I shuffled back to the Mac lab, dumped out my backpack at a IIci, and got to work.

After the usual email check (there was none—I was just logged in eight minutes ago,) I tore through some form letters for the magazine, asking for demos from unsigned bands. The whole operation consisted of cut, paste, and dump to the printer, for 30 or 40 letters I would dump into the mailstream, at 29 cents each. The task, aside from helping the zine, distracted me from the fact that it was Friday and I had absolutely no plans. Even at four in the afternoon, the building seemed vacant as people finished classes and headed home to get ready for parties, bars, dates, or other formidable uses of time. A handful of the people from the chess club convention used the Macs to telnet to machines at other universities. But aside from me, the half dozen people in the lab were all badge geeks. The Union scene would completely peter out within an hour or two, and I'd probably write more letters until dinner, spend some cash at a Denny's or something, then go home and flog off until the fountain at midnight.

In a backgrounded window on the Mac's screen, a session logged into one of the VAXes beeped with a message from Amy. "Hey, I thought you worked until 5?"

"No, 4—I'm at the union now," I typed back. "Working on a mass mail for the zine."

"Sounds like fun," she said. "Any big plans for the weekend?"

"Not much, hopefully I still won't be sick from the meds."

I kept working on the cutting and pasting of addresses during the exchange, something that bitnet made easy. During many of my conversations with Amy, when both of us were working, we'd drift back and forth in the dialogue. We'd both be busy with foreground tasks, and occasionally type in another quick line or two. Although many of our talks were more active than this, the passive exchange was the virtual equivalent of the slow chatting I experienced when working at the factories, where 90% of your attention is focused on putting parts in a box and the other 10% goes toward telling the guy next to you a story, giving him a sentence every three minutes.

"How are you doing with the medicine today?" she asked.

"I think they're really starting to kick in. I mean, I'm not as nauseous as yesterday."

"That's cool. Any headache today?"

"Just a little," I said. "But it's somewhat better now."

"Well, maybe the worst is over," she said.

"I'm really sorry about last night," I said. "I really did want to come over, but I felt and looked like shit."

"I know, I'm just giving you a hard time," she said. "Maybe some other time I'll run into you on campus."

"Yeah, maybe sometime..."

Her slight hinting did manage to distract me from the zine work for a bit, but we both drifted back and forth into our work for the next hour. I thought more about her hinting, her desire to meet me. It felt good to know she wanted to see me, almost to the point where I could deal with it. But I still wanted everything to be perfect. Maybe next week.

5:00 rolled by, and she said it was time for her to close down shop and leave for the day. I told her of my non-plan to stay for a while, wander the campus in confusion, and eventually go to the fountain. We exchanged good-byes, and she logged off, leaving me to print more of my letters. I stayed for another hour, burning away paper and toner, and then did a final wholist—nobody there. I logged off, hefted my stack of printouts under my arm, and wandered back to the Rabbit to head nowhere.

The house contained the same boredom as usual, with no interesting mail and everybody out or getting ready to go out. Reflexively, I fired up my PC and modem, to see if any email had crossed my path in the last ten minutes. I found this message:

> From ARBERGST@ucs.indiana.edu Fri, 31 Jul 92 17:34:05 EST
> Date: Fri, 31 Jul 92 17:34:05 EST
> From: "plus ca change, plus c'est la meme chose" <ARBERGST@ucs.indiana.edu>
> Subject: :(
> To: JCONNER@ucs.indiana.edu
>
> Well,
> I know you didn't want to meet me last night, but I figured the best time to surprise you would be when the whole thing was still on your mind and you were having second thoughts. So I had time to kill before I left for Indy, and I came over here to the IMU to track down the one known as Doctor X. Strangely, he was not logged on. I guess you're always a step ahead of me?
> It's a pretty weird site here. Some kind of CogSci conference is in town and various wild and crazy academic types keep staring at me like I'm a drinking fountain in the desert. However, I had no problem getting a computer in this cluster, for the first time in my college history.
> I'm wondering if I will turn around and you'll be right behind me, logged in with some magical tool that cloaks your location. But, based on the demographic of this cluster, I'm hoping you're not.

Oh well, I guess I'll get caught up on my email, and then head out. Another time? Another place?

-me

Fuck. I checked my watch: 5:36. I fired up a connection to Rose from Bronze—not only was it faster than starting a second session in Procomm, but my Rose session would have Bronze's IP of 129.79.1.15, and she wouldn't be able to tell if I was in the lab or not.

A quick who showed her logged on, at 129.79.110.8, a row in front of where I was sitting a few minutes ago. I fired off a quick bitnet, "Looking for somebody?"

"I couldn't resist—I wanted to see what this John Conner character looked like."

"Maybe I'm disguised as a Cognitive Science lecturer. It's not hard to make a fake nametag in WordPerfect."

"I don't think so. You're a geek, but you can't be this bad. Where are you?"

"Sorry, it got boring there, and I didn't know you were visiting," I said. "I'm at home, flogging off, doing nothing."

"So you're saying I'm out of luck?"

Did I want to go over there and meet her? I had her on the hook—just what I'd been wanting since we first started talking. But what if I fucked it up? I'd be going in almost blind. What if she switched seats so I couldn't find her, so she could get the first look and decide whether to stay or run? I could easily invent some bullshit excuse, log off, and start my miserable weekend. Or I could give it a shot. I needed to think of a decision, and fast.

"Are you going to be there for a few minutes?" I said. "Maybe I could come back, and I could redeem my raincheck? Maybe we could grab a quick drink or something?"

"A coffee at The Spoon sounds great. I'll stay here, but I might switch computers. I know all about your computer genius tricks."

"All right, all right. Stay put, I'll be right over," I said. I made a note of all of the current IPs in the room so I knew which computers weren't her, then shut down the equipment.

Great, I wanted to meet her, but not TODAY. At least now I had an activity to kill a few hours before midnight. I combed my hair a bit, dabbed on some cologne, and rushed back to my car.

Book Three

31

It wasn't hard to find an empty parking spot in front of the IMU on a Friday night, which made it that much easier to dump off the VW after my sub-six minute trip across campus. On the way over, I ran a million different scenarios through my head about what I'd do when I got to the lab. She'd easily be able to spot me coming down the long hall into the computer cluster, and I'd have no sure way to find her until I got on a computer. If she wasn't into me from the first glance, she could easily vanish before I found her. I considered either stealing a name badge from the conference, or maybe finding someone I knew and going in as a pair to throw her off. But with the Friday night IMU abandoned like a mausoleum, I couldn't come up with an accomplice or a better plan during my quick walk from the front door to the Mezzanine hall.

I walked down the long, quiet corridor, feeling like a death row inmate on the way to the chair. I could only hear my throbbing pulse as I put one foot in front of the other, shuffling toward the room. Although every possible fear raced through my head, I also felt the incredible feeling that this would be IT, just like when I met Tammy months before. Every email and bitnet from Amy led up to this scene, which in some sense couldn't go wrong.

I crept into the room and scanned the chairs. About a dozen people sat at the Macs, two-thirds of them males. The consulting machine, my usual spot, was open, but I grabbed a less obvious seat in the cluster, trying not to stare directly at any of the few females in the room.

After a quick telnet session to the Rose VAX, I did a scan of the lab, and...she wasn't logged in. Everyone but me on a VAX from the IMU cluster had temporary usernames provided by the conference, with no other logins from a regular account. What the fuck? I waited, checked again, no dice. Either she left already, or...

"Hey, are you Doctor X?" said a voice next to me.

I turned to see a woman with thick auburn hair in a ponytail, sitting in front of a powered down computer, smiling at me. She was everything Amy told me about herself, and more. My first reaction was that she was far more sophisticated and beautiful than I ever could have imagined.

"Hey! Why weren't you logged in?" I asked.

"I already know you've got the IP numbers in here memorized. That's an unfair advantage. I needed to keep you on your toes."

"Well, you got me," I said. "But if I would've had more than six minutes, the tables would've been turned. I would've stolen a janitor's uniform. Or logged in from the computer behind the counter of the bowling alley."

"Well, at least you finally agreed to meet me," she said. "So, what is there to do in the IMU on a Friday night?"

"Not much, unless you're into bowling."

"Well, how about that coffee at the Spoon? I don't really want to hang out in a computer cluster, even if it is your turf. No offense."

I laughed, "No, that's fine. I've been indoors all day, I could use the walk."

"Sounds great," she said. I logged out, and we headed out of the cluster.

We strolled down the long sidewalk between the gentle flow of the Jordan river and the huge, grassy area of Dunn Meadow, an expanse of several city blocks where people sat in the sun or let their dogs run free. On a Friday evening, we had the place to ourselves, save a handful of people playing Frisbee a few hundred feet away.

"So is the Runcible Spoon a big computer geek hangout?" she asked.

"I don't know," I said. "I don't drink coffee. It's not the drug of choice for most of the CS people I hang out with. We usually go to Discount Den—48 ounce fountain drinks, fifty cents."

"It's nice for me to tap into this alternate culture, see things in another world..."

"I don't think I've ever been to the Spoon before. Isn't it a big poet hangout or something?"

"John," she interrupted. "I think that guy is waving at you."

"What?" I looked over and saw that one of the longhaired Frisbee players was Paul, the senior consultant that trained me the year before. "Hey Paul!" I yelled back, and laughed. "I almost didn't see him there," I said.

"Friend of yours?" she asked.

"Just a coworker," I said. "I can't go anywhere without running into somebody I know. I think I've helped 90% of the student body with a computer question in the last year."

"Too bad you don't work on commission."

"No shit. We'd be going to Italy for a coffee."

The meadow concluded at Indiana Avenue, the end of campus and beginning of the Kirkwood-land of stores and restaurants. We walked a block up from the main drag of shops and restaurants, and continued down Sixth Street, a road populated with old houses converted into departmental offices and parking lots perpetually full of cars, even on a lazy Friday.

"So did you ever think about consulting for a living? I mean, business clients?"

"Yeah, but it would be almost impossible to find clients in town. Everybody uses the same two or three consulting firms, and there's not much room to edge in on them."

"What about Chicago? Or Indianapolis?"

"Yeah, maybe. I don't know, I have an aversion to suits."

"You don't need to dress up to run network cables or do mainframe installations."

"But either I need the degree, or some connections. I'm sure I'll get one of the two soon."

"Well, here she is," she said. We walked up to a place that looked like the typical two-story off-campus dwelling, except with the front yard ripped out and replaced by a gazebo and a half dozen wooden tables and chairs. People sat outside, sipping their Friday cappuccinos and reading from chapbooks of poetry or chatting in small groups.

"Let's go inside," she said. I followed her to the steps that led through a giant portal to more tables and bookshelves overflowing with volumes of obscure literature. Right by the front door, two men hunched over a chessboard, and it looked like they had been playing the same game since 1962. I followed her back, and we found a table for two overlooking the occasional traffic on Sixth Street.

We sat, and I looked around the place, trying to take in all of the infamous campus coffeehouse hangout. Hundreds of exotic coffees and teas sat in jars by the wheezing espresso machines, and a huge glass case of fresh pastries and cookies wrapped around an old cash register, the kind with huge manual-typewriter keys and a lever you pulled each time you entered an item. The pseudo-intellectual crowd huddled over their wooden tables, reading, joking, and praising that was a post-5 PM Friday.

"It's something, isn't it?" she said.

"Reminds me of something out of a William S. Burroughs book," I said.

"Which one?"

"I dunno. Naked Lunch? Interzone? It's definitely a Tangiers association."

A waitress that looked like Natalie Merchant appeared out of nowhere with a order pad. "What can I get you two?" she asked.

"I'll have a caffe latte," Amy said.

"Do you have Coke or Pepsi?" I asked.

"We've got Coke in cans and bottles."

"Bring a bottle," I said. She vanished again, leaving us alone. I glanced around the room again, checking out the people at the tables. Why couldn't I think of a good way to jump into a conversation? I spent all day checking my mail compulsively, waiting for the next sliver of mail from her, but now with her right in front of my face, I waited for something to happen.

"Hey, you're pretty quiet today," she said. "Am I scaring you?"

"Sorry. I'm a lot more talkative over the computer. I'll get over it."

"It is a little weird to put the name to the face. I hope I don't disappoint you."

"No, everything's cool." I said.

Natalie returned with our drinks. Mine was pure heaven for a Coke junkie—a tall, 16-ounce, frost-covered bottle with a trademark fluted glass of ice, and for less than a buck.

I poured Coke over the ice, and watched the head of foam crackle and flow over the cubes. "So," I said, "I was going to ask you a chronology question—if that's not too personal."

"No, not at all," she said, stirring her coffee. "I was about to ask you the same. You go first."

"Okay." I stopped pouring, let the foam subside until my full glass was half full, then carefully poured again. "Well, I wasn't sure if you went to France during high school or college."

"It was the summer between," she said. "One of those package deals where they herd a group of Americans with money into a hostel and show you the sights. It was great though, it really made me realize there's more to life than cornfields."

"I wish I could leave the country sometime," I said. "I had a good friend who was in the army in Germany, and he told me tons of stories about visiting Berlin during Oktoberfest. He was supposed to get out in November of '90, but he ended up going to Saudi."

"That's horrible. Was he in combat?"

"No, he just played a lot of cards, and got more tattoos."

"I could never do that," she said.

"Me neither, I'm pretty much a pacifist. I read this book by Dalton Trumbo..."

"No, I meant the tattoos. I couldn't imagine something on your body forever."

"Different strokes for different folks, I guess. I couldn't do it either, though. I'd be afraid of changing my mind a year later."

I tipped back more Coke, and looked across the table at her. Nervous as hell, my hands fidgeted with the glass, the bottle, the chess table pattern on the table, my hair, and everything else. She was beautiful, sophisticated, down to earth—everything. I couldn't categorize her with just one thing, because she offered so many things at once. I looked at her perfect face, her thick, long hair, her figure, and thought she was just another attractive woman. But then she'd talk like an intellectual, and joke like she wasn't just an honor roll student. Every other woman I dated had flaws and faults that made me realize they were human. But she was a complete package, something that would take years to appreciate. The more I looked at her, the more I realized she had everything I'd ever wanted. But the longer I sat there talking to her, the more I realized I was outgunned.

"My turn?" she asked.

"Huh?"

"Chronology. Can I ask about yours?"

"Oh yeah, sure," I said.

"Did you go to school in South Bend, and then transfer?"

"No," I said. "It's a little more complicated than that. See, I came down here in '89, had a bad first year academically, and then moved back home. Then I went nuts with the parents, and then came back last fall."

"Did you start therapy when you went home?"

"No, no—well, I went to a counselor in my last year of high school, and started Prozac my freshman year down here. Then the lithium when I was home, in '90."

"I'm sorry."

"Hey, it's not your fault. It's electricity, biology, chemistry."

"I mean, I don't mean to pry. I know it's a touchy subject, and I don't know if you're willing to talk about it, especially in person."

"Don't worry about it. The secret's out. I wanted to wait until after we met, but I trust you. I'll tell you anything you want to know about it."

"It's nice that all of our cards are showing, so to speak."

"Yeah, except for my secret life as a pornographer."

We both laughed—she had the kind of laugh that made me feel good, the kind that sounded cute but vibrated like a million-dollar grand piano. I loved to hear her talk, to meld her voice with the weeks' worth of email I memorized. Her messages showed so much caring and humor that I couldn't imagine them as being spontaneous creations instead of carefully crafted replies. But in person, she weaved from topic to topic with so much ease that I could tell she was comfortable with me.

I couldn't fake it with Amy. She wouldn't go for the spaghetti dinner and bottle of cheap wine like the little freshmen women did. She could date a guy who made ten times as much money as me, but she was here with me. I had no games to play this time; all I could do is act like John Conner and hope she'd fall for it.

"So what are you up to this weekend?" she asked.

"The usual," I said. "Filling out those applications for an NSA grant, buying a dozen white linen Brooks Brothers suits for my upcoming trip to American Samoa. You?"

"I've got the big birthday celebration for Mom tomorrow. I'm driving up tonight, and I'll be back Sunday. And when I get back, my roommate will be moved out. I love her to death, but it'll be nice to have the place to myself."

"If only my roommates spontaneously vanished..."

"I'm going to have to get back soon, actually. I still haven't packed, or dropped off my check at the bank."

"Sure, no problem," I said. I dug into my pocket for some cash, but she beat me to the draw.

"Let me put in for mine," I said.

"Don't worry about it. You owe me a drink," she said.

"I can live with that," I said. At least she wanted to see me again.

We ducked out of the cafe, and back to Sixth Street. It still looked so serene and beautiful, just the early start of a great summer evening. We crossed back to Dunn Meadow and headed for the IMU.

"So what do you really do on the weekends?" she asked.

Fuck, I didn't want to tell her that I wandered aimlessly and talked to myself for hours. "Not much. Hang out with friends, have a few beers, catch a movie, whatever. Sometimes I catch a shift with UCS, or go in to the station. Nothing exciting though, I don't have a yacht moored at the lake or anything."

We stopped at the steps in front of the IMU, by the corner of Seventh and Woodlawn. I saw the Rabbit waiting for me across the street, and tried to see which car was hers.

"Sorry about the questions," she said. "I was just curious what made you tick, that's all. And maybe I wanted to lure you to lunch with me sometime. Can I give you a call and see how your NSA grant proposal is doing?"

"Sure, if I can do the same. I mean, you don't have a grant proposal, but..."

"I know what you mean. Let me get something to write with."

We crossed the street, and she opened up her car, a white Corolla, to find a pen. She jotted down her number on a post-it, and then asked for mine. "I don't keep a nine to five schedule, but my roommate does, so watch your timing. I know you keep to nocturnal computer geek hours."

"Okay, I'll stick to email for my 3 AM outbursts."

"Well, it was a pleasure, Doctor X. I hope to talk to you soon."

"Catch you later, Amy. Have a good weekend."

I watched her climb into the compact car and vanish down Seventh Street, then I popped into the IMU cluster to check my mail once again. Nothing new, and I couldn't find a half dozen usernames on the VAX cluster that I vaguely recognized. I hopped back down the steps, to the rusty VW and the great unknown.

I spun down Seventh Street, wishing she would've been in town that weekend. I couldn't believe her. I mean, I couldn't believe the level of beauty she demonstrated in person, the combination of looks, charm, and personality. I don't mean the kind of bathing suit model beautiful, the kind every generic sorority girl with no brain had. I could talk to her for hours about RS-232 cables or Star Wars characters, like she was just another CS geek in Lindley Hall. But when I watched her talk, every movement, every word pierced me her attractiveness.

But there was one obvious problem: what did she want from me? She seemed so in control of her life, from money to grades, to her previous relationship. I knew if she decided to meet me, it would have been a calculated risk. But how could she like me in spite of all of my problems? Was she just looking for friends, or did I feel a vibe that she wanted more from me? I felt helpless around her, without any of my usual defenses. How would it all pan out.

And where the fuck was everybody on campus? I drove past the fountain and down Jordan, and saw absolutely nobody. While she was back at her mom's house, I'd probably be scanning the computer for usernames, and reading interviews from a five-year-old issue of Playboy.

I gunned the engine and then killed the ignition as my tires hit the gravel driveway, so the silver box coasted silently for ten feet into its bay. It was a stupid trick, but I loved doing it when I wasn't in a hurry. Stroll into the house, take two: I knew there would be no mail waiting for me this time.

"It sounds fucking retarded," Yehoshua said to Deon, both of them sitting by the mantelpiece.

"I think it sounds pretty cool," Deon said.

"There's probably a music school party going on. I'm not wasting my money on a movie." Yehoshua stumbled back upstairs to his room.

"Hey John, do you want to go see *Universal Soldier*?" said Deon. "I think it's going to be hilarious."

"I'd have to be pretty drunk to get into a Jean Claude Van-Damme flick," I said.

"That's what I mean!" he said. "We go to Jerry's first, and pick up one of those little bottles of rum. Then you buy a Coke at the theatre..."

"Okay, I think I know where you're going. So how do we get home if we're so fucked up at the theatre? I'm not driving after a pint of Bacardi."

"There's a show downtown. It's only 20 minutes away on foot. That's a pretty short walk if you're plowed."

"I think it sounds fucking retarded!" Yehoshua yelled from the top of the staircase.

"What the fuck, I've got nothing better to do. Gimme a second, and we'll take off." I went back to the bedroom to change into a long t-shirt that would better conceal a hip flask of booze, and we hit the streets for an evening of fun.

I slept like a baby Saturday morning, a pint of rum dissolved through my system from the night before. It felt good to wake without an alarm, slowly drifting out of sleep and enjoying a stretch in bed. The night of drinking and mayhem didn't bring a hangover, or even the slightest wooziness. Instead, the extreme hunger of twelve hours without food pulled me from bed. Deon and I went to McDonald's after the liquor store, and then hid in the seats of the old theatre downtown, pouring our rum into huge, overpriced vats of watered-down Coke. We were lit by the time the previews were over; a good thing, since the movie was pretty much idiotic. We laughed out loud at the fake-cybernetics storyline and corny kickbox-fighting scenes. After the flick, we had enough firewater left to keep laughing, stumbling, and drinking all the way to the fountain gathering, where we hung out with a good turnout of people. All in all, it was a decent night of entertainment.

The computer started with its usual whirring and clacking, the first sounds of the afternoon. I ran my fingers through my hair and watched the sunlight outside the window, waiting for the machine the dial. It connected to the university, and I read my only message:

> From ARBERGST@ucs.indiana.edu Sat, 1 Aug 92 9:35:45 EST
> Date: Sat, 1 Aug 92 9:35:45 EST
> From: "plus ca change, plus c'est la meme chose"
> <ARBERGST@ucs.indiana.edu>
> Subject: from the Indy city
> To: JCONNER@ucs.indiana.edu
>
> Hey you. I bet you didn't think you'd hear from me today, huh? My dad has a modem on his computer, and I learned about dialing in to the Indianapolis number last spring break, when I was bored out of my mind, as I am now.
> Well, it was a pleasant surprise to meet you yesterday. I've never come face to face with someone from the computer, and I didn't know what to expect. But I had fun talking to you. You seemed quiet, but I'm guessing you were put off by the surprise meeting. Maybe next time, I can get you to explain some of your long stories that you keep mentioning...
> I've been promised an afternoon of shopping with Mom, so I better get out of here. Talk to you tomorrow?
> -Amy

At least she wrote back, I thought. And I'd have all day to think about a reply. Fuck, there had to be something for me to do outside, but I couldn't think of anything. I grabbed a towel and thought about a shower, maybe some lunch. Maybe my Saturday night plans were waiting for me. Maybe I'd have to fish for them.

Sunday night. I sat in my bed, reading a years old Guitar World magazine article about the recording of a Joe Satriani album. Back during the school year, Sunday nights were a big deal. IU dorms didn't serve people then; they had a 20 meal per week plan. That meant that everyone gathered together, ordered pizzas, and hung out. Everyone wanted to procrastinate a bit more before trying to get a weekends' worth of studying into the last few hours of the weekend. And even when I was out of the dorms, it was a night to visit with people, go out to eat, or catch up on all of my games of phone tag.

But now, Sunday—nothing. I circled the room, tried to read, tried to work, and tried to do anything except mindlessly fantasize about Amy. I fired up the computer, ran my script to log onto Bronze and Rose, and left the modem to dial while I dug through my CDs, looking for my copy of the new Paradise Lost album. The computer connected and dumped me at a blank prompt, but I kept looking at the stereo rack, trying to decide between the first Dream Theater album and a Sepultura bootleg.

The computer beeped with a message. "Hey you awake?" The bitnet was from Amy. I did a quick who and saw her logged on from Lindley Hall.

"Of course," I said. "Good weekend? How's Mom?"

"It was great—she says hi. Anything exciting here?"

"Not really, unless you consider getting loaded and watching bad movies exciting."

"Well, it can be," she said. "Hey, I haven't eaten dinner yet. You hungry?"

"I was just thinking about that," I said. "How does Chinese sound? Maybe The Grasshopper on Kirkwood? I could meet you at Lindley."

"Sounds good. I'm in the small PC room (as if you didn't know already.)"

"Okay, be there in 15."

"You're not hiding this time?" I said, walking into the PC lab, after a quick ten-minute clip across campus. Amy sat at a computer, wearing a loose t-shirt and jeans. Her hair was down, slightly curled down her neck and onto her shoulders. Her smile looked even better than the image stuck in my head all weekend.

"You know what I look like," she said. "I can't just switch computers."

"There's always stage makeup, costumes, holograms..."

She turned off the computer and got up from the desk. "I don't think I need to hide myself anymore. Unless you want me to."

"No, I'm perfectly happy with you visible."

"I don't know about you, but I'm starving," she said. "I could go for some cheap Chinese food."

"Grasshopper it is, then. Let's go."

We left the battleship gray basement of Lindley and climbed the front steps to Dunn Woods, the small forest between the old crescent and the western edge of campus. The August twilight lit the limestone buildings and dense trees around us, the sky slowly fading into a reddish glow. We strolled down the brick path that followed the arc of buildings and led to Kirkwood.

"So how was the trip home?" I asked.

"Okay, I guess. My folks are pretty obsessed with Tracy and it's bugging me. I mean, I love my nephew Joshua to death, and I'm worried about how things will turn out, but I'm more worried about what I will do next year, you know?"

"Yeah, I know what you mean," I said. "What are your plans, anyway?"

"That's a good question—I wish I knew the answer. I got accepted to grad school in Iowa, but I don't really want to go there, and I got into Berkeley, but I don't have the money. I'm starting the MA program here this fall, but I'm not thrilled with it—I didn't get a teaching spot, and that's what I really want to do. The library still wants me for mostly full-time work, though. It's a mess."

"Hey, you're more organized than me," I said. "I'm still not sure how I'm going to pay for the fall semester."

"I know how I'm paying—loans. I escaped them for four years, but they're in my immediate future."

"Well, you've still got a month of summer until the interest accruing," I said. "And I hope the rest of that month is like this. Isn't this weather incredible?" And it was—the day's heat and humidity slipped away to a cool paradise. The red of the setting sun painted the limestone of Franklin Hall and the Student Building as we approached Sample Gates.

We crossed Indiana and walked down Kirkwood to Grasshopper Chinese, a tiny hole-in-the-wall place next to a bagel shop in a small storefront. I opened the door for her, and we stepped into the small dining area, not much bigger than my apartment. They had Americanized food, the kind of menu where five bucks bought a nice heaping plate of greasy yet tasty food. Primarily a take-out joint, the only place to sit was a counter with high barstools that wrapped around the front window.

"Do you eat here a lot?" she asked, as we grabbed plastic trays and looked at the pots of simmering food.

"Yeah, actually," I said. "It's one of the only places close to Lindley Hall. And there's one vaguely near my house, too."

"You'll never need to prove your bravery to me..." she said.

"Hey there," I said to the Asian woman behind the counter. "I'll have the sweet and sour chicken, and some white rice."

"I'll have stir fry and white rice," Amy said. I grabbed two Cokes from a cooler next to the register, and paid for both meals.

We grabbed a seat at the empty counter; we had the place to ourselves. With the long run of glass in front of the counter, it felt like eating in a fishbowl with the world watching, but it was also nice to watch the people strolling down Kirkwood from the perfect seat. I dug into the sticky orange chicken, and cracked open my Coke. "This is great stuff," I said. "Lots of fat..."

"So when am I going to see your zine?" she asked.

"I don't know—I'm not sure you'd really be into it. It's just a few pages of album reviews, nothing exciting."

"Oh come on, I just want to see your writing. You're so great in your emails. Have you ever done any longer work?"

"I've thought about writing a book, and I've messed around with some short stories, but nothing incredible."

"Well, you should consider taking W103 or W203 sometime. I think you've got the skill to be a great writer."

"Well thanks," I said. "And when do I see your stuff?"

"I'm mostly into lit, so my papers would probably bore you. I have a few short stories, like the ones I used to get into grad school, but they're painful to read. Maybe sometime I will upload them to the VAX and send one to you."

I dug at my food, and scraped the last of the rice together. "So why Berkeley?" I asked her. "Do they have a good program?"

"The best," she said. "A lot of the professors here went to UCB. And California is incredible. Have you ever been there?"

"No, I've never been West before," I said.

"It's incredible—I was just there over Christmas. The weather's great, there's a lot going on, and the campus—it's like Bloomington times ten. More shops, more people, more beautiful buildings, more protesters, more hippies, more writers—it's just a great place. It's too bad it cost way too much, and I didn't get financial aid. I've been spending all summer trying to find a grant, or a fellowship, or something, but I'm not sure anything will come through now. Maybe next year."

We both finished the last of our food. "So, back to Lindley?" I said.

"Actually, I should head out in a bit, but my car's back there."

"Cool, I'll walk you back," I said. We dumped our trays in the garbage and headed back out Kirkwood and the evening sky.

We followed our path back to campus, the moonlit sky casting gentle shadows across the path in front of us. "So do you ever visit Indianapolis?" she said.

"A few times this summer, on the glowstick runs. And I went there a couple of times this summer with...well, with Tammy." Both of us hung silent over the uncomfortable and unmentionable reference.

"Do you still miss her?" she asked.

"Yeah. Yeah, I still do. The distance makes it easier, and the Zoloft. But everything was so perfect, I still wonder if I would've done something different. I wish we hated each other at the end, so it would have been a relief to see her go."

"It's not any easier," she said. "Things were so distant between me and Dave at the end of the year, that I can't even imagine staying with him. But when it was over, I felt like I couldn't breathe for weeks. I was with him for so long, I can't imagine being with anyone else," she said. "How did you manage to date.. what was her name? The Christian?"

"Oh, Jenn. That was sort of a misfire. I don't know, both of us were confused. I don't know how I expected her to go on. It's actually goofy to even think about it now."

"That's good though, right?"

"Yeah, I guess so. I'd hate to deal with any amount of pain from someone I only dated for a few days."

We walked down the row of limestone structures and behind Lindley Hall, to her white Toyota. "Well, this is me," she said. "Do you want a ride back to your place?"

"No, I'm okay," I said. "I could use the walk back." I wanted the fifteen-minute hike by myself, to think about everything and simmer in my feelings.

"Okay, well thanks for dinner," she said. "It was fun. We'll have to do it again sometime."

"You know where to find me," I said.

She unlocked her door and climbed in the car. "Talk to you tomorrow," she said.

"Bye Amy."

I walked away from Lindley, across the long courtyard behind the looming Chemistry building. After twenty paces, I turned back and saw her car pull out of the parking lot and vanish into the darkness. Not bad, I thought. Now I just need to worry about what's next.

I hiked to Jordan Hall and cut to Third Street, to continue home for the evening.

32

Monday morning English went past at a crawl, especially since my head pulsed with a headache that a shotgunned Coke and a handful of Tylenol couldn't help. I calmed my head by thinking of the night before with Amy, the long walk and unexpected dinner date. I also hacked out a final paper proposal, and discussed and debated it with three others in a small working group. It was like stone soup—I brought less than twenty words to the table, and got enough criticism and ideas to stretch it into a real outline. The teacher gave my proposal the green light, and I'd be able to hit the library and start pulling and photocopying articles.

After class, I couldn't find a free computer in Ballantine. There were some lab reservations for classes, and the remaining two rooms had long lines. I thought about heading to the library, checking my mail, and hitting the MedLine search terminals for an hour or two, but it seemed like too ambitious of a plan for a Monday morning, so I hiked home.

With a stolen Sunday paper in hand and Napalm Death's latest in the player, I cleared a spot on my bedroom floor and started a cursory scan of the want ads. Within moments, I found that it was business as usual in the job-barren classifieds, with only a half-dozen listings, all of them sales jobs or telemarketing schemes that didn't pay minimum wage. The need for money went from high-priority to chaotic with the loss of the Dial America job. The scholarship would cover my apartment deposit and the first semester of tuition, but I hadn't heard from the company's scholarship board. The last three years, they cut a check about a month before school started. I felt apprehensive about calling and asking, ashamed that maybe the money wasn't on its way. If it didn't make it, or if it got here late, I'd be up shit creek—I needed to get the apartment lease taken care of, and soon. The scholarship was my only hope. Even with a good job this late in the summer, I'd never get enough to cover the deposit.

Aside from the scholarship, I needed money to keep going until the fall. Even though I had a roof over my head and all the time in the world, I was learning that in America, money equals freedom. I wanted to be happy and run through fields of daisies and write poems all day long, but the ominous threat of fucking bills and deposits and tuition and car problems made me think of nothing but work.

I'd worked a steady job of some sort since I was 15 years old, with no breaks. Even on Christmas vacations, I would sometimes go back to my old job at the department store for two weeks and deal with every fucking degenerate in the tri-state area trying to return presents without a receipt, all for under four bucks an hour. I always dreamed of winning the lottery so I could quit my job and hang out with friends, listen to albums all day, and read books all night. But without any real employment and a pretty open schedule, I found all of my time consumed by trying to make a few bucks.

Ever since I passed the halfway point in my degree, the conflict got worse. Every time I flunked calculus or didn't think I could finish school in under ten years, I fantasized about some consulting firm looking for unschooled geeks with the same eclectic talents as me. They'd pay me six figures to do what I did as a hobby, and I'd automatically get all of the fringe benefits that would transform me from slacker to high-roller: a real job, a parking spot, corporate reimbursements, expensive toys, travel and conferences, health insurance, a company car, and lots of credibility. I'd blow the money on nice clothes, a Beemer or maybe a classic 'Vette, an all out babe lair apartment, exotic vacations, and restaurant dinners seven nights a week. Instead of the geeky kid going nowhere, thousands of beautiful women would see me as a good catch. All through my life, people told me money wouldn't buy happiness, but after a summer with no money, I wondered if that was really true.

I gave up on the paper and alternated between reading an old porno mag and a copy of Thrasher I took from the station. 10 AM, listening to the modern grindcore of *Utopia Banished* on the stereo, reading about pizza delivery boys and recently divorced women and how to build a half-pipe in your backyard, thinking about buying a skateboard and learning how to ride in the church parking lot on the other side of Atwater...The temporary relaxation of freedom took over, and everything else slipped from thought.

About three songs into the disc, the phone rang. I paused the CD and answered. "Yeah?"

"John? It's Amy. Everything okay?"

"Yeah, I guess. Went to English, skipped Econ, listening to some music. Why, is something wrong?"

"No, I was just wondering why you didn't check your mail yet. I thought maybe you got in a car wreck."

"The labs were full at Bal, and I guess I spaced it when I got back."

"Oh. Well, I was wondering if you had lunch plans?"

"Not really," I said. "I've got the afternoon off. What were you thinking? The Bloomington Motel on College has hourly rates. And I-bolts in the ceiling."

"I'm not going to ask how you know that. I was thinking more along the lines of Subway, Garcia's, Noble Roman's..."

"Okay, have it your way," I said.

"Maybe later in the week," she said. "I do have a small request for you. Can you meet me at Sample Gates? I've got to sign some stuff at financial aid, and it would be easier to meet over there."

"No problem," I said. "When does this operation go down?"

"I'll be done by noon, maybe a few minutes after."

"I'll be the one in the white tux, red cummerbund."

"Don't forget your tap shoes. I'll see you in a bit."

"Talk to you later." I threw out the newspaper, checked my money situation ($6 in my wallet, a few more bucks in the bank,) slapped a new pair of batteries in my trusty Aiwa so Motörhead didn't sound like Mudhoney anymore, and headed outside.

I sat on the stone wall next to Sample Gates, listening to the newest Pestilence tape on my walkman and staring at a scene that looked straight out of a promotional poster for the campus. The noon sun baked the limestone gates and lit all of the stone and brick of the campus portal to an almost living tone, better than a truckload of Hollywood lighting ever could. A light load of people trucked to and from classes, and people on mountain bikes darted from the street to the sidewalk and into Dunn Woods. Across the street stood the same row of 75-year-old buildings that were in almost every photo taken of the area. And a handful of other students sat on the low wall next to me, waiting for the A bus to whisk them to the center of campus. I got there early, and watched the scenery.

After a few minutes, Amy emerged from Franklin Hall, wearing a t-shirt, sunglasses, and a pair of cut-off jeans that showed off her long, smooth legs. The noon sunlight brought out the auburn in her long hair, and made her look even more radiant than before. I took off my walkman, and hiked across the red brick sidewalk to meet her.

"Hey," I said. "How'd it go in there?"

"Like pulling teeth. Never tell financial aid your dad's a doctor. It looks like I might get my loans, but it's a real bloodletting."

"You're making me look forward to this process," I said. "I can't wait until my scholarship falls through."

"Don't worry, you've got a summer session to go. You might be able to con that scholarship board for a third time," she smiled.

"So what's our plan here?" I asked. "We just had Chinese, and I'm not really up for Mexican..."

"Are you in the mood for Subway today?"

"After hanging out with Nick, I'm always ready for Subway," I said. "Let's check it out."

We passed through the Sample Gates and down to the same stretch of Kirkwood we walked the night before. In the noon sunlight, the trip felt much more vibrant. I could look at Amy, see her smile, her flowing hair, and the catlike way she moved her body as she walked.

"So, what's up with the paper for this class?" she asked. "Anything I might know about?"

"Maybe," I said. "Susan Sontag wrote about metaphor in illness, first with cancer, and then with AIDS. My theory is that this could also be applied to depression, especially since the Prozac explosion."

"How is mental illness a metaphor?"

"Well, everyone used mental illness metaphors, like when you say something is 'crazy' or 'insane'. Maybe the use of Prozac like candy will have some eventual effect on our vocabulary and remove some of those associations. Maybe not, but it's something I can pad out to fill ten or fifteen double-spaced pages."

"That's cool that you have an interest in English," she said. "I mean, it's cool you know so much about computers, but you can still write."

"I'm glad you think I can write, but I think I need more practice. I've always wanted to write a book, about the depression and everything."

"You should! I mean, you've got a lot of stories to tell," she said. "You just need to get some spiral notebooks, and scribble in them every day. Then you'll eventually start to see pieces of what you want."

"That's almost how I code," I said. "I start with nothing, and start filling in blanks until the framework is there."

"That's why I think you'll make a fabulous writer someday."

Past the sprawl of the main library and Monroe County Bank, we approached downtown, and the location of my new home away from home. "Hey," I said, "the radio station's right up there," I pointed to the run-down office buildings that housed WQAX. "It's in one of the apartments above that art gallery. You should stop in some night during my show."

"That sounds cool, I just might do that."

We continued up the slight hill, toward the square.

The heart of Bloomington was the area squared off by Fifth and Sixth Street and College and Walnut Avenue. The city courthouse, a huge hundred-year-old limestone building, sat in the middle of the city square, surrounded by various commemorative statues and plaques marking various wars and other historic events. Four walls of restaurants and stores surrounded the courthouse, all filled with an eclectic mix of businesses. Some of the older stores, like the Ben Franklin sat next to brand-new urban renewal projects like Fountain Square Mall. The block was one of the only places in Bloomington where you could go into a bookstore that still wrote their receipts on paper, and then walk 100 feet and be in the most yuppified, chrome-trimmed, overpriced clothing store you could find outside of a big city. It was no Manhattan, but it was an interesting change from the strip malls and chain stores that populated most of the state.

We walked over to the Subway, and I followed her into the narrow storefront, which looked a hundred years old on the outside, but still smelled like new paint and wallpaper inside.

The narrow restaurant ran between two bigger offices, with only a small slice of windows in the front. It extended far back into the guts of a building also shared by an insurance company, the kind of sterile offices full of realtors or bankers that you never think about in a college town. The stock Subway wallpaper, with brown-and-white images of old-school New York subway maps, wrapped around the walls, contrasted by real old-fashioned moldings and trim. The ceiling towered over the dining area by at least fifteen feet, and the front windows streamed sunlight over the tile floors. Although it was only a Subway, the whole place look much more exotic than a low-end sandwich shop should be. Much better than the Burger King by the mall, I thought.

At the counter, I saw Brent, a roommate of two other UCS consultants. I knew him vaguely from the VAX—we ran with the same VAX crowd. A big, tall guy, he looked kindof like Nirvana's bass player in a Subway manager's uniform.

"John Conner," he said. "I saw what you wrote on Dent's wall. Pretty funny stuff."

"Yeah thanks," I said. The year before, I was at a guy's house, and he let people write on his wall. He just moved there, so I picked the biggest, most conspicuous spot in the wall, and wrote "I am immortal / I am God / I am John Conner" in foot-high writing. I guess it was still there.

I turned and Amy was already ordering her stuff at the other register. "What'll you have?" Brent asked.

I recited the mantra burned in my brain by Nick's daily Subway visits: "Six inch BMT, bacon, wheat, mayo, mustard, lettuce, tomato, salt," I said. "Oh, and a medium drink.

"You at UCS this summer?" he asked, sliding the bread shell of a sandwich down the assembly line of vegetables.

"When I can," I said. "I'm just trying to pick up hours here and there, you know the deal."

"I've heard," he said. "Times are tough all over."

He sprayed the sandwich with mayo, mustard and salt, and quickly wrapped it into a cylindrical form. Brent handed over the sub and a paper cup, without ringing me up. "Here man, you owe me one."

"Thanks a lot dude," I said.

"No problem. But expect me to bother you sometime when I'm having SSAVAGE utils trouble."

"Hey, my pleasure," I said. Brent disappeared in the blur of lunch customers, and I turned around to look for Amy.

I walked back through the lunchtime bustle of boutique clerks and city workers hunched over their sandwiches, and found Amy at a two-person table, already eating. "Hey, sorry about that," I said. "Ran into someone I knew."

"So you're on a first name basis with the Subway workers?"

"No," I said. "Old friend, sort of. A VAX person."

"You can't go anywhere without running into someone, can you?"

"It's getting harder every day," I said.

I got started on the sandwich, and watched her eat. The BMT tasted good, and the fact that it was free made it even better.

"So it looks like your eating is back to normal now, huh?"

"Yeah, the medicine has eased up a little. I keep getting headaches at night though."

"And you're allergic to aspirin? What happens if you take it?"

"Puffy eyes, trouble breathing. But I found out that Tylenol works okay though. I bought my first bottle the other day."

"That's good. And the depression part?"

"It's better, but not perfect. I should start therapy in the fall, when I can afford it."

"I wish we could get Tracy in some therapy situation that would work. I wish we could find something that works for her."

"Yeah, I've had a lot of trouble finding a good shrink. And it's not like they advertise if they aren't any good."

"Exactly," she said.

"So, is your dad a good doctor?" I asked.

"Of course," she said. "I mean, he's a pediatrician, so I think you're a little old to see him. I think half of his job is just being able to work with kids. He's a man of great patience."

"For my sake, I hope that's a hereditary trait," I laughed.

I finished the last of my sandwich right after her, and wrapped up my trash. "About ready to head out?" she asked.

"Yeah, let's go."

We hiked back Kirkwood in the beautiful weather, watching the slow flow of cars driving around downtown, and the occasional pedestrian strolling the sidewalks.

"I'm parked up here next to the theater, she said. Across the lot, I saw the white Toyota among the rows of cars in the tight parking spaces. "Do you need a lift back home?" she asked.

"Yeah, that would be great," I said. She unlocked the Toyota, and I got in. The interior of the car looked immaculate, without the tapes, papers, food wrappers and books of the VW. All of the plastic and trim still looked untouched, and the car even smelled new, especially for a six-year old econobox. I slid into the front seat and strapped in while she started up the car. "This is a pretty clean set of wheels," I said. "You take care of things better than I do."

"Thanks," she said. "I've had it since I was 16, and we've seen many miles together. Oh, which way are we heading?"

"Towards the mall," I said. "Indiana to Atwater."

We pulled out of the parking lot, and wound down the wide, one-way street bordering campus.

"Are you heading back to the library?" I asked.

"Yeah, I'm trying to sort through a bunch of old terminals we found in storage," she said. "It's pretty dirty work—they have ten years of dust on them. What are you up to this afternoon?"

"I've got this paper," I said. "I might look into a nap first. It's too nice out to sit in bed, but I could use a few minutes. Oh, take a right on Mitchell."

"This is pretty close to campus," she said.

"Yeah, it's not bad. I'm the big gray house on the right—414."

She pulled into the driveway behind the Rabbit. "Wow, this is quite a piece of architecture," she said. "Is it a duplex?"

"It used to be," I said. "Hey, I was going to ask you if you'd want to come over for dinner some time this week, and take the grand tour."

"Is this the patented John Conner home-cooked dinner?" she giggled. "Will it be spaghetti or Chinese?"

"Knock it off. Chinese, nothing spectacular, just a nice evening of stir-fry and amenities."

"It sounds cute. When were you thinking?"

"I've got a show tomorrow, so maybe Wednesday?"

"Sounds good. I'm sure you'll fill me in on the details before then."

"Okay. Thanks for the lift back. I'll catch you later."

I went inside the Mitchell house, scooped up my mail and headed back to my room. At the helm of the computer, I sorted through the prizes of a heavy mail day. I opened miscellaneous letters from two other zines and an unsigned band, and dumped their fliers in a box of other ads I circulated with my outgoing stuff. There was another official looking letter from IU in the stack of mail, under a "have you seen me" postcard. I braced myself for the worst, and tore it open:

Indiana University College of Arts and Sciences
Office of the Dean Kirkwood Hall 104
Bloomington, Indiana 47405
FAX: (812) 855-2060
812-855-1647

August 2, 1992

John Conner
414 S. Mitchell #13
Bloomington, IN 47401

Dear Mr. Conner:

The Scholarship and Probation Committee of the College of Arts and Sciences has read your petition and revised your academic record. The Committee has agreed to re-admit you on strict probation for fall 1992 with the understanding that you will do your work at a quality level which will reduce or eliminate your grade point deficiency.

Your fall registration will not be canceled but the Committee will require you to change your enrollment so that you will be taking less than 14 hours. We also recommend that you review the material from HISP S100 before attempting HISP S150, since it has been several semesters since you studied Spanish.

You will not be allowed to participate automatically in continuing student registrations for future semesters until you have brought your cumulative GPA up to a 2.0. However, we suggest that you assess your own academic performance at mid-semester. If your grades at that point are sufficiently good so that you could reasonable expect to raise your cumulative GPA to 2.0 by the end of the semester, you may make an appointment with an assistant dean to request special permission to participate in continuing student registration for the spring semester. You should bring with you to that appointment actual evidence of your performance in all of your courses, consisting of statements from your instructors of your grades at that time, or the actual exams and papers you have completed up to that point.

If you are not allowed to go through continuing student registration, but do achieve a 2.0 at the end of the semester, you may apply to

Judith Bell in the College Recorder's Office for permission to enroll for the spring semester in January.

Sincerely,
Juan Schwartz
Senior Assistant Dean, Chair
Scholarship and Probation Committee

I almost knew it would happen, but the letter felt like magic in my hands. One thing less to worry about from my long list or current issues, I thought. I didn't really want to take more than 14 hours, but because IU had a flat fee system, you only got your money's worth if you took more than 15. It also didn't look like they knew that I was already above a 2.0 GPA, but that would be easy to fix.

I didn't notice the Brooklyn return address from the last envelope until I tore open the end. A circular metal button fell out, an inch in diameter and black except for the circle and minus that made the Type O Negative logo. I almost forgot that I dropped a line to Type O Negative and told them about the CMJ reporting stunt that Sid and I pulled. Was it a form letter? I pulled out a sheet of paper and read it:

> John-
> Thank you for playing our album, but doesn't your station have any better music to listen to?
> Maybe you'd be interested in an interview some time? Call Ken Kreite at the number below and we can set something up.
> Sorry again,
> Type O Negative

I read and re-read the letter, laughing. This would be IT—my first real interview. Type O Negative were big and would be getting a lot bigger with their next release. I'd be able to tape an on-air interview, and then transcribe it for use in the zine. I paced the apartment, thinking of questions, thinking of how I could promote it on the station. I went to the computer, and got my black book of Death Metal lay across the keyboard—actually blue, it was a notebook with the addresses and phone numbers of every band or label I knew. I transcribed down Ken's information to the book, then gave him a ring.

"Ken Kreite presents, this is Ken."

"Ken! This is John Conner, from WQAX. I heard you were the man to talk to about a Type O Negative interview."

"Hi John, Pete said you'd call. Thanks for playing the hell out of the EP."

"No problem, we love it down here. I hope we can get a crack at the new album soon."

"Well, they're working on it, that's all I know now. Hey, what's your schedule like?"

"Two shows a week. Tuesday and Thursday, 8 to midnight. I'm open for doing anything live then, or I could tape it almost any time."

"Let's try to do it on Thursday, toward the beginning of your shift. I'll have to call the guys, and work it out with them, but they rehearse on Thursdays, so that should work."

"Okay great. I'll let the GM know, so we can run some ads for it."

"Cool—I'll give you a call before Thursday and confirm."

We hung up, and I took a deep sigh. It was easier than I thought, I said to myself. Type O Negative—live on my show. I couldn't believe it, but now I needed to write some questions, plan some ads, and get in the studio for some preparation. I fired up the computer, logged on, and composed a new message to Sid. He's not going to believe this, I thought.

With all of the excitement, I didn't feel like answering mail in the stuffy heat of the room, and it made me feel worse to lie under the fluorescent lights when it was such a nice day out. I wanted to plan this more. There was also that dinner I promised Amy. I'd need to make a grocery trip to Kroger, which would involve some money.

Cash...it was time to weed through my CDs again. They were my currency in times of poverty like now, a way to gather a few bucks until payday. When I was riding high on full-time UCS hours, most of my extra money went to CD stores and clubs, and my collection would swell, both with things I loved and albums I only listened to once or twice a year. Since Tom at CD Exchange gave me good deals on my used CDs, I financed my low times by cleaning out my audio library.

I scanned my bookcase and CD racks, pulling anything useless that would sell. I could live without Led Zeppelin I and IV. Pink Floyd's Animals and Dark Side of the Moon were too depressing to keep around (but I'd hang onto The Final Cut, just in case.) A Billy Joel 2-CD set I ordered from a club, just in case of female visitors would go; ditto for the Police. I could also lose the first Van Halen album. In a few minutes, I found about 15 discs that could go, and dumped them in my backpack. I grabbed my walkman, the latest Shades of Grey tape, a dub of the new Gwar, and hit the road.

The lyrics from the joke-concept band Gwar's latest. *America Must Be Destroyed* rattled through the headphones as I hiked down Third Street's wide sidewalk with a backpack of CDs over my shoulder. I loved coming back from a commercial on the show with the title cut of the album, a weird industrial-sample track that starts with an explosion of sound and drums that always buried the VU needles far in the red. Sid loved to tell me about the time he saw Gwar play at a Holiday Inn in Indianapolis—I guess they completely fucking destroyed the place. He showed me the first video I saw of the Slavepit in action, and it looked pretty nuts: costumes, blood, explosions, violence, and everything else that makes metal Metal. I couldn't wait to get my hands on their latest video, a short movie based on the songs from the new album called *Phallus in Wonderland*. I hit rewind on the Aiwa player and backed up the tape to my favorite part while keeping at the walk downtown.

Walking down Third Street, I saw a guy that looked like an uncle of mine, trotting in the opposite direction. He had bright blonde hair in a seventies haircut like William Macy, short shorts, a stocky figure, like an ex-Marine or Navy vet, and walked at a pretty good clip, just short of breaking into a jog. It wasn't too unusual—there were plenty of power-walkers and joggers on campus, and a lot of them made the Third-Indiana-Seventh-Jordan loop around campus. But I saw this guy every damn day, and not just at lunch; he'd walk at almost random times. He was a regular fixture on campus, and made me wonder if it was his job to patrol the streets, like some kind of undercover cop. Or maybe he was a returning student. Or a prof. One time when me and Yehoshua were at a party, I mentioned this guy, and a dozen people immediately knew who I was talking about. Weird. Maybe someday I'd stop and ask him what his deal was. Oh well, on with Gwar.

"Hey John, how goes it?" Tom said, as I walked in the store. He stood at the counter, going through a stack of CDs. Some kind of slide-guitar music ebbed from the speakers on the wall.

"It goes. Got some stuff for you to look at," I said.

"Sure thing," he said. I put my bag on the counter, and loosed the pile of discs for him to investigate. While he looked at each one for scratches, I wandered around and did my usual scan through the used bins. There were only two or three people that sold back Death Metal stuff, but it didn't hurt to look.

Tom divided the CDs into two piles. "Were you looking at cash or trade today?"

"I'll go with the cash," I said.

"Okay, I can give you four each for these six, and three each for the other nine." $51, not a bad haul.

"Sounds cool," I said.

He put the stacks behind the counter, and opened up the wooden cash till. "How's the show going?" he said, counting out bills.

"Not bad, I'm on Tuesday and Thursday nights. It would be nightly if Sid had his way, but two nights is enough." He handed me a small stack of cash. I folded it and put it in my front pocket.

"Well, good luck with it," he said.

"Thanks Tom, catch you later."

I grabbed my empty backpack, and headed back out to Dunnkirk Square. With the sun in my eyes and the heat on my back, I pulled on my headphones and got back to Gwar for the way home.

33

The cool air conditioning of the Fine Arts lab drifted over my body, another reason to rejoice the noon to four sub shift I picked up the day before. At 11:30 in the morning on a Tuesday, only a few people drifted in and out of the soundless room to check email, leaving me to my own projects. I got to the lab early to bask in the artificial climate and do some playing before my shift. Already situated behind the dual monitors of a Macintosh, I picked through the alt.folklore.computers newsgroup's tales of dinosaur mainframes and ancient ARPANET connections that eventually evolved into the Internet. Even though officially off-watch, I also kept an eye out for anyone in need of computer help. But, at this time of day, answering four questions during my entire shift would be considered a rush. Summer consulting was pretty low key stuff, especially after my experiences during the battles of finals weeks, midterms weeks, and other horrifically busy periods. But, I didn't mind the quiet. As long as I had a network connection, a few mainframes to play with, and maybe a person online to bug, it was fine by me.

The Mac screen flashed to signal a message in another window. I switched from my newsreader session on Bronze to a window containing a connection to the Rose VAX, and saw a waiting bitnet message with Amy. I bitnetted her back, and started a conversation:

> (IUJADE)ARBERGST—Hey
> JCONNER—What's up?

(IUJADE)ARBERGST—Heading out to lunch. Interested in joining me?
JCONNER—I'm working @ Fine Arts till 4 :(
(IUJADE)ARBERGST—Do you always work Tuesdays?
JCONNER—Nope—sub shift.

Bitnet was only quasi-real time; your line wasn't sent until you hit return, and the other person's lines came in slowly, like talking to someone on the moon. I waited for her next return in the volley as my shift crept along. It wasn't like hanging out with her in person, but the air conditioning made it almost bearable.

After work, I stopped in as a last-ditch effort to find anything that would have the slightest positive dent toward my money situation. I still owed the landlord $400 by a week from Friday, and the scholarship check was nowhere in sight. I didn't expect a good job or even a partial solution to my money shortage, but even a position illegally selling dog carcasses to glue factories for a five percent commission would be better than nothing.

The job board at the career center looked like the picked-over, post-vulture carcass of a dead animal in the middle of a desert. On the board, even the half-baked Ponzi schemes and slave-labor waitstaff jobs were gone, leaving only a few dozen leads, most of them futile. I found a card for a busboy job at a resort a few miles out of town, and another for some kind of vague credit card solicitation work. I also noticed a few slips for jobs that I called and found out were filled—further evidence that the whole system was fucked.

I exchanged the cards at the front desk for the actual job information, and headed home. When I emerged back to the sunlight, I saw Gary Gartman crossing the street and making a beeline for the career center. With his bald head and stark white complexion, he moved like a sick parody of a post-apocalyptic underground dweller.

"Hey Gary, what's up?" I played nice—we didn't have any formal conflict, and I felt sorry for the guy, even if he did scam on all of my female friends.

"Not much, I'm going in to look for a job. I'm trying to stay here next year."

"Are you out of cash, or did you get the boot from school?"

"Both. I need to find a place to live, and get something for next year."

"Good luck—there's not a lot there right now. I guess if you're looking for full-time in the fall, there might be something in the papers."

"I tried that, too."

"Well, keep at it. I'll catch you later, man."

"Okay, thanks."

Gartman ducked in the building, and I headed down Jordan. Poor guy, he didn't even know how fucked he really was.

At home, no mail awaited me, job rejections or otherwise. I loved getting checks and demos, but the bills, dismissals, rejections, and other bad news made me wish for more postal holidays in addition to the current 87.

I settled down in the heat of my room, and took another look at my current employment prospects. The busboy job could wait, sort of a last chance thing. Anything involving the removal of half-eaten food is, by definition, a last chance. Instead, I studied the credit card job, and decided to call their 800 number. I'd surely get a recording that would explain the sketchy details a bit more.

To my surprise, a human picked up the phone. "TransAmerican marketing," she said, in a cheery receptionist voice.

"Hi, I was calling about a credit solicitor ad that I found on the Indiana University job board, and I'd like more details."

"Sure," she said. "Our credit solicitors work on a freelance basis, distributing credit card applications. Each returned application earns a one-dollar commission. We provide marketing materials like posters, and applications for a variety of different cards. Does this sound like something you'd be interested in?"

What the hell. I could always put up a few posters with blank applications, and sit in the Mezzanine of the IMU and gather in a few. A buck an app—if I worked a lunch hour, I could do better than dishwashers' wages. "Sure, sign me up," I said.

She took my address and info down. "I'll send you a starter kit and you can call me and keep in touch if you have any questions," she said. "Are you graduating soon?"

"I've got a few classes left," I said.

"Would you be interested in working in Pittsburgh? We're looking for a few people at our main office."

"I'm stuck here for now," I said. "You should've asked me in May."

"Maybe next summer," she said. "I'll get everything in Priority Mail tomorrow. Welcome aboard."

We exchanged good-byes and hung up. I thought of other potential schemes to get the applications out, like buying candy bars in bulk and then giving them out to anyone who finishes an app. I saw it done all the time in the IMU, and even if the candy was three for a dollar, I'd be making money. It could be done, but I'd probably be too lazy to do it. I knew that the package would show in the mail next week, and I'd promptly ignore it and bury it under a pile of dirty dishes.

Their off-the-cuff Pittsburgh job offer bugged me. Based on the context of everything, it would probably be something awful—stuffing posters in mailing tubes for minimum wage or worse. But it bothered me because it was in Pittsburgh, and so was Tammy. I thought about scenarios where I would've had the gig back in May or June, and moved out there. I'd call her, she'd come over and visit me, and it would all be magically restored to what we had before. Or the cynical take on things—I'd get there, I wouldn't tell her, I'd make big bucks, and in the fall, I'd nonchalantly tell her, "Oh, I was in town all summer, but I was too busy high-rolling to look you up."

Either way, the whole thing was stupid. But it made me thing of Tammy for the first time since Amy came around. Amy kept the edge off of the pain, and all of my romantic urges and sexual depravity had a new target. But now, the deeper conflict came back, the addiction to what I had before. It made me realize that even if I was balls-deep in another woman, I'd still cry over Tammy. It made me want to find her number and call her, and explain...something. Or nothing.

I didn't call. I filed away the job slips on the pile of papers surrounding the computer, and thought about a nap before my show, until I realized that I needed food for the dinner tomorrow.

There's nothing like wearing a Napalm Death shirt and some ripped up jeans while you're shopping at Kroger, especially when it's in the middle of the afternoon, when the most pedestrian and geriatric of crowds frequents the place. I wandered the aisles of the College Mall grocery store, grabbing a few things I needed for the dinner, along with a stash of Coke and some other supplies to last the week and a half until payday.

Kroger was something I grew up with, the place my mom would drag us on Saturday mornings when we were kids, the place where Lars and a few other friends worked in high school, and one of the first stores that stayed open 24 hours back in Elkhart. When I first moved into the Mitchell house, my trips to this blue and white store would take hours. I'd wander the aisles and shop for all of the curious brands my mom would never buy. And I'd come in at three in the morning, when nobody else was there, and buy $50 or more of food.

But today, I just had a few things to get. I found the "ethnic" aisle of prefab Chinese/Mexican/Jewish food, grabbed enough bottled seasoning and sauces to make a stir fry and maybe some beef and broccoli, and picked up more chopsticks and fortune cookies. I also hoisted two cases of Coke onto the cart, and browsed the freezer section for more pizzas and burritos, my standard rations.

I whipped through the checkout lanes, loaded the plastic bags and cases of Coke into the Rabbit's tiny hatch, and buzzed back to the house.

A few hours later, I started packing the CDs, tapes and magazines for the show, along with a couple of Cokes and a bag of chips. Of course, it just started to rain, so I wrapped the parcel in a couple of plastic grocery bags and loaded it into the passenger seat of my car. The inside of the Rabbit had a distinct smell, something that I only smelled in other old VWs. A mix of West German technology, shitty wiring harnesses, and the fine black soot of a diesel engine permeated the tiny passenger compartment. With such tight quarters, simplified amenities, and smaller compartments, VWs felt more like planes than cars. From what I read about in books, the old, mass-produced warplanes like the P-51 and B-17 had a unique feel, aroma, and personality. So did the old Rabbits.

The drive across town gave me a good view of Bloomington transforming from a hot and lazy summer afternoon to an evening of lightning and thunder. The smell of ozone and fresh precipitation mixed with the trees and fresh-mowed grass on campus during the eerie in-between phase of clear and rain. The roads glistened as droplets of water mixed with oil and the diesel dust from the campus busses. People ran for cover, ran to roll up their windows, ran to drag their sidewalk sale merchandise to the safety of indoors. Bikes sped to get home before their narrow strip of roadway between the cars and the curb turned into a river. And I hurried to the studio, before the black sky started to pummel the earth with its contents.

I hauled my gear into the booth, and found Andre, this wiry, short-haired punk, playing some obscure records and digging through the vinyl section for obscure fusion vinyl to tape at home. I broke out my stuff and started loading up my stack of discs for the show. From the racks, I pulled all of the usual Century Media and Earache CDs, and thought of how to start.

Andre played tons of his own seven-inch records, something I found phenomenal. Next to cassettes, I found vinyl to be the worst thing to queue up in rapid succession. With a CD, I could drop it in the tray, press hold, and key a track number. Then, with one keypress, I could start the CD whenever I wanted. But a record required such precise aim, and required much more work to play two in a row. With two good CD players, I could queue up a hundred back to back tracks from a hundred different discs without breaking a sweat. Doing a few records in a row on the shitty 1970's turntables seemed like a grueling marathon. With no digital meters for remaining time, and the worry of selecting the right turntable speed (which was a migraine on indie punk records pressed in some freaky mailaway company which almost never labeled them 33 or 45,) I almost never played vinyl. But Andre was good, slamming in and out the wax on the dual tables like a real old-timer. I silently watched as I pulled my CDs from the wall and tried to figure out my play order.

I queued up my first two tapes, a station ID and my first ad, while Andre sat at the console, lining up the last of his stuff and resleeving loose records. Just after eight, he did a signoff and handed me the board. I played the ad while I got in the pilot's seat and swapped for my favorite pair of headphones.

"Good luck with it, man!" he said. "Play some of that speed metal shit!" he joked, pumping the secret devil sign in the air with his free hand, as he dragged a gym bag full of vinyl out the door.

"Catch you later punk rock guy. Go jump on a table and shout anarchy for me," I joked. As he closed the door behind him, the Add Sheet tape just started to close the one-minute slot.

As the last word of the jingle hit my earphones, I punched the mixer from tape1 to tape2, and brought up the microphone. I read the standard disclaimer sheet in my somber, boring radio announcement voice:

"The following program contains material which may be unsuitable for some audiences, including adult language and themes. It may be considered offensive to some listeners. If you have any questions about this policy, please feel free to contact WQAX at 331-9289. Thank you."

In one quick motion, the mic went off, and tape2 went on. "Are you bored of FM radio?" said the zippy, marketing-drone DJ voice, as a radio tuned from station to station. No, I thought, I'm just bored of this station ID.

As the 30-second spot wound down, I clicked the source from tape2 to CD1 with one hand, and clicked the mic with the other.

"It's 8:04, this is John Conner and you're listening to WQAX 103.7 cable FM in stereo. Welcome to Xero Tolerance, Bloomington's only weekly program full of your favorite new Death, Thrash and Speed Metal. I'm going to be bringing you some of the new Unleashed album tonight, along with some Carcass, Entombed, new Deicide, new Dismember and more. But first, here's a song from Type O Negative, from their last studio album, *Slow, Deep, and Hard*. Later in the show, I'll be playing a few cuts from their new live EP, *The Origin of the Feces*, but first, here's 'unsuccessfully coping with the natural beauty of infidelity,' on WQAX 103.7 cable FM."

I bumped the hold release on the CD and clipped the mic in a quick motion, then faded up the CD to a decent level. The spinning disc started its reign, and a rising tone from the intro shook the monitors. A guitar entered, feedback rattling the CDs on the desk, and then an explosion of drums, bass, and Pete Steele started, as he screamed "Do you—believe in forever? I don't even—believe in tomorrow."

With a long song on the player, I had a bit of time to quickly jot down my log files, and get a few more CDs in the stack. The trick was to get a log file down without times and get a decent number of CDs going, so the only real work would be filling in the times, watching the changes, picking the ads and public service announcements, and talking when needed.

As I scribbled the first few songs in the lined sheet, the phone rang. This struck me as odd, since nobody ever called to request anything. An offended listener? Maybe it was Sid or Alex, wondering if they left a record at the console. Sid got into the habit of calling me and requesting Neil Diamond or Linda Rondstat, just to take me up on the offer that I would play anything. Someday, I vowed to buy a copy of "You Don't Bring Me Flowers" to play back to back with Rotting Christ or the Meat Shits.

"WQAX, this is John," I said in a phony DJ voice.

"Hey!" said a female voice, "It's me—can you buzz me in?"

"Umm sure," I said. I could barely hear the person over the music, and it sounded like they were on a pay phone or a mobile, which further distorted the voice. "Come up to the third floor, to the door with all the fucked up Soundgarden posters." I clicked the door button and hung up, quickly realizing I was almost at a song change.

It would be cool if one of my listeners actually stopped by, I thought. Running a radio show typically involved a lot of work in the first half hour or hour, but by the time a stack of disks was queued up and the log sheets were completed, things got pretty boring. Most of the time, I'd bring a notebook and try to review CDs for the zine or dub new albums in the "production studio," a closet full of half-functioning electronics including an old tape player and a single CD player. I'd been inviting almost everyone I knew to come to the studio and hang out during the show. I told people on the computer, from classes, at the fountain, on the air, and just about anyone else that they were welcome to stop by the station to say hi, take a look at the gear, and get on the air if they felt like it. Of course, nobody did. In the summer, everyone's schedule was either geared toward early morning classes or late night mass alcohol consumption. But I kept inviting everyone on a constant basis, hoping someone would finally show up. And now, they did.

Pete Steele's terror quickly came to a halt, so I quickly faded from CD1 to CD2 and clicked the hold release to start the second track from his new live EP. With a more ambient beginning, he monotone chanted "Are you afraid, afraid to die?" I put the first CD back into its case and started an "already played" stack. Since the Type O Negative EP wasn't out yet, I usually played a few tracks in a row, so I had some time to jerk around. I walked through the maze of vinyl stacks and went to the studio door to wait for my visitor.

I opened the door and waited halfway in the hallway to see who would appear. After a minute or two of suspense, Amy climbed up the staircase. "Hey, I found it!" she said, finishing the last flight of stairs.

"Welcome to WQAX," I said. "Don't mind the mess, we aren't exactly high-rent here." I led her into the dimly lit vinyl library, with stacks of records on either side of us. "Here's our vinyl, which I never touch, and up ahead's the control booth. Here, have a seat." I motioned her over to one of the chairs next to the board, and got back at the controls.

"Wow, there's a lot of stuff in here," she said, scanning the gear. "I've never seen this many CDs in one place before."

I tried to jot down the next few songs in the log, before I forgot, and then cut over to the next waiting CD. "Yeah, most of the stuff is junk, but they actually get new music from stations. Sid hopes to go all digital at some point, but some DJs still use a lot of vinyl."

"What is this music? I've never heard it before."

"Unleashed. They're a Swedish Death Metal band. It's not exactly Queensrÿche, but it's interesting."

"Is all of the stuff you play heavier?" she asked. "I mean, like Slayer or something?"

"Yeah, I mostly play Death Metal and Thrash," I said. "No Slayer really, but some similar stuff that's more obscure. Oh shit, I've got to do a song change..." I dove for the board, put on the headphones, and got on the mic.

"That was 'Countess Bathory', a tribute to Venom from Johnny Hedlund and the rest of the Swedish slayers in Unleashed on their new CD, *Shadows in the Deep.* You're listening to Zero Tolerance with John Conner, on WQAX, 103.7 cable FM. Speaking of Sweden, I've got some of the latest Desultory demo and I'll roll that in just a minute, after this announcement."

In a quick swoop, I faded into tape2, cut the mic and went for tape1 to cue things for after the spot. "I hate this ad—I have to play it every hour, and it's driving me nuts," I said. I looked over and saw Amy smiling at me, watching me with great interest. Visitors usually made me nervous, but I felt relaxed with her there. It almost felt like she was interested in watching me run the console.

The one-minute ad wound down, and I carefully clipped the fade to the other tape player, where a waiting demo cassette throttled the VU meters and slammed through the studio monitors. The tape came from a band called Desultory, who hailed from Stockholm and recorded their first three demos in the same studio and with the same producer as bands like Entombed and Dismember. They featured the same sort of heavy, tearing distortion in their guitars, and crisp, defined drum sound with piercing vocals up front. Their drums clipped a faster beat, as dual guitars chugged at a slower speed and did a bit of speedier soloing in time with the drums. The mix resulted in a very energetic and fast-paced song that still held a doomier, slow-ripping guitar sound in the foreground, something that many American bands couldn't master.

"So..." I asked her. "What's been up with your classes?"

"Not much," she said. "I'm taking this polysci class that's pretty boring, just taught from the book. Children's Lit is good though. I've never studied it a lot, but it's a fun summer class."

"A lot of women in there?" I asked.

"You bet. You'd be a happy guy, except that most of them have overactive biological clocks."

I leaned back to the board and pressed a button to switch CDs. "And you?" I asked.

"My nephew is enough for now. I'd rather go to grad school than end up like Tracy."

"Good point," I said. "I'm in the same boat—there's no way I am responsible enough to handle kids. I guess I'm waiting for that ideal woman to straighten me out. Crap—I've got another CD change coming up..."

I slapped on the headphones, pulled the mic to my face and got ready for a quick ID and change. "Okay, that was 'Visions' and 'Twisted Emotions' by Desultory. You're listening to Zero Tolerance with John Conner on WQAX 103.7 cable FM." Bam with the mic, bam with the tape, and another ad played, which would back-to-back with a station ID and then a promo, giving me 85 seconds to get the next two CDs set up and going (minus the two tape changes for the ads, which were luckily cued beforehand.) I backed down the studio monitors to a sane level so we could talk.

"You're so focused," she said. "How do you remember what order you did everything, and all of the titles?" She got up and started to look at the racks of equipment next to the board, the dusty black boxes that pushed signal out of the studio.

"Half the time I don't," I said. "If I get nervous, I try to remember that nobody's listening. It's a lot like playing records in my room—no pressure."

Amy came over and sat in the swivel chair next to mine, right next to me, and leaned over the board to read the yellowing index cards and post-it notes of directions and instructions. The proximity was devastating, just like the time June sat next to me before her party. I could smell her hair, and every part of me wanted to put my arms around her, pull her next to me, and lock my lips against hers. But I didn't know if the closeness was intended or accidental. I'd have to wait for a better sign.

After the next song ran down and I started another change, Amy got up and wandered around the studio, checking out the racks of vinyl and half-dead studio equipment waiting for repair.

"I can see why you like this place," she said. "Lots of music, lots of toys, and the solitude is interesting. It must be a great getaway for you."

"It beats studying for econ," I said.

Amy sat in the window ledge, looking down at the rain-slicked streets below. The storm stopped an hour before, but water continued to trinkle through the broken gutters and from the surrounding rooftops, and a fresh ozone post-rain smell filtered through the windows into the studio.

"This is an incredible view from here," she said. "You can see almost all of downtown."

"Yeah, I like to just look out over the city when I've got a lot of space between my changes. Speaking of which..." I automatically faded and clicked from one disc to another in one sweeping motion, then pulled my headphones and turned back to her.

"Can you let that disc play?" she asked.

"Sure, it's just the new Obituary," I said. I took off the headphones and got up from the board.

"Come over, let's both sit in the window and look at the rain."

I sat next to her at the window to share the view of the water-covered city.

34

Brown beef in 1/4 cup of water and 2 tablespoons of soy sauce. I studied the simple instructions, hoping I wouldn't miss a subtle step that would turn the stir-fry into some sort of botulism experiment or chemical warfare weapon. I still could've used more instruction than "brown beef," like "cook the meat on medium until there's no more pink," but I guess that was the computer programmer in me taking the instructions too literally. I scraped the pre-cut meat from its mod styrofoam tray and plopped it in the pan, where a water-soy mixture already danced from the heat of an electric burner. The beef, proudly labeled "ideal for stir fry!" in an oriental-type font on an orange produce department sticker, sizzled and spat in the aluminum valley, and the smell of soy and frying beef quickly filled my nose. With a wooden spoon, I shifted the pink chunks, leveling and spreading it across the skating drops of liquid.

The frying food was the last step in a busy day of preparation. After morning classes (well, just English,) I scoured the kitchen as much as possible, and washed enough dishes to be able to cook the meal. In the bedroom, all of the books and zines got stacked in neat piles, and I hid all of the dirty laundry in the closet. I even managed to mop the kitchen floor, and run a vacuum through my room. With the floor cleared, the blinds and windows open, and my music collection put away, the tiny apartment almost looked reasonable. I used to do this all the time, the spring before. Before I met Tammy, almost every week that year saw another VAX chick, another dinner, and another quick pass at cleaning up the shithole apartment. I did another quick check, and everything looked cool. Back to the food.

"Knock knock?" said a female voice aside me. Looking up from my cooking project, I saw Amy standing in the kitchen doorway, dressed in a pair of cutoff jeans and t-shirt, highlighting her lightly tanned skin. "I guess I found the kitchen," she smiled.

"Hey, you sure did," I said, holding the wooden spoon up from the pan. "Welcome to the dining facilities in our fine estate. Food's running a little behind, but once this browns, it's almost done. Can I get you anything to drink?"

"No, that's okay, I'm fine." She walked over to the stove, peering at my setup of covered pans, open frying pans, and plastic bowls full of uncooked vegetables and sauces. "Let's see, beef stir fry, white rice—what's in the covered pan?"

"Oh, fried rice," I said. "I fried half of the rice, with some vegetables and stuff. I guess I could've fried it all, but I didn't know which kind you like." I turned the beef again, which was now about half-pink, and drying fast. With a professional-looking twist, I gave it another dash of soy and water. I peered at the meat, now a tender brown throughout. "Looks like we're almost in business here," I said. In went the stir-fry sauce, a brown, spicy liquid that quenched the sizzling sound of frying meat. I dropped the vegetables into the hissing mix of water and meat, and stirred everything evenly. "After this gets up to temp, we'll be ready to eat." I stepped back from the counter, finding my half-consumed Coke. It provided a swig of relief from the stove's scorching heat added to the already sticky summer air.

Amy pulled out one of the old chairs at the beat up dining table, and peered around the kitchen's 100-layer-of-paint cabinets and worn tile floor. "This is quite a place," she said.

"Yeah, well, I hope you don't judge a person by their surroundings. Between this place and the station, you must think I'm a serial killer."

"I don't care what kind of place you life in. It just has a certain...character to it. It's certainly not like all of the prefab dorm rooms."

"It does win points for originality," I said. "I'd love to know the history of this place, like what part was original and what was added on. It's owned by some slum landlord in Kentucky, so who knows what untold tales are here.

I leaned back to the stove and stirred the mix a few times, knocking around the partially cooked vegetables. The first uncomfortable silence hit. It's almost like a benchmark for meetings to me, when the conversation stops. If you meet someone and talk for nine hours straight, you know you're in. If you both freeze eight words into it, find that CIA cyanide capsule you keep in your hollowed-out tooth. It was probably my fault; she was the most beautiful woman to date that had come over for the John Conner Chinese dinner treatment, and I didn't feel the least bit confident about it. I kept poking at the food, and waited for her to start talking again.

"So did you go to the Oriental market down the street?" she asked.

"Oh yeah. I mean, no, not this time. I had to get Coke, and some other stuff, so I went to Kroger. But I love that place."

"Me too, I used to go in there sometimes just to look. I love the packages, all of the paper and Chinese and everything. And the smells, of all the spices. It's so much more fun than a grocery store."

"I know," I said. "I wish I cooked Chinese every day, just so I could shop there constantly. They already know me by name there. I bought a pound of shrimp once, and a week later, they asked me how it turned out."

"That's really cool. I wish there were more stores like that."

"Hey, all the CD stores in town know me..."

I kicked over the stir-fry again, and tested a spoonful. The vegetables tasted cooked, and the meat was nice and hot. "Looks like dinner's served," I said. "Grab a plate, we'll eat in my room. There's a stereo in there, and no roommates."

We loaded up my plastic art-decco dinner plates with plenty of rice, and scooped large amounts of the delicious-smelling stir-fry on top. The rich brown sauce and chunks of bamboo shoots, carrot and bell peppers flowed like lava and fire from the mountains of white and brown fried grains. Balancing the plates, a couple of Cokes, some napkins, and the wooden chopsticks, we went to my room and sat on the clean floor. Eating dinner with a date in the kitchen invited all of the house residents to ogling and later harassment, so I figured my floor would be a more private dining area.

"This room is great!" she said. She sat Indian-style on the carpet, and set up her eating utensils and food in her lap. "It's exactly how I pictured it. I mean, the paneling, the weird ceiling, all of the computers and CDs and stuff..."

"I'm glad you're not completely shocked," I said.

"Oh come on, this is great. There's not a lot of room, but it feels comfortable, like a genie's bottle. You could really get lost in a place like this."

"And I sometimes do," I said. I went to the stereo and slapped in a Chick Corea CD, one I'd been playing constantly for the last few weeks. I sat across from her on the recently-vacuumed carpet, cracked open the fresh can of Coke, manned the chopsticks, and picked up a piece of the beef. It tasted perfect, marinated in the soy and premixed stir-fry sauce, with a rich, permeating flavor. Of course, even an idiot could cook stir-fry. That's probably why I had it mastered.

"Tastes good," I said, assuring her that it wasn't fatal.

She tried the food after me. "Hey, not bad at all. This makes me wish I had a roommate who could cook." We both dug into the food, and listened to the keyboard and sax on the electric pop-jazz CD. She knew of Chick Corea from my constant use of his song titles as process names on the computer. The five-piece sounded like summer, and fit the informal dinner perfectly.

"You know, this might sound forward, but I really like being around you," she said.

"Yeah, well you aren't bad yourself."

"No, really. I guess I've been drifting all summer. It's nice to be around someone so unique. It's very comforting."

"Well I'm glad you appreciate it," I said. "I feel good about it too. A little weird, but mostly good."

"Why weird?"

"It's a 'waiting for the other shoe to drop' weird. I've had a lot of bad luck with the female persuasion as of late."

"Sigh...you should stop worrying, John. You're a great guy. Everything about you is great, except that you don't see it. Live in the now, man!" she laughed.

"Hey, how's your food?" We were both almost done, but I was considering going back for more. "Are you up for seconds?"

"Sure," she said. "This is great."

We both got up, and went back to the kitchen to scoop more food from the frying pans simmering on the stove.

"I really do love this place. How did you end up here?"

"Funny story," I said. She sat down at the dining room table and started eating, while I stood and picked at my food. "When I was back at IUSB, the pit of hell, I applied to the dorms. I thought I could get into that whole low-maintenance, meet-people situation like my freshman year at Collins. I got the contract in the summer, and it was for a single in Willkie. You ever see one of those?"

"Yeah, they're the same as Forest and Read, right?"

"Yeah, pretty much a fucking linen closet, for like $400, $450 a month. And at Willie, I'd get the drunken jock freshmen, bad rap music in every stereo, nightly fire alarms, vomit in the bathrooms, all of that bullshit. So I was dating my ex Lauren that summer. She was here, so I got her looking for a cheap place. She found this, I think on a bulletin board in the music school. She was subletting about a block over on Eastgate, and I visited every couple of weeks. So when I came down one weekend toward the end of July, I looked at it for five minutes, and signed a lease. $177 a month, tons of problems, tons of character."

"It didn't turn out too bad though," she said.

"Yeah, I think it's really changed my life. I mean, being so close to campus, having a few insane roommates but not having the whole redneck teenage beer armada on the floor. It's really made this a different stage in life, you know?"

"I guess I got lucky with the dorms," she said. "It was probably the honors floor thing at Willkie. You had to have a high GPA to get in, so all of my floormates and friends were like super geniuses."

"Well hey, so are you," I said.

"Thank you. Anyway, we were like peas in a pod. I'm still friends with pretty much everyone I lived with my freshman year. It makes apartment life so dreary in comparison."

"So where are you moving this fall?"

"It's a new apartment complex just south of town, near Bloomington South high school. It's actually more of a month-to-month deal I got with two friends who can't afford the place. I had no idea what I was going to do with school next year, so I got a place I could leave if I got more grant money by Christmas. I still don't know what's going on with that, but at least I have a roof over my head."

"That's cool. I've still got to get that scholarship stuff figured out, or I won't have a roof over my head."

"Oh, don't worry about it. You'll figure it out. If not, you can sleep on my floor for a semester," she said. "Hey, is that your zine?" She picked up an issue from a pile on the floor.

"No, that's Cursed Metal, Nick's zine. I write the fake advice column, and some of the reviews."

She paged through the tome, examining the articles. "This type is incredibly small. Is he trying to cram all of this in eight pages or something?"

"Yeah, Nick's got issues about font sizes," I said. "But he always gets a lot of stuff in there, and it's cheap."

"That's cool. How many of these does he put out?"

"Just a few hundred, usually. He sends them to record labels, trades some with other zines, and sells the rest. He never makes any money, but he gets tons of free shit, and meets a lot of bands. It's a good gig, really."

"Are you going to make your zine like this?"

"Maybe, I'm not sure. I want to do more writing—articles and commentary and long-form interviews. But I probably won't have time once the school year starts."

"Well, you do have a knack for writing. You should be doing something."

"We'll see what happens."

She spied around my desk, saw the small pile of prescription bottles and boxes, and picked up the Zoloft package. "So this is the wonder drug?" she said. "It's got such a cute little box. How's it been treating you lately?"

I scraped at the last of the food from my plate. "I got pretty sick there for a few days—nausea, vomiting, general weakness from not eating any food for almost a week. But now the beginning euphoria has kicked in, like when I first started Prozac a few years ago. It's been pretty good to me lately."

"Are all the side effects gone now?"

"I still get bad headaches. I think I'm going back to the doctor, to see if maybe they can adjust the dosage."

I got up, and went for the dirty dishes. "Here, let me get your plate out of the way," I said.

"Can I help with the dishes?" she asked.

"Sure, sure—let me get the rest of this food into some plastic," I said. Wow—help with dishes. Most of my dinner dates would've split by this point, but she was pulling her share. I quickly dumped the remaining stir-fry and rice in a container and filed it in the fridge.

Back in the kitchen, I ran some hot water. "How about I wash, you rinse, and we'll just stack them over here." I dumped some soap into the sink, and started scraping the last bits of food into the trash. Then I let everything soak in the sudsy water, and half-laughed.

"What's so funny?" she asked.

"I don't know," I said. "Nobody ever helps with the dishes. I feel so domesticated."

"I'm sorry..."

"No, no, it's a nice thing, I guess. It's just a cute novelty." I started scrubbing the dishes and smiled.

After the dishes were dried and put away, we ended back in the room, looking at CDs. "What's with you and Chick Corea? I always see these process names of yours."

"I don't know, I just like his stuff. My friend Max got me hooked during my freshman year. I used to listen to the *Eye of the Beholder* CD on repeat for hours, and never notice that it was the same music over and over. And *Beneath the Mask* is becoming the de facto album of the summer."

"I see you've got a lot of metal in the collection." She scanned through the racks of discs on top of my bookcase, pulling out the occasional title.

"Yeah, not as much as I'd like. I dub a lot from the station."

She pulled out my copy of Pink Floyd's *The Final Cut*. "I thought you were getting rid of all your Pink Floyd?"

"Yeah, well..." I said. "Old habits are hard to break. Especially that album."

"Well, be careful," she said. "Put on some happy music, like—what's *Edge of Sanity*?"

"Swedish Death Metal. Very well produced, good stuff."

"Hmm, okay." She finished looking at the rack of CDs, and looked at her watch. "Hey, it's still pretty early. Do you want to go get some dessert? My treat."

"Sounds good," I said. "Where to?"

"We could drive down to Ben and Jerry's on Kirkwood."

"Drive? It's pretty nice—we could hike it. It's only like fifteen minutes."

"That sounds like a good idea. Let's do it."

I shut down everything, locked up my room, and we headed out the door toward downtown.

"This is such a great day for a walk," I said. We strolled down Third Street, on the path I usually took toward Lindley almost every day, the sun streaming down from the sky and a light breeze cutting across the path. "So how does it feel to finish a degree, anyway?"

"Technically, I don't finish until August. But I went through all of the hoopla last May. It doesn't feel much different, especially when you've potentially got many more years ahead of you."

"At least you've got good grades, and some direction. I'm not sure I could ever get into grad school."

"Yeah, but you're a computer genius. You'll probably find something with a bachelor's that pays more than what I'll get with a PhD. But I really want to teach somewhere, and that takes grad school."

"Hey, at least you've got it narrowed down. I'm not even sure I'll make it back to computer science next fall. I mean, I'll probably get back in school, but I don't know what I want to do."

"I'm sure you'll be okay. If you can't do computer science, maybe you can get an individualized major or something, or finish a generic degree in philosophy or history or something."

"Yeah, there are possibilities," I said. "I'm just scared about what to do next."

"You and me both," she said.

We continued the walk to the main drag on Kirkwood, and went to the brand new Ben and Jerry's store. With fresh paint and new cow patterns everywhere, the place flowed with customers enjoying a break from the heat. We went to the counter and ordered two chocolate chip cookie dough cones, and headed back outside.

"Thanks again for the ice cream," I said, licking at the dripping cone. We strolled down Kirkwood, past the new Streetside Records and the rollerblade place upstairs.

"This place is my salvation," she said. "Nothing beats a late night visit here after studying for ten hours straight."

"I'll try to remember that if I ever study that much at once," I said.

The sweet ice cream tasted like heaven, with thick chunks of dough and a crunchy and sweet cone. Even though Ben and Jerry's was a standard commodity across most of America, I hadn't even heard of them until the store appeared a year ago. Last year, I'd often hike there and buy a pint of the stuff and dig through it during a night of hacking.

We finished the ice cream on the walk back to my place. Her Toyota sat waiting, parked in the gravel driveway of the Mitchell house.

"I'm going to have to get back," she said. "I've got homework to finish for tomorrow. Thank you for dinner though—it was great." She leaned over and gave me a quick hug. Even though our first embrace was quick and friendly, it felt so good to hold her in my arms for two seconds, and feel her body pressed against mine.

"Hey, thanks for the ice cream, and the visit."

"We'll have to get together again, especially if you cook."

"Anytime," I said. "You know where to find me."

"Yeah, on the computer," she laughed. "It's been a few hours—I didn't know you could go this long without being on there."

"Neither could I," I joked.

She opened the car door and climbed inside. "Well, send me mail."

"Okay," I said. "I'll catch you later."

"Bye John," she said.

I watched her car pull away, and walked back to the house. I went back to the clean room, and crashed down on the bed, dreaming of holding her in my arms. With that thought in mind, I drifted off for a short nap before my evening of wandering the campus would begin.

35

Late the next morning, the phone dragged me awake just after ten, interrupting a dream about going to a senior prom with Michelle Pfeiffer dressed up in a leather Catwoman suit. I stumbled with the phone, trying to grab the receiver before the four-ring deadline when the machine picked it up. I knocked it onto the floor, and managed to grab the cord and reel it into bed after a few tries.

"Check's in the mail," I mumbled into the phone, re-burying my head under the pillow.

"Hey, its me," Amy said.

"Oh yeah. How did I know it was you? Hey, what day is it? Do we go to the prom today?"

"Why are you still in bed? Didn't you have English class this morning?"

"We had the day off," I said. "Research day, for our papers. I researched what it would be like to sleep eight hours." I pulled with my foot at the worn vinyl shade over the window, letting the sunshine streak in over the bed. "Whoa, didn't know it was nice out," I mumbled.

"Yes, it's a beautiful day," she said. "So, are you gonna sleep all day, or are you interested in lunch?"

"I was thinking about sleeping until it was dark out, like most people."

"Most people sleep at night, John."

"No wonder I can never catch the fucking bank when it's open."

"Okay, okay, I can eat lunch all by my lonesome then..."

"Wait, I'll get my ass in gear. I need to take a shower, get dressed..."

"I can't help you there, but I did drive today. How about I swing by your place at noon? That's an hour from now."

"Sounds great—I'll see you then."

I fell out of bed, floundered for my glasses, and got moving on the showering routine.

11:53, I managed to finish early. I stood in front of the house, the August noontime temperature above 100 degrees, with the thick humidity making it even worse.

I saw the white Toyota round the corner from Atwater to Mitchell, and waved to her to pull in next to the Rabbit. She unlocked the passenger door, and I hopped in.

"Hey you," she said. "Glad to see you made it to the land of living."

"It sure felt good to sleep eight hours," I said. "Too bad my room isn't air conditioned. I'm used to napping during my class in Ballantine."

"Poor baby. So where are we going for lunch?"

"How about Macri's?"

"Oooh, a place with actual silverware," she said. "Macri's it is." She backed the car and headed toward the mall. The scenery of Second Street scrolled by the passenger window—apartment complexes, the elementary school, and cross-streets that led over to Third Street and the gradual buildup of small shops and strip malls. It was weird for me to the in the passenger seat of a car; I was always driving alone in the Rabbit, or hauling around people. I never got a chance to sit back and look at the view. I missed being in control, but it also felt relieving.

We pulled up to College Mall Road, where the mall and its many parking lots lay straight ahead of us. We hung a right and followed the road, which snaked next to the fast food joints, the Target, and other disjointed stores. A stoplight later, she turned into the Kroger parking lot and found a space in front of the restaurant.

"Here we are," she said. We hopped out of the car, and walked inside.

The dividers between the booths, the sturdy wooden table, the menus and homemade fries and brown paper napkins all reminded me of the last million times I'd brought a woman to Macri's. As we followed our server to a table, I could only think of the last time I'd been there, when I bombed out with June.

I stared at the plastic-coated menu and tried to decide on a reuben or a club until the waitress took our orders. It led into an uncomfortable silence, one that I guessed I was supposed to kill.

"So..." she said.

"Hey, tell me a story about the devil," I said.

"What?"

"Do you know any stories about the devil?" This was a test, one that Nick laid on me a while back. Possible responses included stories about witchcraft, mythology and human sacrifice (good) or bible scriptures, attempts at religious conversion, or general confusion (bad.) I figured she'd land in the former, but I wasn't sure.

"This isn't about the devil, but it's a weird fact. Okay, *Rosemary's Baby* was filmed in the Dakota, right?"

"Okay, I guess."

"Well, Roman Polanski directed it, right? And he was married to Sharon Tate."

"Right."

"She was killed by Manson, and he was into the White Album, the Beatles..."

"...And John Lennon was shot in front of the Dakota."

"Exactly. Pretty weird, eh?"

"That's fucked up," I said. She passed the test.

The waitress appeared with our sandwiches in record time, mine hot and overflowing with sauerkraut. I disassembled the reuben and carefully removed some of the excess, to lower the height of the sandwich to something more manageable.

"So, are you doing anything on Sunday?" she asked.

"Not really, why?"

"I'm thinking about breaking out the grill, and doing some barbecuing. Are you interested?"

"Will there be any lighter fluid?"

"I'm not sure if I should let you play with fire. Didn't you blow up your car last year?"

"They totally couldn't pin that one on me. Besides, fire is your friend."

"Okay, it looks like I'm running the grill and you're making the salad or something."

"I promise I won't blow anything up."

"Let me write out the directions to my place, and we'll say this happens at about fivish. Have you ever been to Colonial Crest?"

"No, I don't think so."

On the back of a receipt, she fashioned a crude map to her apartment. "It's not too hard to find, but if you have trouble, just give me a ring."

"Okay, great," I said. I pocketed the map, and got back to work on my sandwich.

After lunch and a quick ride back to the house, I opened the front screen door and shuffled inside, just wanting to take a nap. I didn't find any new mail waiting for me, so I grabbed someone's local paper from the mail shelf, and flipped through the want ads, hoping for something new. There wasn't much, just the usual Cut-All knife door-to-door sales gigs, and telemarketing spots.

The message light blinked urgently at me as I swung open the door. I took off my shirt, went over to the computer desk, and hit the play button on the answering machine:

"Hey John, this is Ken Kreite. I talked to Peter and it looks like the Type O Negative interview is definitely a go for tonight. They practice until about eight, and they can call you from there. Give me a ring back and confirm that time and your studio number, and we'll be set. Thanks."

Shit, I almost forgot about that interview. Actually, I figured on several more rounds of phone tag, pushing back the event by a few more weeks. I didn't really think Ken would call back so fast and get everything in place. I dug around for my all-important notebook of Death Metal contacts and labels, tore through the pages, found Kreite's New York phone number, and nervously dialed.

Two rings, three, no answer…"Hi, you've reached Ken Kreite presents…" I tried to pull myself together—my hands were shaking I was so nervous that I'd somehow blow it by not getting the studio number to him. I heard the beep, and thought for a half-second about what I'd say. "Hi, this is John Conner, from WQAX in Bloomington, Indiana. I'm responding to your message earlier today—eight tonight would be great for the interview. The number at the studio is…" Fuck—my mind was completely blank. I absolutely could not remember the number for the station. I immediately looked around the room for a piece of stationary, an ad, a business card, anything. "…Um, hang on a second…" Finally, in my wallet, I found Sid's business card. "Sorry about that—the studio number is 331-9289. I'll talk to you, or to them, at eight. Thanks."

Motherfucker—I screwed that one up, I thought. I hoped I didn't blow the whole interview. Why couldn't I remember the number? Oh well. I just hoped they would get the message before the show.

The room almost felt cool after the heat and sun outside. A slight breeze shook the blinds on the windows and felt relaxing across my bare skin. I stood and looked at the stream of sunlight coming into the half-dark room, then went to the bed and laid down for a short nap.

When I woke, the sun still filtered through the blinds on the far side of the room, as the breeze knocked it open and closed. I felt fully rested, and lost in the tranquil serenity of my room in the afternoon. I stared at the frame of light that trailed across the floor, on some of my tapes and books, carrying thin particles of dust. I must've been asleep for about an hour, and although I was fully awake, it felt good to lie in bed for another ten or fifteen minutes and think about absolutely nothing.

I found my glasses and looked over to the answering machine—no calls. No Kreite. I hope he got that fucking number. I got up, pulled on a Megadeth shirt and a pair of shorts, and went over to the computer to check my email. I had almost five hours to kill before the interview, and I hoped for some entertainment online.

With all of my demos and other underground shit in the back seat, the VW whirred toward the mall. It was just before five, which gave me hours before I went on the air, but sitting around the house was driving me nuts. I had the final Carnivore album in the tape deck, with the song "Jesus Hitler" booming through the car's tiny speakers.

What would I ask them? I wasn't ready for an interview this fast. Me and Nick joked around about some various questions, and I did think of a few things based on history and liner notes that would make good questions. But the band seemed pretty over-the-top and intimidating from the little I knew of them. I hadn't spent years seeing them on MTV or something— they were pretty much unknown in Indiana. At least I was familiar with the albums. I had memorized every single note of *Slow, Deep, and Hard* from the year I spent with it in the walkman, stumbling across campus depressed at three in the morning. At least that would help me.

I pulled into the McDonald's, and shut down my car. In my wallet, I had enough green to afford a good tray of carbohydrates and caffeine before the interview. I locked up the car, and went in.

Fuck, fuck, fuck...I fumbled with the lock box on the station door, and then knocked it open. Nobody was at the board, and the small apartment was completely silent. Shit, that's a bad omen, I thought. Maybe they've been trying to call for hours. I pulled all of my stuff in the door, and ran to the console.

Ten minutes before, there still wasn't a message from Kreite or anybody else at my house. If he tried to call the station, he would've gotten a pre-recorded message with no way to leave a reply. It was set up that way in case a DJ had the ringer off during their show. Fuck, fuck, fuck—is he going to call, or not? I thought. I paced the studio, trying to figure out how I would start the show without knowing whether or not they would call.

Fuck it, I won't announce it, I thought. I'll start the show like normal, but play the beginning of the EP until I got a sign or something. With silence around me, I went through the usual hurried procedure of pulling CDs from the wall and stacking them on top of the players. I also loaded some blank tape into the deck behind the console that was connected to the outbound signal rig, and arranged my notes next to the desk, just in case.

7:57. Still nothing. I made sure the phone ringer was on, then went to the station start instructions and began the procedure to kick over the console and outbound rig. Life breathed into the lights and gauges, and power supplies hummed with energy after I flipped all of the switches. I was now broadcasting dead silence across the city. 7:59. I loaded the EP into the left CD player, dropped a promo tape into the deck, and hit the mic.

"Hello, and welcome to WQAX." I didn't know when the station was brought down, so I skipped the intro speech and went right to the disclaimer. A moment later, I had the promo going, and tried to think of what the fuck I'd say.

"Hey, this is John Conner, and you are listening to Xero Tolerance, Bloomington's only all-extreme metal radio show. I'm here until the witching hour to bring you the latest Death and Thrash Metal, plus some news, demos, and more. A special guest is supposed to join us on the air tonight, but I haven't heard from them yet—more on that in a bit, I hope. For now, let's start with some Type O Negative, and spin their latest EP,

The Origin of the Feces. Here's the first track, 'I Know You're Fucking Someone Else.' 8:01, WQAX, 103.7 cable FM."

The sound of a crowd chanting "You suck! You suck! You suck!" filled the studio, with Pete Steele yelling "You paid fifteen dollars to get in here, and we're getting paid for this shit. Who's the real asshole here?" Then the grind began—a slow, grating, feedback-filled sorrow that worked like a soul-eating industrial machine designed to pull all of the good from the air. The song broke into a gallop, with Steele singing lyrics—it wasn't as good as the carefully produced and deathfully heavy studio version, but the EP traded precision for variety; in a few places the band improvised or changed around riffs, which worked well. And it was funny when Steele stopped the song to sing "I'm in the Mood For Love" a cappella, with a clubful of people chanting "Fuck you! Fuck you! Fuck you!" in the background.

The song, as always, made me think back to last fall, when I listened to their first album several times a day, and thought every word was about my life. I absolutely knew my girlfriend back then was fucking everyone else in sight, and every time Pete Steele screamed "You! You make me hate myself!" the words rang true.

8:16. The first song came to an end, and it went into the slightly Gothic and new-to-the-EP track "Are You Afraid?" It had a good sound, but was just a short intro before the song "Gravity." I was hoping their new album would be more stuff like this.

The phone rang. Probably Sid, wondering what the hell happened, I thought.

"QAX," I said.

"Is this John Conner, on WQAX?" said a voice, thick with a Brooklyn accent.

"Yeah, this is him."

"This is Peter Steele. I was calling to complain about the music you've been playing lately."

"Hey, I'm playing the EP right now," I said. This was really him! It felt so weird to be talking to the guy who sang the shit I practically worshiped for the last year.

"Don't you have anything better to play around there? Maybe some Perry Como?"

"Some asshole stole all of our Percy Faith singles last spring," I joked. "So are you ready to go on this interview?"

"Yeah sure. Hey, Josh, our keyboard player is here too. He'll answer some questions. Is that cool?"

"Yeah sure, I'll introduce him too."

"Is there anything I can't say on the air?" he asked. "I mean, can I say fuck, shit, or whatever?"

"We're losing our license in August. Say whatever the fuck you want. Hang on a second, let me get my tape recorder rolling, and I'm just about at the end of the third track, so I'll introduce you after that."

"Okay, we'll be here," he said.

I quickly got the tape recording on the broadcast rig, so everything would be saved to cassette. As I fumbled with the controls, I thought "I've got Type O Negative on hold!" I worked fast, and got back to the console.

"Okay guys," I said into the phone, "I'm going to patch the phone into the board so you can hear the signal. You won't be able to talk until you hear me talk, so sit tight. I'll introduce you, and then we'll start. Our equipment is shit, so you won't get the best sound over the phone, but it works."

"Okay, do what you gotta do," said Pete.

I patched in the phone, and could now hear Pete and Josh fiddling around over the studio monitors. There were only a few seconds left on the track, and I let them play out before clicking on my mic and bringing up the phone tap.

"It's 8:18 here on WQAX, I'm John Conner, and that was Type O Negative's new EP *The Origin of the Feces*. And I've got a special treat for you—Pete and Josh from Type O Negative are on the phone with me here to answer a few questions. Okay Pete, Lets talk a little bit about your new EP, *The Origin of the Feces*." My first question was obvious—I knew the CD was not recorded live, but rather in a warehouse with some crowd noises added. But, I wanted their opinion, or cover story. "Now this said it was a semi-live recording. Exactly what does that mean?"

"What it means exactly," Pete said, "is that we did this recording to rip off the record company."

"Was it actually recorded live at Brighton Beach?"

"No, of course not. We totally made everything up, we got a $100,000 budget, and we spent approximately $2,000 on this piece of shit recording and we went out and we all bought Harley Davidsons and we're gonna kill ourselves just like in *Cyclemania*. You ever see that cool movie?"

I hadn't, but I had to lie. "Oh yeah, I based my life on it..."

"That is the agenda. We did this not just to rip off the record company, but to rip off the fans as well, because we know the average person is a moron...Sorry fans, but we had to rip you off because we need your money."

I already knew the interview would get weird, but I hoped it would be as offhandedly funny as their lyrics. I knew they had an upcoming LP, so I thought I'd go there next. "Now you guys are working on a new LP right now, is this gonna be a similar setup there?"

"Well, this LP is gonna be much worse than anything else that we've done before...If people don't hate us already they'll hate us after this next LP. And right now its titled *Things Worse Than Death (And Other Acts of God.)*"

"Any songs done for the LP yet?"

"Well, we have them all written...Right now we're trying to find the best way to scam the record company out of a lot of money, so until we figure out just exactly what our plan is...We've got two or three plans we might go with, we're gonna narrow it down and see which way we can get the most bucks out of 'em and then give them some piece of shit, some piece of garbage that they'll try to push on people like bad dope or something."

I didn't know where to go next, so I went to my list and saw COVER ART at the top. The EP's cover was a pixilated picture of somebody's ass, which got them a lot of controversy. "OK, you had a little difficulty with the cover art on the EP. Did anything inspire you to do that? How did they approach you on that, did they say no right away or what?" I asked.

"I dunno Josh, how did that come up, how did we think of that?"

Josh chimed in, "Well, I dunno, we figured it looked a lot better than our faces so we went for it."

"Well, that is my best side," Pete said.

"We didn't have trouble at all," Josh said. "The record company loved it."

"They loved it," Pete said. "And I think right now that thing is banned in Germany, and England."

"I know some US distributors refuse to carry it," I said.

"Well," Pete said, "they don't know art when they see it."

"Exactly..." I said. I thought to Nick's questions, and remembered he wanted to know about Carnivore cover songs. "I heard rumors you were thinking of recording a Carnivore song for the EP or, do you plan on playing any Carnivore stuff live?"

"Yeah, well, see there were one or two songs in the set, and we were gonna do one on the EP, but we're really trying to push the Type O Negative stuff now. If people want to hear Carnivore they can go and buy a Carnivore disc, but right now we just wanna stick to our stuff. Maybe some time in the future if we pull some other scam maybe we'll do a Carnivore song, or maybe a Partridge Family cover or something."

"As for your live touring, do you know what's going to go on after the album supporting it, are you going to do a headlining tour or a split bill?"

"Yeah, we're just going to do a New York tour, we're going to do a five borough tour, and make it expensive and like a year long, and spend like a month or two at each club."

"Will you do anything elaborate on stage, like killing anyone on stage?"

"Killing ourselves...No, we don't like to do much on stage. Sometimes if we come out and we don't like the looks of the audience, we don't even play. We just walk back out and say 'Well, you paid your 15 or 20 dollars and that's too bad, so, goodnight.' And then there will be like a riot. Or sometimes we'll actually play one or two chords. We just like to say 'We don't feel like playing, so we're not gonna play. And if you don't like it, that's too bad, because you already paid us. And you can go home, and you can think we're assholes, but we'll be out tomorrow spending your money and laughing at you!'"

"Let's talk about musical influences," I said. "Do you look toward anything for musical inspiration?"

"I guess when I was younger I did. But now, I don't, ya know, I like to write how I feel, I mean, I don't try to follow in anybody's footsteps, and nobody in this band tries to sound like anybody. We are just trying to establish our own crummy identity. Just like even though vomit has the same basic smell, if you put four cups of real hot vomit next to each other, they would smell slightly dissimilar depending on what was eaten for dinner, or lunch or breakfast, too, with all that shit in your stomach."

"Do you look toward any movies or books or political sources when writing lyrics?"

"No, I just look into my Swiss cheese soul, because my soul is very blackened and has many holes in it, and there is a lot of powerful things lurking inside of me, following me everywhere I go and I don't have to look to TV or books or anything for any really bad ideas because I'm full of them."

"OK, you did mention you're trying to get everyone to hate you..."

"Umm, let me clarify here. We aren't trying to get everyone to hate us, we're just trying to be really honest with people, trying to tell people we are only in this for money, and that we are trying to rip you off. If you want to come along for the ride, and laugh with us, or at us...It doesn't matter, as long as we get to spend your money."

"Have you been approached by any censorship groups?"

"Actually, if I had kids, I would not let them listen to Type O Negative, so I guess I'm totally for censorship."

That question threw me for a loop, and my list was pretty much exhausted. I had to think of something fast, and I knew any of the "standard" questions would quickly be turned into a joke or ignored by Steele. I needed to make something else up. "I talked to a few people who wanted to write-in Pete Steele for presidential candidate in the fall. If by some freak chance you got elected in the fall, what would be your agenda?"

"I would kill anyone under six feet six inches."

Where the fuck was he going? I thought. "Why?"

"Because I'm six foot six and a quarter, and I like to look up to people."

"Do you still have the same day job?" One time Nick told me he worked as a garbage man or in the sewers of New York, but I wasn't sure which.

"Yes. I am a human feces remover. I make $100,000 a year on my job, I do not have to use my mind on my job, so I get to dwell on the things that disturb me greatly, I let these things torment myself and I let them burn holes in me like acid dripping on me, so by the time I get home, I'm really pretty wound up and looking to hurt myself, not so much the other people around me, but because I don't have the balls to kill myself yet, I must supplicate, and I must take these aggressive feelings out in socially acceptable ways, such as transforming these thoughts and feelings into music."

"I noticed reading through your liner notes mentions of Prozac, Xanax and Doctor Whittaker. Is this mention to actual psychotherapy?"

"It is. He was my psychotherapist, who did not help me. He told me I was crazy and threw me out of his office. I won't waste my money now, because I have come to the conclusion that I am not fucked up, this world is fucked up, I am the sanest person I know."

"If you really hit it big would you move out of New York?"

"I think ultimately I would like to be real rich so I can get out of this city, because I don't like what is going on here too much, as far as what is going on with crime and where my tax dollars are going to. I don't think I would move until I made my fortune and then I would move somewhere isolated like Iceland and never be heard from again."

"Going back to touring, you toured with a few bands.. What happened on last tour, it got cut a little short..."

"What happened is we were out with Exploited and Biohazard, two bands that we were good friends with and like very much, but we felt it wasn't a very good matchup because we're not a punk band and we're not a hardcore band, we're more like a Gothic band, and a lot of the skinheads we encountered on tour didn't like us too much, and we had problems with them, and over in Germany and Austria we had problems with the left wing over there. But, ultimately that turned out great because it was kindof planned, and we had set the whole thing up ourselves...We had spread rumors that we were the Fourth Reich coming over to Germany to retake the country, and we took plenty of time to make preparation, and when we got there we phoned in bomb threats to the clubs that we were supposed to play at so the shows got canceled and we got paid for nothing. We just went out chasing German women, Austrian women, we just went chasing women."

"If you tour with any bands on the next tour, any ideas on who?"

"I don't think anybody in their right mind would tour with us, so it would have to be someone very desperate."

"We're gonna have to wrap up here...Is there anything we should look forward to on the new album?"

"It's gonna be worse than the other stuff, no doubt about it. And I'm sure its gonna be overpriced."

"Any last words to your fans?"

"Yeah, I think you should get your hearing checked," he said.

"OK, we're gonna cut back to the next track on *Origin Of The Feces*."

"No I don't think you should. Don't you have anything better to play?"

"Well, let's go into the next track here, and later we'll go into the actual music portion of the show. I'd like to thank Pete and Josh for talking to me."

"I'm sorry I wasted your time."

I clicked off the mic and picked up on the next track of the EP. "Hey thanks for calling in," I said to Pete.

"You okay man? It sounds like you're pissed off or something."

"No, not at all. I just have to concentrate to hear on that shitty phone tap, and it's like 400 degrees in here. This station is in a punk squat, and has the worst equipment in the world."

"Sounds like a great place to work."

"At least I get to steal a lot of CDs. Hey, I am going to print this in my zine, I talked to Ken about it. I'll send a copy when it is done."

"That's cool. Don't waste your time if anything better comes up."

"Thanks again, though. I've got to split. I'll keep in touch with Ken."

"Okay, later on." He hung up, and I turned up the monitors to hear him singing "Pain" on the EP. It still felt too weird to actually talk to the person who worked on such a great album. I grabbed the tape out of the deck, and stared at it in my hands. This interview will turn my zine into something huge, I thought. This was my ticket to much greener pastures...

The rest of the show went without incident, except for the usual rain shower. After I played my end-of-show music and brought down the station, I sat in the silence and darkness, and thought about everything and nothing. It always felt good to be in a place designed to produce sound and noise and send it to thousands of people, but hear nothing but the wind outside and the dripping of rain flowing through the gutters. I packed up my tapes, and drove home, listening to nothing in the player.

When I pulled in and dragged my stuff back to the apartment, I found a note on the door, written on small post-it notes with a fat marker. It read something like this:

"Hi. You are not here. At the radio station? I was trying to find out if you had eaten dinner yet, and I thought I would stop by and torment you, but you aren't here. Since I'm here and you're not and it's your house I better go. Sweet dreams. Send me email. -Amy"

At least I knew I was wanted. Maybe my plan of wearing her down was working. I flipped on the lights, dropped all of my stuff on the floor, and fired up the computer.

36

The Friday lunch routine always brought a feeling of elation, even when there wasn't a fresh paycheck burning a hole in my pocket. I still had a few dollars left to carry me through the weekend and the next week, and would maybe sell a few CDs to pull in some more green. It wouldn't contribute to the looming rent situation, but it meant I'd be able to keep up the lunch dates with Amy. And since I had a few bucks to spare, I could still celebrate the weekend with a decent meal of greasy pizza.

Minutes before, I popped into Lib102A to check my accounts, and got a quick email from Amy about lunch. I wanted to see her, but I had a million things to do before noon. I wanted to make it to Garcia's for pizza before a 12-2 shift at Lindley. Somewhere in there, I also had to finish a shitload of photocopying and research for English. She said she was going home for the weekend, which meant I didn't have a shot at seeing her until next week.

I went to the reference room in the basement of the library and got to work. Years' worth of hundreds of periodicals rested on shelves and racks around the reading room, waiting to be collected, bound, and deposited in the stacks. Since a few of my articles were in recent issues of Time, Discover, and Scientific American, I needed to find and photocopy everything I needed to write my paper.

I went to work, tracked through card catalog and MedLine search printouts, and found my magazines in the alphabetical stacks of back issues. There were so many odd titles there—periodicals on woodwind instruments, poetry from Vermont, gastroenterology, and historical reenactment.

I wished they let people check out periodicals, just so I could take off a few weeks in December and browse through a few hundred different magazines.

After feeding a pocketful of dimes into a beaten copier, I had a stack of articles, hot and ready to dissect. At one of the reading tables, I spread out all of my findings and hunted through the articles with a yellow highlighter, searching for bits and pieces I could use to prove my thesis. It felt good knowing that most of this research paper lived within the pile of photocopies, and all I needed to do was string it together into nice double-spaced pages. I felt like a sculptor, looking at a solid block of marble and seeing the statue inside.

The research work made me think about what it would be like to be a full-time student in some arcane grad program, where I'd dig up refs in the stacks, collate together papers with the information and some third-party interpolation, and publish them in obscure academic journals. Fuck this suit and tie crap, I thought. Instead of chasing Amy, I could straighten out my academics, lie my way into some kind of sociology PhD program and write about the parallels of Frank Zappa and Japanese monster movies. I could stay in school indefinitely, date nineteen-year-olds forever, and do something I loved. But after thinking about this for more than a few minutes, the tangle of problems related to grades, funding, and everything else made it just as much of a headache as my thoughts of making big money without a degree.

I got back to the articles, then went to the stacks to find a copy of the DSM-3R, the latest version of the Diagnostic and Statistical Manual for psychiatry. After wandering one of the upper floors of the undergraduate library, I found the big, red manual, and sat on the floor to page through its contents. Back in high school, I used to read through the symptoms of almost every disorder listed, thinking "I have that, I have that..." I had thought of some research-related task photocopying statistics, but after I finished, I got lost in the gruesome reading.

The sex problems were the funniest. Imagine having to go to group therapy for frotteurism. No furniture, I guess. And I couldn't think of a male my age that didn't suffer from hypoactive sexual desire disorder. Maybe I could file an insurance claim, and include a log of my email as proof.

After a few minutes of browsing, I turned to the old faithful, the page with my name on it. I had my guesses before, but earlier this year, I caught my number on a prescription form for a blood test, and quickly looked it up. My very own section of the DSM looked like this:

296.65 Bipolar I Disorder, Most Recent Episode Mixed, In Partial Remission

Maybe I wasn't considered in partial remission, since I had such a bad freakout in the spring. I didn't really know how to tell the difference between remission, full remission, or anything in between. I knew that other manic-depressives would have very long periods in their cycle—they would spend 18 months locked in their rooms, unable to hold a job, and then they'd get divorced, married, divorced again, work up a daily blow habit, sell everything they owned for coke, move to Europe, etc. For me, it hit all at once and with much less clarity. When Tammy left and I had what this book would describe as an "episode," I gravitated from wanting to bury myself alive to wanting to drive across the country in my VW naked and start a cult in Wyoming, but it happened in the same day, several times. So I agreed with the mixed assessment, and I guess the partial remission made sense.

It was always so eerie to me to see it spelled out in black and white in such an official way. It felt like being able to read one line of your obituary before you died. Or, seeing some hidden owner's manual to yourself that only the aliens were supposed to be able to look at, like one of those old Twilight Zones where the kid falls and breaks his arm and there are transistors inside. I was proud that I could take care of myself and learn about my disorder, but even two years after my diagnosis, it was all new to me.

I shelved the book, and stayed sitting on the tile floor for a minute, thinking about how weird it was to be ten stories above the campus, but completely enclosed by concrete. After enough of that, I grabbed my shit, and headed for the elevators.

The sunlight outside attacked me, making every part of my skin sweat and every piece of clothing heat to an uncomfortable warmth within a few seconds. Even my shoes started to char against my feet as I walked down the library steps and toward Seventh Street. It made me wish I didn't have my thick prescription lenses so I could toss on a pair of shades and be comfortable in the August heat. But there was some degree of comfort in having a backpack that contained enough research to finish off the last of a 300-level class.

The walkman also helped make it feel like Friday. I listened to an obscure project band called Project Driver, a one-shot 80's super-group featuring guitar virtuoso Tony MacAlpine. Although dated, the hard guitar riffs and power-rock vocals had a real edge that said Friday all over it. It wasn't exactly Death Metal (Rudy Sarzo from Quiet Riot played bass!) but it was a secret pleasure that I loved to hear while walking. In a similar vein, I still played the Guns N Roses *Use Your Illusion* albums almost constantly while walking around campus. I couldn't admit it with a straight face to anyone, especially considering their audience demographics and regular schtick on MTV, but the two albums were a sonic trademark for everything that happened last spring. I didn't dig the more commercial tracks, but a few of the longer and deeper songs made some sense during my depression.

I passed Woodburn Hall and followed the unnamed road that led past Ballantine and behind the Union. It swept past the open field known as Mad Max field, named after the apocalyptic minister who preached on the hillside to passers-by, telling women and Catholics that they were going to hell. Allegedly a Purdue math professor that finally snapped one day, he looked like a threadbare Pat Robertson, and allegedly commuted between three or four major campuses in Indiana. Everyone hated the guy, but it made for good entertainment. In a month or two, there would be a circle of people around him as he pranced back and forth and waved his bible in the air until he was red in the face.

Mad Max didn't mean much to me, but he did symbolize the fall—the time when his audience was at a peak, when the weather was nice and the novelty was still there for his stupid sermons. By November, he wouldn't even be able to draw crowds. One cold December day I bumped into him outside the IMU, and said "Hi Max," just to see if I'd get a rise out of him, to see if he'd yell at me and call me a sinner or recognize me from all of the times I sat in the circle and taunted him. He just said "Hey, how's it going?" and kept walking, business as usual. I felt ripped off, like a little kid who saw a Macy's Santa Claus at a bar drinking a vodka-7, and realized it was all a sham.

All of these thoughts ran through me as I passed the empty field. I felt the heat and loneliness of summer, but sometimes appreciated the desolation. In some ways I wanted the fall to start, the new crop of freshman girls and the new classes, like the new box of 64 Crayolas you got as a kid, each with a sharp new point. But in a few short months, the crayons would be rounded and blunt and snapped in half. And who knew where I would be by December.

Part of me feared that there would be no new feeling to the fall semester, since I'd been on campus all year. Every time I started a new fall schedule, it was after spending the summer laboring in factories. For three months, I'd be running a punch press and wishing I was back in the library, studying Spanish vocab words or going over calculus problems and trying to reverse-engineer someone else's problem sets. By the time I endured a quarter-year of the rednecks and their nigger-nigger-this, nigger-nigger-that mentality, I was so starved for intellectual discourse that a week in an LD reading class would be sheer bliss. Now I feared that without that torture, the new semester would be old hat to me. I hoped the influx of new faces would do the trick.

I passed the IMU, and cut back past the Student Building to the brick path toward Kirkwood. A quick glance at my watch showed 10:54. Gotta hustle, I thought. I passed through Sample Gates, took a left, and headed up Indiana toward Garcia's.

I got home after two, done for the day with ten hours to kill until the fountain, and only a couple of bucks in my pockets. I felt ripped off that things were going so great with Amy, but she would be gone that night. It wasn't like she was with another man, but I wished I could've invited her to a movie, or a long walk or something. No mail waited for me, but inside my room, the answering machine's impatient light blinked at me. I sat at the computer and pressed the button to play the message.

Message one:

"John, this is Bruce...I was wondering if you were open tonight. We've got a sort of last-minute event going on, tonight only, and I'm looking for two people with some experience to send down there. I know this is short notice, but give me a call if you're interested."

Message two:

"John, it's Donna. I'm at Carrie's right now, it's about 1:30. I think we're going to the IMU in a minute though. We're trying to find something to do tonight, maybe go to a bar or get a movie or something. Give me a call, or...no, call here at Carrie's or send one of us email. Or find us in the IMU. You really should come, stop worrying about that woman. Bye."

I thought about who to call first, and went with the more pertinent issue: money. I dialed Bruce, and got through on the third ring.

"Bruce, this is John Conner. What's this about a glowstick run tonight?"

"Are you up for it?"

"As long as you don't send me to some middle of fucking nowhere carnival or something."

"No, there should be a lot of people at this—it's the Bean Blossom festival. It's a motorcycle thing."

"What, like Harleys and shit?"

"Yeah, it's held by the Abate, a biker organization. It's a swap meet, arts and crafts shit, food, some bands, and a lot of people on bikes."

"Sounds cool. Is this a solo event?"

"No, you're going down with another guy. I talked to someone down there, but it could get a little hairy—that's why I need experienced people."

"It can't be more rowdy than the 500," I said. I thought of a worst-case scenario with a bunch of eight foot tall, mindless Hell's Angels, frothing at the mouths and pounding me to a gel.

"It should be okay," he said. "I'm not sure about the weather tonight, but if it gets too bad, we'll just call it off."

"Okay, when do you need me?"

"Stop by around six, and we'll go from there."

We said our good-byes and hung up. I fired up the computer, connected, and made a connection to Rose. Before I could start a wholist, Donna bitnetted me. "Are you at home?" she asked.

"Yeah, I just got here."

"Log off and call me at the IMU cluster. Do you have the number?"

"Yeah," I said. I knew the numbers to almost every cluster on campus, and had the others written down just in case. "I'll call you in a second."

I disconnected, and gave the number in the IMU a ring.

"John?" answered Donna.

"Hey, what's up?" I asked.

"Not much, we're taking a computer break before we get started. Me and Carrie are going to try and clear out the rest of our homework before the weekend. What about you?"

"Just got out of work, and I did most of my research this morning," I said.

"So are you interested in doing something later on with us?"

"I told Bruce I'd sell glowsticks tonight, and I could really use the cash."

"Where are you going?"

"Bean Blossom. I think I should be back around 10 or 11, not too late. I was thinking about heading to the fountain at twelve, but if you guys are just hanging out at the IMU or Carrie's or something, I could catch up with you."

"Okay, that sounds cool. Call there, and if we aren't home, try the computer. Then we can get some food and beer and stuff and go back to her place."

"Sounds good, I'll see you then."

"Okay, later John."

Bikers. Fucking bikers. My first thought was classic Motörhead, like the *No Remorse* double LP, songs like "Killed By Death," "Iron Horse," "Overkill," and "Bomber." But these guys probably weren't into Motörhead. I vaguely knew a few biker-types from living in Elkhart, and they were more of the Jack Daniels and Hank Williams types. Bruce said it could be gold, but I imagined a lot of barefoot and pregnant types who have never seen three dollars, let alone had three bucks to hand over to a street vendor for some glowing plastic.

I hoped for the best, which was anything over minimum wage, and a free meal. I checked my watch—just past three. That gave me a few hours before I had to take off. I hit the lights, and crawled to the bed for a quick nap.

"Have a seat. Do you want a beer or anything?" Bruce's wife led me into the living room/waiting area.

"No, I'm fine," I said. I sat on one of the three couches in the room.

"He should be out in just a minute," she said, before vanishing into one of the other bedrooms. Her side business, some kind of medical testing scheme, took up Bruce's old offices in the front of the house. The glowstick operation now took the rear part of the house, since people were coming in the front door for piss tests or blood draws.

"Hey John, come on back." Bruce poked his head through the kitchen. "Let's get you some product so you can hit the road."

I went to the back room, where a Rob Lowe-looking guy was counting through the tubes of a glowstick holder. "Hey, this is Rob," Bruce said. "He's gonna drive. It's just the two of you, I don't think it will be much bigger than that." He sat at his desk, grabbed a clipboard with some paperwork, and handed it to me. "Eighty of each color," he said, looking into the tubes of a glowstick holder on the desk. "That's probably overkill, but you never know."

I signed each page of the paperwork without reading it. "And we're allowed the sell there?"

"Something like that. Nothing you can't handle, and if it is, give me a call back here. I don't think it will be a rough crowd, but watch your back."

I grabbed the holder, checked the contents of each tube, then dropped the completed paperwork on the desk. "I'll be careful, dude," I said. "Come on Rob, let's get the hell out of here."

When I say the guy looked like Rob Lowe, I'm not stereotyping him because he was a clean-cut fratbrat type. I mean he looked exactly like Rob Lowe—dark hair, the same haircut, the underwear model's muscular body, the piercing eyes and a slightly Nordic, squared chin. We hauled our equipment out to his car, which was a generic, Republican grandfather model Buick four-dour, and loaded everything in the trunk. Before I got in the car, I took a last look at the sky. Dark swirls of clouds made it look a lot closer to nightfall than it really was, but there wasn't any rain yet.

"Here we go," Rob said, as he started up the car. "Have you been to Bean Blossom before?"

"I don't even know if it's a town, the name of the fair, or some kind of geographical nickname."

"Bruce gave me a map, it's right here." He produced a photocopy and handed it to me. I quickly spied his instructions; Bean Blossom was a small town, about a dozen miles down state road 45. Rob drove into town and toward the mall, where we'd pick up 45 and head into nowhere.

"So do you go to school at Indiana?" Rob said. His use of an incorrect name for the school (instead of Indiana University or IU) tipped me off that he was from out of town, or maybe followed a lot of NCAA basketball.

"Yeah, I'm here for summer school. Originally from Elkhart, up north. What about you?"

"I'm not from here, Denver originally. I go to the University of Colorado at Boulder, business school."

"What the hell are you doing out here selling glowsticks?"

"I got an internship with the university, selling ads in the yellow pages for the school phone book. It's pretty good cash—we get paid on a commission-only basis—but I've got nothing to do in the evening, so I figured I'd pick up some extra beer money. What about you?"

"I work in the computer clusters during the year, but the hours really dry up in the summer. I've done this a few times for the same reason, a little cash to run around with."

"Are you a CIS major?"

"No, no—computer science. I don't think I could handle the business classes."

"I've got a lot of friends at the business school that are CIS. It's supposed to be the next big thing."

"I think you can make just as much programming, and you don't have to wear a suit and tie. I could be wrong though—I know a lot of people who went to Procter and Gamble and made tons of cash."

I sat on the couch-like bench seat and watched Rob navigate the car down Tenth Street, under the railroad bridge, and toward Wrubel. Just past the computing center, the road became State Road 45, the next major artery in our trip.

"Hey," I asked, "what other events have you worked at?"

"A fair in Kokomo where we didn't sell too much, and the Fourth."

"Where were you for the Fourth?"

"Indianapolis. We were right downtown—a bunch of us went, but there were people all over the place. I was carrying twice as much as tonight, and sold out in about an hour. What about you?"

"I was in Zionsville, and we sold most of our stuff in about 15 minutes. I was laying out piles of glowsticks, and people were grabbing them and shoving money in my face faster than I could count it. I wish every night was like that."

"No doubt. You had any really bad experiences?"

"The Indy 500 was pretty wild, and it rained on the way back to the car. And I worked a carnival that was a total bust—I didn't sell anything."

"That sucks. I hope it doesn't start pouring tonight."

"You just jinxed us," I said. "I hope you have some towels in the car."

The two-lane road twisted and turned, rising over hills down a pathway between beautiful and tall treelines. Although it was only a dozen miles to the event, with the speed limits and winding roads, it would take twenty minutes to get there. I still wondered about the crowd, and if Rob Lowe was going to have a rough time selling sticks to a bunch of Harley dudes. He was the most clean cut guy I'd ever spoken more than ten words to in my life. He looked like he should be modeling something in a Brooks Brothers catalog, not wandering among the rednecks. But maybe he was a natural born salesman. I'd know in a few short hours.

And the jinx began—a mist of droplets started to pelt the windshield. "Fuck me," I said, "this isn't going to make things fun."

"Maybe it's just misting," he said. As quickly as they began, the droplets stopped, and then started again. "This is pretty weird. As long as it doesn't soak in, I think we're okay."

The road broke through the trees and into typical Indiana rural landscape: acres of farmland, with square treelines every mile dividing properties. The skies didn't look as ominous, but I knew they'd turn against us sometime in the evening. And I was wearing a nice pair of new 501 jeans, too.

"Hey, I think this is Bean Blossom up here," he said. Outside, there was a small IGA market, a tavern, and a gas station. All three buildings looked pre-WWII and straight out of a John Cougar Mellencamp video. Rob pulled the car into the lot behind the market, and put it in park.

"Okay," he pulled out the map, "the event is in a big field down this road, the one that goes down the hill. Bruce's map doesn't have that much detail, but I think it's less than a mile. Do we want to go down there and park, or find something here?"

"It's going to cost a lot of cash to park there," I said. "And there are going to be a lot of people staying all weekend, so you might get stuck down there. Do you think it's legal to park here?"

"I don't see any towing signs, and I don't think we'll be here for more than an hour or two. We could give it a try."

"Okay, it's your car," I said. "Let's get down there."

We walked through a tunnel of trees and down a steep hill, following the slick pavement on narrow road to the event. With my carrier slung over my shoulder, I felt like an infantryman carrying his M-16 into combat, preparing for the worst. I expected Bruce's directions to be completely wrong, with this being the wrong road, or possibly five miles from the event. But we did see some hand-painted signs aimed in this direction, which removed some of the anxiety.

"I think this is it," Rob said. After half a mile, the treeline broke, and a huge field opened to our left, filled with cars and campers. We followed more signs, and came to a dirt road—or rather a mud road. Once we left the pavement, we found that all of the rain from the last week kept the field watered until it was a bog. The two narrow strips of dirt that usually formed a trail for cars and trucks turned into a thick muck in more places than not. I tried to find a dry patch with each step, but soon found out I wasn't getting out of this without totaling my shoes.

The first thing I saw entering the field was the huge, impromptu parking lot. There weren't any big RVs in the field, just rows of older cars and trucks. A few trailers and truckbed-camper littered the parking lines, but the motorcycles were further in. I couldn't gauge the crowd from the trickle of people walking from their cars, but it didn't look like the type that would blow a ten-spot every time their kid whined for something. It would be a hard night.

After a hike of a few blocks, we found the admissions booth, a ramshackle structure that was nailed together from some secondhand plywood around a temporary frame, like a big lemonade stand. Bruce gave us each an extra twenty to get into the event, so we both stepped in line to get a wristband and start the show. After a few minutes, I got to the head of the line, handed over my cash to the grandma-type lady working the booth to buy a non-member admission, and she strapped the plastic band around my wrist. All right—ready to sell, I thought.

"Hey," the lady said to me, as I walked away, "are you going to sell those?"

"Yeah," I said.

"You can't sell those in here if you're not a member."

"But my boss said..."

"No. No vendors unless you're an Abate member."

"How much is a membership?"

"It's $40."

"Okay, hang on—let me talk to my partner here."

I pulled Rob out of line. "What the fuck are we going to do?"

"We could try to sell them anyway," he said.

"That's not going to work if we can't get in the event. I don't think there are enough people hanging out in the parking area to sell much."

I thought over our money situation. He had $45 and I had $25, which wasn't enough to buy two memberships and still make change. "Hey, what if we bought one card, and one of us sold in the parking lot, and the other sold outside? And afterwards, we could split the difference or something."

"Maybe with one card, we could both get in somehow."

"I don't think that will work. Give me $30 of your money, and I'll get one card. Do you think you could handle the parking lot?"

"Yeah sure." He dug out his cash, and handed me $30. "Let's try to work for an hour, and then come out and see how I'm doing."

"Okay, that sounds good. I'll see you then."

He vanished back into the parking lot, and I hoped that he was a natural salesman like I expected. A minute later, I went back to the booth, explained that my partner went home, and bought a one-year membership to the Abate. She handed me a plastic card, and wished me luck.

I kept walking in the field of mud as the sky went from twilight to darkness. On my way into the field, I saw a guy with the German helmet and the biker bitch and everything drive an *Easy Rider* chopper into a lake-sized puddle of mud over a foot deep, and then drop it in the deepest part. The chopper went down with a huge splash, and half of the people at the damned event turned to look and gasp in horror as most of the bike went underwater. The little guy emerged, drenched in water and topsoil, cursing at the machine while his bitch cursed at him. Seeing that was almost worth the $40 card.

Inside, a handful of covered booths housed the food concessions and a honky-tonk band playing square-dance music through a distorted PA. All of the other vendors were set up in trucks or on the dirt and mud. Aside from the usual face painting, bratwurst, and t-shirt booths, there were mostly people selling motorcycle gear. I walked around the circle, and tried to scope out the crowd more. Most of the people were anonymous working-class redneck types, like the people I worked in the factories last year with. There were no Hell's Angel types or other stereotypical bikers—just poor families, some dragging behind their kids, having a good time in the mud. These weren't the kind of people that had the disposable cash to spend on junk.

I found a dry spot next to one of the trails and away from the other vendors, and set up shop. It was dark already, so I cracked open three sticks, made a little necklace, and tried to switch into active mode. People walked by and looked at me as I tried to say hi or otherwise get passers by to notice me or ask questions, but most of them ignored me. They were sinking to their ankles on the trail, half-drunk and ornery.

Then it started to rain. And not a gentle mist, but a real motherfucking downpour, like getting pelted with buckets of water. People tried to run to the closest shelter, which was the food pavilion. I thought about moving there, but was sure bad things would happen if I tried. So I stuck to my position. After a few minutes, the rain eased to a trickle, but it was still enough that it would completely fill my glasses every few minutes, and I didn't have much in the way of dry shirt to keep rubbing them clean.

I got a few disparate sales, but not enough. The crowd ignored me, and after a few minutes, I stopped looking at the people walking by, and tuned out. It was really a very beautiful field, even in the rain. The treelines contrasted the open pasture and reminded me of all of the corn farms in northern Indiana that I used to play in when I was a kid. That was the only positive thought that I could focus on as the sky pissed on me. I also kept thinking that I should've called Donna before Bruce and made plans with her instead. My dry patch of hill slowly melted into mud, and as I paced back and forth, my high-tops sunk lower into the bog with each step.

Suddenly, a giant, seven-foot tall biker guy ran up to me, and grabbed my glowstick holder from me. "You can't sell these here," he grunted.

"What do you mean? They said at the..."

"You can't sell these. You need a vendor pass to sell anything here." The guy towered over me, and I knew I would be stomped by a dozen Hells' Angels, arrested for trespassing, or both.

"I talked to the lady at the admission booth. I'm an Abate member—she said I could sell if I was."

"We've got people out here that pay $600 for vendor passes. I can't have you selling these. Come with me."

He marched me back to the front booth, still holding all of my gear. "Hey, I'm going to need my stuff back," I said.

"No, we have to keep it."

"What? You can't keep it. What if I just leave now?"

"Let's see what they say at the front desk."

We got to the front desk, and the lady that sold me a membership was gone. The ogre and the new cashier went back and forth a few times, before she told me, "You can't sell these here without a vendor's permit."

"Well I don't have $600—you guys took my last $40 on a membership and promised me I could sell here. Now what am I supposed to do?"

The lady backed down, and hesitated. "Well, you could stay for the music. We've got four more bands going on."

"Look, just give me my shit back, and let me use the phone to call my boss."

I was amazed that there was a working pay phone strung up near the porta-potties, a stone's throw from the booth. I didn't have any change, but I learned long ago to commit Bruce's 1-800 number to memory just for occasions like this. I did a quick dial, and got his office.

"Bruce, this is John. I just got busted."

"Cops?"

"No, just the people putting on the show. They wouldn't let us sell unless we joined the Abate for $40, and after we put together our cash for one membership, they told me I needed a $600 permit to sell anything."

"That's bullshit. What happened to Rob?"

"He went to sell commando, and I haven't seen him. I'm assuming he didn't get caught, or I'm fucked on a ride back to town."

"Don't worry, if you get stuck out there, I can send somebody to get you," he said. "What about the product?"

"They took it, but I just got it back. I only sold maybe $10. Did I mention it's pouring rain, and this field has turned into the fucking planet Dagobah?"

"John, I fucked up on this one. Both of you guys will get some hazard pay for researching this one for me. Just find Rob, and get back here, Okay?"

"Okay. This has really been the highlight of my glowstick career."

"Hey, look at the bright side: now that you're an Abate members, bikers are going to be calling your house every time there's a proposed helmet law, trying to get you to sign their petition."

"...and I'll remember this night every time they ask for a favor."

"That's the spirit. I'll see you two in a little while."

"Okay, later."

I hung up the phone, and went back to the information desk, where my gear awaited me, next to the lady selling wristbands "Did you see another guy selling glowsticks who looked like Rob Lowe?"

"Rob who?" she asked.

"Never mind, you probably didn't see *About Last Night*. You didn't catch someone else selling these?"

"No, just you."

"Okay, thanks." I grabbed my gear and headed back toward the row, scanning the people. At least he wouldn't be hard to spot in the crowd. After almost fifteen minutes of wandering in the rain, I found Rob, still selling near the entrance to the field. He still looked like a Brooks Brothers model, and had almost no mud on him at all.

"Rob!" I yelled over. "Hey man, we got shut down. We've gotta get out of here."

"We did? Nobody's said anything to me."

"Well, they know about me now. They lied to us earlier—you need a $600 permit."

"That sucks. I sold about $50 up here."

"Well, you did better than me. Come on, let's get the hell out of here."

The solid pavement felt wonderful under my feet, even if my shoes did squish with every step. The walk back would be uphill, and demoralizing.

And moments later, the sky unleashed the worst of the rain. Water dumped from above, even through the trees. I was sure the cardboard tubes of my glowstick carrier were going to disintegrate. My clothes were so wet, it felt like I jumped into a swimming pool.

We hiked back to the Twin Peaks town, and were overjoyed to find the car still in its spot. The store closed early, dispelling any ideas about finding a Coke, a roll of paper towels, and a public restroom with a warm air drier. The tavern was open, but I didn't want to get into any hillbilly versus city boy, *Easy Rider* antics. Instead, we wrung out our shirts and socks as much as we could, and poured the water out of our shoes. Rob got us back on SR 45, and we waited for the car's heater to kick in.

An hour later, I slumped in the shower stall back in my apartment and let the hot water wash away all of the mud and dirt that I took home. After spending so long in the cold August rain, the steamy drizzle in the shower felt great. I washed my hair twice, got out, and used my biggest, thickest towel to dry off.

Outside of the shower, in my plastic bus tray, my newest jeans soaked in hot water and Woolite. I already tried to spray off the mud from my shoes, but it would take another dry-wet cycle to chip off the dirt. And for all of my troubles, Bruce gave me a twenty. That was still more than minimum wage, but it convinced me that my glowstick days were over.

I grabbed my bucket of toiletries, walked back to my room, and took my time getting dressed into new clothes. It was only a little after nine, so I'd have plenty of time to find Donna and Carrie. The evening was not lost.

37

Books, photocopies, CDs, and floppy disks surrounded my Macintosh in the IMU cluster, like some kind of fortified bunker. At 2:00 on Saturday afternoon, I was one of the few not enjoying the beautiful sunny day outside. A couple of others were with me, pulling it in to the last minute, and hacking away at work for the end of the summer session. The business of sacrificing a good Saturday would normally be out of the question. But I had nothing to do anyway, and I wasn't in the position to spend the last of my cash finding a diversion. So there I was, slamming the keys and trying to finish my damned English paper.

This was actually the furthest from last-minute work I'd ever done in my college career. The paper wasn't due until Wednesday at five. But, out of boredom, I figured I should work out the whole thing over the weekend, and hand it in early. That would give me a chance to worry more intensely about the econ final without having to take off from my radio shifts.

With the portable CD player on the desk, the power supply plugged into the strip on the floor, and the remote a foot away by the mousepad, I had the complete sound system going through my headphones. Chick Corea, as always, worked through the system, but I had some Entombed awaiting the next spot in the player. On the Mac, I had WordPerfect in the foreground, and my telnet sessions to Bronze and Rose in the background. Every few minutes I switched programs, checked my mail, did a quick who on the VMS machines, and maybe said hi to somebody. But I spent a good deal of time on the paper. It was quickly going from a page-long outline to a decently fleshed out piece of work. I dropped all of the quotes and citations into place, and then worked around those to tie everything together. It's almost too easy, I thought.

I took a hit from my Coke hidden strategically under the desk, and did another quick who. Despite the caffeine, I was still tired from the night before. After the glowstick fiasco, I met with Carrie and Donna at the IMU. We drove around and talked about going to a late movie, but it eventually turned into a night at Waffle House, drinking Coke after Coke and talking about nothing. I enjoyed it, though; whenever I was around Donna, she treated me like a computer god, and built up my ego so much with affirmations that I'd me rolling in cash someday because of my skills. I didn't exactly believe that, but it was always nice to get her perspective on things.

The Chick Corea CD spun out, and I switched to Entombed's recent album, *Clandestine*. The low-tuned Death Metal guitars and speedy drumbeat helped me get back to the paper and start grinding through the words. All of the quotes from my sources were in place and properly cited, and all that awaited was my explanatory mumbo-jumbo as a mortar for the mix. I fired away in the gaps of the paper, jumping all over from the easiest to the most difficult spaces to fill.

By the time I got to the last track of the CD, I had a solid eight pages of writing, with no real gaps. I ran it through the spellcheck, read it from start to finish, saved a copy to the disk, and sent it to the printer. It would need to ferment a bit, to make the mistakes more obvious. I planned to read the printout later that night, and red-pen the obvious problems. On Monday, I'd run through it one more time on the computer, then hand in a final draft.

I picked up the output from the printer, closed down the computer, and packed up all of my shit into my backpack. It was going on four o'clock, and I had no idea what to do for the rest of the evening, but it felt good to get the paper close to done. I thought about the fountain, and maybe some other general wandering and killing of time before then. I had nearly eight hours, with nothing to do except dinner, and nobody on the computer. A few longshot schemes ran though my mind, but I knew it would be another boring Saturday night in Bloomington. I hefted the backpack over my shoulder, restarted the Entombed CD in my player, and headed for the door.

The VW crawled up the hill on 17th Street, as I looked for Kinzer pike, following Amy's directions neatly printed on the back of a receipt. The lazy Sunday afternoon felt like one of the vacant days I remembered forever from my childhood, full of sunlight, potential, and nothing to do but sit in the middle of it. The night before deteriorated into the usual course of low-grade depression and loneliness that forced me to walk around campus with a tape of doom in the player and in my ears. I went to bed late, woke up late, and laid in bed half-awake for almost 20 minutes killing time and thinking about the dinner. I showered, shaved, and dressed in lightning time, trying to be careful of every last detail. I'd been looking forward to this event since the invite, and the weather and my state of mind were perfect for it.

I hung a right at the next light and shot downhill on Kinzer, a rollercoaster ride of a trip past a handful of apartment complexes. Amy lived far enough north of campus that there weren't many older buildings, just prefab communities built in the last ten years. I saw the sign for Colonial Crest, opposite to the entrance for an ancient and forgotten IGA grocery store. After a hard left, I cruised the quiet development of two-story townhouses, built in rows like army barracks. Each light tan building stretched for a dozen or more apartments, with identical, institutional dark trim and apartment numbers above each door. Parking spots lined the front of each building, half of them abandoned for summer.

I saw her apartment, #144, after a few turns through the maze of identical buildings, and pulled the Rabbit into a spot. Now I just needed to worry about what happened next. I ran through the scenarios in my head, and tried to think of what I would do, how I would recognize a window of opportunity, and how I would try to take advantage of it. Even though I wanted to make the first move, I knew that it was all her decision, and I'd either walk into a firefight or a dud. No pressure.

I flipped down the sun visor mirror, checked things out, and went over the mental appearance checklist: hair straightened, shirt OK, shoes fine, shorts zipped, breath fine, everything cool. I grabbed a CD, pocketed my keys, and headed for her apartment.

The collegiate feel of the apartment complex hit me as I walked across the parking lot to the townhouses. It was a cross between the off-campus houses like mine, the yuppie stylings of a condo community, and the institutional feel of a hotel resort. With people lying around a full-size swimming pool, the heat from the blacktop, the smell of the fresh-cut grass and Chemlawn fertilizers, the odor of gas grills and charcoal briquettes, everything fit my image of the nicer off-campus communities.

I knocked at the door, one of a dozen in front of virtually cloned front stoops. A moment later, Amy appeared, her hair up, wielding a pair of tongs and wearing a cook's apron. "Hey! Come on in," she said. "You know about charcoal grills, right?"

I stepped into a large living room, with sunlight streaming through the front windows, and a stairway leading to the second level. Boxes littered the area, with a TV sitting on a small rack and a long couch against one wall. Pier One-esque framed artwork and small glass and wire tables covered with knick-knacks in strategic locations.

"Yeah, I know this neat trick," I said, "You light the grill, then you spray a whole bunch of the lighter fluid on it..."

Amy went back through the living room and attached dining room into the kitchen, to mess with the food more. I passed the couch and entertainment center in the living room, stopping for a second to glance at copies of Harper's and Cosmo on the endtable. Plenty of halogen ambient torchlights and Ikea-type prefab furniture made the place look like a college-girl apartment, which is just how I'd pictured it.

"This is a pretty nice place you've got here," I said.

"Thanks, but it's pretty tore up right now. Tracy moved out already, and Cindy and I have been juggling around our furniture until we both move out at the end of the session. What were you saying about the grill? I can't figure out if it's ready or not."

"Let me take a look at it," I said. We walked out the patio door in the dining area, to a small slab of concrete. There wasn't much of a yard; across the way sat another row of tenements, also using the same rectangle of grass as a back yard. I could see other students with their barbecues or laying out on chairs and beach towels, also enjoying the day.

In the center of her patio sat a small metal kettle grill on foot-high legs, holding a pile of half burned charcoal briquettes smoldering unevenly. I poked at the coals with a pair of tongs, rearranged a few of them, and gave the pile a quick jolt with the squeeze bottle of fluid.

"See, it's burning all weird." she said. "Why haven't they invented a microwave grill yet?"

"That wouldn't be any fun," I said. "There's something about playing with fire..." I rearranged the coals a bit more, trying to get the coveted pyramid of briquettes to turn a uniform gray. "Hey, where's Cindy anyway? Do I get to meet her?"

"No such luck today. She's visiting her parents in Carmel for the next few days. It's just us. Hope you're not worried about that," she said.

"Yeah, I'm pretty worried actually, you look pretty sexy in that apron. I might not be able to help myself." I stopped messing with the fire, which looked like it was burning again. "Hey, do you have anything to drink?" I asked.

"I got you some Coke in the fridge," she said. "Let me get this food ready to go."

I followed her to the sterile cookery, and examined the food she was preparing. The carefully sculpted poultry sat in plastic, painted with a bright red barbecue sauce. The table was already set with real plates, matching flatware, and cloth napkins—something I hadn't experienced in years, except in restaurants.

She opened the fridge, and set a glass casserole tray full of chicken on the counter. "Here's your Coke," she said, pulling a red can from the fridge and tossing it to me.

I caught the can, the condensation slick on my hands. "Thanks much," I said, cracking open the top. "So do you barbecue much?"

"Not really," she said, wrestling with a roll of aluminum foil. She carefully wrapped each cutlet for the grill. "I borrowed this setup from my folks for Memorial Day, and we haven't used it since."

I watched her methodically pack the chicken pieces into foil, folding each corner exactly like a Martha Stewart Christmas ornament. It almost made me laugh, how precise she could be with something as trivial as a chicken dinner.

"So what did you do this weekend?" she asked.

Not the dreaded question, I thought. "Not a lot," I said. "I worked on Friday, the glowstick thing."

"Didn't it rain on Friday?"

"Yes it did," I laughed. "We were in Bean Blossom, at this biker convention. They gave us a lot of shit about selling anything there, and I thought we were going to get our asses kicked. Then it started pouring, and we were up to our ankles in mud."

"That sounds horrible. And I'm guessing you didn't sell anything?"

"Not in the least. Bruce gave me twenty bucks as a consolation prize, which I guess isn't bad for killing a few hours of my time. Better than minimum wage, anyway."

Amy loaded the foil-wrapped chicken onto a plate, grabbed her cooking utensils, and headed back toward the patio. "Keep talking," she said, "I've got to throw these on the grill."

"Okay," I said. I followed her back outside. "After the glowstick thing, hooked up with Donna and Carrie and hung out with them for a while. And yesterday I mostly finished my English paper."

"How's it look?"

"I think I'll finish. It's boring as hell though."

"Well, W350 isn't a high-entertainment class, really."

"You'll have to let me check it out once you're done. I'd love to read it."

I took another hit from the soda, and lifted the lid of the grill, to check if there was any progress. Inside, the food steamed and cooked, smelling incredible.

"So," I asked, "what did you do this weekend?"

"Not much," she said. "I've been working on packing things up, and I put some stuff in storage at the folks' house. The big move is Friday, and as you can see, I'm not ready yet."

"So where is the new place?"

"It's south of town. It's a new townhouse, two bedroom, two bath—about same size as this, but a better layout, a little wider, and there's a basement. Have you ever been to Brownstone before?"

"Yeah," I said. "I went to a Little 500 party there this year."

"Well, it's the same floor plan, except these were just built, and there aren't many students there. It's mostly families and professors."

"Let me know if you need any help moving. I might go out of town next weekend, but I can help otherwise."

"Be careful what you volunteer for. You haven't seen how many books I have upstairs..." She opened up the steaming kettle again, pried up a corner of one of the foil-wrapped parcels, and stuck it with a fork. "I think these are done," she said. "I hope they aren't too dry..." She snared each piece with a pair of tongs, dropped them on a plate, and went back inside.

I closed the lid of the grill and spun shut the air holes, smothering the orange-gray coals within before I followed her to the kitchen. "Grill's shut down," I said. "I'd let it sit overnight before you clean it out."

"Great, thanks," she said. "Grab a seat, and let me get everything set up here."

I went to the table, and set my Coke down, while I watched her unwrap the chicken. She put the pieces on two plates, along with a salad and fresh watermelon she'd prepared earlier. It almost seemed unfathomable to watch Amy work in the kitchen. It's not that I found the work beyond her, it's just that I was waiting to see something she couldn't do.

She carried the two plates to the table and the awaiting silverware and napkins. She then untied the apron, hung it next to the counter, and went back to the fridge.

"Another Coke?" she asked.

"Sure, thanks."

She pulled another red can from the refrigerator, along with a bottle of water. "I think we're all set," she said. After putting the drinks down on the table, she sat across from me, and scooted in her chair.

"Well, dinner is served," she said. I watched her carefully slice into her chicken breast with a knife and fork, while I stabbed mine and pulled loose pieces of flesh. "Is the chicken too dry?" she asked.

"No, no—it's excellent," I said, my mouth full of food. Everything tasted delicious, probably just because I ate with real silverware from real plates, instead of from a bucket or a box.

"It's no John Conner dinner, but I don't cook much," she said.

I smiled, and looked across the table at her. I always enjoyed eating with her, watching her meticulously pick apart her food and eat it like an accountant working through a tax return. She was so dainty and precise, especially for a woman that seemed so much like me. And today, we weren't in a fast food place, battling the rest of the lunch crowd for a small spot in a sea of tables. Today, she was mine.

With my last meal was over seventeen hours before, I ravished everything on my plate, practically inhaling the green salad after the chicken was vaporized. The watermelon tasted so good; seedless, pure red water melting in my mouth with each bite, the juice running down my hands. "This is incredible," I said. "Where did you get this? I haven't had watermelon in years."

"They sell it at Kroger, you know. It's not in individually wrapped, plastic-sealed bachelor packs, though. You have to buy the whole thing and slice it up."

"Damn, I'm going to have to remember that or something," I said. I plopped the last bit into my mouth and savored the final taste.

"Done with your plate?" she said.

"Oh, no. I mean, let me help you." I grabbed both plates and carried them over to the sink. "Let me help with the dishes," I said.

"Why thank you," she said. "Let me just rinse them off. I'll wash them later.

I handed the dishes to her one by one at the sink, watching her scrub the food into the disposal. I stood close to her, like she sat next to me at the station earlier in the week, almost as a challenge to see if she would back away or move even closer. She didn't move away, but I still couldn't tell if I should make a move. I kept imagining an opening where I could have grabbed her, bent her over the counter, and started ravaging her with kisses. Maybe my imagination was working overtime, but I felt she was dropping more than subtle hints at me that it was time for action.

After the dishes were taken care of and she put the leftovers in the fridge, the air was heavy with a "what's next" feeling, both of us awkwardly grabbing for the conversation or activity that would continue the evening. I wanted to go in for the kill, and I was almost certain she did too, but I didn't want to blow it. Then I remembered the CD I brought, which was sitting on an endtable in the alcove.

"Hey," I said, "Where's your stereo? I brought a CD to listen to."

"Well, actually, it's in Indy," she said. "I usually use Cindy's, and it's already packed up. I think the parts are all in the living room, though."

We dug through the boxes in the minimalist room, and located a tiny low-end bookshelf system and two small speakers amid the ruin. While Amy continued to re-stack and rearrange things to clear more floor-space and hide some of the junk, I plugged the unit into a wall and fumbled with its speaker wires. A quick glance revealed that it had the most basic, rudimentary CD player I'd ever seen in my life. As long as it worked, I thought.

"What CD is this?" she asked, still moving around stuff.

"It's Shadowfax," I said. "Jazz/New Age sort of instrumental music." I considered this particular disc of instrumental background music my secret weapon in situations like this. At least it worked with Tammy, so maybe it would be okay with Amy, too.

I sat on the floor, fed the CD into the player, and got things started. The first track, "Angel's Flight," filled the room, a quiet number with guitar and lyricon, a gentle, wind-based synth. She sat next to me on the floor, and we bathed in the fading sunlight, both wondering what would be next. I hoped the music would create a mood, and it did.

"So, would you like a backrub?" she asked.

"Yeah, that would be nice," I said. "Are you sure you're not taking advantage of me?"

She just laughed. "Here, lie on the floor over here."

I got on my stomach, and she kneeled next to me, kneading my neck and shoulderblades with her soft hands. It felt good, not because her fingers were slicing through my tense muscles, but because I could feel her body so close to me. And I knew that this had to be more than just a friendly gesture. There was no way things couldn't escalate from this point.

Her massage got more involved, her hands navigating down my back and under my shirt. It was hard not to hide my excitement as she touched my bare skin, and this made her get even more involved. She straddled me, a knee at either side of my hip, and put her weight into each push against my muscles with the heels of her hands. Her pelvis ground into my ass with each repetition, and she kept rubbing me, not afraid of showing her intentions.

She slowed her rhythm, but I wanted to keep things going. "Is it your turn now?" I asked.

She smiled, and we traded places, but I skipped the sweet and innocent part. I straddled her, gently moved her silky hair away from her shoulders, and gently plied at her shoulders. I leaned close to her, my breath on her neck, my body hovering just above hers. It didn't take much imagination for me to see her naked under me, and my massaging turned to slow grinding, my hands stroking the tanned, bare flesh of her back. Each rub brought my hands against the lacy purple strap of her bra, and I had to suppress the uncontrollable urge to pull loose the fastener.

Then without warning, she rolled over, and our lips locked in fiendish passion, an intense kiss that made me forget everything else. My lips explored hers, my hands tearing at her shirt. Her nails dug at my bare back as my tongue darted into her open mouth. My mouth moved to her jaw, her ears, the soft, tanned skin of her neck, her supple collarbone. Her fingers ran through my hair as we rolled on the floor, our bodies locked together. From her gentle moans, I could tell she was enjoying this as much as I was.

She pulled up from me in mid-kiss. "Let's go upstairs," she said, half panting with excitement. I stood up, took her hand, and pulled her up to me, where our lips met again. I never wanted to move away from her arms again; I wanted to taste her lips forever. We stumbled backward toward the stairs, still kissing passionately. I backed her into the wall, and started nibbling on her shoulder. We went up one or two steps, and then she backed me against the wall and attacked my ear with her soft tongue. We bounced from wall to wall, one or two steps at a time, until we got to her room. It must have taken us fifteen minutes to climb the stairs, but neither of us were complaining.

We pushed through boxes and furniture with each step. "Be careful, there's junk everywhere," she said. She flipped on a light, and we stumbled into her room. I backed her toward the bed, but she stopped me first and broke our kiss.

"We...we need to draw a line somewhere," she said.

"Okay, what about the 'no removal of undergarments' rule?"

She unbuttoned my jeans, and pulled at the zipper. "Okay, I can live with that if you can."

Clothes flew, and we collapsed on top of each other on the bed. My almost-naked body pressed into hers was about three pieces of clothing away from complete paradise.

We ravaged each other for hours. Although we were traumatically close, we stuck to the 'no removal of undergarments' rule, and didn't have sex. As things slowed down, my mind raced with thoughts about where this would leave things, and how we'd continue. But we didn't discuss future repercussions or plans. I liked that, even though I was hoping to somehow seal the deal with our physical actions.

Hours later, we curled together in bed, our sweaty and exhausted bodies pressed tight. It felt so good to have her head lying across my chest, to smell her hair, to feel her skin against mine. I'd spent so much time imagining a moment this comfortable with her, and the real thing felt several orders of magnitude more complete.

"How are you doing?" she whispered.

"Fine. Drowsy."

"You can stay if you want. The alarm goes off at six. Can you manage?"

"Not a problem."

She snuggled up closer to me, and I pulled a sheet over our bodies. Within moments, she fell asleep in my arms, and I wasn't far behind.

At six, I walked out to my car, carrying my CD and watching the sky turn from dark black to a pre-dawn blue. It was cold, much colder than a summer should be. All of the car windows outside were still fogged over and covered with condensation. As I walked back to my VW in the row of other cars in the parking lot, I saw a familiar face also returning to their vehicle. It was Brecken!

"Hey Brecken!" I yelled. "Have a good night, you scammer?"

"Conner!" he said. "Man, this is a weird coincidence."

"Yeah, I know. We've gotta stop planning these things like this. It's like we're a bunch of women with synchronized periods or something."

"Holy shit, does that really happen?"

"I don't know, man. I don't even pretend to know about that shit. So what's your deal here? You scoring or still shopping around?"

"I've been dating someone for about a week," he said. "Well, moving in place for dating, you know what I mean. She works at the gas station just down the road from Bruce's. She's just in town for the summer though, from Iowa."

"Sounds like you might have some roadtrips ahead of you this fall."

"Yeah," he said. "We'll see. What's with you? Another VAX chick?"

"Sort of. I mean, she's not the typical type."

"No 19 year olds this time?" he said.

"No, not really. It's going okay, but still confusing."

"I hear ya," he said. "Hey, I've gotta go get some sleep while I still can."

"Me too, I'll catch you later dude."

Brecken drove off in his Jetta, and I fired up the VW. Inside, I rubbed the dew from the windshield and cranked the tiny heater motor to clear the glass more. I pulled onto Kinzer and drove toward my house, watching the sun start its ascent from the horizon, painting the city with its orange glow. The evening's actions still spun in my brain, and I wondered if it really happened, and what was next. I need to forget about this for now and get some sleep, I thought, as I drove back to the student ghetto.

38

The drive home felt like the moments after I met Tammy for the first time, the minutes I felt she was the one I dreamed of for my entire life. I still felt Amy in my arms, smelled her on my clothes, and imagined everything falling into place. Still, a lingering feeling made me think not everything was ready for prime time between us. I'd need to know what happened next, how she reacted the day after.

But before that, I'd have to worry about finals. During the short drive back to my house, with the sun streaming into the VW, thoughts of my final paper and econ test overtook my system. In about five hours, the final econ lecture would take place, probably some sort of review session that went over the entire summer session of material. As a master truant, I learned that if I skipped an entire semester of classes, I could often skim past the final by going to the last lecture. The problem was that I'd probably sleep through this session. And I also needed to finish the last of the work on my English paper. Without some serious sleep deprivation, I would be fucked.

I hauled ass into my driveway, shut down the car, and practically ran into the house and to my room. I set my alarm for 9:00, which would give me almost four hours of sleep. I stripped back out of my clothes, turned the box fan on high, and hit the bed. My mind still raced with thoughts of Amy, but a complete lack of energy pulled me unconscious in only a few minutes.

By noon, I ran a mostly complete paper through the spellcheck two more times, just in case. The econ review helped, but it also made me realize how little I knew. I wrote down everything the prof wrote on the board, and followed along as best I could, but still felt lost. I hoped that a few dozen hours with the text and my new notes would make things clearer.

After two hours of labor in Ballantine 308, my paper looked much better. I read through it again, fiddled with obvious mistakes, and played with the fonts to get my pagecount above ten, and printed off a first copy to the LaserWriter to take a look at things on paper.

When I got back, the window logged onto the Rose VAX beeped. "Hey, you awake?" said Amy.

"Barely," I said. "I had econ, and now I'm finishing a paper. What about you?"

"I made it on time. It's not that hard for me to pretend to be awake here, so I'll survive. I still feel a little weird, though."

"How so?" I asked.

"I don't want to scare you or anything, but I was just thinking about last night. I mean, I don't think it was bad, but I don't want to rush things. But I don't want to tell you this and discourage you."

"I know what you mean." Really, I didn't. I wanted to leap right into something with her without even looking, but I feared that she felt otherwise.

"Well, I'm doing a show tonight. Want to stop by?"

"I've got to go to a study session tonight. Will you be around later? I can give you a call before five."

"Okay, sounds good. I'll talk to you then."

About last night...the words hung in my head while I trudged through the rest of the paper. I felt confident that she wouldn't call and tell me to get the hell out of her life forever, but I also knew she wouldn't be waiting with open arms so we could immediately dive into a full-blown relationship. Shit, I needed to worry about more important things, but I couldn't.

After another hour of nitpicking, the ten pages of paper turned into 13, and it looked solid enough for a final draft. I read over it a few more times, trying to fine-tune some of the small details. The whole thing seemed too easy, and it didn't feel right handing in the work this early. But all of the sources checked, the sentences read okay, and everything was in order. I sent a copy to the printer, shut down the computer, and gathered up the last of my stuff. After a staple in the corner, the paper went up to the fourth floor English office and into the teacher's desk.

Halfway there, I thought, as I climbed down the stairs and back to the outside world. Now I just needed to learn a semester of econ in less than four days. I headed back to the house with plans to immediately study and reverse-engineer the econ notes until I knew at least some of the basics. But after checking my mail (none,) I crawled into bed and fell asleep.

I couldn't tell what time it was when the phone rang and pulled me from my nap, but it was still light out. I stumbled for the handset while trying to put on my glasses and look at my watch. 4:40. "Hello?"

"John? It's Amy. Were you asleep?"

"Yeah, but I gotta wake up," I said. "I've got a show at eight."

"It sounds like you've been out a while. I hope that means you got some sleep."

"Yeah, I'll be awake for the show. How are you doing?"

"Tired. I'm going to a study group for polysci tonight, and I hope I stay awake. Time for some coffee."

"So, about last night..." I said.

"Yeah, about last night..." she said. "I don't know, that sounds so terrible. I don't regret anything we did. I mean, I really had a great time with you."

"I did too," I said. "I just hope I didn't confuse things."

"We confused things, not you. It's not your fault. I am a bit worried, about how things will go. I mean, I don't want to mislead you about anything. I'm not sure I can be what you need right now, and I'm not even sure where I will be in a year. I like you a lot, but I worry how things line up."

"I know what you mean, but I don't know what to do about it."

"I know...I care about you, John. And I've had a lot of fun with you since we met. And I'm hoping to keep spending time with you. But I don't want to hurt you by making you think I want to be what Tammy was. I just got out of this relationship, and..."

"I know, I know. I don't expect you to be my girlfriend or whatever. But I do want to spend time with you. You're incredible to me...I don't want to screw that up."

"Sigh...I wish we could not talk about this, and just...be. Know what I mean?"

"Like a 'don't ask, don't tell' policy?" I said.

"Exactly. We might be fooling ourselves, but I think it's the best plan for now."

"Agreed," I said. "Hey, I've gotta get out of bed and get some food together. You interested?"

"I really need a nap before this study session. But I'll send some email later, okay?"

"Okay. Have fun with world government."

"Have a good show. I'll talk to you later."

"Bye Amy."

I tossed the phone into the small sea of laundry and sighed. It could have gone worse with her, but I wanted it to go much better. I crawled back into bed to stare at the ceiling for another hour or two and try to digest the conversation, but I fell asleep within minutes.

Rain poured from the sky. The hard trickle leaked over the decrepit building from rusty gutters and onto the city street below, drizzling and hissing white noise through the battered window. The rain hit the summer pavement below like B-52 Arclight strikes against the North Vietnamese, never slowing, never relenting. I stared down at the city from a three-story altitude, with a unique view that the average Joe on the sidewalk would never see. The town square's trimmed shrubbery, sterile white walkways, immaculate statues and monuments stretched across the horizon, lit by bright, ever-burning floodlights. A block away, older buildings full of ghetto housing, punk squats, and tons of graffiti made up the bleak neighborhood I inhabited.

Even though I constantly bitched about the summer heat, I still wasn't completely into the sudden outburst of rain that coincidentally happened every time I had a show. I hated dragging my stuff inside when it poured out, and the leaky ceilings in the studio weren't too convincing, but having my own radio show on a station that let me do whatever I wanted was worth the waterlogged sneakers and muddy pant cuffs.

The ancient mixing board, covered with cigarette burns, carved graffiti and peeling band stickers, glowed from its peaking VU meters. The tapping of the meter's needles against the far left of the glass was inaudible over the peaked studio monitors. Vibrating Death Metal drums and guitar riffs of the new Carcass album shook the creaky wooden floor and bounced from the walls, wallpapered with torn and faded band publicity posters sloppily scotch taped one over another. The mosaic of ancient promo pictures and murals featured bands ranging from MC Hammer and Madonna to Soundgarden and Grave. Almost all of them faded and ripped before something else covered them up, and comments and profanities scribbled in by bored DJ's littered the glossy paper. On top of the console, one of the three CD players hummed and clicked away the time, second after second, on a green-blue LCD display.

The drums shook and the guitars continued in their detuned grind as the chorus passed, as Bill Steer's ice-smooth guitar leads hovered over the dragging power chords. The new Carcass CD was sort of a concept album full of sickly medical terminology. It sounded like Bill and the rest of the band smoked about a pound of hash and started reading *Gray's Anatomy* the night they wrote the songs. But it still had incredible production, and a heavy, unrelentless sound that didn't sound like the million other bands that came out of Europe, all ripping off Entombed.

Last words on the disc...the music did an about-face and slowed down to a crawl with a final death knoll from Steer. With Michael Atom's guitar pounding a low rhythm bam-bam-bam-bam, bam-bam, bam, and Steer's eerie, scalpel-sharp guitar tone telling me that the massive opera of a perfect Death Metal CD was just about at final curtain.

The time remaining counter on the CD player dipped below ten seconds. I slammed to the board and grabbed the pair of headphones, quickly fitting them on my head while anticipating the conclusion of the song, with a finger waiting on the mic switch. Three seconds. Two. On one, I clicked in.

"All right, that's 'Lavaging Expectorate of a Lysergide Composition,' the grand finale on the new Carcass release called *Necroticism—Descanting the Insalubrious*," I said, simultaneously turning off the player and fumbling with a log sheet. The large foam-screened mic dangled from a Frankenstein boom stand, capturing every syllable and relaying them back to the electrical maze. "It's 11:42 here at WQAX 103.7 FM, and you're listening to Beneath the Remains with John Conner. Hey, speaking of Carcass, they've got a new EP out that contains some stuff from the new album, a re-recorded old song, and a new one for the title track, called *Tools of the Trade*. We just got that one in, and I'll be playing the whole EP in its entirety next time I'm here. But tonight, if there's anything you wanna hear before I shut down for the night, give me a call at 331-9289 and I'll see what I can do. In a few minutes, it'll be time to freak out and dig up your grandmother's body while we listen to a little bit of Haunted Garage, but first, this message." I slapped the mic lever back to off and hit play on the cart machine for the obnoxious Ad Sheet commercial I had to play far too many times during the course of a show.

The next sixty-second change went by without thinking. I ejected the two disc players and grabbed a CD in each hand, quickly slapping them into a pair of waiting jewel boxes on the console. Then, I popped a CD from each of the two cases next to those by pulling on it with my thumb and middle finger while popping the center hub with the index finger, and carefully set them in each cradle, giving them a gentle tap to close the doors. The quick, precise movements jumped like a Swiss watch made to play Swedish Death Metal, carefully engineered and designed to perform mechanical tasks exactly. I could gauge how much time I had to cue up the next two songs because I'd memorized the entire jingle from constant exposure to the commercial.

On the last line of the spot, just as the mother was exclaiming how she loved to find good deals in the Ad Sheet, I snapped in the switch to the left disc player and clicked out the cart player with one motion, then cranked up the levels. The song started with a sample: "We are their cattle; we are being bred for slavery," and then the UK grindcore guitars pegged the VU needles into the red zone. The speedy, pounding drums that started the Napalm Death song sharply contrasted the previous Ad Sheet commercial so much it made me chuckle. I loved totally butting high-speed grindcore right against that pathetic commercial. And the lyrics of this song, "Awake (To a Land of Misery)," were so anti-consumer, it made it even better.

I punched the eject button and the cart machine presented the plastic cartridge with the commercial. After dropping it with a slight spin into a rack to the right, I quickly logged the song. Rolling back in the squeaky office chair, I grabbed the super big giant colossal gulp I bought from the gas station down the road hours ago, sloshing with melted ice and long-flat, watered down cola and took a short drag from the plastic straw. I got up and started reshelving a stack of discs I used earlier, carefully sliding the plastic jewel boxes into the wall of numerically organized shelves.

The Napalm Death song was short, so I let it play through to the last one on the disc, and the most depressing. But I didn't argue—I felt every word of the sludgy, grinding finale. The disc spun out, and I tripped the second player to start. I almost forgot about the Haunted Garage disc, and it was an abrupt 180 from the heavy-duty grindcore. Haunted Garage were a shock-joke-horror band, vague cousins to Gwar with several Troma Film alumni in their ranks. I spun up their song "976-KILL," and went back to the window.

If this was a real job, I'd be set. If I could jock for 20 hours a week, make my rent, and actually be heard...I didn't even know the procedure or training to become a real DJ on real radio stations. I imagined it involved a telecom degree, a bunch of experience, a ton of ass kissing, and some unpaid internships involving lots of coffee making and photocopying. I couldn't go from the mixing board to the bottom rung of some anonymous million-watt AOR station. It wouldn't happen.

I wanted some kind of revolution from within, just like I did in the computing vocational field. During the summer station meetings, there were no staff members present, just the temporary DJs and other assorted slackers that kept QAX on the air from May to August. With no meeting agenda, we talked about changing everything at the station. Plans of mutiny and anarchy were commonplace, as we talked about moneymaking schemes that would pull control of the place from its current hippy-trippy communal status to a full-blown commercial station. We wanted to get the money from all kinds of hair-brained schemes—DJing parties, selling airtime, selling compilation CDs, selling t-shirts, having fundraisers, whatever we could do. And the list of needs and wants always came up—better equipment, more music, more on-air appearances, syndicated shows, salaries for DJs, a better studio, better furniture, and everything else. And of course, everyone wanted to get off of cable and hit the airwaves. Some people (mostly Sid) wanted to go pirate, but others (like me) thought that within a year, we could get some idiot to match funds and help us get going. Maybe we watched the movie *UHF* too many times.

In reality, the station probably wouldn't finish out 1992. Although every show was required to have a monthly sponsor, almost nobody could find one, including me. Almost nobody listened to cable FM, except the other DJs. And because of everybody bailing for the summer, there was no money coming in. The rent was paid until September, but everybody was expecting a fire sale after that. I thought about going back to WIUS, or trying some other way to fake a broadcasting resume. If I heard about a job announcing news part-time at a honky-tonk station in Oklahoma, I'd probably take it. Anything with some kind of meaning would be better than this.

I loaded another CD when the Haunted Garage song ended. After a brief moment of silence, the pounding, slow guitar chords of the Swedish Death Metal band Dismember's song "Dismembered" slammed the walls of the studio like an explosion aftershock. The distorted rhythm repeated, as a smooth, almost melodic lead guitar circled above, surrounding the slow groans of the lead singer Matti Karki. The intro climaxed with Matti whispering "dismembered…" and then screaming a death cry, as the drummer, Fred Estby tore apart the soundscape and sent the track hurtling to hyperfast speeds. Karki then started grumbling the lyrics, about dismembered flesh.

I took a look at the album cover, of the members of the band standing against a wall, covered in pigs' blood. Just a week before, British customs seized a shipment of their newest picture disc on the grounds that it was "brutally obscene." I looked at Matti clutching a human heart in his hands, and laughed thinking about some old, uptight, religious customs officer slicing open a box of CDs and finding this jewel.

Almost midnight. I gathered up the rest of my stuff, put away everything except the playing CD, and finished the log sheet. I thought about hitting the fountain after my show, but the weekday meetings had been redundant, and I hadn't been to one since the Amy situation started. I didn't feel like spilling my guts about my dating bullshit with all of the regulars until I knew if she was a friend or more than a friend, or neither. No use in jinxing it, I thought.

The song came close to an end, and I put on the headphones for the last time of the evening. I put Morbid Angel's album *Blessed Are the Sick* in the CD player and cued up the last track. I got in place in front of the boom, manned the controls, and right after the Dismember track ended, I clicked over to the mic.

"Hey it's John Conner, and it's 11:58 here at WQAX 103.7 cable FM. You've been listening to Beneath the Remains. You were just listening to Dismember, the track 'Dismembered,' from their album *Like an Everflowing Stream*. It's almost the witching hour, which means it's time for me to split and shut this place down for the evening. First, I'd like to thank my pal Nick at Cursed Metal zine for all of the demos and news he's sent my way. Also a big thanks to Tom at CD Exchange for getting me the newest and latest, and Pete the Freak for the demo of his band Shades of Grey. As always, Xero Tolerance will be on Thursday, so you'll have a whole week full of metal. So stay evil, and see you tomorrow."

I clicked off the mic and hit play on the waiting CD. The track "Desolate Ways" played, a soft and sad yet sinister acoustic guitar track that I used to end all of my shows. It was the perfect farewell, and after four hours of brutal Death Metal in my ears, sitting in the dark and listening to the desolation of the track felt like the perfect closure.

But it wasn't, at least for the station. After the CD played, I found the yellowed notecard on top of the console contained the fading typewritten words that I monotonously read to close up shop. I turned on the mic one last time and mumbled in my semi-official voice about shutting down for the day, mumble mumble starting the broadcast day tomorrow, 8 AM, mumble mumble, for more information about the station, write to this PO box. The signoff script was one of those things I had to do every night, but I never paid attention to it, like the instructions on the back of a bottle of shampoo. I shut down the heavy-duty switches to the transmitting rig, put away my last two discs, and shut down the board power before hoisting my stuff on my shoulder and heading out.

The studio seemed strange, ominous in the midnight darkness, with all of the gear frozen in suspended animation, their gauges and lights in a quiet sleep. It reminded me of when I worked in the theatre, and there was a musical or a play, and the seats were full and the stage was jumping with song and dance and drama and people. Then the curtain fell, the people left, and when we moved all of the scenery and I was the last one there, mopping the stage floor, it hardly seemed like the place it was only a few hours before.

I locked the dual bolts on the door to the studio, and headed down through the hallway of coldwater flats. I saw the resident tabby, a little cat I nicknamed Satan, sleeping by the top of the stairs. She stretched but didn't wake when I reached down and gave her a quick scratch on the back. Tough day chasing mice, I thought.

The rainstorm stopped, but the street glossed with an even coating of dampness that made it look like an asphalt river. Water dripped from awnings and ebbed to the flowing streams of the gutters. I crossed over to the bank's parking lot where I routinely parked the Rabbit. I unlocked the small door to reveal the smell of molding carpet from a leaky floor, something that would remain until the summer heat dried out the damp interior again in a few days. When I drove in the rain, little droplets of water would hit my ankles, which must've been wonderful for the fuses and electronics under the dash, and the metal pan under my feet. With tapes and CDs hefted to the passenger seat, I cranked over the diesel and headed back to my house.

The gravel driveway crunched under the tires of the VW as I guided in beside the other tenant's cars. I killed the buzzing diesel engine and picked up the box of CDs and tapes, but got lazy and put them back down—they could stay in the car until morning. The large duplex cast a dim shadow over most of the moonlit parking area, the light from a half-mounted light fixture gone because of a burned-out bulb.

The house seemed quiet, and there wasn't the usual greeting party of Deon and/or Yehoshua looking to be entertained. All the better, I thought. The rain had me in such a weird funk, that I didn't really feel like dealing with anyone. I grabbed my mail, walked to door thirteen, and scraped my key into the lock. Inside, the first thing that I noticed was that one corner of my shitty, acoustic-tile ceiling, the squares absorbed water from the storm and continued to drip into a plastic cup I'd strategically placed on top of a metal bookcase. All year, the quadrant of tiles slowly melted toward the floor, rotting and turning yellow, then brown. The landlord gave me some mumbo-jumbo about getting a roof guy to find the leak but he'd have to come out when it was raining, and that was the trick. I should've faxed the guy a copy of my show schedule.

I tossed the parcels onto a flowing pyre of mail that I'd eventually sort and answer when I was feeling more industrious. The only thing to do before bed was to check email and see if anything important was going on. I sat at the helm, fired up the modem, and got to my Bronze account. There were only two messages waiting, both of them mindless replies to email I fired off to people earlier in the day. The modem clicked as I dropped carrier and shut off the computer.

After prying off shoes and drenched socks, I collapsed in the unmade bed. DJing wasn't exactly manual labor, but it felt good to lay on my back and stare at the slowly atrophying ceiling above me. The show ran through my mind: the order I played songs, the parts I flubbed, the quality of the news segments. I wanted to perfect everything, but in less than 20 hours, I'd be back on the mic again. And I had a lot of other things to worry about in the next 20 hours.

Heavy sigh. I didn't feel depressed, but a strange solitude ran through me. It was only a few steps removed from the feeling you get when a job is finally done, but you don't feel any closure from it. Maybe it was the rain, maybe it was Amy. I felt like there was something I should be doing, but I didn't want to get up from the bed. All I could do is feel the heaviness, the hollowness in my chest, and...Take a heavy sigh.

I peeled off my shirt and pants and threw them down onto the pile of dirty clothes on the floor. After my nightly dose of lith, I clicked off the light, got back into bed, and pushed back the sheets so my skin could feel the humid air and ozone in the darkness. I stared at the ceiling, wide awake.

One of my worst habits was interrupting the peaceful, worry-free period in the morning right when I woke up, and filling it with sheer terror and paranoia about my worst worries. Wednesday morning, the focus was that I only had until Friday to make the deposit for the apartment for another year, and because I left Dial America and was too sick to get another job, I didn't have any of the money. My scholarship money hadn't materialized, and there was no chance my parents would give me the cash. I needed to call the scholarship board and find out my fate.

I got out of bed, and stared at the phone for what seemed like an hour before digging out the BrassCo phone number. The whole procedure would be a tad less embarrassing if I hadn't worked there the summer before. Now, instead of dealing with an anonymous entity like the financial aid office, I was speaking with the place where I went to the summer picnic the year, and packed boxes full of copper tubing pieces for three months straight.

I dialed the number, and got transferred nine times, having to tell my sob story, complete with grades and GPA numbers nine times. After each repetition, my intestines wound around themselves again, and I wondered how much blood I'd shit after getting off the phone. After an eternity of the religious lite-FM radio station, I got transferred to an accounting droid that I'd have to send in a transcript for Summer II, and then they'd make a decision and cut the check. They hung up as quickly as possible after the kamikaze explosion hit, and I sat on the floor with phone still in hand, unable to move.

Fucking great. No check. Well, there could be a check in September, but I'd be on the street by then. I gambled everything on that fucking money: my apartment, my tuition, my books, even my groceries for the next few weeks. I needed that money, and now there was no way in fuck for me to get it.

I put down the phone and crawled in bed, hoping for a sudden heart attack or airliner to crash into the house and destroy me. No such luck. I tried to think of any other options to gather the cash. Short of selling my car and all of my CDs, which would be impossible in Bloomington and still wouldn't scrape together enough for my rent, I had no idea what to do. I had to start thinking about my long shots and last hopes. Who owed me money? Nobody. Who owed me favors?

I picked up the phone again, and called Peter. Last time we talked, he'd been making decent money, and had a surplus above his school payments for next fall. I helped him out last year once when his cash situation was fucked, so maybe it would work out again this time.

I talked to one of his sisters, who bounced me to a number in Goshen where he was temporarily staying. I gave the number a dial, and he picked up on the third ring.

"Hey Peter, what's up? It's John."

"John! What the fuck happened to you? You sound like shit!" he said. "What's wrong?"

"Look, my situation here has totally come to a head. Can I ask you a massive favor?"

"Yeah, yeah!" he said, "What do you need?"

"What's your money situation like right now?"

"I totally paid off the school for fall, and I've got some money sitting in the bank until winter term comes up. Why?"

"Look, I need to borrow $400 for my apartment deposit. My scholarship hasn't come through, and I'm fucked in a big way if I can't pay this fast."

"Yeah, I can definitely loan you the money. I can send it down there registered. When does it need to be there?"

"Friday, but I think I can stall until Monday. I was thinking about coming up for the weekend, for the required parental visit."

"Shit man, I'm house-sitting at this totally cool place in Goshen. Why don't you stay here?"

"You mind company? I don't want to impose."

"Fuck, you can stay here. I can cook us up some food, we can get some beers, hang out and stuff. Get a pen, and I'll give you directions to the new place."

I scribbled out a map from Peter's dictation, and we agreed on a time to meet that Friday. I thanked him profusely for the help, and we hung up. At least that's taken care of, I thought. Now I'd be able to worry about Amy full-time.

When I arrived at the station after a McDonald's dinner Thursday night, the cheap wooden door was already open, its heavy lock box undone already. Before I even walked in, the sound of the new Nirvana album blared from the studio. I crept in past the vinyl room and its stacks of ancient, dusty, unused records.

"And that was 'Lithium,' by Nirvana," Sid said. "Speaking of lithium, John Conner is in the studio, getting ready for his show."

"Ha. Ha ha. Pretty funny, poserboy," I half-laughed sarcastically. "Make yourself useful and throw on one of those Sloppy Seconds singles you have," I said.

"Well dude, after this Ministry cut, its all yours," Sid said, as he grabbed a stack of vinyl singles and carefully stashed them in a brown paper grocery bag.

After Sid left, I ran through the usual news and concert dates, and started assaulting the airwaves with Unleashed, Desultory, Malevolent Creation and Obituary. I tightened up the playlist, and reduced the chatter between songs to blitzkrieg as much raw energy as I could. Listening to Death Metal with this much volume and power was my only weapon against the loneliness of being in the studio by myself. I temporarily forgot everything I didn't want to dwell on, but it slowly came back, as the music became more routine. And I knew in a few hours, I'd be wandering in the rain and darkness, wishing everything with Amy could be just slightly more in my favor.

I sat in the window, while the last hour of the show approached. With my right leg dangling over the edge, I thought about how to wind down the show and step back into my boring and sometimes confusing life. I wanted it to be Sunday again, to sleep with her in my arms. And I didn't want to go to Elkhart for the weekend and miss another chance with her. But even though I felt she could be my closest friend in the world, my paranoia made me think I somehow screwed everything up by getting too close.

A clap of thunder echoed across the buildings. The thick clouds overhead started to drop streams of rain down on the streets again. The view of rainstorm starting over the city was great, but all I could think of was carrying all of my crap back to the car in the summer rain. Again.

39

The sun trickled through the window while I tried to memorize what made up the Gross National Product from the econ workbook. This is going to look pretty stupid someday, I thought. It was my third attempt at remembering an essentially trivial formula, and the third time I tried to stay up all night and burn it in my head hours before the final. I couldn't even study it all the way through in a straight shot; at least twice an hour, I would crank over the computer, check my mail (there would be none) and then try to find something to do, to waste my last few moments of time before the exam.

It wasn't clear whether or not this test would completely kill me. Since the polysci class last summer session brought be back to a 2.0, I just needed to keep balanced this session. I had a good feeling about the English class, and it had to be worth an A or B. That meant econ would have to pull about a D. Maybe I'd remember enough of this from the last two times. Maybe it would be multiple choice.

I was riding the caffeine wave of the summer, and I knew I was about 12 ounces of Coke away from crashing hard. I needed to keep going, but I already knew the fridge was devoid of any further soft drinks. I paced the room for a second, checked my wallet for cash, and hit the door.

The reddish light of dawn and the almost cool temperature outside reminded me of the time I walked back from Carrie's in the morning, half hung over with my contacts fused to my eyeballs. That evening seemed so long ago—was that even this summer, I thought? It felt like years before. I stumbled across Atwater, and toward Third and Jordan.

The infrared sensor buzzed as I walked through the front doors of the VP. Behind the counter, the clerk sat against the register and read a copy of the Ad Sheet.

"Hey man, you're up early," he said, not looking up from the paper.

I walked over to the wall-to-wall cooler, opened a glass door, and pulled out a cold two-liter of Coke. "I've been up all night," I said. "I've got an econ final in a couple hours."

"Good luck man, I hope you don't fall asleep. I did that once. I stayed up all night, taking NoDoz and drinking pots of coffee. It was for a calculus final. I fell asleep an hour before the test. I was out for like 18 hours."

"That sucks," I said. "I think I'll make it, though." I grabbed a pack of Hostess mini-donuts from a rack, and put everything on the counter. "I've got to drive to Elkhart later tonight, though. That's gonna kill me."

He punched the keys of the register. "If you take a nap, make sure it's longer than three hours. Otherwise it's not worth it," he said. "That's $2.09. You need a bag?"

"No, I'm cool." I dug out some change and two bucks, and slapped them on the counter.

"Take it easy man," he said. "Have a good trip."

"Thanks." I grabbed the stuff and headed out the door.

On the way home, I thought about the odd fact that at that exact hour, Amy was probably getting ready to go to class. Then I remembered she was wasn't going to class—she was moving into a new place that afternoon. Maybe I could catch her for lunch after the final, I thought.

It became more difficult to get her out of my mind and think about anything else lately. I knew that I'd soon need some definition or clarity from her in the relationship, or I'd need to get out. No sense in having a half-broken thing with her when a new infusion of freshman chicks was just weeks away, I thought. It sounded pig-headed, but I couldn't stand on one leg forever.

I couldn't stay awake forever, either. I got home, took a quick look at my econ notes, and realized this whole plan wouldn't work. I needed a couple of hours of sleep before this test, or at least before the drive to Elkhart. I put the Coke in the fridge, and did some quick math. I could sleep three hours, take a shower, and make it to the test. Just to make sure I didn't snooze-alarm my way into a fatal situation, I set my alarm clock across the room, which would require me to get out of bed. Then I put my computer chair right in the middle of the room, meaning that I would trip over it while trying to shut off the alarm, stubbing my toes and bruising my shins, also causing me to wake up faster. I also took a roll of tape and taped the alarm's "on" switch into position, which would require me to spend ten minutes disarming the piece of shit while it blared its siren at me.

I got everything in place, turned my fan on high, and got into bed. I was unconscious about 15 seconds later.

After what felt like another 15 seconds, the alarm started blaring its klaxon at full volume. I jumped from bed, charged across the room, almost impaled myself on the wooden chair, and tore at the tape blindly until I got the damn thing off. Not only did I never enter a dreamstate during the three hour nap, I don't think I even moved. I frantically checked both the clock and my watch to see what time and what day it was. I still had an hour and a half before the final, plus the two-liter and donuts for breakfast. This might work after all, I thought. I grabbed my stuff and went to take a shower.

I almost ran to Ballantine after another 45 minutes of intense studying, hoping I wouldn't forget the goddamned GNP formula before I got to class. Finals week always provided a strange outdoor scene. During the fifteen-minute schedule breaks, a steady stream of people flowed from building to building. But during the marathon finals blocks, the pathways would almost be empty. I knew in a few more days, the campus would be this barren all the time, until classes started again.

I climbed the stairs to the fourth floor, grabbed a seat in the back, and hoped none of the regular attendees noticed that I was there for about the fourth time all session. From the looks of a few other people in the back, I wasn't the only one in this situation. I kept at my book, and tried to force the last few pieces of information into my brain before the test began. I hoped that the teacher didn't stray too much from the text during his lectures.

The Michael J. Fox lookalike teacher came in, with a stack of photocopied tests. I ditched my books, got out my pencils, and prepared for the onslaught. The papers made their way down the rows, and I nervously awaited my fate. "You'll have ninety minutes to finish the test," he said. "But you probably won't need all of it. If there are any questions, let me know."

I got my test, handed the rest back, and got to work. I prayed for multiple choice, but this was a mixed bag, also containing some fill in the blank and a couple of draw-a-graph type problems. I got on it, hoping I could bullshit this one.

A half-hour later, I walked out of Ballantine, the summer session complete. I didn't know a damn thing on the test, even with the studying. But I knew that a supply/demand curve would always get some partial credit, and Doc Hollywood didn't look like he'd be that tough of a grader. With a good curve, I'd at least hit a D. Now, I had a fat paycheck waiting for me, an empty day ahead of me, and a roadtrip later in the evening. I headed toward the library to get my cash.

After walking the grand circuit of the main library, the bank, and Garcia's pizza for lunch, I walked back to 414 and prepared for a heavy-duty nap. Once inside the front door, I went to get my mail inside, where I saw the landlady talking to Yehoshua.

"Oh, there you are," she said. "I was just looking for you about your lease. Are you re-signing for next year?"

"Yeah, I am."

"I'm going to need you to pay your deposit by today to keep the room."

Fuck. Without Peter's money, I couldn't do this. I got my biggest paycheck of the summer from UCS, but I was still at least $150 short, even if I gave up my food money for the rest of the month. "I don't have the money today, I'm going home this weekend to get it. Is there any way I could write you a postdated check today?"

"Yeah, I'm sure we could do that," she said.

"Okay, hang on, let me get my checkbook."

I hope Peter comes through, I thought. I ran back to my bedroom, noticed a message on the machine, and grabbed by checks and a pen. Back at the mantelpiece of mail, I scrawled out a rubber check, tore it out, and handed it to her.

"There you go," I said. "Thanks for letting me do this. I haven't been able to get home because of finals and everything."

"That's no problem." She pulled out some yellow triplicate papers from a binder. "I've got your lease here. It's the same as last year, I just need you to sign it."

"Sure thing." I took a quick read, and noticed that it was the same exact paperwork as before, except for the date. I jotted my signature on the bottom, and handed it back to her.

She tore off the top copy and handed it back. "Okay, it looks like we're all set. Thanks a lot—have a good trip this weekend."

"Thanks again," I said. I took the lease, and headed back to my room.

I clicked the play button on the answering machine. "Hi, it's me," said the message, from Amy. "I'm home getting grimy, packing boxes, and cleaning stuff. If you're alive after your final, give me a call."

I didn't feel like calling—I didn't even feel like staying awake for another minute, but I wanted to hear from her. I picked up the phone, sat on the floor, and gave her a ring at home. On the fourth ring, she picked up.

"Hey, where were you?" I asked.

"I've only got one phone in the kitchen. Everything else is in boxes. How was the test?"

"I'm not gonna blow the top of the curve for everyone else," I said. "At least it's over. I feel like shit though. I'm running on about three hours of sleep."

"Do you want to come over for lunch? I look like hell, but we could get some sandwiches and come back here and eat on the patio or something."

"I'm feeling pretty screwed up right now. I think it's sleep deprivation, or stress, or something."

"Why don't you take a nap, get some rest?"

"I've gotta make this damn drive to Elkhart. I'm afraid if I pass out, I won't wake up until tomorrow."

"Poor baby—get some rest, you'll be okay. I'm going to get back to work, but call me if you need anything, okay?"

"Okay," I said. "I should be okay."

"If I don't hear from you, I'll talk to you Sunday."

"Okay, good luck on the move."

We hung up, and I tried not to think about anything but sleep.

The post-dated check bugged the hell out of me. I should've told the landlady to go fuck herself, but I knew that if I got the weekend out of her, something else would happen and delay the cash from Peter even more. Now that I was relying on the money to be there this weekend, it was like I almost knew something would happen and it wouldn't. I expected the car to blow up, some accident or illness to keep me in town, or some financial disaster on his end.

Money, money, money. I had a few bucks in my pocket, but that would all go in my gas tank for the trip north, plus some cash in the bank for groceries and to make it through the pay period. Maybe it was the lack of sleep, but all I could think of while sitting on my bedroom floor was cash. I'd been hustling all summer, and now it was down to the line. I fooled the scholarship board twice before, but I didn't think it would go through the third time. And no tuition money meant dealing with parents and their conditionality. It's easy to change majors and do what you want to do when it's on your dime. But with them bitching about the bill, it only meant more stress.

And I hadn't even told them about this latest eighty buck a month prescription. They never understood the depression or the medication. Every time I got onto something new, my mom asked if it was an upper or a downer. They thought antidepressant meant speed or goofballs or something. And they also thought each prescription was a temporary thing, like a round of antibiotics for a bad cold. They always asked when I would be "done" or "better," and I always explained that it didn't work like that. Fuck, I was just glad I wasn't a diabetic or something. I had to float so many of my prescriptions when I had zero cash—if it would've been insulin, I never would've made it past my first year of college alive.

The rush of thoughts ran my body out of control. My breathing went from heavy to hyperventilating and I couldn't slow it down. I looked around the room, found an empty paper bag, and started breathing into it, to slow things down. I curled up on the floor, the blood pounding through my temples, and tried to think of anything else to get me away from the stress and depression.

Before I took off my shoes and crashed, I set the alarm for 4:00, knowing I'd be out cold before I even hit the bed. Between the late night with econ and the day's stress, my body was in knots. I got in bed and started to make a mental checklist of stuff to do in preparation for my trip back to Elkhart. I passed out after thinking about the first item, fueling up the car.

The alarm jarred me from a sleep so heavy, I didn't know if it was day or night, even with sunlight creeping through the blinds. I didn't even know why I was waking. For a few moments, I was stuck thinking I had to go to class, or maybe to the factories. I stared at the 4:00 on the clock and still didn't know what the hell was going on. The two-odd hours of sleep were thick and dream-free, and I couldn't shake the sludge from my brain. But it felt good—I knew that after a Coke or two, the four hours on the road would be no problem.

I packed quickly—a couple shirts, a couple pairs of jeans, clean underwear and socks, and all of the medicine and toiletries I'd need to survive until Sunday. I pulled a few CDs from the rack, and froze at the stack of demo cassettes, trying to figure out what I needed for the road and what Nick hadn't heard yet. I dumped everything into my gym bag, grabbed a pillow just in case Peter didn't have extras, and headed out.

After a quick stop on the north side of town for a tank of diesel and the biggest cold Coke they had, the VW hummed north on 37, on the part of the road that always reminded me of the movie *Breaking Away*. The fields of crops were now golden, and in the process of getting mowed down acres at a time by huge farm equipment. I cracked open the sunroof and kept my eyes on the road, even though I was still trying to awaken from my nap. I knew traffic would start to get heavy, and I'd probably hit Indianapolis just after five. Great fucking timing.

This was probably my quickest planned trip up north, I thought. The summer before, when I dated Lauren and went to Bloomington every few weeks, I made many visits on the drop of a hat. But I had enough gear stashed away at her place that I could stay there a whole weekend without bringing much more than my meds. It was such a regulated system, that it didn't require much thought. But during the school year, whenever I went home for a break or a holiday, I had the whole thing planned the week before. This time I just knew I needed to make the trip, and I left.

Why was I going home? I needed to pick up that check from Peter. And I wanted to hang out with him, since I didn't make it to Elkhart all summer. There was also some sort of parental guilt, like it was required for me to see them between each school term. I didn't need to beg them for money, and I didn't need to crash there for a week or two like when I was a freshman and they kicked us out of the dorms during the Christmas break. Seeing them would be an incidental.

And I wouldn't see them much. Since I'd stay at Peter's, I'd only make a quick visit, maybe on Sunday. It would be cold, impersonal, and either they'd be glad to see me and they'd avoid talking about bullshit like money and grades, or I'd leave. Since I wouldn't be staying in their house and eating their food and using their phone and everything else, the pressure would be off, I hoped.

My last trip home seemed like it happened ten years ago—Tammy, deciding to stay for the summer, my last trip to Elkhart. 1992 was no longer a year or an era; it felt like I had to further divide it. Thinking of both Tammy and Amy in the same year was like thinking about Napoleon and aircraft carriers in the same time and place—the two seemed so radically different. And when I thought about Lauren AND Tammy AND Amy all happening in the same year, it seemed impossible. What if Amy didn't work out, and I was single again soon? I imagined a TV infomercial announcer saying "But wait, there's more!"

I kept driving on 37, closer to Indy, and downed the last of my Coke.

The red and white smokestack appeared on the horizon, but I already knew I was close to Indianapolis by the traffic. It felt like I was going into the belly of the beast, with the cars packing closer together and slowing down. Hopefully, the loop around town on I-465 would provide some relief, I thought. I changed to my trusty copy of Motörhead's *1916*, and kept at it.

Normally, I'd pull into a truck stop on the south side of town to refill the tiny bit of fuel I already used. I could make it from Bloomington to Elkhart and back on a single tank, but if I did a lot of driving in Elkhart, the extra gallon or so would help. It was more of a ritual than anything else, a place to stop, use the can, grab another Coke, and stretch out. Plus, I'd go across the street to McDonald's and grab a burger for the road. But I wanted to make good time, and Peter said he'd have dinner ready for me.

My stomach was just starting to relax from the caffeine overdose of last night, and it was hitting me that I ate nothing more than the pack of donuts today. But, I'd forego my hunger, and maybe stop at the halfway point north of Kokomo for that second drink and bathroom break.

I pulled through the on-ramp to 465 without incident, although it looked like the inlets were stacked pretty deep with cars trying to commute home. I hit the highway with as much speed as I could edge from the VW and took off like a bat out of hell, whining through the gears and edging to the outer lanes. Although 465 got a lot of use, it always seemed like at least one lane was wide open, and traffic almost never came to a complete stop. I hoped this trend would continue, and pushed my car to about 75.

By the time I got past the airport and Speedway and into the lazy drive through Northwest Indy, the traffic thinned out and I felt awake enough to stop paying attention and drop into autopilot. I did feel more awake than I did a bit over an hour ago, when the alarm brought me back from the dead. And most of the stress-related coronary bullshit from earlier seemed to be gone. It felt good to cruise 465 with Motörhead in the player and the small rectangle of sunroof opened to the sunny skies above. I relaxed, and let the road slide under me.

When I cruised the north side of Indy, I wondered where Amy's parents lived. Amy...I still wasn't sure what the hell was going on with her. Every time I convinced myself that she had no interest in me or a relationship, she did something that made me think she wanted to spend the rest of her life with me. I was too used to running with 19 year old airheads that were very binary in their feelings for you—either their legs were spread open, or their boyfriends were beating the shit out of you because you emailed them too much. Amy told me how she felt, a new situation for me. But I didn't always feel comfortable asking about the truth.

I knew she wouldn't jump into something with me after her last relationship. What a mindfuck—dating the same guy since she was practically a kid. She didn't seem the type—she was so together, sophisticated. But how could I go next after such a long relationship? I was about as opposite from him as a person could be. Maybe that's why she kept talking to me.

It wasn't that I didn't know if I liked her. I did; maybe I even loved her. I felt the same kind of spark I felt with Tammy months before, the kind of feeling that extinguishes everything else and tells every cell of your body that nothing's wrong. I was completely infatuated with Amy before the first kiss, when I thought I had no chance and I was just chasing her to injure myself even more. But now, maybe there was a chance.

Either way, it bugged the fuck out of me. When I thought that she loved me, I also thought she'd transfer to another school. When I thought she'd stay, I'd realize that I probably couldn't corral her into a long-term relationship. I couldn't win. I could just try to focus on any evidence that she did care about me, and keep my eyes on the road.

Kokomo came up fast, but the Friday night rush hour traffic slowed me down to a crawl during the dozen or so stoplights on the alleged US 31 bypass. I looked out the window at the rows of fast food joints, and severely craved a Beef, Bacon and Cheddar from the Rax roast beef restaurants. But Peter promised dinner, and I kept at the traffic.

After fifteen minutes, things lightened up, and the real jump northward on 31 started. Bored of the sound of wind, I cranked shut the sunroof, and swapped in the latest Judas Priest tape. This was where the boring part begins.

It's amazing how a loud diesel engine and an hour and a half of straight, empty blacktop can make you disassemble, inspect, and reassemble every individual component of your mind several times, revealing every flaw, imperfection, and possible upgrade. I couldn't avoid thinking about Amy, comparing her to Tammy, wondering if she was the last woman I'd ever want to date (both in the good and bad way) and what aspects of my life, depression, studies, career and hobbies would impact her role in my life.

Pretty heady stuff, but this type of low-level introspection is something I've mastered after years of factory jobs and boring weekends. I spent a good deal of the drive through Peru and Grissom trying to reconcile a summer where I missed every single intended goal. I didn't visit Tammy, or save money, or fix the Rabbit, or save the scholarship, or do any amount of computer programming. I guess I did pass my classes and get back into school, but how could I explain this scorecard to a parent or a scholarship board?

I dug around for a Jello Biafra spoken word tape for almost 40 minutes, and tried to push the double-bind dialogue out of my head. Someday, I thought, all of this is going to seem stupid and life will be okay.

The 90-minute spin across nothingness slowly pulled me out of the no-man's land of central Indiana. I hauled out of the cornfields, past the Culver military academy and toward Plymouth. This trip, I wouldn't take the brand new US 20 bypass into Elkhart. Instead, I'd break east on US 6, and then take 19 and 119 into Goshen. It probably only saved me a few minutes, but it would mean leaving the current road a little bit earlier, which would seem a lot faster. Before the bypass, this was the preferred route to Elkhart, although it was all two-lane roads with lots of oncoming traffic, and I'd always get behind some idiot going 30.

Civilization finally appeared for a brief moment at the intersection of 31 and 6, in the form of gas stations and mini-marts. I thought about making a quick stop and getting some cheap diesel, but decided to hang the right onto 6 and keep barreling toward Goshen. There were many fond memories of those 24-hour plazas, their coolers full of Coke and racks full of cheap cutout tapes. Many a time the summer before, I dumped some fuel in the tank, took a quick piss, and picked up a copy of *Sabbath Bloody Sabbath* on tape for $3, along with a big bottle of Coke and some junk food for later.

Traffic didn't look bad on US 6. It amazed me that forty years before, every major superhighway was as small and shitty as this concrete death-trap. Just give me a half an hour, I thought. Thirty miles and I could let the VW cool off, and finally get something to eat.

40

The VW hurtled down State Road 119 in the dusk sky, toward the tiny city of Goshen. With Queensrÿche's *Empire* in the player, I smoothed the folded up map of instructions Peter gave me on the phone and tried to visualize where I'd need to turn off. The house was in the area near the college and right on Main Street, which wouldn't be too tough to find.

It felt weird to be cruising down 119 again. Two summers ago, I worked at BrassCo in Goshen, with my dad. Every morning I took a shortcut during my drive in from Elkhart, and followed the last part of the same two-lane route on some days. My drive totally depended on if there were trains blocking my path. Either way, I was so asleep every morning, I drove the dozen or so miles without even realizing it.

Although it was the county seat, the city of Goshen wasn't much more than a small satellite of Elkhart located about ten minutes south on US 33. The metropolis consisted of two intersecting streets, an industrial park, a Wal-Mart, and maybe ten thousand people. Goshen College, a Mennonite school, ran on the south end of campus. But with the puritan attitude of its students and administration, the usual bars and activities of a college campus weren't around. Peter went to school there because he got some decent scholarships, and he liked the small theatre program. I spent some time there a few years back when a former girlfriend lived near the campus in a sublet. Although I'd never purposely planned to be there, I found myself hanging out in Goshen a fair amount in the last couple of years.

The road came to an end at Main Street, and I hung a left. This was the area before the typical "Main Street" two-story brick storefronts and streetlamps—mostly shaker-style homes and the occasional gas station populated the road. Within moments I found the street address—a small, two-story house just like every other one for miles. I swung into the drive, and saw a familiar figure sitting on the porch of the house.

"Johnnn!" Peter set down his beer and jumped from the lawn chair, running to the car. "You made it, man!"

I powered down the car and extricated myself from the tiny cockpit. "Hey man. This place looks great!" I said.

"Yeah, and it's free! This house-sitting crap is very cool. Lemme help you with your stuff."

"Sure, thanks, man. This is a hell of a deal," I said. "Sure beats the parents."

"No shit," he said. I unlocked the hatch and pulled out my duffel bag and pillow out of the car. "I did the parent thing until the end of July, while I was at the factory. What a fucking nightmare."

"I'm glad for once I missed it."

"Lucky bastard," he said. "Come on inside, I'll get you something to drink."

We dragged my gear up the porch steps and inside. The place was half of a small house, one of the types that was built 80 years ago so all the staircases were only two feet wide and you could barely walk in the tiny kitchen and bathroom. But the solid wooden floors and nine-foot ceilings reminded me this wasn't suburbia.

From the few clues I got, it looked like Joe was the Tokyo cowboy type, or maybe the far East James Dean poseur. He had a motorcycle out front, and pictures on the fridge of him in full leathers, long jet-black hair down to his ass sitting on this Kawasaki like a new-age Marlon Brando or something. Nothing wrong with that, I thought it was pretty cool to see a mix of this nostalgia thrown in with the traditional Japanese influence on the place.

"Man, this place is far out," I said. "I take it Joe's from Japan originally?"

"Yeah," Peter said. "He's just a student here. He goes back every year for a month or so."

I tossed my bags in the living room, and took another look around. The apartment looked like a gray-market importer's wet dream. High-end Sony audio equipment with all-Japanese characters on the dials and switches littered the place, probably stuff he got for almost nothing over in Japan, but it kicked ass over the most expensive rig you could buy in the states. I saw a word processor on the floor that looked pretty high tech. I opened the lid and saw it was actually for typing in Japanese or English. I randomly plunked on this totally random Kanji keyboard that had some weird system of five or ten shift keys, and an LCD display lit up with perfectly formed characters. I didn't even know they made something like that, outside of the movie *Blade Runner*. And to contrast all of the high-tech stuff, some beautiful Japanese art covered the walls, between pictures of the Budweiser girls and Harley hogs. Beautiful.

"Hey, before I forget, I have something that should calm you down a bit," Peter said. He walked in and handed me a check for my rent.

"Hey! Holy shit, thanks a million man."

"Just get it back to me whenever you can, after your scholarship bullshit settles down."

"Okay man. You're a lifesaver—the fucking landlord was on my case this morning about it. This does calm me down greatly..." I carefully put the check in my bag with my checkbook so I wouldn't misplace it.

"Hey, how about that drink?" he said. He reached into the fridge and grabbed a cold Coke. "Here, I went to the gas station and got some of these, I know you're an addict," he said, handing me the condensation-covered can. I clicked open the tab and chugged back the drink, sweeping out the taste of diesel and road heat and replacing it with the smooth coolness of the cola.

"Thanks, that hits the fuckin' spot," I said relaxing against the staircase in the living room. "Man, it sure is good to see you again."

"I'm glad I could get you back up here."

"Well thanks for the place to stay, I appreciate it."

"Anything to help you escape the parentals. Thank Joe for the pad though, I'm lucky to get the house-sitting gig. What do you think of this place?"

"Pretty fuckin' cool," I said, finishing another hit of Coke. "It'd be cool to have a place like this, full-time. Sure beats the dump I've got now."

"Yeah, from what you say, it sounds like a real hole. But at least you got out this summer."

I sat down on one of the futons in the living room, and he followed suit. "Yeah, I don't know. It was nice to get out, but there were so many problems."

"Dude, you survived. And you'll be back in school this fall. You're not trapped, you avoided the factories, and you missed the parents. You won."

"Yeah, but I feel like I lost, too. I mean, the depression, the loneliness, the money, I don't think I gained any ground on any of that stuff."

"But you're still alive. And you've still got everything ahead of you. No worries."

"Yeah, maybe. We'll see what happens..."

I got acclimated and checked out the apartment a bit more, while Peter started on one of his kick-ass Chinese meals. "I cook this stuff almost every day," he says. "Joe's got a high-end rice steamer and all of the other tools, and I learned all of this great recipes in China. It's a hell of a lot cheaper than eating at McDonald's. And there's nothing else in this fucking city."

"Are you still working at the soda shop?" I asked. During school, Peter bussed tables at a retro soda fountain place just off of campus. It wasn't the best pay in the world, but there weren't many options in a town like Goshen.

"Yeah, that's all I'm doing until school starts," he said. "Thirty, forty hours a week. I've actually got a shift tomorrow night, so I don't know what the plan is there."

"That's cool," I said. "I've got stuff to take care of—I'll probably run into South Bend."

"Are you going to hook up with Nick?"

"Yeah, maybe. I haven't talked to him about it yet."

"Captain brutality," he scoffed. "Has he calmed down any lately?"

"Not really. He's okay, though."

"Yeah, well..." I knew I wasn't going to win Peter over on Nick—we'd all known each other for years, and even though I grew closer to both of them, they drifted further apart.

"Hey, when are you seeing your parents?" he asked.

"At the last second," I said. "Maybe Sunday afternoon. It will be a quick mission."

"That's cool. Hey, can you drink? I was thinking we could go to the pub later."

"The pub's okay, but I can't drink anything—new medicine."

"That's right. How is that shit going?"

"I got really sick, but that's gone now. I might have to go off of it though. I'm talking to the doctor about it on Monday."

"Why, what's up?"

"I keep getting really bad headaches and nausea. And I'm not sure it's totally helping. I mean, I don't feel like my mind has gone completely fucking sideways, especially with all of the shit going on right now, but I don't feel like it's a miracle cure, especially with the side effects."

"That's fucked up man," he said. "I hope it works out. Hey, I'm about done with the food, you wanna grab a plate?"

I got up from the futon and went to the kitchen. The delicious smell of Hunan beef and stir-fried vegetables filled the room. "Damn, this shit smells good," I said. "At least you learned something in China," I said.

He scooped some rice onto his place from the cooker, which was also labeled in Japanese. "I learned how to take showers with no hot water, and I learned you're the fucking slowest person in the world in answering their letters."

"Shit man, you shoulda had email," I said. I piled my plate with food, and grabbed another Coke from the fridge. "Are we eating in the living room?" I said.

"Sure, grab a seat in there," he said, grabbing another cold beer.

"I appreciate everything here," I said. "I mean, the food, the place..."

"Shit, stop thanking me," he said. "You've been around for much worse times. Plus you've been my fucking chauffeur since 1987."

"True..." I shoveled in some food, and it tasted as good as it smelled. "This is some good shit," I said, my mouth still full.

"Thanks," he said. "I asked for the freshest dog meat they had," he joked.

I didn't care if it was dog meat or worse. I was so hungry, it tasted incredible. I cleaned my plate in record time, and went back to the kitchen for seconds.

After dinner, we drove into downtown Goshen, a town like something out of an old western. A single main street ran for about ten blocks, with a courthouse on a town square, and a single row of storefronts and apartment buildings. I found a place to park, and we went to the pub. It was a narrow drinking tavern squeezed between two bigger buildings, with an upstairs loft and a real bar, made of hundred year old wood and solid as steel. We found an open booth and grabbed a seat. Peter ordered a beer for himself, grabbed me a Coke, and got both of us a basket of popcorn.

"Thanks man," I said, cracking open the red can.

"No problem," he said. "So what's up with this chick you were telling me about? The older one?"

"She's not that much older, just a year. I don't really know where it's going, though."

"You fuck her yet?"

"No, close. I don't know how much closer I'll get though. It's really fucked up. I mean, I like her, she's really awesome. Great looks, great body, fun to hang out with..."

"But..."

"But I don't know. It's like we've connected, but nothing has fallen into place. I feel like I should be doing more to get things moving. Or maybe I shouldn't. I can't tell."

"You don't need to put up with that shit," he said. "Just stand your ground, let her know what you want."

"I wish it was that easy," I said. "I'm just afraid of screwing things up. I'm hoping I can either sort it out or get the just friends speech before the new shipment of freshmen."

"I hear you," he said. "At least you don't have to deal with the Mennonite factor down there. It's like roulette on this campus."

"Yeah, but they seemed a lot cooler, at least the ones I met the last time I was here. In Bloomington, the chicks can be damned vindictive. Rich parents, sororities, you know what I mean?"

"Yeah, well. Alcohol's the lowest common denominator. Find the right parties or bars, and everything else will follow."

"Maybe so," I said. "We'll see next fall."

Peter and I stayed for a couple of drinks, and then headed back to the apartment. Since all of Joe's couches were too short, I slept on the floor of the bedroom upstairs, with a sleeping bag and a couple of pillows. It reminded me of the times during my senior year, sleeping on the floor of Peter's dorm when I couldn't deal with the parents and wanted to briefly experience the college life. During those visits, everyone was Peter's best friend, and the small campus was like a warp field into an area of tolerance amid my world of horror. While everyone else in Elkhart listened to bad rap, I could vanish into a place where everyone could name the first five Yes albums and old Genesis wasn't a bad thing. It was one of the things that helped me hang on until college. And although Goshen was significantly different than Bloomington's huge campus, it was also so far removed from Elkhart that I could get lost in it forever.

The floor wasn't comfortable, but it had been a long day, and my schedule was already full tomorrow. I drifted to sleep quickly, still thinking about those first nibbles at collegiate life.

The VW burned down US 20 and toward Mishawaka, with Bolt Thrower's latest Death Metal in the deck. The two-lane road curved west, past small houses and wide-open areas of nothing. In a few minutes, I'd be hanging out with Nick, on a world destruction tour starting with Grape Road. He said to meet him at work, and we'd grab a late lunch. After he got back to his job, I'd also have some time to travel around alone and take in some nostalgia before returning to Goshen.

I called my mom before leaving Peter's, and coolly told them I was already in town and that I'd catch up with them tomorrow. She acted almost freaked out, or worried. I knew it was because I did everything on my own, and had control of the situation. It felt good, much better than the amount of bullshit I went through on my usual visits back to Elkhart.

The open spaces of US 20 turned into more businesses, including the AM General plant, with its parking lot full of Hummers. This was a different route than what I took every day last year, commuting to IUSB, but I drove in on 20 enough to remember every shop, restaurant, and small detail on the trip.

I cruised in until the road became McKinley, the big thoroughfare with fast food and strip malls everywhere. Last night's menagerie of high school flashbacks made me recall the Pizza Hut just down the road. For some reason, I used to visit that restaurant any time I was with a girl during my senior year (which was about three times.) There was an identical Pizza Hut in Elkhart, and another in Goshen, but I always seemed to end up at the same one. I hadn't learned much about women in the last three years, but I had learned.

I kicked the car right, into the shopping center past the Chuck E. Cheese and Arby's restaurants. After ditching the car in the crowded and bustling lot, I walked into the glass doors of World, passed through the alarm system panels and saw Nick at the counter, simultaneously dealing with a customer and the Jeordi CD in the store's player.

"Hey Nick, what's up?" I said, walking to the counter. "Do you have a copy of that new MC Hammer cassette single?"

"I'm going to kill you..." he said. "I'm going to beat you to death with the Ticketmaster machine..."

"Did you eat lunch yet?"

"No, I've been waiting for you. Let me finish ringing this up, and then I'll clock out."

I took a look at the racks of used CDs in the front of the store, skimming over the generic top-40 has-beens and looking for any good Death Metal. I didn't have the cash for a good spending spree, but I wanted to make sure I wasn't passing off some promo-only item that was long out of print. No such luck, though.

"Come on, let's get the hell out of here," Nick said, emerging from the back of the store with his car stereo bag in hand. "Any lunch preference?" he asked.

"Rax?" I said.

"Sure, let's go. And put down those used CDs already. You wouldn't believe how much of a profit the store makes on that shit."

We headed out to Nick's maroon Escort. Once inside the car, he unloaded the stereo into the rectangular slot in the dash, and turned on Motörhead's *1916*.

"What an album," I said. "It's got summer '91 written all over it."

"It still kicks ass though," he said, pulling the car out of the spot and nailing the gas.

"No shit," I said. "I still listen to this constantly."

"Hey, when did you get into town?"

"Last night. I'm staying out in Goshen with Peter."

"So did you see your parents yet?"

"Nope, tomorrow. I'm keeping away from them as much as possible."

"That's the way to do it," he said. After a quick zip down McKinley, he turned left into the Rax lot and found a space. He shut the car down and we went inside.

This was a Rax where me and Nick used to eat the year before, when he didn't want to go to his usual default restaurant of Subway. It hadn't changed at all, and it was mere months since we last went there, but it felt like it was decades before. I still remembered the days we split classes at IUSB, sat in the restaurant's lobby, and talked about comic books and heavy metal over roast beef sandwiches. Many crucial decisions about his zine were discussed in this red and brown eatery. It somehow made me feel good to return there and eat lunch with Nick.

We got into line in the maze of people-herding railings and waited for a cash register. "I wish I could get rid of my parents," he told me. "I thought it would get easier, but they keep making me want to buy some fucking explosives and level the place."

"I'm telling you man, move to Bloomington," I said. "Chicks everywhere. No parents. You can't go wrong."

"I'd do it in a second if it wouldn't completely destroy the zine," he said. "It would take every last cent to get down there."

"I know what you mean," I said. "Hey, when is the next issue coming out?"

"Shit man, I wish I knew. I've been so busy with summer classes, work, answering mail, helping my dad with stupid fucking errands—the other day, he woke me up at five in the morning so I could help him build a fence. A fucking fence. Can you believe that shit?"

"Jesus christ," I said. "I'm glad I don't live with my folks anymore..."

We got to the front of the line, and placed our orders. I got my usual, the BBC, and we went to grab a seat. The front of the restaurant had a glass solarium, with a wraparound view of the strip and an incredible amount of sunlight. We found a place to sit by one of the glass walls of the atrium.

"So what's up with the radio station?" he asked. "Any chance it might survive?"

"Not really," I said. "Everyone is supposed to find a sponsor for their show, to help pay the rent. I don't think anyone has one, including me."

"Shit man, I'd sponsor your show if anybody listened to it."

"That's the problem. Nobody's shelling out cash for a cable FM station. A couple of us talked about a hostile takeover, doing some other stuff to get money together to go broadcast. Like DJing parties, holding dances, promoting concerts, something like that. But there wasn't any organization, it was just a crazy idea."

"That sucks. It would be cool to broadcast whatever you wanted over the airwaves."

"It would be even cooler to do that for a year and then get a job at a real radio station."

"No shit," he said.

I dug into my food, and the sandwich was as good as I remembered. It was a throwback to my days as a kid, when it was the first non-burger place to roll into Elkhart. Now, the roast beef joint was just an occasional novelty, usually when I was back north.

"So did you get back into school?" he asked.

"Yeah, everything's cool but the money. But I think I can figure it out. What about you?"

"I'm thinking of dropping out of computer science for English. The math's killing me. I haven't given my parents the speech yet."

"Yeah, I'm thinking of going to this computer-philosophy split degree. Calculus I and II only. I have to take a bunch of logic classes though."

"Good luck on telling your parents. That seems like the toughest part to me."

I picked at my french fries, my sandwich complete. "I find it best to keep them in the dark on things," I said. "Take this scholarship thing. I might not even bring it up when I talk to them tomorrow."

"I wish it was that easy for me," he said.

"Maybe you can find your own place in South Bend."

"I've thought about it. Maybe after the next issue of the zine is out, I'll have some more money to think about it."

"That sounds cool," I said.

"Yeah, we'll see. Hey, I've gotta get back. I've only got a half hour."

I downed the last of my fries and washed them down with the rest of my Coke. We dumped our trays in the garbage, and headed for the car.

Nick drove back to the parking lot, removed his stereo, and headed back. "I've got to deal with this insanity until closing."

"Good luck with it, man. I'll give you a call when I'm back in Bloomington."

"Hail Satan. Let me know if you steal anything cool from the radio station."

"Okay, later man."

Nick vanished back into the store, and I went back to my car, for a long, time-killing drive of South Bend.

It wasn't just the Pizza Hut on McKinley; so many other parts of metropolitan South Bend reminded me of my senior year of high school. I guess that was when I first started exploring the city every weekend. It was when I didn't have a curfew, when I had my first couple of dates, where I drove when I got sick of Elkhart. Back then, I thought it was a massive city, with buildings taller than three stories, the Century Center, the Notre Dame campus, two big shopping malls. Now it was all a joke. But at the time, it provided some reliable escapism.

I cruised down Michigan, home of everything from adult bookstores to mammoth music stores to the Studebaker museum. I thought of the day I skipped school in my senior year. There was a bomb scare, and as they evacuated people before first hour, I drove west, thinking about going to Chicago for a day. Instead, I went to University Park Mall and slept in my car for a few hours. Then I walked the streets of South Bend, like some scaled down version of *Ferris Bueller's Day Off.*

And my prom was at Century Center, a huge, multi-leveled convention center used for trade shows, business seminars, and of course, proms. I brought a girl I liked from my piano class. By the day of the event, we couldn't stand each other. But driving past the center brought back all of the memories of a time that seemed decades ago.

I drove to the mall, and walked the concourses for an hour or so. I also went to Notre Dame, and walked across the campus for a while. It seemed so small compared to Bloomington. I remembered back in high school when I would wander around and get lost, wondering how students knew how to get from one place to another on time. Now, even though it was beautiful, it wasn't stunning. And where were all the people? Notre Dame students must never leave their rooms.

The random drive continued. I buzzed the old IUSB campus, went to Scottsdale, and then headed back to Elkhart. By nightfall, the memories became boring, or at least the driving did. I pointed the car back at US 33 and headed back to Goshen for the night.

I woke up before ten, and took a shower while Peter slept. Outside, the sun danced and made it far too nice of a lazy Sunday to deal with my parents. But I had to see them before I left. Actually, I didn't even know why I needed to see them, or why I had to make these visits every semester. They never came to Bloomington, and I probably wouldn't need to show up and beg for money anymore. Holidays became less and less of an issue as my extended family scattered and never held centralized gatherings. The death of my grandmother pretty much ended the Christmas dinners I knew since I was a child. I liked to see Peter and Nick, but they would have more fun visiting me at IU. Everything else was a distant ghost to me. Maybe I'd stop coming back every semester, I thought. Maybe there was no need.

"Did you get everything out of the bathroom?" Peter said.

"Yeah, I'm all packed up, I think." At my feet in the living room, my trusty duffel bag held the weekends' worth of gear. "Now I've just got to deal with THEM," I said.

"Don't sweat it, man," he said. "At least you aren't asking for money."

"True," I said. "But there's still this fear in my gut..."

"I know what you mean," he said.

"Hey, thanks again for letting me hang out here. I owe you one."

"Well I'm gonna have to get to Bloomington soon, and sleep on your floor."

"If you can find any room, you're more than welcome."

"Sounds like a deal," he said. "Here, lemme help you load up your car. I don't want you to be late or anything."

We hauled the gear and dumped it into the hatch of the VW. I opened the driver's door and climbed into the cockpit.

"Thanks a million again," I said. "I really appreciate everything, man."

"No problem. So when do I see you again?"

"Christmas? I wish I could stay down in Bloomington for the holiday, and shuttle you downstate. I'm getting sick of coming back to this ghost town."

"I'm almost done here," he said. "Maybe someday we'll be in the same place again."

"I'll drink to that," I said. "Okay, wish me luck."

"Break a leg, hopefully one of theirs."

I fired up the diesel engine, rolled open the window and moonroof, and shut the thin door.

"Green hell man, I'll give you a call when I'm home again."

"Green hell, dude."

I hit the gas, pulled backwards on the road, and pointed the car toward Elkhart. He stood at attention in his drive, saluting me with a goofy look on his face. I snapped him a quick return salute, then took off, laughing.

Hours later, I hurtled down US 6, away from Elkhart. Despite my worries, the parental visit went without a hitch. My mom asked me hundreds of worried, paranoid questions that I didn't answer: was I okay, was the medicine okay, did I get good grades, when would I hear about the scholarship, was my car okay, and so forth. The house had a new couch and some new wallpaper. I got a lunch out of it, and managed to escape by five.

Before dark, before supper, I reached 31 South and the first real road on the trip south. I cranked the latest Ozzy in the player, the perfect music for leaving Elkhart and returning to my home. I'd made this trip so many times before, and this was my favorite part. Back on the twin ribbon southbound, I put my right foot into the VW Rabbit, and headed for Bloomington.

41

"So, you are having problem with the Zoloft," the doctor mumbled, sitting behind his cluttered desk and fussing with my bright red medical folder.

"Yes, sort of," I replied from the deeply sunken leather seat in the psychiatrist's office. Ambivalence pretty much summed up my relationship with the little blue pill. It provided more happiness and stability than just taking lithium, and the euphoria was better than any I'd experienced with an antidepressant. But the bliss was wearing off, my moodswings were slowly returning and breakdowns were starting to happen again. Zoloft was a good Band-Aid, but I had a wound that needed sutures. Also, it made me constantly sick, shaky, gave me headaches, and most of all, it just made me feel dependent. And it cost $2 a day, a habit that really added up over a month's time. After great internal debate and discussion with Amy, I found myself in the doctor's office, trying to find another option.

"What do you mean? Does it not work?"

"A lot has been going on lately, with relationships and money and school and a bunch of stuff, and it works good with some of that. But I still get depressed under a lot of stress. And it has a lot of side effects. It worked good at first, but now its tapering off."

"What side effects were you having?"

"A lot of nausea, some tremors. Some insomnia, but that could be my schedule. A lot of problems with diarrhea, or constipation. And also some really bad headaches."

"Hmm," he paused. "I could prescribe you to another medication, longer term antidepressant that might not have the same side effect. Would you want to try?"

"I'm not going to take Prozac again, but if you have any other suggestions, I would be willing to try them."

"No, no Prozac or Zoloft. Have you tried Trazodone?"

"Yeah, it made me sleep 20 hours a day."

"Hmm..." He flipped through a large tome, scanning down the pages. "Have you had history of epilepsy? Anyone in your family?"

"No, none at all."

"Anorexia? Bulimia? Any in family?"

"Not at all."

"Head injuries with seizure? Other problems with seizure?"

"None."

"Are you taking any other medications besides the lithium?"

"No."

"We could try older medication, called Wellbutrin. One problem, that you will have to take three doses, one in the morning, one at lunchtime and one in the evening. Would that be a problem?"

"No, I don't think so."

"Okay, I will write prescriptions. Please ask pharmacist for a list of warnings and read them. There are no food restrictions, but you must not drink any alcohol when you take this, and you have to contact me if you need to take any other medications, even cold medications. Do you understand?"

"Sure."

"You will need to stop taking Zoloft today, and not take any medication except the lithium until..." he dug around the desk, found a calendar, and quickly studied it. "...until one week from Wednesday. Ten days from now."

"Okay."

"Also, I am writing a prescription for Klonapin, a muscle relaxant. If you have problems with mania, insomnia when you start this medicine, take Klonapin. I'll give you a prescription of 15, which should be enough. And make an appointment to see me again in a month, we will see how this is working for you and discuss the dosage." He scribbled on the pad. "Are you taking music classes in the summer?"

"No, I'm not."

"That is right, computer major." He finished scrawling on the paper with his fountain pen and tore off four sheets. "Here is lithium, Klonapin, morning Wellbutrin and afternoon and evening. There are different pills, the labels will explain it. Start a week from Wednesday."

"Thanks, thanks much."

"Remember, no alcohol, no other medication, see me in a month."

I walked down the hall, trying to decipher all of the sheets of paper he gave me.

"Hey Amy, it's me. How's the library?" I laid on the floor with the phone, opening the stapled top of the white paper bag from the pharmacist.

"You know, slow as usual. How was the doctor?"

"I didn't ask how he was. I was going to ask him if he was still studying cello though. Anyway, he stopped the Zoloft."

"That's good, isn't it?"

"Maybe. He put me on a different medicine that's supposed to be better for me. I'm sort of worried about it though, he just acted weird when he gave it to me."

"I thought he always acted weird."

"Yeah, but this was even weirder. He usually doesn't give me any warnings on this stuff and just hands out Prozac like candy. Today, he was telling me all sorts of things and asking me all sorts of questions first."

"What is the stuff? I'm sitting next to a wall of reference books—I could look it up."

"He said the stuff is older, it's called Wellbutrin. No generic name, I don't think."

"Okay, just a second," she said, shuffling through pages.

"Yeah, he gave me some medicine in case I..."

"John, are you sure it's Wellbutrin?"

"Yeah, I've got two bottles of it right here. Why?"

"Wellbutrin was banned by the FDA in the seventies, it was just recently re-released for limited use. They pulled it because it caused seizures in a high percentage of people."

"How many people are we talking here?"

"Well, under one percent, but even if it was only a tenth of a percent of the people and easily documentable, that's enough lawsuits to shut down a major drug firm."

"How the hell did they re-release it? Did they add something to it?"

"Nope. It says seizures correlated to epileptics, bulimics, anorexics, alcoholics, and with drug interaction. And the thing about 10 warnings saying not to mix alcohol with it. Looks like you're not drinkin' anymore, bud. Was this stuff any cheaper?"

"They charged me $80 for the first month. No wonder so many people had seizures—they looked at their bill."

"You'll survive. I'll see if I can dig up any MedLine articles for you."

"Thank you very much—you're a sweetheart."

"No problem. Hey, I'm supposed to hang out with the roommates tonight, but do you want to go to dinner tomorrow?"

"This sounds like a date..."

"It is a date," she said. "And you never know what will happen after dinner..."

"Actually I do—I've got a show. But I'd love to see you before then."

"Okay. I'll talk to you later..."

We hung up and I went to see if the mail had arrived for the day. It hadn't.

I rolled out of bed the next morning, the damned sun streaming through the windows and preventing any further sleep. The day would be longer than the night before, I thought. I'd need to kill the hours as they pulled by slowly, until Amy got out of work and I could see her again. Now that the physical precedent had been set, I missed her even more between visits. I spent all my time waiting to kiss her, hold her in my arms, hold her hand again. It was maddening torture to be away from her, and it made me wish I could have her all to myself. But I couldn't.

I pulled myself out of bed, made the usual rounds at the computer, and then hit the shower, with absolutely no plans for the afternoon.

The day ebbed on, in a series of long, random walks and too much critical self-evaluation between sessions at the computer. It felt like a dozen hours passed, even worse than a hellish Saturday with no plans or money. Every detail of the day hung through my mind. I looked at the buildings and the cars passing by as I walked across the campus and back. I knew I would regret wasting the day later. I thought about sleeping an extra ten hours just to add to my reserves, but I learned long before that you can never catch up on sleep.

I got home at five, checked the computer a few more times just for sport, and then started to put together everything for the show. Tuesdays were usually worse, because half of the new tapes were still in the car, and the other half were spread all over the room. I got my trusty cardboard box that served as a briefcase, and piled in the zines, fliers, notes, and music. The new Dismember EP spun in my CD player, while I dug around to find some random cassette. Someday, I'll have my music collection organized, I thought.

"Hey you," said Amy, standing in the doorway "Heard you had a hot date tonight..." She wore a nice, tight sundress that covered a lot of her legs but hugged her figure tight enough to keep my imagination going. She also smelled of fresh perfume, not like something she'd be wearing at the office.

"Hey..." I got up, pulled her close, and gave her a long kiss. "Yes, I have a hot date, with a sexy librarian."

"That's library technician to you, sir." She looked in at the boxes of tapes and zines sitting around my computer. "I can't believe how many people from Norway or Sweden or whatever send you tapes."

"I'm sure the post office is investigating me for mail fraud."

"So, about dinner...I think we could grab some food and get you to your show on time," she said.

"Sounds good. Any idea on where you want to eat?"

"No, but let's not sit around here talking about it though. Let's hit the road and figure out where to eat."

"I'm not sure if we'll have time to get back here and then get me to the station."

"Well, can you just pack your stuff up and throw it in my car? I can drop you off at the station after we eat, but I've got to run after that. How can you get home?"

I thought for a second. "Don't worry about it, I can walk back home. It's no big deal."

I was wearing a black t-shirt for the band Cianide, with a picture of a rotting christ hanging from a cross, the arm torn off but still nailed in. "I'm going to just grab another t-shirt real quick, okay?"

"Can I watch?" She lifted the shirt over my head and started ravaging my chest and shoulders with bites and kisses.

"We're never going to make it to dinner on time now..." I laughed, looking around the room for a clean shirt while I fought to keep my balance.

We hurtled down Third Street toward the mall. Her perfume battled it out with the Eternity I sprayed on my neck before I left the house, making the small car into some kind of cosmetics testing ground. I realized that our entire relationship would be based on the olfactory sense, and for years I'd get a raging hard-on every time I walked through a department store fragrance counter.

"So what's the plan, Stan? I mean, Amy?"

"Have you ever eaten at Billy's? It's that Tex-Mex place just before the intersection with 446?"

"I don't get out here too much," I said. "Is it any good?"

"If you like Tex-Mex, it is. Way better than Chi-Chi's."

"Fine by me," I said. "As long as I can tell the waiter that it's your birthday."

We pulled into the restaurant, a big place that looked like it was made with stones and boulders like some Southwestern adobe, even though it was built three years ago by general contractors out of plywood and lumber like any other building in town. Inside, they had the usual decor of fake Mexican paintings and rugs, with high ceilings, dim lights, and lots of unfinished timbers. We got a small table for two with only a few minutes' wait, and got menus right away.

"It looks like we shouldn't have any problem getting you to your show," she said.

"It's not a big deal if I run late," I said. "It's not like anybody's listening. If I don't show up at eight, the DJ before me either locks everything down or leaves it for the squatters to steal. It's all going to the dogs in a few weeks anyway." I eyed the menu, looking for something with steak—fajitas, pizza, anything.

"I know, it's just I don't want to impose or anything," she said. "I know your show is important to you, and I don't want you to think I'm infringing."

"Don't worry about it," I said. "I'm glad I got to see you tonight."

The waiter came around after a few minutes. Amy got the taco salad and a margarita, and I got some kind of bizarre Tex-Mex steak combo with lots of sour cream, and a Coke.

"So, how have you been?" she asked. "I mean, the new medicine and stuff?"

"It hasn't started yet. I went off the Zoloft, though. I haven't crashed heavily, but I can feel the difference. I can't wait to get back on something."

"So...I have some news," she said.

"Good or bad?"

"Both, I think." She took a drink of her margarita. "I had lunch with my grad school advisor, and talked to her about my predicament. I mean, I pretty much flat-out told her that I didn't want to be in the program at IU, and I had my sights set on Berkeley."

"Yeah, what happened?"

"Actually, she went to Berkeley, back in the seventies. But she still keeps in touch with a lot of people there. She said she could try to pull some strings, talk to some people, and maybe see about a fellowship or a teaching position or something."

"So what's the bad news?"

"All of this could fall into place faster than I thought. I mean, I was hoping for a year from this fall, but it's possible I could get out there after Christmas. And…I just don't know how you feel about this."

"Amy, just do what makes you happy." I wanted to tell her more, to get her to stay here forever, in my arms. But I knew from the Tammy experience that all I could do is watch and wait until all of this unfolded. "Once you know the facts, we'll figure out what happens next. Okay?"

She sighed. "Yeah, I guess. I just wish this was easier."

The food came out fast, mine still sizzling in the hot iron pan. It smelled great, and it felt good to be eating prime steak on a day when I thought I'd be on ramen noodles again. Not long after we got situated and ate our dinners, we had to pay up the check and hit the road. Outside, the sky raced with heavy clouds, and lightning flashed across the horizon.

"This is going to get interesting," I said. I climbed into the car, and we started back toward town.

"What time is your show over? Maybe I could pick you up later?"

"Don't worry about it. This happens every night. It will probably stop by midnight. If not, I've got an umbrella. Or I'll get Sid or somebody to drag me home."

"Are you sure it will be okay?"

"It's fine, don't worry about it. I need the walk."

By the time we got to the station, it was pouring—the kind of rain that exploded against a windshield like tiny rocks instead of water. She double-parked in front of the station, while I pulled my stuff from the back seat.

"Thanks again for the dinner," I said.

"Don't worry about it. Thanks for hanging out with me."

"No problem." I leaned over and gave her a kiss. "Have a good evening."

"Thank you. I'll talk to you tomorrow."

"Okay, later."

I bolted from the car to the front entrance of the building, with my tapes and other gear in tow. I hope the rain stops by twelve, I thought.

The downpour continued through the first two hours of my show. It almost fit, the darkness and desolation of the storm and the evil, Satanic music coming through the soundboard. If they made a movie about the show, I thought, it would HAVE to have weather like this. It was strange to listen to Dismember pounding away through the studio monitors, and then have a round of thunder that belted even louder than the Death Metal, shaking the whole building.

The weather calmed down by the end of the show. After I played my final song, read the closing announcements, and powered down the board, I had the windows open and was enjoying the fresh smell of the storm. Although I'd get wet on the walk home, the downpour no longer trapped me. I packed up my abbreviated stash of equipment, and headed out.

The streets were glazed black with the remains of the downpour, slick like bodies of water instead of asphalt. Rivers of overflow, unable to escape into the city's poorly designed storm sewers, rushed next to the sidewalks, dumping into puddles and pools at backed-up drains. With no cars on the road, and most of the strip shut down, I had all of Bloomington to myself.

I wanted to ask Amy for a ride home, to spend more time with her. But I also wanted to see this. There were times when I needed the long walk, the loneliness, just to escape. I spent a lot of my time alone, but trapped in a world where everything around me was together. It's difficult to deal with depression in a sunny, cheery world full of couples in love and people who enjoy their jobs. But in this world of darkness and nothing, it felt good to feel as bad as I did. I could revel in my darkness, with a perfect landscape behind me.

I walked down an empty Kirkwood, got out my walkman, and headed back to Mitchell Street at my own pace.

The next day slowed down even more, as I hit a no-Zoloft wall of depression. It didn't help that every spare cycle in my mind was consumed by thoughts of Amy moving across the country forever. To appease me, she promised a home-cooked dinner if I met her at her apartment after work and help her cook it, and I couldn't pass that up. I guess she felt sorry for me, because I was dead broke and practically down to my last dollar, although I did have enough frozen pizza to last me until next Friday. I hurtled down Henderson avenue in the VW, with the latest demo from the Swedish Death Metal band Desultory in the tape deck.

After a run down a hill that took me past Bloomington South High school's buildings, I brought the car down to a three-way stop just before her place. I pushed in the clutch, and when I hit the brake, the pedal went down to the floor without slowing the car down. There were other cars moving through the intersection, and my heart suddenly jumped about a hundred beats faster. I jammed the stick into second, and let the clutch tear town some of the speed. I laid on the horn and hit my emergency blinkers, and another car barely missed me as I slid through the intersection.

What the fuck? I checked all of the idiot lights on the dash, which didn't help much. There was one brake light, and it wasn't glowing. I felt like I was in an airplane disaster movie, the only passenger who didn't eat the chicken, now auguring in a 747 full of people and trying to find an open spot on the ground. Luckily, I only had a few hundred feet to go until I was at her apartment.

With more creative shifting from fourth to first, I got the car to her parking lot. I couldn't completely stop it though, and had to brace myself and take a hit as the concrete curb divider punched the car like an anchor being thrown out of a moving boat. I popped the hood, and tried to look for anything obvious. The smell of burning brake components wafted from the front rotors, and a small pool of leaking fluid seeped from near the right tire. It's probably not a temporary fluke, like overheated brake pads, I thought. Leaking fluid usually means a broken line or rotor, which meant money I didn't have.

I went inside, and found Amy boiling pasta. "Hey," I said. She turned around and kissed me, but I kept my arms away.

"Watch out," I said. "Brake fluid." I went to the sink and started scrubbing my hands.

"Something up with your car?" she said.

"Yeah, it's DOA. I think there's a broken brake caliper, or hose or something. Can I keep it here for a couple of days until I can get it to the shop?"

"Sure," she said. "We're going to be using both of our spots, but it should be okay for a few days in a guest spot. Is it serious?"

"I'm not really sure," I said. "I'll have to look at it later, and see if it's anything I can mess with." I knew that it was probably something I couldn't fix, though. It would almost certainly require dropping a big chunk of cash I didn't have.

I finished washing off my hands, and checked out the dinner.

42

After Wednesday night's dinner with Amy, I wanted to stay there with her in my arms all night. But she had work the next day, which meant she brought me home by midnight. There was nobody online. There was no fountain gathering. And I didn't even have a car, which meant no wandering drives across town or on SR 37 to beat the boredom.

This was dead week—or dead weeks, rather. The two weeks between summer session II and the beginnings of the fall semester were more vacant than one of those 80's post-nuclear apocalypse sci-fi movies. The dorms were boarded up for two weeks, as a minimal cleaning staff scrubbed and sandblasted everything down in preparation for the mad rush of students. It meant that any full-time dorm dweller had to go back to mommy and daddy for two weeks, or find some other place to live.

Even many of the full-time residents of the city vanished during the dead weeks. It was one of the few chances for faculty members with a full load of summer teaching to take a vacation. The same went for staff members and all but the lowest rung of custodial workers and rent-a-cops. Offices closed, buildings closed, and even some restaurants and shops shut down for a week.

Apartment leases were designed to fuck people into leaving during dead weeks, too. Many contracts finished right after summer II, and a lot of leases started right before the dorms opened. The only way to stay in Bloomington during the dead weeks, short of buying your own house or sleeping in the streets, was to sign two leases back to back, like I did.

I awoke alone on Thursday, and for the first time in a long time, I had absolutely nothing to do for an entire day. I knew Amy would be nowhere to be found—she had to do some off-site bullshit at the IUPUI library in Indy all day long, and planned to see her folks that evening. UCS was down to barebones staffing for the next week and half, which meant nothing there. And there were no classes. This would be my first completely empty weekday in years, maybe since I started college.

I checked my computer and took a shower, just like any other day. My mind ran through a checklist of everyone in town, or rather everyone not in town. Alex and Renee went to visit their respective parents; Sid ran off to Indy to cool out for a while; Derrick moved out, and said he'd be in another slum landlord house across town in a week or so. Donna stayed hidden at her place in Spencer; Carrie went home; Bill vanished to points unknown, and Brecken took off to Iowa to chase after his latest interest for a few weeks. Who was left? What would I do?

I got dressed, rummaged around my dresser for spare change, and got on a pair of shoes. The concept of not having a car still bothered me. Ever since the summer after my 16th birthday, I almost always had a set of wheels. A car meant independence to me. It meant that whenever my surroundings disturbed or bored me, I could find a good tape, pop it in the deck, and take a long drive into nowhere. When I lived in Elkhart, this was my only salvation. Although I hated commuting to IUSB the year before, I enjoyed having 45 minutes each way to listen to a good album and forget about my house, my parents, and everything else.

Today, I would be on foot. Unless that scholarship money showed up, I would be hoofing it for a while. I was now counting on using a couple hundred bucks of that cash to get this brake bullshit fixed on the VW. I hoped it was just the caliper or something else cheap. I needed that car back. Even though Bloomington was a nice place for pedestrians, Indiana as a whole was a very car-centric state. I used my car too much, from grocery shopping to laundry to food. When I had a staff parking pass, I even used it to drive across campus and go to classes. I didn't have my car with me during my freshman year, and I remembered how much of a bitch it was to do simple stuff like get to the mall with a crap bus pass and a ten speed as your only tools of survival. I didn't want to spend the next year like that.

With the Desultory demo in my walkman, I hit the streets looking for something to do. Despite the sunlight and beautiful day, I could feel a heavy, low-grade depression start to pull through my system. I was four days into my Zoloft fast, and the euphoria felt washed away, leaving me with the usual, depressed me. I had another six days to wait until I could start the new stuff, presumably so the two wouldn't mix and cause some horrible reaction.

The long and boring walk made me think and rethink things with Amy, probably in the most unhealthy way possible. For me, the period between the first kiss and the first sex were the most ambiguous and panic-generating of any relationship. With Amy, it felt like I was on third base, with no control of the situation, watching batters strike out and waiting for someone to tip me in. I usually struggled greatly to get to the first kiss, with awkwardness and a lack of self-confidence preventing me from making the first move until I lucked into it. And usually once I got to that point, the rest of it fell into place. I'd always stumbled into dating situations so full of energy that it was like playing with matches in a TNT factory—after a few seconds, the entire thing exploded. With Tammy, we kissed in the afternoon and she spent the same night. But with Amy...

Part of me wanted Amy as a full-time gig—being in love, being her boyfriend, seeing her exclusively, the whole thing. But I also wanted all of the fringe benefits of a girlfriend with all of the excitement of the chase. If we settled down and signed up for the long run, maybe things would change. But then there was the whole California factor. I didn't know what to think.

I walked the usual route to Third and Jordan, and headed down Third toward Lindley. I knew the 24-hour labs would be open and well air conditioned, even if I had no email to read. Some vague programming projects crossed my mind, but I knew I'd probably stop there for fifteen minutes, get bored, and keep wandering.

Even though it was Thursday, I had no more radio show to keep me busy. Sid emailed me on Wednesday, and said to stop going in. The station missed their last rent payment, and would soon be melted down for scrap. This meant I already did my last show and didn't know it. I had vague ideas (but no plans) about closing out my short tenure with something sick, disgusting, and packed with 100% Death Metal, but that wouldn't happen now.

The tearing Swedish metal ground through my walkman, but I still couldn't stop the depression consuming me. It weighed me down on the short walk across the south of campus, even with the sun out and almost nobody around to bother me. In the heat of the semester, when I had 30 hours of classwork to do a day plus my job plus my fucked up relationships, I would've killed for a day with absolutely nothing to do.

I crawled into the basement lab of Lindley, gave a quick hello to the two consultants in the hub office, and went down to the SPARCstation lab. Every machine was open, so I plopped down at the one closest to the door, logged in, and fired up an X session. The new lab, with bright white furniture and modern trim, seemed almost spooky without a dozen grad students living at the consoles. During the year, people would have stacks of books, printouts, backpacks, drinks, lunches, coats, everything short of pillows and sleeping bags, all piled on the low-slung desks. Now the place looked like a hospital's ER trauma room right before an accident—clean, orderly, and awaiting the worst.

No new mail—I knew that. I poked around, started a game of solitaire, and then gave up and logged back out. No use in wasting my time inside, I thought. I walked past the other four labs, with a total population of maybe three users, and headed back to the door and sunlight outside.

The empty labs reminded me of last year's end-of-summer dead week, when I was also here. Lauren helped me get my place on 414 Mitchell, and I pulled into town when she was visiting her parents. I got moved in, bought a ton of new stuff from Target, ran to Kroger for some food, and populated the apartment nicely in about a day. I had nothing to do then either, and sat around the Library labs. I'd done everything short of murder to leave the boredom of my parents' house and get back to Bloomington, and when I arrived, absolutely nothing was happening.

It baffled me that the brief memory took place a year ago. It seemed like twenty. I flipped over the tape in the walkman, and wandered toward the IMU.

By Friday afternoon, the heights of boredom and depression engulfed me. I woke up after noon, with no Amy to bother me online. She had to drive to Indianapolis for the day to deal with some financial aid stuff at home, and see her folks. She did email and tell me to keep my schedule clear that evening. No problem there—with no money and absolutely no obligations, I was practically deaf, dumb and blind with extreme boredom.

After the usual shower and no-email computer time, I hiked to the library stacks, which were amazingly open. I went to an I/O card catalog terminal and did a "S=JIM JONES MASSACRE" search on the graduate stacks. With a printout in hand, I found the spot in the colonnades of books where the bulk of the Dewey decimal numbers landed. Instead of being a good student and bringing the volumes of interest to a reading table, I sat down on the floor, fired up my walkman, and pages through the books. For some reason, I only knew third-hand what happened at Jonestown, and I was just a kid when everything went down. So I stared in grim fascination at the bloated bodies, and skimmed through the stories of cyanide punch and egomania.

When that got boring, I found another I/O terminal and did a search on "S=DEEP THROAT." After hitting a ton of surgical articles about larynx cancer, I redid the string as "S=DEEP AND THROAT" and hit a handful of articles. Once again. I found the tomes and sat down for some more reading. There were no pictures this time, but I did find some interesting stuff on the various legal battles surrounding the film. It also talked about earlier porno work where Linda Lovelace fucked a dog in a short film. I started laughing so loud, I was afraid someone would find me, but nobody did.

After killing a few hours in the library, I hiked back home, and did some quick cleaning on my place. I'd still have an hour or so until Amy found her way back into town, maybe more. The cleaning work slowed down until I found myself siting in bed, then lying down. Within moments, I drifted off into a light nap.

The phone pulled me out of bed abruptly, just as heavy sleep started to pull me under. 4:24. I grabbed it before the third ring.

"Hello?"

"Did you miss me?" Amy said.

"Hey, you're back. How was Indy?"

"Same old. Were you asleep?"

"Sort of. I spent all afternoon at the library doing research."

"I thought you finished your paper?"

"Yeah. Just looking up useless trivia, conversational banter, nothing too unusual."

"I see. And how is your health situation?"

"This depression is a relentless motherfucker. I'm glad I'm starting new drugs next week, or I'd have Pink Floyd's *The Wall* permanently stuck in the CD player by now."

"So," she interrupted. "Are you free this evening?"

"Some chick said she had something lined up for me. I wasn't expecting her to get back to me..."

"I understand you are depressed, and I thought maybe some seafood would help?" she said. "Are you a lobster fan?"

"Steak and shrimp sounds like a great idea. What's the plan?"

"It's Bloomington—all we've got is Red Lobster. But I'm buying."

"Sold. Umm, my high priest of Satan garb is at the cleaners. I'm assuming nice jeans and something with a collar will do?"

"Something like that. You don't even need the collar. Really, you don't even need the jeans..."

"Okay, okay," I said. "What time should I be ready?"

"I'll swing by around six-thirty."

"See you then."

By 6:30, I wore the traditional John Conner impress-the-date uniform: the nice pair of light button-fly Levi's, the collar shirt, casual boat shoes, and the required Eternity cologne. I even swapped out the regular white briefs for a pair of nice silk boxers, just in case. At the computer, I fiddled with a DOS Tetris clone, when the knock at the door came.

"Hey there," she said. She wore the a loose-fitting t-shirt and baggy jeans, a relaxing uniform for dinner.

"You look great," I said. I quit the game, and gave her a hug and kiss. "You feel very comfy."

"I recognize that outfit," she said. "Are you expecting something tonight?"

"The worst," I said.

"Very funny," she said. "Okay, let's hit the road."

Red Lobster was just a quick spin down Third, near the mall. I'd only been there once or twice—most of my seafood experience was the deep-fried, high-fat junk at Long John Silver's. The dead week crowds meant we got there and got a table in no time flat. A waiter whisked us to a booth in the corner, and we settled in with our menus.

I looked through the menu for something heavy, with lots of fat to absorb my depression. "I love shrimp, I love steak..."

"You can get both. Do you like salmon?"

"I can't stand it. When I was a kid, we had a cat that would only eat salmon cat food. It's a horrible association I can't shake."

"Well, it doesn't smell like cat food to me," she said.

Our waiter returned, and I got a steak and shrimp combo, while Amy got a smoked salmon dinner. After we ordered, Amy fidgeted with her napkin and silverware, and we sat in silence.

"You're awful quiet tonight," I said. "What's up?"

"I feel like every time we go out to eat, I give you more bad news."

"Oh come on. What's wrong?"

"I heard from Berkeley. I got a fellowship."

"That's great!" I said. "It covers your tuition?"

"Plus my dorm. And a stipend."

"So what's the bad news?" I said. "Do they have to take one of your kidneys?"

"No. It's for this semester. This fall. I would have to leave in a matter of days."

"What did you tell them?"

"Nothing yet. I mean, I need to talk to my parents, and I have a million things I'd need to figure out. I might see if they will let me defer until January. But..."

"I know, you want to be there. It's a hell of a deal."

"I just don't want to spend the rest of my academic career explaining that semester-long hole in my resume. And I don't want to waste my time."

"I understand. Look, I know I'm not making this any easier. But if you need help, I can help you...you know, packing, cleaning, whatever."

"No, John. This is bad enough for you. I'm not going to force you to help me leave, too."

The waiter arrived with our food, steaming hot, delicious, but completely inedible to me. I knew it would only be a matter of hours before I lost her forever.

The dinner ended somberly; the food hung in my gut like lead. We shuffled to the car and drove aimlessly, trying to find something to do. After a few minutes that seemed like hours, we silently cruised back to Amy's apartment. Inside, half of her stuff was still in boxes, ready to move back home and then to California. I felt like all of this had been planned for months and I just found out about it, even though I knew inside the surprise was shared by both of us.

We stumbled to her room, and she threw her arms around me and held me tightly. Before I could react, I heard her sobbing against my shirt. I pulled her closer, and held her head against my chest.

"I'm sorry Amy...I'm sorry I'm making this so difficult."

"No, I'm sorry," she said. "The last thing in the world I wanted to do was hurt you. You don't deserve this..."

"Amy, please don't do this. I know you didn't want to get involved. But we did."

"I know. I just wish there was another way."

She sniffed, almost done crying.

It felt good to wake with Amy in my arms, to smell her hair and see her curled sound asleep next to me. I enjoyed a few moments of this reverie before I started to remember that my days were numbered, and she'd be across the country and gone forever in a little over a week.

Amy rolled over and grumbled. "What time is it?"

"It's almost nine."

"I've got to get up and take a shower," she said. "I'm supposed to bring a carload of stuff to my parents' place before lunch. I don't suppose you want to go and meet them?"

"I'm not sure that would be a great idea," I laughed.

I rolled her over on her back, and pinned one of her arms to the bed. "Wake up, cutie!" I kissed her forehead, and then gave her a slow, careful kiss on the lips.

"Thank you," she said. "I'm sorry again about..."

"Hey hey...let's not talk about it. Now get your cute butt out of bed before I have to leave."

She smiled, and pulled herself up from the mattress. "I'm going to miss this," she said.

I got back to my place Saturday morning, smelling of Amy's bed and wishing I was still in it. After the joy of spending the night with her faded from my system, I remembered it would probably be the last time I'd be with her. This thought, plus the lack of anti-depressants in my bloodstream, made me feel like knocking down peoples' doors or making dozens of random phone calls until somebody would listen to my idiotic sob story and offer some sympathy or advice that I would later ignore.

But nobody was home. And I had an entire weekend to kill, with no money, and no plans. I climbed into bed, stared at the ceiling, and tried to think of a time in my life when I was more alone. I couldn't.

43

There wasn't a lunch date with Amy on Monday, or Tuesday. And although we talked about hooking up both nights, nothing became of it. Every time I called, something came up—packing, transferring of records, doctor's appointments, car maintenance, travel plans. The email wasn't as prolific as usual, either. She sounded apologetic when I talked to her, but deep in my paranoid mind, I knew she'd be leaving forever. And I wanted her to either comfort me, or hurt me, but I didn't thing I'd get either.

I couldn't find anybody else to lay this story on. The second dead week meant more isolation and emptiness for me to wallow in. I went through two sets of Duracell batteries in the walkman just wandering back and forth across campus, listening to all the depressing songs on Guns 'N Roses' *Use Your Illusion* that made so much sense during the tail end of a boy-meets-girl situation. I tried to find something to do, or at least something that didn't involve money, which was in scarce supply. I started at least three overly ambitious programming projects in C that never got past the first two dozen lines of code. And I kept thinking about the zine, or maybe writing my regular column for Nick's zine far in advance. Although I was down to my last few dollars, I thought about spending it on a matinee, to pull away my mind for a couple of hours. But I feared spending a fiver on something and then imagining that all of the perils and problems of the protagonist were just like mine. I kept to free diversions, even if they didn't work.

I couldn't bury myself in a project. I couldn't get more than 15 minutes into something without thinking, "what did I do wrong this time?" I wished I could confront her and say "what was it?" and then rewind the tape a week and redo all of my actions. When I sat in bed, or walked across campus trying to run into someone I knew, I could replay these thoughts until they brought me to a frenzy.

By Tuesday night, I felt like I'd been mentally tortured for weeks. I cruised Lindley and the Library, the only two places with open computer labs that week, with no luck. I was ready to give it all up—her, I mean. I wanted to forget that she ever happened, but I knew I'd spend months wishing I could have her back. With my depression at full boil, I spent the evening at home, waiting for sleep.

The red pills looked big, ominous—more like a sweet tart than something you swallowed whole. I woke early, to get on a regular schedule with the three-time-a-day administration of the new medicine, and now stared down at the dosage. It's going to be a bitch swallowing these horse pills every day, I thought. And I'm going to have to walk around with a clipboard tied to my ass to keep track of what I've taken and what's up next.

I kicked back the new meds, along with the old standard lithium tablets, and went to the bathroom to start the regular shave, shit, shower routine. I didn't have anything to do today, but I figured I might as well try to stay awake, review some cassettes for the zine, and maybe go for a decent walk.

It was Wednesday, the beginning of the end of dead week. Residence Halls would open for business again, allowing the first early adopters to move into the dorms and start their school year. This would mean moving trucks, parents driving the wrong way down streets, and double- or triple-parking everywhere. At least the bulk of the move-ins wouldn't happen until the weekend or next week. It seemed like 90% of people waited until the last minute to get back to campus. But the first 10% would change the scenery dramatically.

I finished brushing my teeth and started the shower. I guess the returning students didn't bother me too much. They'd breathe life into a dying campus, and I always enjoyed meeting the new people and seeing lots of beautiful women on campus again. The return of regular shifts at the computing clusters wouldn't hurt, either—I could use the regular paychecks.

The problem that bothered me is that this meant the summer would soon be over. When I started, I wanted it to go by so fast—I wanted to get back to dating Tammy, working in the clusters, and hanging out with my big group of computer friends. But once Tammy left and I drifted, I guess the mission plan changed. And now I felt like I needed an extension on that three-month mission to get everything completed. I wanted to stabilize things with Amy, or at least ride things out and see what happened in the end. And even though I spent the summer starved, depressed, suicidal, and alone, I felt like I learned to see. It wasn't the kind of transformation you hear about on dopey evangelical religious stories, but something noticeable happened over the summer, and I wasn't ready to give it up.

I got into the shower, and let the hot water jet over me. It felt like if I stayed in there for long enough, I could wash away all of it, the thoughts about the summer, the problems with Amy, everything. I stayed in for twenty minutes and tried to see if it would work. It didn't.

On Thursday, I took my regular lunchtime walk across campus, toward Kirkwood. Tomorrow would be a decent payday, with plenty of money for groceries and more. And I still had about $12 and change in my pocket, plenty to walk into town to grab some fast food. I headed down Third and toward Indiana Street, the divider between campus and the off-campus world of tiny shops and restaurants.

There were more people on the streets, walking to Kirkwood, to the sororities and fraternities across the way or just strolling in circles around the campus. It felt good to have an infusion of new faces around after surviving dead week, even if they would eventually steal away the summer tranquility I'd enjoyed for the last three months.

I walked to Grasshopper for a quick bowl of sweet and sour chicken. While in line at the register, I thought of the date where I met Amy at the same restaurant. I sat at the front counter, watching the new students stumble by like tourists, and thought about that night that seemed years ago. I nursed my food, and tried to think of a plan for the afternoon.

Back in my cell at 414 Mitchell a few hours later, I listened to the new Obituary with a notepad next to me on the floor. I needed to finish some reviews for the next issue of the zine, which I wanted to put out before school started. I would possibly have the cash for all of the photocopies after payday tomorrow, but I wasn't sure I'd have enough material to review for a few more weeks. Better early than late though, I didn't want to be stuck with a hundred things to review and no time to listen.

The intense, guttural growls of the Florida band reminded me of their earlier stuff, when their were no lyrics, and the rasping Death Metal growls were improvised. Now, they seemed to have more structure in their tunes, but it was still rough and grating in a good way.

I heard a knock at the door over the CD, and hit the mute button. Probably somebody pissed at the music, I thought. I got up from the floor, and walked over to see who it was.

Amy stood in the doorway. "Hi, what's up?" she said. "Did you eat dinner?"

"Hey stranger," I said. "No food yet—I've just been reviewing records."

"Well I'm going to J. Arthur's for dinner. Are you interested? My treat?"

The 'my treat' part sounded great, considering my day-before-payday situation. "Sure, that sounds good," I said. "Lemme change shirts real quick."

I was wearing a Napalm Death shirt, and I looked around for something more apropos for a sit-down restaurant. After digging through my laundry, I found a clean shirt with a collar, and changed.

"How's this look?" I asked.

"Pretty good. Let's go."

It bothered me that she didn't kiss me, hug me, or even come near me at all when we were back at my place. Even though I picked up a confused, apologetic vibe from her, I thought she was keeping her distance. Maybe she was—or maybe my paranoia was just getting the best of me.

A few minutes later, we reached the square downtown, and found a parking spot. I'd never been in J. Arthur's before, but knew it was some kind of yuppie steakhouse bar and grill. This was a town where 90% of the restaurants were pizza places or cheap Chinese food, so I guess the Thirty-something crowd needed a hangout, too.

"Are you sure I'm up to dress code here?" I said, as we crossed the street.

"Don't worry," she said. "You look fine."

We walked past the old-school storefronts, bookstores and boutiques with picture-window displays, and entered the grill, a place that smelled of money. Inside, varnished wood trim, brass railings, and low lights made the place look like an exclusive men's club from the fifties. No wonder I've never been in here, I thought. This was the place you took your rich parents when they were in town and they wanted to take you to a nice dinner, not the hangout of a starving student.

A server brought us to a table for two, and I sat across from her, a small light above shining down on us like an interrogator in the back of a police office.

"Are you okay with this?" she said. "We could go somewhere else."

"I'll be cool," I said.

I paged through the menu, and tried not to gasp at the cost of a good steak. I found the default hamburger platter, and stuck with that.

"I'm sorry about the last few days," she said. "It's been so busy with packing and getting stuff into storage. I'm sorry I haven't been around. What have you been up to?"

"Not a lot," I said. I couldn't even think of a tangible event that happened since I saw her last Saturday. And I knew she wasn't breaking my balls with the question—absolutely nothing took place, except for excruciating depression and loneliness.

"Oh, I started the new medicine," I said. "The Wellbutrin."

"How's that working out for you?"

"Not bad. I don't feel that different. I have to take the pills at the same times each morning and night though. It's a real pain in the ass."

The waiter arrived, thank god, and took our orders. She got some kind of pasta dish, and I ordered my hamburger.

I thought about telling her more about my week, or at least a fake story. Maybe I could make her jealous, I thought, hint at some other interests, or make my life look more exciting. I didn't know if I needed to win her back, or calm her down, or simply vanish.

After the waiter left, I dug in for the long and boring wait for our drinks and appetizers.

"So, have you found out any more details about school?"

"Yeah, some." she said. "Their semester already started, so I'm showing up late. I'm just doing a writing seminar and an independent reading slot, plus teaching and some research for this fellowship."

"That sounds cool. How are you getting out there?"

"Flying, on Tuesday. My parents are shipping some stuff out via UPS, and the rest will stay at their place in storage. The car, too. I was lucky enough to get a single dorm room."

"It sounds like everything's figured out," I said.

A waiter showed up with our drinks, and carefully set down the glasses in front of us. I took a long sip from my Coke, waiting in the silence.

"John, you know I didn't plan it to happen like this. I feel horrible..."

"I know. I do too. I mean, what am I supposed to do? I feel like I'm telling you not to follow your dreams or something."

"And I feel like I'm Tammy all over again."

"I just wish I knew what would happen, is all. I mean, with no real definition or anything..."

"This is where 'live in the now' becomes a problem. I can't tell you what will happen to me when I get to California. One of the reasons I'm going is to get away from everything here, to have a fresh start."

"I know, I know. It's just..."

"John, I wish I could promise you anything. I wish I could promise something. I know that next fall..."

"Please, let's not talk about this," I said. "I don't want the 'you're a great guy' talk, or whatever. I just want to remember what happened, and...I don't know, try to go from there."

We both sat in silence and waited for our food.

An hour later, I was back at the house, picking at my wounds. For a split-second during dinner, I thought the conversation would pick up and I would be able to steer her into coming back to my place for a bit more, but it fell flat. Nothing. Confusion. Awkwardness. And no resolution.

We made vague plans again, but I knew they'd fall through. And I didn't know what would happen over the weekend. I would get a paycheck on Friday, and I thought of all kinds of projects involving the cash. I wanted to get my room into order before the fall semester started, and maybe do a few small things so it wouldn't seem like the same old place. I guessed that would be my weekend—cleaning the room, buying crap at the mall, and checking the email.

I got on the computer, and tried to think of some way to kill a few hours before bed.

I woke up suddenly, with a tearing at my temples like a sinus headache, but without any of the headache, just the strange pressure like someone massaging my inner brain with a water pic. With the doctor's ominous "no other medications" speech, I had no idea what I could take alongside Wellbutrin. With two pillows clamped over my head, I tried to think of anything but my brain in an effort to calm down.

After several minutes of deep breathing, I concentrated on a nice, ideal summer vacation in upstate New York, visiting the mountains and clear lakes and small towns and deep forests, and spending hours floating in a cool swimming pool. The pain subsided slightly after a few moments, which seemed like hours. I put on my glasses and looked at the clock. 7:40 AM. After some rapid fidgeting in bed, I realized I was too awake to doze off again. I crawled out of bed and took a long shower to prepare for the Friday with two hours of sleep.

After the shower, some fiddling on the computer, and a long walk across campus, I headed out to sign for my paycheck. UCS finally had a real check for me; I accumulated forty hours over the last two weeks, which would score a decent haul of groceries and leave some money to burn. On the way up the hill to the library, I felt awake, maybe too awake for so little sleep. It was probably a good thing though, I had a lot of things to do now that I had some cash.

Since I'd be staying at the same house for another year, room improvements became one of my big priorities, and I planned to make it more presentable to visitors. My intentions weren't too ambitious: hide the hole in the ceiling, hang some cheap miniblinds and tape up a poster or two to make the place look civilized.

With check in hand, I headed off to Kirkwood. Steve Vai's album *Passion and Warfare* was in the walkman, the complex and upbeat guitar instrumental genius reminding me of a year and a half ago, when I listened to it constantly. It brought back memories of the summer before, driving in the VW, wishing I could play guitar like him or be in a band or something. But now, I wished for a good day, a short line at the bank, and some errands to be crossed from the list, now that I had money to throw at them.

I also had a 12-4 at Lindley, which was a rare find during a dead week. It would remove any chances of a lunch with Amy, but I didn't think that was much of a worry. I'd fire her off some email after I got to work, and maybe see what her weekend was like. But with the check burning a hole in my pocket, I was mostly just thinking of all the stuff I could finally get done that weekend.

I got home from the mall around ten that night, lugging two miniblinds, a quart of paint and painting gear for the room's window trim, some cleaning chemicals, and a Monet poster to hang near the bed. Even though I got almost no sleep the night before, my eyes were wide open and my blood surged like the caffeine of a thousand coca trees surged through my veins. With my new supplies, I felt like getting some stuff done in the room.

With my favorite Chick Corea CD spinning on the stereo, I started cleaning the room. Clothes went to their drawers or the laundry basket, and I tore through the mess of papers on the floor and near the computer, sorting or pitching everything in sight. I felt possessed, jerking through the cleaning, putting away odds and ends, meticulously arranging my tapes and CDs in their racks, and sorting through a year of debris and making quick treasure/trash judgments on everything. Like a whirlwind, the room regained order, and I foraged beyond the typical clean state and started to decide on new ways to store things, to make more room or get things aesthetically pleasing.

I didn't stop for breaks, procrastinate, or multitask between the computer and cleaning. Spasmically, I jumped all over the room, switching to macrovision and taking care of even the smallest of details. I tried to envision what a perfect, new apartment would look like, then focus in on all things that varied from that plan. I looked for wires that could be re-run, shelves that could be re-organized, surfaces that could be scrubbed or sprayed down with cleaners to restore them to like-new status. Everything was scrutinized, and the small changes started to add up.

Then I broke out the new stuff. Poster, wall, done. Cleaning stuff, dirt, done. I scrubbed the baseboards, the walls, the dresser, the door, my chair, and anything else that wouldn't move. I went through a second time with warm water to remove the cleaning residue, then I found an old toothbrush in a junk drawer and carefully worked at the dust and lint in corners and crevices. The dishpan of water turned black several times, and I had to flush away the layers of dirt several times in the kitchen sink. Sterile, I felt an overwhelming urge to make it all sterile.

Next, the paint. I broke out some newspaper, covered the floor by the one windowsill, and got out the steel wool. After tearing down the old window shade, I stripped the window frame faster than a power tool, maniacally scrubbing with the steel in my bare hands until they bled. Then I hit the smoothed trim with the water and rags, and quickly dried it. Masking tape and more paper covered the glass panes, and within moments, I had camel hair and latex slapping wood, coating the old layers of faded stain with bright white pigment.

Paint, done. Brush, clean. Paper, removed. Blinds, hung. Glass, cleaned. I quickly surveyed my handiwork, then started cleaning out the junk drawers after alphabetizing my CDs.

During my sorting, I went to the kitchen to look for something, and saw Deon in the hallway, sleepy-eyed and wearing his bathrobe.

"Hey man, what are you doing up?" he said groggily. "Are you painting or something?" he asked, poking his head in the room.

"Yeah, I was doing a little cleaning," I told him.

He looked around the room, gazing at the cleanliness. "What the fuck, man? How long did this take? I've never seen a room in this house that was this clean!" He walked in, surveying the work. "Wow, these are pretty cool blinds!"

"Thanks. I just did a little work since I got back from the mall a little bit ago," I told him.

"What do you mean a little bit ago? Didn't you get home around nine or ten or some shit?" he asked.

"Yeah, something like that."

"Dude, its 3:30. Are you on coke or something?"

I checked my watch: 3:37. "I guess it's just insomnia."

"I'd say, man. You should try drinking a warm beer or something. You're gonna start going into convulsions or some shit."

"I'll be okay. I need to get back to work though."

"Okay man, I'll catch you tomorrow." He closed the door and went back to his room.

3:37? It didn't feel like 6 hours had passed since he started cleaning, but things definitely felt abnormal, the constant twitching rush through my nerves making me feel like I was crawling out of my skin. It was the same unnerving feeling that comes when someone scrapes metal on metal, but constant, and more intense. I sat down and tried to figure out what to do next, but I wanted to still work more, I wanted to get everything that had to be done completed. The room was clean, painted, and set. I thought about what the next task would be.

The car.

Twenty minutes later, I found myself hiking down a dark back road toward Amy's house. With Godflesh's *Slavestate* EP slamming through my walkman, I kept an automated pace down the road, trying to figure out how long the walk would take. She lived a couple of miles away, so I figured I could get there in an hour if I kept a decent pace. The temperature was in the low to mid sixties, so I wore a thin windbreaker, but it was now drenched in sweat as the machine of my body churned away, propelling me down the road.

I no longer felt human. I didn't know if it was the medicine, my mood, the music, or the excitement of the moment, but it made me feel like some kind of robotic terminator killing machine, out to recapture my car. The weird buzzing feeling in my head went away as I became removed from the animate piece of myself formerly known as my body. I watched myself marching double-time on the dark road, hovering over and driving myself forward. It felt as if something else controlled me, pumped my body with energy and convinced it to do the work, the compulsive labor and slackless devotion toward tasks.

The Godflesh EP repeated on auto-reverse at least three times, until I got to the surreal lighting of Amy's subdivision. The VW peacefully rested in its space, awaiting its next roadtrip to parts unknown, forgetting its prior injury. I unlocked the door to the Rabbit and tossed my balled-up jacket and walkman in the front seat.

The plan was to drive on the back roads from her house at about 20 or 30 MPH, and carefully downshift to roll through the stops at a slower speed. With no cars on the road, I'd be able to safely return the car to my driveway, and maybe get out my tools and bang out a repair over the weekend. The brakes would work once or twice before losing most of their fluid, so I could save their power for an emergency. Plus, I could always downshift from fourth to first and work the clutch to jerk the car to a stop if needed.

The diesel engine fired up almost immediately, and I carefully jockeyed it from the spot and onto the main road. Everything felt normal with the engine purring and the moonroof open to the August night sky, but I had to carefully remember not to hit the brake, or get into a situation where I needed to hit the pedal.

It felt weird to drive again, especially since I covered the terrain I had just walked, carefully crawling uphill to my house. Once I found how easy it was to slow the car down to a crawl, I started thinking about groceries. I wanted to shop earlier, but didn't want to limit myself to a couple of bags that I could carry on the bus or walk home with, and I didn't feel like paying for a cab. But now, I could easily drive to the 24-hour store, fill the VW with food, and limp back to Mitchell Street. I pulled away from my current route and set a course for the Mr. D's grocery at Eastgate plaza, by the mall.

I didn't even see any other cars on the way over. Nosing into the lot, I shifted from fourth the second, then down to first and managed to slowly coast the car across the length of the lot to a near stop, like a plane crash-landing and skidding down the whole field with no gear and sparks flying from the hull. But, I'd be able to fill the hatchback with groceries and not have to drag them home on foot.

Inside the store, the three or four clerks had a radio blasting a local AOR station as they tore through stacks of boxes, stocking the shelves and joking around while Bachman-Turner Overdrive and Kansas jerked through the speakers. I grabbed a cart and headed down the aisles. With about $180 in my pocket and the thought that I might not have a car for a while, I would have to make this a good trip.

I crept through each aisle, dumping stuff into my cart like one of those shopping race marathon TV shows. Need this, need this, need this, need this. Need bread, need pop tarts, need Coke, need flour, need fruit roll-ups, need dried banana chips, need soup, need instant gravy mix, need cornbread mix, need need need need. The cart started to overflow with items. I kept vague track of what I put in it and the price, but the trip still bordered on psychotic.

After a record haul through all 12 aisles, I hustled one of the night clerks to a register and had him scan and bag the whole affair. I never thought the UPC scanning would end. The clerk had to grab another helper to wrap up the dozen bags of food. And the grand total: $178.13, almost all of my cash on hand. OK, here, money, change, paper, thanks, load up the car. The groceries took up the entire hatch of the car, plus the back seat and a couple of bags riding next to me up front. I put back the cart, fired up the Rabbit, and tried to figure out how to get home safely.

At home, it took 20 minutes just to drag all of the stuff into the kitchen, without even putting any of it away. When I started cramming things into cabinet and refrigerators, I got the odd urge to leave Amy a phone message explaining the car incident. I knew she was going to Indy the next day, but I also knew she usually turned off the phone in her room and let the machine pick it up at night.

Fuck it, I'm not going to call. I went back to the kitchen and finished putting away everything as the sun rose. Then I took my morning doses of the medicine and crawled into bed to try and catch some sleep.

A knock on the door made me jump from bed, and search for a pair of pants and a dirty shirt. "Hang on a second!" I fumbled across the room, pulling on the clothes with my shaking hands. I tore from sleep quickly, feeling like I was twenty minutes late for work. My heart beating at quad-speed, I remembered it was Saturday, and I had all day to sleep. I picked up the clock from the dresser and held it to my face to read the numbers. 6:51. I must have slept less than an hour, but I didn't feel like I could drift back with any amount of effort. I sat in bed, hoping that at least staying in one place would make up for the lack of sleep.

I unlocked the door and swung it open to reveal Amy. "Hey, what's up?" I said. "I thought you were going to Indianapolis?"

"I am, I'm on my way up there right now. Why did you get your car in the middle of the night? I thought it didn't have brakes?"

"Oh yeah," I said. "Sorry about that. I thought I could drive it back when nobody was on the road."

"What time did you get to bed anyway?"

"I don't know...maybe five?"

"John, you're running full-blown manic. Did you already take your medicine? Can you call a doctor?"

"Don't freak out. I'll be okay."

"I am freaked out. You could have hurt yourself, and I'm leaving town in three days, and I have no idea what to do with you."

"Calm down. I'll be okay. I'll crash eventually. I promise I won't wander."

"I've got to go. I'm supposed to meet my family for brunch."

"I know," I said. "I'm sorry I'm confusing things."

"I'll try to call you later," she said. "I've got to go."

She rushed out of the apartment, obviously confused by my condition. What the fuck was I supposed to do now? I got back in bed, and tried to get back to sleep. I couldn't.

44

I couldn't go back to sleep, even though I got back in bed and laid there for hours. It must've been around 11:00, and I felt like taking a shower, getting dressed, and walking to Dagwood's for a sub sandwich with extra cheese, bacon, and anything else bad for the health but good for my mood. But I also felt like staying in bed until the earth opened up and swallowed the entire house down into the pits of hell. I hoped that the sleepless night would catch up with me and I'd be unconscious for eight or ten hours, regardless of the amount of heat and sunlight in the room. But the medicine kept my brain fully functional on no sleep. And that kept me staring at the ceiling, and thinking.

My situation kept me in a chokehold indefinitely. I thought maybe I could probably take the anti-mania drugs, sleep for a day or two, and then come back to her and plead insanity. But she'd be gone by then. And it sounded like she didn't want to hear from me until after she left, which meant all of the conflict would have to stew in my mind infinitely. How can everyone else in the world but me leave things unresolved like this? I thought. I couldn't handle this for fifteen minutes, but I'd need to put my feelings on hold for what seemed like forever.

I sat on the edge of the bed, and stared at the floor for a while, with my head in my hands. After a few dozen deep breaths, I still couldn't straighten the jumble of thoughts in my head about her, about what to do next.

A shower might help, I thought. I wasn't getting any sleeping done. I checked my email first—nothing. I almost half-expected some kind of mail from her, but all I got was a mail from Brecken asking me something about forwarding email from Iowa. I powered everything down and hit the shower.

Saturdays were usually slow, but the constant processing of everything the night before and the potential endgame of the relationship made this day seem weeks long. I did take the next dosage of medication, and hoped that I'd ride through the mania after the weekend, and maybe make use of the untapped energy on some other projects around the house or on the computer. With the VW damaged, I'd need to waste the day as a pedestrian, which made it all seem that much more futile. I hit the streets with my walkman, and brought a mostly empty spiral notebook, formerly earmarked for econ, and a pen. During the height of my depressive episodes, I always found that writing some diary-type essays helped clear up my thoughts, sort out my ideas, or at least distract me from the current issues. Onward to Kirkwood, I hoped to find something to do or a nice place to write.

The second floor of the Kirkwood McDonald's made a decent Saturday afternoon retreat. Without any room on the strip, the store expanded upward, adding another dining area with huge bay windows looking outward at the streets below. Bathing in the sunlight, I sat at a brown and red plastic booth, watching the pedestrians below, and adding to my open notebook. I picked up my pen, and scrawled down some more thoughts to the depressing entry:

> "I wish there was an easier way out, another option. If I had a spine, I would've walked away a long time ago, stopped talking to her, went to something else. I need something more conventional—me loving someone who loves me back, with none of these bullshit games.
>
> "I can't believe I'm still around her, but I am. She makes me feel complete, but I can't have her. Maybe she wants me. She picked me,

she stayed close to me. But she's going to be gone—how can I change that?

"It seems like everyone before her was so simple. I meet a woman, we spent a bunch of time together, we fall in love, we have sex (maybe those two are reversed) and we're boyfriend and girlfriend. When it happens faster, it's more fun, but the brighter it burns, the faster it's gone. I don't think I can correct this easily, though.

"I want her to come back, say this was all a mistake, take me back, and make it all better. But I know that won't happen. I know this is a mess. I want her to do what makes her happy—I can't deny her the dreams she has. I feel like I need to rip a Band-Aid off, and I wish it would happen fast and be over with. But I like her. And maybe I even love her. This is fucked up..."

I closed the notebook, and looked back out the window again. The agony is killing me, I thought. I just wanted it over, no matter how it was going to end.

No new mail. It was my tenth time checking it in the last 90 minutes, but I still felt a need to go to the VAX machines and see if she logged on to check her mail. I hadn't sent her anything—I would have to wait for first blood before I could do anything.

It was almost dinner, and I still hadn't slept. My body felt physically exhausted, but I was still wired, the sick kind of mania that overdrove my senses and left me with a shivering feeling that kept me from sitting in one place too long. I kept thinking about the antimanic drugs, and wondered if they would push the depression even further, or make me sleep for days. I wanted to go completely blotto and forget about everything, but I also wanted to be ready in case she came around to deliver some sense of closure to the situation.

I went through the cycle again: kickstarting the modem, checking Bronze for mail, checking Rose to see if she'd logged on. Nothing. And nobody was around either, another Saturday night of desolation. At least every other Saturday night alone this summer, I was able to drop some Death Metal into the CD player and work on some record reviews or a C program or something. But now, I could only obsess.

It would be dark soon, and then the long stretch into the evening would continue. I knew I had to get out of the house and do something, find some way of distracting myself. Instead, I crawled back to the computer, fired up the modem, and waited for a login prompt. I didn't expect to find her there on a Saturday night, but I thought I could dig around through some old email, and wait until anybody else logged in. Maybe there would be people at the fountain at midnight.

The ominous darkness of Union Street on the east side of campus matched my mood. I slowly crawled through the blocks of university-owned houses, with Type O Negative's first tape grinding away in my walkman.

I was always nervous about girlfriends cheating on me, and the album helped me wallow in those thoughts. It gave me a good, temporary excuse that didn't involve blaming myself, although I still did. I practically fantasized about her being with another man all weekend, just to torture myself. I almost wished she would call me up and say there was someone else, just so I could say "I told you so!" I couldn't believe how worked up I could get with this scenario.

Fuck, I didn't know what to do. Ten minutes into the walk, I realized I was instinctively going to the Village Pantry to buy beer, and I didn't even think about getting drunk. The doctor told me not to drink at all with the new medicine, but common logic told me I should never point a loaded gun to my head, and every part of me wished I still had shells for that shotgun in my room. I just went to the pharmacy and got refills on everything—I could easily drop all of my lithium, a bottle of antimania pills, and the Wellbutrin along with a fifth of rum and call it a day.

I guess part of me wanted to go on, even though I tormented myself and thought about blowing my brains out constantly. I knew that when she was over, there would be others. And that started me thinking about the ones before her. I feared my past—I started running through the lineup, the women, the problems and the breakups. Even though they were completely different types of people, it all went down the same way. Regardless of age, hometown, major, height, weight, or anything else, there was a point where they were off fucking someone else and I was wandering the streets of Bloomington like an idiot. Maybe it was a me problem. All I knew is that I'd never figure it out.

I got back to 414 Mitchell at a little after 3 AM, still wide awake. The wandering of campus confused me more than it solved any problems, but it was still essential. If I could deal with Sunday, I'd probably hear from her the next day. Either things would be all better, or they'd completely fall apart, but I felt ready for either situation.

I got on the computer one last time: no mail, nobody on. My only answer were the pills the doctor gave me for mania. I needed the downtime, and hoped the things would do something for me. I found the bottle, and popped one of the tiny, dark blue tablets. Then I sat down on my bed, and waited for sleep.

Through the thickness of the drugs, I heard a banging on the door. I looked at the clock: 2:37 PM. What the fuck happened? "Hang on, hang on a second," I yelled, stumbling toward the door. I was still wearing a pair of shorts, a t-shirt, and socks from the night before. Somehow, I managed to remove my shoes before losing consciousness. It felt like I was 15 minutes into a nap after staying awake for two days. I had been awake for two days, but I couldn't figure out how twelve hours had passed.

I unlocked and opened the door, to reveal Amy, looking depressed and tired, like she hadn't slept all weekend.

"Hey, can I come in?" she said.

"Sure, sure. Do you want anything?" I asked. I got a Coke out of the fridge.

"No, I'm fine." She sat down at the chair in front of the computer. "Did you sleep?"

"Yeah, Klonapin. It hit me like a truck full of bricks. I feel like I'm hung over." I sat on the floor, and cracked open the Coke.

I went to clear a space in the middle of the floor and sit down when she started sobbing. I got up and put an arm around her. "Amy, honey, it's okay. What's wrong?"

"Everything's wrong. I'm sorry...I'm sorry John, I feel so awful."

"Calm down," I said. "It's okay."

"John, I don't know how to do this..." She sniffed back her tears and wiped her eyes with her wrist.

"Do what?"

"This is it, John All of my stuff's out of my apartment. I handed over my keys. I'm driving back to Indy from here, and my flight leaves on Tuesday. This is it. I just wanted to see you before I left."

I put both of my arms around her, and held her sobbing face against my shirt. When I felt her hair in my hands and her body next to mine, the tears burned in my eyes and started to run down my face.

"This is so hard, to say I'm done here. Everything reminds me of my past, and I've spent the last year trying to get away. I thought I'd be married by now, playing house and wanting kids, but now I have to do something else, and get away from this. I've never felt this way before, and now I need to go to California and make it happen."

"I can't blame you," I said. "If I had the money, or a job, or grad school, I'd probably leave too."

"John, I wish I would have met you years ago. You would have changed my life, and I could have helped you so much. You're everything I want, and I know big things are going to happen to you. You're the biggest individual I've ever met. I know you'll escape."

"I just wish it was with you. You're everything I ever wanted. Maybe..."

"Maybe someday, I don't know. But not now, I can't promise anything or keep you waiting forever. You need more than I can give you over the phone, or through e-mail. I've spent years trying to help my sister, and failing because I wasn't enough. I don't want to do the same thing to you."

"Part of me wants to say you're wrong, that you are enough. But I know you're right."

"I'll be back someday. My family still lives just up the road. And Until then, it's still jconner@indiana.edu, right?"

"You know it," I smiled. "I better hear from you."

"You will. You know you will." We both got up and hugged, a tight embrace that would etch into my brain forever. I wanted to think she'd be back, or I'd follow her out there, but I almost knew this would be the last time I would see her.

"Goodbye John," she said. "I'll miss you."

"I'll miss you too. Talk to you later."

"Bye Doctor X."

She walked out the door, and looked back to force a smile and wave. I watched her car pull out of the driveway and vanish. I wiped my eyes dry, got a glass of water from the kitchen, and went back to the dresser to my ever-growing collection of pills. I took my usual lithium and the new Wellbutrin horse pills with a few swigs of water. Then I looked at the anti-manic drug, Klonapin, and shook two of them from the childproof bottle. Better to stay down than to think about this, I decided. I downed the tiny pills, took off my socks and shirt, and got back into bed for another marathon sleep session. Within moments, I was unconscious in a thick blanket of nothing.

1:47 AM. When my eyes first opened, my head was still full of sludge. I sat up, and tried to fight through it, like a prizefighter going against a punch to the head. After a minute, the sleep caught up to me, and I felt awake. The mania was still there, at a low level, but it felt manageable. I'd be awake until sunrise, but I'd sleep eight solid hours after that.

I got up, and rubbed my hands through my hair. A shower would help, I thought. And my stomach rumbled with a lack of food. I still had a house full of groceries, and a few bucks in my wallet. I just need to get moving, I thought.

The hot water of the shower rinsed away the last of the sleep and heavy drug crud from my head, and gave me a chance to get back up to speed. It already seemed like weeks since Amy left, but I knew it would hit me soon. The next time I was home during lunch, I'd expect an email invitation to meet at Sample Gates, and there would be nothing.

I got out of the shower, dried off, and put on a robe. I felt pretty decent, but my whole body ached for some high-fat food. I combed out my hair, and walked back to my room.

In the kitchen, Yehoshua sat at the table, playing with a cigarette lighter. "Hey man," he said. "What's up? Did you just wake up?"

"Yeah," I said. "I took some fucked up medicine and slept all day."

"That's cool," he said. "Hey man, I saw you had that chick here earlier. What's up with that?"

"It's over with her man," I said. "Kind of stupid bullshit," I said.

"That's too bad," he said. "She was okay looking. Hey, did you eat dinner?"

"I'm about to. What about you?"

"Not really. Are you going anywhere?"

"No, I think I'm going to make a frozen pizza. You want to split it?"

"Yeah, that would be cool."

"Fire up the oven, I'm going to get dressed."

After the 2 AM lunch/dinner and random conversation with Yehoshua, I grabbed the trusty walkman and hit the road outside for another walk across campus. It felt better now that she was gone, I thought, but it would still take time. She was a grand experiment in trying something slightly different, someone who wasn't the typical 19 year old girl from the

VAX. I didn't think it would work, and it didn't. There was a lesson in there somewhere, but I knew I wouldn't understand it for years.

I headed toward the Main Library, a very symbolic walk in an odd, convoluted way. It was just like the walks I took a year ago, which felt like an era decades old. I couldn't full explain why a mere twelve months ago felt like 1963 to me, except that so much happened. College life is like dog years sometimes, with the passing of people and changes every semester. In so many ways, I felt I'd grown up tremendously since the first time I pulled my VW into the gravel driveway of 414 South Mitchell and unloaded my shit into room thirteen. In other ways, I felt like I would be starting over that semester. I guess breaking up with someone always did that to me.

I climbed the steps of the library like it was Mount Olympus, and entered into a main lobby that had a few more people than it did in the weeks before. The dorms were already open, the next round of freshmen had their VAX accounts, and the old regulars were returning to the labs to read months of old email and find their friends. Pretty soon, people will be emailing me with stupid computer questions. Pretty soon, beautiful women will be emailing me with stupid computer questions. Maybe it gets better after it gets worse, I thought.

A Zenith PC's green and black screen awaited me, and I logged on. Over on the Rose VAX, I did a quick who. I saw Shannon logged in from the Mac cluster in the next room, so I logged off and walked over.

"Hey, what's up?" I asked. I sat down in the chair next to her.

"Not much," she said, typing in the last of a message while talking. "Just catching up on email. You?"

"Not a lot. Just split up with Amy Bergstrom today."

"That's too bad. You think maybe you'll get back together?"

"No, we won't. I'm pretty sure."

"You never know. Maybe it's just a mood."

"No, really, I know. It's not going to happen. She's leaving for California."

"Sorry to hear it," she said. "You okay?"

"Yeah, I'll be okay."

"Well, if the liquor store was open, I'd offer to get you drunk and take advantage of you."

"It's a rare opportunity. I'm only like this about four times a year."

"I know what you mean," she said. "It's amazing how you can be so close to a person and then a month later, they're throwing everything you own out of a three story window."

I laughed. "I hear you. Hey, I should probably get back. I've got to stop this nocturnal shit before classes start."

"Okay, try to feel better," she said.

I walked out of the limestone castle and back into the darkness, thinking about her offer. There will be others, I thought.

The VW sat in the gravel driveway for the weekend, slowly leaking brake fluid. Monday afternoon, I played phone tag with a few brake places to see how I could get the car somewhere for a free estimate. The exhaust and brake place where I got some work done the summer before offered a free estimate if I could get the the car in the shop, and said they had plenty of openings for the rest of the day. It sounded like a deal, as long as I could find a way to get the car there. I hoped they didn't turn up anything worse than a bad caliper or a busted hose. I couldn't afford more than about $100 in repairs, and that was assuming that I didn't eat for the next eleven days.

I spent some time mentally thinking through the trip, and decided to drive over there sans brakes that afternoon. I thought of a back route that took me to their branch south of town that only involved three or four stops. I got my checkbook and a city map, and went to the car. I topped off the brake reservoir and put the rest of the brake fluid inside the car with me. From my experiment the night before, I could fill the thing and get one or two shaky stops before all of the fluid was on the ground. But, that would help in an emergency.

It felt good to drive the car again, to hear the engine crank over and feel the diesel vibrate in front of me. But I didn't have as much of a manic buzz of bravery as I did a few nights before. It felt like I held my breath for the whole trip across town. I kept the car at a low speed, and carefully downshifted through the gears to slow me down to a roll at the stops.

At the repair shop, I coasted into the lot, ran through the paperwork, and dropped the keys on the front desk. A mechanic told me there was an empty bay, and they'd pull it in and check it out in a minute. I sat in the small, bare waiting room, which had three chairs, some kind of Knights of Columbus candy display with an honor-system change box, and a single copy of *4x4 Magazine*. There was also a glass window where you could watch the cars being hoisted in the air and torn apart by impact wrenches and welding torches.

I started to read the magazine, scanning the pictures of trucks with five-foot tall tractor tires, when the mechanic came back in with my keys. Maybe he couldn't get it started, I thought.

"Everything okay?" I asked.

He shuffled through my paperwork, and started writing on my chart. "Can't do an inspection on that car."

"What do you mean?" I asked. "I thought when I talked to you on the phone..."

"Your floor pan and subframe is almost rusted through on the passenger side," he said. "That car's a unibody—almost no frame at all except the floor. If we put it on a four-point hoist, it would punch right through the rust."

"Can't you jack it up with that lift?" I pointed to a car on the type of drive-up ramp lift. "You did that when you replaced the exhaust last year..."

"We can't do that if we need to pull a wheel. And from what you told us on the phone, you've probably got a bad caliper."

"And you can't lift it from the side, or the bumper?"

"Not safely."

"So what do I do now?"

"I don't know. Find another VW with a bad engine and a good frame for a couple hundred bucks, swap over your good parts. Or sell it to someone who's looking for a good diesel engine. There's always someone in town with a few dozen of these old VW's looking for a solid fuel injection setup."

"Okay, okay," I said. "Do I owe you anything?"

He tore off the top sheet and handed it to me. "No charge today. Sorry I don't have better news for you."

"That's okay, thanks."

I slouched out to the VW, which was again sitting in the parking lot. The engine leapt to life on the first crank, and purred like it was still on the assembly line in West Germany, 1980. This could be the last time I drive this car, I thought. Even when the engine blew up the year before and it was shooting oil on US 31 and making sick internal cranking noises that were obviously very wrong, I didn't think that the car was a complete write-off. But you can't replace the body of a car, unless it's a classic and you're willing to dump thousands into restorative welding and new custom sheet metal. This was the end of the road for the VW. At best, I'd find another straight Rabbit and transplant the engine. At worst, I'd be driving a 1978 Monte Carlo with no exhaust that I picked up for 300 bucks. Or I'd be walking.

I carefully drove the car back, pulled into the gravel drive, and turned off the key. I probably sat in the car for another twenty minutes. It felt like I was sitting over my best friend's corpse.

I sulked inside and checked my mail. Amid the junk, there was a letter from BrassCo. I tore it open, knowing there would be a "we regret to inform you" letter. Instead, there was a check—for a thousand bucks. The enclosed letter said if I got good grades, they'd cut another check for the other thousand in January.

Close enough, I thought. Some quick mental calculations told me I'd be able to pay my part of my tuition bill, give back Peter his cash, and have enough money left over for a value meal at McDonald's. I'd originally hoped that with two grand, I could buy a $500 VW with a blown head gasket and swap engines, or pick up a $500 beater and sell the VW. My pedestrian era was beginning.

45

The campus transformed almost overnight, like a dead and gray transplanted kidney instantly pinking up and jumping to life again when the surgical clamps are magically removed from the connecting veins and arteries. Moving vans and annoying parents arrived in droves for a few days, and left behind 30,000 people on campus, half of them unable to tell the difference between Jordan Street and Jordan Hall (or Jordan River, or former President David Starr Jordan, or Michael Jordan, or the country Jordan...) The dorms that were largely vacant all summer now welled with new loft beds and posters and cube refrigerators and computers. I saw freshmen everywhere, carrying maps and brand new book bags, wearing new blue jeans that were BLUE. I couldn't walk from home to work during the day without getting asked directions. I guess I looked like a veteran. It felt great the first few times, then got old fast.

And the freshman women—there was a bumper crop of cute little 18 year old girls away from home for the first time. They looked even younger this year, but that didn't discourage me. I knew all of the pain of Amy would fade, and I'd start trawling the computers, running into people at work and cooking the infamous John Conner dinner, just like old times.

I managed to level my bill with the bursar, get all of my probation papers in order, and register for classes. I got into a 400-level class on graphical user interfaces, and audited an intro computer class to pick up another programming language. I also enrolled in a philosophy class, to scope out my options in case this whole computer science thing didn't work. Oh, and I picked up a music class on the history of rock and roll. Even though I kept at the Obituary and Malevolent Creation and planned to keep chugging on the zine, I started listening to the Beatles. Who knows, maybe it would increase my odds with women.

The Rabbit was gone. After I put an ad in the paper, a couple of guys showed up in a six-color Jetta that looked like it had been rolled in an action adventure-movie and put back together on a zero-dollar budget. They ponied up a hundred bucks, and drove away my car with no brakes. I couldn't even watch them leave—it hurt so much to see that car go. I took the cash and bought a decent ten-speed from a coworker. It meant going to the mall now involved hopping a bus or throwing on a backpack pedaling my bike down Third Street for a mile or so. I missed the Rabbit like a friend, but it would mean a new era of spending more of my time at home or in the labs, which wouldn't be that horrible.

I didn't know what would happen next semester, money-wise. After the bursar, I had enough cash to buy my books, and barely afford two pair of jeans and some new t-shirts at the mall. I'd save a couple bucks on fuel and maintenance for the car, but it looked like student loans were in my near future.

Speaking of money, all of the computing centers were open and fully staffed, which meant I got as many hours as I asked for. I'd spend almost every weeknight for the rest of the year in the basement of Lindley Hall, the nerve center of all of the public facilities. And with a new wave of freshly hired consultants, I got to help teach training courses. It also meant I'd be working in labs with newer people in my command. I even picked up some odd hours helping the education division of UCS teach some of the intro to computing classes and seminars they held for freshmen and others trying to get a jumpstart on computing.

I'd be at Mitchell Street for another year. Deon moved to another house owned by another slum landlord, on the other side of campus. I still ran into him all the time, though. Yehoshua stayed in the house, but got bumped from his primo room in the front to a space not much bigger than a closet—something about not paying his deposit fast enough. Almost everyone else left, and a new rotation of freaks and weirdos moved in. My new neighbor was a 15 year old cellist from Spain who spoke almost no English, stole a bunch of cash from my room once, and moved out a few weeks after I got a copy of the new Dismember EP and started listening to it constantly with the volume at 11. The tenants changed, but the atmosphere was still the same.

Amy did email, as she promised. She told me about her classes, her profs, her dorms, and everything else. California sounded like a dreamland from her emails, the kind of place I'd like to visit someday. I spent a few weeks wondering if I could swing a Christmas visit, a spring break trip across the country in a rented car, or some other way to see her and this mythical paradise of sun and intellectuals. It hurt that I couldn't drop everything and see her again, but I couldn't do anything about it.

I sent Amy lengthy emails almost every day, with details on new classes and the updates on my returning friends and life on Mitchell Street. I missed her, but I didn't tell her. I also omitted the brief encounters I'd been having with the new freshmen, even though none of them had been successful. I thought if I dumped all of my real emotions into a message, the pure despair and confusion would scare her out of ever writing again. As it was, I got an email from her for every five or six I sent, each shorter and shorter, mentioning her teaching load and busy schedule more than anything else.

Amy slowly faded into the distance, and I didn't even notice it. As my trolling for new women picked up steam and I prepared to make more John Conner dinners of spaghetti or Chinese, my email updates became less frequent. Then one day, around Halloween, I ate lunch at Macri's Deli with Michael, and realized I hadn't talked to her in over a month. Every once in a while, a small detail reminded me of her, and I remembered when I never thought I'd be able to live without her in my life. But somehow she vanished just as quickly as she appeared. I wasn't devastated, but I didn't feel a hundred percent better, either. I'd never forget her, but life went on.

And then I saw Tammy. Just once, but I saw her. I was walking home from C201 one afternoon, down the alley of a parking lot behind Wells quad. My usual route home from Ballantine took me down the lot, where I then ducked between the music school and the old education building, and emerged right outside Third and Jordan. But this time, I saw a group of people coming out of the glass doors of the music building, and I saw her.

And she saw me—our eyes met from a few dozen feet away, and I didn't know what to do. After her email, I never wanted to talk to her again—I never wanted to acknowledge her existence in any way. But she looked as beautiful as the first time I saw her, when I drove up to Forest last spring and saw her waiting for me, when I instantly knew I wanted to be with her forever.

I wanted to drop my books and run to her and pick her up and hug and kiss her, like the ending of some sappy chick-flick where the couple is magically reunited in the final minute. I wanted to go to her and bitch her out for hurting me so much. I wanted to say hi, and act all cool and tough and phony, like I was over her and my life was all together, even though it wasn't. I wanted to make up some lie about another woman, or a new job in California, or an internship at NASA, or a sudden inheritance of a billion tax-free dollars, or something that would make her realize she made the wrong choice. I spent three months rehearsing in my mind exactly what I would do if I had this chance, and now that it was happening, I couldn't think of what to do.

And I didn't do anything. She smiled, and awkwardly waved, but I blew it. I gave her an quick, impersonal smile, and kept walking. I didn't even process the event until I got home, and then the floodgates opened with all kinds of ideas. I counted up the last of my money, and contemplated going to the liquor store and buying a fifth of Everclear and washing down all of the pills in the house. I read the Wellbutrin pamphlet and did the math on the overdose studies. I thought about the gun, the ammunition, how long it would take me to ride my bike to a sporting goods store to buy a box of 16-gauge deer slugs. I sat in bed with no music on, staring at the ceiling for hours, paralyzed by the whole encounter. I'd spent three fucking months thinking of what I would say to her, and in the end, all I could do was walk away.

A few weeks later, on an evening after my history of rock and roll class, I stammered into a computer lab on the first floor of Ballantine Hall to check my email. I went to classes even though the depression still tore through my body. The slight feeling of accomplishment of attending, doing the homework and taking sporadic notes helped me feel more complete, even though I still didn't know which way to go with life. Without Amy, all I knew was work and school, the romantic aspect of life severed and dead. But, taking full-time classes got me thinking about computers, filling requirements, and a possible, distant career. It kept me out of the house, anyway.

Clicking through my correspondence, I scanned my new emails. More work stuff, nothing interesting. Nothing happening.

"Hey!" flashed a quick message on my screen. "Wake up! I'm at the sorority and can't talk long. Where are you?"

Tricia! I hadn't talked to her since last spring. I wrote a few letters, and got a quick postcard in return, but she was otherwise in the dark about everything that happened over the last few months. I quickly jumped to the VMS prompt to reply to her message.

"Hey! I'm in Ballantine, just got out of class," I said.

"How are you doing?"

"The truth?" I said. "I still feel pretty numb. A lot's been going on since you were last here."

"Hey, I have to get off of here—someone else has to use the computer. You wanna meet up and go to the Waffle for some chocolate shakes and a talk? I'll drive."

"Great, I'd really like to catch up," I said. "Meet me in front of Ballantine in about 5 minutes?"

"See you there," she said.

I logged out of my accounts, grabbed my stuff, and headed out of the lab. I'm glad she can still read minds, I thought.

The mighty eleven story classroom building stood over me in the September night sky, a limestone marker of the campus that housed my love and trouble. The evenings always made me remember my freshman year, where I was so depressed because I lost my first girlfriend, my home, my pride and my life as I transported to the new and alien campus. I spent my nights wandering the cool Indiana autumn breeze, wondering and crying and feeling and blocking and absorbing the falling leaves and the gentle hills and brightly lit buildings and monuments. Reborn and refreshed, I spent the rest of that year and future years around the buildings and territory that became burned into my mind, but always felt a strange deja vu at times, when the leaves rustled and the wind blew and I felt like it was still orientation week 1989 and I was still wondering how things would end up.

The same feeling of nostalgia and fall swept over me again as I thought of the summer passing. The heat and sun and green trees and grass would quickly subside, as golden leaves and cool September breezes would steal away the hot summer nights, only to lose it to the quick attack of chilling frost and winter. In only a few weeks, winter coats and the future promise of snow would symbolize the coming of winter, and only the quick blast of heat from a fireplace or heater would remind me of the nights at the fountain or after-class naps in the sauna of 414 South Mitchell, cell 13. Autumn overtook my system slowly from the first day of classes. On nights like this one, when I walked home from Lindley, I felt the chill and saw the falling leaves, and knew it was time to let it all go and prepare myself for a long winter. Suddenly, like a picture coming into focus, it all made sense.

A familiar blue Mercedes rounded the corner and pulled up to the building. I ran over and opened the passenger door.

"John!" cried the beautiful brunette in the driver's seat. "Come on in, let's go try to get something fattening." I got in the seat and closed the door. She gunned the car up the twisting road to Seventh Street. "It's so good to see you! How are you doing?"

"Better," I said, watching the trees and buildings as they whirred by the window. "I'm doing a little better."

About the Author

Jon Konrath has written two books, *Summer Rain* and the upcoming *Rumored to Exist*. The former editor of *Air in the Paragraph Line*, he also writes a regular column for *Metal Curse* zine, and his work appears in numerous other zines. A technical writer by trade, he has contributed to several unix-related publications. Raised in Indiana and a former Seattle resident, he now lives in New York City.

Printed in the United States
106165LV00001B/101/A